American Made Music Series

DICK WATERMAN

A LIFE IN BLUES

Tammy L. Turner

Foreword by Edward M. Komara

UNIVERSITY PRESS OF MISSISSIPPI • JACKSON

The University Press of Mississippi is the scholarly publishing agency of the Mississippi Institutions of Higher Learning: Alcorn State University, Delta State University, Jackson State University, Mississippi State University, Mississippi University for Women, Mississippi Valley State University, University of Mississippi, and University of Southern Mississippi.

www.upress.state.ms.us

Designed by Peter D. Halverson

The University Press of Mississippi is a member of the Association of University Presses.

Manufactured in the United States of America

First printing 2019

∞

Library of Congress Cataloging-in-Publication Data

Names: Turner, Tammy L., 1967– author | Komara, Edward M., 1966– author of foreword.
Title: Dick Waterman: a life in blues / Tammy L. Turner; foreword by Edward M. Komara.
Description: Jackson: University Press of Mississippi, [2019] | Series: American made music series | Includes bibliographical references and index. |
Identifiers: LCCN 2018042678 (print) | LCCN 2018045536 (ebook) | ISBN 9781496822703 (epub single) | ISBN 9781496822680 (epub institutional) | ISBN 9781496822710 (pdf single) | ISBN 9781496822727 (pdf institutional) | ISBN 9781496822697 (cloth)
Subjects: LCSH: Waterman, Dick. | Concert agents—United States—Biography. | Blues (Music)—History and criticism. | LCGFT: Biographies.
Classification: LCC ML429.W348 (ebook) | LCC ML429.W348 T87 2019 (print) | DDC 781.643092 [B]—dc23
LC record available at https://lccn.loc.gov/2018042678

British Library Cataloging-in-Publication Data available

CONTENTS

FOREWORD

THERE ARE VERY FEW, IF ANY, BIOGRAPHIES ABOUT THE MANAGERS AND promoters of bluesmen. Tammy Turner's biography of Dick Waterman is a rare account of how blues and early rock acts were managed in the 1960s and 1970s, how they traveled on the road, and how their concerts were booked with land-line telephones and postal mail before the days of fax, e-mails, and texting.

Of course, the anecdotes told by Waterman to Turner about some of the most highly regarded Mississippi bluesmen of the 1960s, namely Son House, John Hurt, Skip James, and Bukka White, illuminate their reputations with their personalities. A few stories may dismay or even horrify some readers. But blues people are real people, and these stories should be taken not as good or bad, but as characteristic of how these men, women, and Dick himself acted within their cultures and situations.

The managerial tasks that Dick executed with aplomb were initially undefined, as before 1963 there was virtually no awareness of elder bluesmen yet. They were also laden with pitfalls—some financial, some legal, some personal—that could be crippling if they were not treated carefully by the manager. Not every person who encouraged an inactive African American musician to return to public performance was capable of getting a fair profit for that musician. Phillip Ratcliffe's biography *Mississippi John Hurt: His Life, His Times, His Blues* (Jackson: University Press of Mississippi, 2011) gives, in its later chapters, a cautionary tale for a revived career—and Hurt was one of the more appealing artists on the circuits for blues and folk music.

There have been only a few secondary accounts of Waterman as a manager, some kind (Bruce Cook's *Listen to the Blues,* cited in Turner's text), some downright wrong and hostile (Stephen Calt's *I'd Rather Be the Devil,* also cited in the text). He may be seen in the 2016 film documentary *Two Trains Runnin',* which contrasts the search for Son House that he took with Nick Perls and Phil Spiro with the Philadelphia, Mississippi, murders of three civil rights workers committed during that very same week. Some of the tales that Waterman tells for this book were written previously in the form of his newspaper columns for the *Oxford (MS) Eagle* and, later, its weekly entertainment supplement *Oxford Town*. Waterman provided some short essays to accompany his photographs in his 2003 book *Between Midnight and Day*, which went out of print all too soon. It is a joy to have this biography, so we can read about Waterman again, this time in conversation with Turner.

I see two keys to Dick's style of management. One was a watchfulness for the reputations for the musicians he managed, even after their deaths. A leading example was Son House, whose alcoholism Dick remained discreet about, even in his January/February 1989 obituary in *Living Blues* magazine. Only in 2008 did I hear Dick describe House as a "major league alcoholic," and that occasion was for a Catholic charity event for the Rochester, New York, homeless, which, Dick went on to say, House would have been one if not for his wife, Evie—and, if I may add, if not also for his blues career. In the present book, Dick admits more than ever before the efforts, responsibilities, and burdens involved in managing the Indian summer career of this great bluesman. The depiction of House's weaknesses is meant to show that he was a human being, not a legend on old 78s, and Waterman was careful to maintain the humanity of House and those of the other artists he worked with.

The other key to Dick's managerial style was his absolute insistence that his musicians refer to him all inquiries for booking performances, even if it was easier, quicker, or more profitable for the musician to deal directly with the club owner or the record label owner. When a musician broke this rule, as did Booker White in 1966, Dick could no longer trust him and retain him, knowing (as he puts it to Turner) "he was going to poison the well" of his other Avalon agency artists. The shame of the instance of White was that he was a first-rate bluesman (I agree with Peter Guralnick's appraisal in his classic book *Feel Like Going Home* that White's 1940 Vocalion label session "rivals even the Robert Johnson." Sometimes I think that Dick, more than any other manager, could have helped him in wringing the most dollars from this reputation. But as Turner tells in this book, Robert Pete Williams and Fred McDowell were among those who remained loyal to Dick, defended him to White, and continued having careers with him that now seem to be more highly regarded than White's, perhaps even more beloved, by today's blues fans.

I first met Dick in 1993, when I was the newly arrived blues archivist at the University of Mississippi. The blues boom heralded by the 1990 2-CD reissue of Robert Johnson's recordings was underway. Also, for reasons described in the book, the 1990s was a transitional decade for him, as he was having to become a public figure. He was no longer managing talent, but he knew that his photographs of bluesmen could be a new way during this blues boom of trading his public visibility into a new source of revenue.

One distinctive trait of Dick's photography is how differently his subjects pose for him than for other photographers. I first realized this difference while viewing his large art-quality prints in Jim Weems's frame gallery in the late 1990s. The usual pictures taken by many photographers of one or another elder bluesman often look formal, perhaps a bit too stiff. But for Dick's camera, his subjects were often relaxed and at ease. The glint in Son House's eyes suggests that, as a young man, he had more problems with women than with the bottle. Arthur Crudup, Robert Pete Williams, and Fred McDowell, all great bluesmen, are horsing around as friends. And miracles of miracles, Dick caught the often dour-looking Skip James actually smiling!

During the 1990s, I took every opportunity to listen to Dick speak, whether at a noon lecture at the university, at a summer presentation at the Delta Blues Museum in nearby Clarksdale, or during a chance encounter on the Oxford square. Also in Oxford was Tammy Turner, then studying toward a DA at Ole Miss, who was discovering blues music and gaining an understanding of Dick's importance as a living primary source about the blues. In 2001, I left Mississippi for New York State where, in Son House's Rochester, I had family and friends. Tammy now shuttles regularly between Kentucky and Mississippi. Her friendship with Dick has helped her jog his memory for stories old and new, and not just those he had told in *Between Midnight and Day.*

One of the keys to Dick's early success was his humanity to his friends in the blues. Later, he rediscovered his own career by saving the photographs he took of those friends. Thanks to Tammy, we all now have Dick's friendship in the blues.

EDWARD M. KOMARA
State University of New York at Potsdam
April 2018

INTRODUCTION

WHILE COMPLETING A DOCTORAL DEGREE IN MUSIC HISTORY AT THE University of Mississippi, I enrolled in African American musical traditions class. During one of our class sessions, the professor announced he had invited a special guest to share his photographs with us. With minimal introduction, he presented Dick Waterman.

At the time, my knowledge of the blues was limited. My recognition of Waterman's name came solely from having seen his column, "On Thursday," in the local newspaper. The class was small and seated around a table, so he placed his notebook binders in front of us and opened them, revealing a collection of 8 × 10 photographs in sheet protectors arranged in no particular order. He spoke quietly and briefly as he identified the individuals in each photo. Muddy Waters, Bonnie Raitt, and a host of iconic blues musicians filled the pages. The photos were not posed: they were candid, personal, and "real."

The class ended and, being a graduate assistant with classes to teach, there was no time for a conversation. Eventually, I graduated and moved away from Oxford to continue my collegiate teaching career. The African American musical traditions class I had taken proved particularly beneficial when I began teaching jazz history and rock and roll history. As I studied blues more intently, I was reminded of Dick Waterman and his photographs. When I saw his book, *Between Midnight and Day*, at a bookstore after it was published in 2003, I eyed it wistfully, thinking again how I had missed such a rare opportunity to talk with him.

Years later, as I pondered ways to bring fresh ideas and perspective to my classes, I decided to take a brief trip to do some research and immerse myself in the blues. Memphis, Clarksdale, and Oxford were my destinations. Out of curiosity, I searched online to see if Dick Waterman still resided in Oxford and was pleasantly surprised to find both his photography website and a listing with his address and telephone number. Perhaps this was a second chance to have a conversation with him.

Following some internal debate, I picked up the phone and dialed his number. Upon hearing the recorded greeting on his answering machine, I searched for the words to succinctly offer an explanation of who I was and the reason for my call. The resulting message was more akin to a hurried, babbled monologue of how we had met many years before and a request for an interview than the concise, eloquently worded query for which I had hoped. Despite my message, he returned my call and graciously invited me to his home to meet with him.

After arriving in Oxford, I followed his directions, which led me down a quiet street to an unassuming house beneath a canopy of trees. The door opened and he said, "Hello, I'm Mr. Waterman," with the patient, knowing demeanor of a man who has welcomed no small amount of researchers, interviewers, and blues fans into his home for decades.

We spent a delightful afternoon talking and looking at his photographs. I noted his impressive collection of music albums and asked if he still listened to all the old blues artists he had worked with early in his career. I was genuinely surprised when he said that he did not. As explanation, he made a single comment that was so profound it left me speechless, and I have never forgotten it. He said, "The music brings back to me their aftershave lotion, their laugh, the way they cooked hamburgers. It's the people." I understood.

Before I left, he mentioned that he occasionally gave informal lectures at exhibitions of his photography, but had never held an exhibition in the area where I lived. I had some ideas for possible venues and said I would contact him after I returned home. After some research and a few meetings, I proposed a venue. He agreed and enlisted me as a sort of local liaison to assist with media and other details.

As I researched his career, I was fascinated. His life was an amazing and unpredictable journey. Following an affluent Jewish upbringing in Plymouth, Massachusetts, he served in the military, earned a college degree, and began a career as a sports and freelance writer. While working as a writer, he joined two other men on a fateful trip that led to the rediscovery of Delta blues musician Son House in 1964. In an effort to revive House's music career, he became his manager. He soon founded Avalon Productions, the first management agency of its kind, dedicated to representing black blues musicians. In addition to booking and managing, he worked tirelessly to protect them from exploitation, demanded competitive compensation, and fought for royalties due them. During the early years of his career, he documented the work of numerous musicians through his photography, a passion that was rekindled following his retirement.

In working with him, I found he was quick to laud the talents of those with whom he worked, but was disinclined to speak of his own contributions. His name appeared in various books and articles, yet there was not a single source that brought all of the disparate pieces together into one cohesive narrative. His was a story that needed to be told. I had never written a biography, but realized that his was one I wanted to write.

His lecture and exhibition, which was well received, afforded us the opportunity to visit several times over the course of a few days. During a conversation, I asked if he had ever considered writing an autobiography. He thought for a moment and then replied, "Oh, I'm not certain if I have that much of a story to tell." I was stunned. He had an incredibly interesting story that was integral to blues history.

I told him that if he ever decided to allow someone to write about his work and career, I hoped he would consider working with me. I would not do it without his consent and participation. Days after returning to Mississippi, he called and said, "I thought about what you said. I'm in."

He routinely comments that, although he is a seasoned photographer, "Access is everything." Certainly, that is true of this project. Dick enthusiastically granted me complete access to his life and his archives. As those who know him will attest, few people recount stories better than Dick. For this reason, I have drawn upon our countless hours of interviews to allow his own words to chronicle many of the events in his life. For ease of reading, if the speaker is not identified immediately before a quoted passage, the speaker is Dick Waterman. The remaining quotes from his friends, colleagues, and family members are gleaned exclusively from original interviews I conducted. The title of each chapter are lyrics from songs recorded by Son House, the first blues artist Dick managed.

One of the unexpected, but delightful, aspects of this project was the wonderful people I met and the friendships I forged. I am grateful to each person who agreed to be interviewed, allowed access to their private archives, and contributed photographs.

I wish to thank Craig Gill for guiding me through the submission and editorial process. Thanks also to the talented staff at the University Press of Mississippi for all their work on this project.

I am indebted to Edward Komara for devoting a significant amount of time to proofreading my manuscript and for providing invaluable advice. He is a gracious friend and mentor.

Heartfelt thanks to my husband, Charles A. Gibbons, who is and always has been an unwavering source of love and support. I am grateful to Amy Cash-Allison, my beloved friend and confidante, for always being there to listen and offer encouragement.

Thanks to Dick Waterman for the countless hours he has given to this project. He has become a cherished friend. My hope is that this work will honor his contributions and achievements and preserve and celebrate the rich history of the blues.

Above all, I give thanks to God.

DICK WATERMAN

CHAPTER 1

I Didn't Have No BLUES

ON A SUNDAY IN LATE MAY 1965, DICK WATERMAN SAT BEHIND THE wheel of his 1964 red Mustang. The last rays of sunlight were dropping low on the horizon as he sped along the toll road near La Porte, Indiana, headed for Rochester, New York. His traveling companion was elderly Mississippi Delta blues musician Son House, who had faded into obscurity over two decades prior. Waterman was one of the three men responsible for House's rediscovery in 1964. In the following months, he had worked diligently to revive House's career by booking him to appear at festivals, coffeehouses, and other venues. House had recorded an album for Columbia records in April 1965 and began a tour across the country from New York to California following the recording sessions.

They had been traveling for over five weeks and were making their way to Rochester, where House had resided since 1943. Neither was inclined to lengthy conversation, so they passed the time in silence, House staring out the window at the passing landscape, or listening to the radio. On this particular evening, Dick had tuned the radio to Boston AM station WBZ. Disc jockey Jefferson Kaye was hosting his folk music program called *Hootenanny*, which aired each Sunday at 6 P.M. Just before a commercial break, Kaye announced that when he returned, he would be playing some new music from an old blues artist. Waterman's heart skipped as he knew that Kaye was referring to Son House.

He waited anxiously and, when the commercial break ended, he heard the first chords of the recording of "Death Letter" House had made the month prior. A feeling of exhilaration swept over him. He immediately pulled the car onto the side of the road and stopped. The day had been warm and the windows were down, but as trucks roared past shaking the car, he quickly rolled them up so he could clearly hear the sounds emanating from the speakers. Interestingly, House did not recognize the song as his own until Waterman informed him they were listening to one of his recent recordings.

All the months spent writing letters, making phone calls, negotiating a recording contract, and driving House around the country to performances had culminated in this triumphant moment. Waterman had never been more excited or prouder of an accomplishment, though it was not a scenario he had ever imagined as a young Jewish boy growing up in New England two decades earlier.

Richard Allen "Dick" Waterman was born on July 14, 1935, in Plymouth, Massachusetts, to Isidore H. "Earl" and Hattie Waterman. His father was the second of four children from a hardworking, blue-collar family in Chelsea, a tough, poor section of Boston. A devoted student, he graduated from high school at the age of sixteen. He worked multiple jobs while earning a degree from Harvard University, and then graduated from Tufts Medical School.

Dick's mother, Hattie Resnick, was a native of Plymouth, Massachusetts. She was the oldest of six children born to parents who were cattle traders and dairy farmers. Following high school graduation, she enrolled in college in Boston to study fashion.

In 1921, she met Earl. He spied her across the courtyard of the apartment building in which she lived, later confessing he was absolutely smitten and fell in love immediately. Though engaged by 1922, they waited six years to wed, on October 28, 1928, so he could complete medical school and a year of internship in 1927 before assuming the responsibility of supporting a family.

They settled in Plymouth, "America's hometown," where he founded the highly successful small-town medical practice "I. H. Waterman, M.D." From a young age, Dick was aware of his father's work ethic and had an abiding respect and admiration for him, both personally and professionally. "My father woke up early, by 6:00 or 6:30 A.M. His feet hit the floor and he'd reach for the phone. He'd call the hospital and check on people. He went out and made house calls. Sometimes he came home for lunch and then went to the office because he had a waiting room and office hours from 2 to 4 P.M. He made house calls again between 4 and 5 P.M., came home for dinner, went back for office hours from 7 to 8 P.M., then came home. He worked a *very* long day. He didn't hunt, fish, or garden. He got up in the morning and made sick people not sick. That was his calling; that was what he did.

"He was beloved in that town. His patients would sit in the office for long periods of time. It was really one on one and they would come in and tell their stories. There was no 'move the patient in, move them out' mentality. They treated my father as a wise man who would give them sage advice, and he realized this responsibility."

Dick and his sister, Rollene, who was three and a half years his senior, enjoyed privileged childhoods. They grew up in an upper-middle-class neighborhood in Plymouth, a city that boasted a population of over 13,000 inhabitants. Although the Jewish population was relatively small, most were upper middle class.

The family lived in a stately red brick Georgian colonial home with a pineapple, the symbol of hospitality, ornamenting the front door. Built in the 1930s, it was centered atop a hill with a spacious, rolling backyard and beautiful garden. Dick's leisure time was spent playing baseball games until dark with neighborhood children at the local grammar school and football with friends in his backyard. He was a well-behaved child, never one for indulging in mischief. His parents were proud of their Jewish heritage and insistent the children do nothing to dishonor the family or the Jewish religion. While Earl managed his medical practice, Hattie stayed at home with the children.

Dick had a passion for movies, but he had little to no exposure to live music performances. There also was little music to be found in the Waterman house. "We had a phonograph player and a small collection of LPs, but the stereo was in the parlor. It was off limits to us kids, so we really never had music in our house. My mother and father were not big music fans."

He occasionally played recordings of Calypso music. Among his favorites were Harry Belafonte and groups such as the Mighty Zebra and Mighty Sparrow. Along with a limited number of recordings, he owned a small radio. At night, he lay in bed, hidden under the covers with his radio, and listened to broadcasts from the West Virginia station WWVA. Through the radio he was introduced to the music of singers such as Red Foley and Hank Williams, which began his longstanding affinity for country music.

Though his sister was a model student, Dick was not particularly fond of school. Rollene remembers, "He wore glasses at a very early age, maybe four or five [years old], and he was kind of a loner. He was not much of a student in the early grades."

The problem was not a complete disinterest in school, but an insecurity fueled by an impediment he had grappled with his entire life. He stuttered. It wasn't intermittent. It was pervasive, obvious, and horribly embarrassing for a young boy. "I'm a lifelong stutterer, and stuttering is like alcoholism. It's always there. You never get away from the fear of stuttering. Stuttering is terrible. With me it had nothing to do with 'put your tongue here' or 'make this sound.' Stuttering meant knowing you were going to stutter. It can be helpless. Your throat seizes up, and you can't breathe. I *knew* I was going to stutter."

His teenage years passed in much the same fashion as his childhood. There was no flagrant flouting of parental authority or rebellious attitudes. It was the 1950s, the Eisenhower era, a time when most of the teens he encountered maintained the status quo.

"I didn't know any rebels when I was a kid—never mind rebels without a cause. I didn't know *any* rebels. Good Jewish kids were not rebels in the '50s. I never knew anybody who had a phony ID. We were forty miles from Boston, which could have been four hundred. To go to Boston on those small, curvy roads and traffic lights before there were interstates was a good hour's drive away. That was a big deal, so you went to Boston with your mother and father. Everything just seemed to be very low-key."

Desiring the best education for their son, his parents enrolled him at Clark School, in Hanover, New Hampshire, in 1950. He remained there, unhappily, for only a year. The following year he attended Williston Academy in Easthampton, Massachusetts. Again, it proved an utterly miserable experience primarily due to his stuttering, at its peak during his teenage years, and the accompanying feelings of awkwardness and isolation. Dick had few friends and was taunted by classmates.

After suffering, disconsolate, through two years at the preparatory schools, he returned home to finish his education at Plymouth High School. Unfortunately, the preparatory schools had not offered a comparable number of courses to that of the public school, so he entered the high school a year behind students with whom he had attended junior high school. Being placed in a class with the younger siblings of some of his former classmates resulted in even more shame and withdrawal.

His return to the local high school did little to expand his social circle. "I didn't have any social life. I didn't date at all. I was small, I was skinny, I had ticks and mannerisms, and I stuttered a lot." His sister's popularity served as a constant reminder of their profoundly different positions in the social hierarchy. Rollene was attractive and intelligent, and she excelled academically. Sometimes, Dick was the target of disparaging remarks from teachers in whose classes Rollene had been enrolled because they felt he was not living up to her academic precedent. Not only did this cause a certain level of resentment toward his sister, but it compounded his insecurities.

Imbued with his father's strong work ethic, he began working while in high school to earn extra income. Living on the East Coast where fishing was plentiful, he easily secured a job as a bait boy on a sport fishing boat that ferried tourists about an hour out from shore to realize their dreams of deep-sea fishing. Later, he worked as a pin boy at the local bowling alley and as a golf caddy at the Plymouth Country Club. Interestingly, the job as a caddy led to the publication of his first article. Following the Plymouth Country Club Golf Championship, he penned a short article and submitted it to the *Old Colony Memorial*, a Plymouth newspaper. "They printed it exactly as I wrote it, so I figured if those editors could look at my stuff and print it unchanged, then I might want to go this way [with my career]."

Encouraged, he began honing the skills that soon led him to his first vocation. His lifelong battle with stuttering had resulted in the realization that he greatly enjoyed writing. "When you stutter, you learn to express yourself in the written word. Stutterers are better writers. You go to the written word and you shine it and polish it until you get the written word to say *exactly* what you want."

After completing two years at Plymouth High School, he graduated in spring 1954. There was little debate whether he would attend college, so in the fall he enrolled at American International College in Springfield, Massachusetts. His family was not surprised when he chose writing as his course of study. He was an average, somewhat unfocused student earning only passing grades.

Though not always passionate about his studies, he greatly enjoyed writing fictional works. He joined the staff of the college magazine printed on campus, and soon his stories were appearing in print. He became the editor and, when one of the staff members tasked with writing some stories resigned just before a deadline, Dick quickly produced a trio of one-thousand-word stories to replace the missing content. "My mind was just exploding with ideas and plots; the well was very deep. I wrote well, I wrote easily, and I wrote a lot. I was very prolific, and my writing was good."

Feeling a lack of direction, he contemplated enlisting in the military. Although the United States had signed the armistice agreement with Korea on July 27, 1953, the draft remained in place for many years. Fearing being drafted, some men volunteered for service as a means of ensuring their choice of military branch and garnering a greater chance for preferential or less dangerous assignments. After some deliberation, Dick left college and enlisted in the United States Army in September 1956.

His goal was to gain admittance into an elite group, so he tested for the Army Security Agency, which specialized in cryptography. He scored well on the test, passed the rigorous security clearance process, and was assigned to the agency to work as a counterintelligence cryptographer. Following basic training at Fort Dix in New Jersey, he was stationed at Camp Gordon in Augusta, Georgia, where he began his training as a cryptographer. He also received another education, of sorts, while there. He found racial tensions and discrimination far more pervasive in the South than anything he had witnessed growing up in an area somewhat cloistered from such attitudes. A performance in Augusta given by jazz musician Louis Armstrong was his classroom.

The main floor of the venue was a large room, crowded and thick with smoke. There were no chairs, so many people were standing, some chatting and laughing, as one of the world's greatest jazz trumpet players performed a few feet away from them.

"Too many people were moving and talking and being inattentive, so I turned and looked and saw a balcony. Great! I went back into the lobby and walked up the stairs into the balcony. There were seats up there, and I was able to get a seat in the front row. I walked down to the seat, and there were a lot of Negroes upstairs. The word at the time we used was 'Negroes.' We were looking down on Louis, and the sound was *so* much better. He had a *fabulous* show and everybody was moving to the music. When the show was over, I went downstairs. One of the guys I knew said, 'What the hell were you doing up there?' I said, 'I don't know. I went up there to get a better view. Why?' He said, 'Because that's where the niggers sit.' I said, 'What do you mean?' He said, 'This is segregated. That means the niggers sit upstairs.' I said, 'Really? Wow! They got the better seats!' That was my introduction to segregation."

The military offered cryptographers the option of indicating their preference of assignment location—the United States, Europe, or Asia—following completion of the training program. His choice was Asia, and in spring of 1957 he was sent to Tokyo where he spent the remainder of his three-year military career. "We had a small base because I was in the Army Security Agency, which is not part of the regular army. The local post commander where we were had no jurisdiction over us. We didn't take our orders from US Army Japan. We took our orders from DIRNSA, the director of national security in Arlington, Virginia. We were a small, independent, elite group."

Dick completed his military assignment and was to be discharged at the end of July 1959, though he returned home over a month early. The army allowed anyone who had served over two years and planned to return to the United States to be discharged rather than reassigned if they had less than ninety days of service remaining.

He arrived in Plymouth to begin a new chapter in his life. Needing income, he took a job during harvest season picking corn on his uncle's farm. After doing backbreaking work for minimal pay, he decided to enroll in college once again and complete his degree. In the fall of 1959 he entered the School of Public Relations and Communications (SPRC) at Boston University majoring in journalism and took an unpaid staff position with the student newspaper, the *Boston University News*, as a sports writer. With a renewed sense of direction, he completed the remaining coursework within a year.

Anxious to secure employment, on the last day of classes he stood before a campus bulletin board scanning advertisements for job openings. One posting caught his attention. A newspaper office, *The Town Crier*, in Westport, Connecticut, was seeking a general reporter. He immediately called to inquire. Following a brief conversation, he was offered the job at a salary of thirty-five dollars per week, which he readily accepted.

The newspaper was published biweekly, and he quickly realized he had found a job that provided him with both excitement and gratification. His job entailed covering general news such as police, fire, and court cases along with his favorite assignment, a regularly recurring sports column. He also was tasked with taking photos to accompany his articles. Though he had no experience as a photographer, with practice he became more proficient and flourished in his new position.

Unfortunately, he faced a life-threatening health condition just a few months later. Experiencing a progressively worsening chest pain over the course of a few days, he finally sought medical treatment from a local physician. Following a cursory examination, he was rushed to the hospital in Norwalk, Connecticut.

A remarkable series of events led to a confirmed diagnosis and recommended course of treatment. A young physician at the hospital had read an article in a recent issue of the *Journal of American Medical Association* concerning a rare condition known as Idiopathic Spontaneous Hemopneumothorax. Dick presented symptoms identical to those detailed in the article. Untreated, the condition would result in death.

The article detailed a surgical procedure that had been performed successfully as a treatment. "The doctor who wrote the article, because he had done the surgery, was in Darien, Connecticut, which was the next town to Norwalk. *There's* a coincidence. In the whole of North America, this guy's in the next town."

It was after midnight when the doctor was contacted, but he immediately drove to the hospital. Thankfully, the surgery was successful and Dick's hospital stay was brief. Within a few days, he was released with a prognosis for full recovery. The pressing issue was that his lungs were not fully healed and in a fragile state. It was autumn, and there was concern about his ability to recover during what would, no doubt, be a cold winter in Connecticut.

His aunt, Hattie's sister, lived in Miami, Florida, so it was decided he should spend a few months convalescing in the warmer climate. He resigned his job in Westport and traveled to Miami, where he rented a room in a rooming house in an area known as Six Corners in Coral Gables. Earlier, Rollene had moved to the same city to take a position with the *Miami News*, a subsidiary of the much larger publication the *Miami Herald*. Dick soon secured a position in the same office working part-time as a freelance sports photographer.

CHAPTER 2

Gonna Get Me a RELIGION

AFTER RECOVERING FROM HIS ILLNESS, DICK MOVED FROM FLORIDA TO Bridgeport, Connecticut, in 1961 to work as a general news reporter at the *Bridgeport Post*. The new location resulted in a new passion. There was a rising popularity of folk music, and he took an immediate interest.

"I was hearing folk music. It was unlike anything else being played on the radio. This was the time of Perry Como, Joni James, Connie Francis—very bland stuff. About 1963, the Rooftop Singers had a big hit with a Cannon's Jug Stompers song called 'Walk Right In' and folk music exploded. It really appealed to me."

His increasing fascination led him to Greenwich Village, New York. He made a couple of trips there each week. "I used to go to Greenwich Village at night, so I hung around in the Village. I would either drive in or take a night train. I'd get there around 9 to 10 P.M. and then come back about 3 to 4 A.M."

He heard a wide variety of performers at the various venues, many performing topical songs based on events that unfolded before them on a daily basis. "The music was Greenwich Village contemporary folk. Things like injustices would inspire a song. If an event had happened socially or racially, people wrote songs about it immediately. They were what we called protest songs. Every Sunday afternoon at a place called the Village Gate the contemporary songwriters came and sang their new songs for each other. It was a big deal."

The Village Gate was established in 1958 by Art D'Lugoff and located at the corner of Bleeker and Thompson Streets, not far from the Café Au Go-Go. It was an important jazz venue where legendary artists such as Billie Holiday, Duke Ellington, and Dizzy Gillespie performed. It was the "open mic" Sunday afternoon sessions that attracted young folk artists such as Phil Ochs, Mark Spoelstra, and Eric Andersen. "Phil Ochs would come in on Sunday having created the best and newest song that week about an injustice like the Kitty Genovese murder."

The Gaslight Café and Gerde's Folk City hosted some of the most traditional folk music in the Village. The Gaslight Café, opened by John Mitchell in 1958 and purchased by Clarence Hood three years later, was a coffeehouse that seated approximately a hundred patrons located in a basement on MacDougal Street. Beat poets were some of the earliest performers there, but shortly after a shift in management, folk music became the primary entertainment.

It was a modest venue, long and narrow, with a dressing room that was a little alcove separated from the stage by a hanging sheet. The interior was dimly lit except for stage lighting that spilled onto the main aisle leading from the back of the room, past the stage, and into the kitchen. Initially, it was a "basket house," where musicians were not paid by the management, but instead passed a hat or basket through the audience at the end of their set hoping to collect tips.

Although the Gaslight was a popular venue, the owner did not have a liquor license. Performers and patrons desiring drinks stronger than coffee usually went upstairs and next door to a neighborhood bar called the Kettle of Fish. It was at these local establishments that Dick came to be friends with performers such Phil Ochs, Tom Paxton, Dave Van Ronk, and Patrick Sky.

"We used to drink at the Kettle of Fish, so we knew the bartenders and the waiters. Whoever was playing at the Gaslight, they went upstairs between sets. The Kettle of Fish had a bar on the left and a middle aisle all the way back to the restrooms, with four or five tables on the right. At the end of the tables was a big wall air conditioner. Bob Dylan and his manager, Albert Grossman, always sat at the back table with their backs against the air conditioner looking at the room. We would sit there and say, 'What are they saying? What are they doing?' because Albert was so powerful, and he was just beginning to manage Dylan. Dylan was going to skyrocket, we knew that, but no one ever knew what they were talking about. It was a great mystery.

"Phil Ochs lived only a block away from the Gaslight and Kettle of Fish, on Bleeker near MacDougal, so sometimes I would go over to Phil's apartment. He was married to Alice Skinner. He often had people there playing guitar like Eric Andersen and Mark Spoelstra. It was like chaos. The apartment was *filthy.* The kitchen was just filled with pizza boxes and roaches. Meegan, their daughter, was maybe a year and a half old and walking around with a dirty diaper. Phil was so wrapped up in his music that he would be just playing his songs or writing songs, oblivious to the fact that his child was wandering around with ashtrays and cockroaches everywhere. He was totally into the music, writing and creating."

Located on a corner of West Fourth Street not far from NYU was Gerde's Folk City, a coffeehouse established in 1952 by Mike Porco. In 1960, it became a traditional folk music club that hosted a hootenanny each Monday evening that soon became one of the most popular in the Village. The Bitter End, located on Bleeker Street, was one of the most prominent nightclubs on the Village folk circuit, offering a more commercial fare and catering to a slightly more mature, upscale crowd. Founded by Fred Weintraub, it boasted acts such as Odetta, Judy Collins, and Bill Cosby. It also became a locus for aspiring musicians such as the folk trio, Peter, Paul and Mary, who debuted there in late 1961. Dick attended a number of the club's famous Tuesday night hootenannies.

"In the '60s, a hootenanny was a music show where talented amateurs, people who thought they had something to say and sing, could come up and do a certain number of songs. It was called an 'open hoot.' You brought your instrument and played three or four songs. Sometimes if there weren't a lot of people who wanted to play, a professional who might be in the club would get up and do a few songs."

In the 1960s, "folk" was an umbrella that covered a wide range of music, including the blues. An impressive array of bluesmen including Josh White, Brownie McGhee, Sonny Terry, Jesse Fuller, and Reverend Gary Davis frequently performed in the Village. Following their rediscovery in the mid-1960s, Mississippi John Hurt, Son House, and Skip James performed there, as well.

Dick lived in Bridgeport for a few months until he was assigned to cover stories in some local towns with which he was unfamiliar and not particularly interested. Unhappy, he decided to return home to live with his parents. Despite the drive from Plymouth to Cambridge being over an eighty-mile round trip, he traveled there each night to hear music. "This folk music thing was really happening, and I wanted to be a part of it. I went to Cambridge and started to go to folk clubs. I was there in the folk scene." Although there were a number of folk performers, Eric von Schmidt, who had been performing in this style since the 1950s, was the one Dick considered the forerunner of the folk scene.

Located in a basement at 47 Mount Auburn Street behind the Harvard Coop was Club 47. Though the acoustics were a bit lacking due to the brick walls, they served good coffee and baked goods, and catered to a clientele composed largely of Harvard students and local residents who enjoyed listening to acoustic folk and blues music.

"Jackie Washington played every Monday, and Tom Rush played every Tuesday. They had big followings. The Jim Kweskin Jug Band was a popular band at the time, and in it were Geoff Muldaur and Maria D'Amato, who later became Maria Muldaur."

Dissatisfied with his position at the *Bridgeport Post*, Dick soon sought other employment. In 1963, he began working as a freelance writer for the *National Observer*, the Sunday edition of Dow Jones and Company's *Wall Street Journal*. The publication's specific focus was financial matters, but Dick's interests were sports and folk music, so his articles were only occasionally included. "I knew the entertainment editor, but I still had to pitch and sell every story."

Desiring to be closer to the burgeoning folk music scene, he moved from his parents' house into a modest apartment in Cambridge. "When I saw Clara Ward, Sister Rosetta Tharpe, or Fanny Lou Hamer, who were huge in the civil rights era, I was aware. When they use the expression 'Cambridge in the '60s' to mean a certain amount of intellectual liberalism both artistically, literature, et cetera, I was aware. I used to say to people, 'Pay attention because we're going to look back on this time as being an important time. Remember this.'"

The time he had spent in Florida heightened his cultural awareness. "I had worked in Connecticut, I had worked in Florida, but Cambridge was so different. It had a real energy, and the energy didn't need anything external. Cambridge in the '60s had its own vitality and its own force. When somebody like Judy Collins or Dave Van Ronk came in from New York, we wanted to know what was happening in the New York scene and who was writing and who was singing and who was new. When Tom Rush came back from Detroit and said, 'Chuck Mitchell's wife, Joni, she's not performing but she's a great writer,' we knew that Joni was a great songwriter, and we knew from people we saw at Newport that Jackson Browne was really coming. We didn't need anybody to read it to us or show it to us on television.

"I was three or four years older than the people who were playing in the Club 47 and other places. They were twenty-two to twenty-three and I was already twenty-six or twenty-seven. I knew that these people like Tom Rush and Eric Von Schmidt were really important.

"Eric's father had founded the Famous Artists School, a studio of artists in Westport, Connecticut. Eric grew up around art and music, illustrating, and painting. Eric was the really wise head. He's known because Dylan gives him a spoken intro [in one of his songs], so his claim to fame is being mentioned in a Dylan lyric. He was just a really great guy and a great songwriter. We kind of looked up to him.

"My point is we were aware that we were the forefront. We were the leaders. We were maybe not groundbreaking, but the stuff that we were doing was important. It wasn't just by rote. We had some really creative people among us."

Although folk music was popular in both Greenwich Village and Cambridge, there were distinct differences between the two. "In Greenwich Village everybody was earning a living or trying to earn a living. If you wanted to make it in folk music, you went into the Village. The Village was a place where you had to work at the Café Wha? or wherever, and then you worked your way up to the Gaslight, the Bitter End, or Café Au Go-Go. People came there to get recognition, recording contracts, and begin a career. Cambridge was just more for the music. There were a whole lot of people who were happy to live and work in Cambridge, and maybe get a recording contract and never go to New York City because Cambridge and its energy was not so much a path or a midway point in the journey, it could be a destination all by itself."

Needing supplementary income, he began working as a freelance writer for *Broadside of Boston*. The publication had been founded two years earlier, in 1962, by David Wilson and focused on the thriving folk music scene in the Cambridge and Boston areas. It was a weekly publication, and Dick's job was to provide the cover article. "It helped me a lot musically. If there was going to be a bluegrass cover, or a gospel cover, or a cover on Bob Dylan or somebody else, it helped me diversify and learn about different kinds of music because I would immerse myself in order to write the cover article."

His passion for folk music led to his proposal that he attend and report on the 1963 Newport Folk Festival in Newport, Rhode Island. He was persuasive, and his editor agreed to the story. The festival was conceived by the Newport Folk Foundation as a means to generate income for the foundation. George Wein, along with his partner, manager Albert Grossman, worked together to transform their idea into a reality. The inaugural festival was held on July 11–12, 1959, in Newport's Freebody Park and featured twenty-eight performers, including Pete Seeger, Odetta, the New Lost City Ramblers, and little-known young folk singer Joan Baez. In the wake of its initial success, another festival was planned for the following summer.

Unfortunately, rioting among the crowd during the 1960 festival halted subsequent festivals for a few years. "In 1960, the people way in the back, for some reason, rushed the stage and it became like a tsunami. By the time it got to the people in the front, there were just hundreds of people pouring all over them into the area in front of the stage. It was very disruptive, and they called the police. The city of Newport pulled the permit, so there was no festival in '61 and '62."

The festival was reinstituted in 1963. "In the two years of no folk festivals in Newport, the Rooftop Singers, Peter, Paul and Mary, and Ian and Sylvia emerged. This whole folk revival was just a groundswell. Newport was the right timing. If you look at pictures, it was all white kids wearing madras, Bermuda shorts, and sweaters, with crew-cut hair. Folk music was 'in,' and Newport drew big crowds. The capacity was around fifteen thousand. The idea and timing were right. Newport '63 was a great event."

The festival was expanded to three days, from July 26–28, and featured approximately a hundred performers from a variety of styles including songwriters from Greenwich Village in concerts and workshops, bluegrass, Appalachian music, blues, Canadian musicians, and many others. A sunny weekend helped entice an audience that numbered approximately forty-five thousand. "A tremendous amount of people brought their own guitars and banjos. There were little impromptu gatherings of people just sitting around playing for their own amusement. They sat on the lawns of Newport and in front of the stores in groups of three, four, or five. People came from all over. I wouldn't say that 1963 was a national festival, but folk music was basically in the Northeast. People came just to play and swap licks."

Of the performers Dick saw at the festival, a single blues player became the object of his fascination: the newly rediscovered blues artist Mississippi John Hurt. Hurt's 1928 recording of "Avalon Blues," named in honor of his hometown, had served as a reference point for Tom Hoskins, who rediscovered Hurt, still in Avalon, in 1963. Witnessing Hurt perform was a life-changing experience for Dick.

"I was totally captivated by him. I just fell in love with him. He was a small man, maybe 5'6" with kind of a rolling side-to-side gait, and a derby hat. His music was totally accessible as opposed to Son House's Delta music, which could be difficult. His music was just hypnotic. He was the whole package. John Hurt was lovable and friendly, so everybody simply took to him. He was just a really happy man. He was all these contradictions. He was a naïf, a complete innocent, but you couldn't underestimate him because you could be talking around him and forget he was even in the room, and he would simply look up and say something and you'd realize that he had been in the conversation all the time. He would say something that was so insightful that it just decided the whole discussion. He was very wise.

"John had 'vanished' about 1928–29 and then was rediscovered in 1963. He was in his mid-sixties then. The songs he was doing, 'Frankie and Johnny,' 'Stack O'Lee,' things like that, were absolutely identical [to his 1928 recordings]. Except for the quality of the recording equipment, you really almost can't tell the difference. His dexterity was exactly the same. He just played brilliantly well.

"If you had to have an entry person for people who didn't know blues and would like to have a starting point, Mississippi John Hurt was then, and still is, the best way to bring people into the blues. Some like Charley Patton or Blind Lemon Jefferson or Willie McTell, but they can be fairly difficult, not confrontational, but a torrent of emotion. With John, you just felt that he was a terrifically nice person. There was the sense that he could connect with you as an individual.

"They introduced John, and he came out, sat down, and started to play. By the first song, everyone was quiet. By the second song, they were leaning forward and hanging on him. When he finished fifteen minutes later, they came to their feet. They would *not* let him go! He had them in the palm of his hand. They just fell in love with him. They brought him back for an encore. I never saw anything like it. A little, old, black man with an acoustic guitar went out in front of fifteen thousand people and brought them all up on the porch with him. He was magic.

"Everybody at Newport was completely approachable, if not in the backstage area, then as they walked to or from the backstage. 'Backstage' may have been indicated by a string or something painted on the grass, but there was really no high-level security. There were no boundaries around Pete [Seeger] because as long as he had been in the folk music movement, he had always moved among the people."

The 1963 festival stands as a monument in Newport Festival history, and even though those attending may not have grasped its full significance at the time, there certainly was some understanding of the importance of what was happening. "I think when the Freedom Singers got on stage with some of those people who were right out of the civil rights front lines, and everybody linked hands—Dylan, Baez, Seeger, the Freedom Singers—and sang 'We Shall Overcome,' it was really powerful stuff. To put this in historic context, it was about five weeks before Martin Luther King's 'I have a dream' speech, which was August 1963."

Though freelance writing about the music he loved was gratifying, Dick was drawn into the music business when he was hired by Manny Greenhill at Folklore Productions. Greenhill was inspired to pursue managing and promoting after hearing Pete Seeger and the Almanac Singers perform in New York. He soon became involved in promoting concerts in the Boston area in the early 1950s. In 1957, he established Folklore Productions, an artist management company in Boston, and worked with some of the foremost folk artists, including Joan Baez.

When Dick accepted the job, he had no idea he would learn valuable lessons that would play an indispensable role in his career. "I worked in Manny's office every day booking his folk artists, so I knew how to book.

Manny was the only person I ever worked for in the music business. He was my mentor. He was a terrific man. He had an incredibly high standard of ethics. While working there I got to see Dylan and all the traditional folk musicians. Manny managed Reverend Gary Davis and Jesse Fuller, so I saw them often."

Dick also came to know Dylan on a more personal level during this time. "I liked Dylan. I had seen him and photographed him. November 2, 1963, he played a concert in Boston at Jordan Hall. I went backstage and shot a roll of film, standing maybe three to four feet from him while he lit a cigarette and changed strings. He was totally camera accessible and friendly. The Dylan I knew was not a rock icon."

His admiration for Mississippi John Hurt led to his first venture in music promotion and management. Following Hurt's engaging performance at Newport, David Wilson contacted Hurt hoping to book and to promote him for six nights at Café Yana in February 1964. The café, located adjacent to Fenway Park, was a small, dimly lit coffeehouse that seated approximately seventy-five patrons. The management required a monetary guarantee in advance, so he needed a partner to supply half the financing for the show. He approached Dick with the idea, and he immediately agreed.

A seemingly random event just days prior to the shows bolstered attendance. "In some crazy fluke that people find hard to remember, Mississippi John Hurt was on *The Tonight Show with Johnny Carson*, which broadcast from New York. He did a song and it was charming. Then, he stood up as they went to commercial. In those days they had huge cameras, seven to eight feet tall. Each camera had huge cables. As John was walking he got lost in the cameras and the cameras kept following him as he's walking over the cables, befuddled and confused. They didn't cut to commercial, they stayed with him for about twenty seconds as he's holding his guitar and wandering through the cameras. This little black man with a derby hat was lost among the big cameras and technology. It was just funny and captivating. It made him all the more lovable. That John Hurt had done *The Tonight Show with Johnny Carson* makes you look back and ask, 'How is that possible?' but it was great!

"Everything in Boston in February is terrific risk. From Tuesday to Sunday we had perfect weather, which you never could have dreamed of in February in Boston. There was not a grain of snow, not a drop of rain, and temperatures were in the 40s and 50s every day. We sold out every seat of every show. We made some real money. We made a couple hundred dollars. Being close to John all week was just wonderful. His music was so captivating when he played that no one talked."

Phil Spiro was in the audience during one of the performances and met Dick for the first time that evening. Spiro was a junior computer programmer who worked for the Itek Corporation. He was also an amateur musician with eclectic musical tastes who hosted a couple of folk music radio broadcasts each week on MIT radio station and occasional live broadcasts from Club 47. His roommate Al Wilson, an aspiring young musician, was accompanying Hurt on the harmonica for a few of the performances that week. Spiro points out the importance of that week of concerts. "That gig was a watershed moment for traditional music in Boston. John was an excellent musician, an engaging performer, and had an enchanting personality. Everyone who saw him perform felt at once they had known him all their lives. If anyone ever opened the door for other traditional musicians, it was John. We had David Wilson and Dick Waterman to thank for bringing John to Boston at a time when such events were still rare."

As a trained journalist, it was not unusual for Dick to bring a camera along to a performance. That week was no exception. "I worked the door every show, every night. On the last show of the last night, I took my camera and crouched down next to him. There was only one light over him. I opened the shutter wide open, f2.8 and I just shot 1/60th [of a second], 1/30th, 1/15th, 1/8th, all the way down. I finally got an image at 1/4th of a second. I took about half a roll of film and my photograph of him, called 'Café Yana,' is a still shot of him with the light on his face and the front of the guitar, and the rest is all dark. That's always been a particular favorite photo of mine."

The unusually good weather ended with the closing of the final show of the week. One of Dick's friends, folk singer Dave Van Ronk, had performed all week at the Unicorn, a coffeehouse located in a basement on Boylston Street. His final show concluded slightly earlier than Hurt's, so he came to the Café Yana to watch the end of Hurt's set. Following the performance, Van Ronk accompanied Dick and Hurt on their drive to Roxbury.

"When John finished the last song of the last set on the last night, it started to snow. I got us to John's place in Roxbury, an apartment where he was staying with a relative, and we got snowed in for two days. Dave had a full bottle of bourbon, and we sat around and drank bourbon and played guitar for two days. It was great! The love between Van Ronk and John was very real."

CHAPTER 3

I Grabbed up My SUITCASE and TOOK OFF Down the Road

ENCOURAGED BY THE SUCCESS OF THE CAFÉ YANA PERFORMANCES, DICK soon embarked on another venture. In April 1964, he and a partner booked a show with Delta blues musician Booker White. White had been rediscovered in Memphis in 1963, the same year as John Hurt's rediscovery, by Ed Denson and John Fahey. He was the cousin of Riley King, who became legendary blues performer B. B. King.

They scheduled Booker to perform for three nights at the YMCA on Huntington Avenue in Boston. Unfortunately, this endeavor proved less successful than the Mississippi John Hurt performances. The revenue covered little more than their expenses. Despite being financially unsatisfying, this set in motion an unlikely series of events that became a turning point in Dick's life and a catalyst for a new career.

White needed a place to stay while in town, so Phil Spiro and Alan Wilson happily volunteered to host him at what Spiro described as their "rattrap Cambridge apartment." Spiro remembers, "Between the two of us, Al and I had a single fork and no dishes, and we could not afford a telephone. Any spare cash went into records, and we had few of those. For us, seeing Booker White play in the here and now, in Boston, in 1964, seemed not at all possible. Yet it was, and we were there."

While at the apartment with White one day, David Evans, an undergraduate at Harvard, and Wilson played tapes of blues music and discussed with him the music and musicians. Evans turned the topic of conversation to Son House. White mentioned that his friend, blues singer Lillian "Memphis Ma Rainey" Glover, had seen House exiting a movie theater in Memphis the previous year. They were astounded by this revelation because Son House had vanished from public view over two decades earlier. No one was certain if he was still alive. When Spiro returned home that evening, Wilson enthusiastically related White's comment that House had been seen in Memphis.

Son House, a Delta blues musician, had made a few commercial recordings in Grafton, Wisconsin, in 1930. In 1941 and 1942 he was recorded again by Alan Lomax for the Library of Congress. Few were familiar with his music outside the region where he lived, for his recordings certainly had not brought him great fame. The early recordings by House and other blues artists eventually made their way into the hands of devoted collectors of 78 rpm records. These originals were used by the companies of Origin Jazz Library (OJL) and Records, Books, and Film Sales (RBF) to create reissue LPs, which led to greater appreciation for both the artists and recordings by folk and blues enthusiasts. Even so, the audience for such music was limited.

Spiro explains, "In spring 1964, House's name and music were unknown outside of a small number of people who knew of his few Library of Congress cuts from the 1940s, and the smaller group of country blues fans who collected 78s or who bought the reissues of country blues 78s on LPs from RBF and OJL. Al and I belonged to this last group—all reissue LPs, and heavily indebted to the record collectors for our information about the music we loved and the people who had played it some thirty years earlier. There were certainly excellent contemporary blues musicians like Fred McDowell, Howling Wolf, Muddy Waters, Big Joe Williams, Robert Pete Williams, and John Lee Hooker, and we liked their music as well. But the old 78s had mysteries, voices from the past, which were often more compelling than an LP recorded last month or last year. Before the OJL reissue LPs came out, I doubt that there were more than a hundred people worldwide who had heard of Son House as a musician, and by the time we found him, that number might have doubled or tripled thanks to the OJL reissues."

Intrigued, Spiro made some telephone calls. He contacted Lillian Glover and, although she did not know where House was currently residing, she confirmed White's story. White and John Hurt had been rediscovered the previous year, so perhaps Son House was still alive. Some vacation days from work, youthful exuberance, and a desire to meet one of his music icons resulted in plans for a road trip.

Spiro occasionally saw Dick at local coffeehouses and was aware of his interest in folk music. Knowing he was a journalist and photographer, Spiro decided to invite Dick to accompany him on the trip. Although Dick certainly had heard the music of many folk and blues artists, he was not familiar with House's music. He viewed the invitation as a rare opportunity for a news story. As he still was freelancing for the *National Observer*, he approached his editor with the idea and was told, "If you find him, you've got a story. If you don't find him, there's no story." Dick then notified Manny that he would be out of the office for a few days.

Al Wilson was an obvious choice as an additional traveling companion, but he was a struggling musician with a performance already scheduled at Club 47, which he was unwilling to cancel. Spiro called Tom Hoskins, who had rediscovered Mississippi John Hurt. Although Hoskins had no interest in the trip, he suggested an acquaintance from New York, Nick Perls, mentioning that Perls had both a car and a tape recorder.

Despite the fact that neither of them knew Perls, Spiro contacted him. Perls was interested and provided their transportation in the form of a red Volkswagen Beetle. He had an enviable collection of 78 rpms and reel-to-reel blues tapes along with a large Ampex tape recorder and microphones that he brought along on the trip to capture music by any willing blues musicians they encountered. Unfortunately, issues of personal incompatibilities emerged almost immediately.

"Perls had gone to a few colleges and was in his twenties. His parents were very rich, and he just smoked dope and listened to blues. We spent two weeks in a Volkswagen together, so we got to know each other pretty well. I hated Perls by [the time we reached] the Lincoln Tunnel. He made racist remarks. He was just arrogant and spoiled."

Since White's friend had reported seeing Son House in Memphis, this was their initial destination. Otherwise, there was little prior planning. Spiro says of their impromptu journey, "We had a lead to a great musician who hadn't been heard from in twenty-odd years, and we thought it worth a few weeks' time out of our lives to follow it up, just to see what would happen. We were in our twenties, an age when you will follow hot tips just for the hell of it, as indeed we did, but we were not complete fools. We were looking for a person and were not out for a career for him or for us. Thanks to Dick, Son did get a career, and Dick built a career for himself, and so, in his way, did Nick. But none of that had been in the air when we started out.

"We certainly had the specific goal of finding Son, but that's as far as it went. We had no idea how old he might be or what kind of health he might be in or if he still had all ten fingers, or if he had gone over to religion and forsaken music entirely. And even if he had been seen in Memphis in 1963, he might not still be alive in 1964. Just finding him was the goal. We'd have been happy to meet him and shake his hand and be on our way if it came to that." Dick, too, admits, "I didn't know what we were going to do if we found him or didn't find him. We just weren't thinking that far ahead."

In the mid-twentieth century, locating an individual was often a painstaking process. Many living in impoverished areas had no telephone. In some instances, the only method of finding someone was to simply ask people if they knew or had seen the individual and where they could be found. In

Memphis, the trio was directed to the homes of two elderly blues musicians, Will Shade and Furry Lewis. Upon arrival, they encountered an environment far removed from that to which they were accustomed. Despite racial tensions, neither Lewis nor Shade seemed apprehensive about admitting the three young strangers into their home. "They knew that if they played some music they would get some money. We didn't have much money, five or ten dollars, but enough to buy a bottle of whiskey. We just got in on the local blues scene in Memphis. We never felt we were in any danger, but the slums of Memphis were just ghastly. It was so hot.

"We were in the black community in Memphis with Furry Lewis, who had recorded blues, and Will Shade of the Memphis Jug Band. We met Furry at his house on Beale and Fourth, which was really a slum. It was the next building over from Will Shade's, who was very famous in the 1920s in the Memphis Jug Band. He was the leader, vocalist, and songwriter. He and his wife, Jennie Shade, were in real poverty. She'd been one of the most beautiful women in the 1920s and Will Shade had won her [over] and married her. Now, forty years later, she was just an old, shrunken lady who sat in a rocking chair and chain smoked Pall Malls and dropped the butts in a Maxwell House coffee can. She sipped Calvert's whiskey out of a coffee mug. She didn't say a single word all the time we were there.

"We interviewed him and he played a few songs for us. When we left, Phil and I each took out a five-dollar bill and put it in his hand. He thanked us, and we thanked him. As we were leaving, Nick was driving, Phil was in the passenger's seat, and I was in the back. Perls said, 'You gave him money, didn't you? I saw you give him money.' I said, 'Well, yeah. He gave us his time and his music. Ten dollars really isn't a lot of money.' Nick said, 'You guys just missed the point. You don't understand. It isn't what he gave us. It's what we gave him. We gave him immortality. We recorded his music. His music will live forever, because long after he's dead, we have these tapes of his music. He just gave us a few minutes out of a night that he wasn't doing anything anyway.' I looked at Phil, and Phil looked at me. We just couldn't say anything beyond that."

They met with Lillian Glover because she was their initial source of information regarding House's whereabouts. They also contacted Reverend Robert Wilkins, who had known House earlier in his career. Wilkins was a country blues musician who had recorded in the 1920s and became an ordained minister in the 1930s. He had been rediscovered in Memphis in the early 1960s by Dick and Louisa Spottswood and then booked to perform at various festivals. Spiro found his name in the Memphis telephone directory and placed a call to him that met with a favorable reception. Arrangements were made to visit him at his home on McLemore Avenue. They soon arrived at his house, which was situated in a middle-class African American neighborhood with impeccably clean lawns and streets.

They were delighted when he agreed to join in their search, and, ultimately, he proved a fortuitous addition. He was from the area, had friends there, and knew people who remembered House. Spiro credits Reverend Wilkins's participation as a key factor in the success of their trip. "Everyone we met who had known Son in the old days was glad to help us locate him once they had decided to trust us. Son appeared to have left only good will behind after he left Mississippi. With Reverend Wilkins's presence as our bona fides, we were able to tap into that good will. Without him, we encountered a moderate degree of mistrust that was appropriate to the situation."

Their trip coincided with the increasing unrest of the civil rights movement. Despite the turmoil, Dick and his friends were not fearful for their own safety perhaps because they did not fully grasp the potential implications for their own lives. "The mistreatment of Negroes in the 1960s was certainly well known. If you were in folk music, [this fact] was well established. I think we were just feeling that nothing bad was going to happen to us. That was *their* conflict. We weren't involved. We weren't integrating or registering voters, we were looking for bluesmen. It was a little naïve, but in the long run, that's how it worked out. We were protected by our own foolishness."

Spiro's assessment is similar. "We certainly encountered a level of hostility from local white people, but not as much as I had anticipated before the trip. I had lived in New York until age ten and went to unsegregated schools there, but I had also lived in Miami from ages ten through seventeen, and segregation was a way of life there as much as any other place in the South in the 1950s. Thus I was expecting problems, but nothing like what was actually going on elsewhere in Mississippi while we were there. I had thought about the issue beforehand and had felt that looking for a black musician to record was nothing new to southern whites and would be an acceptable situation. Luckily, we never had to put that questionable idea to much of a test. If we were not in direct danger ourselves, it was still a very dangerous time and place, and we were fortunate not to have run into serious trouble. It was pure dumb luck."

They stayed in the southern suburbs of Memphis and made a short drive into Robinsonville and Tunica, Mississippi, each day accompanied by Reverend Wilkins, who served as a buffer between them and the local residents. They drove down rough, dusty roads and plodded through cotton fields in the sweltering heat of the Mississippi summer. They carried taped recordings of bluesmen such as Charley Patton, Robert Johnson, Skip James, and Son House to play for the people they encountered, asking if they had heard of the performers or if they knew House's whereabouts.

Despite the heat, humidity, and dusty rural settings, Reverend Wilkins always was impeccably dressed and stalwart. Each day he met them attired in a dress shirt, tie or bow tie, suspenders, trousers, and a jacket, his eyes peering out through gold-rimmed glasses. Spiro and Waterman took their places in the backseat while Perls drove and Reverend Wilkins navigated their route from the passenger's seat, an act that was potentially dangerous to everyone in the vehicle given the racially charged climate. Wilkins also was the one who stepped out of the car to hold conversations when they needed information from local residents.

"One time there was a pickup truck stopped and two white guys were standing outside of it talking. We stopped, and Wilkins got out and stood up and talked across the Volkswagen to them and said, 'I'm looking for the house or store of X' and they looked at him and went back to talking. Wilkins repeated the question, and they looked at him longer and then went back to talking to each other. Wilkins just looked at them and said, 'Looka here, I'm talking to you' and he repeated his question. They turned around and stared at him, he stared back at them, they told him what he wanted to know, he nodded his head, and got back in the car. He was like that. He was not going to be intimidated or ignored.

"I don't really remember having a lot of hostility. These [white] people, obviously, held this well-dressed black man in contempt, but Wilkins had very erect posture and as a minister he was not going to talk up to anyone. He was used to being treated as an equal, and he demanded that. He was very forthright, not confrontational, but he just stood up straight, looked you in the eye, and demanded an answer."

Finally, their efforts yielded a potential clue to House's whereabouts. One of the musicians they met and recorded while in Mississippi was Fiddlin' Joe Martin. He was a direct link to House, since he had performed with House in the 1930s, and they had been recorded together by Alan Lomax on his trip to the Delta in 1941.

Martin urged them to contact a man named Benjamin Brown Sr. They visited Brown in a Memphis hospital, and he verified Martin's information that his son, Benjamin Brown Jr., had once been married to House's stepdaughter and that his son might know how to contact her. Martin located the son and accompanied them on their visit with him. Indeed, Benjamin Brown Jr. knew the name of the mother of the man to whom his ex-wife was married and directed them to her. She, in turn, informed them that her son and daughter-in-law resided in Detroit and offered their telephone number.

Since Dick stuttered and Spiro was more knowledgeable about blues artists and music, they decided Spiro should place the call. When she answered, he explained they were searching for Son House and asked if she knew him. She said, 'Yeah, he's married to my mother. He's my stepfather." With increasing excitement, he asked if she had seen them recently and learned that they had visited with her in Detroit two to three years earlier. The foremost concern was whether House was still alive and, if so, where he was residing. They learned he was living with his wife, Evie, in Rochester, New York. Spiro requested his telephone number but was told he did not have a phone. She said their friend, James "Jim" Knox, had a phone, and he brought them to his house whenever they needed to make a call. Before ending the conversation, he asked for House's address and Knox's telephone number.

Assuming Knox was a next-door neighbor, they sent a telegram to House with their telephone number and asked if he would make a collect call to them. No call ever came because the telegram was incorrectly addressed. After waiting for a while, they contacted Knox. Once more, they explained the reason for their call.

Knox confirmed that he knew House. Spiro inquired when last he had seen House and he replied, "Oh . . . it was early afternoon yesterday." They were elated! They asked if he would mind to bring House to his home so they might call again the following day and speak with him. Knox agreed.

Anxiously, they waited another twenty-four hours and called again, but their excitement quickly gave way to disappointment as Knox admitted he had forgotten about the call. Spiro impressed upon him their need to talk with House. Once again, he asked if Knox would help and, when he agreed, Spiro said he would call again an hour later.

"We knew he was 'E. House,' so there was the assumption that it was 'Eugene House.' Phil said, 'Is this Eugene House?' He said, 'No.' Phil said, "We're looking to find Son House, the one who recorded for Paramount, the one who knew Robert Johnson, the one who knew Charley Patton, the one who recorded for Alan Lomax and the Library of Congress at Clarksdale in the early 1940s. Are you that Son House?' So he said, 'Say, who is this anyway?!' And then he said, 'Yeah, that's me. I done them things.'"

Understandably, House was both surprised and perplexed by the questions since he had left behind his life as a musician decades earlier. Phil asked if he still played guitar, and he responded that he could although it had been some years since he had last played. Knowing he was alive and living in Rochester, all that remained to complete their journey was to meet him in person. They asked for his address, told him they would leave immediately, and asked him not to go anywhere until they arrived.

The day they made contact with House was noteworthy for multiple reasons. "That was Sunday, June 21, 1964. It was Father's Day, and it was the day Jim Bunning pitched a perfect game for the Phillies against the Mets, which was very rare. It was also the day civil rights activists Goodman, Schwerner, and Chaney were let out of jail in Philadelphia, Mississippi, and murdered."

They quickly loaded into the Volkswagen and departed that same day from Memphis bound for Rochester. Based on information they had received while in Mississippi about another old bluesman, Skip James, they decided to try a route that would take them through Poplar Bluff, Missouri, to search for James. Upon arrival in Poplar Bluff, they spent the day searching for anyone who could provide information about him or his whereabouts. When their inquiries yielded no results, they realized their information had been erroneous and resumed their journey to New York.

On the evening of Tuesday, June 23, they arrived in Rochester. The area was a modest, middle-class African American neighborhood with several apartment houses interspersed with patches of grass and trees. "The apartment house had a low stone wall. A well-dressed man in a white shirt and tie and his wife in a neat dress were sitting there by the wall. We said, 'Is this 61 Greig Street?'

"'Yeah, it is.'

"'Do Son House and his wife live on the fourth floor?'

"'Yeah, they do.'

"'Okay, thank you.'

"So we walked on by and the man said, 'But he ain't up there now.'

"'Really? How do you know?'

"He looked at me and smiled, and said, 'Because I'm him!'

"At that point I set my camera and gave it to Mrs. House. There's a photo of Son with the three of us, which she took with my camera."

The group walked upstairs to the House's sparsely furnished, but meticulously tidy, apartment and played some of the recordings of Skip James, Robert Johnson, and House's old friend, Charley Patton. He recognized Johnson and Patton, and reminisced a bit about the latter, but did not recollect ever hearing James's music. They played some of his 1930 Grafton recordings, but he did not recognize them as his own. "He listened to it with some interest. Then he said to us, 'That guy got some of my words.' Mrs. House said, 'That's you.' I said, 'Yeah, that's you with Paramount in Grafton, Wisconsin, in 1930.' That was a knee-slapper to him. He said, 'Yeah, that's me, baby, me and Charley.'"

Obviously, they were anxious to hear him play and sing. They wondered whether he would sound the same as he did on those old recordings. Initially, he declined their requests to play saying it had been a number of years since he had played. On their second day in town, they coaxed him into playing on a borrowed wooden guitar and recorded his efforts. His hands shook, and he asked if they would purchase a bottle of wine and bring it to him. They left and returned shortly with the bottle he had requested.

His first attempts were ragged and halting. "As he drank, he got better. He hadn't played in many years, so he had no calluses. He was playing this very lightweight, flimsy, wooden guitar. He played so forcefully, so aggressively, attacking the instrument. He was having trouble fretting with his left fingers, so we put the slide on, and he was much better. He would start a song and clear his voice several times and, ultimately, he found his register—that low, heavy, majestic voice.

"He played, and of course, not being musical, I didn't know what I had in front of me. Perls knew because he had the original Library of Congress recordings, and Phil played blues guitar, so they realized that, although he hadn't played in many years, the essence of it was there. I'll tell you, when he sang he filled up that room. We were in his living room and that deep, rich Delta voice was pretty awesome stuff."

They spent the night in Rochester and then drove to House's apartment for a final visit the following day. He performed for them again and, having played the previous day, his dexterity was slightly improved. The next morning, they began the trip home, tired but elated at having located and met Son House during a ten-day adventure none of them could have predicted.

In finding House, Dick also found the story he was seeking for the *National Observer*. He had no way of knowing at the time that House's rediscovery was to become one of the most pivotal events of his life. His article detailed their trip, but primarily focused on House. He related the story of how House had disappeared from the blues scene and lived in anonymity for over two decades in Rochester, New York, following his 1930s Library of Congress recordings. The photo taken by Mrs. House with Dick's camera appeared in the article. Spiro authored another article for the July 22 edition of *Broadside*.

They had accomplished their goal of locating House, and Dick had gotten his article, but he also felt an obligation to assist in reviving House's music career if he was amenable. Spiro had a full-time job in computer programming that he enjoyed, and he was not interested in pursuing music management. Perls was neither suited for nor interested in such an endeavor, so Dick assumed the task of finding work for House.

"Nick and his family owned a five-story building in the art district of Manhattan/Madison Avenue in the '60s, which is a very upscale neighborhood. The art gallery was the bottom floor, and the stories above it were the residence. He had an extensive tape collection and headphones. He would smoke marijuana, get high, put on his headphones, and listen to tapes of Charley Patton and Robert Johnson. He had all this wealth, but listened to the music of poor black people. For him, as with other collectors, it was just music frozen in time. Those people were forever young. It's always 1928 with Charley Patton, and it's always 1937 with Robert Johnson.

"He didn't much like Son as a person. He didn't much like any living blues person. Son was just an old human being and had to be taken care of. Nick only wanted the Son House that lived in his headphones from 1930. The living, breathing Son House had no place in his life. Nick had absolutely no interest in the post-rediscovery Son House."

Spiro adds, "Nick did his share of the work on the trip, and I have no complaints about that, but he was best suited to working by himself with things like records, rather than dealing with people. And that's what he ended up doing, working with records." Indeed, Perls went on to become founder and owner of both Yazoo Records and Blue Goose Records.

Several of the old bluesmen who were rediscovered had not simply lived out their lives as performers and then retired. Most had recorded in the early twentieth century, but due to the economic woes of the Depression and a somewhat limited audience, their music had faded into relative obscurity, save for a handful of blues enthusiasts. They were forced to abandon their music careers and seek other employment in order to support themselves. House worked various jobs before moving to Rochester and finding work with the New York Central Railroad. When Dick and his companions found him, he was retired from the railroad and surviving on a monthly pension.

"He was bemused, if not bewildered, as to why, having played all of his music in and for the black community, now after he had been retired or semiretired for twenty years or more, suddenly three young white guys track him down in Rochester, New York, and tell him that his records and songs have been issued, reissued, and there is an audience waiting for him to come out and play, and he can earn money."

Dick continued to write freelance articles as he set about finding work for House. One of his first calls was to Ralph Rinzler, who booked for the Newport Folk Festival, in hopes of having House added to the program despite the fact the festival was only weeks away. Dick forwarded tapes they had made in Rochester to Rinzler and received confirmation that he was scheduled to perform on the evening of Thursday, July 22, the opening night of the four-day event.

During their conversation, Rinzler related an amazing story. Bluesman Skip James, who the trio had searched for in Missouri on their way to visit Son House in Rochester, had been rediscovered on the same day as House and was scheduled to appear at the festival. "I asked where he had been rediscovered, and he said, 'Tunica.' I said, 'We were just there! We were literally in Tunica!' Three guys from Boston and New York came to Tunica and Robinsonville, and three guys [John Fahey, Bill Barth, and Henry Vestine] came to the same place, and the two blues guys were found on the same day! The coincidences were just mindboggling."

In preparation for his appearance at Newport, Dick scheduled some performances for House at small venues in the Boston area including Club 47 and the Unicorn Coffeehouse. Dick had seen him play in the familiar setting of his Rochester apartment, but Club 47 was the first time he saw House perform for a live audience. Eric Von Schmidt also performed that evening and introduced him. The setting was not acoustically ideal because House was sitting directly in front of a noisy espresso machine throughout the performance. It was a modest but crucial first step in the revival of his music career.

Al Wilson also assisted House in preparing for the festival. It had been many years since House had actively performed blues and his recollection of his earlier pieces was sketchy.

Dick remembers, "Al sat in front of him, knee to knee and guitar to guitar, and said, 'In 1930 when you recorded *My Black Mama* you played it like this.' He played it, and Son nodded his head. He said, 'Eleven years later when Alan Lomax came to you in Robinsonville, Mississippi, you played it like this.' Son would sit there listening and looking at Al's hands. Then Son started playing with Al, their two guitars facing each other. To Al's credit, he never slowed down for Son. He kept it at the original tempo so Son had to pick it up. Through a period of days they went through Son's earlier repertoire, which was not much. There were a few songs from 1930 and perhaps a dozen songs from Lomax in 1941. Al helped get Son's dexterity back: his ability to play guitar and to recall those earlier songs and lyrics. Once Son got up to speed, he was all right. Without Al at the beginning, we wouldn't have had any comeback career, because Al knew how to play that material exactly as Son had played it."

Unfortunately, House's scheduled debut at the Newport Folk Festival the following month was not to be. House traveled to Newport but became ill while there. He was taken to the hospital by Spiro, where he remained for several days. Despite his absence, the blues workshop was a landmark event. "The blues workshop of 1964 remains one of the great gatherings of traditional bluesmen all in one place at one time. Son was sick and didn't participate, but virtually every other great rediscovered bluesman performed. It was fabulous."

Sam Charters hosted the workshop and considered it the most memorable event of the festival. He comments, "It was just unbelievable. A moment that had never happened before and never happened again. They were all living together in an old schoolhouse that had been converted. There were cots in bare rooms that had white walls. I'd walk by and there was Sleepy John Estes wearing a coat, tie, and hat, and there would be Mississippi John Hurt sitting on a bed exchanging licks with Fred McDowell. Really, I did feel absolutely that I had died and gone to heaven. Here they all were. The only one we missed was Son, who didn't make it."

Dick, and others, referred to it as "the Blues House," but it was the Miantonomi House. "The house was downtown, away from the festival field. Anybody could walk in as it was just a house. Nobody needed an invitation. The word just spread. Skip, Sleepy John Estes, and Robert Pete Williams were all there, and everybody had their own room. If you went down the hall, in each room there were about fifteen or twenty people inside listening to a bluesman. Every room was packed. It was wild! It was the greatest collection of blues players. What happened was that we [the blues folks] got killed by liberals. They said, 'You put the Negroes in a ghetto house instead of integrating them with white artists. You've created a fancy Newport ghetto by putting them together.' Well, the truth of the matter was they [bluesmen] *loved* it. It was a blues fan's dream. You could go from Sleepy John Estes's room to Mississippi John Hurt's room to Skip's room. It was only that one year, though."

Due to the timing of his rediscovery, Skip James also was a late addition to the Newport 1964 roster. There was no advance advertising of his appearance, but his performance was well received. "When Skip came to Newport 1964, that was really big news. You'd had to have been a blues fan to know this guy had recorded in 1931 and was coming out of a thirty-three-year void. Nobody knew anything about him, what he'd done, where he'd worked, or anything. There were only scratchy 78s [of his music], and a couple of them had been included on LP anthologies.

"He came to Newport, and the fact that he played well and had that incredibly high, wavering, eerie voice and strange guitar tunings was totally unique. No one had heard anything like it. He played on a day workshop, but the night concerts had been set by May or June before he had been rediscovered. His workshop was so dynamic and electrifying that word swept across the festival grounds. They rearranged a couple of things and found him ten or eleven minutes. He came back and repeated the songs he had done in the daytime workshop. Fabulous! He was charismatic and thrilling, and people loved him."

Bruce Jackson, American folklorist and author, points out the almost impossibly perfect timing of this gathering of bluesmen at Newport. "The folk boom wasn't that old then, so the audience for it hadn't existed previously. The audience in black communities was interested in a different kind of music. If you look at the pictures of who was at Newport, the audience is almost entirely white. There are very few black faces in that audience. There wasn't a big venue for it, so whoever put that together, I think it was an act of programming genius. And it couldn't have been done a few years later. Skip was dead a few years later and so was Mississippi John Hurt. It was the one time those guys had just been found, there was an audience that was willing to pay to get them there, and there were people who were enthusiastic about it who were willing to put it together without making any money on it."

While backstage at Newport, Dick spied blues musician Robert Pete Williams sitting near the stage during the blues workshop and walked over to him. His introduction to Williams's music was through the recordings of Williams, Robert "Guitar" Welch, and Matthew "Hogman" Maxey made by Dr. Harry Oster, a professor at Louisiana State University, at Angola Prison in the late 1950s titled *Angola Prisoner's Blues.* "The Robert Pete Williams cuts on that are just breathtaking. You have a man who is doing life for murder (for shooting a man to death in 1956 in a club, although he always contended it was in self-defense) and when he does a 'Prisoner's Talking Blues' about being free again and how much he misses his wife and children, it's just wrenching. It's incredibly emotional music.

"He had been paroled (his sentence was commuted to twelve years) and he had been allowed to leave Louisiana in the custody of the Newport people just for his performance under the condition that he be back in the state of Louisiana less than twenty-four hours following the completion of his performance. That was his first time out of Louisiana.

"It was July and he was wearing a black wool suit with a shirt and tie and pork pie hat. From under his hat, he had lines of sweat coming down the sides of his forehead. Around his neck he had a kazoo in a twisted, bent coat hanger. Like most of the black bluesmen, he called the kazoo 'the jazz horn.'

"Now, if you think Son House and Skip James and the others had a tremendous gap between being in the black community and suddenly having these young white people talking about their music, it was even more so for Robert Pete because his recording had been done while he was incarcerated. He had come from virtual social isolation. Robert Pete didn't read or write; he was a functional illiterate. Because of that, he was very shy, very hesitant, and very withdrawn. He was extremely guarded and suspicious.

"He was in this backstage area where everybody was white. He was sitting down. I stood up next to him and said, 'Hello, Mr. Williams, nice to see you. I have a copy of the album that Dr. Harry Oster recorded in Angola Prison. I liked it very much and am looking forward to hearing you perform.' He just nodded his head. After that, I didn't know what to say. I was trying to make some kind of small talk with him, and he obviously wasn't saying anything to me because he had absolutely no idea what to say to some young white guy that he was just meeting. I'm really stupid and innocent, so I said to him, 'I enjoyed your music and the guitar music of Guitar Welch and Hogman Maxey.' Then I said, 'Mister Welch and Mister Maxey, where are they now?' He had his head down, and he was smoking. He lifted his head up, looked at me, and just said, 'They still there.'"

Although Son House missed an important opportunity at Newport, Dick scheduled another performance for him after he recovered from his illness. His first public appearance before a large audience came at the Philadelphia Folk Festival in August 1964. Dick accompanied him, which became standard procedure. "In those days, 1964–65, he wouldn't get on a bus alone. To get him to a performance, I had to drive from Cambridge to Rochester, pick him up, and we went to the destination. Then, I drove him home."

House's repertoire, though never extensive, was particularly limited immediately following his rediscovery. He performed three songs, approximately fifteen to twenty minutes. "There are so many random floating verses that simply rhyme, so Son House might start a song that had three or four set verses, and after that he simply let the emotion take it wherever it was going. He never really developed a full repertoire. He might have had as many as a dozen including some a cappella gospel songs such as 'This Little Light of Mine' and 'John the Revelator.' He reached a point where it became more emotion than material. When he went into an open G tuning and was playing something like 'Sundown Blues' or 'Levee Camp Moan,' the songs were virtually the same, but he got so into it with sweat coming off of him and the audience just being totally captivated by it that nobody was going to nitpick and say, 'Gee, that song was pretty close to one he did earlier in the program.'"

House also performed for an afternoon workshop and an evening concert. Despite the abbreviated length, Dick found the latter unforgettable. "I put Son on stage and I was sitting out in the audience to watch. He had a steel body National [guitar] at that point. He took the slide way down at the end of the neck, and he took a deep breath and sighed. He was talking very softly, saying, 'This is a little piece of blues and I hope you like it' and things like that. It was really self-deprecating, but not intentionally so.

That's just the way he was talking. Then he would give this deep sigh, and he would kind of inhale and exhale. Suddenly, he would rip the slide up the neck, and the whole weight of the steel body would come pulling up off of his lap, and then it would come down. He was slashing the slide, playing the strings with a backhanded slap that started somewhere over his left shoulder. He was *wild.* I looked at this and my eyes just burned open. Then Son started singing, 'I got a letter this morning, how do you reckon it read?' It was awesome.

"Right from the very beginning, he absolutely was a physical force unlike other people who were subtle or enticing or cerebral. Son House was a slashing attack. He was a full-frontal assault. He just battered it. He did his three songs and got an astounding standing ovation. As we left the backstage area it was totally a flood of people. People didn't know what to make of him."

House was equally perplexed by the attention he was receiving. Decades had passed since his early recordings, and even then they had not fared particularly well. He had changed careers, relocated to another state, and no one had shown any significant interest in his music during the intervening years. Certainly, he was unaccustomed to the venue and type of audience he found in front of him. He had known only house parties and juke joints within black society, a world away from the predominantly white, middle-class audience at the festival.

More performances in small coffeehouses followed including some in Cambridge and at the Orleans on Charles Street situated at the base of Beacon Hill in Boston. It was there Dick first met Peter and Alexandra Guralnick. Dick approached their table, introduced himself, and told Alexandra that House had been inspired by the hat she was wearing. They chatted briefly, and Dick returned to his duties.

Though he had gained valuable experience working for Manny, Dick had never handled the myriad duties of management on his own. Nevertheless, he was determined to find more work for House. The process proved challenging and time consuming.

"I wrote letters to the few festivals that existed, folk song societies, and schools. I had an old Underwood open-top manual typewriter. I typed with two fingers. I wrote letters and organized a fall 1964 tour. We opened on Friday, the thirteenth of October at Antioch College in Yellow Springs, Ohio. We played some small schools in the Midwest: Ohio, Indiana, and Illinois. Those were the first dates. He wasn't really well known because he didn't have any reviews. We had the *Newsweek* article and through my journalistic training I could write a pretty good press release, so I wrote one for the tour."

The tour was short, encompassing only six concert dates, yet crucial in reigniting House's career. Dick accompanied him to every performance.

"The first year, I sat next to him on stage just giving him song titles so he would remember what to play next."

The increasing amount of time on stage spurred his creativity. "He was great. As he got more comfortable performing, he didn't do more songs, but he did longer songs. When he finished his set, I would take the guitar, and he would encore by singing a cappella gospel songs like 'John the Revelator' and 'This Little Light of Mine.' It was a logical way to lengthen his set without overexerting him. I look back and listen to those 1964 and 1965 performances, and he was stronger and had a lot more hand speed than I remembered. By the time we got to 1970–71, his hand speed had slowed down a lot. From 1964–65, I was surprised at his dexterity and speed. It was pretty good."

Eventually, he played longer shows that included a couple of one-hour sets separated by an intermission. Even though his repertoire was limited, there was the frequently alternating appearance and disappearance of various verses within the songs, and his accompaniment on guitar varied as well. These were some of his early performances before a white audience, and he used them to hone his skill of entertaining with stories and witty comments.

In November, Pete Seeger contacted Dick to inquire if House would make a guest appearance at a concert he was performing at the Eastman School of Music. It was a great opportunity, so Dick immediately accepted. House played a few songs to open the show and was well compensated by Seeger, who paid him one hundred dollars.

House was booked to perform at the Gaslight Café in New York City in January 1965. By this point, it was apparent that an increasing amount of time was needed to properly manage his career. Dick made a necessary, yet difficult, decision. He walked into Manny's office, told him of his plan to book a tour for House, and then resigned his position.

"I was the competition, and the market was pretty small, so to have somebody else come in was tough, but Manny was incredibly ethical. Manny gave me a lesson in management that I never forgot. He said, 'Anybody can find some dates for an artist, but that's not management. Management is a promise and commitment that you can support this man, his wife, his children, and his extended family. Anybody who looks to him to support them is now dependent on you. It's a commitment that you can find the work to support this person and everyone he supports for an open-ended period of time. It's a heavy responsibility and one that you can't put down. Once you pick it up, it's yours to carry.' He was a great man."

Dick also resigned one of his freelance writing jobs. "David Wilson ran *Broadside* at his house. In those days you wrote something on your manual typewriter, got in the car, and drove it over. I was writing for almost nothing.

I had a day when I ran into insane traffic. Instead of being there at 4 P.M., I got there at 4:05 or 4:06 P.M. He exploded at me, saying I had been late, I was unreliable, he couldn't count on me, and he wanted things done on time. I stood there and listened to that, and I said [to myself], 'You know what? I don't need this shit. I really don't. I'm doing it for nothing. I work hard every week to immerse myself to write the cover story, and all I get is abuse. I don't need this, and I don't need him.'" When Wilson finished his diatribe, Dick unceremoniously informed him that he would no longer be writing for *Broadside.*

CHAPTER 4

I'm a-Preach THESE BLUES

LEAVING TWO JOBS TO DEVOTE HIS TIME TO HOUSE'S CAREER RESULTED in a Spartan existence. Writing volumes of letters in search of performance dates eventually could prove fruitful, and it did, but he needed a more immediate source of income to survive. The logical choice was to continue freelance writing. It provided him a flexible schedule and supplemented his income, so he sporadically contributed articles to the *National Observer* for over another year.

He lived in a small apartment, subsisting on a diet of coffee and soup, using the meager proceeds he earned to cover the expenses of his management endeavors. "I remember pretty much living on air. My belongings all were in a duffel bag and that was everything. The money wasn't big, but I didn't need anything. Any money I made went into stationery, postage, and typewriter ribbons."

With a steady supply of coffee to keep him going, he sat at the typewriter day after day creating letters of inquiry. Finally, his persistence yielded incredible results. Among the multitude of letters he had written was a singular missive addressed to the titan talent scout and record producer, John Hammond. Hammond had been involved in the discovery and careers of many important artists for the Columbia record label, and he possessed a special interest in blues and jazz music. Dick hoped Hammond's affinity for the blues would prove beneficial in finding a company interested in signing a recording contract with House.

Given the relatively small market for blues music, Dick realized securing a recording contract would be a challenge. A small recording company was an option, but there was less probability a major label would be interested in signing with an elderly blues musician. Hammond, however, had been instrumental in Columbia Records' reissue of Robert Johnson's recordings in the 1960s, and Son House was one of Johnson's mentors. Dick had nothing to lose.

"If John Hammond was head of signing talent at Columbia, and he loved Robert Johnson, why wouldn't he love Son House? It wasn't that difficult to contact him. Nobody made phone calls in those days. We wrote letters. So, I wrote him a letter and got an instant response, saying, 'We'd love to have him. When can he record?' It was as simple as that.

"I was very naïve in record company dealings, and I took the first offer on the table. This was the biggest, most famous label in the world, so just his presence there meant we weren't going to argue about money. Son House being on Columbia was a big deal. It was not only a big deal to the other bluesmen, it was a big deal in the blues world."

Their initial meeting with Hammond was not what Dick expected. An ardent enthusiast of Robert Johnson's music, Hammond welcomed them and immediately launched into recounting his quest to secure Johnson for his *From Spirituals to Swing* concert at Carnegie Hall in 1938. Dick sat patiently, but House was blatantly apathetic toward Hammond's enthusiastic tale and simply stared out the window. Confronting an imposing personality such as Hammond was daunting, yet a trait Dick would have to hone to survive in this business. Finally, he intervened by gently pointing out that House had known Johnson in an entirely different context than a blues enthusiast. Johnson, several years House's junior and overly eager to hang around with other blues musicians, on several occasions had been little more than a nuisance to House and his friends. Dick finished by saying, "Son is a great artist in his own right, and it's a little insulting of you to bring us here and then talk about someone else." Hammond quickly refocused and assured House that Columbia was honored to have him sign with them and that, together, they would produce great recordings.

Hammond offered an advance on royalties payment of one thousand dollars. Even after the extensive amount of work he had done to secure the contract, Dick kept none of the funds, insisting House receive the full amount. He was careful, however, to entrust the money to Mrs. House. Though Dick managed to keep it hidden from the public, he had discovered early in their working relationship that House was an irrecoverable alcoholic and irresponsible with money. Either he spent it on alcohol, became drunk and gave it away, or passed out from drinking and awoke to find it had been taken from his pocket.

Though most would have viewed a recording contract with Columbia as a career-altering opportunity, House seemed decidedly indifferent about the matter. "He really didn't have a lot of enthusiasm for anything. If I said, 'Son, we're going on tour' and I picked him up, then we went on tour. If I left him alone, that was okay, too. He didn't have any real thoughts about a career, about a vertical movement up into popularity. He just did what was set in front of him."

After scheduling the recording sessions for April 12–14, 1965, Dick set about attending to other matters. In order to protect House's rights and royalties, Dick formed a publishing company named Sondick Music. To help him prepare for the sessions, Dick scheduled two performances a few days prior in Washington, DC, at the Ontario Place club. Musician Al Wilson journeyed from Cambridge, Massachusetts, at Dick's request to aid in the preparations and to play on a couple of the recordings.

All the recordings were accomplished during the first two evenings, with alternate takes recorded on the third evening. Hammond's vision was to do some of the recording in front of a live audience, so approximately fifteen people were seated in the small studio. An audience presence, regardless of size, seemed to have no effect on House.

"He was the same everywhere. If you had five people in a room or fifteen thousand in a stadium, he did it the same way, which was with his eyes closed and full emotion, sweating, and pounding away on the guitar. He never played for light entertainment. He totally immersed himself deep into the music. He only had one way to do it. He was sometimes really scary to watch.

"He would lose himself in each individual song, right from the first song in Philadelphia all the way through his career. He would introduce the song in soft, hushed words, he would pause, put the slide on, and then get himself settled into the chair. He would put the slide way down on the neck, and suddenly it was like a charge, a voltage. Something would happen, and he was just roaring, his arms flashing aside. His eyes would close, and when they opened it was like his eyes rolled back like he had just gone somewhere else and was not of this time and place. He emotionally put himself into some self-induced trance so that he would not be aware of where he was and what he was doing until he was spent and exhausted. The storm would last anywhere from four or five minutes up to twelve to fifteen minutes. Then he would slump back in the chair, his eyes would open, and he would drink and refocus. He would reach with his right hand and take the slide off his ring finger and put the slide in his shirt pocket. Then he would lean forward, reach into his left rear pocket, take out a handkerchief, sit back in the chair, mop his brow, and wipe his face really slowly. He would open his eyes and chuckle or smile sheepishly.

"He would talk a little bit about the next song—a little anecdote, a little story—and then he would lean forward, put the handkerchief back in his left rear pocket, sit back in the chair, reach his right hand in his shirt pocket, take the slide out, put the slide on his ring finger, and then 'pop-pop' at the end to put the slide on. Then he would kind of rise up and sit up a little straighter in the chair. He would put the bottleneck down at the neck of the guitar, and he would drape his right hand on the top of the steel body. He would look at the people, then he would smile and sigh. Then he would just close his eyes, reach way to the bottom of the neck, and then suddenly *Boom! Slash!* He's off again."

When he performed in Cambridge, he always stayed at Dick's apartment. Neither had sufficient funds for him to stay at a hotel, and even if they had, he required constant supervision. During one of his stays, Dick took him to a local music store. House had been playing a steel body National, but another guitar at the shop caught his attention. Someone handed an electric guitar to him and urged him to try it. As his fingers deftly strummed the strings, his eyes widened with delight, and he smiled approvingly. "Somebody said, 'You sound pretty nice, Mr. House.' He said, 'Ah-hah.' I said, 'Don't even think about it.' He said, 'Aw, Dick. Here's me, working so hard, mashing my fingers down, and I take this, and I just go easy and sound go jumping out of that box, man. I got to have this. This is so easy on my fingers. I can just play this instead of mashing down on that old guitar.' He really loved that guitar. He wanted it, but no way was I letting him have it. The musicologists and traditionalists would have run me out of town. Lightning Hopkins was already electric, but Son was Delta. He was with me, and I wasn't going to buy it for him. No way. It would have been interesting, yes, but no cameras please."

One occasional purchase was guitar slides. "We would go to a hardware store and into the pipe fitting section where they had hundreds of yards of copper, steel, and brass pipe. I would say, 'I want a piece of brass tubing.' They would ask, 'What size?' I would say, 'Son,' and he would stick his ring finger in them and find the right one. The guy would ask how many feet I wanted, and I'd say, 'Give us about three inches.' The funny thing was that I should have bought three or four of them, but I didn't. We always carried just one. It was always a real dilemma if he had misplaced his slide. Looking back on it, they were thirty cents each, so we should have bought a bunch of them."

Even though House was fascinated with the electric guitar and was earning money from performing, he never saved money to purchase one. Even the Nationals he received as gifts did not remain in his possession for long. "He wouldn't have spent his money on guitars. He would have spent it on liquor. Stefan Grossman gave Son a National at some point, maybe 1965 or '66. Every National he ever took back to Rochester he pawned."

Dick planned a tour immediately following the Columbia recording sessions. They departed Cambridge heading to destinations including Chicago, Denver, and the UCLA Folk Festival. Though House was amenable to travel, touring with him was challenging. The greatest obstacle was his affinity for liquor. He would drink anything available, consuming it in minutes regardless the size of the bottle.

"We knew he had a problem right from the beginning when we found him. We got him a bottle of liquor, and he drank too much. He would drink *any* liquor. If he was buying it, he would drink cheap wine. I only gave him bourbon. If he had money, he was going to buy liquor. If he had a lot of money, he drank a lot of liquor. I knew it had to be regulated."

Getting help for his alcoholism was out of the question, for like other alcoholics, House did not consider it a problem. Dick's solution was to give alcohol to him in measured amounts. He purchased half gallons of bourbon and filled a few small airline bottles each evening.

"I would carry the little ones on me in my pocket. I knew how much he could have to get through a performance. I would give him one maybe a half hour before stage time and then another one just before he went on. One little bottle too few, and he couldn't play. One little bottle too many, and he couldn't play. It was extremely difficult. It was precarious, and you were always at risk. He was never at the point where he would say, 'Okay, that's enough. I can play now.' It was always, 'I just need one more, and then I'll be right.'

"He walked out of the hotel, drunk, in San Francisco and decided to walk home to Rochester. I didn't even know what way he went out of the hallway, so I'm out on the street in San Francisco trying to find him. The same thing happened in Ann Arbor, too.

"Son was an alcoholic long before I ever met him. Either he was in his room alone, or I was with him. He couldn't be out of his room alone without me. He would borrow money. He would take money. He would ask people to buy him a bottle. We had some scenes where he got his hand on somebody's bottle, and it was a horror show. It required vigilance, always guarding the public from knowing that this man could absolutely ruin a performance in the flash of a wrist. We had a couple of times when we had a real physical confrontation. He got a bottle, and I had to get the bottle away from him before he absolutely drank himself right out of the performance. He was angry. These are not good memories. He thought I just didn't want him to drink because I didn't want him to be in a state of happiness or satisfaction, but we had a performance."

Given their common interest in music and House's earlier associations with blues musicians such as Charley Patton and Robert Johnson, the assumption would be that he and Dick discussed blues as they shared countless hours together. This was not the case, however.

"I can ride in silence for hours. I do some of my best thinking and planning then. Son would not initiate a conversation. He wouldn't turn to me and start talking. He would respond if I talked, so if I had been really inquisitive about him and his time and his contemporaries, I would be one of the world's great experts on prewar blues. It just comes under the heading of missed opportunity.

"I'm a quiet guy, so we would often just drive in silence. We'd drive for days, weeks. He had no interest in current events. We never talked about music or women or people. We certainly didn't realize that Robert Johnson would become such a world phenomenon."

During their stay in Los Angeles, Dick had the opportunity to reunite House with an old friend. He had learned Howling Wolf and the Rolling Stones were performing on an episode of the ABC variety show *Shindig* on April 28, 1965. Although prior clearance was required to gain access, Dick was not deterred. He arrived with House in tow and managed to negotiate his way onto the lot, into the building, and, finally, onto the set.

House had not seen Wolf in over two decades but assured Dick he would recognize him. They made their way onto the set through the back of the stage and found Wolf sitting alone. "We came down the steps, and Wolf looked up. He got up out of this small theater seat like an elephant coming out of a phone booth." House was surprised at Wolf's size, as he had been much thinner when they last saw each other. He turned to Dick, wide-eyed, and proclaimed, "Man, he sure has got his growth!"

The two old friends were excited to see each other after so many years and immediately were engrossed in conversation. Dick stepped back to allow them some time together and took a few photos to commemorate their reunion. As he stood watching, he felt a tap on his shoulder. He turned to see Rolling Stones guitarist Brian Jones. The band members, who had been watching as Wolf greeted House, were curious as to the latter's identity. Dick informed him the man was Son House. Instantly Brian replied, "Ah, the one who taught Robert Johnson and Muddy Waters!"

On May 4–9, 1965, House played a series of dates at the Ash Grove, a folk and blues club in Los Angeles. One of Dick's clearest memories from that week was a quiet moment with House as they relaxed from the tour. "We were staying out at a beach house in Pacific Palisades, which was very expensive real estate. I was sitting there reading and putting logs in this big fireplace. Son was playing the guitar, just kind of noodling away on it. Then he turned to me and said, 'Well, I just did it.' And I said, 'Did what?' He said, "Clarksdale Moan." I said, 'What?!'

"He had recorded that song in 1930, but he had totally lost the recollection of that song. I said, 'You just played "Clarksdale Moan?"' He said, 'Yes, sir. It came back to my recollection, and I just played it.' I said, 'Wow, that's fabulous! Now you can start playing it in concert.' He said, 'Play what?' I said, "Clarksdale Moan." He said, 'Oooh, I played that *years* ago.' I said, 'No, you just played it now.' He said, 'Played what?' I said, "Clarksdale Moan." He said, 'Oh, I haven't played that in forty years.' I said, 'But you just played it for me.' He said, 'I couldn't have. I don't have no recollection of that.' It was just incredible. The song came back to him while I was reading and inattentive, and he played it, and then lost it out of his memory. Just totally forgot about it. It came back, he sang it, and then he forgot it again, and never played it again."

After reaching the West Coast, they began the long return journey, playing more concerts along the way. The highlight of the tour for Dick, and one of the highlights of his career, came during the trip home. "We're driving back on the interstate. We had passed Chicago and were in Indiana on the turnpike. We were listening to WBZ out of Boston, a fifty-thousand-watt station, to a two-hour Sunday folk music show with a guy named Jefferson Kaye. Before they went out for a commercial, he said, 'When we come back, we're gonna have some new sounds from an old bluesman.' I knew it was going to be Son.

"Jefferson Kaye came back from commercial and said, 'Son House, an old bluesman recently rediscovered, this is the first track on his new album, *Death Letter*,' and he started to play it. Son, as we drove, always had his head slightly to the right looking out the window. I heard him on the radio and it was like POW! I did it! I did this! I made this happen!

"WBZ could be heard from England, Scotland, Ireland, down to South Carolina, Georgia, way up into the Canadian Maritime Provinces, and we were listening to it in the middle of the country. The potential population that could be hearing him was into the tens of millions. I had no thought that tens of millions of people were listening, but it was that this station was so big, so powerful, and was playing Son House. I had done this. I found him. I got the recording contract. I got the album done, and now listen to *this*! I pulled the car over by the side of the road on the interstate. The tractor trailers were roaring by, and the car would shake. I said, 'Son, listen to this!' He said, 'Hey! He got some of my words!' I said, 'No, Son, that's you! That's the record you made for Mr. Hammond.' He turned to the radio and listened to it, and he kind of nodded his head. He was interested, but he wasn't an excitable man. He was happy because I was happy.

"I had a surge of just being elated. This wasn't just driving a guy around the country. I had accomplished something. It was real, tangible. This was mine. I had done this. I had looked for him, found him, got him a contract, got him into the studio, and now he was on a fifty-thousand-watt station on Columbia Records. It was like the greatest three minutes of my life. It was just a triumph, over the top beyond anything I could have dreamed possible. It was one of the high points of my life to sit on the Indiana toll road and listen to Son House's 'Death Letter.' Wow!"

As was House's way, he remained as impassive as he had been during the initial meeting with John Hammond. He never engaged in conversations with Dick about success or fame. He was not impressed or excited about such matters. He simply took things as they came.

CHAPTER 5

Wouldn't Mistreat Nobody Not for My Weight in GOLD

THOUGH HOUSE WAS DICK'S SOLE CLIENT UNTIL THE SUMMER OF 1965, Dick became increasingly aware of the obstacles encountered by many black blues musicians. Some were managed by jazz or folk agencies, but there were no management companies dedicated solely to blues. Most dates for the older bluesmen were booked through recording companies. Although the companies wanted the artists to perform in hopes of selling more records, they had no interest in handling booking and management responsibilities nor were they equipped for such tasks. Securing concert dates for the artists was tedious and time consuming, and the recording companies were only interested in making and selling records.

There was little communication between the companies regarding the fees paid to musicians for a performance, so talent buyers used this to their advantage. The buyers frequently offered blues musicians no more than thirty-five to fifty dollars per evening. If a musician lived near the venue, this amount could be reasonable. If the performance required traveling a significant distance, lodging, and meals, as was the case when he traveled with Son House, the amount remaining after expenses could be quite small. Dick realized the buyers were taking advantage of the musicians, and some were not even aware of it, or those that were did not have the power to fight against them.

"Nobody knew what the other [companies] were doing, so the talent buyers were just lowballing everybody. The money was really terrible. There wasn't much money in the folk circuit anyway, but I had Son out there for a while before we broke into three figures [per performance]. We got one hundred fifteen dollars at Wayne State University in Detroit, and I thought it was bonanza time! We were doing whole shows for fifty to seventy-five dollars."

On June 17–20, 1965, the New York Folk Festival was held in famed Carnegie Hall. Dick was in attendance as both Son House and Mississippi John Hurt had been invited to perform. Though the festival was a success, Dick learned afterward that the bluesmen had been the last performers added to the schedule using the meager sums of money remaining after all the other artists had been booked. This served as the catalyst for a decision that would not only change his life and career but have an incalculable influence on the lives and careers of numerous blues musicians.

"It was June 25, 1965, at the Henry Hudson Hotel on the West Side. We were sitting in the lobby. I made up my mind that I was going to launch Avalon Productions. I formed Avalon to find work for the old bluesmen because they were the last ones hired with leftover dollars. I wasn't going to stand for that. I hated that."

He ordered business cards and stationery, and within a few weeks was operating his newly founded business. His agreement with Son House was that he would receive a 10 percent commission from House's earnings. In reality, on only a few occasions did he ever collect his 10 percent, as he usually gave the full amount to House.

Although there had been a few booking agencies for popular blues artists on the "chittlin' circuit," Avalon Productions was the first booking agency established during the folk and blues revival to represent black blues artists. The name of the company was a tribute to his friend Mississippi John Hurt. Avalon, Mississippi, located on Highway 7 between Grenada and Greenwood, was Hurt's hometown. The company was the solution for some of the problems faced by recording companies and blues musicians.

First, he contacted the recording companies to make them aware of the services he could provide. "I said, 'I'll book your artists. You make the records, and I'll find them work on the road. We're going to solidify a base price of two hundred to three hundred dollars [per performance]. I'll provide photographs, biographies, itineraries, and arrivals. I'll bring structure and organization, tell you where they're playing, and you get records in the stores. We're going to do this in a professional way.'"

The record companies, having always disdained the chore of booking, were impressed with his ideas and delighted by his proposition. By the opening of the Newport Folk Festival, July 23–26, 1965, word had spread about Avalon Productions, and he was being approached backstage by blues artists. Representatives from various recording companies were in attendance and urged their artists to seek him out. "They knew that Son House had an album on Columbia Records, which was a big deal. That made him different and very special. I guess my reputation for honesty was out there. Other bluesmen who didn't have managers came to me and asked me if I would handle their work."

One of the first to approach him was Skip James, the Mississippi blues artist whose 1964 Newport Folk Festival performance following his rediscovery had captivated the audience. Those who had assisted him had not capitalized on this success to secure a recording contract or bolster his career. Following the festival, he had spent months working as an opening act at Mississippi John Hurt performances and hoping for the type of success being enjoyed by Hurt and Son House.

Dick had seen James perform and had met him. Backstage at the festival, someone mentioned to Dick that James wished to speak with him, so he walked over and sat beside him. James shook his hand and said he knew of Dick's work with House. James was keenly aware that his career could have been handled differently following his mesmerizing appearance at Newport the previous year. He asked if Dick would become his manager, and Dick agreed. "Skip created a sensation in 1964. By 1965, he was just an ordinary guy who didn't have an album out. At that point, I did the best I could, but by then he had lost his momentum from 1964." By this time, James also was suffering the debilitating physical and psychological consequences of cancer.

For many attendees, the most memorable event of the festival was Bob Dylan's "electric" trio of songs, which charted both a new course in music history and Dylan's career. "Dylan going electric is really the major, overwhelming memory. The point I always make is that nobody was caught by surprise. He had an electric amplified sound check in the afternoon and that's when everybody freaked out. Newport had quiet, acoustic workshops close to each other. These were maybe a couple hundred people here and there in little groups about fifty yards apart out on the grass going simultaneously.

"Dylan came in and set up and did his electric sound check at about 4 P.M. When Bloomfield hit that first note, everybody turned and said, 'Turn it down! Turn it down!' So, there were no surprises that night because everybody knew he played electric amplified rock and roll that afternoon. Some people booed, some people didn't. I don't think it's fair to say there was a consensus. You can't say Dylan played amplified and was booed off the stage. There were thousands of people, and everybody's got an opinion.

"I'm a Dylan fan, but I'm a lyricist foremost, so I didn't like the fact that you had to shout over the sound because that's a distortion. I had already heard the Paul Butterfield Blues Band and the Chambers Brothers, so hearing blues played amplified wasn't new to me. The reason for the volume was not Dylan, it was Bloomfield. He was playing a Fender Stratocaster. It was a straight out rocking guitar. Dylan without Bloomfield would have been a plugged-in folkie with a rhythm section.

"Dylan played an electric guitar [during the first three songs], and some of the crowd booed with their unhappiness. After he left, Peter Yarrow had to come to the microphone. Peter was in a very embarrassing place that Dylan had left the stage after only three songs. It was painful [to watch] because he was not a professional emcee. He was just doing it that night. He had to keep the audience calm while Dylan got an acoustic guitar and decided to come back up the steps to the stage."

Dick also witnessed the backstage altercation between famed folklorist Alan Lomax and influential manager Albert Grossman. Lomax appeared on stage to introduce the Paul Butterfield Blues Band and took the opportunity to publicly criticize the use of electric instruments in the performance of folk and blues music, an obvious rebuff to the band. Grossman, who had agreed to manage the group, was incensed by the critical remarks. As Lomax exited the stage, disparaging words were exchanged between him and Grossman, and a fistfight commenced.

"I arrived as they were rolling around on the ground. It was the only fight where nobody said, 'Break it up!' They were both furiously disliked. Everybody's thinking, 'Let 'em fight.' I had no feelings one way or the other. I had no dealings with Grossman. In the folk world, he was the giant manager. He had Dylan, Peter, Paul and Mary, Paul Butterfield Blues Band, Richie Havens—the cream of the crop. He was really a formidable person. He was really a genius, but he could be a real bully. Lomax was regarded as being one of the great contributors to American culture."

The reception of Avalon Productions at Newport from the artists and recording companies was quite different from what he encountered from owners at clubs. The majority were opposed to the idea, not because they personally disliked him, but because they considered his work an interference that affected their profit margin. Most did what they could to thwart his efforts by attempting to circumvent him entirely.

They were accustomed to calling the bluesmen at home and negotiating a price, always as low as possible. There was resentment at the thought of having to pay a few hundred dollars more than they had previously paid to book musicians because Dick had solidified price ranges for their work. At first, they tried to intimidate the older performers.

"They would call them at home and say, 'I'm not booking you through any guy in Cambridge, Massachusetts. I've been booking you directly, and if that's over then I'm not going to use you anymore. I've been paying you a hundred dollars, and this Waterman guy wants three hundred, so I'll give you one hundred and fifty dollars.' It was just maddening for these club owners. They had been ripping these guys off."

The manner in which he gained clients was unplanned and variable. Many simply sought him out, and then a verbal agreement was made. "I never had contracts with anybody. If you want to be with me, you're with me. If you don't want to be with me, then I don't want to be with you."

One aspect of the deal that was not negotiable was loyalty. His management of their careers would not work without it. It could not have been easy for a poor blues musician to turn down an offer that was higher than they were normally paid, yet lower than Dick's base price, when club owners were threatening to rescind the offer if they refused. "I'm big on loyalty. I give loyalty, but I want it back. To their credit, the guys who were really poor, like Robert Pete Williams and Mississippi Fred McDowell, said, 'No, you got to call Dick Waterman, and if he says I can play for you, then I'll go, but if he don't say, I'm not coming.' I was getting loyalty from people who couldn't read or write. They just totally trusted me."

There was perhaps one unintended consequence of Avalon Productions' management of some of the blues artists from the rural South. Dick told the artists they were always free to schedule performances at juke joints or clubs near their homes. Some, including Mississippi Fred McDowell, chose not to do this. As they began earning more money for performances booked by Avalon, they were less inclined to perform for far less pay at rural establishments.

Though obstacles were many, he found ways of overcoming them. Dick usually obtained suggestions from managers at the venues regarding appropriate accommodations for the artists. Receiving payment following a performance also could be a challenge. The prospect of taking a check from another state, especially one thousands of miles away, back to Mississippi and cashing it was not advisable, so he often asked the venue manager to have the artist endorse the check at the venue and pay them the amount from the proceeds that evening.

He taught Sleepy John Estes, a blind blues musician, a system for handling cash at a Newport Folk Festival. Estes was not an artist he managed, but Dick was sitting backstage with him when he received a check for his performance. "It was for four hundred dollars, so I went and got it cashed for him. He was sitting down, and I bent down on one knee in front of him. I said, 'Okay, put your hand out, Mr. Estes.' He put his hand out. I said, 'These are one-dollar bills. Now put these in your right pants pocket.' He put them in his right pocket. Then I said, 'These are five-dollar bills. Put them in your left pants pocket.' He said, 'Okay.' I said, 'Do you have a wallet?' He said, 'Yes.' I said, 'Take your wallet out.' He took his wallet out, and I said, 'These are ten- and twenty-dollar bills. Take these, and put these in your wallet. Okay, now what do you have in your right pants pocket?' He said, 'One-dollar bills.' I said, 'What's in your left?' He said, 'My five-dollar bills.' I said, 'And what's in your wallet?' He said, 'My ten- and twenty-dollar bills.' I said, 'You have a total of four hundred dollars. You be careful now, and have a good trip home.' As I stood up, his hand went out, and he took me by the wrist. He said, 'Mr. Waterman?' I dropped down on one knee again and said, 'Yes, Mr. Estes?' He said, 'I want to thank you for doing that. Nobody ever fixed my money for me before.'"

Travel required precise planning, and communication with the artists was often tedious. "I would write them a letter and tell them I had a date and a time. Then they would call me, and I would give them the info. Those who couldn't write would have somebody take the phone and write it down. Mississippi John Hurt could read and write. Son could, but needed glasses. Skip could read. I was never really sure about Mance [Lipscomb]. I always traveled with Son, but most of the others could go on their own. They often went by bus. I always knew they had to have rest upon arrival, and they had to know where they were, who was going to meet them, who was taking care of them, and who was going to send them on their way to the next place.

"Robert Pete Williams, who lived in Louisiana and was illiterate, had to know that if he went to the Baton Rouge airport that there would be a ticket waiting for him. He would fly to some city and someone would meet him when he came off the plane and would take care of him. He had to know when he was going to be playing, and where, how much money he would be paid in cash, taken back to the airport, and somebody would meet him back in Baton Rouge. He had to hear this from my voice and, somebody had to write it down, and he would carry it and my phone number.

"We're talking about a man who doesn't read or write. Now *that* is a leap of faith to totally trust you that when they get off the plane in a city where they've never been that somebody is going to say, 'Mr. Williams, hello. Dick Waterman told me you would be coming.' It's amazing that they would do that. Robert Pete, Mississippi Fred McDowell, and Mance Lipscomb were illiterate, but they did it. They believed me. They trusted me."

When a concert was scheduled for a venue within a reasonable distance of Dick's apartment, he brought the performer to stay with him. This allowed them to take home more money. Older blues artists were certainly not being paid enormous sums to perform, and his apartment was an environment in which they felt safe.

Williams stayed with him on multiple occasions. During one stay, he decided to do something for Dick to show his appreciation. "Robert said to me, 'You are always bringing home the food. Tomorrow, I'm going to go to the store, and I'm going to do the cooking. I'm going to buy the food.' So I said, 'Okay, sure.' I came back, and he had bought a big frozen macaroni and cheese. I said, 'That looks good, Robert. I like that.' He said, 'Yeah, that's going to be good.'

"I baked it up and I could smell this macaroni and cheese. It smelled good. We take it to the table, and I spoon half of it on his plate and half on mine. I sit down, and he's poking at it. I said, 'What is it, Robert?' He's really distressed and very agitated. He said, 'Where the meat?' I said, 'There's no meat.' He said, 'This is cooked-up meat.' I said, 'There's no meat, Robert, this is cheese.' He said, 'It got meat on the picture.' I went and got the package out of the trash. The little ridges in the cooked macaroni on the top looked like meat in cream sauce to him, and he was very upset. He thought they had fooled him at the store. I said, 'This is wonderful, Robert. I like macaroni and cheese, and I haven't had it in a long time.' It took me a while to calm him down. He had tried to get something that would please me and his inability to read the packaging had fooled him, and he thought I would be disappointed."

He had heard Williams play many times, but during his visit Dick overheard him playing a different music than he performed on stage. "I had a one-room apartment. I had one major room and then had a bedroom and a small kitchen. Robert would sleep on a mattress in the big room, and I had the bedroom. I got up in the morning, came out of the bedroom, and was going in to make coffee. I could hear music coming from somewhere. I looked, and it wasn't in the bathroom or the main room, and I was confused. I made coffee, got dressed, came out, and down in the stairwell leading up into the apartment was Robert sitting down at the bottom of the stairs. He was playing very gentle and soft. His fingers were barely brushing the strings, but because he was down at the bottom of the stairwell the sound came up. It was mixed and amplified so it was a full sound.

"I got my camera and took some pictures. I was up on the top step looking down on him, and I must have popped three or four pictures. He heard the shutter, and he suddenly stopped and turned around. He said, 'Aw, Mr. Richard, man, I woke you up. I was playing too loud. You heard me. Oh, I'm sorry, Mr. Richard. I tried to be quiet.' And I said, 'No, Robert. Look what time it is.' It was probably noon time. I said, 'You didn't wake me up. That was really beautiful. What were you playing, Robert? I really liked that. I thought it was soft and gentle.'

"He said, 'I wasn't playing no kind of music. I was just talking to Hattie Mae (his wife). I said, 'Really, what were you saying?' He said, 'Oh, I was just talking to her. I said I'm staying here with Mr. Richard and having myself a good time. I said I just got one more job to do, and then I'm on the bus in the morning, and I'm coming home. I tell her to tell them chilluns that they better be doing their schoolwork or I'm going to take a strap to them. I said, I just miss you a lot, I love you a lot, and give them chilluns a kiss for me. I'm here with Mr. Richard and I'm doing just fine. I just got the one more job, and I'm coming home to you tomorrow morning.'

"I said, 'Robert, that's really beautiful. You should play something like that this evening at the show. Something soft and gentle just like that.' He said, 'Oh, no, no, no. I wasn't doing no kind of music. I was just talking to Hattie Mae. Now, the people spend their money and they want to get entertained. They come to see me play. They want to see a show. They don't want to get no kind of that sad talk that I was doing. They want to hear me play some blues. That's just total different. I just wouldn't be doing that kind of music.' That was the paradox. That was the irony. What he felt wasn't really music, just his sending words off to his wife, was really beautiful. It was such a sad lament.

"On stage, he played almost staccato notes. He didn't play chords, just individual notes. It's a very harsh, almost guttural style. It was hard on the ears. He was not easy to listen to. His voice rose and fell and was very hard to understand even if you were right in front of him while he was singing because his voice was so high and his Louisiana dialect was so difficult to understand. That, along with the fact that he wasn't playing gentle, easily accessible chords, made him commercially difficult to book. You could listen to Robert Pete for about ten or fifteen minutes, and then he just lost you."

After spending some time with him, it became apparent that Williams was superstitious. He believed in the blues mythologies of John the Conqueroo, mojo, spell casting, and divining the future, but was particularly fearful of spirits and cemeteries. "He wouldn't walk in front of a graveyard. If he was being driven past a graveyard, he would turn his head. He even had series of rituals and incantations for such occasions: spitting on his hand, slapping his hands together, waving his hands, turning in circles, turning back around the other way."

Williams's past, eccentricities, and guarded personality did not dissuade Dick from forging a close relationship with him. "As the years went on I got to know Robert. I think Robert was the one that I personally cared for most. I spent more time with Skip James, and John Hurt and Fred McDowell were outgoing, friendly, lovable people. But Robert Pete, I really liked him a lot. He was just a very gentle man. He was terribly misunderstood because the fact that he had killed someone always came into the room before him. *Robert Pete Williams is coming in. He killed somebody, you know. He was in Angola for murder.* When people met him, that always preceded him."

On August 6–8, 1965, Dick accompanied Son House to the fifth annual Mariposa Folk Festival in Innis Lake, Canada. While there, Dick met Richard Flohil, who was hosting one of the workshops. Immediately, they became friends and, eventually, business associates.

A few weeks later, Dick booked Mississippi John Hurt to play at the Gaslight in Greenwich Village. Dick's sister, Rollene, was out of town, so he and Hurt stayed at her spacious apartment on Central Park West. One morning they stood staring out the window down onto the park and talked for a few moments. "With all the stupidity of the white liberal, I said to him, 'John, do you ever wish you had been born white instead of being born a poor Negro in the South?' That was a dumb question. He had his head down, and his hat was shaking. I thought for a moment that he was sobbing. He lifted his head, and he was *laughing.* He couldn't even control himself he was laughing so hard. He shook his head, with tears running down his face, and said, 'Woohooo! Woohoooo! Man, you white people don't know how to let it all out. When you're feelin' good or you're feelin' sorrow, you keep it all inside. The black folks, we let it all come out!' What John said is like what Rufus Thomas said about what Beale Street was like in the 1930s and '40s. He said, 'If you could be black for one Saturday night on Beale Street, you'd never go back to being white again.'"

Dick had made no plans for the day as they were not due to arrive at the Gaslight until evening, so they decided to see a double feature at the movie theater that afternoon. That night, Dick was standing off the side of the stage watching as Hurt sat in the warm glow of the spotlight tuning his guitar between songs and talking with the audience. Casually, he mentioned, "Me and Dick went to the movies this afternoon." Someone asked, "What did you see?" He looked up, thoughtfully, and said, "Well, I don't recollect, but the same boys was in both of the movies." Turning toward Dick, he said, "Dick, what was the name of them boys?"

Dick stood unmoving and speechless for a few moments. The movies they had seen were the Beatles' *Help!* and *A Hard Day's Night.* Dick had no idea how he would explain this as every eye turned toward him waiting for an answer. After a few seconds of tense silence, Hurt repeated his question. "Them boys that was in that movie. What was the name of them boys?' Finally, Dick managed to answer in a hushed voice, "The Beatles." Hurt exclaimed, "Beatles! That's what it was! The Beatles! They were playing guitar out in the snow, but I know they was funning because them guitars weren't plugged into nothing."

There was a collective gasp as shocked expressions quickly spread through the audience, and they turned to stare at Dick in disbelief. "You've got to realize that in those days there were purists. Real purists. It was blues; it was folk music. It had to be unamplified; it had to be traditional. They were very fussy, very particular. Acoustic, traditional, ethnic blues was a little island connected to nothing, certainly not four mop tops from England playing rock and roll. It was so alien. This was just heresy. It was a total bastardization of cultures. It was going to be communicable, like he was suddenly going to burst into 'Please Please Me' or something like that."

Thankfully, the audience enjoyed Hurt's music, and the remainder of the evening was less eventful for Dick. After the show, they went upstairs to the Kettle of Fish for a drink. The bartender, Tommy, knew them well and poured a shot of bourbon for John. "Tommy said, 'John, this is going to be the last time I see you because I'm leaving and going back to my father's funeral home.' John said, 'Well, I certainly do wish you well.' We finished our drinking, walked to the doorway, and Tommy called, 'See you later, John!' John said, 'Yeah, but not *too* soon!'"

A few months later, Dick received a call from a renowned manager and had the opportunity to assist a young musician in launching his career. "There was a New York manager by the name of Harold Leventhal, who was one of the old veterans in the folk management world. He managed people like Pete Seeger, Judy Collins, and Theodore Bikel. He was really a benchmark of integrity: quiet, dignified, but a really brilliant negotiator, and never raised his voice. I didn't see him but maybe every two or three years when we'd cross paths. He called me up and said, 'Dick, I need a favor.' I said, 'Anything for you, Mr. Leventhal. What can I do?' He said, 'You know, we've got Woody's [Guthrie] boy working here in the office just doing paperwork and odds and ends. He's got that itch to perform, just to put his foot in it and see if he likes it. I figured that you would know a good place. It's got to be something that's professional, but it's got to be really low level so that if he doesn't like it he can just try it and then step back and nobody ever knows.' I said, 'Okay.'

"I thought about it, and I called a club in Springfield, Massachusetts, called the Pesky Sarpent. The guy said, 'Is he any good?' I said, 'I don't know. Number 1, he's Woody Guthrie's son and Number 2, he's got Harold Leventhal's name behind him. Harold is really the gold standard among managers and agents. If Harold says, *Can you find him a weekend?* I'd do anything for Harold.' The guy said, 'Okay, I'll make you an offer of two hundred dollars for the weekend.' I said, 'Okay,' and I called Harold. Harold said, 'Yeah, that sounds fine.' So, Arlo went off and played the Pesky Sarpent."

"The next week I called Harold and said, 'How did he do?' and Harold said to me, 'To be honest with you, he didn't say much about it, but it went okay.' I said, 'Okay.' The end result is that, apparently, Arlo liked western Massachusetts because he's lived in a town called Washington, Massachusetts, ever since. He moved there shortly after, made his home there, and has raised his family there. I think Arlo has never heard of how he got his first professional date at the Pesky Sarpent."

CHAPTER 6

I Just Wasn't SATISFIED

IN APRIL 1966, SON HOUSE AND MISSISSIPPI JOHN HURT APPEARED TOgether in concert at Oberlin College and the University of Cincinnati. Dick structured the shows so both played a lengthy set during each half of the show, thus giving them time to rest between their respective sets. At the Oberlin concert, on April 15, House finished his first set and exited the stage. Dick walked to the microphone to introduce Hurt, speaking enthusiastically about him and his music. As he concluded, he turned, expecting Hurt to join him on stage. He quickly looked around and, not seeing him, began improvising more commentary. Nervously scanning the auditorium, he spied Hurt sitting in the balcony.

Dick finally said, "John, you've got to come down here." He quietly stood up, walked to the stage, and performed his set. Afterward, Dick approached him backstage and said, "What was going on? It was your turn to play. You knew you were playing. How come you weren't ready to play? You were up in the balcony listening to me." He replied, "Dick, you were saying such wonderful things about me, I just didn't want to come down [to the stage] and you stop [saying nice things about me]."

Dick was protective of the artists and quick to intervene when there was a problem. He adored Mississippi John Hurt and was concerned when he learned about the old bluesman's situation. Hurt was living on a farm tending the farm owner's cattle near Avalon, Mississippi, in 1963 when Tom Hoskins, with direction from Dick and Louisa Spottswood, met him. Hoskins had traveled to John's home, knocked on the door, introduced himself, and said he was from Washington D.C. "John had a little still in the back, and he thought Tom was a revenuer who had come to bust him." He was relieved to learn Hoskins's interest was in his music. Hoskins urged him to come to Washington D.C. to pursue a performing and recording career. "I think John was such an agreeable person he didn't want to say 'no' to anybody proposing anything." A contract was signed by the two men, and soon Hurt and his wife, Jessie, moved to Washington D.C. As Dick's relationship with Hurt grew, he learned the details surrounding the signing of the contract.

"John said to me that he really liked the man on whose farm he worked. The farmer said to John, 'If you want to leave, John, and go off and play music with this man, that's fine. I want you to know you've always got a home here. You can always come back here. I'm really fond of you and Jessie.' I remember this really well that John said to me, 'The farmer said to me, *If they ever give you any papers to sign and you don't understand them, you just bring them to me. I'll look at them and I'll have my lawyer look at them, but don't be signing nothing you don't know. I don't want them to be taking advantage of you.*' Then John said, 'Oh, Dick, my heart like to break when he said that because I had already signed a contract with Tom.' I actually saw the contract once. It's a couple pages of single-spaced type. I thought the terms were heinous, vulgar, and unacceptable."

The situation culminated in a confrontation in May 1966, involving Dick, Jerry Ricks (a musician and friend to Dick), Hurt's niece "T," and Hoskins, following Hurt's performance at Central High School in Philadelphia. Ricks had seen the contract, contacted some of Hurt's relatives in Philadelphia whom he knew, and shared his concerns about the document. Though Hoskins had not booked nor attended the performance, he appeared backstage afterward to collect his usual fee and was met by Hurt's niece. She confronted him and stated they were unhappy with his management of her uncle's career. Throughout the conversation, Hurt sat silently watching. Although he was not in disagreement with his niece, he was distressed by the discord.

"John wanted everybody to get along. He'd say, 'Why can't everybody get along? People fightin' over me and yellin' and mad and hard feelings, it stirs up my heart to have all these people do all this bad talkin'. Don't be like that, please.' The point is that John loved Tom as a person: he was from the South, he picked guitar. Tom really was easy to like, so when people would go to John and say, 'You should hate him because he's robbing you and stealing your money,' John would basically say, 'I don't want to go that way.' He hated conflict, he hated confrontation." Though Hoskins walked away, the contract between him and Hurt remained. Even if the confrontation had resulted in subsequent dissolution of the contract, it would have had little effect on Hoskins's future earnings from Hurt's performances because, sadly, the show in Philadelphia proved to be one of his last performances.

Booking for an increasing number of artists posed greater challenges. Not only was there a large amount of paperwork involved, working with some of the musicians proved difficult. One of them was Little Walter Jacobs.

"I knew he was going to be a whole lot of trouble. Fred Below, who wore a beret at a rakish angle and was drumming for Junior Wells, once said to me, 'If you gonna be workin' this scene man, I gotta put you hip to Walter. Walter will mess with you. Walter will mess with your gig, he'll mess with your car, and he'll mess with your woman. Walter will mess you around. You cannot trust that cat, so if you come in here and Walter messes with you, you can't complain to me because I set you hip to Walter.'" Dick soon learned Below's warning was justified.

Jacobs had been playing with Muddy Waters's band, and Junior Wells had been playing with a group known as the Aces. Then, Wells left the group to join Waters, and Jacobs left Waters's band to join the Aces.

"I had Walter with a trio called the Aces, which was Louis Myers on guitar, his brother, Dave Myers, on bass, and Fred Below on drums. I had booked them on a West Coast tour and the last date was at the Keystone Club in Berkeley. There was a Keystone in North Beach, San Francisco, and another one in Berkeley at the top of University Avenue near the campus. Walter was opening for somebody, and at the end of the gig, Walter says, 'I'm going upstairs to get the money.' The other guys are shooting pool. The headliner goes on and then off, the janitors are sweeping up, and finally someone comes and says, 'That's it, guys. You gotta get out of here. We're locking up.' They said, 'No, we're waiting for Walter. He went upstairs to get paid.' The guy said, 'The harmonica player? He's gone, man. He left hours ago.'

"'What you talkin' about? He went upstairs to get the money.'

"'Yeah, well, he's gone.'

"'Gone! Where'd he go?'

"'Well, he got a ride to the airport.'

"'Airport?! What you talkin' about?'

"'Yeah, he was taking the red eye back to Chicago.'

"'Chicago?!'"

Walter took the money, went to the airport, went back to Chicago, and left them stranded. They had to sell something to get money to ride the bus home. It may have been Louis's amplifier. They spent two days on the bus knowing they were going to rip him apart. They got back on Monday night and they knew that on "Blue Monday" he would be at a certain club. They walk in and Walter's sitting at the bar. They are ready to kill him. Walter turns, and Walter stutters, and he says, 'M-m-man, am I g-g-glad to see you guys! What happened to you, m-m-man? I was afraid something happened to you.' They looked at him, they looked at each other, and said, 'He messed us up again.' They just fell out laughing at all the stupidity. He did it again!

Walter was such a nasty, unlikable person. He was just evil, but he was evil to the point that he was consistently evil. He was totally untrustworthy."

Unfortunately, more incidents followed. "There was a club opening in the Back Bay section of Boston. This club wanted to hit the ground running with somebody who hadn't been to Boston in a while and would make the public pay attention. They were opening with Little Walter, and I had arranged the booking. I sent Walter the money for him and the guitar, bass, and drum players.

"I went to meet the flight. We were cutting it close by meeting at like 7:00 or 7:30 P.M. and going right to the gig. I go to the gate, and Walter comes off the plane. I said, 'Hi, Walter. How ya doin'?' We hug, and then we stand there until there are no more people coming off. The crew and pilot come off, and then they lock the door. I turned to Walter and I said, 'Walter, where's the band?' I'll never forget what he said to me. He said, 'Man, it's a messed-up thing.' I said, 'Messed-up thing? Where's the band?!' He said, 'Man, you can't count on them people, you know.' I said, 'There's no band?' He said, 'Nah, man. No band.' *Ack!* I ran to a payphone, called the club, and I said, 'He's got no band. Get a guitar, bass, and drum [player]. Find them somewhere. We're on our way over!' The guy said, 'Dick, it's Friday night! Every good musician is already working tonight.' I said, 'Just find me guitar, bass, and drums because we're on our way.'

"Walter's totally relaxed because that's just the way he worked. We get to the club and by showtime, 8:30 P.M. or so, I've got three strangers that don't know each other. One plays guitar, one plays bass, and one plays drums. I introduce them to Little Walter. Walter says to them, 'Do you know "My Babe?"' It's a basic 'Bar Band 101.' They said, 'Yeah.' He said, 'Do you know "Juke?"' It's an instrumental piece. They nod. Walter looks at me and says, 'It's cool, man.' Somebody says to Walter, 'What key do you play "My Babe" in?' Walter says, 'Whatever. I go with you.' They get on stage and hit it, and it's raggedy, but because of the fact that Little Walter is there, the crowd doesn't care. They played a set, and by the second night, they were good. He wasn't stretching anybody, he was just doing down-home Chicago blues right out of Muddy's band.

"He gets paid in cash, and then he and I go to the Swarthmore Folk Festival [April 1–2, 1966, featuring Son House and Tom Rush]. He goes and plays, and then he's going to a party. I'm not up for partying on the college level, so I said, 'I'm going back to the room.' We were staying in dorm rooms. I go back, and I was sleeping when there was banging on the door. It was about three o'clock in the morning. I open the door, and it's Walter with some guys. He said, 'I lost my money!' I said, "What do you mean you lost your money?' He said, 'Coming back from the party I had to take a piss, so they stopped [the car]. I was out in the bushes, and when I got back in the car I had lost my money.' I said, 'What money? The money from Boston or money from tonight?' He said, 'Both.' *Great.* It's almost four in the morning and I'm out there walking through the Pennsylvania landscape looking for a shiny leaf that Walter pissed on. We didn't find the money."

Sometimes the logistics of travel and idiosyncrasies of the performers proved complicated and tedious, even when the person was a dear friend. Dick booked Mississippi John Hurt to play at the Café Lena in Saratoga Springs, New York, on the weekend of July 8, but getting him to the venue was far more difficult than he had imagined.

"This is so unbelievable. I had a flight booked for him from Memphis to Philadelphia and then we would go to the café. I spoke to him in the morning [the day of the performance]. I said, 'Okay, just get the bus from Grenada to Memphis, take a cab to the airport and your flight will be ready.' He said, 'I can't do that. I never did that before.' I said, 'Do what?' He said, 'Ride in a taxi cab by myself.' I said, 'It isn't hard,' but he wouldn't do it. He couldn't do it. He said, 'You got to come get me.' I said, 'What?!' He said, 'You got to come and get me at the bus station.' Craziness! John took cabs with people but apparently he never took them alone. Maybe it was a social thing. It was just something that he had never done.

"I bought a ticket from Philadelphia to Memphis and took a cab to the bus station. I got there just before he arrived. I grabbed him, took a cab back to the Memphis airport, and flew to Philadelphia. We got in my car and drove from Philadelphia up the Garden State Parkway and then connected to the New York Throughway. I got in the left lane and went about eighty-five or ninety miles per hour all the way. It's over two hundred and fifty miles. I raced, driving like crazy all the way to the Saratoga turnoff. I knew where the club was, so we drove there and got a parking space. I grabbed John and the guitar. We walked across the street, walked in the door, started up the stairs, and at the top was Lena. She was a crotchety, old fuss-budget lady. She spoke in a high, nervous voice. She looked down and said, 'Now, Dick, we like to have our acts come a little early and not show up at the last minute like this.' And I said, 'Yes, ma'am.' We got there *just* at showtime."

After the show, they were pleasantly surprised to find a soul food restaurant, Hattie's Chicken Shack. It was located on the first floor in the same building as the café and was still open. They were tired and hungry after a long day, so they decided to have a late dinner. "John got to talking with the old black owner and his wife. They really hit it off. I brought the guitar in, it was only a little bitty place, and John sat there and did a couple of songs for them."

As Dick's reputation grew, he received more calls from festivals and venues searching for acts. He often helped promote artists' work who were not Avalon clients. "It was just always very loose. If I got a call from a festival and was asked to put together two nights with four or five acts per night, then I called guys I didn't ordinarily manage. I was kind of benevolent about spreading the work around."

He also was generous in regard to the commission he earned from them. If he booked a club date for them, he took no management fee. Only when he booked them at venues, mostly festivals, where they would earn several hundred dollars did he accept any compensation. Such was the genesis of his professional relationship with Booker White. Unfortunately, he did not receive the same loyalty from White as he did from most of his regular artists.

Dick had invited White to stay with him at his Cambridge apartment before departing on a short tour. Beginning in Springfield, he would play a few dates and conclude the tour in Memphis. Dick was careful with routing to avoid an exhausting travel schedule. White would earn three to five hundred dollars per concert, totaling a few thousand dollars by the time he returned home.

Typically, Dick received feedback from venues regarding performances, but there had not been a single call regarding White by the end of the tour. He found this peculiar, but dismissed it. During a conversation with a friend from Massachusetts following the tour, he learned that White had another performance scheduled at a club he had recently played during the tour. Surprised, Dick contacted the club owner. The owner said White had requested to be called directly for future booking, and complained, "Dick Waterman don't play no music. Dick Waterman wasn't the one sweating on stage. Dick Waterman didn't do anything but stay at home and take 10 percent of my money." White handed the man his home address and telephone number. After a few calls, Dick learned he had done this same thing in every club he played during the tour.

While Dick was booking the tour, he had arranged for White to appear in a CBC production titled "Festival Presents the Blues," which was being booked by Manny Greenhill. After agreeing that White would be paid five hundred dollars for his performance, Dick also requested that he receive an additional payment of five hundred dollars if a subsequent show was ever produced from the video footage. Greenhill believed a second show highly unlikely, so he agreed to Dick's request.

The first show was so successful that a second show soon was in production. White, being the only artist whose contract contained an agreement stipulating additional compensation, received another five-hundred-dollar payment. The check was sent to Dick, who deducted his 10 percent management fee and forwarded the remainder to White. Dick was pleased that his forethought had resulted in White earning twice as much as had been expected and assumed White also would be happy with the extra funds. Unfortunately, that was not the case.

White, disgruntled that Dick was receiving a percentage of the money he considered to be his, found an audience for his complaints. In an era when many white liberals suspected all white people managing black artists of exploitation and thievery, it required only a few disparaging remarks from White to incite a letter of complaint to the CBC in Toronto insisting White be paid the money withheld from him. Immediately, the letter was forwarded to Dick since the CBC was not privy to the managerial arrangement between him and White, and they were not interested in becoming involved in the dispute.

The letter arrived approximately the same time Dick learned of White's request for club owners to bypass Dick and call him directly. Dick was offended and angry that White would be so disloyal. He decided to settle the matter and knew exactly where to find White because he had scheduled him to appear at the 1966 Newport Folk Festival the following week.

Dick spotted him performing at an afternoon workshop. He strode across the grounds, stood directly in front of White, held up a fifty-dollar bill, and placed it in the pocket of White's shirt. "I said, 'Here is your money. Don't you ever speak my name again until they throw dirt over your dead body.' I made myself stare at him until he turned his head away. I never spoke to him again. I just couldn't trust him and, if I had people I could trust, I couldn't have Booker around. He was going to poison the well. He had to go."

Their working relationship was severed, but White soon faced hostility from other musicians who were loyal to Dick. One of Dick's friends witnessed two heated encounters, which he relayed to Dick. A few months after Dick had confronted White at Newport, White was in Berkeley, California, performing at a festival. Robert Pete Williams also was one of the scheduled musicians. The two were in a backstage area lounging on couches across the room from each other. White commenced loudly denouncing Dick. Williams had been drinking, and after witnessing a few moments of the tirade, he came to Dick's defense, shouting back at White. Within moments, a loud, angry exchange was in progress.

"They got up off of their couches. They both were very big, muscular, heavy, older, black men. They started at each other. Robert was saying, 'Don't you say a word against Mr. Richard! Mr. Richard is my man!' Robert wore cowboy boots. He reached down into his boot, came up, and snapped open a long straight-edge razor. He lifted it up head high and said, 'You dare not talk a bad word on Mr. Richard!' There was silence in the room, because Robert had killed before. He had shot somebody with a pistol. No doubt Robert was capable of it. He had been drinking and was under a full head of rage. [Booker also had served time in prison for murder.] Booker made a quick evaluation of this and backed down. He said, 'I ain't got no time for this.'"

Weeks later, this same scenario was repeated at another festival. White was playing at the University of New Hampshire in Durham along with other artists including Mississippi Fred McDowell. Once again, he was sitting backstage complaining bitterly about Dick to anyone who would listen.

"Fred hears him and says, 'What you saying about Dick? You can't be talking bad about Dick!' Booker started to give him some mouth and Fred got up off the couch and headed at him. Fred was small and wiry, like a bantam rooster. Booker headed at him, and Fred went into his boot and pulled out a screwdriver sharpened to a needle point. Booker must have thought, 'I'm never going to get rid of Dick Waterman.'" Onlookers realized the exchange was rapidly deteriorating into a dangerous situation, so some fellow musicians stepped in and pulled the two away from each other.

The entire matter was regrettable on multiple levels. Dick had been unwavering in his efforts to assist White's career and steadfastly loyal to him, even to the point of defending him during a confrontation with Peter Guralnick a few weeks prior. Guralnick was at Club 47 one evening when he saw Dick approaching. Anticipating Dick's usual genial greeting, he was stunned when Dick's demeanor darkened and he abruptly said, "I ought to punch you in the face." He stood, perplexed, as Dick proceeded to question him regarding comments he had made that had appeared in the British publication *Blues Unlimited.*

Guralnick explains, "I was in touch with the editor of *Blues Unlimited,* the first blues magazine [founded in 1963] in England. The editors were Simon Napier and Mike Leadbitter, but I had never seen the magazine before, despite many efforts. I sent in my subscription. I would write letters back and forth, but there was some glitch in their subscription system, which was basically there was no subscription system. There was Simon and there was Mike, and they did a ton of different things. So, it took a long time for my subscription to become an active one even though, in the end, I got all the issues.

"I'm writing these letters, and I would tell them what was going on in Boston. I wrote about seeing Booker White and what a disappointment it was because he was a fat, garrulous old man. Now, this was in a letter which I had no thought of ever being in print or I would never have written that way. It turned out that during the many months when I was corresponding and never seeing the magazine, they were running portions of my letters as news from the Boston blues scene. So, Dick came up to me and said, 'Did you write in *Blues Unlimited* that Booker White was a fat, garrulous old man?' I said, 'No,' having no concept of having done that. He said, 'Well, that's what I read in *Blues Unlimited*.' I was really taken aback because it never occurred to me this would be in print or that I would be responsible for something I didn't write for print."

The animus was fleeting, as the matter was resolved and became a source of humor between the two. Dick later confessed to Guralnick that he shared some of these same sentiments regarding White, passing off his initial hostility as, "He may have been a fat, garrulous old man, but he was *my* fat, garrulous old man."

The encounter with White at the 1966 Newport festival, held July 21–24, was only one of a series of frustrating events that week. Dick and Son House were standing on the festival grounds when they saw Alan Lomax. Lomax had recorded House in Mississippi in both 1941 and 1942 while on research trips for the Library of Congress. Afterward, House's whereabouts remained unknown in the blues world until his rediscovery by Dick and his companions in 1964.

"I knew Lomax on sight but I don't think we ever had a conversation. He was a famous man because the Lomax family was very famous, and he was on the Newport board of directors. I was just a lowly guy out of the folk world, and there was no reason for us to cross paths."

House recognized Lomax, leaned toward Dick, and said, "There's that old booger, Lomax." Lomax approached, extended his hand, and said, "How are you, Son? Still living by the bridge in Rochester?" Shaking his hand, House nodded affirmatively. Dick was speechless. Finally, mustering the courage to question Lomax, he asked if Lomax had known where House had been living in the years since those 1940s recordings. Lomax admitted that, indeed, he had known, and House nodded again.

Shocked, Dick wondered why Lomax had known his whereabouts all along and had not assisted him in furthering his musical career. When Dick asked him, Lomax shrugged and simply replied, "After I recorded him, it wasn't any of my business what he did with his life. My job was to record him for the Library of Congress. I didn't care what he did after that." He turned and walked away as Dick stared after him in disbelief. Dick did not know at the time that Lomax actually had offered to assist House in joining with a music group in New York many years earlier, but House chose instead to take a position with the railroad.

Unfortunately, the encounter was a harbinger of a troubling situation resulting from personnel changes in the Newport administration that year. The advisory team served three-year terms. Thus the years of 1963–1965 were governed by the same board. A new regime was in charge of the 1966 festival, which gave control of the blues performances to Lomax. Lomax scheduled Booker White, Skip James, and Son House to appear on stage simultaneously at one of the evening concerts. It was not intended as a collaborative performance, but rather a competitive one.

Still in the early years of his management career and intimidated by Lomax's reputation and the power he wielded at the festival, Dick was both vexed and wholly uncertain how to rectify the problem. Neither Lomax, nor anyone else for that matter, had discussed with Dick the matter of the three men playing together. He was informed only of the minutes allotted the performers and was expected to have them on stage at the appropriate time.

He sought out Pete Seeger's wife, Toshi. After a lengthy discussion, she assured him she was sympathetic to his plight, but did not have the power necessary to circumvent Lomax. He approached several others, but the response was the same. The blues portions of the festival were Lomax's domain, and no one was willing to overrule him.

The bluesmen also were unhappy with the arrangement. Dick expressed his disdain to House but did not mention it to the others. From an artistic perspective, Dick knew it was ill conceived and, ultimately, ill fated. The three men had diverse playing and performance styles. Each primarily created his own material and they had never rehearsed together. Nevertheless, Dick's attempts to thwart what he knew would be a debacle proved unsuccessful.

House, James, and White filed onto a raised pallet on the stage, with White standing on the right, James on the left, and House between them. "Skip was playing an acoustic, wooden guitar. Skip picked very lightly and very fast. Son played a steel body guitar, but played slowly, dragging the slide. Booker, very strong and muscular, was playing on a steel body National guitar also. He was playing very loud and fast and singing very loud."

The trio finished the first song and had begun the second when House quietly, but unmistakably, demonstrated his contempt for the entire matter and signaled his refusal to continue. "Son stood up, moved his chair, and stepped down from the pallet onto the back of the stage. He came around behind Booker, in front of Booker, three quarters of the way across, and sat down on the pallet with fifteen thousand people to his left. He put his guitar down, crossed his left leg over his right, reached for a cigarette, and sat there and smoked a cigarette in front of fifteen thousand people with his back to the others."

"Most blues artists weren't interested in hearing other blues artists. They took pride in writing their own material. They had passed through all of life's battles, and they had come out the other end as survivors. They took an amount of pride in their own creations. The songsters, like John

Hurt and Mance Lipscomb, liked to listen to others, but the really intense bluesmen—Son, Skip, Booker—they didn't have any interest in the songs of another bluesman. If they were seated in a semicircle around the stage, they *might* listen or pretend to listen.

"When I look at it now from the viewpoint of forty-five to fifty years in the blues business, a member of the Blues Hall of Fame, and with some degree of influence and respect, I think, 'Why didn't I just say my guys are not going up?' Because he was Alan Lomax and I was Dick Waterman. My voice was like a strand of wheat in a hurricane. He was not going to be denied. I was so intimidated by Lomax."

House was scheduled to perform at a blues workshop the following day. Unfortunately, he was away from Dick's watchful eye just prior to the performance, and his alcoholism spiraled out of control. Dick was staying at a different location during the festival than House and his wife. The Newport Foundation had vehicles to transport performers to the grounds, so House was to arrive by van for his workshop on Saturday. John Koerner, of the music trio Koerner, Ray, and Glover, was the driver.

Dick was already on the grounds when the van arrived. Koerner exited, visibly upset, and approached Dick saying he had made a mistake and apologizing profusely. Confused, Dick listened as Koerner related the story of their short trip to the grounds. "He said, 'Son said that it was okay if we stopped at the wine store and I gave him . . .' I said 'Oh, shit. Don't even finish the story.'

"I turn around, and Son was getting out of the vehicle. He was leaning up against the door. He had this goofy smile on his face, and she [Evie] was wild. Son was standing there swaying, and he's pointing his finger out and saying, 'I fooled you this time. I got me some rye.' He was just plastered. He absolutely *couldn't* go on. He was falling down. He was just totally drunk. Mrs. House was clucking at me, 'How could you let this man do this? It's your fault.' I said, 'I wasn't even there!' I turned to Koerner and said, 'Look, man, performing is the way we make our living. This is a big-time fuck up.' Koerner was totally crushed and beside himself over what he had done."

Dick was concerned because House's inability to perform could hinder future bookings. Few television shows at the time featured blues artists, so they relied largely on live performances for their livelihood. "You got your bookings playing live by doing well at the major festivals, and the biggest festival of all was Newport. If you went up and laid down an incredibly great fifteen minutes at Newport, you could get enough bookings to do very well for many months or through the whole year."

Arrangements quickly were made for Muddy Waters to serve as his replacement, and he even played a couple of House's songs. Those sitting in the audience eagerly awaiting House's appearance on stage were told he was ill. It was suggested he be added to that evening's lineup of performers, but scheduling proved problematic, so a decision was made that he should appear alongside Skip James on Sunday at the Religious Music Concert.

Perhaps the most disturbing situation at the festival was the performance, of sorts, Lomax arranged. It included Son House, Howling Wolf, Skip James, Booker White, and Reverend Pearly Brown with the intention of recreating a juke joint atmosphere. Although Dick was managing some of the artists, Lomax never spoke with him about the evening before or after it occurred.

"The Newport Festival board had brought the bluesmen to Newport at their expense. Lomax got an empty mansion or something that had a room, and he sent cars to bring the bluesmen to this room. He put out bottles of liquor and just filmed it as it happened. I didn't even know about it until decades later when the film was released. I never watched it from beginning to end. I know that Son is very drunk, and Wolf scolds him.

"It happened at night after everybody had gone back to where they were staying. Lomax had them picked up and brought to the location. They just thought it was part of the festival. I later spoke to a friend who was a major festival organizer, and he said the board didn't realize it until decades later, and they were upset that Lomax had used their bringing of the men to Newport as an opportunity to profit."

Over time, a few artists were added to the Avalon roster, but Dick continued doing freelance writing whenever possible. His management earnings were modest at best, and he was aware this venture might continue only for a short time. "I was going to go back to being a sports writer. I was going to give this management thing a year or two." His situation began to change as the result of a conversation he had with Bob Koester, founder of Delmark Records in Chicago. Koester pointed out that, although artists like Howling Wolf and Muddy Waters toured, there were several young blues musicians who were not touring, but would welcome such an opportunity.

"I said, 'Okay, you find me one who's honest, talented, motivated, really wants to get out there, and is somebody I can trust.' He said, 'I just released an album called *Hoodoo Man* [*Blues*] by Junior Wells, and he's the one. He's really good. He's honest and hardworking.' I made an agreement with Koester that I would book Junior, so I booked three or four dates for him." Without having met Wells, Dick scheduled performances for him at the 1966 Philadelphia Folk Festival, a club in New York, and Club 47 in Cambridge, Massachusetts.

The Philadelphia Folk Festival was in August, so he planned to meet Wells there to give him the contracts for the remaining performances. Upon arrival, he walked to the backstage area in search of Wells. "There were four or five black guys standing around in long trench coats and looking very serious. I started to talk to them about contracts, and one of them said, 'You gotta talk to Junior.' I said, 'I thought *you* were Junior.' He said, 'No, *he's* Junior,' and pointed back over his shoulder."

Wells was sitting alone at the back of the tent smoking a cigarette when Dick walked over and sat down. "I said to him, 'Do you want to sign a contract?' And he said, 'Do you want one?' I said, 'I don't care, it doesn't matter to me.' He looked at me and said, 'Koester says you're a righteous dude, and I can trust you. You make a dollar for me, and I make a dollar for you.' We shook hands and never had paper [a contract] between us."

Junior Wells's band was the first band Dick managed, and it was the catalyst for a significant shift in his financial situation. The older bluesmen played in venues such as folk clubs and coffeehouses, most of which did not serve alcohol. Wells, however, performed mostly in bars and lounges. Patrons came to drink and dance, and artists generally earned more money playing these venues. Wells also was considerably more popular with younger crowds than Son House, and he had just recorded *Hoodoo Man Blues.*

"When I got Junior Wells, I was suddenly booking a band for a thousand to fifteen hundred dollars per appearance. Holy shit! Making 10 percent of that, I was making *hundreds* of dollars! If I put Junior out and he worked a couple of nights in succession, I'd make two or three hundred dollars. I could live for months on a couple hundred dollars."

A pivotal moment in his career came during a backstage encounter with a blues legend. Shortly after Wells became a client, a few other bands signed with Avalon. One was scheduled as an opening act at a concert at Notre Dame. To his dismay, they arrived late, and their performance was underwhelming. Upon exiting the stage, they walked to a communal dressing room where other performers were waiting to go on stage. Exasperated, Dick stomped over, stared at the leader, and said, "When you go up there, all of my artists go up there with you. Son House goes up. Junior Wells goes up. Your success is our success, and your failure is our failure. You screwed up. You weren't ready to play."

There was little the young man could say as he knew Dick's words were justified. As the musician dropped his head and walked away, Dick felt the eyes of everyone in the room on him. He realized they had witnessed the exchange and the embarrassment of a fellow black musician. Although what he said was true, he was dismayed by the manner in which it had transpired.

As he turned to leave, he caught sight of a lone figure sitting at a table calmly shuffling a deck of cards. It was Muddy Waters. Waters looked at him and motioned for Dick to join him at the table. Though they were not well acquainted, Dick walked over and sat down beside him. Waters placed the deck of cards on the table, leaned back, and stared directly into his eyes. With his familiar vocal cadence loud enough to be heard by all those standing nearby, he said, "Now, I heard what you said to the boy, and the boy had it coming to him. Boy didn't show no respect for the people. Boy didn't come ready to play. You done right. You told the boy what he needed to hear. Now, I been watching you, and you just keep on keeping on like you been doin,' and you'll be just fine." In that instant, Dick knew he would never return to the life of a newspaper reporter. Waters's words were all he needed to convince him to pursue this career. "If I was all right by Muddy Waters, I was going to do just fine."

Although Waters had given Dick his blessing, it would take time for him to earn the trust of others, including aspiring young blues artist Taj Mahal. His first encounter with Dick was in the mid-1960s at Club 47. Mahal, who was pursuing a bachelor's degree in animal husbandry at the University of Massachusetts, was playing at a Sunday evening hootenanny. Dick was the unofficial photographer at the club, so he was there almost every evening. Though Mahal was a relative newcomer to the blues scene, he had access to many of the older black blues musicians of the mid-1960s and quickly developed friendships with some of them. Consequently, he was aware of the ill treatment suffered by some of the older artists, so he assumed the mantle of protector. He kept a watchful eye on the white people with whom they had business dealings, and that included Dick.

Mahal comments, "Oftentimes, the handlers didn't really know how to work with these people. I never failed to say to Dick, 'How are you treating the folks these days?' I didn't realize he was intimidated by the whole thing. I just was saying that because I was concerned, and I spoke directly to him because I felt that if nobody spoke up then I sure was. I guess, looking back, I did take it upon myself to make sure that I looked out for them as much as I could."

Despite the fact that Mahal was an intimidating presence, Dick did his best to appear unruffled. "Taj would say, 'I'm watching you. I'm checking on you.' He was big. I would always say, 'I do what I do, and your presence isn't going to change me.' I wouldn't see him for a while, but it was always the same. He would get right up to me, chest to chest, and he'd say, loudly, 'What are you doing for the folks?' He never smiled. He stayed right with me. Once we passed about 1995, he backed off a little, but the first thirty years were tough."

Mahal admits that, over time, Dick earned his respect. "Little by little, he separated himself from the other people by the fact the people he had cared for were taken care of. He was extremely attentive and, ultimately, very knowledgeable. A lot of these other guys you couldn't get close to, and you couldn't get close to the people that they were handling either. He was somebody I could really talk to. Dick was one of the people that I kept a really sharp eye on, and he never disappointed me. Not one time."

On the return trip from the Philadelphia Folk Festival, Dick and Son House stopped by the Gaslight in Greenwich Village to watch John Hammond Jr. perform. Like his father, Hammond was an admirer of Robert Johnson's music. "John knew that Son had been rediscovered and that I was coming to New York with him on the way back to Rochester. He'd never seen Son [in person]. The Gaslight is a long, narrow club and the aisle to backstage went right along the edge of the stage. It was all dark, but there was a little pool of light over the stage. As you walked backstage, you walked into the pool of light. I was walking, and Son was behind me. John was between songs, and he looked up. His eyes got big, and he said, 'Is it?' I said, 'It is.' I introduced them later. It totally blew John away."

On November 2, 1966, Dick experienced a sudden and profound personal loss when Mississippi John Hurt suffered a fatal heart attack and died. Almost a year earlier, Hurt had moved from Washington, DC, where he had been living with his wife, Jessie, and two of their grandchildren. He had never felt comfortable raising the children in that environment, fearing the negative influence of crime, violence, and gang presence, so he returned to Mississippi and settled in Grenada, near his hometown of Avalon. The man who had inspired Dick's explorations in the world of the blues and, most importantly, who had become a beloved friend, was gone.

"I didn't have money to go to his funeral. I've always regretted that. I went to my father and asked if I could borrow the money to fly to Mississippi and my father said, 'You know, this just doesn't seem to be worthwhile.' My father did not refuse me anything I really wanted, he just didn't understand this.

"John had the ability to communicate one on one. He could look at you and you would melt. He had a wonderful smile. His speaking voice was very low and husky, very gravelly, but his singing voice was very high and clear. He also had the ability to be a little bit risqué and naughty. He could slip a double entendre lyric past you, and then you suddenly realized what he had said. He had that sly wink naughtiness. Like he would really talk about it, but he wouldn't really do it.

"John's personality was so outgoing, compelling, and winning that you just fell in love with him. He was beyond age, race, demographics, anything. Everyone loved John Hurt and those musicians who met him were profoundly moved by him. He was just a sweet man. Nobody could ever say anything negative about him. He was a great musician, and he told wonderful stories."

CHAPTER 7

CHANGE My Way of LIVING

THE FOLLOWING YEAR WAS A FLURRY OF ACTIVITY AS THE CLIENT LIST of Avalon grew. "About 1966–67 things started to happen really fast. The psychedelic ballrooms, the summer of love, Hendrix in London with the trio, Junior was out on the road, Buddy was out on the road, then Junior was going overseas on the State Department tour."

He booked Junior Wells to play at the Fillmore Auditorium, a psychedelic ballroom in San Francisco, on January 13–15, 1967, alongside the Grateful Dead and the Doors. Such venues were different from the bars and clubs to which the blues artists were accustomed. The ballrooms were an amalgam of swirling lights and colors projected onto screens, creating stunning visual effects. Some also featured mirror balls, strobe lighting, and "floating" dance floors, which served to heighten the hallucinogenic experience for patrons who indulged in LSD.

At the same time, Dick was working on a new venture. He had been asked to book musicians for the Swarthmore College Folk Festival in Swarthmore, Pennsylvania, scheduled for March 10–11, 1967. As the dates drew near, one of the musicians canceled, so he hastily searched for a suitable replacement. A few days later, he saw Richie Havens.

"I first met Richie Havens when I was bringing bluesmen into Greenwich Village, maybe around 1964 or so. He was the house opening act at the Café Au Go-Go on Bleeker Street. He got five dollars a set, but he never knew if he was going to get a second set because it depended on whether enough customers wandered into the place and owner Howard Solomon decided to let it [the music] run a little longer.

"I had a late cancellation for the festival, so I asked Richie if he wanted to do the gig. I told him that I'd pick him up in New York City, drive down for the gig, and come back later that same night. He asked me about the money, and I told him that I had four hundred dollars set aside for him. He moved his lips but no sound came out. I looked at him, and he nodded his head. On the night of the gig, I picked him up in the Village, and we drove down for the festival. He played a magnificent set, ending with a stunning version of 'Follow' as he got up from the stool and slowly sang his way toward the edge of the curtain.

"I had arranged for him to be paid in cash, and he got 20 twenty-dollar bills from my hand into his. He looked at it and just started to laugh. It was a totally wonderful full-body laugh with his head back. He had a roadie friend with him, and we were driving on the New Jersey turnpike. I hadn't eaten, so we stopped at a rest area restaurant. We went in, and I ordered a meal. I don't think Richie had anything at all. Richie went over to the cash register and asked the cashier if she had small bills because he wanted to change the twenties. She broke the money down into fives and tens, and Richie went off to sit by himself while I ate a meal. I looked over and he was just sitting there counting the money over and over. He would shuffle it together and count it again. He lifted it, put it back onto the table, and stared at it. We were there maybe twenty minutes and then got back into the car. He was just joyful."

Following his performances that January in San Francisco, Wells played a series of dates in Old Town, an area on the north side of Chicago with an entertainment district that was popular among white audiences. A representative from the US government approached him and Dick with an offer for Wells to play at Expo '67 in Montreal, Canada, the city chosen to host a world's fair coinciding with Canada's one hundredth anniversary.

It was an impressive event located on two islands in the St. Lawrence River and open from April through October. Wells's performances at the American Pavilion, a stunning geodesic dome designed by Buckminster Fuller, garnered him a much more substantial offer. The representative was so pleased with the band's performance, Wells received an invitation to appear on a US State Department tour of Africa scheduled to begin in November 1967. He accepted without hesitation.

While Dick watched Wells perform one evening, a young blues musician entered the club carrying a guitar. Dick had heard his name before, Buddy Guy, and it was not long until he secured Guy as a client. A native of Louisiana, Guy had relocated to Chicago and worked as a mechanic and tow truck driver by day. In the evenings, he was a studio musician at Chess Records in Chicago playing with such artists as Etta James, Little Esther Phillips, and Little Walter. Though he enjoyed playing, music was only a part-time job. "Buddy had a wife and kids and a job. If he had a night off, he didn't want to go play in the bars. Buddy was never an eager participant in the Chicago club circuit like Junior Wells or Otis Rush. They would play three or four nights each week. He had better things to do than hang around in clubs."

Blues fans were introduced to Guy's work through his Chess singles such as "Stone Crazy" and "When My Left Eye Jumps," but he had never recorded an album of his own work. He and Wells were friends, so he had played on Wells's 1965 Delmark album *Hoodoo Man Blues.* At the time, Guy was under contract with Chess and, although Leonard Chess gave his approval for him to play on the sessions, he would not agree to Guy's name appearing in the credits. Thus, he was listed as "Friendly Chap" on the album.

Initially, Guy was content to earn a secondary income as a musician. Dick was arranging increasing amounts of work for Junior Wells. He believed that Guy could succeed as a full-time musician. He just needed to convince Guy. "He wasn't looking to travel, and he wasn't looking to expand his career. He didn't have a lot of ambition. He was living an okay life. He had a day job and was picking up money with sessions at night. I think it was Junior's success that showed Buddy that money could be made on the road."

Guy remembers his first meeting with Dick. "I had heard about him 'cause Junior and I were friends. He had found out that I did quite a few records with Junior and Muddy as a studio man. He came and found me, and I was up under one of those big ole tractor trailers. Well, this truck was too big to jack up, so I had to use a creeper. Some guy bent over and said, 'You know you could lose a finger doing that.' And I say, 'Well, I'm not going to rob and steal,' because I'm not ready for no conversation with nobody 'cause I was working anyways. So he said, 'I'm Dick Waterman. I manage Junior.' I said, 'Oh yeah, I know who you are.'

"He invited me to lunch. We sat down, and he kind of explained to me what he wanted from me. He wanted to know how much I was making, which was $2.11 an hour, and he invited me on the road. Well, I was skeptical about going on the road 'cause I had done tried two or three trips before I took my day job. Some promoters would invite you out there, and you wasn't paid. Texas, Louisiana, the few places I went, percentage-wise I got paid less than I got paid all the time [at his day job]. Well, he said I'll write you a postdated check if you want to go out on the road and guarantee you as much money as you'll make in a year at this thing. I still was skeptical about it so I said, 'I tell you what, I'm going to take a two-week vacation in September, and I'll give it a try.' We agreed, and he booked me in Ann Arbor, Toronto, Boston, and, I think, Rochester."

The audiences at the venues Dick booked for him were different from those to which he was accustomed. Guy had no idea blues music was so popular with white audiences. "When I got to Ann Arbor there was 98 to 99 percent white [people]. I had never seen that before. It went over pretty well and I'm saying, 'Wow! I didn't know this many white people knew anything about the type of blues we play,' 'cause we were playing around here [Chicago] and if I saw a white face *I* thought it was a cop because they would come in the black joints. A lot of times it was Paul Butterfield, Michael Bloomfield, Charlie Musselwhite, or Steve Miller. These guys were just coming over picking up what we were doing."

When Guy played the Mariposa Folk Festival at Toronto on August 11–13, 1967, he again found himself before a predominantly white audience, but this time it was far larger than he expected. "We left and went to Toronto and, of course, I had never seen that many people listening to music before. It was like thirty thousand people!"

The larger venues, particularly the festivals, were sources of unprecedented income for him. Playing club dates, Guy often earned little more than thirty dollars per night. "Those places where the blues festivals were coming up, he [Dick] would put us in and we made a few extra bucks more than we were making at the colleges. I had never made five hundred to six hundred dollars a gig before in my life!"

Unlike Son House, Guy did not require Dick's undivided attention when they traveled. Working with House, however, was a learning experience that had forced Dick to become more skilled at handling issues faced by some of the older performers. While at the Mariposa Festival, Dick was asked to assist Reverend Gary Davis, who was not one of his clients. Dick had met Davis years earlier in Greenwich Village and was happy to oblige.

"He [Davis] was from South Carolina and on the New York scene before I was there. By the time I came along, he had a lot of albums out, mostly gospel. He was a great guitarist with a unique style and a powerful vocalist. He lived in Astoria, a suburb of Queens, and he took private students. The fact that he gave lessons was pretty important. People like Danny Kalb of the Blues Project, Dave Van Ronk, Stefan Grossman, Rory Block, and others took lessons from him, so the Reverend's style was really stamped in the Village in the 1960s. Jorma Kaukonen of Jefferson Airplane and, later, Hot Tuna was wild about Reverend. People who like John Hurt like Reverend Davis because it's the same attraction of the finger picking style.

"I got to Mariposa with Buddy, and he was playing on Saturday. It was a three-day festival, and the Reverend had played on Friday and had gotten very drunk. He had really embarrassed himself. The woman running the festival, Estelle Klein, came to me and said, 'You've got to help me. The Reverend got very drunk last night and played very badly. We're all very nervous because he's got to play again on Sunday. He needs somebody to take care of him.' I said, 'Okay.'

"He was Manny Greenhill's act. I loved Manny and would do anything for him. In those days there was no competition. You didn't want the other guy's artist to do badly. You wanted everyone to do well because there weren't that many of them.

"I went in the room where he was sitting and said, 'Hi, Reverend. It's Dick Waterman. How are you doing?' Then I said, 'I understand you had some problems last night?' He said, 'The devil got to me. The devil tempted me, and I fell to temptation. I drank the devil's liquor last night.' I said, 'Okay. Who gave it to you?' He said, 'It was a minister from the devil.' I said, 'Well, we've got to make sure that minister is not around here. Who was it?' He tells me who it was and I'm blown away. It was Roebuck 'Pop' Staples! Now, Pop could take a drink and hold his liquor, I guess, but he gave the bottle to the Reverend. Anyway, the Stapleses had done their show and left. I said, 'Well, you'll have such a good show tomorrow night that no one will even remember what happened. I'll be right here with you.'

"I said to Estelle, 'How much stage time does he have on Sunday?' She said, 'Give me a token, maybe twelve or fifteen minutes.' I said, 'Okay, that's what you'll get.' I sat down with the Reverend and said, 'Okay, Reverend, you are going to do four songs. What are you going to do? How about "Twelve Gates to the City" and "Samson and Delilah?"' So, we worked out four songs before leaving the dressing room tent to go to the stage area.

"Now, this was a high stage with a steep set of stairs and there were no handrails, so it was just a 'walk straight up' situation. I said to the emcee, 'How long is it going to take to introduce him?' He said, 'How long do you want?' I said, 'We're not waiting. When we hit the door at the top of those stairs, then it's showtime. Take twenty or thirty seconds to introduce him, then get out of the way because we're coming through that door.'

"I've got his guitar in one hand and him with the other. We're going up the stairs, and when we're about fifteen steps up, I look down and *Fuck!* We were out in the darkness because all the stage lights were up out front. We were just going up the stairs in the dark. I see the door in front of me so I say, 'Okay, Rev, I'm going to open this door and here we go.' The emcee was still talking *way* too long, so I open the door, and the light pours out. I say, 'Come on, Rev.' We hit the top step, and the emcee turns around and says, 'The Reverend Gary Davis!' We went right out onto the stage. He began to play, and he was *magnificent*!

"The Reverend was one of the few blind musicians I knew who played standing up. Most played sitting down. As he played, he had a very slight rock to the left. It was like he would move three inches to the left and then come back two and a half inches to the right. Gradually, over a period of several songs, he would be off the mic. After fifteen or twenty minutes, he would be facing stage left. In those days, nobody—liberal white people—wanted to do anything critical of a black person, so nobody wanted to touch a black blind man on stage and tell him he's doing something wrong. Occasionally at a festival, and especially at the Mariposa Festival, he wandered over from the mic and had turned left. I came up behind him and touched him on the shoulder and said, 'Hey, Reverend, put your hand up. You're off the microphone. Turn right.' He put his hand up, I turned him around back to the mic, and he was fine.

"He did his four songs and there was a standing ovation. He totally redeemed himself. I got him by the hand and said, 'Come on, Reverend. Let's get out of here.' We start down and go from glaring light into pitch black again. I'm feeling for the step, taking a step, feeling for a step, taking a step. The Reverend is leaning on my shoulder trudging down with me. We get down to the bottom and there is Estelle Klein. She said, 'Dick, that was wonderful! Could you take him back up for an encore!' I said, 'Estelle, this would be a very good time to quit while you're ahead.'

"Later, Estelle said to me, 'Will you fly back with the Reverend?' I said, 'That's fine.' She said, 'We'll change your ticket from Toronto to Boston and buy you one for Toronto to La Guardia to Boston, and you take him home.' We had a really early flight, around 9 A.M., so he gave me his room key. I said, 'Reverend, I'm going to come and bang on your door at 7:30 A.M., so you gotta be ready.' He said, 'Okay.' I go to his room the next morning, knock on the door and say, 'Reverend, it's Dick Waterman.' I unlocked the door and went in. I thought *Jeez! How can he sleep in here?! Every damned light is on.* Then, I realized, *Oh, it doesn't matter. He's blind.* He's dressed and ready, so we get a ride to the airport. It happened to be my day to get messed around by customs. It's like 'Who pulls the short straw today? The guy with the long hair, fringed jacket, and black hat with the old guy with a guitar. Let's give him a hard time.' They went through *everything*: suitcases, shoulder bag, camera bag, the guitar, my boots. They weren't going to find anything, because we were both clean. They took an incredibly long time. Finally, they let us go through.

"Our gate was the *last* gate on the concourse, and we had only a few minutes to get there. I had the Reverend's guitar in my hand, the Reverend's bag under my arm, my bag hanging on my arm, and I've got the Reverend by the wrist. I said, 'Come on, Reverend, let's go!' The Reverend was wearing a suit and tie, hat, and dark glasses, and we are *running.* I start to yell, 'Get out of my way! I'm running with a blind man! Running with a blind man!' People just flattened up against the walls. The Reverend and I ran the length of the concourse. That was so politically incorrect in those days! We get to the counter, gasping for air, and handed over our tickets. The worker looked at us and said, 'Oh, no worries, we're on a delay.'"

Amid his hectic schedule, Dick occasionally found time to go to clubs to hear blues performers other than his clients. When he learned B. B. King was scheduled to perform at Louie's Lounge, he made plans to attend. "The mass white audience did not get B. B. until he crossed over with 'Why I Sing the Blues' and 'The Thrill Is Gone,' but he had a lot of black hits like 'Sweet Little Angel' and '3 O'Clock in the Morning.' His LP *B. B.: Live at the Regal* was a solid hit, and we all loved him."

Louie's Lounge was located on Washington Street in the Roxbury area of Boston. Elevated train tracks ran past the entrance, and the roar of passing trains echoed through the club. Inside was a small room with an archway leading to a larger room in which was located a stage. Due to its location, the club was patronized primarily by black clientele, so Dick sometimes was the only white patron. Over a period of time, King came to recognize his face and, eventually, his name.

One of Dick's favorite clubs was the Scene. It was located in a small basement owned by Steve Paul and located on 46th Street off of 8th Avenue around the corner from Madison Square Garden. The Scene was a favorite after-hours meeting place for musicians who had finished their nightly gigs elsewhere and wanted to socialize or jam with fellow musicians. Venues such as the Fillmore usually closed around midnight, so the Scene was bustling by the early morning hours. It wasn't specifically a blues club, so the only act Dick ever booked there was Buddy Guy, but sometimes he rode the train in to spend an evening there.

"There weren't really shows. It was just really loose. Sometimes there would be nobody booked but a lot of people on stage. It was an atmosphere very conducive to jamming and playing. Everybody liked each other. Sometimes there were English musicians who didn't cross paths in London but would cross paths in New York at the Scene. Steve Paul was such an important guy because he brought a creative atmosphere to his club. Musicians were welcome. They weren't going to get pestered by autograph seekers or cameras. They could come in there, they could hang out, be themselves, and sit at a table. Nobody bothered them."

It was at the Scene in August 1967 that Dick made the acquaintance of a young musician who would become one of the most influential guitarists in rock music. "About 1967 we first heard a reference that Buddy was copying the moves of Jimi Hendrix. He knew nothing about Hendrix. Buddy was a wildly flamboyant, exhibitionist guitarist. He played in a club called Pepper's, which had the heating pipes wrapped in asbestos right over the stage about seven feet [overhead]. Buddy would jam the guitar into the asbestos and take out a handkerchief and whip the guitar. Then he would come down and play it with the microphone stand or behind his head. He was just totally wild. He was being Buddy.

"We heard that Hendrix was a black guy in London with a trio. He had an album called *Are You Experienced?* and he was coming to America on tour. Hendrix was at the beginning of his rise to fame in the United States. He played a wildly successful set at the Monterey Pop Festival in June, and Bill Graham booked him at the Fillmore East just weeks later.

"Hendrix had come in, and he had on military epaulets. He wasn't really famous. It was his first US tour for his first album. I went up to him and said, 'Hi, I'm Dick Waterman. I manage Buddy Guy.' Everything was 'cool man.' I said to him, 'You don't have an accent.' He said, 'Why should I have an accent?' I said, 'I don't know, you came from London.' He said, 'Yeah.' I said, 'I thought you were from like Jamaica, Trinidad, or Barbados.' He looked at me and said, 'No, man, I'm from Seattle.' Wow! I was just totally surprised.

"I don't think anybody was inaccessible at that point, maybe the Beatles, because this was already post-Beatles. Of the working, touring, living musicians, there wasn't anybody up behind a gate in those days. Hendrix was friendly, low-key, accessible, and incredibly curious. He loved to play, he loved to jam. Since most of the people that were sitting in played guitar, he would always go to bass.

"I've always said he was probably one of the most inventive, original bass players I ever heard because he played the rhythm instrument, bass, with lead guitar mentality. He didn't play so much a rhythm bass, but he played a melodic line. He loved to play bass, and guitarists loved to have him sit in on bass because his sense of rhythm was rock solid. He started from a great musician's sense of having great rhythm on bass, and he added to it the ability to be musically creative. I saw him jam with the Chambers Brothers, Albert King, and Buddy.

"He listened to a tremendous amount of other people's music. When you would see him at the Scene and he'd be talking to another recording artist, he would mention to them, 'Hey, man, I heard your new album.' He'd go specifically to a cut, like the first cut on the second side, and say, 'Man, I loved the way the organ comes in after the guitar' or whatever. He really had listened to it and had great admiration.

"He was fascinated with blues players, particularly Albert King and Otis Rush. I found out later it was because they were left handed. He was left handed. He loved to talk about Albert King. He wanted to know more about him. I was managing Buddy, but Albert was with Associated Booking Company. They were a big, powerful agency. Albert was much bigger than Buddy in that his agency could get him on bigger shows, so I was getting crumbs off the table. The pie wasn't that big, so I was always trying to hustle for Buddy, and I had Hendrix, who just wanted to talk about Albert King.

"I think Hendrix's curiosity would have led to an incredible number of great collaborations. That's the important thing about Hendrix. You can just envision Hendrix and Miles Davis, or Hendrix and Sun Ra, or the one I always envision, my favorite, Hendrix and Bob Marley. I think anything would have been possible. He was a willing collaborator. He had the ability of all great sidemen, which was to totally subordinate all ego just to be in a supporting role to enhance the playing of the other person."

In September, Dick saw his friend, Alan Wilson, again. Wilson had moved to California not long after he played on the Son House recording sessions in 1965 and became a founding member of the group Canned Heat. The group was scheduled to perform at the Boston Tea Party in early October 1967, and Wilson had arrived early for an extended visit with family. While in town, he and Dick attended a concert given by the British group Cream at the Psychedelic Supermarket. It was a rather unusual venue with atrocious acoustics because the structure was originally a concrete parking garage.

"Al had really no social graces at all. He wore cracked glasses. He took cotton batting, rolled it in his fingers into long sticks, and he stuck them in his ear. So, he had about two inches of cotton sticking straight out from his ears. Cream was incredibly loud, and Al turned to me at one point and said, 'He [Eric Clapton] can really play!' He was able to decipher Clapton's ability to play when it was just a solid wall of sound to me."

Earlier in the evening, Dick had packed a tape of the complete outtakes from the Robert Johnson recording sessions that he planned to share with Clapton. Following the concert, he and Clapton adjourned to the latter's room at the Somerset Hotel on Massachusetts Avenue near Kenmore Square. Dick set up his Wollensak reel-to-reel tape recorder, and they listened over and over to the pieces. Clapton, with his acoustic guitar in hand, played along trying to recreate Johnson's distinct sound.

Clapton, a great admirer of Johnson's work, was enthralled by the alternate renditions of some of Johnson's released work. Clapton remembers, "I had gotten used to listening to *The King of the Delta Blues* for a few years by then. I'd probably been aware of it six years and was studying it, and then to know that there were, at least, the same amount of tracks again [alternative takes] was pretty mind shattering really. I mean, it was a treasure trove. It really was like finding buried treasure."

Dick remembers, "We were there for hours. There was a king-size bed, and we were sitting on the foot of the bed. At some point, I saw movement out of the corner of my eye. I turned my head and there was this extraordinarily beautiful naked girl. She slipped out of the bed, walked naked over to her dress, which she pulled over her head, she stepped into her shoes and walked out the door. Eric glanced up and put his head back down. It showed his priorities—or something. She was so pale skinned and blonde that I had never even seen her, being just a few feet from her. I guess our music making woke her up, so she got up at two or three o'clock in the morning and walked out the door." The two continued listening until almost dawn and, before leaving, he gifted the tape to Clapton.

"I had gotten a bootleg from the Columbia Records vaults in Bridgeport, Connecticut. The first Johnson record had been out on Columbia, and all of the masters and alternate takes were in the vaults. I don't remember who I got it from. It wasn't really widely circulated, but the Robert Johnson fans had it. They dubbed it for each other. I had it and then gave it to Eric. He went back to England and, in turn, dubbed it for the Robert Johnson freaks over there who, within a couple of years, would go on to be famous musicians."

Less than a month later Cream performed in New York. Dick also was in New York with Skip James and Son House, assisting them with preparations for the American Folk Blues Festival tour in Europe. Instead of listening to early blues recordings with Clapton, this time Dick wanted to introduce him to the old blues musicians.

"There was no doubt in my mind he would want to meet them because Son was so important and they [Cream] had recorded Skip's song 'I'm So Glad.'" He called Clapton at his hotel, said House and James had free time before their departure, and he would like to introduce him to them. The trio had checked out of their hotel, so Dick arranged for them to meet Clapton at the Vanguard Records offices at three o'clock that afternoon.

The Vanguard reception area was small and contained only three chairs that faced the elevator. Dick, House, and James were waiting for Clapton when he arrived. Stepping out of the elevator into the diminutive space, he found himself face to face with two Delta blues legends. Dick made the introductions and offered his chair to Clapton so he could talk with the two bluesmen.

Of this impromptu meeting, Clapton comments, "We [Cream] had cut 'I'm So Glad,' which is Skip's song. I had only heard Skip James on an Origin Jazz Library album and, later on, discovered all of the rest of his catalog. He was such a hero to me, more than a lot of the other guys because he had a unique way of singing in a very high, almost falsetto voice. I was attracted to him for some reason because of that gift. His songwriting, too, was very unique, unusual, and very different from the standard kind of country blues stuff. I was really overwhelmed. I do remember being incredibly moved by them.

"I had become a pretty avid student of most of the regional country blues artists and was trying to educate myself on what style belonged to what area and who was playing with whom, and who had learned from whom. I was trying to piece together my own little blues history. I saw Son, too, I think shortly after that. He came to play in London, and I went to see him at Hammersmith Odeon on his own. That was pretty phenomenal."

James, aware that Cream had covered his recording, removed his guitar from its case and performed the song. House downed a shot of bourbon, took the guitar, and also played a song. He then offered the guitar to Clapton and asked if he would like to play something, but he politely refused.

The intimate performance became a lasting memory for Clapton. He recalls, "It was unique. I always felt, back then, that I was a bit of a fake because I was English, and I was white. Yet, I was also aware that there was some kind of connection that drew me to these guys rather than modern pop music or modern rock and roll. I was also quite confident in my knowledge of what they had already done so I wasn't intimidated or anything. I just felt very, very privileged and honored to have that kind of experience. I don't know what they thought about the whole thing. It must have been unusual for them to be experiencing a reawakening of what they'd done—this kind of comeback thing that happened for both of them. I imagine it might have been nice or interesting at least for them to meet a young white kid from across the ocean who knew who they were.

"You know, there was a great thing about the fact there could have been, on his [Dick's] part, a certain amount of alienation, because how dare I or these white kids come in? It has happened to a certain extent where the white culture has bled the black culture to line its own pockets. I never really saw it. All I ever really wanted to do was pretty much what Dick did, which was to make people aware of this stuff. The greatest joy for me was to record something like 'I'm So Glad' and insist on putting Skip's name as the writing credit so that those who were interested could see that it was written by him and make their own little journey into the history."

The trip to the blues festival in Europe was the only time since House's rediscovery that he had been unaccompanied by Dick at a performance. Dick was leaving on tour with Junior Wells and could not reconcile the scheduling. The day after their meeting with Clapton at Vanguard, House and James arrived in Europe the next day to begin the tour. At the time, there were special restrictions on the airline tickets. Travelers were required to stay no less than fourteen days and no more than twenty-one days. The performers opted for the latter. The tour organizers, Lippmann and Rau, attempted to schedule as many performances as possible during their twenty-day stay. Scheduling cycles of five concerts followed by a day off was typical, so they were not surprised to learn they would be performing seventeen evening concerts. This proved challenging at times due to the sheer amount of travel and the fact that most of the bluesmen were elderly, and one musician, Sonny Terry, was blind.

There were other obstacles such as illiteracy. Restaurants were particularly difficult as some required assistance with menus. "Unless they had someone help them with food, they had to have little cards that said 'ham,' 'eggs,' 'hamburger,' et cetera. These guys couldn't do restaurants." This was mitigated in part by a travel schedule so rigorous they seldom had an opportunity to visit a restaurant. Sometimes the venue or local business would provide food, and there were always blues fans eager to buy a meal for the artists. "Older black people in their sixties and seventies also are reluctant to change money [exchange currency]. If you were only going to be in a country for two or three days and you don't spend it, that money was wasted."

The tour was profitable, as each performer earned between fifteen hundred and two thousand dollars. Before the tour, Dick had negotiated a slightly better compensation for Son House than initially had been offered. Typically, the musicians were paid a certain amount per week or a lump sum for the entire tour. Dick insisted House's contract stipulate he would do a set number of performances per week at a specific amount per show. If he did any more than the specified number of shows, he would be paid a stated amount per show. Since a television show usually was taped in the afternoon followed by a live performance in the evening, House earned substantially more money. Dick was able to make this deal because House's health was considered more fragile.

While House and James were in England, Dick finalized paperwork for the State Department tour for Junior Wells. More extensive than any of the previous tours, it was scheduled to begin in November and conclude approximately fourteen weeks later. They would visit many countries, spending only a few days in each. The preparations presented various challenges because everyone had to have a birth certificate and passport with their full name, but some who were born in the South did not have a birth certificate.

There also were medical issues requiring attention. Dick immediately placed a call to his father. "When Junior Wells and the band were going to Africa, we had to have a whole series of shots: tetanus, typhoid, diphtheria, smallpox. My father gave all of them their shots. As a matter of fact, he gave all the bluesmen their shots when they traveled overseas.

"Going overseas was a winner in so many ways. The money was good. The per diem was generous. They also gave us money to get a sound system and have it put into fancy air travel cases that were very expensive. They had the crates built, and we got to keep the cases for the amplifiers and sound system. It was fabulous!"

Airfare for the band and Dick was included as part of the package. One other attractive concession was that Dick was allowed control of the dates of the tour. The winter months were chosen because the weather was unfavorable for booking extensive travel in the United States, and most festivals were held during warmer months.

Although they stayed in hotels similar to those found in the United States, not all of the venues were quite so modern. Some of the smaller towns were little more than hillsides covered by huts with fires burning for light and heat. "We went into areas that were so remote that we had the only electric line."

The culture was different, but the music was universal. The attendance at some of the remote concerts was impressive. However, one of the instruments was perplexing for many of the native population. "The African audiences understood the drum. They understood the saxophone. They understood the harmonica if Junior held it up and showed it to them before he put it up to the microphone. What they did not understand was when a man holding something that was around his neck touched silvery strings and noise jumped from a box. They couldn't comprehend the electric guitar. That was black magic. They were a little afraid and fascinated by it."

They encountered unexpected situations during their travels. After Wells performed in Timbuktu, the group prepared to depart. Upon arrival at the airport, they went inside to find a man in a uniform and cap waiting to check them in and take their tickets. He instructed them to go outside and wait for the pilot. "We stand there, and the same guy came out, and he had on a different hat. He was the pilot! He goes down and puts a rope around the front wheel strut. He turns the rope over his shoulder and drags this plane up to where we're standing and unties the rope. He had said to us, 'No extra weight.' There are six of us, and we got on the plane. As we are getting on, I've got a paperback book, a pretty thick one, and he takes it from me and says, 'I said, *No extra weight!*' It was kind of scary."

Audience members spanned the range of social classes. While in Liberia, Wells was invited to perform at an event celebrating the reelection of President William V. S. Tubman, who held the position of president longer than anyone else in the country's history. The group was surprised to learn the US vice president, Hubert Humphrey, was in attendance.

"Junior, as was his wont, would come away from the microphone blowing a harmonica, sing a verse, blow the harmonica, and walk around. He was walking toward the vice president, and everybody is watching Junior. I'm watching the secret service men as Junior comes within twenty feet, fifteen feet, then ten feet. They got a little edgy. They didn't like him coming too close to Hubert Humphrey."

Due to the timing of the tour, the Thanksgiving, Christmas, and New Year holidays were spent in Africa. Dick received a rather unexpected, and altogether unforgettable, Christmas gift from Wells's drummer, Fred Below.

"I'm alone in my hotel room, and I hear a knock on the door. There's this absolutely gorgeous coffee-colored skin young woman, maybe seventeen or eighteen years old. She says, 'Merry Christmas from Fred.' So I say, 'Thank you. Tell Fred *Merry Christmas*.' She walks past me into the room and says, 'Merry Christmas from Fred.' So I said, 'Fine.' She goes over, sits on the bed, and looks at me. I look at her, and she says, 'Merry Christmas from Fred.' *Great.* She stands up, reaches her thumb into where the fabric is hooked in the front of her dress, pulls the fabric, and the dress comes off. She says, 'Merry Christmas from Fred.' I said, 'No, no, no! We can't have this!' So, I grabbed the fabric and wrapped her up. I grabbed her by the hand and ran down the hall. I banged on Below's door. Below opened the door and said, 'What can I do for you, my man?' I said, 'Talk to her, Fred. Say, *no, I'm not interested. Thanks anyway.*' Below stood there rubbing his chin and said, 'I cannot do that, my man.' I said, 'Why not?' He said, 'It took me a half hour to teach her to say, *Merry Christmas from Fred.*'

"I was freaking out. I was in Africa. I thought maybe she had a tribal father who was going to come after me. Fred just thought it would be nice to give me a Christmas present. I don't know if he gave her money or what. He had taught her that line and sent her to my door."

Socially, Dick found himself in an unfamiliar situation. "I was the only white person. We played for black audiences, and in every country the embassy personnel that came out to host us was black, so you learn a little reverse discrimination. I knew the local businesspeople were not really friendly to me, but that was okay."

After every concert, in every city and country, the local black businessmen would invite Wells and the band to posh, private parties complete with women and liquor. Dick was never informed or invited. "They were always wanting Junior [to attend] because he was the star. Junior would say, 'What about Dick?' and they would say, 'No Mr. Charlie.' In other words, *no white people—he's not welcome.* Junior would nod and say, 'He's part of the band. If he's not going, I'm not going. If the band wants to go, that's up to them.' Junior never attended a single party on the tour." It was over two decades later when Dick learned the details of what had transpired. Dick was fiercely loyal to his clients, and Wells had repaid him in kind.

CHAPTER 8

He's a Traveling HORSE

SHORTLY AFTER RETURNING FROM THE STATE DEPARTMENT TOUR, DICK was contacted on behalf of Van Morrison. Though Dick lived on Franklin Street, just around the corner from Green Street where Morrison resided, they had never met. Morrison had released his successful single "Brown-Eyed Girl" produced by Bang Records the previous year but was unhappy with the label and wished to extricate himself from them. In addition, he knew Warner Bros. was interested in signing him, but they could not approach him since he was under contract with Bang. His contract stipulated he must produce one more record with Bang but he was reluctant to do so, and a stalemate ensued. A meeting between Dick and Morrison was arranged at the home of a friend whose father was a professor at Harvard.

"It turned out to be a very big house with a huge library with large rugs and tapestries and *many* books. There were also a couple of huge leather chairs, so we sat on the arms of the chairs with our feet in the middle. He had an acoustic guitar and just started to play. It was so intense that I couldn't even comprehend that level of talent. 'Madam George' played with intense emotion at a distance of two feet is a lifelong memory."

Morrison asked Dick to be his manager. Dick was working on scheduling a short tour for Son House and busy with booking for his other clients He declined because he knew managing Morrison's career would be complex and time consuming, but he offered advice on obtaining both a lawyer and a manager. The songs Morrison performed that day for Dick eventually became the album *Astral Weeks*, his first release on the Warner Bros. label.

Dick planned to accompany House on his tour, traveling to each venue by car. House arrived at his apartment and stayed overnight before they departed the following day. The prospect of having a blues legend as houseguest might seem appealing, but the reality was another matter. "It was a full-time job because he was a real alcoholic. If you didn't watch him, he would be out on the street getting a bottle. It's really 24/7 maintenance."

The most viable solution was to find ways to keep House occupied. Occasionally, he enlisted a friend to stay with him for short periods of time. One of them was Jack Viertel, a student at Harvard University. He remembers, "I met Dick in a funny way actually. I had a very good friend at school, Liz Spelke, who was fascinated with the blues and particularly with Son House and wanted to either become a producer or promoter. We were sophomores in college, but she was very excited about this. I said to her, 'Well, you know Dick Waterman manages Son House, and he lives in Cambridge. I don't know where he is, but I bet you can find him.' I left it at that and she did find him, I'm not sure how, and introduced herself to him.

"Then, at some time after that, maybe a month, she called me up on the phone and said, 'Come on over to Dick's house and meet Dick.' I went over to meet Dick, and Son was sitting there in the living room, which, to me, was like having God sitting in the living room. It was a wonderful shock. We all sat around and drank coffee. Son played a little, and we talked and just got to know each other. After that, Dick and I became friends.

"It was really shocking. Son was actually not that old at that time. To me, he was a very old man, but this was 1968 probably, so Son was probably sixty-six. He was shockingly handsome and charismatic looking although he had almost no teeth. He was dressed the way he always was dressed, with his little red bow tie with the ribbons hanging down from it. I idolized him as such a mythic figure, not as a human being. The thing was, as a human being he actually existed. I mean, I'd seen him on stage and seen him perform, but to see him close up and shake his hand and just be there was really a sort of life-changing experience for me.

"Son was worth listening to, but not necessarily fun to talk to. He didn't absorb much of what you said. He was very deferential. I don't think he ever really trusted that a white person didn't have the power to make his life more difficult and might not use it under some circumstances, but he was fun to listen to because he told stories. When he was reasonably sober, they were coherent stories about his life in Rochester, working on the railroad, and working as a tractor driver in Mississippi—stories about life in general and philosophical points of view about life. They weren't complex, but they were interesting."

Viertel made subsequent visits to Dick's apartment when House was there and even learned to play slide guitar under his tutelage. Over time, he was entrusted to watch over House when Dick needed to leave the apartment. Constant supervision of House's alcohol consumption was imperative. Jack remembers, "It was a learned skill. I watched Dick do it, and Son really did need to have a certain amount of alcohol in him virtually at all times. It had to be meted out very carefully or he would simply go completely around the bend. Son would always say, 'Let me have a little nip.' That was his way of letting you know he needed some more. Dick would probably respond positively on the third or fourth request. The first three would go ignored, and he would tell him, 'Not yet.' Son wasn't difficult about it. He clearly was on a leash, and he knew he was on a leash."

During one of House's stays at Dick's apartment, Viertel called to ask if he and a friend could come for a visit. Dick always welcomed a reprieve from watching House, so he invited them over, planning to leave for a short time. "Having Son with me 24/7 was really stressful. If people gave me the opportunity to drop him off [or came to Dick's house], it was like a weight off me for a few hours. I would certainly take advantage of that."

Dick was pleasantly surprised when Jack arrived at his apartment accompanied by a young Radcliffe freshman he was dating named Bonnie Raitt. Dick recognized the name immediately as he was an admirer of John Raitt, her father. During his youth, Dick had been impressed by the elder Raitt's work in Broadway musicals and films such as *The Pajama Game, Carousel,* and *Oklahoma*. He was immediately enamored of Bonnie.

He still struggled with stuttering, but by this time it posed more problems during telephone calls and public speaking than in a small group setting. "As long as we were talking about music, movies, or things like that, I was all right." Before their visit ended, he asked for her telephone number. "I don't know if she was immediately smitten. I think that I was like an entryway into a world that she really liked. I was certainly not any rakish physical figure at that point. I was a skinny guy with huge hair."

Raitt had become aware of Dick's work when she moved to college. She remembers, "When I heard country blues, I heard it on a Newport record and didn't know about Dick Waterman, but later found out that he was working with Mississippi John Hurt. Around the time that I went to college, I was able to find my own subculture of blues freaks. At the same time that I came to college, in 1967–68, is when I found out who Dick was and the fact that he lived in our town. I was just a freshman and listening to the Harvard radio station blues show. Son House was on, and my friend, Jack, called me and said, 'I hear he's going to be at Dick Waterman's house. Would you like to meet him?' That's how Jack took me over there, and that's when I met Dick.

"I'd grown up in a show business family. Although we didn't hang out in those circles that much, I had been around Broadway stars and some film stars. I had a little bit of exposure to that world, but, for me, this was the first legendary figure. Out of the past, this guy [House] just loomed so large in terms of those of us who loved Robert Johnson and all the great old blues records. To actually meet someone in the flesh that was the father of Delta blues was life altering. I'd have to say I was more stunned and impressed by that. Of course, as when you meet people, he was just a man, but he still had so much mystery and dignity. I don't know how much was projection and how much was just him. He just had a lot of charisma."

Although her initial interest was in meeting House, a friendship and romance quickly grew between her and Dick. "I was enamored of him and looked up to him, and I guess he was attracted to me. I don't really remember how long it took, but it was definitely a mutual attraction. He was quite a bit older than me, so when I eventually told my parents that I was dating somebody that was fifteen years older than me, it didn't go over so well."

The day after Viertel and Raitt's visit, Dick and House flew to San Francisco. He had scheduled a tour for Buddy Guy and his band, and House was to be a guest performer at the February 23–24, 1968, concerts at the Avalon Ballroom. Guy and the band traveled by car, with plans to meet Dick and House at the motel.

Guy comments, "We're in this motel, and it's six dollars a night. I had to get the one room for six dollars and put my whole band in there. Shows you how much money I was making. When he [Dick] flew out, he checked Son House in. He wrote a big note on a piece of paper and stuck it on my door, 'cause I was out. It said, 'Do not go over there and give Son anything to drink.' I'd never met him, so I said [to myself], 'I want to meet Son House 'cause my music was from Muddy and Wolf, and Muddy and Wolf got it from Son House.

"I heard this acoustic guitar in the next room. He [Dick] had booked his [Dick and Son's] room next to mine, and he was in there singing at about ten o'clock in the morning. I don't know it's Son House. I just hear this acoustic guitar, and I think it could be anybody that is playing guitar and singing. Maybe an hour or two later, I took a shower. I was beat. I said [to myself], 'I'm gonna lay down and get a nap 'cause we gotta play tonight on the same show as Son House.'

"I got a knock on the door and, if you know Dick, he stuttered a little bit. He came in, pushed his glasses up, and said, 'I . . . I . . . I told you, left a note, for you to not give him nothing to drink!' I didn't say nothing because I hadn't been over there. So when he finished, I said, 'When you're finished, I would like to meet Son.' He looked at me, and walks over to the door, got a key, and he opened the door. Son was sitting on the bed with his bottle of whiskey. As soon as Dick walked in the door, he [Son] said, 'See, you think you slick. When you got on the plane in Boston, I had went out and got the bottle of whiskey. And I knew you was gonna go in my suitcase and find it, but I put it in *your* suitcase.'"

They were invited to appear on a CBS show, *Camera 3*, which was filmed at the CBS studio in Manhattan and aired at 10:00 on Sunday mornings.

Guy reminisces, "You know, the first time I'd ever been on television in my life was *Camera 3*. I was so excited. I'm saying, 'Why am I playing with this legendary guy? I'm up here trying to keep up with him when I should be sitting out there listening so I could see what I could learn from what he was doing.' When I saw him, I always wanted to say, 'I don't even want you to know I'm here. I just want to watch you play so I can see what I can learn from that.'"

During the show, Dick learned the tedium sometimes associated with such productions. "Son was on a riser, up about four feet, and he was sitting on a little frail chair. He had rocked forward so that one of the feet of the chair was close to the edge. I said, 'Stand up a minute, Son, I gotta move the chair back.' Son stood up and I took the chair and pushed it back. Then, somebody blew a whistle, and everybody froze. He said, 'Man touched a prop! Man touched a prop!' Everybody was running around, and they all came down [front].

"The directing producer came out of the booth and said, 'What happened? What happened?' The man said, 'He touched a prop!' They looked at me and the guy said, 'What did you do?' I said, 'Well, Son's chair had danced up close to the edge, so I just pushed it back a couple of inches.' He said, "Oh no! Aww man, you can't do that. You gotta ask somebody to do that.' I said, 'But I just moved it . . .' He said, 'No, that's why they have unions. A union man had to move that. You touched a union man's prop.' I said, 'What happens now?' He said, 'Now I gotta go into conference with the shop steward, and they're going to get concessions from me before they go on with the taping.' I said, "But I just moved it three or four inches!' So they went in, and we just stood around. They came out, and everybody was unhappy. He said, 'Okay, is the chair where you want it now, Mr. Waterman?' I said, 'Yeah.' He said, 'Okay,' and the show continued. That was a scary memory! Son performed alone, and then he performed with Jerry Ricks. Buddy and the band were also on the show, so at one point Buddy and Son sat side by side and did an acoustic duo."

After returning from California, Dick received a call from Bob Koester at Delmark Records. Koester was recording the album *Look on Yonder's Wall* with Arthur "Big Boy" Crudup and was searching for a booking agent for him. Crudup had recorded a number of songs in Chicago during the 1940s and 1950s for Lester Melrose at RCA/Bluebird, but like many others, fell prey to exploitation by the recording industry. Others, including Elvis, recorded covers of his music, but with little education or understanding of copyright law, Crudup was unsuccessful in collecting royalties owed to him. Disheartened and unable to earn enough money with his music to support his family, he did not record for several years. The Delmark recordings eventually reinvigorated his career during the last few years of his life. At Koester's request, Dick agreed to meet with Crudup. "I wasn't as knowledgeable as I should have been, although I knew he had written 'That's All Right,' which Elvis recorded. I went to Chicago for the recording sessions and met Arthur, who was big, quiet, stoic, very gentle, low-key, and passive."

Like many early bluesmen, his life had been difficult, and he held little hope of it changing. Dick liked him and agreed to work with him. Although Crudup wrote some great songs, he was never a charismatic performer and not particularly popular with audiences. Nevertheless, Dick managed to book some festivals and other appearances for him. "He was a very uninspiring live performer. He was a good songwriter, but fairly boring. He was just a big man who stood up very straight, played a little guitar, and sang in a big, strong voice."

Junior Wells and the band were booked to play five nights, May 7–11, 1968, at the New Orleans House, located on San Pablo Avenue in Berkeley. Desiring some time away from the office, Dick decided to accompany them. "While in Berkeley, I had found an incredible soul food restaurant right on the Berkeley-Oakland line. It was a very tough part of Telegraph Avenue. One end of the avenue dead ends at the university, but if you take it back the other way, it goes through a very tony, upscale part of Berkeley. The neighborhood gets bad again, and it goes into Oakland. The restaurant had iron bars. Any place where they give you the food through iron bars is going to be good food.

"When Junior and the band got there, I said, 'Hey, I found you a great soul food restaurant. The chicken's to die for.' Fred Below, the drummer and the authority on everything, said, 'I don't know about that, man. You can't be trusting that. They could spice it up or spice it down. You can't go wrong with the Colonel [Kentucky Fried Chicken].' I said, 'What do mean the Colonel? What's with going to Colonel Sanders? You can go to Colonel Sanders anywhere. This is home food. This is soul food, man. This is to die for.' Below said, "Don't mess with the Colonel. He's got them herbs and spices down.' I looked at Junior and said, 'What are you going to do? Is he crazy? Colonel Sanders?! This is down-home soul food! Junior, tell him.' Junior looked at me, dead serious, shook his head, and said, 'Listen to Below. Below knows what he's talking about. Some of these places, they be messing around with different spices. You never know what you're gonna get. If Below says we're gonna eat with the Colonel, then we're gonna eat with the Colonel.'"

A few weeks later, Dick traveled to Beloit, Wisconsin, with several of his Avalon artists. A couple of months before, he had received a call from Leroy Pierson, a student at Beloit College, hoping to book performers for an event he was organizing. Pierson had attended the New York Folk Festival at Carnegie Hall in 1965 and was mesmerized by Son House's performance. While there, he also discovered and purchased several issues of *Sing Out!* in which he saw Dick's Avalon Productions advertisement and learned he was representing Son House and Skip James. Soon, he was obsessed with blues music. In early 1968 he had written a short book for an English class on the core themes of blues and how they were poetically expressed in selected works by various bluesmen. His professor was so impressed with the work that he began to explore blues music and, consequently, approached Pierson about being an organizer for one of the college's "Convocation Cluster" weekends.

These events were held each semester, with the weekend devoted to a specific theme and, depending on the subject matter, contained speeches, readings, workshops, and performances. All students were required to attend at least one such event per academic year so a sizable audience was guaranteed. Along with the professor's interest in blues, a tragic event earlier in the year also influenced the choice of subject matter for the weekend. Shortly after Pierson submitted his English project, Martin Luther King Jr. was assassinated. Pierson explains, "That was such a huge shift in a lot of thinking on college campuses. A lot of campuses that had paid no attention to black folk in terms of their programming and studies began to think, 'We should really be concentrating on doing something about this.'"

He excitedly agreed to organize a weekend event and already had ideas about which performers he wanted to include. The dates of June 27–29, 1968, were chosen, and he called Dick to ask if he could book Son House, Mississippi Fred McDowell, and Junior Wells. Arthur Crudup was added to the roster, as well.

Dick had mentioned to Pierson that Son House usually rose early to sit in his room and play gospel tunes. On their first morning in Beloit, Pierson made his way to House's room to hear him play. Soon, McDowell and Crudup came to the room, and the three began singing together. Pierson quickly rearranged the evening's performance schedule, shaving a few minutes from their respective solo performance times and adding a gospel set to feature the three of them together.

At the concert the trio embarked on the gospel set while Pierson and Dick stood in the wings of the stage. Pierson was stunned when House came over, took him by the arm, and led him onto the stage to sing with them. He remembers, "That was the first time I was ever on stage doing music, and I'm up there with freaking Son House! It was terrifying, but it was one of the greatest things that ever happened to me."

Junior Wells delivered an engaging performance, though it was not exactly what Pierson had hoped for or expected. He explains, "When Junior Wells was performing, I was somewhat concerned because I had seen Junior a lot in the clubs in Chicago. I knew that he was really good at blues and blues harmonica, but I also knew that he could get up and do a James Brown imitation that would last two hours and not even touch the harmonica. I said to Dick, 'I guess he knows this is a blues festival and he should play blues?' He says, 'Well, I'll be truthful with you, Leroy, I haven't talked to him about it. Why don't you go back and see what he says?'

"I go backstage and Junior is back there in a shower stall snorting cocaine. I walked up and said, 'Hey, Junior, how are you feeling tonight?' He says, 'Good.' I said, 'Well, I know you know me, so you know I really want you to do a lot of harmonica and the blues stuff tonight. If you don't mind, leave out the James Brown stuff.' I could tell instantly I had made a bad mistake because Junior got angry that I would have the temerity to ask him to do one thing or another. So, he came out and started doing the James Brown thing.

"Dick was sitting next to me. He had a check in his pocket for Junior for two thousand dollars, and he was taking a percentage of Junior's pay, so at least two hundred dollars of that was going to be his. Junior did three numbers in a row of this stuff. Dick reached in his pocket, pulled out that check, and tried to hand it to me. I said, 'I'm not going to take that back.' He said, 'No, I want you to take it back. He's not giving you what you want.' I said, 'Yeah, but we can't not pay the guy.' Dick says, 'I'll pay him.' I said, 'No, you won't. Put the check back. He's doing a good show. It isn't what I wanted, but look at the kids. They're enjoying it.'"

Following Dick's return to Philadelphia, he was asked to book musicians for an upcoming Eugene McCarthy presidential election rally scheduled for July 25, 1968, at Fenway Park in Boston. Dick immediately called B. B. King to ask if he would like to perform, and he agreed. He was to play a half-hour set prior to McCarthy's speech, but things did not go as planned. King had finished his set and exited the stage when Dick received news that the McCarthy motorcade had been delayed en route to the stadium. King was asked to return to the stage and continue playing until McCarthy arrived, which turned out to be well over a half hour later. King played brilliantly, so the delay provided an excellent showcase of his talent to the largest white audience for which he had ever performed. The forty-thousand-seat stadium was completely filled, with many standing outside in the street listening as the proceedings were broadcast through loudspeakers.

McCarthy finally arrived and delivered a lackluster speech. Dick paid little attention because his thoughts were elsewhere. "I remember B. B. sitting on the dugout bench with me, looking at McCarthy, listening and paying close attention to what he was saying. He was very involved in McCarthy's speech."

Although people had come to hear the speech, it was King's performance that was the highlight of the event. "'Why I Sing the Blues' did not come out until the following year and 'The Thrill Is Gone' didn't come out for two years. The rally was before his white crossover, but it got people ready for him."

The following day, July 26, 1968, Dick, B. B. King, Junior Wells, and Buddy Guy were at the Newport Folk Festival. Dick had brought his camera along to capture images of the performers both on and off the stage. One of his subjects was Janis Joplin. He had met her less than three months earlier, in April, when she performed at the Winterland Ballroom in San Francisco. "I was in the dressing room at Winterland with her a couple of times. She was okay. You could talk to her about movies, restaurants. In other words, she was just Janis. She was a normal girl. She created the persona 'Pearl', which was reminiscent of 'Destry Rides Again' with the whore with a heart of gold, who was tough and brittle with an edge. She had a soft heart, and someone had to find that soft heart. That's what Pearl was, it was Janis's exterior."

One of Dick's favorite moments at the festival occurred backstage. "I remember a card game on a hood of a car. It was so awesome. They were playing five card stud, one down and four up. It was B. B., Buddy, Junior, and me. After four cards dealt, it ended up that Junior had three hearts showing and a hold card. The fifth card is called 'fifth street.' Junior was just running his mouth in a monologue. He said, 'If I get a heart on fifth street, you'd better look out because I've got a flush.' Well, Buddy hit two pair, which is a very good hand. B. B. hit three of a kind, which is an even better hand. Either one of them could have a full house, which would have beaten Junior's flush. So we come around on fifth street, and *Shit! Junior gets a heart!* Junior said, 'That's it!' and reaches into his pocket and takes out a *wad* of hundreds.

"Buddy looks at his two pair, then at Junior. B. B. looks at his three of a kind, sure that Junior doesn't have a heart as his down card, and that he's full of shit. Junior starts counting hundreds out there [on the car hood]. He said, 'I know you don't have the full house because I got my flush. I'm all red. When that heart hit on fifth street, you were dead.' Buddy said, 'You don't have it, motherfucker!' B. B. just shook his head because he couldn't believe he was going to fold over three of a kind. Junior just keeps running his mouth and throwing money down. The end of it was Buddy and B. B. folded, and Junior took all the money. Buddy said, 'Show me that down card! Show me you have it!' Junior said, 'I don't have to show you shit!' and he never did. We never found out if he was bluffing. I don't know the card, but I know Junior. He was messing with their minds. I was gone out of the hand. They started reaching for hundreds, and I was out of there. I just supplied the car hood that they played on."

A few months later, Dick saw King again. Dick's apartment was situated at the edge of an African American neighborhood not far from Pep's Lounge. "It was kind of funny. I walked in, and I was the only white person there. I sat at a table and couldn't get a waiter to bring me a drink. So, I sat there alone in this pretty big club."

The stage was a lowered area in the center of the room surrounded by tables and chairs on graduated tiers. Dick sat at a table not far from the stage and soon realized the absence of a waiter was an indication his presence was not wholly welcome. "He [B. B.] was with a band called Sonny Freeman and the Unusual. They came out and opened, and B. B. did 'Every Day I Have the Blues,' which was his theme song, and then he did another song. Then, he squinted into the audience and said, 'Hey, Dick! What are you doing here? Nice to see you!' and I waved. Suddenly, I had waiters running at me because I knew *the man,* and *the man* knew me."

Junior Wells's tour of Africa the previous year had been so successful that he received a second invitation to participate in a State Department tour in Asia. The tour would be slightly longer than the previous one, and the circumstances were different. "The African tour was much tighter. Being in Asia in the middle of the Vietnam War, no matter where you went—Cambodia, Laos, Vietnam—the atmosphere of war was just everywhere."

They departed in November 1968, with Fiji as their destination. "When we were in Fiji, Junior was such a triumph that he was honored by the government of Fiji. They gave him a large shark's tooth on a gold chain in a box of purple velvet. After the presentation, which was on our last evening, word swept across the island, and the Fijian people came to the hotel by the hundreds. They came up the driveway. and they were chanting, 'Junior Wells! Junior Wells!' Junior came out and held up the velvet box with the shark's tooth. This had rarely been given and was presented to people like the governor general of Australia and visiting British royalty. He was the first nonwhite person to ever get this. It was an amazing honor. The people of Fiji just went wild."

Although Fiji is comprised of several small islands, there are two main islands, and the band traveled by plane between them. One trip across was particularly memorable. "I'm sitting there and the pilot is in the cockpit. He opens the door and says, 'Junior Wells, you want to come up and sit with me?' I'm reading a magazine, and the next thing I know the pilot is walking down the aisle talking to people. Okay. Suddenly, I think, *If the pilot is standing here, who the fuck is flying this thing?!* I looked up and Junior's in the cockpit. Junior was afraid of flying! I say, 'Junior is flying this plane!' And the pilot says, 'Don't worry, don't worry.' *Don't worry?! Whoa! Get back up there!* When you flew with Junior, he sat and looked out the window and never talked. He was petrified of flying, but he never closed his eyes."

Departing Fiji, they flew to the Philippine Islands. The concert was scheduled for the Araneta Coliseum in Quezon City, but they received a request to perform at an additional event. A beauty pageant was being held that same week in Manila, only a few miles from Quezon City, so they accepted the invitation. The band was delighted to be surrounded by the pageant contestants during their stay.

Christmas was spent in Vietnam with the war raging around them. The band was scheduled to perform at schools, but upon arrival they were invited to play at a military hospital. "When we were there, they asked us to play for a hospital. We really couldn't say 'No.' So, we did. Junior did what I thought was a great show, but we couldn't get any reaction. Afterward, the guy who had organized it said it was fabulous and a huge success. We said, 'Are you kidding? We didn't get any reaction.' He said, 'Oh, those were shock and trauma patients.'"

The hospital concert was so successful they received an additional request. "There were so many black soldiers, and they never had a prayer of getting blues, soul music, or R&B. When they asked us if we would give up a couple of open days and go play for the troops, we said, 'Yes.' We thought it was going to be in Saigon, way down south and safe. We went to Da Nang, way up north and dangerous. They laid out steaks and bottles of whiskey for us. Obviously, liquor is not supposed to be in a combat zone, but they had cases of it."

For their protection, they were housed in military barracks. The sounds of gunfire overhead were ever present. "At some point, three or four o'clock in the morning, we hear shooting. I got out of bed and put on my pants, and I go to the top of the stairs leading down to the outside. At the bottom of the stairs was the guard protecting the building, leaned back and sound asleep. So I thought 'Okay,' and I went back to bed. I wasn't going to go down and wake him up. I'd have probably gotten shot!"

Less than a month before the end of the tour, Dick had an accident, the effects of which lingered long after he returned home. He and Wells had gone out into the countryside and were standing near the edge of a cliff. Dick had brought along firecrackers for entertainment. "I smoked in those days, so I would light firecrackers from a cigarette. To make it last longer as it fell down, I wound the string tighter. Stupid me, instead of turning it counterclockwise, I turned clockwise, which didn't tighten the fuse, it *loosened* the fuse. I have this big firecracker, and I lit it with a cigarette. It went off [in my hand] right by my ear. I clutched my hand, and I couldn't hear anything. All the muscles in my hand were just frozen. I couldn't open my hand for six or eight hours. When my hand finally came open, I had Chinese characters burned into my skin." Upon realizing he wasn't seriously injured, Wells looked at him and said, "That's one of the stupidest things I've ever seen."

The tour took them into other areas including Laos, Cambodia, Malaysia, and Singapore before returning home. Thankfully, Dick's injuries eventually healed. His hand suffered no permanent damage, but it was months before the hearing in his right ear returned.

CHAPTER 9

I's Thinkin' 'bout the GOOD TIME

WITH DICK'S ASSISTANCE, BONNIE RAITT'S PERFORMING CAREER FLOURished in 1969. A local band, Sweet Stavin' Chain, was performing at the Second Fret in Philadelphia and Bonnie was the opening act. "She got 10 percent of the door [proceeds], and they got 50 percent of the door. The door was about five hundred fifty dollars. Sweet Stavin' Chain was a big band, eight pieces with horns, so they got about two hundred eighty dollars, which they split eight ways. She got fifty-five dollars and thought she had found nirvana. That was big money for her. I think the first gig for which she ever had a paper contract was a place called Pennypack Park. She got seventy-five dollars.

"I introduced her to a lot of authentic blues players, but she had learned off of blues records before I met her. She was mature for her age to the extent that she understood there wasn't really a lot of glamour in the entertainment world. She knew that from her father's career ups and downs, which made her a lot easier to work with professionally."

It was through Dick that Raitt met the inimitable Howling Wolf at one of his performances at the Scene in New York City. Meeting him left an indelible impression on her. She remembers, "I was young and absolutely floored by Wolf. I was scared, excited, and thrilled. There was something about his music that appealed to me so much; the epitome of what makes your parents wish you weren't listening to it. All that sex, all that danger, all of the rhythm was absolutely intoxicating.

"In the foyer of the club, as in a lot of '60s and '70s clubs, there was some black light. When he came off the stage, he was just pouring sweat. His white shirt was drenched. He stepped into the [alcove] to meet us away from the crowd. All I could remember was the size of the guy and his sweat and shirt were like fluorescent purple [in the lighting].

"He reached out his hand, which was more like a paw. Dick and I have laughed about this because I'd never met anybody that gigantic before.

He said, 'Hello, dahlin,' in this kind of wolf voice, and I was buckling at the knees. I was so thrilled to meet him!

"Afterwards, I didn't get to see him a lot, but he was one of my absolute favorites of the blues artists. Like a lot of us that loved the blues, everybody was quite intimidated by the magnificence and the magnitude of Wolf as a man. Physically, he seemed intimidating, but he was very thoughtful and self-aware of his place in the business. He was always very nice to me."

After the introduction, Wolf returned to his dressing room. "I turned toward Bonnie who was still standing frozen with her hand extended. 'You okay?' I asked. She turned to me slowly and said, 'That is the sexiest man that I have ever met in my life.'"

It was during this same time that Dick and Raitt met Dion DiMucci at the Main Point, a coffeehouse on Lancaster Avenue in Bryn Mawr, Pennsylvania. It was opened in 1964 by Jeanette and Bill Campbell and offered an intimate setting with good food and performances by legendary musicians at a reasonable price. DiMucci, formerly of Dion and the Belmonts, had released his hit single, "Abraham, Martin and John" a few months earlier. He was playing a few performances, with his guitar as sole accompaniment, on the coffeehouse circuit. Darryl Hall and John Oates were his opening act that evening.

Dick and Raitt came to the show and soon were backstage chatting with DiMucci. Raitt and DiMucci began playing blues tunes and later, onstage, he performed a few blues songs. DiMucci comments, "We bonded around this music, and we started talking. I mentioned Fred McDowell, and he knew Fred McDowell! One thing led to another, and I ended up at his house playing all night. He was playing records of Fred McDowell and a few other guys. He told me, 'Dion, you're at your best when you're singing the blues. It's a natural thing for you. You should do a blues album.' Bonnie Raitt agreed with him."

In early 1969, Dick booked a tour for Mississippi Fred McDowell in England. Transatlantic Records arranged for McDowell to come to a London recording studio on March 8 to record some tracks. The result was the release of two albums, *Mississippi Fred McDowell in London, Volume 1* and *Volume 2*, which initially were available exclusively in Europe.

While on tour, McDowell routinely had inquiries both from people in the music industry and from reporters regarding personal contact information. He did not have a telephone in his home in Como, Mississippi, so he gave them the telephone number of a local business where he often visited with friends.

"Stuckey's is a chain of gas stations and restaurants. They're at interstate exits so there was, at the time, a Stuckey's in Como at I-55. Fred would just go and hang out there. A promoter or interviewer from England would call him, and one of the employees would say, 'Fred, come on in here. You've got a call.' He would take calls there.

"The word came around [to me] that Fred needed money so badly that he was working at a gas station pumping gas at Stuckey's. I called him up. I said, 'What's this I hear that you've got no money, and you're working at Stuckey's gas station? You just came back from England. You made an album there. They paid you in cash. The money was good. I mean, it looks bad on me that I'm managing you, and you're so poor that you've got to be pumping gas.'

"He said, 'Dick, I got to tell you, I get up in the morning, and I go there 'cause all my friends hang out there. I just sit with them and we're just talking. When they [the gas station] get busy, they yell, 'Hey, Fred, give a fill up on pump three to the Cadillac with Illinois plates!' I go down there, fill it up, and that's all. I got nothin' to do and I'm sittin' around there. Dick, they paying me thirty-two dollars a week, and I am flat out stealing that money!' Fred was Fred. He was just a sweet guy."

Weeks after McDowell's tour, Dick accompanied Buddy Guy to England. He had received an invitation to perform in an event labeled "The Supershow" in London scheduled for March 25, 1969. It was held in an area known as "The Slough" near Heathrow Airport. Artists including Eric Clapton, Stephen Stills, Jack Bruce, Rahsaan Roland Kirk, John Heisman, Modern Jazz Quartet, Dick Heckstall-Smith, and Buddy Miles were the featured performers. Although Jimi Hendrix was invited, he was not present.

"I think I was the only still photographer there. I shot three rolls. I was shooting color and I only had one roll. I stupidly and impatiently shot Clapton adjusting the controls on his Marshall amps with his back to me. Why didn't I wait with the last couple of shots until he turned around? I don't know."

While in London, Dick received a call from the Beatles' office. They were interested in signing Buddy Guy to their Apple label and asked if Dick would stop by to discuss the details. "I went to the Beatles' office on Baker Street and met with Peter Asher. I remember they had a gatefold album of a guy I'd never heard of named James Taylor. Peter and I talked, but we never got around to money. They liked the idea of having Buddy, but I never knew which Beatle was for this idea. It was probably George." Unfortunately, after initial negotiations, they never managed to work out a deal.

After returning, Dick gained Delmark artist J. B. Hutto as a client. When possible, Dick went to clubs to watch his artists perform. One evening when he was in Chicago he headed to a club where Hutto was playing. "I went to see J. B. at a place called Turner's Lounge on Chicago's south side. J. B. wore a fez and played slide guitar just like Elmore [James]. The music was *way* loud. This place had like a sandy floor. I got on the end of the bar, and the floor was kind of muddy. I leaned over to the bartender and said, 'Where's the men's room?' The bartender leaned forward and said, 'Say what?' I said, loudly, 'Where's the men's room?' He said, 'You're standing in it!'"

The circumstances that led to the addition of Lightning Hopkins to the Avalon roster were an amazing coincidence. "I wanted to book Lightning Hopkins, but I didn't have an address. All I knew was that Chris Strachwitz had recorded him at Arhoolie. Hopkins had made a film with Les Blank, which was called *The Blues According to Lightning Hopkins* [1968]. I wrote him [Blank] a letter and said that I was trying to book Lightning. I asked if he had a name, phone number, or any way that I could get in touch with him.

"I came down from my apartment. The mailbox was on the right corner, and on the left corner was a bar. We called it the 'Peanut Bar' because everybody cracked peanuts, and the floor was inches deep in peanut shells. I consciously said to myself, 'Should I mail the letter or should I go have a drink first?' I said, 'I'll have a drink first.' I walked in the door, and there were hardly any customers. The bartender and I knew each other as friends. As I walked in, the bartender said, 'Hey, here he is now! Dick, come here. We were just talking about you.' I walked up to the bar. I put the letter down, and the bartender turned to a guy and said, 'What did you say your name was?' The guy said, 'Les Blank' and extended his hand. I put my finger on the letter and said, 'Here. This is for you.'

"He had been to Philadelphia to show his films at a film festival. He had gotten on a random bus for no real reason, gotten off on a random corner, walked into this bar, and struck up a conversation with the bartender about being in town showing his film about blues. The bartender said, 'I know a guy who lives right here in the neighborhood who does a lot of work with blues singers.' That's when I walked in."

In spring 1969, Dick embarked on the first of many crusades to secure royalties for a blues artist. Reverend Robert Wilkins had played a crucial role in the quest to locate Son House, and Dick wanted to return the favor. In 1968 the Rolling Stones recorded their album *Beggars Banquet*, which included "Prodigal Son," a song composed and recorded by Wilkins utilizing the guitar part and melody of one of his earlier compositions, "That's No Way to Get Along." The original cover bore the image of a filthy bathroom stall and quickly was banned. A new cover, a photo of a simple but elegantly scribed invitation card, took its place. Unfortunately, an error was made when the credits were added to the new cover. On the original, Wilkins had been credited for his work, but on the new cover, all songs were ascribed to Jagger and Richards. When Dick learned of this, he contacted Atlantic

Records. He informed them Reverend Wilkins was alive and should be receiving royalties. "They said, 'Okay. Do you have an address?' I gave them his address, and money started to flow. If a group wants a guy to get the money, he's going to get the money."

In August 1969, a new festival dedicated solely to blues music was held in Ann Arbor, Michigan. John Fishel, a junior at the University of Michigan, and self-professed admirer of "black music," responded to a flyer advertising a meeting for students who were interested in organizing a music festival. At the meeting, he volunteered to co-chair the entertainment committee and was tasked with booking the artists. Sponsorship was provided by the university and Canterbury House, an Episcopalian students' group. Though most of the students on the committee had little or no knowledge of blues festivals, university officials left the production and programming to their discretion. Fishel turned to Bob Koester, whom he had met in Chicago at the Jazz Record Mart in late 1968, for assistance. Koester suggested he enlist the services of Dick Waterman.

A significant aspect of the festival was that it was the first to offer commercial wages to the performers. Fishel was committed to ensuring fair compensation. This was important for the older bluesmen who were trying to earn enough money to survive. They also made a way to provide lodging for artists who needed to stay overnight. Fishel explains, "We housed many of the artists at the Ann Arbor League, which, until that time was a residential center only for women. We convinced them to open it up so we could house our artists there."

Fishel's younger brother, Jim, who had recently graduated high school, assisted him by chaperoning Arthur Crudup and Mississippi Fred McDowell. With Dick and Koester's help, Fishel scheduled what Dick considered one of the greatest assemblages of blues musicians of the time.

"It was like the blues hall of fame in the backstage area: Muddy, Wolf, Freddie King, B. B. King, Lightning Hopkins. There were ten or fifteen of the greatest bluesmen alive. Mrs. House was there with Son. She was a dour, serious woman who laughed at nothing. She came up to me and said, 'Dick, do you know that Lightning Hopkins man?' I said, 'Yes.' She said, 'Could you take me over and tell him my name, and I could shake his hand?' I was surprised, but said, 'Sure' and brought her over to him.

"Lightning, who wore shades [sunglasses] at night, was talking to somebody. He turned his head and saw me coming with Mrs. House. He's sitting down, but he stops what he's doing and looks up. I said, 'Lightning, I want you to meet my friend, Mrs. Son House. This is Evie. Evie, this is Sam *Lightning* Hopkins.' He lifts his glasses, peers at us, and then lowers them again. He took her hand in his, reached out with his other, put his hand past her elbow, and slid it down to her wrist. He said, 'What's a sweet chil' like you doing here all alone?' She giggled and put her left hand over her mouth. I didn't want to be party to any of that, so I turned and walked away. She came back in a couple minutes and was still grinning. She said, 'That Lightning, he sure does say some pretty things to the ladies.' He was just a charmer. Lightning never raised his voice. He was very soft spoken and *very* smooth around women."

Mississippi Fred McDowell spent an evening socializing with some of the college students. "Bonnie and I had a room in the student union. We came back about 11:00 P.M. She said, 'I want to knock on Fred's door and say *Goodnight.*' I said, 'Leave him alone. Fred is fine.' She said, 'No, he's probably sitting there all alone.' I said, 'Fred's a big boy. Fred will take care of himself.' She said, 'Well, I'm going to knock on his door and make sure he's okay.'

"She knocks on the door, but no answer. She knocks louder. No answer. She knocks even louder. The door opens, and the smell of marijuana rushes into the hall. Holy shit! There are two beds in the room, and there must be at least fifteen people in there! They're smoking, they're drinking, they're on the floor, they're on the bed, they're on the desk, they are everywhere! They are partying. All of them were white college kids between [the ages of] nineteen and twenty-three. Bonnie's eyes got big. Fred, who called her Bunny, said, 'Hey, everybody, that's my friends, Dick and Bunny. That's my booking agent. Come on in.' We step in, and now there are seventeen people in this small room. I looked at Bonnie, and she just shook her head. It was great! Fred was the ultimate people person. Fred made friends with everybody."

Raitt remembers, "There were all these college kids, a lot of pretty girls, just sitting at his feet, and he's holding court. I was completely floored. I thought this guy was so lonely, and he was just entertaining a lot of young college girls. He had a terrific personality and a great sense of humor. Nobody enjoyed being rediscovered more than he did. You can imagine after being ignored for so long what it was like to suddenly be brought into this international scene."

The festival was incredibly successful, with approximately twenty thousand in attendance. "It was very important in the world of blues. It was the first stand-alone blues festival where blues was not a part of a folk festival. It proved that blues alone could sell enough tickets to sustain its own festival."

It was a triumph for Son House. He was scheduled to appear on the last concert, directly preceding James Cotton, who was the final performer of the evening. During his stay in Ann Arbor, House had gone to Detroit to visit relatives. As the concert began, he was nowhere to be found.

"I saved Son House's career at 1969 Ann Arbor. John Fishel said, 'We gotta cancel Son. We'll let Cotton close, and that's the end of it.' Cotton went out, and as Cotton was playing, Son showed up in the backstage area. I grabbed Fishel and said, 'Son will close.' He said, 'He can't follow Cotton,' because Cotton was extremely physical. He did somersaults and barrel rolls, jumping all over the place. I said, 'I'll make it happen. Trust me. Son will close the festival.' He said, 'Okay.'

"Now, I'm a stutterer, and I've got to go out and handle fifteen thousand people, but I've got to save the gig for my guy. I had to save him and his money. Stuttering or no stuttering, I had to walk into that lion's den. When Cotton came off, they set a chair and a microphone for Son, and he went out. With some amount of stuttering, I said, 'It's been three days of great music. You've heard great bluesmen from all over the world. Keyboard players, horn players, harmonica, electric guitar—it's been a great weekend for blues. But, let this festival end as the blues began: one man, one guitar. From the Mississippi delta, the great Son House!' I pulled it off.

"He came out and played a great set. I had people say to me, 'After Cotton, we took our blankets, our handbills, and our coolers, and we started to walk into the parking lot. Suddenly, we heard that voice and slide guitar over the loudspeakers and we just turned, looked up, and walked back.' I saved him right there, and that closing led to a lot of work for him, including a big West Coast tour in late 1969."

Despite the stuttering, Jim Fishel was impressed with how Dick handled an unruly audience member while on stage. "I'll never forget someone yelled something from the audience, and Dick yelled, 'Shut up, Dummy!' That stuck in my mind because it was Dick at his best and he was right. He was more or less saying, 'You drunk, stoned, idiot, you're in the presence of history and you'd better just sit back and enjoy every minute of it.'"

In October 1969, Dick learned of the passing of Skip James. "I think he had cancer when he was rediscovered because in the original rediscovery photos of him in 1964 he's thin and gaunt. In later photos, 1965 and '66, he gets round faced, and I think that was the medication bloating him up. It came back out of remission, and he just slowly died of cancer. I was in Philadelphia with him when he died. He was a hard man to get close to, so I spoke to him and visited once in a while. He was very vain and very difficult so there wasn't a lot of small talk. I went to his funeral and, some years later, went to the funeral of his wife, Lorenzo. She was John Hurt's niece and he [Skip] married her late in life."

A few weeks later, a young man named Bruce Iglauer contacted Dick about booking an artist to perform at a concert in November 1969. Iglauer was a college student in Appleton, Wisconsin, with limited funds but a burning desire to make a first attempt at concert promotion. The artist he wanted was Luther Allison. Although Dick had reached a position of prominence in the blues world, he was only a few years removed from his own early ventures in promotion and management, so he was willing to help others on this path.

Iglauer recalls, "I called up Dick, whose name I knew because I'd been a folkie, and I had seen little Avalon Production ads in *Sing Out*. I remember the conversation with Dick because I was so nervous. I didn't know anything about negotiating. I just knew that I had six hundred dollars, and that was *all* I had.

"I said that I wanted Luther Allison and I had a specific date. I think he said, 'What can you offer?' I said, 'I've got six hundred dollars' and he said, 'Okay.' I assume there was a contract issued. I don't remember anything about that, but lo and behold, there was Luther Allison. [He] had a hugely successful show, because I had promoted it so well. It was based on the success of that show that I convinced Bob to give me a job because Luther, at that time, was a Delmark artist." Koester appreciated Iglauer's passion and on January 2, 1970, he began working as the shipping clerk in the basement of the record shop.

"Prior to Dick, there was nobody presenting the blues artists to the public, and especially to the performance situations—clubs, concerts, festivals—in a way that was professional and straightforward and simply made them available. Dick was advertising. Anybody with the least bit of interest knew what Avalon Productions was. He provided such an essential bridge to carry the artists to their potential listening audience. I can't begin to tell you how little concept the blues artists of those generations had about how to reach this group of hippies, who they knew were out there but had no concept of how to get to them, how to make a career, or how to get on a stage in front of them. The only person who was doing this day in and day out was Dick Waterman. For the record companies, like Delmark, Dick's work to get the artists in front of audiences was essential, and it created the sales.

"Muddy, Wolf, B. B., and maybe Albert King had legitimate booking agents, but they were booking agents who didn't book other blues artists. Dick was the guy with this unimaginably fascinating roster of artists. He was not only the standard of the industry for booking blues, he *was* the industry for booking blues."

Given the great success of Junior Wells's two State Department tours, it was not a surprise when Dick received a call regarding another State Department tour of East Africa. This time, they wanted to feature Buddy Guy. After some negotiation, an agreement was reached and the tour was scheduled to begin in late 1969. Son House also had an upcoming tour. Dick knew he needed to accompany him so he called his friend Jerry Ricks in Philadelphia, and asked if he would be willing to travel with Guy. Ricks agreed to serve as road manager for the tour. Guy invited his younger brother, blues guitarist Phil Guy, to accompany him as part of the band.

After finalizing preparations for the Africa tour, Dick and Son House began their cross-country journey. House performed in several cities, including Bellingham, Portland, Eugene, Seattle, Berkeley, and Oakland. While in Seattle, he filmed a television production sponsored by the Seattle Folk Society.

Taj Mahal was in Seattle that same week performing at the Eagle's Auditorium on November 15, 1969, and had an opportunity to visit with them. "Dick brought Son by [for the concert]. On the encore I brought him out and played with him. There was no way in the world that I wouldn't have this man on stage. This is why I was able to be doing what I was doing. I was really excited."

The concert in Berkeley was held on November 21, 1969, in Zellerbach Hall on the university campus the following week. Mance Lipscomb, Lightning Hopkins, and Booker White were scheduled as guest artists. Despite the excellent roster of musicians, the day before the performance, Dick was concerned by low ticket sales. An article by Ralph J. Gleason, contributing writer for the *San Francisco Chronicle*, dramatically changed the situation.

"The auditorium holds about twenty-two hundred people. We had sold about six tickets by the morning of the show. Ralph wrote a column that morning that said [paraphrasing] there are lots of things happening in the Bay area tonight. Janis is here, Mike Bloomfield is there, Santana, Country Joe, Steve Miller, et cetera. There are lots of music choices, but nothing is as important as the four great bluesmen that will be at Zellerbach Auditorium. This is not only great blues, this will probably be the only time that four bluesmen of this magnitude will ever play together in the Bay area. You can see Janis or Carlos or Country Joe some other night. It is a blues concert for the ages, and nothing in the musical sphere in the Bay area is more important than your being at Zellerbach tonight." Within hours, the event became a sellout.

The concert was a success both financially and musically, but Dick was concerned about House's dexterity. "He was starting to lose it a little bit. There was a gradual decline. When I go back and listen to stuff from 1964–65, he still had his hand speed, and he could play guitar well. By 1967–68, he was starting to go into decline."

Typically, when House performed on college campuses, Dick scheduled him to speak at question-and-answer sessions for classes on the day of the concert, though Zellerbach was an exception. "I encouraged interviewing of the older bluesmen. If people knew the blues and they wanted to know more about the 1920s and '30s, they could ask questions that might not occur to me to ask Son. When I would have him play on campus, I would send in a Son House album, photos, and biographical information in advance. We would come to campus and, in the daytime, he would go to the class and answer questions about the depression, Mississippi, the 1920s, black people and white people—things like that. There was no music; this was just conversation. We'd do this for a half hour or so.

"He had a soft voice and he spoke in a self-deprecating way. He was never boastful and always very modest. He didn't understand this fame thing or why people were making a big deal out of him. He would talk about driving a tractor and working from sunup to sundown, why they worked five and a half days [per week], why they kicked up [their heels] on Saturday night because it was their only free night and how they would party on all night: things about the agricultural life of the Delta in the 1930s. Afterward, the students would be at the concert and see him perform. After we had left, if they listened to the music, they would perceive or interpret it on another level because they understood him as a person and knew what motivated his music."

Less than two months after the death of Skip James, Dick lost another friend when Sam "Magic Sam" Maghett suffered a fatal heart attack on December 1, 1969, and died at the age of thirty-two. Bob Koester had introduced them a year earlier when Maghett was searching for a manager. Dick had booked a New England tour for him, which was to begin in December 1969. Sadly, it never came to pass.

"Out of all the musical losses in that time period from 1968–70, I think probably the greatest loss was Hendrix, who I think was enormously creative and probably the most curious individual musician I ever met. Out of all the people in rock music who died young—Hendrix, Joplin, Mama Cass, Keith Moon, Brian Jones—I put Sam's loss at least the equal of any of those in the blues world. He may have been one of the great blues talents of all time. Sam was really brilliant. If he had gone on to have a full life and release an album every two or three years, I think the body of work that he would have left over the next twenty to twenty-five years would have marked him as one of the really great blues figures as a singer, a guitarist, and a fabulous showman. He was an incredible live performer. Whatever is that ability to communicate live, he had it. He connected with the audience. He had charisma, a great smile, and could really sell a solo. He loved to communicate with his music. Just magic!

"His Delmark album, *West Side Soul*, is a really great album. It's in the Blues Hall of Fame and deservedly so. It's one of those albums that you love so much that you give it to your friends. I did that a lot with *West Side Soul*.

"One thing I point out with Sam is that when someone dies young with a very limited discography available, people come to the marketplace with inferior tapes—things that would never be issued with the artist's permission. Sam had a couple of 45 rpm singles released on local Chicago labels, some of them very good, and two LPs on Delmark. Just about the time he died, the second LP, *Black Magic*, was released. A year or two after he died, a lot of inferior stuff came to the marketplace. It's really too bad because if people hear the posthumous stuff first, they shrug him off and never go any further, whereas *West Side Soul* is mandatory blues listening."

Shortly after returning from his tour, Son House's pervasive alcoholism put his career in jeopardy. While inebriated one evening in January 1970, he staggered around his neighborhood, lost consciousness, and fell into a snowdrift near his home. He was found by a snowplow driver and taken to a local hospital. The doctors saved his life, but his hands were severely frostbitten. There was concern he would never regain the use of his fingers. Dick was notified of his condition, though he did not learn the details of how it had transpired until later. A long period of recuperation followed during which House missed some important performance opportunities, including an invitation to play in a concert at which Eric Clapton was to perform.

Clapton was a member of the group Blind Faith in 1969, and from mid-year they performed as the opening act for Delaney and Bonnie Bramlett. The group disbanded in August 1969, and Clapton joined the duo, which was renamed Delaney & Bonnie & Friends. Rock promoter Bill Graham booked them to play on February 6–7, 1970, at the Fillmore East in New York and decided to invite Son House to open the shows.

"Bill Graham called me and said, 'Delaney and Clapton are huge Robert Johnson fans.' I said, 'I know that. I gave Eric the Robert Johnson tapes about five years ago.' He said, 'If I could have Son House do a short set in front of Delaney & Bonnie & Clapton, it's win-win. If Clapton and Delaney look at Son House performing before their show, they are going to be so motivated they'll just go crazy. The audience will get a fabulous show.' I said, 'His hands are frostbitten, and he can't play.' Bill said, 'I don't need thirty minutes or even twenty. Give me fifteen. Just let me have two or three songs, twelve or fifteen minutes. I'll pay you whatever you want. I'll give you five hundred dollars a night.' In those days that was just amazing.

"I called Rochester, and they said, 'No, he's not even moving his hands. He's not going anywhere to make any music for a long time.' I called Bill back and said, 'Listen Bill, I would really love it, but it just can't happen.' Bill said, 'I'm really sorry because the audience would have loved it. Clapton and Delaney would have played just inspired music to follow Son House.' That's absolutely true. That was a career opportunity lost. He would have been seen by almost three thousand people each night."

House's performance at a concert scheduled for two weeks later also had to be canceled. Richard Flohil and Dick had decided to co-produce an event they titled Blue Monday scheduled for Monday evening, February 23, 1970. It was to be held at Massey Hall, the Canadian equivalent of Carnegie Hall, in Toronto. Like a house of cards, one thing after another collapsed, conspiring to ruin the evening. "We got a very bad night of the week so the thing was really cursed to begin with." Flohil concurred, "I had the idea of having four people in the show, but it was like it was jinxed. The whole bloody thing was jinxed."

The local musicians' union required the hiring of a local musician or group, so Whiskey Howl was booked as the opening act. "So then, I booked Magic Sam, but he died. Then I booked Son House, and he fell in the snowdrift. Then I booked Otis Spann, who had just left the Muddy Waters band for a solo career, and he went in the hospital and didn't come out. Three days before the show, he canceled. His wife called up and tried to get the gig, but I wasn't interested."

Finally, Bobby Bland was hired as the headliner for the event, leaving only three performers for the evening. Amazingly, they managed to glean a fourth performer, blues guitarist Lonnie Johnson, from the audience. Johnson was living in Toronto at the time. He had relocated there with the assistance of a local businessman and secured a job playing in a local club. While walking down the sidewalk one day, he was struck by a car. A hospital stay and reconstructive surgery followed. Unfortunately, during his recovery he suffered a stroke.

Flohil remembers, "Lonnie was kind of managed by a woman I knew in Toronto. In the show we brought Lonnie out of the audience, sat him on a stool, and he sang three songs. Buddy Guy came out and played every Lonnie Johnson lick you've ever heard down cold, brilliantly done, and Lonnie never sang again. [He died on June 16, 1970.] There was a big party afterwards at a local club. The day after, I woke up and thought, *Cripes! I just lost twelve hundred dollars I don't have!*"

While Bonnie Raitt continued classes at Radcliffe, Dick booked gigs for her whenever possible. "Bonnie was still going to school. She was playing coffeehouses, but she never played the Boston coffeehouse circuit. There's a city about forty miles away called Worcester, so she would go there and play college concerts at Holy Cross, Clark, Worcester Tech, and another school or two. She was making seventy-five to a hundred dollars to do little college concerts. The other folkies were playing down on Charles Street in Boston for twelve to fifteen dollars. She would ride the bus to Worcester, stay with friends, pick up a hundred bucks, and ride the bus back.

Boston and the surrounding areas were home to several institutions of higher learning and, consequently, young people yearning to hear folk music. The area boasted several coffeehouses and other music venues in the early 1960s that catered to such audiences. By 1970, things had changed. Few clubs in Boston and Cambridge featured blues acts on a regular basis, although there were still blues fans in the area. In an effort to promote blues music, a handful of young enthusiasts came together to form the Boston Blues Society. They contacted Dick to enlist his services.

Peter Guralnick, a founding member, describes some of the work of the society and the crucial role played by Dick. "We brought in Fred McDowell, Son House, Robert Pete Williams, Johnny Shines, Joseph Spence, a double bill of Hacksaw Harney and Houston Stackhouse, Hound Dog Taylor, and Otis Rush. We all put in a great deal of work to make the concerts happen. [We] put out publicity, took tickets and such, but without Dick we never would have done it. Dick was the one, not just with the connections, but with the ability to reach out and get people to do things: to drive the distance from Chicago to Boston for not a great deal of money.

"All the shows we did were at Harvard. We started out at the Freshmen Union. I remember we went down to one of the houses for the Hound Dog Taylor and the Otis Rush concerts. In some cases, like Fred McDowell, he had played here before, but in many cases this was the first time [for] artists like Hound Dog Taylor and Otis Rush and Hacksaw Harney. We introduced Joseph Spence. We would have a meeting over at the Harvard radio station, WHRB, and decide who it was we wanted to bring in and strategies for being able to set up other gigs."

The station was a logical choice as it was where fellow members Cal Markley, Jack Viertel, and David Gessner were employed. Though the society only lasted a couple of years, their work was important not only to blues fans but also to artists who otherwise might never have played in that area.

Dick again assisted Leroy Pierson at Beloit College to expand the Convocation Cluster event from two years prior to create a blues festival. The idea surfaced when one of Pierson's musician friends mentioned the college was considering booking Frank Zappa and the Mothers of Invention for a concert at the cost of seven thousand dollars. Pierson felt certain he could create a weekend-long blues festival for the same amount or less and immediately called Dick's office.

Dick offered to assist in placing advertisements and articles in key publications if the festival was approved. He suggested Pierson contact the administration and emphasize the amount of publicity such an event could generate for the college. He followed Dick's advice. The idea immediately appealed to the administrators, and the Wisconsin Delta Blues Festival was scheduled for March 27–28, 1970.

Pierson shares his memories of the festival. "Dick booked the majority of these acts. I think we had sixteen, and he booked about twelve of them. The other ones were Chicago acts, guys that I knew and could just call straight away. Peter Guralnick came out to the show and so did Jeff Titon and Bonnie Raitt. Even better than that was when Dick came into the O'Hare airport, and I went down to pick him up. As their luggage is coming off the carousel, this old-looking guitar case comes off the carousel. He says, 'Leroy, pop that guitar case open. Tell me what you think. I brought this for Son to play.' I popped it open, and it was this beautiful Style O National [guitar]. It was not only a Style O but it was fourteen frets to the body, which was an unusual Style O, the kind I always desired. I said, 'That thing is beautiful!' He said, 'I bought it this morning, and I got it really cheap. I got it for one hundred dollars. If you will commit, for the foreseeable future, that if Son House is within three hundred miles of you that you will go to the show and take this guitar with you, then it's yours.' I almost died. Of course, I would have been going to any Son House show anyway. If it was five hundred miles away, I would have been going. If our relationship needed a cementing, that guitar was it. That blues festival was the greatest weekend of my life. I just enjoyed it so much."

In April 1970, Dick produced his first concerts, which featured James Taylor. Two shows were scheduled on consecutive evenings on the Harvard campus at Sanders Theatre in Memorial Hall with Bonnie Raitt performing the opening sets.

"His father, Dr. Isaac Taylor, was at the show. He was dean of the medical school at the University of North Carolina. His father sat with my father, and neither one them had a clue what their sons were doing. Dr. Taylor said, 'You know, these are the songs Jim's been playing out on the porch with his brothers and sister, and now he's making a living at it apparently. My father said, 'Richard's been managing these Negro blues singers for years. It's nice to see he's putting on a concert with your son, and it's very successful.' The tickets were $3.50 to $4.00 each. The capacity was about fifteen hundred twenty-five per show, and I had a double sellout."

Less than two months later Son House began a European tour accompanied by Dick. One of the first concerts was in Switzerland at the Montreux Jazz Festival held at the Montreux Casino near beautiful Lake Lucerne on June 17–21, 1970.

He was scheduled to play at 10:00 on the final evening. The auditorium, which held approximately two thousand people, was full, and Dick was hoping for a warm reception to House's music. Things did not go as planned, however. "About 9:35–9:40 P.M. people are starting to move to the aisles. At 9:45–9:50 P.M. the crowd gets up and walks out. By 9:55 P.M. we look out and there's nobody. We've got maybe thirty or forty people. Son begins playing and I think, '*What the hell is happening?!*'

"I walk out into the lobby, and it is packed. There are two thousand people in the lobby! There were TV monitors, and the whole crowd is watching Italy play Brazil for the World Cup broadcast live from Mexico City. Some of the crowd is shouting, 'Ee-ta-lee! Ee-ta-lee!' Others are shouting, 'Pe-le! Pe-le!' The great soccer player, Pele, was playing for Brazil." Brazil prevailed and House finished his set unfazed by the disappearing crowd.

England was the final destination on the tour and the last time House would perform abroad. The advertisements for the dates touted "Final English Tour." Dick had witnessed a slow, steady decline in House's health, exacerbated by the severe frostbite, paralleling a decline in his musical abilities.

Chris Trimming and Ron Watts, who had produced Arthur Crudup's record from his London studio sessions only months earlier, served as promoters for the tour. The performances were held in a series of pubs, with two evening shows of approximately thirty-five to forty minutes in length. The level of interest in blues music there helped bolster the tours, and House was well received by the audiences. "There were English publications like *Melody Maker* and *New Music Express*, which all wrote about rock, but they did a lot of writing on blues. When a bluesman went over, there was a lot of publicity. Major articles were written about them before they got there."

The June 30, 1970, concert was held at the 100 Club in London. Al Wilson was on tour with Canned Heat in Europe and came to the club to see House perform. He came onstage and accompanied House for two songs on harmonica. The performance was taped and later released as an album titled *John the Revelator*. The album was dedicated to Wilson, who died two months after the performance.

Tony Russell, British music historian and author, attended both a public concert and private performance afterward that was videotaped. "I had been to the concert at the St. Pancras Town Hall that Son had given. The word had gone 'round a few people in the know that there was going to be this filming. They were a young audience, sort of hippie-ish kind of people. I don't believe I saw anybody else there that was known to me as a blues person.

"It took place in Holland Park, which is a district of West London, not very far from the center of town, in a loft that I think belonged to or was borrowed by one of the people involved in the filming. It was all set up, obviously, at very short notice. It started about 10:15 in the evening on July 13, 1970. They managed to assemble quite an audience, maybe a hundred to a hundred and fifty people in this large loft space where an informal stage was set up. Son just performed five songs, two unaccompanied spirituals and a few blues. There was also an interview, which, as the most supposedly knowledgeable person present, I did. I conducted it, which was just really prompting Son to talk about happenings in his life.

"The thing that stayed with me is that, at one stage, a dog who'd been brought in by somebody wandered onto the stage while Son was either doing the interview or actually performing, and was just let to do so. I remember Dick coming forward and saying, 'No, stop right here. We don't want this. This is not cute.' I forget the exact words he used. A nice little dog was not in the spirit of this performance. The thing would have become sentimentalized perhaps, he felt, by this animal wandering around. I was rather impressed by this sort of aesthetic decision that he promptly made."

One of the primary problems of the tour was finances. "The promoters were very slow to pay, and I wasn't getting my money. We got to the last two dates, and I told them, 'Unless we get paid in full, tonight and tomorrow night there's not going to be any last show because he's not playing,' because once we did the last show, I'd have no leverage." Finally, he collected the money owed, and House finished the tour.

Jack Viertel flew to England to perform with House on the last dates of the tour. Viertel recalls, "I have locked in my memory the experience of going out to dinner either before or after one of these concerts and Son refusing to sit at the table with us because he felt that somebody might start some trouble. I don't think he had an understanding that in London there was even less racism than there was in New York or Boston where there was even less racism than there was in Mississippi. He was just uncomfortable in a foreign place, and he insisted on sitting at his own table."

After returning from England, House performed at the second Ann Arbor Blues Festival on August 7–9. "Son came back to the 1970 Ann Arbor festival with more stature, because in 1969–70 he had toured to great acclaim. He had been to England earlier that year, so by the fall, he had come into a preeminence as being among the leading acoustic bluesmen."

John Fishel again contacted Dick for assistance with planning and booking the festival. It was a more ambitious endeavor than the previous year. Despite memorable performances by an impressive roster of artists, the festival did not fare well financially.

The Goose Lake International Music Festival, a rock festival akin to the Woodstock Festival held less than a year earlier, was planned for the same weekend as the Ann Arbor festival. Held in Leoni Township, Michigan, the rock festival was less than forty miles away from Ann Arbor. Though Goose Lake promoters anticipated a large attendance, they were overwhelmed when three to four times more fans arrived than were expected. A significant number of hopeful festival goers had to be turned away. Unable to gain entry, some drove the few miles over to Ann Arbor. Unfortunately, they were an entirely different crowd from those who had come specifically for the blues festival. Soon the rambunctious, and at times inebriated, rock fans began jumping the fence without paying. Ticket prices had been reduced by 30 percent at the second festival in hopes of attracting a larger audience, yet the budget for performer compensation was greater. This, along with the loss of income from those who crashed the gates, resulted in a deficit of tens of thousands of dollars, a crippling amount.

Disappointed, but still hopeful, Fishel planned a benefit to help mitigate the financial loss. "We did try to recoup it. Dick played a role in that as did Koester. We did a benefit in November or December of 1970. We had a lot of artists that had played the show and people like Johnny Winter who had come to the show and who wanted to see a third one, but we couldn't raise enough to actually get the sponsors to do it again."

Though there was no festival in 1971, Fishel points out the influence of the first two festivals. "Some of the festivals in Newport had used some of the artists whom Dick worked with. Most everything had been folk and blues. I think Ann Arbor was the first solely blues festival of that scale to use as many artists as we could identify. At that point, after the 1970 show, I think these two festivals, in some way, began to really have an impact in terms of the creation of a marketplace for a lot of the artists that he [Dick] was managing. You started to see more and more blues festivals."

Shortly after returning from Ann Arbor, Dick received an unexpected call. "My phone rang and it was Ahmet Ertegun from Atlantic Records. Ahmet asked me if I wanted to put Buddy Guy and Junior Wells into the same band and go to Europe to open for the Rolling Stones. Ahmet is one of the gods of music, so when Ahmet calls, you don't say 'No,' so I said, 'Okay.'" I was a good agent. I worked really hard. Other than that call, I didn't get many gifts dropped in my lap. There was a lot of competition, a lot of blues bands out there."

The tour was scheduled for August 30 through October 9, 1970, and opened in Malmo, Sweden. Dick accompanied them on the tour and was especially impressed by the way the Stones prepared for the opening concert. In the late afternoon, the performers assembled in the venue that would soon be filled with approximately fifteen thousand screaming fans.

"The place is empty. Chip Monck, who was the voice of Woodstock, was the stage manager. He says, in his distinct British accent, 'Ladies and

Gentlemen . . . the Rolling Stones!' They come running out. They are going up the stairs and, because it's dark, the stairs have luminescent tape on them so that they can run in the dark and see the steps. They go up in the order of their instrument. First one up is the bass, which is Bill Wyman. The next one up is Keith Richards on guitar, and next is Mick Taylor. Charlie, at the top of the stairs, turns left because he comes to the drums from the back. In the darkness, Mick runs straight ahead to the front of the stage. The light hits him [as he is] waving his scarf. As the bass and guitars reach their spots, a roadie hands them their instrument, and plugs them in so there is no lost time, because the first thing you see is Mick running out of the darkness. You never see anybody fumbling for a guitar cord or putting a guitar on, because the roadies do that in the split-second of Mick holding their attention with the scarf.

"The Stones do their entire show: all of the dancing, the choreography, the piano playing, the horns playing, and Mick spinning. They had a big patterned rug across the stage so Mick could look down and always know how close he is to the front of the stage. They do about seventy-five minutes to an absolutely empty hall, aside from a couple ushers and sound guys. They do the lights, they do the sound—everything. The crowd is gathering, and you can hear the crowd in the parking lot outside. They do the entire show all the way to the last song. They finish the last note of the last song and Mick comes to the microphone. You can hear the sound reverberate out all the way. Mick is satisfied and says, 'Okay, let them in.' No sound check, no rehearsal. They did the show, all seventy-five minutes, to an empty arena."

Unfortunately, at some of the concerts, Junior Wells and Buddy Guy were ill received. "In Italy, booing is done by whistling. The house lights went down, and the crowd is roaring—and five black guys walk out. They started to whistle fiercely, wildly. They didn't stop! They hated us. Junior and Buddy weren't advertised, so the audience didn't know they were going to be there. Italian audiences are very tough. This was not Puccini, this was rock and roll. They didn't expect it. I think if they had known we were coming it would have been better. It just surprised them.

"The Stones listen to every night's show after the show. Always. They take about an hour and a half with a tape recording off the soundboard and sit around and listen to it. They don't back up the tape to hear every single thing, but they do a running critique of the show. If they liked something, then they don't say anything. If they don't like something, they'll mention it. They sit and listen and make plans of where to go to dinner, because some restaurant has been contacted to stay open past regular hours."

Navigating the customs office at the airport proved problematic in virtually every city. "We always got hassled at customs. Customs took searching the Stones as very serious business. We had short flights, thirty to sixty minutes, yet when we landed, the Stones were isolated from other arrivals. All of the luggage was put together in a big circle. They released dogs, and the dogs would go leaping and bounding just to see if there were any drugs. As Charlie pointed out to me, and I never knew Charlie to do drugs, [theoretically] why would they travel with drugs if all they had to do was stay clean for forty minutes? They could have friends who give them drugs all the way to the airport and friends who could meet them at another airport with drugs [if they had wanted]. Did I ever see the Stones do drugs? No, never. I don't know if they do drugs. There was always hard liquor and good wine. We were traveling through Europe, so the best German and French wines were always there, as well as cold beer."

Since everyone on the tour spent most evenings at concerts and dinner afterward, they pursued individual interests during the day. Dick had invited Bonnie Raitt to accompany him on the tour, so after performing at the Philadelphia Folk Festival on August 29, she had flown to meet him in Europe. When time permitted, they strolled through the towns stopping at points of interest and sampling local cuisine. Dick brought his camera on the tour, taking several candid photos backstage and during the performances. This was the last time he photographed musicians for at least two decades. The self-imposed hiatus was not the result of a conscious decision specifically to abandon photography. He simply became increasingly busy with work and ceased to carry the camera with him.

Having traveled extensively with musicians, he was accustomed to doing a number of tasks, so he helped backstage during the concerts. "On the song 'Midnight Rambler,' they needed an extra set of hands, so I would pull lights for them. Bill [Wyman] was far left on the stage. I'm offstage with my camera at the light board and, all of a sudden, I hear someone talking. I turn around, and there was Bill next to me. He was playing onstage with a long cord on his guitar. He looked around and saw behind them that they had a big backdrop, and there were people sitting up behind there. Still playing, in the middle of the song, he said, 'Dick, do they sell those seats up there?' I said, 'Yeah.' He said, 'That's a bloody shame! Those people can't see.' Then he walked back onstage again."

Traveling together for several weeks resulted in the forging of special friendships. "I loved Charlie [Watts]. Charlie is different. Charlie was my favorite. I was sitting next to Charlie on a plane as we were flying out of Germany, and he had a picture book. He said, 'I got this for my daughter.' I looked at it, and it had really beautiful photographs. I said, 'It's in German, Charlie.' He said, 'Oh, you're right. It is in German." I said, 'Does your daughter read German?' He said, 'No, but it's the pictures. Aren't they lovely? It's the beauty of the photographs. She'll understand that.' I thought, 'Well, he's right. So what if it's in German? It's got beautiful photographs.' He was just a really nice guy."

Bill Wyman had brought a pair of mustard-yellow-colored suede pants on the tour. For weeks, Dick admired the pants and jokingly commented to Bill on several occasions that he should purchase a pair for himself. Bill always smiled and assured him that he would help him purchase a pair once they returned to England.

"The day we get back to London, I go by the Stones' office to settle money. Bill is there. He said, 'The pants! We've got to get you the pants!' I said, "Well, I'm up for that.' We walked out, walked a block or two, and went in the store. The woman said, 'Hello, Bill!' He said, 'This is my friend Dick Waterman. He's come for a pair of trousers.' *Great!* I'm trying on pants, and Bill says, 'I'm going back to the office. See you later!' I say, 'See you later!'

"I get a pair of faun brown suede pants with a stripe down the side. They were satin lined and really exquisite. I tried them on and they fit. As I'm leaving, she said, 'Will that be cash or charge?' I said, 'I thought Bill was paying for these.' She said, 'Oh no, he didn't mention anything to me about it.' It was like one hundred seventy dollars, and I was freaking staggered! She's got the pants in a box, wrapped, at the register, looking at me, and Bill is gone. I gave her my credit card and paid for those super expensive pants. After talking about it for two months, I thought Bill was buying me the pants. Boy, they were great! They were really classy pants."

Unfortunately, three gifted musicians whom Dick counted among his friends passed away during the tour. The first occurred on September 2, 1970. "I heard that Al Wilson of Canned Heat had died. Aw, man, he was my Cambridge buddy. On September 18, we are doing four or five nights at the Olympia in Paris, and Hendrix dies. From Paris to London is a brief flight, so they think we should cancel a date and go over for the funeral. There's a lot of confusion. The word comes back that there will be no funeral in England, maybe a memorial later, but his body is going back to his family in the United States. So, we go on.

"About a month later, in October, we're in the last dates of the tour. We get to Berlin or Frankfurt. As we check into the hotel, on an English language radio I heard the words 'was found dead between the beds of a Los Angeles hotel. She was twenty-seven.' I didn't know who it was, so I stepped out into the hall and two or three others had stepped out into the hall. Someone said, 'Who was it that just died?' Someone else said, 'Janis. Janis just died.' What a cursed tour that was!" Buddy Guy had to leave before the tour concluded. He was notified that his son had been hospitalized following an allergic reaction to a vaccination, so he boarded a plane for Chicago immediately.

Being on tour with the Stones had a profound effect on Bonnie Raitt. She explains, "I was planning to go back to college. I had taken a semester off to hang out with Dick and meet all those blues people. That was my opportunity to hang out with these older people who wouldn't be alive for a long time, and I was going to take it. Then, Dick calls up and says, 'There's room on the tour for you if you want to come.' I was kind of helping road manage a bit for Buddy and Junior, who were opening for the Stones.

"I wasn't planning it, but it was like a dream come true. It was one of those fortuitous moments. The tour was extended, and I missed registration at college for the fall semester, so I decided to go back in January. I would just graduate a year later, because it would be a full year that I'd taken off. My parents said to me, 'We're not going to support you. You have to get a job if you miss registration.' So, I did, and then I started playing live. Otherwise, I probably wouldn't have gotten those gigs. That Stones tour had more of an effect on my life than just having fun."

After a few early performances in Philadelphia, Raitt became the opening act for Mississippi Fred McDowell at the Gaslight Café in Greenwich Village. "It was her first 'big-time' engagement. Lots of famous blues people played there like Skip, Son, Mississippi John, and others. I knew the owner, Clarence Hood, who was from Mississippi. I don't know why they gave me the gig because I didn't have any leverage at that point. I just had the old blues guys, but they gave Bonnie a chance. She was seen by some people who gave her reviews. She made it look so easy. The problem with Bonnie was she would retune between every song. She would capture the audience with this magnificent voice and guitar playing and then retune between songs. They would become disinterested, and she would lose them. Then she would sing and get them back again. She got a good review from Kit Rachlis in the *Village Voice*, a very prestigious weekly [newspaper] in New York City."

As a result of the Stones tour, Dick became involved in an album project with Buddy Guy and Junior Wells. Luminaries, including Ahmet Ertegun, founder and president of Atlantic Records, and Eric Clapton, attended the Stones' concert in Paris. "Clapton got on stage with Buddy in Paris and played with him. They both played really brilliantly. In the backstage area, Eric turned to Ahmet and said, 'You should sign him, Ahmet. He's just absolutely incredible.' Ahmet was then, and remained until his death, one of the most powerful visionaries. To show how fast Ahmet's mind worked and what a visionary he was, he immediately looked at Eric and said, 'Will you produce the album?' Eric was caught, so he said, 'Okay. Yes, I will.'

"A few weeks later, we were in Criteria Studio (founded and owned by Mack Emerman) in north Miami Beach making an album. We had all chiefs and no braves. In the control room were Ahmet Ertegun, Jerry Wexler,

Tom Dowd, Ron Albert, and Eric. Buddy and Junior were just playing their standard Chicago stuff. On the first day, it was just very ordinary stuff. There was no real fire to it. On the second day, obviously, Ahmet was just getting basic Chicago blues so they made noises about how it didn't really have fire.

"Ahmet said to Eric, 'You go in the studio, and give them some leadership. Get them to tighten up. Let's go!' Eric said, 'Me? I'm not going to go in there and try to bring any discipline to Buddy Guy. He's my idol!' Eric went in, and they ended up playing a couple of duets. Buddy got in two or three songs. We were there three or four days.

"Eric took the tapes back to England with him to mix them. He was in his drug phase, so he kept them for months. Then, Ahmet took the tapes back and kept them for a while. Finally, Peter Wolf, of the J. Geils Band, got the tapes in Boston when Buddy and Junior were playing there. He brought Buddy and Junior into the studio, and they added a couple of tracks to finish it. One of them was a Joe Liggins song, 'I Don't Know.'" The album *Buddy Guy & Junior Wells Play the Blues* finally was released in 1972. Unfortunately, the interest in blues music sparked by Woodstock had begun to wane. "If it had come out in 1970 or '71, it would have had real fire to it and would have had a promotional wave."

CHAPTER 10

A Good FRIEND Is Hard to Find

ONE FUNDAMENTAL TENET OF DICK'S BUSINESS WAS A GUARANTEE TO his artists that if he booked a gig for them, they would be paid. If necessary, he would pay them from his own account, and then pursue the promoter who refused to pay. This was one reason his clients trusted him implicitly. He had never experienced a major failure of payment to an artist until 1971.

Arthur Crudup's tour of England in 1970 had been successful, so Dick scheduled another British tour to begin in late January 1971. Complications arose when British postal workers went on strike on January 19. Due to the strike, Dick was unable to exchange contracts with the British promoters prior to Crudup's date of departure. Ron Watts, who had promoted the previous tour, as well as Son House's 1970 tour, was one of the promoters. Dick considered him trustworthy and continued with plans for the tour. Given the circumstances, he had little choice but to rely on a verbal agreement, yet felt a lingering sense of unease. "There were two promoters and I liked and trusted one. I realized it was the other guy who was going to be taking care of Arthur and taking him around to the gigs. I didn't trust the promoter."

Dick stayed behind in Philadelphia while Crudup flew to England, and was waiting at the Philadelphia airport to meet him when he returned. "The first thing I said was, 'Show me the money they paid you, Arthur.' He showed me some American dollars, some English pounds, and a check. This smelled bad immediately because the English pounds and American dollars didn't come to much, maybe a couple hundred dollars. A couple thousand was due. *Fuck!* The check was made out in pounds on an English bank, so I rushed to my bank and said, 'Can you send them a wire to put an immediate hold on these funds and I'll pay whatever it costs?' They said, 'No, you can only deposit it and wait for it to clear.'"

Dick confided to Crudup that he feared there could be a problem with the check. Crudup left the matter in Dick's hands and returned home. Not long after, the check was returned for insufficient funds. "My fears were realized when it turned out the account had been closed after putting Arthur on the plane to go home. He was cheated out of his money. Arthur was very philosophical that things like this were just destined to happen to him."

Though disappointing and frustrating, something even more disastrous soon followed. In February, Dick suffered the most financially debilitating blow of his management career up to that time. Compounding the damage was that it was caused by a musician he trusted.

The National Entertainment Conference held its annual convention in Philadelphia on February 14–17, 1971, at the Ben Franklin Hotel. Dick lived in Philadelphia at the time, so it was an excellent opportunity to showcase his business. The cost for a large booth, the type usually rented by prominent entertainment companies, was five hundred dollars, but he decided it would be worth the cost. He called John Fishel, organizer of the Ann Arbor Blues Festivals, to ask if he would help staff the booth. Bonnie Raitt accompanied him, because she was scheduled to perform a short showcase during the convention in an effort to secure future concert dates. He planned to showcase Luther Allison on Saturday night. He was at the booth constantly Thursday through Saturday handing out flyers and other promotional materials hoping to attract a large audience and, ultimately, many bookings following the showcase.

A man from Ohio Wesleyan University, who was the coordinator for the Ohio colleges, approached Dick. He wanted to discuss the possibility of booking Allison for a block of shows and negotiate a price, provided he was pleased with the performance on Saturday evening. Dick informed him of the usual twelve-hundred-dollar fee, so the man countered with an offer of a thousand dollars per performance. Dick replied that he would consider it if Allison was guaranteed a block of performances at a minimum of eight to twelve schools. Having reached an acceptable compromise, they agreed to meet at Dick's booth following the showcase to finalize the details.

The performances at the convention were brief, but Allison played an impressive set. On Sunday, Dick was surprised when no one stopped by the booth to discuss booking him. Finally, he packed away all his promotional materials and returned home, perplexed and disappointed at the lack of interest.

"Luther had a lawyer friend in Madison, Wisconsin, who was sucking up to him because he wanted to be his lawyer. Luther wanted everybody to like him. He was spineless like that. He didn't want to disappoint anybody. Luther called me a couple of weeks later and said, 'I need the month of October off.' I said, 'Wow, that's full of football weekends. That's a good touring time for colleges. Having October off is really difficult.' He said, 'I've got a guy in Tulsa going to give me some land. I've got to go down there and take title on it.' I said, 'You need a whole month?' He said, 'Yeah.' I said, 'We'll talk about it, but I really can't spare you to be off the whole month.'"

Two months later, Dick received a call from a man offering congratulations. Utterly baffled, Dick professed his confusion. The man replied that he was referring to the situation with Luther. "He said, 'You got the biggest block in the history of the N.E.C.' I said, 'I did?' He said, 'Yeah, congratulations! You broke all the records.'"

When the conversation ended, Dick immediately placed a call to the Ohio coordinator with whom he had negotiated at the conference. An assistant answered and proved evasive. Unable to glean any information, Dick insisted the man come to the phone and speak with him, threatening to call the chancellor of the university. Finally, he acquiesced and picked up the phone.

"I said, 'Tell me about the Luther Allison block.' He said, 'Don't blame me. I don't want to be caught in the middle here. I just did what I was told to do.' I said, 'What were you told to do?' He said, 'After Luther played, we went into the dressing room and shook hands. I said, *Congratulations! We're buying dates. We'll see Dick in the morning.* Luther said, *No, don't do that. I've got a lawyer in Madison. Get in touch with him.* He gave me the lawyer's name, address, and phone number.' The lawyer didn't know anything about management or booking. He just liked Luther, and Luther was impressed because the guy was a lawyer.

"The set went over so well that schools from western Pennsylvania to southern Michigan and eastern Indiana all wanted in on the Ohio block. He got something like thirty-two concerts in thirty-five days, driving an hour each day to a different college. Incredible! It's your dream! I had spent five hundred dollars for the booth, and that was an incredible sum of money. I also had the cost of flyers, brochures, a showcase fee and hotel. I put a lot of money out there. Luther played the dates for the other guy, and I got nothing out of it. *Nothing!* If Junior and Buddy had been with me for years, why should I not expect that this guy was going to treat me well?"

Allison began his tour, but Dick had no intention of letting the matter pass. He drove to Allison's concert at Tufts University in Massachusetts to confront him. "The black expression is 'you went into the alley on me.' I went up to him in the dressing room and I said, 'You went into the alley on me with this guy.' Luther said, 'Hey, man, I just want everybody to get along. I want you and Bill to like each other. I like you, and I like him. We can all be friends in this.' I said, 'No, we can't, man. I worked hard on that. They went in the dressing room, and you told them not to come to me but to go to Bill. That's it. We're done. Take a walk!'"

In late spring, Dick worked with the Boston Blues Society to bring Joseph Spence to the eastern United States for a series of concerts. Spence, a Bahamian guitarist and vocalist, was known to a small constituency of blues fans via two of his albums. Sam Charters recorded him in 1958 in his native country for a Folkways release. In 1964, he had recorded *Happy All the Time* for Elektra Records.

"A Cambridge record producer named Paul Rothchild, who later went on to do some of Bonnie's albums, Janis's last album, *Pearl,* and a lot of the Doors' stuff, was working for Elektra. Fritz Richmond, who was the bass player and jug player for the Jim Kweskin Jug Band, went down to Nassau to see if he could get Joseph Spence to sign with Elektra to make an album. Fritz was from Cambridge. He saw Spence and asked Spence what he wanted [compensation] to sign with Elektra. Spence said he wanted three sets of Black Diamond guitar strings. Fritz wired Rothchild and told him. He said, 'Okay,' so Spence made the album. Spence, as a musician, is really out there. He is really unique. It's tough to take an hour or so of his music because his voice rises and falls, and his diction is so guttural, Bahamian, and his guitar style is contrapuntal."

Dick arranged for Spence to come to the United States for a tour, which included a recording session. On May 16, 1971, he recorded the album, *Good Morning, Mr. Walker,* released by Chris Strachwitz on his Arhoolie label. One of Dick's photographs served as the cover art.

Dick paired Spence with Mance Lipscomb for the tour. Spence, at times, proved a trying traveling companion. "I had a Pontiac LeMans. It was a two-door, so the seats pushed forward so the person in the back could get out. When Joseph was sitting in the front passenger's seat and we would stop and he would get out, as the person in the backseat pushed the seat forward to come out of the car, he would slam the door on their head.

"If there were four people sitting at a table and there was a platter with four pieces of chicken, someone would take the platter, take one piece, and pass it to the next who would also take a piece. When the platter passed to Joseph, and he was hungry, he would take the two remaining pieces of chicken and put the platter down. He didn't think 'One for me and one for the last guy.' If he wanted them, he just took them. That was just him.

"They were playing somewhere in northern New England. On the way back, we stopped at a Howard Johnson's. Neither of them read, or, at least, read very well. I read off the menu: hamburger, cheeseburger, hotdog, fish sandwich. Joseph said, 'Fiss!'"

Joseph was sitting across from me and Mance. Between Mance and I was the back of a woman with big, bouffant hair teased very thin and away from her head. Joseph and Mance agreed on fish sandwiches. I'm not a fish eater, so I got a burger. The fish was a square, deep-fried patty, which is what I knew it was going to be. The food arrived, and Joseph takes this big bite and immediately spits! It went right by my head between Mance and me. It hit this lady's hair and stuck, so she had a big wad of fish, roll [bread], and spit in her hair. As it went by, it hit me and Mance in the face. No warning! Joseph said, 'Dis fiss?' I said, 'Yeah.' He said, 'Dis no fiss come fumdy sea!' Nobody sitting with the woman saw it hit. I'm eating my hamburger, and I keep glancing at her head. We got out of there before she left."

The year was a milestone in Bonnie Raitt's career. An arts and repertoire representative from Capitol Records was in the audience one evening at the Gaslight in Greenwich Village watching her on stage. Impressed by her music, he approached her with an offer for her to fly to Los Angeles to meet with other executives at Capitol and arrange a showcase in which she would perform. She immediately agreed.

She was scheduled to perform an opening set for Tony Joe White at the Troubadour. She and Dick decided to explore their options while there. "Bonnie loved Warner Bros. because they had Randy Newman and Ry Cooder. In the afternoon, Bonnie and I drove out to Warner Bros.' offices to talk with them. Tony Joe White happened to be a Warner Bros. act. We told them that Capitol Records flew us out and she was playing an opening set for Tony Joe White that night at the Troubadour. The Warner Bros. executives had tables at the Troubadour, so no one would have been surprised if they came to see the show that night.

"Bonnie did a guest set in front of the opening act. She did four songs solo, folk, and her voice was just great. As we walked by, Joe Smith, head of Warner Bros., reached up and touched my wrist and said, 'Call me in the morning.' I nodded, and we walked on." The Capitol representatives were also impressed by her performance, but Raitt eventually signed with Warner Bros.

Raitt enlisted Dick's lawyer, Nat Weiss, as her own lawyer to handle contract negotiations. She explains, "Nat Weiss was representing George Harrison and Eric Clapton, and they both wanted Buddy Guy on their labels. That's how Nat met Dick. He represented me and got me a great deal with Warner Bros. with a lot of artistic control, so a lot of my position in the industry was because I had such a great lawyer."

Dick was elated by the terms of her contract with Warner Bros. "Nat got her an extraordinary contract. She had control over everything. Basically, it was that they were distributing the music she gave to them. An independent production deal was the kind of deal that didn't get popular until artists became superstars thirty years later. Her older brother was living in Minneapolis, so she went out to Lake Minnetonka and made the album there. Willie Murphy produced the album." The album was recorded during the summer of 1971 and released as the self-titled debut, *Bonnie Raitt.*

Her career and professional relationship with Dick were thriving, but they were growing apart as a couple. "We went to play a date in Montreal. I got a plane from Philadelphia to Boston. I got off the plane and came around the corner of the concourse. She didn't see me, but she was walking toward me, arm in arm, with some guy. She gave him a big kiss before she turned to come to the gate. She was twenty, in college, and dating. Why not? I waited until we got to Montreal, and then I told her what I had seen. She was hurt that I was hurt. And I *was* hurt. It was really a very dreadful, ugly night."

For Raitt, the decision was rooted in practical matters. "I was living in Cambridge and he was living in Philadelphia. I think it was the separation, probably, and possibly the age difference. If you're never around somebody, eventually you grow apart. What we had in common were the blues artists. I never expected to do this for a living. Dick was able to get me my first couple of gigs opening for some of his blues artists. At that point, I was beginning to play a little bit, and he was my booking agent. It became more of a professional relationship and a friendship."

Despite their personal differences, Dick chose to continue as her booking agent. "The transition from personal to business was very tough, and it took a long time. I'd call for business and some guy would answer. She would be going off to play some date, and a guy would be with her, driving her. I sent a songwriter over to give her a song, and they ended up living together. It was very hard on me."

Amid the personal turmoil, he realized his apartment lease would soon expire. He considered a new location, thinking a change of scenery might be beneficial. A definite decision to relocate came after being robbed at gunpoint while walking to a nearby restaurant.

Shortly after the robbery, he moved to Somerville for a short time before renting a beautiful carriage house on the Cambridge-Somerville city line, where he remained for several years. This house also served as his office. There was a door on either end of the house, so there were two possible addresses: one in Somerville and one in Cambridge. The latter was a more prestigious address, so it was used for all business correspondence. After converting an extra bedroom to an office, he had everything necessary to run his business from his home.

One of his first business ventures at the new location was booking performers for a bar in Cambridge called Joe's Place, which opened in 1971. "Joe Spadafora was a really crude guy. All he wanted to do was get laid, so he wanted to have a club to bring in a lot of chicks. The club brought in about three or four hundred people per night. He didn't know anything about music. Nothing! People came in for the music. They didn't even know Joe was a real person."

Joe needed a partner who could book performers, knew the business, and had connections. Dick was the perfect choice, because he either managed or was acquainted with many prominent blues players, particularly those in the Chicago blues scene. "There were a lot of them out and touring, so getting somebody fresh every week was no problem. I also had a lot of white kids sitting around, like George Thorogood and Bonnie, who wanted to be opening acts."

After beginning work at Joe's, Dick met the manager, Mark Krantz. Krantz describes the bar by saying, "This was a strip with lots of bars. Before we took it over, the place was just another Irish bar. It wasn't anything special. It was one big room with a stage in the corner. Not that we made it special, but we painted it black and put a lot of blues pictures on the walls.

"It was amazing because it had a two-hundred-person capacity, and we brought some of these artists who had never played in front of white people. If they had, they had played for them at schools [colleges]. This was like an old roadhouse. There was lots of beer, lots of drugs, and craziness. It was also plopped down in the middle of south Cambridge, so you had a couple of adversarial things going on here. You had these crazy college kids coming in to this Irish Catholic family neighborhood, all of these amazing artists like Lightning Hopkins and Hound Dog Taylor, and this whole other contingent of the Rolling Stones, James Taylor, and J. Geils Band hanging out at the club. It was pivotal. It was an experience, and the best place to be was behind the bar because you called the shots. You got to know the musicians."

Dick's managerial expertise and extensive blues connections led to a successful opening week and a thriving business. "We hit the ground running. We were a hit right the first week! Real blues, *Chicago* blues. We ran a phone line from the club to the biggest, hottest radio station in Boston, WBCN. On Saturday night from 10:00–11:00 P.M., we had *Live from Joe's Place.* Whoever was performing would play an hour. WBCN plugged *Live from Joe's Place* so people who came into Boston went to Joe's place. We did a lot of these shows. The next thing I know, this is incredibly successful! My pay was supposed to be 10 percent of the door [proceeds], which, for some weeks, was hundreds of dollars. In those days, for the lifestyle I was living, it was a lot of money for me."

It was at the club that Dick first met a young waitress named Katherine Tierney. She soon became known simply as "KT," a nickname he gave her to abate the confusion created by having multiple waitresses with the same first name. Dick was considerably older than KT, and his worldliness appealed to her. Although Joe had a policy prohibiting dating among employees, they did not allow it to deter their relationship.

She remembers, "I think that I was drawn to his charisma. He knew amazing people, although I didn't really even realize the depth or quality of his life at that point. He was fascinating and knowledgeable, and it was kind of like opening a good book. We regularly would get fired along with the rest of the staff because the owner was always drunk. He was an alcoholic. Every Friday night he fired everybody, and every Saturday morning he had to call back and rehire everybody. Our reason for being fired was always because we were going together."

Dick did not want to reduce his client list, but it was an option he was forced to consider. "I went overseas with Son, came back, and then I went overseas with the Stones. I was also gone for months at a time on State Department tours. It was very difficult for me to run an office, keeping track of all the booking and routing, when I was gone for months. I was getting into Bonnie's career. She happened very fast. By the time her second album came out, she was very popular. My phone was ringing, so I had to drop some of the lesser ones [performers]. Although, by that time, Son, Fred, and Arthur weren't touring as much and Skip and John had died. It was a process where the roster was getting smaller anyway."

What began as a collaboration to present a single concert quickly grew to something much greater. Although blues had not been a particularly popular genre in Vermont, Dick worked with H. P. Albarelli Jr. and Margaret "Peggy" Ladd to present Bonnie Raitt and Randy Newman in concert at the Flynn Theatre in Burlington. The show was so overwhelmingly successful, the trio decided to work together to present a blues festival in Burlington.

"I did the Vermont Blues Festival where Buddy and Junior headlined, and Bonnie was sixth on the bill and opened the show. We did three or four Vermont blues festivals, and they got bigger and more successful. I did festivals at Notre Dame, Swarthmore, which is outside Philadelphia, and Bryn Mawr. I did a wonderful one at Beloit. The Beloit blues festival was a gathering of ten blues artists, five each night. I think practically every single one of them is in the Blues Hall of Fame now. It was just mind-boggling. We were riding a wave of blues popularity from Ann Arbor 1969–70."

In addition to Buddy Guy, Junior Wells, and Bonnie Raitt, the roster for the first Burlington festival included Son House, Mississippi Fred McDowell, Robert Pete Williams, and Arthur Crudup. Every ticket sold, and the performances and festival were lauded in multiple reviews.

Along with his regular clients, he continued to do bookings for some of the other blues musicians who traveled and performed less frequently. The festivals were excellent opportunities to showcase their talents. "I always tried to balance men, women, piano players, harmonica players, guitar players to get a balanced festival." One he occasionally included was Elizabeth Cotten. "It was a case that I listed her [on Avalon's roster] and when I got a call from a college or university, I'd try to book her. I knew she wasn't going to travel much. It was mostly a regional representation. She didn't work very much, and she didn't want to work very much. I think I met her at either Howard University or Newport. That little woman got out there in front of fifteen to seventeen thousand people and performed. 'Freight Train' was her big song. She also played folk songs that had been around in her family for many years.

"She was a maid in the [Charles] Seeger household. The Seegers had guitars all over the place, so one day one of them was walking by the kitchen, heard guitar playing, looked in, and Elizabeth was sitting there playing guitar, left handed and upside down. They listened and realized she was really good. She was afraid she would get fired because she had gotten caught playing someone else's guitar, but they were very encouraging that she should play. The Seeger family, especially Mike, was very protective of her."

Shortly before the end of 1971, Dick contacted Bruce Iglauer to schedule Hound Dog Taylor for some performances. Dick was involved with the Boston Blues Society, and they were scheduling blues concerts for the holiday season. In the two years since he had assisted Bruce Iglauer in booking Luther Allison, Iglauer had founded Alligator Records and released its inaugural album, *Hound Dog Taylor and the Houserockers.*

Iglauer explains his excitement, saying, "Dick called me up out of the blue and said, 'We'd like to bring Hound Dog Taylor for some dates in New England.' I was floored, because I'd been doing a little bit of booking for the band and I was not a good booking agent. He's calling me up the first or second week of December with Harvard, Yale, and University of Massachusetts. I'm thinking, 'This is a step up from Florence's Lounge on the Southside. It's Harvard! We're going directly to the big time here!' It was four hundred dollars per show and a place to stay. This was big money. It was a really important break for me to have this tour.

"I suggested that we were getting airplay at this station, WRTC at Trinity College, and he should call the blues deejay there and see whether they would do a show. Lo and behold, we got four nights in a row! The only show Dick was at was the Harvard show. Hound Dog and his band played in front of the Christmas tree in a cafeteria. Dick showed up with a jug of Wild Turkey for the band, who were extremely distressed when, at the end of the night and there was still some Wild Turkey left, Dick screwed the cap back on and walked out with it.

As Dick's workload increased, it became clear he needed a full-time assistant in the office to help with financial bookkeeping, processing contracts and documents, and a plethora of other duties. Jeffrey Hersh, a blues fan who had seen Dick briefly at a concert, proved the solution to his problem.

Hersh relates his first impression of Dick and the events that led to working in Dick's office. "Sometime prior to 1971, a friend took me to a life-changing event: a Son House concert at Harvard's Paine Hall sponsored by the Boston Blues Society. A somewhat tall, thin, scraggly-haired man in his mid-thirties wearing a broad-brimmed black hat and Frye boots strode out on stage to make the introduction. Despite his stutter, he gave a riveting and incredibly emotional ten-minute tribute to Son that affected me deeply. As he finished, the audience surged to the stage as the curtains opened to reveal the legendary bluesman, 'the tractor king,' playing his steel-bodied guitar."

In December 1971, Lloyd Segal, a local Boston music agent and personal friend of Hersh, suggested that Dick invite Hersh over for an informal dinner at his home. It would provide an opportunity for them to meet and assess whether they would enjoy working together. Dick's initial response was, "Yeah, he can come over, but I can't afford him." Money was not an obstacle, however, as Hersh was willing to work for free. Dick was happy to have an unpaid intern at his disposal.

Hersh's skill set was a perfect complement to Dick's. "Jeffrey did all the numbers and all the paperwork. He did no bookings and no negotiating. I did all of that, so we offset each other. *Great!* He worked for me for months and never actually got paid. I thought, 'This is great! I've got a slave!' Finally, after about nine or ten months, he came to me and said, 'My unemployment ran out.' It occurred to me, 'Oh yeah, that's how I got a slave.' So, we worked out a money deal, and he came to work for me."

Dick always maintained a practical approach for routing tours. "I was probably one of the best routing agents of all time. You don't have to be a genius to know if you're going from Cleveland to Cincinnati, you're going to go through Columbus, but you'd be surprised at the number of people who *don't* know that. I knew the geography of this country from driving it with Son from 1964 through 1967. By the time Bonnie had a band, or I was routing Buddy and Junior, I had that knowledge. It was just a matter of knowing that there was a club or a talent buyer in that area.

"I had Bonnie on tour, and we had a bus driver who got paid a certain minimum per day plus mileage. He wanted two to three hundred miles per day, and I was giving him fifty to seventy. Finally, after ten days to two weeks, he said, 'I love you, Dick. You are one of the nicest people I've known, and Bonnie is just a sweetheart. I love this whole band, man. This is the nicest bunch of people I've ever traveled with, but I can't make any money with you. I'm driving sixty or seventy miles a day. I got to get three or four hundred miles a day. I got to quit this tour.' He called and asked them to send another driver, and they did.

"Bonnie opened for Little Feat in the early to mid-70s, and Premiere Talent, which was Little Feat's agent, had some powerful women routing agents. One of them was routing this tour. She was doing her job, which was to get the maximum amount of money for the bookings. She did what she was supposed to do. They went from Lansing, Michigan, to Jackson, Mississippi, to some place in New Jersey and then came back down to Atlanta.

"The problem was the band was traveling in the bus, but the crew members had their own vehicle. While the band was sleeping in the bus as some guy drove, my crew had to chase along in their own vehicle. I said to the agent, 'This is brutal routing. This is killing my crew.' She said, 'Then get another crew. Crews are a dime a dozen. Just pick up another one. We've got to go where the money is.' Of course, with the big agencies, that's very true. You've got to go where the money is: big act, big facility, big money. I just couldn't do this. I went to the crew and said to them, 'I apologize. I was wrong. I gave the routing over to Little Feat's agency, and you guys are paying the price for this. I'm sorry. I promise you it'll never happen again.' They shrugged and said, 'Okay. We know this isn't something of your doing.' I was responsible for the hard work and the burden they were going through. I never let it happen again."

Will McFarlane, a guitarist with Bonnie's band for several years, comments, "Dick was always about the music and the people. It was never as much about success at any cost. I used to kid people back in the day because Bonnie's tour routing was magnificent whereas a lot of people were just wherever the gig came. A manager would just put you where the door opened. He [Dick] was so concerned. There were so many times where it was a three-hour bus ride. It was unbelievable how he would work it out so that the players weren't beaten up."

In early 1972, Dick accompanied Buddy Guy and Junior Wells on a trip to Toronto to perform at the Riverboat coffeehouse. Opened by Bernie Fiedler in fall 1964, the establishment had grown in popularity and was known for hosting prominent folk singers, Canadian and American, as well as blues musicians. During the trip, Dick and Wells perpetrated a ruse on Guy.

Wells had made a deal to purchase a leather coat from a man for a hundred dollars. Since he didn't have that much money with him, he asked Dick if he could borrow the money and pay him back at the end of the evening when he was paid by the club.

"I had a hundred-dollar bill I kept in my wallet, so I put it in my shirt pocket. I'm talking to Buddy as Junior came down the narrow aisle. I reached in my pocket, held out the money, and Junior, without breaking stride, took the hundred and kept walking. Buddy looked at me and said, 'What was that?!' I said, 'What was what?' He said, 'You just gave Junior a hundred-dollar bill!' I said, 'I gave Junior a hundred-dollar bill?' He said, 'Don't be fucking with me, man! You just gave Junior a hundred-dollar bill!' I said, 'Whoa, man! I work too hard for my money. I'm not gonna give my money away. You must have imagined it.' He said, 'Don't be fucking with me! You just gave Junior a hundred-dollar bill!' Months later, we finally told him. For the next year or two, when Buddy would be onstage and see me, he would say, 'Dick Waterman, give me a hundred-dollar bill!'"

A year after the opening of Joe's Place, the bar was thriving. Dick was booking an impressive array of blues artists. Among them was Big Mama Thornton, who came for a week of performances. She was not one of Dick's regular clients, but he persuaded her to do a tour of the Northeast beginning at Joe's, followed by appearances at various clubs, colleges, and the Siena Blues Festival in Latham, New York.

Dick arranged to meet her when she arrived in town, and Jeffrey Hersh accompanied him to assist in going over the details of her tour. Hersh remembers, "Big Mama met us at the Midget Café on the Arlington line for an early dinner. Dick laid out the fine details of the tour and discussed how and when rehearsals would begin. Big Mama sat quietly staring right at Dick waiting for an opportunity to make demands and generally drive us crazy with unpredictable orders. Dick and I would take a quick glance at each other occasionally to see who would start laughing first. Well, this time, Dick broke first and choked on his dinner.

"He jumped up from the table, turned a shade of blue, pounded over his shoulder onto his back and charged down the stairs to the bathroom. Fortunately, he recovered. I didn't want to be stuck at the table with her by myself. Big Mama sat there nonplussed. When Dick returned we headed off to get her situated at the Astor Motor Inn. She camped out for two weeks cooking anything and everything she wanted in her Crock-Pot.

"Dick put me in charge of keeping her out of his hair during the day and out of trouble, if possible. She'd call about ten in the morning after a late night at the club wanting to go shopping and drinking. Usually, she'd polish off a bit less than a fifth by about 2 P.M. while we'd drive around town. She'd bark orders. It was fun, and we got along just fine. Dick would then take the late-night shift at the club. I'd punk out earlier to get some rest and wait for her morning calls."

Big Mama's culinary explorations rapidly became a source of irritation to the management and other hotel guests. Dick was left to rectify the situation. "In the morning, I got a call from the manager. He said, 'You the fellow that booked that Thornton woman with me?' I said, 'Yes.' He said, 'You'd better get out here.'

"I went over and parked. I knew what room she was in. I opened the door to the hall and *Pow!* The smell hit me! As I walked down the hallway, people were hanging out the doorways of their rooms with wet facecloths over their faces. Someone said, 'Are you walking toward that smell?!' I said, 'Yes.' They said, 'It's room 234!' I said, 'Yes, I know. I put her in there.' I knock on the door, throw the door open, and the funk just hit me in the face and rolled down the hall. I staggered back. She looked at me and said, 'Nothin' like chitterlings and hog maws cooking in the morning.' She was cooking with a huge kettle on a hot plate. I said, 'Are you going to be doing that every day?' She said, 'Nah, that's enough to last me all week.'

"She broke my balls every damned night she performed. She would do a couple songs and then stop and say, 'Now I know you people work hard for your money. You pay a ticket price and you deserve to see Big Mama at her best. I come in here, and I need a band. I say to Dick Waterman . . . Whar [where] Dick Waterman?' Everyone turns to me, and I look up. 'Dick Waterman say to me he gonna have a good band. Now, I got me a *band* back home. Them boys can play. I'm not saying this band here not tryin.' They tryin' their best. But, you folks deserve Big Mama at her best, and you ain't gettin' what you paid for because Dick Waterman he give me this band, but I got boys in California where you'd hear me at my best."

Dick was shocked and horrified. She had embarrassed him, but worse, she had humiliated the band. Though they stood stunned and speechless onstage during her diatribe, they were irate. "I thought, 'Okay, that's it!' At the end of the night, I go into the dressing rooms and say, 'Rehearsal at 4 P.M. tomorrow. Be on time!' She looked at me and said, 'What for?' I said, 'You just torched this band on stage.' She said, 'These boys is *good.* What are you talking about?! This band is all over my California boys. They can flat out play. I love this band. This is the best band I ever had.' I said, 'Now, I don't want any more criticism then.' She said, 'Nah, these boys is good. This is the best band I ever had.' I said, 'Okay, you're happy? You don't want to rehearse?' She said, 'Nah, this band is good.'

"The next night, about two or three songs into the set, she stopped and said the same exact thing she said the night before. She did it to me *every* night. Why would she do it? It was because she was ingratiating herself to the audience so that they would feel sympathy for her, that they would feel

Dick Waterman with his parents, Dr. Earl Waterman and Hattie Resnick Waterman, at La Guardia Airport, 1957. Courtesy of Dick Waterman.

Al Wilson at Club 47 in Cambridge, MA, 1963. Courtesy of Dick Waterman.

Bob Dylan at Jordan Hall in Boston, MA, November 2, 1963. Courtesy of Dick Waterman.

Bob Dylan at Jordan Hall in Boston, MA, November 2, 1963. Courtesy of Dick Waterman.

Mississippi John Hurt at the Café Yana, Boston, MA, February 1964. Courtesy of Dick Waterman.

Mississippi John Hurt at the 1965 Newport Folk Festival. Courtesy of Dick Waterman.

Dick Waterman onstage with Son House while he performs at the 1964 Philadelphia Folk Festival. Courtesy of Dick Waterman.

Dick Waterman with Son House in Philadelphia, PA, 1964. Courtesy of Dick Waterman.

Son House at UCLA, April 1965. Courtesy of Dick Waterman.

Son House at the Blue Beat in Hermosa Beach, CA, April 1965. Courtesy of Dick Waterman.

Nick Perls, Dick Waterman, Son House, and Phil Spiro in Rochester, NY, June 23, 1964. Courtesy of Dick Waterman.

Reverend Gary Davis at the 1965 Newport Folk Festival. Courtesy of Dick Waterman.

Mississippi John Hurt, Skip James, and Son House at the 1965 Newport Folk Festival. Courtesy of Dick Waterman.

Susan Jackson, Skip James, and Dick Waterman at the 1965 Newport Folk Festival. Courtesy of Bruce Jackson.

Dick Waterman at the 1965 Newport Folk Festival. Courtesy of Bruce Jackson.

Phil Ochs in the dressing room of Club 47 in Cambridge, MA, 1966. Courtesy of Dick Waterman.

Mississippi Fred McDowell at the 1967 Newport Folk Festival. Courtesy of Dick Waterman.

Dick Waterman at the 1967 Newport Folk Festival. Courtesy of Bruce Jackson.

Dick Waterman with Son House at the Golden Gate Bridge, 1969. Courtesy of Dick Waterman.

Arthur Crudup, 1970. Courtesy of Dick Waterman.

Mick Jagger and Keith Richards, 1970. Courtesy of Dick Waterman.

Bonnie Raitt by the Seine River in Paris, France, 1970. Courtesy of Dick Waterman.

Bonnie Raitt and Dick Waterman at the Sunset Series on the Common in Boston, MA, July 26, 1972. Photo courtesy of Michael Dobo/Dobophoto.com.

Dick Waterman, Bonnie Raitt, Claudia Angelos, Katherine (KT) Tierney, and Bruce Smith, 1973. Courtesy of KT Leary.

B. B. King, Dick Waterman, and Duke Robillard in Suffolk, MA, August 13, 1973. Photo courtesy of Michael Dobo/Dobophoto.com.

B. B. King and Dick Waterman at the Sunset Series on the Common, Boston, MA, July 26, 1972. Photo courtesy of Michael Dobo/Dobophoto.com.

Son House in Toronto, Canada, July 14, 1974. Courtesy of Dick Waterman.

Dick Waterman with Son House at the 1974 Mariposa Folk Festival in Toronto, Canada. Courtesy of Dick Waterman.

Robert Pete Williams and Dick Waterman at the State Theater, Ann Arbor, MI, November 1, 1975. Photo courtesy of Michael Dobo/Dobophoto.com.

Dick Waterman and Robert Pete Williams at the State Theater, Ann Arbor, MI, November 1, 1975. Photo courtesy of Michael Dobo/Dobophoto.com.

Champion Jack Dupree, 1991. Courtesy of Dick Waterman.

Dick Waterman with B. B. King in California, 2005. Courtesy of Tom Davis.

Dick Waterman with Mississippi Fred McDowell's guitar in St. Louis, MO, June 2013. Photograph by Tammy L. Turner.

Dick Waterman with Dorothy Moore at the Rhythm and Blues Festival in Jackson, MS, August 2013. Photograph by Tammy L. Turner.

Dick Waterman receiving a Keeping the Blues Alive award for Photography in Memphis, TN, January 2014. Photograph by Tammy L. Turner.

Dick Waterman receiving a Brass Note on Beale Street in Memphis, TN, October 2017. Courtesy of Charles A. Gibbons.

that this was a woman who was being burdened with inferior musicians. They were *not* inferior musicians. They played magnificently behind her, and she damn well knew it. She just wanted sympathy, so she burned me every night.

"We get to the Siena Blues Festival, and Mance Lipscomb went on before her. Mance was just a heavenly sweet, gentle man. He was thin, reedy, and wore a flat hat. She sat there drinking from a pint of whiskey, and the longer he played, the drunker she got, the madder she got. She was mad because she was waiting for him to get the hell out of there.

"Mance hit an audience that just loved him. *Magical!* He finishes up, comes off, and the crowd is saying 'More! More!' He started back [to the stage] and looked at her sitting in the chair. She hit the bottle, looked at him, and said, 'You goin' back out?' He said, 'Well, they wants me, Big Mama.' She said, 'You goin' back out?' They were still yelling, so Mance goes back out and does another song or two. Fabulous songs. He comes off, and they are on their feet screaming, 'One more! One more!' She's still drinking when he comes off. He stands with the guitar, thinking of going back, and he looks at her. She says, 'You through, fool!' He looked at her and said, 'You right, Big Mama. I is through.' He was afraid of her. Everyone was. She was not only big and belligerent, but drunk as well. Jeffrey and I have a lot of memories about her. None good, but they're all funny."

Hersh recalls, "Big Mama was in the middle, with Mance Lipscomb opening and Willie Dixon's band closing. Big Mama could, on occasion, be lazy on stage, but not when she thought she should be the headliner. We showed up in the early afternoon and found that she was steaming and was going to make someone regret this 'affront.' This time it was directed at Willie. She breathed a blues fire set for forty-five minutes with an attitude of . . . 'try and follow this!' She was fantastic. Meanwhile, Dick had to navigate between the two big egos and keep peace.

"About six months after the end of the tour, with us safely back in Cambridge and Big Mama in California, some of the club owners called to report that Big Mama was contacting them directly, trying to re-book her dates without contracts and looking to save the agency commission. They wouldn't deal with her since it was unprofessional, and they knew her reputation for being ornery. Eventually we'd talk about this and laugh hysterically about the stories of her overall riotous behavior. Dick would say, 'Why am I laughing? She's ruining my reputation!' I doubt she ever thought she'd done anything wrong."

Dick was not particularly surprised by her behavior because he had witnessed it a few years earlier. "I'm in a club in San Francisco on a street called

Divisadero Street [the Both And Jazz Club] in the late '60s. Big Mama's on stage and Janis [Joplin] walked in. She was with a guy and they sat down at a table right in the front. Big Mama glanced down and saw her.

"Big Mama finishes her song and then starts a rant. 'Some people, they know the blues, and write songs, and ain't got but ne'er [nothing] to show for it. Some other people, they come in and start singin' at the blues. They think they know what they're doin' but them people, they don't know. They don't write no songs at all, and they got big, fancy homes up in the hills. Now I wrote me a song called 'Ball and Chain,' and I ain't seen no money comin' to me from my song. But now that some people done that song, they livin' high and singin' about gettin' themselves a Mercedes Benz.' Janis and the guy she was with got up, dropped a twenty-dollar bill on the table, and walked out. Big Mama was just a real handful."

The success of the early Ann Arbor festivals led to an increasing number of colleges and universities hosting festivals, so Dick frequently received requests to assist in booking artists to perform. One of the subsequent festivals was the Midwest Blues Festival sponsored by the University of Notre Dame in South Bend, Indiana. Dick attended and, while there, he was shadowed by Bruce Cook, an author and writer for the *National Observer.* Cook was working on a book about blues music. When he arrived at the festival, the name he heard again and again was "Waterman." He questioned one of the promoters, Perry Aberli, about the planning of the festival, so Aberli offered to introduce him to Dick. Cook spent a significant amount of time talking with Dick and then arranged to meet with him again at the upcoming Vermont Blues Festival in Burlington.

Dick handled the majority of booking for the festival in Vermont, which was scheduled for the weekend of April 14–16, 1972. "At that point I was putting together college festivals and blues festivals. I was pretty much the 'go-to guy' if you had some money. I could put a festival together with very little money. Big rock acts were getting ten to twenty-five thousand dollars, but I could put together a whole festival for seventy-five hundred including two bands and some soloists."

Buddy Guy, Junior Wells, Bonnie Raitt, Arthur Crudup, Mississippi Fred McDowell, and Son House were featured at the festival. Given House's advanced age and health issues, Dick had not booked him at the Midwest Festival. He made it a practice not to book the older, southern bluesmen for concerts in the north during the winter months as it was generally too taxing for them. Bruce Cook met with Dick, and stood beside him offstage watching as Son delivered a fine performance that evening. He later recounted his experiences with Dick and the blues artists at the festivals in his 1973 book, *Listen to the Blues.*

Bonnie Raitt comments, "Dick was really aware of how long it took to drive from this place to that place and how tired they were going to be. He knew how much rest they needed. He knew what kind of foods they liked. He knew how many shows to do a week."

Dick's work extended beyond booking performances. He regularly worked to ensure royalties for both his own clients and others. In the spring of 1972, he negotiated a settlement for Mississippi Fred McDowell. On their 1971 album, *Sticky Fingers*, the Rolling Stones had recorded a cover of "You've Got to Move." Dick filed a copyright claim on behalf of Fred, but Manny Greenhill immediately filed a contesting claim on behalf of Reverend Gary Davis. Neither artist was the original composer of the song, but both had claims to their separate arrangements of it.

"The Stones said that they had done Fred's version. Keith Richards used to play it on a tape player when I was with him in 1970, so I knew it was Fred's version. Chris Strachwitz, founder of Arhoolie Records, who held the copyright, accepted a settlement that Fred got 75 percent of the money, and the Reverend got 25 percent for doing nothing. If anybody ever did the Reverend's version, which was unlikely, Fred would get 25 percent for doing nothing, and the Reverend would get 75 percent."

Fred had been diagnosed with cancer before the agreement was reached. All of the negotiations proved a futile task when Reverend Gary Davis died suddenly of a heart attack on May 5. Fred received a check for the royalties due him but, sadly, it would be the only one he received for use of the song.

"I knew he was sick, and they were taking him to a hospital. On July 3, 1972, my phone rang and it was his doctor. He said, 'Mr. Waterman, I'm calling from Memphis. I wanted to tell you that your friend, Mr. McDowell, fought very bravely against cancer, but he passed away this morning.' I said, 'Thank you very much for calling, doctor. I appreciate it.' How many old, illiterate black men can befriend and influence a doctor to the degree that he'll pick up the phone and call a stranger in Massachusetts to tell him that this old black man had died? That was Fred.

"Fred was so outgoing, friendly, and beloved. He made friends with everybody. Nobodys, kings, and emperors, they all loved Fred. He was a people magnet. He loved everybody. He was a functional illiterate, but he got it done. He used his ability to make friends to cover up for his illiteracy. He would get on a bus and say to the bus driver, "Looka here, old buddy, my name's Fred McDowell. I'm going to Rochester, New York, to play a concert. Now, I don't read too good, and I ain't got my glasses with me. When we get to Rochester, you come on back and shake me, and say, 'Hey, Fred, this is Rochester. This is where you get off.' You come to the show, and I'll get you a ticket.'"

When Dick received the call, Bonnie Raitt was in Woodstock with producer Michael Cuscuna recording her second album. "Fred always pronounced Bonnie's name 'Bunny.' He used to say, 'Me and Bunny is *natural* friends.' 'Natural friends' means we don't have to pretend to be friends, we're just really friends.'

"I called Michael and said, 'Fred died. You're going to have to tell Bonnie.' He said, 'I can't. We finished the recording, and we're doing the mixing. We are at the most crucial stage of mixing. Give me another couple of days.' I said, 'You don't have another couple days. Somebody could walk into that studio, turn to Bonnie, and say, *I heard your friend Fred died.*' This was in the morning, so he took Bonnie aside and told her. She nodded her head, turned around, walked away, and went to the cabin where she was staying. She stayed there all day and all night. The next day she came out and finished the album [*Give It Up*]. It's dedicated to him."

A couple of weeks later, Dick visited with friends he had not seen in almost two years. The Rolling Stones were on tour in the United States and scheduled to perform two concerts in Boston on July 18 and 19, 1972. Knowing he had toured with them, some friends jokingly questioned him about whether he planned to call them while they were in town. "I said, 'No. I've seen the show. If they want me to be there, they'll call me.'" His response met with both amusement and incredulity when they realized he was serious.

"In the afternoon of their second day in Boston, the phone rang. It was Charlie Watts. He said, 'Are you coming to the show?' I said, 'I don't know. I guess so.' He told me the hotel where they were staying. I went, and they were glad to see me. I rode to the show with them. After the show, they all came back to the hotel, and we went out to eat.

"I had a tiny Austin Healey Sprite. It was a two-seater. There was a jazz club about thirty miles away, and it was freezing outside. I've got me, Charlie, and Ian Stewart in the car, with the two of them mashed into one little seat. We went to a place called Sandy's Jazz and Blues Revival, a jazz club in Beverly, north of Boston. Roy Eldridge was playing. We arrived just as he was finishing a set, so we sat at the bar and were talking.

"A guy on my left, who was a little tipsy, said, 'What do you do?' I said, 'I work with musicians.' He said, 'Really? I'm a drummer. I gig all over the place.' He leaned forward and said to Charlie, 'Hey, man, what do you do?' Charlie said, 'I'm a musician.' The guy said, 'Where are you playing?' Charlie said, 'In Boston.' He said, 'Really? Where?' Charlie said, 'Uh, I don't know.' He looked at Ian and said, 'Stew, where are we playing?' Stew said, 'The Boston Garden.' Charlie said, 'That's right, the Boston Garden!' The guy said, 'Oh man, I'll come over and see you, but you can't be playing at the Boston

Garden because tomorrow at the Boston Garden is the Rolling Sto—,' and he froze right there. He realized who Charlie was and said, 'Hey, I know you . . .' Charlie said, 'Shhh . . . just a moment now, Roy Eldridge is coming back on stage' and turned back around to the stage. It was a great moment."

CHAPTER 11

I Done EVERYTHING I Could

FOLLOWING THE SUCCESS OF THE BURLINGTON FESTIVAL EARLIER THAT year, Dick helped to organize the first Sugarbush Folk Festival in Warren, Vermont, held the first weekend in September 1972. Several of his clients, including Buddy Guy, Junior Wells, Bonnie Raitt, and Maria Muldaur were featured performers. The Ann Arbor Blues Festival also returned in September 1972, though in an altered form from the 1969 and 1970 festivals. In addition to blues artists, the new format included an impressive list of jazz musicians including Sun Ra, Miles Davis, and the Art Ensemble of Chicago. "It was a very bad idea. If you had that combination, there was going to be somebody you'd love and somebody you absolutely loathed."

Bonnie Raitt, who had just finished recording her second album, was scheduled to perform at the festival on Sunday afternoon, September 10. Her performance included a special guest, 1920s blues singer Sippie Wallace. "In 1968, Bonnie had gone by herself for a summer to Europe. While in London, she stopped by the famed record store, Dobell's. She found a record by Sippie Wallace on the Storyville label that she'd recorded in Europe in 1965 [during the American Folk Blues Festival]. Bonnie was enamored of the album."

Raitt covered some of her songs, which eventually led to their first meeting. She recalls, "I had recorded a couple of her songs on my first album in 1971, and Dick was looking for a way to find a family to pay some royalties for the publishing. She had been rediscovered in the '60s, done a tour in Europe, and made a record, which is how I found out about her, but we didn't know she was still alive. We found out that she was alive and living in Detroit. She'd had a stroke, and she wasn't going to play blues anymore."

When Raitt was invited to perform at the Ann Arbor festival, Dick made a suggestion. "I said, 'You know that Sippie lives in Detroit? She could easily be brought to Ann Arbor, which is less than an hour away.' Bonnie was dying to meet this woman, so I got in touch with Ronnie Harwood, who was a young guy managing Sippie. He brought Sippie to the festival and that's where Bonnie and Sippie met. They had an instant connection."

Despite Wallace's plan to no longer perform blues, Raitt hoped she could be persuaded to join her onstage for a song. She explains, "We agreed to reach out and see if she would come to the festival. I could meet her, and then I was going to see if she would sing. After saying she wasn't going to do any blues because she didn't do blues any more, she said she'd do a gospel song. One of my favorite stories is that she was in our trailer backstage and I was warming up. I did this kind of deliberately. I had us play 'Woman Be Wise' with my guitar and the saxophone player that played on the record played soprano sax, so it was really like a 1920s version. She started swaying back and forth. She said, 'That's a really good one, isn't it?' She agreed to sing 'Woman Be Wise' on the stage with me. That began our long friendship. From 1972 to 1986 we toured together. We did everything from the *Mike Douglas Show* to *Letterman* and many concerts together. She was my virtual grandmother. We were just very close."

Following the success of their previous tours, Dick scheduled Buddy Guy, Junior Wells, and Arthur Crudup for a 1972 Australian tour, on which he accompanied them. "The Australians are not wild and rowdy. They're polite. It was a good tour and made money. On the way back, because of the way I had a ticket, I decided to get off the plane in Fiji just for a short vacation. The plane stopped for an hour or two. I said, 'I think I'm going to stay here for a day or two,' so I got my suitcase, and I got off the plane."

Fiji was one of the stops on Wells's previous tour of Asia for the State Department. The impact of Wells's presence on the local citizens became clear when Dick returned to the hotel where they stayed during the tour. "I went back up the hill to the same elevated hotel. You could look down on the airstrip and see the airliner. I walked in and registered at the hotel. As I turned, someone pointed to me and said, 'Junior Wells is back! Junior Wells!' He was running all over saying, 'Junior Wells is back!' I was saying, 'No, no! He's not!' The funny thing was, from the elevated hotel I could see the plane, and Junior was in the plane. Almost five years later they recognized me and immediately started to yell, 'Junior Wells!'"

After forming a close friendship with Dick while working at Joe's Place, Mark Krantz eventually began working for Avalon Productions. Jeffrey Hersh managed the paperwork in the office, but Dick needed someone to handle outside issues. "If somebody had to be met at the airport or had to be taken somewhere for a radio interview, he did that. He was good at it, too."

Krantz remembers, "I think Dick kind of created a job for me to get into music and out of that other life. I was a twenty-four-year-old white kid and it was all just amazing. I'd go out on the road sometimes with the guys to do college tours. I'd pick up Hound Dog Taylor or Lightning Hopkins, and we'd just drive from college to college. It was great! I remember he asked me to go find Hound Dog Taylor because the car broke down. He told me, 'You've got to go get him. He's at a gas station.' I picked up the phone and said [to Taylor], 'Where are you?' He said, 'I'm on exit 22 on the M—A—S—S. . . . I think it's Massachusetts . . . P—R—K. . . . I don't know what that word is.'"

In February 1973, Dick, accompanied by KT and Krantz, traveled to the University of Miami Blues Festival. Dick's friend, Dion DiMucci, was living in the area at the time. "Dion used to come by my apartment in Philadelphia. I always had somebody there: Arthur Crudup, Fred McDowell, Buddy Guy. Dion would play guitar with them. He regarded me as being the like 'godfather' of the blues world."

Krantz was an ardent fan of Dion's music, so Dick planned a surprise for him. Krantz remembers, "I used to love Dion. I'd never met Dion, so Dick said, 'Watch this.' He called him and said, 'Hey, Dion, it's Dick. I'm in town for the festival. I want you to say hello to a friend of mine.' Of course, Dion is from the Bronx and when I get on the phone he says [in his Bronx accent], 'Hey, this is Dion. Who is this?' I'm thinking, *I can't believe he just got Dion on the phone*!"

As in the previous year, Dick assisted in booking the talent for the Vermont Blues Festival held on April 27–29, 1973. Unfortunately, transportation to the festival proved disconcerting to older bluesmen Mance Lipscomb and Lightning Hopkins. "Mance had a guy who found him work on the West Coast and I found him work on the East Coast. My arrangement with Lightning was the same. I flew from Boston to Burlington with Mance Lipscomb and Lightning Hopkins in a prop plane that held six people. Neither of them liked to fly. Burlington is now a big city with a big airport, but in those days you came in on a prop plane. When we came in over pastureland, Mance and Lightning looked out the window and the cows were looking up at them. That was just a little too small for them.

"Mance was a very gentle, sweet man and very quiet. He couldn't read. He had a guitar on the upper plate of his false teeth and he would be quick to take it out and show it to you. As with all the bluesmen, they had a favorite song that they knew I liked. 'Alabama Jubilee' was the song he would play for me.

"Lightning lived in Houston. In order to get in touch with Lightning, I had to call Dr. Cecil Harold. Lightning trusted him [to assist with his career] because he was literate and a physician. I always had to do the 'racial walk' with Dr. Harold. He was always scolding me for the way that white people treated Lightning. He talked very slowly. He'd say, 'Now people have not been doin' right by Lightning for so many years. Now comes the time when people come callin'. They want Lightning to come and play after such a long time that he wasn't gettin' the respect that was due him. The wheel has turned now. You have to come to me.' I would say, 'Dr. Harold, you've known me a long time. I've helped Lightning out. I'm a good guy. Why do I have to get this lecture every single time?' He just liked doing it. I really just wanted to say, 'Could we move this along, please?' The answer was *no*! You had to get the lecture every time.

"I'd give him the date and money [amount]. He'd call, and Lightning would say, 'Okay.' Lightning was paid twenty-five hundred dollars plus airfare, so I would say, 'I see that Lightning is playing a show in New York in two months. For the airfare from New York, I'd be glad to pick Lightning up the next night so he could come up, play another gig and in two nights make five thousand dollars instead of twenty-five hundred. I'll take him the next night if he's coming up to the northeast.' That was something which Dr. Harold could not fathom. He may have been smart in some ways, but he couldn't really follow that he should take advantage of the fact that Lightning was already coming up into the northeast and book another show. Lightning was a difficult businessman. He didn't take a lot seriously.

"He recorded a lot of product over a lot of years with a lot of other bluesmen. Lightning had a habit of having so many songs that he had no songs. He had a couple of familiar guitar runs and he'd just use them to make up songs. When you tried to find a Lightning song on a record, it was like every song was [made up of] all his songs and there were no distinct songs. Hypothetically, he could be recorded in New York six times playing a song called 'Comin' to New York,' and they'd all be different. He just winged it! He had a couple of basic songs like 'Going to Louisiana and Get Me a Mojo Hand.'

"Lightning was never going to be a slave to remembering songs. He'd just make them up. That's an old blues tradition. Booker White use to call them 'sky songs'—songs up there in the sky. He'd just reach up and pull them down. Alternately, Son, on most of his songs, started with two or three standard verses and then, depending on how he felt, he would just bring in [verses of] songs from somewhere else. They weren't other people's songs, but just random floating verses."

Dick also had an unstructured arrangement with Otis Rush. "I got Otis when Buddy and Junior were otherwise busy. Otis was so difficult to work with. One of the greatest managerial feats I ever did was when I had him booked in Rochester. About 6:00 P.M., before the show, my phone rings. Otis says, 'Okay, I'm here. Where's the gig?' I said, 'It's at the university.' He said, 'Okay.' I said, 'Where are you?' He said, 'I'm in Westchester.' I said, 'No!

Not Westchester! Rochester!' He said, 'Oh, I thought you said Westchester.' I said, 'You're a long way from Rochester. Get on the New York Throughway now. Go north! Fast!'

"He gets on the New York Throughway, and I call the people at the university and say, 'He's going to be a little late. Have the opening band play longer.' They said, 'How much longer?' I said, 'A lot.' They called me about 10:30 or 11:00 P.M. and said, 'The opening act has been on for three hours, and people hate them.' I said, 'He's on his way.' He played at 1:00 A.M., but I saved his gig and his money."

Dick booked Rush for a double show at Larry Blake's Restaurant and Bar in Berkeley, California, and it did not go according to plan either. He took Rush aside prior to the show and asked him to play for approximately fifty minutes for each show that evening. He agreed and walked away.

"Otis smoked weed before the show. The band starts without Otis. He comes out and stands there with his eyes closed. He's a beautiful guitarist. He plays a liquid, warm, soothing, beautiful guitar. He plays ten to fifteen minutes. He starts to play songs, and I realize he's really stoned. By the time he's at the end of the show, I've got my late-show audience lined up along the building. He does some incredibly long eighty- to ninety-minute show, and he comes wandering off. He looks at me and says, 'There you go! Fifty minutes, right to the minute.' You could go crazy from these guys!"

Dick was watching him perform at the I Spy Lounge near Comiskey Park on Chicago's south side one evening when violence erupted. "Otis's drummer was in an argument with a woman. He basically told her to get out of his face, and she turned around and walked off. Otis liked to smoke a little marijuana before he went on stage, so he's up there opening the set with an instrumental. A woman walks in, comes right down the middle aisle, pulls a gun out, and just starts to fire at the drummer. The bass player went over the amp, the guitarist dove off the stage, and the drummer went off the back. The only person who didn't move was Otis. People are flying all over the place, and Otis is just playing. She got off all eight shots, threw the gun at the drummer, turned around, and walked out. Otis was still playing.

"Otis couldn't get out of his own way. He was real hesitant and low-key. He couldn't keep a band together or get a regular gig. He wasn't lazy, just totally unmotivated and had no business sense or drive. I booked him sometimes, but he was just impossible to work with. It was like pulling taffy or working with a cloud. You couldn't really get through to him. Buddy and Otis were Chicago guitar rivals. Buddy was motivated, focused, and wanted to get out there and make money. Otis was in dreamland."

Booking for Buddy Guy was easier because he wanted to perform as much as possible, but his motivation was from more than just a strong work ethic. He was concerned for his family. "Buddy made no bones about it. He came to me and said, 'Get me out of Chicago. I gotta get my wife and kids out of there. I can't have my kids out on the street with the fucking gangs. I don't give a shit what you gotta charge for me or what I gotta do, just get me out.' He was completely fixated on money and getting out of that area."

As a manager, it was necessary for Dick to understand the personality and concerns of each performer. Whereas Guy was trying to provide financial stability for his family, Bonnie Raitt's motivation and attitude toward ticket sales was quite different. She explains, "I grew up in a family where my dad was in show business, and a lot of the details of the business he wasn't interested in, but I was very interested in it. Being a left, progressive-leaning person, I always wanted to use my ability to raise money, as well as expose people to older blues artists who had gotten ignored and be able to pay them better than their agents were sometimes asking for them. I wanted to keep the ticket prices a little bit lower because I knew I didn't have a hit record. I thought it was a good idea to make sure that more people could come."

Dick understood her convictions, but they sometimes presented challenges. "She wanted to keep ticket prices several dollars lower than anybody else, and she didn't want to play for big promoters. She wanted to play for the small, independent promoters, but they weren't hard-nosed commercial moneymakers and really not professional. They might have banana bread and flowers for her, but forget to rent a piano. They might be politically correct and antinuclear, but forget to bring in food for the crew. My road manager would call me and say, 'The rider calls for eight stagehands and they've got three! Where are my stagehands?!' That was the way Bonnie wanted it. She had no regard for money at all. She was giving it away and wanted to be politically correct. I suffered because lower prices equal lower commission, but my crew was really hindered by working with amateurs. I had two opposites [Buddy and Bonnie]. I was managing people simultaneously who had totally different commercial views. That was very difficult."

When booking the older bluesmen, he frequently had them stay at his home because it was both less costly and more convenient than a hotel. Additionally, some of the musicians did not drive, so Dick often assumed the role of chauffeur. KT had moved into the carriage house with Dick a year after they began dating, so she assisted him in making each guest comfortable.

She remembers, "They would come to stay and he would have to pick them up at the bus stop. He would be very detailed in his arranging of how they were getting around to their gigs. He explained that they [some] don't read or write, and they don't trust people they don't know. It was very important for him to be caretaking. I think of all the bluesmen I met, Mance was my favorite. I always thought he was so sweet, and such a kind man.

"One time when he was staying with us, I made french toast for him in the morning. He had never had french toast or maple syrup, so he was totally infatuated with it. I told him how to make it. He said he was going to go home and tell his wife about it." The next time Mance came, Dick asked if he and his wife had made french toast and if he enjoyed it. "He looked at me in all seriousness and said, 'We messed it up so bad, the dawg wouldn't eat it.'"

By late summer, Bonnie Raitt was touring with Randy Newman as her opening act. While they were in Detroit for a concert, they received news that musician Jim Croce had died in a plane crash following his concert in Louisiana on September 20, 1973. He was a close friend of Newman's, so there were questions regarding whether Newman would leave to attend the funeral, but he opted to continue the tour.

They arrived in Philadelphia for their performance at the Schubert Theatre where Newman gave a particularly poignant performance. "Randy was working solo. He was on stage and I was by the edge of the stage. He got to a song called, 'I Think It's Going to Rain Today.' He got to the line 'Tin can at my feet, Think I'll kick it down the street, That's the way to treat a friend,' and his tears were falling on his hands as he played. It was just really moving."

After returning from the tour, Dick resumed booking for Joe's Place. He spent many evenings there, and one night he was involved in a dangerous fight. A group of local teenagers caused a commotion with their loud, obnoxious roughhousing, so they were promptly escorted outside. A short time later, they returned and disorder erupted again. Mark Krantz describes it as "surreal and self-fulfilling. It was like it could have stopped at any point, but it didn't. It just kept going on and on."

Dick watched as an employee confronted the offenders. "Lee, the bartender, said, 'That's the second time, assholes! There's not going to be a third time. Get the fuck out of here!' It was pretty crowded, but three or four of them came back and began throwing stuff. Lee said, 'That's it!' and he went over the bar. We had a door with a crash bar, and he hit the bar and ran outside. I looked up. *Fuck!* There were about ten of them out there on the street! I shouted, 'Hey! Lee's in trouble! Come on!' I hit the crash bar and went out. Then I heard a bad sound. I heard the door slam behind me. *Whoa!* Nobody was behind me. Now it wasn't ten against one, it was ten against two.

"I jumped the guys that had Lee and pulled them off. Then, I got hit with an iron bar across the face, and I went down. I kicked the guy that had Lee, but he had about four or five guys on him. I was pretty thin in those days, so I got under a car and grabbed the manifold and held it fiercely. They were whacking at my feet and ankles with iron bars, clubs, and hammers. I was not going to let them pull me out. They were going to have to lift that car. I don't know how long I was there, maybe minutes, then there was flashing lights. Lee got beat up pretty bad. I got pulled out from under the car and taken to the hospital. I called my mother and father and they drove in. I woke up in a hospital room. I had tape across my face and a plastic holder to hold my nose in place." His nose was broken, and he was hospitalized for several days. Months passed before the injuries fully healed.

"Lee recovered. He came by to see me at home, and he was still bandaged. He said, 'I'd have been dead if you hadn't come out.' The kids got arrested, but nobody could identify them. They brought them in court and asked, 'Do you recognize them?' I said, 'I don't know. I hit a crash bar, and went out into a dark street. The next thing I know, I have three guys on me.' For the next year or more, I would go into a bar in Cambridge or Boston, and they would say, 'No money.' I would say, 'No, it's okay.' They said, 'You went into the street to save a bartender. Your money is no good. It will never be good. You don't have to pay for a drink.'"

The calamitous bar fight notwithstanding, Joe's Place continued to thrive. Musicians who performed there were usually booked for six consecutive evenings, offering the opportunity to earn a considerable income. Bruce Iglauer, who was still in the early years of his career, understood the significance of such an arrangement and used it to the advantage of the artists. He comments, "That was an iconic club. It became tremendously important for a period of time. You could base a tour on it. Since you'd be starting at the beginning of the week, you could play the weekend before somewhere else on the East Coast. Boston was a really good blues market for us, and Dick opened that door with this club. There was really nowhere else like it in the country where you could book six nights. Joe's was booking almost all road artists. Dick certainly knew a lot about the road and how exhausting and potentially dangerous it is. It was like a gift from heaven for the blues world for artists who were desperate to make money to be on the road and be able to go into a city for a week and play the same place. People came out. They sat on the floor. Hound Dog Taylor [one of Iglauer's clients] became a big artist there."

Two employees at the bar, George Thorogood and Spider John Koerner, were also musicians. Thorogood loved blues, so they gave him a day job at the club. Later he performed occasional solo sets to open for other artists. Koerner was one of the bartenders.

Bruce Springsteen, a young musician who was friends with Joe, was a frequent performer at the bar. "I wouldn't say he [Springsteen] was the house act because he went home to New Jersey, but he would play there for weeks at a time. He had incredible energy. He just did marathon sets. We couldn't get him off the stage, but we turned off the outside lights."

Joe's became *the* place to hear great blues music. T-Bone Walker played there for two weeks. Brownie McGhee and Sonny Terry, Freddie King, Buddy Guy, Junior Wells, and Big Mama Thornton were other featured performers. The price was reasonable because the cover charge was a mere two dollars. Most of the musicians performed three sets per night. Howling Wolf performed during the week of October 9, 1973, and proved to be one of their most financially successful acts. People flocked to hear the musicians, and Joe amassed large profits. "I raised the cover charge from two dollars to three dollars for Wolf. The week began on Tuesday night and I had Wolf paid for by Wednesday night. It was all profit after that.

"Wolf had a reputation for being very hard on his sidemen, but I got along with him fine. I got along with all of them because I was in the business of green [money]. I didn't play an instrument, and I didn't want to play an instrument. I didn't want to be onstage or sit in. I didn't want any part of their stage fame at all. I wanted to make money for them and make money for me. You've always got a friend when you want to do that."

Interestingly, blues icon Muddy Waters never played at Joe's. "I booked Muddy on some shows, but never at Joe's Place. Muddy played for Fred Taylor. Fred had dual clubs, the Jazz Workshop and Paul's Mall. You walked down a set of stairs, and one club was on one side, and one was on the other. I didn't approach Muddy about playing at Joe's because he had a working relationship with Fred, and I was friends with Fred. I never interfered in that relationship. Sometimes if I did a festival in Vermont or someplace else I would hire Muddy by going to his manager and agent. It was just a hiring situation. I had a deep friendship with Muddy. He had great affection for the older bluesmen, especially Son, who was his mentor. Muddy liked me, because I took care of the older bluesmen. I had Muddy's respect.

"Muddy talked in a cadence. His voice came up at the end of the sentence. I was talking to him one day, and he said, 'I hear you got yourself a club.' I said, 'Yeah.' He said, 'I hear you're doing good.' I said, 'Yeah.' He said, 'You know I can't play for you.' I said, 'I know. I never asked you.' He said, 'I play for Fred. He played me when nobody else would play me. Now everybody wants to play me, but I play for Fred. I got to show the man some consideration.' I thought that was one of the greatest lines I'd ever heard! Isn't that the greatness of Muddy Waters? 'Consideration' was an important word in the black lexicon. Money couldn't take him away from Fred. He played Monday to Sunday, with a Sunday matinee there. Now *that's* a workweek! Try to get somebody to do that now for maybe fifteen hundred or two thousand dollars a week."

In October 1973, Dick began a long, complicated battle for royalty payments on behalf of Arthur Crudup. Although Crudup had never achieved great renown as a performer, some of his songs had become famous. A young Elvis Presley had covered a trio of Crudup's songs, beginning with "That's All Right" in 1954. By the early 1970s, other popular artists also had covered some of his songs. One day Dick questioned him regarding his receipt of royalties. Crudup's reply was both surprising and deeply disturbing. Despite the large amount of money being made by the cover artists, he only had received occasional, small sums.

Dick contacted John Carter, the director of the New York City office of the American Guild of Authors and Composers. "I had worked with him to get some money for St. Louis Jimmy Oden for a song called 'Going Down Slow,' a beautiful blues anthem. The song was covered by a couple of people, including Aretha Franklin. He had brought a sizable check down to Jimmy at a black blues festival they held at Howard University. I knew John, and I was very fond of him, so I brought the Arthur situation to him."

Many of Arthur's early songs had been recorded on the Bluebird label. The publishing rights were held by Wabash Publishing, a subsidiary of RCA Victor, which was owned by Lester Melrose. Before Melrose retired to Florida in the 1950s, the Hill and Range publishing company obtained control of Wabash Music. In 1968, Melrose passed away. Carter approached Hill and Range in hopes of securing the royalties that had been withheld from Arthur.

"They worked out an agreement that Arthur was to get sixty thousand dollars. We arranged the date for the signing. In order to have the signing, they had to have the heirs to the estate sign and say they wouldn't sue after their father died." Dick and KT drove to New York from Cambridge, while Crudup and his children made the long drive from his home in Virginia. John Carter was there to meet them when they arrived.

"We met at the Hill and Range offices in Manhattan. We went into the office of the lawyer, and Arthur signed the papers. The guy was going to go upstairs, have the papers signed by the company president, then return with a check. The guy goes upstairs, but he's not back in fifteen minutes, or twenty."

Tension in the room mounted as the minutes passed. Dick tried to remain hopeful as Arthur sat in silence. Finally, after more than a half hour had elapsed, the lawyer returned. He was visibly upset and had no check in hand.

"He walks behind his desk and sits down. He looks up and says, 'He wouldn't sign the agreement.' Nobody says anything. He says, 'This agreement gives away more in settlement than you could win in litigation.'" Despite heated protestations by Carter, the company's position on the matter remained unwavering. They knew Crudup did not have the financial means to file a lawsuit against them.

"Arthur looks at me, because he knows I'm going to explain to him what has happened in a way he can understand. I said, 'They're not going to give you any money, Arthur. If you want money, we're going to have to sue them.' Arthur nodded his head."

Realizing the futility of further discussion, the group left the office in stunned, dismayed silence. "I went out on the street, and Arthur's kids were huddled out by the building. I stood in front of him and told him several times how sorry I was. I told him over and over that we would get them and make them pay for what they had done to him. Arthur took my hands and folded them in his and he said, 'I know you done the right thing. I respects you, and I honors you in my heart, but it ain't meant to be. These people in the big building, they got their ways to keep money from people like me. If they put green money in my hand and said, '*Take this and close up your hand,* Arthur,' then I'd know I had me something. Naked I come into this world and naked I shall leave it, but it ain't meant to be. I know you done your best and I honor you in my heart because of what you tried to do.' Then he looked over at his kids and said, 'I 'spect we best be going. We got us a long drive.'" There was nothing more to be done, at least for the moment, so Dick and KT returned to Cambridge.

Though Dick had declined Van Morrison's request for management a few years prior, he promoted a show featuring Morrison on March 14, 1974, at Harvard Square Theatre. "When the Harvard Square Theatre was just a movie theater, Van Morrison lived in Cambridge. He was my neighbor. He signed with Warner Bros., released *Astral Weeks,* and then moves on. He hadn't played Boston in years, but he was touring and had an opening in his schedule. Jeffrey and I get the idea to co-promote him at the Harvard Square Theatre. The biggest promoters in Boston, including Don Law and others, wanted the show. The theater basement was a bunch of rooms that had rugs and drapery that had been in there so many years they had mildewed and molded. We brought in a crew to make dressing rooms where none had existed.

"When Van came in he was unfriendly and standoffish. The horn player who played on *Astral Weeks* showed up at the afternoon rehearsal to see if Van wanted him to play, and Van snubbed him. That was the way Van was. That was my view of the professional Van Morrison. He's very standoffish, aloof, and unfriendly, but he was a professional to work with."

The venture was tremendously successful. Ardent fans clamored for tickets, resulting in an almost immediate double sellout of the shows. They were not disappointed, as Van delivered great music at each performance.

The denial of Arthur Crudup's royalties continued to weigh heavily upon Dick, but he had not abandoned hope of obtaining the full payment due him. Sadly, before further action could be taken, Crudup suffered a heart attack and passed away on March 28, 1974. Dick and KT traveled to the funeral in Exmore, Virginia. At the request of Crudup's family, Dick spoke at the service.

While they were away, a friend called and left a message for Dick. Unfortunately, it was more bad news. "I called back and asked what had happened. He said, 'There was a fire at Joe's Place last night. It burned down everything.'

"Joe was such scum. He ended up owing me thousands of dollars, and he never paid the bills. The man was making so much money. The phone line was like twenty dollars a month, and he didn't pay it, so the phone company pulled the line. How dumb is that?! They turned the electricity off, too. I said, 'You've got one of the most successful clubs in New England. People want to come here and spend money on food and drinks. We were making a couple thousand dollars per night just from door profit. That's not even including the first beer. How can you not pay the electric bill?! What is it, like sixty or seventy dollars?' He actually ran a cord out the back door, down two buildings to a restaurant owned by somebody we knew, in their back door, and jacked into their box. How stupid!

"The last act that played there was Freddie King, who was a large-shouldered, thick-necked Texan. I'm sure he was a nice guy, but he was a heavy presence. He had a white guy from Boston, Dave Maxwell, come and play piano with him. Joe said, 'I don't want any white guys on stage in my club. This is black blues.' Freddie looked at him and said, 'You run your club, I'll run my bandstand. I'll have up there who I want.' So, Joe took a nickel or a quarter out of his pocket and flipped it off his thumb. It hit Freddie in the forehead and fell down to the floor. Freddie just looked at him. Freddie could have broken him with one hand. When the club burned down, Freddie's equipment was in it."

Dick and KT left Virginia following the funeral but decided to take care of some business on the way home to Cambridge. "On the way back, I stopped in Nat Weiss's office. He had taken on a woman partner named Ina Meibach. I started to talk to her and, I just talked for about two hours. I unloaded *everything* that had happened to Arthur. She said, 'Okay, I'll look into it.' The first thing she did was get a list of all the Crudup songs. Then, she notified every record company that had a Crudup song and told them to stop paying royalties to Hill and Range. She said, 'There will be a legal action, and if you continue to pay Hill and Range, you will be a co-defendant.' They all stopped paying Hill and Range.

"It stayed that way for a short time. Then, Chappell Music came in to buy Hill and Range. They saw that they had this grievance with Crudup. They said, 'We're not going to buy you and inherit this festering thing. You've got to get that settled.'

"I think the settlement was with Chappell and not Hill and Range, but Ina negotiated it. The estate would get back royalties and ownership of the songs when they came up for copyright renewal. We got one big check and then royalties after that. Most lawyers will take 30 to 40 percent, and most agents also take 30 to 40 percent. Ina took 10 percent, and I took 15 percent of the original settlement and then 10 percent in perpetuity. I was in the office when the first check was issued. The first settlement was over four times what Hill and Range had refused to pay Arthur."

Less than two months after the successful Van Morrison shows, Dick booked and promoted Bonnie Raitt at Harvard Square Theatre. He scheduled two shows, 6 P.M. and 9:30 P.M., on May 4, with Bruce Springsteen as her opening act. Raitt had lived there while she was a student and, not surprisingly, all the shows were sellouts.

"The story of this show is long and complicated. I met Bruce at Joe's Place. He had been very popular there but had outgrown Joe's. Then, his album *Greetings from Asbury Park* came out. Bonnie had played a show with Bruce earlier that week in White Plains, New York. It was a double show with a third act on the bill. They started at 6 P.M. and got out about 5 A.M. The next day in Boston I said to Bonnie, 'How's this Springsteen kid?' and she said, 'He's long.' I said, 'What do you mean *long*?' She said, 'You'll find out this weekend.'

"The first show starts at 6 P.M. He's supposed to do forty-five minutes. He goes on and passes forty-five minutes. I have the audience for the second show beginning to line up outside the building. He did about an hour; screwed my timing up. We did a fast turnover and got Bonnie on. I've got the full second show waiting outside, so I went to Bruce and said, 'Look, Bruce, you're very talented. You're going to be a headliner someday . . . but not tonight. This is Bonnie's town. Bonnie is headlining, so you played too long.' He looked at me and said, 'I'm really sorry, Mr. Waterman. I really appreciate this. Opening for Bonnie in concert is a big break for me. Tell me what to do.' I said, 'Okay, do forty minutes and an encore. Got it?' He says, 'I really appreciate this, Mr. Waterman. I promise you. Thank you.' I think, 'What a nice kid!'

"The last subway is going to leave at 12:40 A.M., so I had timed it that the shows would end about 12:15 A.M. The Harvard Square Theatre and the subway kiosk are located right across the street from each other. If this thing ends at 12:20 A.M. or so, I've got fifteen minutes to get them out, and

I'm okay. We get the second crowd in and Bruce out on stage. He waves at me. Minutes pass; momentum is building. Forty minutes pass. *Holy shit!* He comes to the front of the stage and does a song called 'Rosalita (Come Out Tonight).' They rush the stage! Fifteen hundred people got up and rushed the stage! He's at forty-five minutes and they are going *crazy.* He's at the front on the stage playing straight down at these adoring fans. I suddenly realize I've got somebody standing next to me in the wings. I say to myself, 'Please, God, don't let it be the redheaded girl.' I looked, and it was her. She looked at Springsteen, looked at me, looked back at Springsteen, then turned around and walked away. I was in big trouble.

"He did about an hour or more. Now I'm really screwed because it's 11:00 P.M. We do a fast turnover, and Bonnie is going to go on, but I can't get her on until almost midnight. She did every song she knew, thought she knew, might have known, could have known, should have known, and made up new ones. What happened was that at 12:20 A.M. people looked at their watch, got up, and started to leave. By 12:30 A.M., her audience is streaming up the aisles to get the last subway. She was pissed. This is her hometown. She's headlining a double sellout in Harvard Square, and her audience is walking out on her. She played until almost 2:00 A.M. Bruce and Bonnie became good friends. I don't think they ever discuss that Harvard Square thing."

On June 28, 1973, Dick traveled with Buddy Guy and Junior Wells to a performance at the Montreux Jazz Festival in Switzerland. Their band was comprised of an impressive group of musicians including Bill Wyman, Dallas Taylor, Pinetop Perkins, and Terry Taylor. The performance was taped, but did not receive immediate release. Eventually, Wyman obtained the tapes. His search for a studio to mix them brought him to Los Angeles where he and Dick met to discuss the album.

"Bill was with Astrid [Lundstrom, his girlfriend]. She was Swedish and talked with a pronounced accent. I was up in his suite at the Beverly Wilshire hotel, and we were talking about the album. I said, 'Geez, Bill, why do you stay here? This is so far from Burbank where you are doing business.' Astrid said, 'He likes to stay here because everything here has his initials on it.' I didn't know whether these people were serious or not. It's a good story, though."

After a significant amount of time and effort, Wyman succeeded in finding interest at Pye Studios in London. The tapes were mixed there in March of 1980 and released in 1982 as the album *Drinkin' TNT 'n' Smokin' Dynamite.*

Over time Dick had noticed a decline in Son House's health and performance abilities. By the time Dick returned from Switzerland, the deterioration had become painfully obvious. "He would finish a song, and then sit there for a long time, and then look at me. There would be a long, embarrassing silence, and then he would strum the strings to see what tuning he was in because he couldn't remember what he had just played. It looked like he was being abused and didn't like being up there. He could still play okay and sing very well, but he was becoming very forgetful and fairly weak. When he didn't have the guitar and just sang gospel, that was really the best part of the performance. The gospel singing at the end was very strong."

House's last performance was at the Toronto Island Blues Festival on July 13–14, 1974. Each day they took a boat across to the venue, but the day of his final performance proved trying when he refused to board the boat. Jeffrey Hersh and KT stood on the boat dock and watched as Dick tried, with great difficulty, to coax House onto the boat. "It was an unpredictable thing because I think he had been over onto the island the day before. I said, 'What are you talking about? We went on this boat yesterday!' He said, 'Noooo, I'm not gonna get on no boat.' It took me two little airline bottles of bourbon to get him on the boat. He didn't like the idea of the boat in the first place, and I think the water was a bit choppy that day."

This trip was the first time KT had met House, but Dick had apprised her of the situation beforehand. She remembers, "Dick had told me so many stories about Son throwing [liquor] bottles out of the car when they traveled. While we were there, Dick had been really careful about not letting him get anything or letting anyone hand anything to him. Just before he went onstage, a young man came into the backstage area and handed him a bottle. He drank it right away."

As Dick watched House on stage, he knew it was time for his music career to come to a close. For over a decade he had managed House, and now he wanted to protect his musical legacy. "There was deterioration, and it continued there. I thought, *That's it. I don't want it to go any further.* I had to make the decision. I wanted him to step back at a time where his greatness would be appreciated." Dick stood by the stage and shot an entire roll of film of the performance. When House finished playing his set and prepared to leave the stage, Dick walked over and embraced him.

"After the show, which was on my birthday, I brought him home and sat down with Mrs. House. He was there in the room. I said he had become quite forgetful, and it was becoming kind of an embarrassment. He'd had a good run for about eleven years. I wanted him to be remembered as a great bluesman who left on top." Mrs. House understood and agreed.

House had been amenable to performing, but he never called Dick to request dates or initiate tours. If a concert or tour was booked, he would be ready when it was time to depart, but he was equally content to stay home. Perhaps this was the one aspect that made the decision regarding his retirement easier.

He listened to Dick's conversation with Mrs. House, but made no comment. It was not surprising, as his initial reaction a decade prior to Dick's suggestion that he pursue a music career was much the same. "I said, 'Do you want to come back and make music again?' and he just shrugged. When I said, 'That's it, Son. I don't think you should play anymore,' it was okay. He was more or less ambivalent. He had no reception to wild praise. When people thought he was really great and wanted to tell him, he would just put his head down and kind of scuff his shoes. He had no conversational participation in people praising him."

CHAPTER 12

WALKIN' BLUES

SON HOUSE'S RETIREMENT ALLOWED DICK TO FOCUS SOLELY ON HIS work with Bonnie Raitt. As her career flourished, she felt it necessary to relocate to California to be nearer Warner Bros.' offices. It was a logical and wise career move and, though they would be living on opposite coasts, she chose to retain Dick as her booking agent.

She was scheduled to perform again at the Troubadour, but unlike her previous performance, this time she was the featured act. Dick flew to California to visit and attend the concert. Afterward, Dick found himself in a dangerous situation.

"We had gotten paid, so I had her money. It was maybe twelve to fifteen hundred dollars. I went to La Brea Boulevard to a twenty-four-hour restaurant. That's a very busy part of the city. I'm sitting at the counter. I had a newspaper, and when I read the sports section, I *really* read the sports section. I'm reading the sports section, turn around, and the guy on the stool next to me is sitting with his hands up in the air. I fold the newspaper down and there's a guy on the other side of the counter, maybe two feet in front of me, with a ski mask and a shotgun. He points it at me and says, 'Welcome to the party.'

"This is a big, crowded restaurant. Apparently, he had come in, dropped down to one knee, and was robbing the cash register. I turn to the guy next to me and say, 'How long has he been here?' The guy said, 'A while.' He gets up, turns the gun, and says, 'I'm coming around with a paper bag. Put all your money into it.' I think, *Holy shit! I've got Bonnie's money!* I reached into my pocket. I had all the money folded over, so I put my finger into the middle of the roll and slide out two bills: either two dollars or a one and a five. Then, I put my other fingers on the rest of the roll. I'm sitting, and he's on the other side of me, so he can't see me from my chest down. I take the roll out of my pocket, drop it next to my foot, put my foot on it, and bring up the two bills. The bag comes around, and I make a big deal of sticking my hand in the bag and my hand coming back up empty. He robs everybody, walks out with the shotgun, and runs off through the parking lot. A woman behind me went ballistic. She was screaming, 'You didn't give him your money! You dropped your money under your foot! You could have gotten us killed!' I said, 'I'm not in his business, I'm in my business. Robbery is not a voluntary process.'"

Maria Muldaur also had moved to California the previous year and was faced with the same difficult decision of whether to continue with Dick as her booking agent. She had met Dick in the mid-1960s in Cambridge at the Club 47. The end of her marriage to musician Geoff Muldaur in 1972 signaled the demise of their musical partnership, so she was left to forge a solo career. Realizing the challenges she faced, Dick offered to help with some booking and put together some shows featuring her and Bonnie Raitt.

Warner Reprise offered Maria an opportunity to record a solo album. The self-titled album *Maria Muldaur* was released in late 1973 and was more successful than she could have imagined. She recalls, "I went out to California thinking nothing more than that I was going to get out of the bitter, freezing, cold weather of Woodstock for the winter. I thought I'd make a little album, get some session scale pay for it, avoid shoveling myself out of the driveway, and that was about as much of a vision as I had for that little endeavor. Much to everyone's surprise, everyone just immediately took to the album and it started being played as an album."

Her single, "Midnight at the Oasis," climbed the charts. A few months later she was featured on the cover of the August 1974 edition of *Rolling Stone* magazine and nominated for three Grammy Awards. She also received invitations to perform on the *Johnny Carson Show* and the *Midnight Special.* Warner Bros. was delighted with all the publicity, but there was concern about her management.

Muldaur explains, "My exposure and popularity continued to grow. At a certain point, Warner Bros. called me into their offices and told me, 'Listen, we know you love Dick Waterman. We know you have a long-time history with him from the Club 47 days and the Cambridge folk scene. He's doing a great job with Bonnie, but, much to everybody's surprise, your popularity is climbing. You're getting requests to do more and more things. We really feel that as good a guy as Dick Waterman is, there's no way he can handle that level of professional activity. He's just one guy in an office with an answering machine, and he's already quite busy with Bonnie. We're not getting the feeling that he would be able to handle all these offers that are coming in, so we've handpicked for you this other agent, Elliott Abbott.'

"I just sat there kind of overwhelmed. I felt an enormous loyalty to Dick. I said, 'Well, but Dick's a good guy. I've been with him for so long and I trust him.' But they just kept saying, 'Yes, that's all true. We understand that, Maria, but this is your chance to really get on out there and do things you've never dreamed of before. This agency is going to be the one that's going to be able to handle all of that for you.'"

Feeling heartbroken and pressured to comply with the company's demands, she tearfully approached Dick and explained what had transpired during the meeting. Dick listened and gave her his blessing. "I said, 'I love you, Maria. We've been pals for years. This is business. Business comes and business goes. Friendship is forever. Do what you have to do.' And, we have always been friends.

"I had her poised for success, and then she was taken from me. I met Elliott Abbott, her new manager. He had a tennis sweater on over his shoulders with the arms folded over his chest. I looked at him and thought, *You're leaving me for that? Yuck.* She didn't have a single thing in common with this guy. I thought, *This isn't going to last.*"

Unfortunately, Maria's concerns proved well founded. She remembers, "It wasn't very long after that I came to regret the move. Bonnie's career continued to climb because Dick was doing it old school. He would really pay attention to which markets she was popular in and book her maybe one, two, or three times at a venue of a certain size. If her popularity really exceeded that, then maybe the fourth time she came into the particular city he'd bump her up to a bigger venue. Whereas, unbeknownst to me, they [the agency representing her] had a lot of acts. They just would do something that agents do, which was to say, 'You want Randy Newman? Well, then you have to put Maria in a big auditorium this month.' I got out on my next big tour and now I'm on the cover of *Rolling Stone*. I ended up playing a lot of markets in big venues where I was only maybe, with luck, half filling them. The venue would pay me per the contract, but made an immediate mental note 'Let's not have her again. She's not very big in this market.'

"Instead of building slowly, they went for the big grab of quick money and, consequently, the way my booking developed just was very short lived because they hadn't done it the old school way that Dick Waterman did it. Dick did it with great love and care. He truly loved the music of the people he was presenting. Everything he's done for all those old blues artists is invaluable. It was a labor of love for Dick. He didn't try to parlay Mississippi John Hurt against Son House. He really cared. He really knew what each artist was about, and he booked them appropriately and really built their careers."

Although Dick spent most of his time working, he sometimes hosted an all-night poker game for friends, which often lasted from late evening until the following morning. "I don't think it was a regularly scheduled game. You should only play poker with people you know because so much of poker is bluffing, not bluffing, or only betting when you have a good hand.

You learn habits and tendencies. To get into a big-money poker game with strangers is just really dangerous."

KT remembers one evening when Phil Ochs stopped by to join the game. "It was an amazing evening. It seemed like everyone had a creative side. By the early morning, Phil had made three predictions about the year to come. He said the war in Vietnam would be over, Nixon would be out of office, and there was one other thing. To this day, none of us can remember what the third prediction was. The guys all laughed and said there was no way that this stuff was going to happen. The war was in full swing at that point. They kind of took bets on it, and Phil wrote his predictions down on a piece of paper. Within a year, Nixon was out of office, and we were out of Vietnam.

"Who could have known those things ahead of time? Phil did, and he was willing to put his word on it. Dick had explained to me that he had a dark side and he was depressed a lot. He committed suicide not too long afterward [April 9, 1976]."

Phil was a frequent guest at Dick's house. "He stayed with me all the time when he played in Cambridge and in other clubs in 1963 through 1966. If he was playing north of Boston at the Kings Rook or at Club 47, he would come and I would drive him. He was rehearsing or writing new songs all the time. We had a lot of time together. I helped with a couple of songs—a line here, a word there. He got stuck writing the song, 'Here's to the State of Mississippi.'

"To hold a conversation with Phil was like the expression 'sixes and sevens.' It means they don't quite connect. We in Cambridge were involved in civil rights, voter registration, the Negro in the South, and 'We Shall Overcome.' Phil was into right wing terrorist execution squads in Central America. I would say, 'Phil, it's just folk music. It's just fucking folk music.' But, he would say, 'No. It's your world. It's all connected. We're an evil country. We're propping up dictatorships all over the world. We're oppressing hundreds of thousands of people through military regimes and dictatorships. We're enslaving people all over the world.' I would just give up. I couldn't make the connection and he couldn't get me to understand this on his level. He was *way* out there. He was so far ahead of everyone else.

"He was really nervous, twitchy, and agitated. He had all kinds of ticks and mannerisms. Phil's mind was just different from other people. He had severe issues. He was probably bipolar but he wasn't the kind of person who would have taken his meds regularly anyway."

Dick had booked Buddy Guy and Junior Wells to perform July 3–6, 1975, at the Bottom Line in New York City. Muddy Waters had been the featured artist for a few days prior, and Bob Dylan sat in with him for an evening. Dick and KT arrived early to have a drink and watch Guy and Wells perform.

"Dylan, at that point, had just sat in with Muddy, so he had the itch to play. He came up to me at the bar and asked me if he could sit in. I went backstage and said to Buddy, 'Bob Dylan wants to sit in. He's a very famous musician. He'll be able to fall right in.' A. C. Reed, the horn player, said, 'If he don't know the changes, he can mess you up. Can't be bringing strangers up on stage.' Buddy looked at me, and I said, 'It would do you good because he's really famous. He writes fabulous songs. He was sort of retired for a while, but him playing with you would be front-page music news. It would be a big deal if he got on stage with you.' Everybody looked at Junior for an opinion. Junior, normally, would be all for publicity. Junior said, 'We gotta listen to A. C., man. If the guy don't know the changes, he can mess you up.' Buddy nodded his head. I said, 'What are you talking about? This guy is incredibly famous. This would be headlines all over the music world if he sits in with you. This is freaking Bob Dylan! This would be huge!' He said, 'No, if he don't know the songs and just messes it up, I don't want that.' Period. End of story. I had to go back and tell Dylan that he couldn't sit in with Buddy and Junior."

Later that summer, promoter Bill Graham was organizing a performance for his Days on the Green concert series in Oakland, California. Initially, Led Zeppelin was to be the featured act at a concert scheduled for August 23–24, 1975. Dick had a client he felt would be a suitable choice as an opening act for Led Zeppelin, so he contacted Graham's office. He left his name and his parents' home telephone number because he was leaving for a visit with them. The return call resulted in frustration for both Dick and his parents, exposing generational and cultural gaps between them.

"The phone was in a little hallway with a little vestibule. The kitchen was adjacent to it, and around the kitchen, out of sight, was the dining area. My mother and father had gone in for dinner. My father was sitting down, and my mother was getting ready to take dinner off the stove. The phone rang, and I answered. The woman said, 'I have Bill Graham for you.' I said, 'Fine,' and Bill came on the line. He said, 'You want to put this artist on with the headliner?' I said, 'Yeah.' He said, 'The act is perfect. The price is right, the music is right, and the building is right.' His voice came up, and he said, 'But I *can't* do it! The sons of bitches managing the headliner have restricted my right to choose the opener. They want to put their own act on. Sons of bitches! They're the wrong act and the wrong money. Your act is the right thing.'

"He's getting louder and louder. I can't take the phone off my ear or the sound will go shooting down the vestibule into the kitchen. He's yelling and it's really hurting my ear. I finally lifted the phone off my ear about an inch, and my mother, in the kitchen with a plate in her hand, just froze. Bill is really yelling how his hands are tied about what to do. He can't put a support act on that he wants because of the manager, Peter Grant, with Led Zeppelin. Bill and Peter hated each other, and it went unabated until their deaths. Bill is just screaming and hollering about the injustice of how he can't control his own show. My mother and father are hearing this, so I said, 'Okay, Bill, whatever you say.' He says, 'I can't do what I want!' Then he slams down the phone.

"I walk in and sit down. Everyone is really quiet. My father is eating. He said, 'Is this a way to make a living, to let a man yell at you like that?' My mother said, 'Such a terrible thing to be in a business where people yell at each other like that.' My father said, 'Why do you have to take this abuse from this man?' I said, 'No, no, he's my friend. He wants to help me; it's just that the circumstances have his hands tied. He can't help me. He's really not a bad man.'

"The phone rang again and everyone was quiet. I got up, went down the hall, picked up the phone, and the woman said, 'I have Mr. Graham for you.' I said, 'Yes, Bill,' and he said, 'I'm sorry. I didn't mean to blow up at you. It was my fault. I shouldn't act that way.' I said, 'Okay.' Then, it all got to him again. He said, 'It's just that these sons of bitches, they get power, and they think they know what's best for booking! They don't care what the audience should see. They don't care about the right act. Your act is the right act. They don't care about building a show. All they care about is power and lining their pockets. Money, greed, power! Those sons of bitches!' He just kept right on steamrolling over the whole thing. I said, 'I understand, Bill. We'll do it next time,' and hung up.

"I went back in and sat down. My mother was looking at me, not saying anything, but just shifting her weight. She was really agitated that her only son was being buffeted around and taking such punishment. I said, 'He's a nice man, and he's trying to help me. It's just that other people have control over the show. He can't use my act like he wants to.'

"My father had been a doctor in our small town since the 1920s, so he only had sick people who came to him in their time of need. He had tremendous respect and prestige. No one yelled at my father. He was thought of as being a wise man and a leader. He couldn't understand this kind of abuse. He never gave it and would never take it. He said, 'What kind of Meshugana business is this that people would yell at each other? And you say he's your friend trying to help you? Do you have to do this? Do you have to let people yell at you like that?' Meshugana is the Yiddish word which means a crazy person who makes no sense. I said, 'No. Nobody yells at me. This is just one incident.' My father said, 'You know, you have your pride, you have your self-respect, but you don't want to have people yell at you. This is a terrible thing.'

"It was very complex what was going on. You have Jewish people who have worked their way up from poverty to being a strong, respected, healthy, well-liked, powerful family in town. Now their son was beaten down and taking such terrible abuse on the phone from someone he'd said wasn't angry and was a good guy. My mother and father were just bewildered. It was another culture where someone could yell and scream at me, and I just held the phone and took it. That was not anything that had come into their lifestyle. They couldn't understand why I let a man yell at me.

"I knew that Bill loved to craft a good show. Bill was happiest when the headliner sold the tickets and people left talking about the opening act. That was Bill's glory. If the opening act came in and stole the show from the headliner, Bill loved that because that meant he had crafted the right show."

KT, who had visited his parents' home, comments on the cultural conflict within their family. "I think a lot of what Dick was about was searching for his parents' approval because it wasn't immediately clear in their minds that what he was doing was valuable, as opposed to his sister who had a more mainstream career in publishing. I think it took them some years before they could acknowledge that they should be proud of their son. He had multiple careers: he was a sportswriter, he did some photography, he did managing, but he was managing lesser-known artists because Bonnie wasn't big at that time. They were older and pretty rigid. They valued different things. Probably some of that lack of understanding had to do with when he was booking for Joe's Place. They thought, 'What are you really doing? You're hanging out in a club, and you've got a younger girlfriend.' I think they didn't respect that. I'm sure that was not their initial hope for him. I think they dearly loved him in spite of the fact they didn't understand his career decisions, and there was disapproval. I definitely felt the disapproval personally, and I felt it for him."

Despite their differences, Dick often introduced his friends and the artists he managed to his parents. "My mother and father met, at one point, almost all the bluesmen. They would say to my mother and father what a good boy they had, how good I was, how honest I was, and that I took care of them. My mother felt because they [the bluesmen] were quiet and didn't talk very much that she had to speak extra loudly to them. I even had Son and Evie House down to their house. My mother made the guestroom nice for them."

Rollene attributes Dick's unquestioning acceptance of others to their father, saying, "One of the things that I can remember [was] my father was a very 'class-less' person, meaning that in the best way. My father's patients could be what were known locally in town as 'deadbeats' or [they] could be a banker's family. I think that there must have been something in that atmosphere that my brother grew up with. My brother, I guess the expression was, 'had no side.'

"I think my brother had a very strong identity with his artists whether he was taking their photograph or whether he was traveling around the country [with them]. I think there was a lot of my brother, either culturally or personally, that was 'other.' It was 'different from' and he identifies very strongly with people and talent which is not mainstream.

"He brought Son House, among others, to our beautiful, elegant, Georgian colonial house on the hill. That was just a natural thing for my brother. They [parents] went along with that. Whoever my brother brought home, that was good. My dad would take care of them medically, and my mother would be sure there was always a great meal."

His parents developed a fondness for several of the artists with whom he worked. "They liked Buddy and Junior. When Bonnie became popular playing places like the Music Hall in Boston or the Cape Cod Melody Tent in Hyannis, she would always stop the show and dedicate a song to them. They really liked that a lot. That meant a lot to them to receive that type of recognition."

Unfortunately, Dick's romantic relationship with KT ended later that year. She remembers, "I walked into Jack's, a club on Massachusetts Avenue in Cambridge, while he was with someone else. It was really clear to me that something was about to happen based on the body language. I moved out the next day. There wasn't any question of working it out or talking it out. It was just me going. I was heartbroken."

In late 1975, Dick received an unexpected call from Phil Ochs requesting help with booking. "He called me and said, 'Listen, man, I'm broke, and I need work. Help me find a gig somewhere.' I called Allen Pepper, who was a co-owner and booker of the Bottom Line, a well-known folk club in Greenwich Village. I said to Allen, 'I got a call from Phil Ochs, and he really needs some help. Do you have any kind of show that you could put him on?' There was a pause and he said, 'I can't help you, Dick.' I said, 'Really, Allen? Nothing at all?' He said, 'Look, he's fallen a long way. He came in here and was totally disruptive; getting drunk, starting fights, just being a real distraction. He just made it crazy for everybody. The employees couldn't handle him, so I had to bar him.' I said, 'Phil Ochs is barred from the Bottom Line?!' He said, 'You don't understand, Dick. He's not the same. He's just out of control.' I said, 'Thanks, Allen. I appreciate you being candid with me.' He said, 'I don't know what to do. I love him, and I've played him for years, but I can't play him the way he is now.'"

This revelation shocked Dick because he had not seen Ochs in some time. He had always known Ochs had problems, observing some of his struggles in previous years, but it appeared they had become severe and debilitating. Ochs's alcoholism had worsened, and he was struggling with mental illness. He claimed that he was now a man named John Train, and that Train had killed the true Phil Ochs. Just a few months later, in April 1976, he committed suicide.

Dick sadly recalls the years preceding Ochs's death. "He was a real New York person. He went to L.A. and signed with A&M Records owned by Herb Alpert and Jerry Moss. He never should have moved to California. He spent some years there but he never took to that scene. He tried different incarnations, but the original 1963–65 Ochs was great. So brilliant! By the time he got back to the East Coast, he was really messed up. Very clearly, he'd lost his muse."

By fall 1974, Dick was booking Bonnie Raitt's "Turkeys on Wheels" tour. They were finalizing arrangements for Tom Waits to appear as her opening act when Dick received a call from an agent. "He said, 'Do you have an opener for Bonnie's tour?' I said, 'Yes, it's going to be Tom Waits.' The guy said, 'Well, can I at least make a pitch?' I said, 'Yeah, okay.' He said, 'We're representing a guy named Steve Martin.' I said, 'Okay. What does he do?' He said, 'Well, he's a banjo player. He comes out on stage in a white suit and plays the banjo. He's got a fake arrow through his head, and he blows up animal balloons.' So, I said, 'Okay, let me get this straight. A banjo player comes out with a white suit. He's got a fake arrow through his head and blows up animal balloons?' The guy says, 'Yeah, and he's got a new record on Warner Bros. which is about King Tut.' I said, 'King Tut? As in the Egyptian tomb?' He said, 'Yeah, it's really funny.' I said, 'It's about King Tut, and it's really funny?' He said, 'Yeah.' I said, 'Okay.'

"I went to Bonnie and said, 'I got a guy that pitched an opening to the tour.' She said, 'What is it?' I said, 'It's a guy named Steve Martin. He plays banjo. Comes out in a white suit with a fake arrow through his head, and he blows up animal balloons. He's got a new record out about King Tut.' Bonnie looked at me, and I looked at Bonnie. Bonnie said, 'Tom Waits.' That was the whole conversation."

On November 16, 1974, Waits and Raitt played a sold-out concert at the D.A.R. in Washington, DC, their last performance of the tour. The same evening, Little Feat played at another sold-out performance at the Capital Center in Landover, Maryland. The evening was a triumph for the artists and Warner Bros. Records, as both Raitt and Little Feat were signed to their label. In celebration, Warner Bros. hosted a huge party in the Grand Ballroom of the famed Watergate Hotel. Dick was in attendance, but the festivities took an unexpected turn.

"Somebody said, 'Hey, Dick, somebody wants to see you in the kitchen pantry.' I went down the hallway, pushed the door, walked in, and I didn't see anybody. It was a huge kitchen, all metal and tables. I turned around, and I got jumped and knocked to the floor. It was Tom Hoskins and another guy. They were kicking me and beating me. I got up and headed out of there because they would have beaten me to death. I pushed my way up, and they were grabbing me. Finally, I got my legs under me. I made one lunge, knocked the door open, and fell into the ballroom. People turned around and looked as Hoskins and the other guy ran away. They asked me, 'What happened?' I said, 'You saved my life.'

"I'm standing in the ballroom and, suddenly, somebody yelled, 'Look out!' I turned around, and it was Hoskins and that guy coming after me in front of about five hundred people. They came down the stairs and jumped me. People just started to shriek, 'What is it? Who are they?' They grabbed me and were beating me again.

"Bonnie had a black drummer named Dennis Whitted, a big guy, and he reached in with his hands and grabbed them both by the back of their shirts. He pulled them off of me and lifted them up. Suddenly, security guards and police were all over the place. The people standing around said, 'This is the second time these people have attacked this guy.' The police said, 'What's your problem?' They basically said, 'It's none of your business.' I was banged, bruised, and had torn clothes. The police asked if I wanted to press charges and have them arrested for assault. I was so shaken that these guys would rush me in front of hundreds of witnesses in a ballroom. I just said, 'No, just get them out of here.'

"Hours later, we're leaving the Watergate. We came up out of an underground driveway from the hotel. I looked over on the grass near the entrance, and Hoskins was sitting against a tree drinking out of a whiskey bottle. He and the other guy were waiting for me to come out. I don't think they were drunk when they grabbed me in the kitchen, though. That was the last time I saw him. I never saw him, I never really spoke to anybody who knew him or saw him, but he was always out there, somebody who hated me." Hoskins's ill feelings no doubt stemmed from his disagreements with Dick regarding the terms of Hoskins's contract with Mississippi John Hurt and his management of Hurt's career.

Dick, along with the blues community, suffered the loss of two musicians in January 1976. Howling Wolf had suffered from kidney failure for some time, and later was diagnosed with cancer. He passed away on January 10. Sadly, less than three weeks later, Mance Lipscomb died in his native state of Texas on January 30.

"I flew from Boston to Chicago for Wolf's funeral. At the airport, I rented a Lincoln town car with a driver. It had a heated backseat with a blanket to throw over my lap. We drove to the funeral parlor for the wake. Lots of people were there. Everyone was in the front room signing the guest register.

Wolf was in a separate room. The casket was up on a podium, so you had to walk up a few steps to look down on him. Wolf had his arms crossed across his body and he was really formidable looking in his casket. He was the scariest corpse I ever saw. You looked down at him and thought he was going to reach up and grab you. He was really terrifying. He could be in real life, too, but I never had any trouble with him. I was there long enough to sign the register and give my regards. Then, I got back in my town car, went back to the airport, and flew back to Boston. It was a bitter cold winter. I did it right by renting a warm car and driver."

Bonnie Raitt was planning for her fourth studio album, which was to be recorded later that year. Circumstances had changed considerably from her early days when she opened for other blues artists. Now, some of the older bluesmen had become opening acts for her.

Although Raitt's success allowed her to offer the older blues musicians more opportunities to perform, it also put her in a somewhat unusual position. She explains, "It was very awkward. It was a reality where they could have either continued to play for less money to smaller crowds by playing clubs and have to do two sets a night sometimes, or they could double bill with me. I looked at it more as a double bill, but the promoters probably looked at it more as they were opening for me. I could give them a little bit more money and, more importantly, give them exposure to my growing audience. I was developing a really strong following with a national record company and some critical reviews. I had a bigger national presence.

"Dick, very shrewdly, went to the NEC and set up a booth there and had me play at that conference. That's how I got a lot of my college dates. I would say, 'Listen, if I can control who's on the bill with me, let's put some blues artists on.' The first time Muddy and Buddy Guy and Junior Wells opened for me it was very awkward, but I think they understood. In my little, modest way, opening for me in Columbia, Missouri, at a college with a fifteen-hundred- or two-thousand-seat venue gave them places they wouldn't have been able to play otherwise. In my mind, I was helping them get exposure, more regular work, with a better sound system, in a nicer venue, and I think they knew that. They could figure it out. They had a choice of either playing to a smaller clientele or a bigger one, and I always liked to share. I gave bonuses from my money if I didn't think they were getting paid enough.

"We all kind of knew the picture. Whether Dick represented Muddy or not, Muddy could figure out he could make a lot more money playing with me. It was a win-win situation. I was twenty-five or twenty-six years old the first time I drove up to the venue, saw my name above his, and got the better dressing room. It was very hard for me to understand. That I'm not just a blues artist had partly to do with it because I had a little bit broader appeal. The double bills that we did, whether it was folk musicians or blues artists, hands down were the best. I was really pleased to have my heroes on the show with me because also, just for selfish reasons, I wanted to sit in the wings and watch them!"

In regard to the financial aspects of booking bluesmen as opening acts, Dick and Raitt were in agreement that they be well compensated. "In all situations, I said to promoters, 'Pay them whatever they want. Don't quibble with their agent. We'll take it out of her money.' It was fine with her."

They did the same for regional artists who played at her concerts. "As we went from city to city on those tours in the mid-seventies I would say, 'Don't forget he [a particular artist] lives there.' She'd say, 'That's a good idea. Let's put that person on the show.' Bonnie and I gave them a minimum of five hundred dollars. The promoters would say, 'This is *crazy.* This guy plays down the street on Thursday nights and gets fifty or seventy-five bucks. What are you doing?' We would say, 'It's not your money, it's her money. It's a reallocation of the budget. Instead of her getting three thousand and the opener less, she's going to get less, and the opener gets more. It's what she wants.' We both insisted on that. There was no arm wrestling. We discussed it and did it. She loved standing on the edge of the stage watching them. She's a music fan. You'd see this guy, and he's got great sound and great lighting. He's happy to be making great pay, and he's playing really well. What's not to like about that?"

By mid-1977, professional and personal stress from previous months had taken a toll, leaving Dick disconcerted and exhausted. Deciding travel might alleviate some of the stress, he booked a vacation in the Bahamas. Upon arrival, he had an unexpected encounter with a distinguished calypso performer whom he had admired since his childhood.

"I had to get out of town and clear my head. I had loved calypso in the '50s. I listened to Harry Belafonte, the Mighty Sparrow, the Mighty Zebra, and Blind Blake. Blind Blake made ten-inch LPs and they were wonderful. I had a couple. His diction was great. You could understand the lyrics, and he did wonderful songs.

"As we came off the plane, it was a long walk from the tarmac into the building where they processed customs. As I went down the steps I heard music to my left. There was a chain-link fence, and on the other side of it was a shed with a roof over it. There was an old man in dark glasses and a straw hat sitting and playing the guitar with three or four young black men playing with him. As I walked toward the fence, I thought, 'That's a Blind Blake song. He sounds like Blind Blake.' I walked to the fence, and realized '*It is Blind Blake!*' He was maybe fifteen or twenty feet past the fence playing for the tourists. I stood there and the line went by me, and I moved over to the fence. I watched him and was just hypnotized. As I stood there, I felt a tap on my shoulder. It was a Bahamian policeman saying, 'You can't stand here. You've got to process through customs.' I looked around, and I was there all alone, so I went inside. I figured if he was playing in the airport then he was probably performing somewhere else in a club, so I'd go see him.

"I got to the hotel and asked about him. They said, 'Blind Blake? Is he still alive?' Someone said, 'I think the government pays him and he plays at the airport.' I said, 'Yeah. Is he playing anywhere else?' They said, 'No. He's not played for many years. I think only the government puts him out there for a couple of hours a day, but that's all. Most people don't even know he's still alive.' At least I saw him. What a real thrill!"

In mid-1978, Dick received a call from songwriter Doc Pomus. His call was for assistance in hiring a guitarist. Dan Aykroyd and John Belushi had created a band named the Blues Brothers as part of a sketch for an episode of *Saturday Night Live*, which had aired in April 1978. Jake and Elwood Blues, wearing retro suits and John Lee Hooker–inspired hats and sunglasses, had found an audience, and the band moved beyond the confines of the show to become a separate entity. By fall, new band members were needed as plans were being made for a tour and album.

"I helped John Belushi and Dan Aykroyd put the band together for the *Saturday Night Live* tour. It had only been a soul music send-up on *SNL*, but doing it, they decided to put a real band together and go out and play dates. They had been using the *SNL* band, which was very good, but for different circumstances they needed a couple of musicians."

Howard Johnson and Donald "Duck" Dunn had signed on to work with the band, but Steve Cropper had declined, so they were in desperate need of another guitarist. "Doc gave me Belushi's phone number, and we went back and forth. Belushi comes from a town in northern Illinois, so he hung out in Chicago a lot. By the time Belushi got to New York with *SNL* success, he knew the electric blues scene. I had a lot of conversations with Belushi. He was very specific and very knowledgeable about the musical style he wanted. He wasn't looking for Chicago. He was looking for Memphis, Stax Records, Sam and Dave, Booker T, et cetera."

After discussing various guitarists, Pomus suggested Matt Murphy. Dick knew he was precisely the musician they needed. "I knew that Matt was playing in a band called the Zychek Brothers in Connecticut, and he was very loyal to them. He wasn't going to walk out on them for another band. I told him to try this new band for two weeks and if it didn't work, he was back with the Zycheks again.

"Our finding him and convincing him to leave his gig and go play behind Belushi and Aykroyd is kind of a fascinating story. Matt had never seen

Saturday Night Live. The point being, is that if you're a good musician, you are working on Saturday nights. I went over the amount with Belushi, cleared my throat, and called Matt. I told him he was to go to New York on Friday, rehearse for two days, and then go to Los Angeles for a two-week gig. Their first engagement was to play ten days opening for Steve Martin at Universal Amphitheatre.

"Naturally, his first question was about the money. 'Seventy-five hundred a week,' I said. Silence. 'And a hundred a day for per diem expenses.' Silence. My mind was racing ahead. *What if I couldn't make this deal happen?* We got right down to the last week, *literally* the last week. We had come to the point of Matt Murphy. Period. There was no other choice available. I heard Matt breathing on the phone. 'How much that come to for two weeks,' he said slowly. 'Fifteen thousand in salary and fourteen hundred in per diem,' I said. I heard him say softly, 'Man, who I got to motherfucking kill for that kind of money?'

"I exhaled slowly, gave him traveling plans to get to New York, and called Belushi back. I said, 'Matt's good. He knows where to go for rehearsals.' Belushi said, 'I hope he's the right guy because we're fucked if he can't cut it.' That's a hell of a way to break into the business. Nobody ever called me from Los Angeles with a report, but I saw the movie a few years later with Matt playing Aretha Franklin's husband, so I guess that it all worked out for the best." The band's first album, *Briefcase Full of Blues*, was recorded during that series of performances in Los Angeles.

By this time, there had been a significant shift in Dick's workload. Many of the older bluesmen he had worked with early in his career had either died or were no longer able to tour. He had stayed with them, promoting, and, when necessary, protecting, as long as they needed him. Although he occasionally still helped book festivals, his time was spent booking for fewer, better-known artists.

Bonnie Raitt's popularity continued to grow, so an increasing amount of time was required to manage her schedule. His work with Junior Wells and Buddy Guy gradually declined until, eventually, he ceased booking for them. There was no definitive incident that precipitated the parting, but rather a slow, steady deterioration in their working relationship.

"They were really difficult together because Buddy was very focused and work oriented and Junior was not. Buddy and Junior were great, but the shows just got too long, and there was too much liquor involved. The band would go up and play an instrumental or two, then Buddy's brother, Phillip, who was more of a soul-blues singer, would do two or three vocals. Then A. C. Reed, who had made his own records and was really a good vocalist in the Jimmy Reed style, would do two or three. Now we're already twenty to twenty-five minutes into this and we haven't seen Buddy or Junior. Buddy would come up and do an instrumental or two, and then he would do a couple of vocals. Now we're at least an hour into the set, and we haven't seen Junior.

"They were going to do two sets. Junior would be at the bar drinking, and when he comes up for the late set, he is pretty drunk, as is Buddy. Finally, once Junior gets up there, he starts talking and jiving and shucking, and Buddy's had enough liquor that he's talking back at him. The audience, who had been sitting there for an hour and a half to get some really crisp music, is just getting a wandering unfocused show, so it was really not a good mixture. It was really toxic. Junior felt he had to wait too long to get up there, and Buddy felt that when Junior came up he was drunk, and he had to play guitar behind a drunk vocalist. It was bad on both sides."

"As Bonnie's career accelerated, I couldn't lift them any higher. They had become heavy weight. Somebody called and said they had some dates for Buddy and Junior and asked would I mind if he called Buddy directly. I thought about it and said, 'I think that would be a good thing.' We never had a meeting where I said I couldn't do it anymore. Eventually Buddy started to take bookings through other people. They just went off at some undefined point in the mid- to late 1970s. They knew that Bonnie was a major artist and was playing bigger and bigger venues. I think Buddy felt that I got too busy with Bonnie and neglected him."

On October 28, 1978, Dick's family and friends assembled to celebrate his parents' fiftieth wedding anniversary. The festivities were held at a hotel in Plymouth. Searching for a gift, Dick finally settled on a print of Norman Rockwell's famous, "At the Doctor's Office." "We took it out to Stockbridge where they lived. He [Mr. Rockwell] was ill, so it is hand signed with an inscription by his wife. It said, 'To Dr. and Mrs. Waterman to celebrate the 50th anniversary of their wedding,' and it's dated. He died days later [November 8]."

Jeffrey Hersh was in attendance and recalls Dick's part in the ceremony. "The speech he made in tribute to his parents on the occasion of their fiftieth wedding anniversary was magisterial. He was introduced before a dinner party of one hundred fifty or more in Plymouth. He spoke very quietly from a prepared text while the diners were chatting, clinking glasses, and somewhat inattentive. As Dick continued to extol the virtues of his parents, citing a quote from Oliver Wendell Holmes, of family and devotion, his dad's years as a physician in Plymouth, Massachusetts, the crowd grew more quiet, serious, and attentive. He closed with a beautiful poem by A. E. Housman. His remarks were met with a standing ovation.

"His older sister, Rollene Saal, had attained a measure of fame as an editor with Bantam Books and Doubleday, including a brief tenure as Jackie Kennedy's boss. She was a good writer and author on her own merits. After the ovation for Dick, she grumbled, 'I should have known better than to try and follow him.'"

Working with Bonnie Raitt while living on opposite coasts had created serious challenges. Dick was handling the booking while Hersh managed other daily business. Communication was difficult because there was a three-hour time difference, and they relied solely on phone calls and letters.

Hersh recalls how their workload grew as Raitt's fame increased. "With every new album release came more attention and a growing need to construct a more sophisticated foundation to handle the business. Now was the time to learn more of the fundamentals of entertainment law, banking, contracts and riders, accounting, publishing, copyright, insurance, actuaries, and the world of the record company. That was partially my role to process as much of this elementary level traffic as possible while allowing Dick more freedom to concentrate on the higher priorities: career direction, live show bookings, deal making, press, tour routing, and client control."

Although being in the same location was not mandatory, Dick realized that it would be in everyone's best interest to relocate to California because Warner Bros. encouraged Raitt to retain a manager and agent who lived in the area. This same situation had occurred just a few years prior with Maria Muldaur when she was pressured to hire a new agent in California. Since Raitt was his primary client, he knew the move was necessary. Dick discussed the matter with Hersh, and he agreed.

Raitt insisted the management of her career be on her own terms. She explains, "I never wanted to be managed. I represented myself to the record company. I think the record company would have preferred I had a manager that was representing me. I don't think they really liked the fact that I was making decisions, but that was my deal. I said I was going to determine when I record, with whom, and what songs, and it was frustrating for them because everybody else had a manager. I had Dick Waterman in Cambridge, but he didn't fit that mold. I wasn't somebody that needed to be managed. I wanted to control my own direction, so he was basically my office and my booking agent. There were times when, if I'd had a more conventional manager, they probably could have negotiated with the record company about getting my albums in the stores better and for positioning in advertising. Dick was not that kind of a manager. I probably could have sold more records and had a better relationship with the record company had I had someone batting for me there on that level, but that's not the relationship I had and that's not what Dick did.

"I worked with my boyfriend at the time, who formed a management company with one of Jackson Browne's managers, and we went with them in California. I think Dick wanted to make sure he didn't lose me, and that's part of the reason he moved out here. I think he got tired of the winters and wanted to come to California. A lot of his blues artists had passed away, and he wasn't working with Buddy and Junior. I think he felt it was a good idea, business-wise, to come out there and be more of a presence. I actually hired Gary George, who worked at Warner Bros. and oversaw Maria Muldaur's success with her record. There was Maria, Jackson Browne, myself, Annie O'Keefe, and Warren Zevon: we all went with Gary so we could coordinate the publicity and promotion. In terms of overseeing where I toured, that was between me and Dick. They had nothing to do with that."

Hersh assumed the task of searching for office space and housing for both himself and Dick. He spent two weeks in Los Angeles and secured housing for himself. Around the same time, Raitt purchased a new home and offered to rent her other house to Dick. With accommodations in order, he departed Cambridge for California.

The initial plan was to live and work in the same building as he had done for many years in Cambridge, but he quickly learned this was not a possibility. Hersh explains, "We didn't realize that California law required a personal manager to have separate commercial space. A talent agent licensed in California must also be fingerprinted and pass a criminal background check. No home offices! We moved the business to an office at Crossroads of the World [on Sunset Boulevard] in Hollywood. The complex was filled with music industry management offices."

By the late 1970s, Dick's management career had come full circle. He had begun with Son House as his only client and, after working with a number of blues artists for over a decade, Bonnie Raitt was his sole client. "I've always said one is the wrong number. You've got to have more than one because if the artist goes into the studio, you have no income. It they go on vacation, you have no income.

"She was a really great live act. Where we made our money was in the outdoor sheds in summer. You could really rake in some money then, even at the ticket prices in those days, which were relatively low. If the weather was good and we had a good opening act, she could do really well. We would play indoors during fall or spring in different parts of the country. I'd schedule two or three weeks in one place, then take a break, then two of three weeks somewhere else. We tried to build a good show with a good support act."

Occasionally, when she was not on tour, she and Dick found time to attend performances by other artists. "I was living alone in the Hollywood Hills. Bonnie was not hanging out with anyone at the time, so whenever she wanted to see a movie or go to a certain restaurant or hear some music, I got the call to be the designated date. I get a call from her that Etta James was playing at the Palomino in North Hollywood, and she really wanted to go. I said that was fine. I picked her up, and we headed for the Palomino.

"The club is not in a very great part of the city, so your best bet is to park as close as possible. Bonnie and I go in, and Etta has saved seats at the front table. She rocks through the first set and invites us to spend some time with her in her trailer. I suddenly remember that there is a great meat market just a few blocks away. I tell Bonnie that I'm going to do some shopping, but I'll meet her back at the table. I cruise on down the street, and when I reach the block where I think the market is located I slow down to about five miles per hour and look to see if the place is open.

"Suddenly, I have a police car flashing its dome lights right behind me. I freeze behind the wheel, and then I have a cop at my window. He asks for my license and registration. He orders me out of the car and asks if I have been drinking. I tell him that I have not been drinking, but he wants to do a field test on me. He says, 'Stand on one foot, close your eyes, put your head back with your arms out, and then touch your nose with your middle finger.' I arc my finger toward my nose and feel that I have touched my cheek. He drags me onto the curb and tells me to walk the crack in the sidewalk. My balance is not so great under the best circumstances, and I am really nervous. I don't like being around guns, so I hit a couple of lines and then miss a couple. He says, 'Lock your car. Turn around and put your hands behind your back.' *Wait a minute, what is happening here?* He twists my wrist until I am buckled with pain as he handcuffs me, and then I am thrown into the back of a North Hollywood Police car.

"They walk me into the station and say, 'Get down on your knees and put your forehead against the wall.' I look around and it's all Latino gang members. They are stripped to the waist with gang tattoos everywhere. There is a constant roar of profanity around my head. Everybody is yelling in Spanish, and I feel like I'm hallucinating. I am the only Anglo in the place. I have my head down, and I'm freaking out. *What the fuck am I doing here?*

"I lose track of time, but I must have been there for fifteen or twenty minutes when a sergeant walks into the room. He is obviously the watch commander. He nods at me and says, 'What have you got on him?' They told him. He said, 'Bring him over here.' They grab me under the arms and pull me in front of the sergeant. He glares at me and pulls out a breath analyzer. 'Blow into this straw, and I mean *hard*!' I draw a breath and blow as hard as I can for several seconds. He looks at it, resets the machine, and says, 'Blow again.' I pull as much air as I can and blow into the straw until I am gasping. He looks at the dial, and he is enraged. He turns to two policemen and says, 'He blew a double zero. He blew a double zero *twice*. You're wasting my time. Get him the fuck out of here!'

"They send me up to the front desk, but now the guys who brought me in are off duty and it's midnight. They can't find me a ride back to my car, but they know that they are in major trouble if the watch commander walks in and I am still there. They give me a ride back to my car, and I burn rubber getting back to the Palomino. I walk in and can see Bonnie sitting alone at the front table with Etta doing her second set. I walk up to the table, and she is *livid.* As I start to sit down, she unloads on me. 'Where the hell have you been? You abandoned me! I'm sitting here alone and these guys have been hitting on me!' I said, 'I got arrested.' Before she could launch another attack, I showed her my arms where the handcuffs had left welts and deep red grooves cutting into my wrists. Her eyes pop wide open, and she says, 'We've got to call a lawyer and get the ACLU involved in this.' I said, 'No, I just want to go home.' We gather up our belongings, give Etta a wave, and leave."

After many years working together, Jeffrey Hersh decided to take a position with another company. As in the early days of Avalon Productions, Dick again was handling all the business. "Things were really strained with Bonnie. Sometimes I couldn't talk to her for weeks at a time. It was like three independent camps, so I wasn't really surprised when he said he was leaving. Jeffrey had an old friend from Boston University named Lloyd who was starting up a business. He wanted Jeffrey to come and be his partner, so he left me to be with Lloyd."

Not long thereafter, however, Hersh returned to the office complex where Avalon Productions was located, set up his own office, and worked as Bonnie's business manager. "He never said why he left Lloyd, but he wasn't there more than a short period of time. It made for a bad time between Jeffrey and me because we had been as close as twins. Bonnie could always get along with him because he was never confrontational. He never said, 'You're wrong. Listen to me.' He was always lighthearted."

In December 1980, Dick took a trip to New York and, while in town, made arrangements to meet a longtime friend, Jim Gianopulos. Gianopulos, a self-professed "blues geek" was attending Boston University when he met Dick in the early 1970s when Dick was living in Cambridge. Gianopulos was immediately intrigued by him. The two spent many hours together at Dick's house drinking an endless supply of coffee, dissecting articles from the *New York Times* and the *Boston Globe*, and, of course, listening to music.

"When he needed tickets to see something, he would call me and ask if I could get tickets. His expression was, 'Can you make it happen?' So I'd say, 'I'll see what I can do.' He loved the Stones, so I got tickets for him to see the Stones when they were playing in New Jersey. They toured around for a couple of weeks and then they were coming back to Madison Square

Garden in New York. I got tickets for my niece and nephew, Matthew and Theo, who were probably in their early teens at the time. Rollene said that they couldn't go alone. They needed a responsible adult to go with them. I called Jimmy and said, 'I need a favor.' He said, 'Anything for you.' I said, 'I need you to go see the Stones next week.' There was a pause, and he said, 'What's the favor that you want?' I said, 'I just need you to go see the Stones next week. You gotta pick up my niece and nephew, who are really nice, well-behaved kids. Just pick them up on the Manhattan west side, take them to the show, and take them home.' He said, 'That's it?' I said, 'That's it.' He said, 'Sure. I can do that.'"

Though he and Gianopulos lived on opposite coasts, they stayed in touch and attended concerts together occasionally when Dick was in New York. Willie Nelson was booked for two nights, December 11–12, 1980, at the Palladium on East Fourteenth Street in Manhattan during Dick's trip to New York, so he secured tickets and made arrangements to meet Gianopulos at the venue. "I was going to go in the back door. I don't remember why I had backstage access. It was freezing cold and there were about eight or ten people on the back steps. The guy said, 'You're on the list. Go ahead.' I said, 'That's okay. I'm waiting for somebody.'

"I noticed over on the right stairs was this old man in a threadbare topcoat huddled there with no hat. Jimmy showed up, so I hugged him and reached for the door. Jimmy looked over and said, 'Mr. Marks?' The old man looked up and said, 'Oh, hi, Jimmy, nice to see you.' Jimmy said, 'Mr. Marks, are you coming in?' He said, 'Well, I'd like to.' I said to the doorman, 'I've got to bring him in with me.' How did I do it? I don't know. Everything then was so much less complicated.

"We get inside and step into the hallway. Jimmy hugged him and said, 'Good to see you, Mr. Marks. What are you doing here?' He said, 'Well, I'd like to thank Willie for doing my song. I really liked his version of it.' I said, 'Okay.' We walked down a hall and into the room with Willie.

"I said to Willie, 'This is my pal, Jimmy Gianopulos.' Jimmy said, 'This is Johnny Marks. Johnny, I'd like you to meet Willie Nelson. Willie, Johnny wrote "Rudolph the Red-Nosed Reindeer."' Johnny said, 'I love the way you sing my song. It's really a pleasure hearing you.' Willie was kind of aghast because he thought the song was really old. He said, 'I'm really honored to meet you.'

"We stood in the wings for the show, and then everybody said their goodbyes. By the time we left, the streets were abandoned, and it was really cold. Jimmy said to me, 'You wait here with Mr. Marks. I'll go get a cab.' I said, 'Okay.' Jimmy races down to where the street hits the big avenue, and I'm talking with Mr. Marks. He said, 'He's such a nice fellow. Whenever I go into the office, he always has a handshake and a smile for me.' I said, 'He's a good friend of mine. I've known him a long time.'

"Jimmy comes with a cab, so Mr. Marks says, 'Jimmy, we've got to have lunch.' Jimmy says, 'Any place in town?' He said, 'No. *Any place*—London, Paris, San Francisco—any place you want to have lunch I'll be glad to take you.' He said, 'See you later, Mr. Marks!' Isn't that great?! A little old man in a threadbare topcoat, yet so wealthy!"

Though Dick did not often travel with Bonnie on tour, after returning from New York he accompanied her to a performance at the Centroplex in Baton Rouge, Louisiana, in late 1980. While in town, Dick visited his old friend Robert Pete Williams. Their previous visit had been almost two years earlier when Dick traveled through Rosedale, Louisiana, on his move to California.

Never the easiest artist to book, Williams's age and physical health had made the process even more difficult. "I had some really strange things happen. Robert had been on the American Folk Blues Festival. He had traveled through Europe including three or four dates in England. Then, I had a booking request for him in England. I put in for a work visa for him and it came back that they had refused him the work visa. I said, 'Why did you refuse the work visa?' They said, 'Because he was convicted of a felony.' I said, 'Yeah, but the thing is, he was paroled, and since the parole he's been to England. How can you say he can't come in when he *was* in? We have proof he was on the American Folk Blues Festival. How could you have let him in and now say, 'We're not going to let him?' They said, 'Her Majesty's government need not comment on these matters.' He didn't get his visa, and they chose not to comment on it. Crazy things happened to Robert. If you'd told me that incident and said, 'Who fits that description?' I would've said, 'That would've happened to Robert.' Just crazy, bad things happened to him, but he expected it. He knew crazy, bad things would happen.

"I was able to put him on packages. If somebody said, 'We'll give you three thousand dollars, and you give us two bands and two solos, I could put Robert on a show like that.' If they simply said, 'You know the bluesmen better than we do, give us a package, then I could give them Robert where I didn't have to sell him on his reputation or record sales or things like that."

The income from these bookings was substantial, especially for older bluesmen who played for only a few dollars per night many times in their careers. Dick often negotiated three or four hundred dollars per performance. Williams had never requested fewer performances, but during the late 1970s his health had deteriorated rapidly following a cancer diagnosis. Knowing he was seriously ill and would not live much longer, Dick seized the opportunity to see him once more while in Baton Rouge. He hailed a cab and asked the driver to take him to Earl K. Long Hospital.

Dick was no stranger to African American culture in the South, but what he encountered at the hospital was disturbing. "I got to the waiting room, and it was like going into a third world country. Everybody was black, poor, and malnourished. This was in the evening, so they apparently couldn't believe a white person was walking in.

"I went in and said to the admission nurse, 'I'm here to see a Williams—Robert Pete Williams.' She flipped through a list and said, 'We have a lot of Williams here.' I said, 'Well, he's dying of cancer.' She nodded and reached for a little gray box with 3"x 5" cards and flipped through it. She said, 'He's on the third floor.' I went to the elevator, hit '3' and I went up. There was nobody on the floor. I walked down to the big, circular end of the hallway with a nurses' station and nobody was there. I walked around, and saw there was a nametag that said 'R.P. Williams,' so I went in and saw him. He was wearing a white hospital gown and lying on his side. His body had shrunk, but his head looked huge. I stood there and looked at him.

"There were metal trays on legs, and as I turned around, I hit one and it rattled on the floor. I turned back around, and he had opened his eyes. I looked at him, and he looked at me. He said, 'Mr. Richard, is that you?' I said, 'Yes, Robert.' He opened his eyes wide and picked his head up. His head was huge, and in that skeletal head his eyes were big. He said, 'How you doin,' Mr. Richard?' I said, 'Fine, Robert. I'm in town with Miss Bonnie. She's playing here in Baton Rouge.' He said, 'Well, you give Miss Bonnie a hello. Tell her it come from Robert. How Miss Bonnie doin'?' I said, 'She's fine. I'll give her your hello.' He said, 'It hurts bad. Oh, man, this cancer done et [*sic*] me up. I know I ain't got long. When it come your time, Mr. Richard, I want you to know you got a place with me. I save you a seat. You come be next to Robert. Don't be in no hurry, but when your time comes, you come be with Robert.'

"I thought about the scene in *Captains Courageous* when Spencer Tracy is all caught up in the rigging and netting. The only way to save the boat is to cut the nets so the net and sails will go down, and he'll drown. I waited and his eyes fluttered and closed, and I stepped back. Then, I left.

"I walked out of the room, back past the nurse's station, to the elevator, and pushed the elevator button. No nurse or hospital personnel had ever appeared on the floor at any point while I was up there. I took the elevator down and quickly went to get a cab, but a cab would not come. I kept calling, and they wouldn't come. Finally, I was late for the show. I went back inside the hospital and said to the lady, 'I'm calling a cab company, and they won't come. I've called two or three times, and I've been standing out there for a very long time.' She looked at me and said, 'Did you tell them you're white?' I said, 'No.' She said, 'Well, that's it. They ain't gonna come for you in this part of town unless they know you're white.' I said, 'Oh, okay.' She looked at me as if, *boy, are you ever stupid.* I called the cab company again and said, 'Hi, this is a man in front of the Earl Long Hospital. I need a cab and I'm white.' They said, 'Oh, okay, we'll be right along.' And they came right along."

Williams died just a few weeks later on December 31, 1980. Dick returned to Louisiana for the funeral and burial in Scotlandville, a small suburb of Baton Rouge. "I was at the funeral and people came up to me and said, 'You're Mr. Richard. You're Pete's man. You live up in Massachusetts.' I said, 'Yes.' They said, 'Pete, he talk about you. He only speak the highest of you.' I said, 'Well, I'm very honored.' They said, 'Yeah, he speak your praise.'

"He is buried at a beautiful place. It's where the river turns. The Mississippi comes into Louisiana, and from his grave you can see where the river runs east and west instead of north and south. He's buried right on the river bend under a giant weeping willow so that he's there in the morning sun."

CHAPTER 13

With the BLUES THREE Different Ways

BONNIE RAITT'S TOURS WERE SUCCESSFUL, AND MANY OF HER ALBUMS garnered critical acclaim, but Warner Bros.' primary concern was always record sales. "From about 1975 on, Bonnie had some bad years. In 1983, Warner Bros. had a purge in which they dropped about ten artists in a day." Raitt, along with other prominent artists, was suddenly without a record label. The timing was unfortunate as she was finishing her album, *Tongue and Groove*. It was put on indefinite hold by the company. Even for a successful touring artist like Raitt, having no album was detrimental to sales and tour promotion. This quickly became a source of frustration and tension between her and Dick as he worked to maintain a full touring schedule for her.

Significant changes also were occurring in the music industry, which presented new challenges. "We were entering the point where videos were coming out. To make an album you had to be video conscious as well. Video came in fast and like a big monster. The old-timers who went out on the street, heard a band in a club, listened to the tapes, and made deals to put them in the studio were being replaced by guys who were more video aware. The personnel in record companies was changing, and the rosters were changing."

During this time, Dick lost another friend when Muddy Waters died on April 30, 1983. He and Raitt regularly heard news of Waters and would see from him from time to time, but months had passed without any contact. She mentioned this to Dick, wondering if he was simply busy with touring. Concerned, Dick placed a call to longtime friend and Waters's agent, Mike Kappus.

"I said, 'How's Muddy?' He said, 'He's okay.' I said, 'Well, Bonnie is a little concerned. We haven't heard anything in a while.' He said, 'No, he's okay.' A few weeks later, Bonnie again mentioned that still she had not heard anything from him and expressed her concern. "I called Mike and said,

'You know, Bonnie is very tight with Muddy. She cares for him very much. He's been a really wonderful figure in her life. I've known Muddy since the '60s. No surprises here, Mike?' He said, 'He's fine.' Then, he died. It's a manager's job not to put information out on the street, though. I didn't go to the funeral because it caught me on such short notice that I couldn't make plans to attend."

Exactly two months later, on June 30, Dick had a strange and disturbing encounter. "There was a bar called Chadney's directly across the street from NBC Burbank. When I lived in the Valley, that's where I drank. I'd go over and have a drink or two and listen to music. The house band didn't have a name. The drummer was named Jimmy Pugliano. He was from Pittsburgh and was the drummer in a band called Jaggerz.

"Jimmy Gordon would come in, and when they were on set break Pug would always say, 'Do you want to sit in for a couple?' So, at the beginning of the set, Jim Gordon would sit in for a couple of songs. We were all just pals and it was always very loose. He cowrote 'Layla' and what I love most about 'Layla' is the piano coda. I used to have that alone on a tape loop and just play it. It's majestic, and that's Jim Gordon playing the drums.

"We would talk about publishing, foreign sublicensing, and things like that even though I didn't know a lot about it. I was in there one night when he came in, and he was wearing cream-beige slacks. From the ankles almost to the knees it looked like spatters of caked mud, but it wasn't raining, and it hadn't rained. Pugs came up and said, 'Jim, you want to sit in on a couple?' He didn't answer. He just looked at him, and Pugs shrugged and went up to the [drum] kit. I was talking to Jim, but he wasn't really answering. I turned around to get a drink, and he was gone. He had murdered his mother before coming to the club, and what I'd thought was mud was actually blood.

"He was very quiet and would keep to himself. He wasn't an outgoing, jovial guy. He never had the biggest joke or biggest laugh. He was just a quiet guy and a really good drummer, and that was about all we expected out of our friend. I don't remember when the story came out, but I don't think it was a big story."

After considering various business options for months, Dick moved to San Francisco in the spring of 1984 to join Avalon Productions with the Rosebud Agency. The decision came after almost a year of negotiation with founder Mike Kappus. Rosebud's roster boasted artists such as John Lee Hooker, Muddy Waters, and Mose Allison, and other acts that were compatible with Bonnie Raitt. Kappus was a great admirer of her work, and became acquainted with Dick while booking artists to open for some of her shows.

"Mike and I had been good friends for many years. He said if I ever wanted to move there and fold Bonnie into Rosebud, he'd be happy to have her. Bonnie wasn't working much and had been dropped by Warner Bros. She was still touring, though. She's always a successful touring act, only these were smaller venues. The deal was that I would move to the Bay area and keep Bonnie with me. I was only working with her, but he had no artist as big as Bonnie. He had a lot of artists, and he had an organization that was well run."

Dick did not want to close Avalon Productions, so a way had to be found for him to work at Rosebud while still keeping Avalon in business. Kappus explains, "It was a little tricky, so I think what we did was advertise that the Rosebud Agency was representing Bonnie Raitt in association with Avalon Productions. The fact of the matter was that Dick was in our office, he was booking our other artists just like any other agent, but we had a separate special deal with regard to Bonnie's bookings."

After an agreement was reached, Kappus was eager for Dick to begin work. Unfortunately, Dick had not secured living arrangements in advance of his move to San Francisco. Since the Rosebud offices were located on the second floor of a building in an apartment that Mike had converted to office space, Dick, along with his dog, literally moved into the office and lived there for a few weeks until he could find more suitable accommodations.

After a short time, it became clear this business arrangement was not working for either of them. "I'm very fond of Mike. He's a nice guy, but we did business in totally different rhythms. Negotiation is a rhythm, and we were polar opposites and couldn't work together. It was apparent immediately, so I worked there for a few months and then left.

"One of the hardest working agents in the history of music is Mike Kappus. When I worked for him, I showed up at 9 A.M. and he was already in. The next day I showed up at 8:30 A.M., and he was already in. The next day, I showed up at 8 A.M., and he was already in. I thought, *Fuck It!* I went back to coming in at 9 A.M. If hard work will get it done, Mike Kappus will get the job done."

They agreed that the collaboration was not working and parted amicably. Kappus comments, "I was just very happy that there was no negativity. We had a mutually friendly relationship. I'd admired Dick from the beginning. At the time I was representing maybe ten artists. I'd always tried to stay small. He went from representing one artist he knew inside out to suddenly representing ten different artists he didn't have a history with, and was not necessarily connected to people all over the place. He was connected more to the circuit that worked for Bonnie. We just had to produce at a higher rate than he was accustomed."

Dick always maintained a basic philosophy in regard to successful negotiation. "The secret of negotiating is to make somebody else feel what you want them to do is a good idea. You have to enlist them as an ally. You have to make a collaborative effort. Whenever I would be negotiating ticket prices, I would always say, 'I'm not going to tell you what the ticket price should be in your town. You know your town and your economy. I don't. You know what's an eight-dollar ticket or a twelve-dollar ticket. I'm not going to sit here in Los Angeles and tell you what Bonnie Raitt is worth in your town.' They would realize, *This guy is helping me. He's on my side.*

"I always say to agents, 'The most important obligation you have is to make money for your artists. The second most important obligation you have is making money for the talent buyer. If you don't, he's not going to stay in business. If you burn, pillage, and put him out of business, the next time you come to that part of the country [to book], you have to start all over again with a stranger. Make money for the talent buyer!'

"By the time I retired, I had talent buyers that I would call, and they would ask their secretary, 'Who's on the phone?' They'd say, 'It's Dick Waterman.' The guy would pick up the phone and say, 'Okay, I've bought acts from you that I made money from, so what have you got for me?' It was because I always made money for him. I could say, 'I've got a guy coming through. You've never heard of him, and I'm going to ask for more money than you're going to want to pay, so if you say *no*, I understand. I just wanted to give you the courtesy of a call.' That's the way it goes. Make money for somebody, and they want to do business with you.

"There are young agents from big agencies who want to make a big impression and a big price, but the talent buyer loses money. That's shortsighted. I was well liked by talent buyers because I made money for them. It was important to me that they make money and stay in business. You've got to allow the talent buyer who's buying your act to be successful and flourish so that he'll be there when you come into his part of the country with another act. When you call his office, and he hears your voice, it's a positive thing. He thinks, *Hey, I made money with him!*"

One other key tenet was stating costs first so time was not wasted in long negotiations. "I had an expression, 'This is what I have to get for this. I have to get X amount.' I had done the math in advance. I know what it costs for sound, lights, security, hospitality, advertising, radio, and print ads. I know your costs in advance, so I know my cost from the band's point of view. I came in with a figure that I thought was reasonable and not very negotiable. I never came in with a dream amount and assumed they were going to come back with a lowball figure."

Since Dick had maintained Avalon as a separate entity during his brief tenure with the Rosebud Agency, when the arrangement went awry, he went out on his own again. Within a few months he moved to the East Bay/Berkeley area and continued to book for Bonnie Raitt.

In the fall of 1984, Bill Ferris, director of the Center for the Study of Southern Culture at the University of Mississippi, extended an invitation to Dick to present a photo lecture at the university. Raitt was playing the following evening in Memphis and since Oxford was just over an hour away, Dick accepted. He had met Ferris years earlier when he was living in Philadelphia. Ferris was attending graduate school at the University of Pennsylvania. Blues musicians frequently stayed at Dick's apartment. Ferris's interest in southern culture prompted him to contact Dick and stop by for an occasional visit.

The photo lecture, part of a "brown bag" series, was scheduled for November 6, 1984. During Dick's visit, Ferris suggested he consider moving to Oxford, mentioning that there would be a place for him should he decide to relocate. That evening, Dick went to the Hoka, a well-known local establishment, to socialize. Operated by Ron Shapiro since the 1970s, the Hoka was a corrugated tin building that once housed cotton. It had been converted into a movie theater, stage, and restaurant where locals, Ole Miss students, and the occasional famous visitor congregated.

"There was a stocky, round-faced guy who was incredibly drunk. He turned to me, and the first words he said to me were, 'You got a dawg?' I said, 'Yes.' He said, 'What yore dawg's name?' I said, 'Bill.' He said, 'Damn fine name for a dawg; none of them frou-frou fancy names. Where's Bill now?' I said, 'Bill's in California.' He said, 'California?! Nah! Go get Bill and bring him to Oxford. Damn fine dawg shouldn't be in California.' I turned to somebody and said, 'Who was that?' They said, 'That's Willie Morris.' I said, 'Willie Morris?! *North Toward Home* [author] Willie Morris? Oxford Rhodes Scholar?' They said, 'Yeah, that's Willie.' I said, 'Wow! That's like the drunkest human being I ever saw in my life!' That's how I met Willie."

Following Raitt's concert, Dick returned to California. Soon after, he learned Elizabeth Cotten, another older blues artist for whom he had booked occasionally, was not receiving royalties and set about to find a way to assist. Cotten's musical talents had been discovered in the 1950s by the Seeger family, for whom she served as a housekeeper, when she was in her sixties. She performed at blues festivals in the 1960s, but as she grew older, she performed less. Some of her songs, however, were covered by other artists including the Grateful Dead.

A song titled "Sugaree," cowritten by Jerry Garcia and Robert Hunter, was initially recorded for Garcia's solo album in 1971. It later appeared on a

Grateful Dead album. The title, along with some of the inspiration for the song, derived from Cotten's recording, "Shake Sugaree."

"I wrote them a letter and said, 'That's an Elizabeth Cotten song. She's still alive and about ninety years old. Can I get some royalties for her?' That was the way you did it back then. [No doubt, the letter went to their management and the group members never saw it.] I got a letter back from their lawyer showing me eight or ten public domain versions of 'Shake Sugaree.' In other words, 'Fuck off and die. We're not going to give you anything.'

"The matter was closed, but then I saw John Scher from Pasaic, New Jersey. He owned the Capitol, a big rock and roll theater there. I told him the story. He was sort of their East Coast manager, so he said, 'Does Jerry (Garcia) know about this?' I said, 'I have no access to Jerry.' He said, 'Jerry would be furious.' I said, 'Be my guest. Tell Jerry.' He told Jerry, and Jerry went wild. The decision was that 'Shake Sugaree' was in the past, but they would do one of her songs called 'Oh Babe, It Ain't No Lie,' and they would give her a seven-hundred-dollar advance on the publishing.

"They sent her the seven hundred dollars. She was living in Syracuse, New York, and she went out and bought one of those two-door refrigerator-freezers in avocado green. I saw her later playing in Los Angeles at a place called McCabe's. It's a guitar store by day and a folk club on weekends.

"She was in the dressing room and I walked into the room. She was a little bird-like woman. She said, 'Oh, Mr. Waterman, how are you?' I said, 'Hi. It's nice to see you, Mrs. Cotten.' She said, 'I want to thank you for helping me with my song.' I said, 'Oh, that's all right. Did it all work out well?' She was very serious and said, 'Mr. Waterman, people come from all over Syracuse to stand in my kitchen and look at my new refrigerator.' I said, 'That's wonderful. Do you tell them where it came from?' She said, 'I do. I tell them it come from some dead people in California.'"

Unfortunately, not all of the female performers with whom Dick worked were as amiable as Mrs. Cotten. One of his bookings for Etta James devolved into a debacle. He had booked her to perform at Larry Blake's, a club located in a basement on Telegraph Avenue near the UC Berkeley campus.

"I don't remember the ticket price, but it was something like eight or ten dollars. I was going to sell it, take the door proceeds, and they were going to take the bar sales. She came down the steps, waved to people, walked through the audience, shook hands, and signed some autographs. She was lovely and gracious.

"I took her to the dressing room and came back out. Somebody said, 'Etta wants to talk to you,' so I went back to her dressing room. She said, 'I've got to go back to the hotel.' I said, 'We don't really have much time.' She said, 'No, no. I've got to do this.' I get the car, bring it around, and she came down.

"We went to the hotel and walked down to the hall. She went in her room and closed the door. I was standing there waiting, so I said, 'About how long are you going to be, Etta? You've got to get back to do that first show.' She was doing two shows that night. I was going to have the second show waiting outside while she finished the first one. We had to start the first one on time, and I was already running tight with time. I knocked and said, 'Etta, you coming?' No answer. I knocked harder and said, 'Etta, come on. Are you coming out?' She said, 'I ain't coming. I ain't doin' no show tonight.' I said, 'You're not going to do a show tonight? You were already there. They were really nice people, and they're waiting for you. Come on and let's go.' She said, 'I can't do it. I can't do it, tonight.' I said, 'You can't do it? Why not? Come on, you can do it.' She said, 'I see I can't.' I said, 'What do you mean *I see I can't*?' She said, 'My third eye sees. My third eye tells me I can't play tonight.' *Wow. Okay.* I said, 'What does your third eye want? Would your third eye like to see a little more money?' She said, 'No, no, I ain't playing tonight. Don't be asking me no more. Go away! I ain't gonna play tonight!'

"I had to go back to Larry Blake's, find a parking space, and go down through the crowd that was already forming for the second show. The bartenders and manager are all looking at me and asking, 'What's happened?' I said, 'You don't want to know.' I had to go to the microphone—stuttering me—and say, 'I'm really sorry, ladies and gentlemen, but Etta isn't going to perform tonight. If you get in an orderly line we will refund your money.' A guy right in the front jumped up and said, 'What the fuck are you talking about? I just shook her hand a few minutes ago!'"

The formerly genial crowd quickly became a roomful of irate patrons, but Dick managed to avoid any physical altercations. In a single evening he became persona non grata for some time thereafter in the Berkeley club scene. Thankfully, the "third eye" never manifested in any of his future bookings for James. He also never booked her in Berkeley again.

On August 24, 1985, Dick traveled to Houston with Bonnie Raitt. While there, he learned Townes Van Zandt was scheduled to perform at a club called Anderson Fair. A fan of Van Zandt's music, Dick stopped by the club that evening, but missed the end of his set by mere minutes. Blues guitarist John Campbell had been the opening act and, soon, he and Dick were engaged in a conversation.

"We got to talking about blues and other things. I didn't know much about him, but he had heard of me. He was leaving the next morning to move to New York City. I gave him the name of my friend, Mark Krantz, who was managing the Lone Star Café. I said, 'Give him a call. He'll help you out.'"

When Campbell arrived at LaGuardia, he called Krantz at the club. Krantz invited him to come by that night to sit in on a jam session. Campbell went to the club, sat in, and met a musician named Teo Leyasmeyer, who went on to manage the original House of Blues in Cambridge.

"Teo was a white keyboard player who spent many years on the road with Freddie King and James Cotton. Teo said, 'Hey, we sound pretty good together. I got a gig tomorrow night. Do you want to come with me?' Campbell said, 'Sure.' That led to a gig, so the two of them gigged together regularly, and Campbell got to play at the club a lot. He always said that he was one of the few people that never had an unemployed day in New York City. He went there and worked from the first day he got there. When I saw him later at Memphis in May, he hugged me and said, 'Man, everything opened from that first doorway. It just all tumbled together: the work, the recording offer, the career. I hear all these horror stories of people in New York who go through their money and can't get a gig. I just tell them Dick Waterman gave me a name, and I worked from my first day in New York.' He was a sweet guy. It's too bad he died very young."

Bonnie Raitt continued to tour without signing with a record label. Raitt and other popular artists such as Arlo Guthrie, Van Morrison, and T-Bone Burnett, had re-signed contracts with Warner Bros. Then, amid financial concerns, the company opted to drop their contracts along with those of a few other artists. Raitt had always maintained control of her career, with Dick serving as her booking agent. Despite her desire to be self-managed, the need for retaining a management company to negotiate with record company executives on her behalf became apparent. The frustration of the situation contributed to tension between her and Dick. Over time, both realized changes were necessary.

"I don't remember what the catalyst was. I just think that we were running out of markets. She was playing smaller places, and it was harder to put together tours without an album. The record business was going to CDs at that point. Her format of putting out albums had become outdated, but she wasn't with anybody [record company] putting out CDs. It was no longer really lucrative. I made the decision. I said, 'I've got to get out of here,' and it was okay with her. I went down to meet with the guys at Monterey Peninsula Artists. They were good guys, a good agency, and a good fit for her. I asked if they would step up and take her. She still had her voice and a good reputation."

Raitt was amenable to the idea. She explains, "I still drove my career, but when Dick decided he wanted a change, I wanted a change as well. I was trying to represent what I wanted artistically, but I wasn't getting anywhere. I needed to get a management company that would go to bat for me and knew how to talk to those executives. The industry had changed. It was a bunch of accountants running the business, and I needed a hard-hitting manager who knew how to work with the record companies. I made a decision to go with somebody that could negotiate for me. I wasn't going to keep doing it myself. I decided, for career reasons, when I got dropped that I needed to get somebody that could go in and get a better interface between me and my record company or else it wasn't really worth it to keep doing this.

"I think Dick was a great booking agent, but the business was changing. The 80s were a terrible time for people managing blues and roots artists. There were just less and less opportunities until the late 80s. College radio and VH1 were coming up, and then there were different forms of radio. FM radio, as we knew it, and the club and blues festival scene was making Dick's situation very awkward because he was so aligned with those older blues artists. He was somewhat adrift, so I understood. I felt for him. At the time, I almost wished he would go somewhere where he didn't have to be sullied by the business types. I didn't want to see him change, nor would I think he'd change. I wanted him to be happy."

Jeffrey Hersh, who continued working with Raitt for many years, describes the steadily mounting tension that ultimately led to her and Dick's decision to end their working relationship. "The interaction between Bonnie and Dick was slowly deteriorating and getting tricky. Bonnie insisted she was self-managed. This didn't work well if she was up all night recording and sleeping a good part of the workday. We needed decisions and lots of them. Measuring the right time to get a positive answer demanded a certain skill set. This was not exactly an intellectual pursuit as much as the ability to carefully read the emotional thermometer. Mainly, we'd try and determine when the mood was light enough to get papers signed and business moving forward. We used to say: 'If you want a *yes* on Monday, you better get a firm *no* the previous Friday.'

"Dick was finding this whole deterioration in the communication process to be a bit untenable. I ran interference for years when they weren't in the mood to talk to each other. It didn't help with the changes in record sales, consumer taste, radio formats, the attitude of the record company, and a general frustration between them. After quite a bit of unhappiness on both their parts, Bonnie decided it was time to make a change."

Desiring a change of location, Dick contemplated several options. He remembered the conversation two years earlier with Bill Ferris in Oxford. "I thought I would have an affiliation with the university, but it turned out when I got here, I was on my own. I moved here, and there was nothing. I had moved down expecting to find something waiting for me. I ended up with no work and no income. I had brought all of my belongings from California and very little money."

Returning to California or making any other long-distance relocation was not a viable option given his financial situation. The other issue was that he had no job elsewhere. He faced the critical decision of how he would support himself. One thing was certain; he knew how to manage and promote artists. Given the circumstances, this seemed the most logical choice.

"I produced shows with Mose Allison, Dr. John, Taj Mahal, Charlie Musselwhite, and Marcia Ball. I was bringing them into clubs in Oxford, such as the Gin. I thought I could promote a show each month, but it turned out that people wanted college alternative rock. They weren't interested in what I was bringing in. I brought in four or five shows, and I realized I did not want to learn college alternative rock. I had spent over two decades learning blues. I wasn't going to learn something else at that point in my life. The acts I promoted in the clubs just didn't work."

In a conversation one day with Walter Liniger, who was working at the University of Mississippi Blues Archives, he learned some surprising news about Son House. "He told me that somebody had visited Son in Detroit. I said, 'Who was Son visiting in Detroit?' He said, 'No, Son *lives* in Detroit.' Evie had a daughter there."

Following Son House's final performance in 1974, his physical and mental health had continued to deteriorate. In 1976, he and Evie had moved to Detroit. Dick's free time had become increasingly limited in the 1970s while working with Buddy Guy, Junior Wells, and Bonnie Raitt. House had no telephone in Rochester so, over time, he and Dick lost contact.

"I don't know what happened. I wasn't calling them, they weren't calling me, and then it just slipped away. Months became years. They didn't tell me they were moving to Detroit. They just went. I was still trying to get royalties for him, but in those days nobody was covering the songs. His sales were very small. The company sent a statement every six months. He may have gotten two or three during the first year or so. Then they just stopped, and the ones he got were very small. We never got any publishing statements although I had formed the publishing company [Sondick Music]. What happened was they [Columbia] ignored my letters."

Following the move to Oxford, Dick was forced to confront a problem he had managed to keep hidden for many years. "I was drugless in the 1960s. I didn't even drink because I don't like the taste of beer. I started doing cocaine in Cambridge around 1973–74. I don't remember who started me on it. It was a little recreational stuff in the beginning.

"As Bonnie became bigger, my commissions became bigger. I had the money to do more coke, and I did more coke. Then, I moved to California, which was insane because of the whole culture. Everybody was wide open.

You'd be around musicians and they were just doing coke right in front of you backstage or at the hotel.

"When I did coke, it never made me social. It made me antisocial. I never did recreational coke with other people. I just wanted to do coke by myself. I would get cocaine, a bottle of Stoli, and a half gallon of fresh orange juice. I'd make gigantic screwdrivers and do lines of coke all night. I did so much coke that I would lie in bed at 7 or 8 A.M. and look down and see my heart beating in my chest. It gives you a rush and exhilaration, but when you come down, you want that feeling again. So, you do more, but you never quite get that high, until finally, you're doing a lot of coke, and you're not getting high anymore."

Despite his drug habit, he knew the responsibilities of his job and remained focused at the office. He was able to hide his use from most everyone except KT and Jeffrey Hersh. "My workload wasn't that big. I didn't have a whole lot of artists, but I would go in and do my job. I *always* did my job. I was never on coke at the office. I did coke at night. I also didn't want to be pulled over in a car when I was carrying."

"The year after I moved to Oxford, I was sending cash to a guy in Berkeley who was sending me coke. I didn't get my weekly shipment, so I called him. Some guy answered the phone and said, 'Berkeley Homicide.' I thought, *Hmmm.* He said, 'Who is this?' I said, 'Who is *this*?' He said, 'A sergeant from Berkeley Homicide.' I said, 'Where is X?' He said, 'He's dead. If you know something, come forward. Now is the time to talk. We've got his Rolodex. We know who you are, and we're coming after you. If you've got something to say, say it right now, and it'll go better on you.' I hung up the phone. This was before the days of caller ID.

"I happened to know a California lawyer. I called him and told him what had happened. He said, 'I don't do criminal law, so I'll make a call and get back to you.' He called me back and said, 'Number 1: He's got nothing. He's fishing. He wants you to tell him something he doesn't know. *Never* call that number again. Number 2: Get clean. Number 3: Stay Clean. Got it? Do nothing.' I said, 'Okay.'

"My dealer worked out of his house and he had a screened-in locked porch. Whenever someone buzzed the buzzer, he looked out to see who it was. If it was someone he expected, he let them in. If it was someone he didn't know, he didn't let them in. He got killed because someone he knew got him out of the house onto the street. Maybe they were making a shipment out of their car or something. It was a middle-class white neighborhood. This was no 'gang bang.'"

The incident jarred Dick into full comprehension of the gravity of the situation. He knew he had to take his friend's advice. "I had been using over seven grams per week. I decided if I was going to look around for more, I needed to keep in mind Oxford is the federal jurisdiction for northern Mississippi. This is not just city or state court. This is federal. If I got popped, they would turn me over to the DEA, and I would face federal charges in Oxford. I was too well known. They would've made an example of me. It was time to quit.

"There was no rehab. I just quit. It was very hard, but I have a really strong mind. Drinking was part of drugging, so when I stopped drugging, I stopped drinking. I just willed myself to stop. About the time I quit, I opened a drawer and inside was a supermarket plastic bag. It was bulging full with tiny brown bottles. Every brown bottle had held a gram, and every gram was worth a hundred-dollar bill. It was a whole bag of hundred-dollar bills that I had burned. It was a *lot* of money."

Overcoming his addiction had both physical and financial benefits. Unfortunately, it did not solve his struggle for income or his lack of a job. He earned enough money from promoting a few shows to support himself for a while, but there was no security in such ventures. He returned to the frugality with which he lived most of his early career.

"I was living in a world of hundreds as opposed to thousands of dollars. My rent was low. My expenditures were low. My living was low. I still had my old Volvo and was just living by myself in an apartment. I had some saved money, but not much else."

While on a drive to the Midwest, Dick received a message on his answering machine informing him that Son House had died on October 19, 1988. The funeral was to be held in Detroit, so Dick turned the car around and drove to Michigan. "I went alone to Son's funeral. It was at a huge church which seated thousands. They were scheduling funerals there every two hours. There were a couple dozen people at the service. There were two other white guys, but I never knew who they were. The minister obviously had *never* met Son. He was just the church minister. He said, 'And the deceased, his head was low. Lowly he moved along his path of life. And he lifted up his eyes and said, *Lo, I have seen the holy Jesus. I have seen the Lord. My head riseth up. I see the Lord, and I say, Take me, Lord! Take me in your embrace.*' Oh, great.

"The funeral is over and we go out to the burial. Afterward, food is being served back at the church in the room behind the main auditorium. I'm sitting there with Mrs. House, and I hear the Reverend say, 'And the deceased, his head was low. Lowly he moved along his path of life. And he lifted up his eyes and said, *Lo, I have seen the holy Jesus. I have seen the Lord. My head riseth up. I see the Lord, and I say, Take me, Lord! Take me in your embrace!*' I looked at Mrs. House, and she just said, 'Lovely service.' He said the exact same speech because he didn't know any of them!"

Regarding the relationship between House and his wife, Evie, he observes, "He had been a pest and a bother and sick. They were two bickering people that lived together for many years. They were married forever. I think they got married about 1934. There's an expression called 'jump the broomstick.' It means being married without a church or papers. Two people hold hands and jump over a broomstick, and that's [common law] marriage. It was common in the black community. Once, I was sitting with Son and Evie in their apartment in Rochester and the subject came up about how many times each of them had been married.

"She said, 'He my second husband. I had children before I met Mr. House and he raised up my children like his own. He was married one time before.' Then he said, 'Says you.' She said, 'Say what?' He says, 'Says you I was married one time before.' She said, 'What you mean? You tell me that you were married to Beverly.' He said, 'Uh-huh, and maybe a few others.' She said, 'What you saying to me? What you saying to me? You're married to more women?' He said, 'Man, I jumped the broomstick with so many women before I met you. You'll never know how many times I was married.'

"She went ballistic! They started to fight about how many times he was married. I'm in the middle of this, and *war* has broken out. They were just people who picked at each other. Where was he going? Where was she going? They weren't going anywhere at their age."

Due to her religious beliefs, she never approved of blues music. She loved gospel music and sometimes performed a gospel song with him. "She was, as he said, 'Church-y; she was a church-ified woman.' He wasn't, but he could do gospel songs as his encore, and they were very moving. He would introduce them with great feeling. He sometimes said, 'The Scriptures say you cannot hold God in one hand and the devil in the other because they will not coexist. It is not a thing that is copacetic.' He loved that word copacetic. He'd say, 'You got to put one of them down and pick up with the other. And I put down the Lord, and I picked up with the blues.' He believed he had done that.

"He was very proud of the fact that he was not only an excellent tractor driver, but he used to say that he was referred to as the 'Tractor King.' When a major tractor company had a new model they would bring it into the Delta. The plantation owners would gather around to see if they were going to buy it. Son House would be the one that would take this new tractor out into the fields and show what this vehicle could do. When I was looking for him in 1964, we had some old people that thought they remembered him, but weren't sure. Somebody would say, 'Oh, yeah, he was the tractor king. He sure was the best driver around.' When we rediscovered him and recounted that story, he chuckled and nodded his head. He liked that story. He said 'Yeah, that's true. I was the best there was. I was the tractor king.'"

Weeks after House's death, Dick received a call from the editor of *Living Blues* magazine asking if he would write an obituary to be included in the January/February 1989 issue. "I said, 'No,' and then I got a great piece of advice from a friend. She said, 'He's going to get an obituary written. If you don't do it, somebody else will, and you'll be unhappy with it. Write it yourself.'

"The interesting thing was that I ended the obituary by saying, 'On October 19, 1988, every bluesman in the world moved up one place because there was a vacancy at the very top.' It's a nice line, but it happened that I had read that Jack Nicholson had said, 'Brando is the best, the actor that we all look up to. When he goes, the rest of us move up one place,' so I actually stole the line. Nobody ever knew because they didn't remember the Jack Nicholson quote. Anyway, that line I used was quoted for a number of years as being a very strong, powerful, meaningful line."

Dick comments on his most compelling memory of House with a passionate and unparalleled description of his stage presence. "All of the bluesmen and women that I worked with had varying abilities to communicate with an audience. Son House was absolutely the greatest communicator.

"Mississippi John Hurt would sit in a chair with his little derby hat on and tilt his head forward until the spotlight was out of his eyes. Then he could look down and see a face in the front row, whether it was a club or a big or small stage. He would work to that face. He would talk to that person. He would say 'I'm going to play a song about Stack O'Lee' or 'This is about Frankie and Johnny.' Although he was talking to one individual in the front of the house, everybody felt that one-on-one connection.

"Skip James would just look up out over the heads of the audience out into some distant abstract. He had this untethered attitude, sort of like a balloon in a breeze. It was kind of unconnected and a little bit spacy.

"Son House, of all the traditional bluesmen, could work from the big stage. All of them could work in a club, a one-hundred or two-hundred seater. When you put somebody up on a stage that is six or eight feet high with a twenty-foot photo pit, and there's fencing and ten to fifteen thousand people out on a festival field, the man sitting on the chair in the lights looks very small. Son House had the innate ability to absolutely lock in and communicate with you. He could connect with people. The emotion that was charging through what he was doing could just mesmerize and transfix somebody one hundred or two hundred feet from the stage. You cannot falsify that. You either have the ability to absolutely rivet people or not.

"If there's a pseudo emotion, if you're just making up stories, or chatting at people between songs, then the effect of locking in just dissipates, and they lose interest. Son House would absolutely take people. Going into the parking lot at the back of a huge audience they would hear him, look back over thousands of people at this distant seated figure, and start to move back toward him. He had that ability, and I saw it happen.

"What I would say about Son House is this: If the blues was an ocean and you distilled it into a pond, and then a stream, and then a tub full of liquid, and then a glass, and, ultimately, into a few drops, what you had distilled, the essence of it, that was Son House. Son House was the very essence of blues, and its most basic emotional form of one-to-one communication. He could do it in a room sitting knee to knee with you on two hotel beds, and he could do it ten feet up in the air off the front of a giant stage for fifteen thousand people. He absolutely had the ability to communicate. He could make you feel the sweat, the pain, the anguish, and the hurt, because what he was doing was so devoid of any frippery and artifact. He was the genuine article. He was the bare nucleus. He was the essence of the Delta blues."

CHAPTER 14

YEARS Have Gone Past

REVISITING HIS EARLY CAREER, DICK BEGAN WRITING A COLUMN FOR the local newspaper, the *Oxford Eagle*, in 1990. Titled *On Thursday*, a name assigned by the previous columnist, it was an unpaid position, but one he enjoyed during his eight-year tenure with the newspaper. To earn income, he turned again to booking.

"Jessie Mae Hemphill was a real handful. I got a call to book her into a blues festival in Montreal. We were going to fly up on a Saturday, stay overnight, play on a Sunday, and come back. We got a call that Saffire, the women's group, had canceled a date at a school about an hour west of Philadelphia. They called to see if I had anyone who could substitute. I said I was flying with Jessie Mae to Montreal, so they asked if she could pick up the date on the way. I called the airline and it cost no extra money to change the ticket. The Montreal date was going to pay two thousand dollars. The Philadelphia date was fifteen hundred dollars. For no extra cost in travel, she was going to have a thirty-five-hundred-dollar weekend.

"We go to Philadelphia, I rent a car, we drive to the gig, and she plays the gig. Afterward, I see the guy come up to her and give her fifteen hundred dollars in cash, which I don't like because I have to get my money first. The saying among black artists is, 'You gotta get yours first, 'cause once I get it down in my pocket, I ain't coming back up with anything for you.' They understand that. They're fine with it. If you got yours coming, then take yours, but once I get mine, it's mine. I couldn't pay somebody in full and then expect him to part with his money. They were in the *me* business, not the *you* business.

"When I had the guys out in clubs, I would call the club owner and say, 'He, the bluesman, understands that he is going to get X [amount] and I'm going to get X paid directly to me. Understand?' The club owner would say, 'Okay, I'll give him his and send you yours.' If the money got big, there was no way that somebody was going to go play for fifteen hundred or two thousand dollars and then walk around with my money. It didn't matter if we were friends or not. The friendship didn't matter. It was the way the process went. I had to look out for mine.

"We get to Montreal, and the guy in the dressing room had a huge turkey being carved, and he had a huge slab of roast beef, and a giant filet of salmon. Jessie Mae sits in the dressing room and says, 'I want the Colonel Sanders.' I said, 'Jessie, they put a lot of money into this food. There's anything you could want.' She says, 'I want Colonel Sanders!' I said, 'I don't even know if they have Colonel Sanders here in Montreal.' She went into a fit. She said, 'I get the Colonel Sanders in Italy. I goes to Edmonton, and they bring me the Colonel. I want Colonel Sanders *here*. I want my Colonel Sanders!'

"I go to the promoter with this, and he's bug-eyed about it. He's losing money on the date, and she won't go on. He looks in the phone book, and there is one Colonel Sanders way the hell over in another part of town. He sent somebody out and, with all of this food going to waste, she gets her Colonel Sanders. She puts it on a table, puts a chair facing the door, and eats her Colonel Sanders looking at the door so nobody can come in and take it from her.

"We get on the plane to come back from Montreal to Atlanta, so I said to her, 'Look, Jessie, I've got to get some money from that Pennsylvania date because I had to pay for tickets and other things.' She said, 'I ain't gonna give you shit.' I said, 'Look, I turned two thousand dollars into thirty-five hundred dollars. I'm at least entitled to get the hotel and rental car money back. Give me a couple hundred dollars. I'll lose money but I won't lose as much.' She said, again, 'I ain't gonna give you shit.' We fly from Atlanta to Memphis, and as we're coming out of the airport, she said, 'You're gonna leave me here. You ain't gonna give me a ride home. You're gonna leave me right here, ain't you?' I said, 'Put your ass in the car, and don't say a fucking word to me. Just shut up!'

"It's maybe forty-five minutes to Senatobia. We drove in silence and I did not speak one word to her. I had a Volvo, and it had a bar in front right near the glove box where you could pull yourself up. She puts her hands on it and when we get near her home, she starts to rock back and forth. She says, 'Oh Jesus, Jesus Christ, Savior Jesus!' She's yelling, 'Yes God! Save me, Jesus! Oh Lord, Save me! Save me!' We get to her driveway, and she's saying, 'Save me, Jesus! Deliver me home! Safely, Safely! Thank you, God! Thank you, Jesus! Christ Almighty has delivered me!' I pull into the driveway. I get out, take her guitar and suitcase, march them up to the door, and put them down. She gets out of the car. I say, 'There! Now you're home, bitch. Are you happy? Stay out of my face!' and I left.

"The thing was, when I would go to a casino in Tunica and win money, I'd stop at her house on the way home and give her a hundred dollars. If I lost money, I'd stop on the way home and give her a hundred dollars. She began calling me and asking if I was going to go to the casino in Tunica. I'd say, 'No, I wasn't planning on it.' She'd say, 'You ought to go! Then, stop and see me on your way home.' She was a freaking handful! She was a suck-up to whoever was with her. They were her best friend, and then she would poison it. She was really a terrible person. After her funeral, people stood around outside and most everyone had a Jessie Mae story. Not all of them were good. She was not one of my shining successes."

After a two-decade hiatus, Dick picked up his camera and began doing some photography. The catalyst was bluesman Champion Jack Dupree. Quint Davis had made arrangements for Dupree, a native of New Orleans, to fly roundtrip from his home in Germany to perform at the 1990 New Orleans Jazz and Heritage Festival. Dick saw Dupree backstage, and they exchanged a few words. Before parting, Dick handed him a business card and said if he ever wanted to pursue a more extensive US tour, he would be willing to come out of retirement and serve as his agent. Months later, he received a fax from Dupree's manager inquiring if he would like to book a tour for him. Unhesitatingly, he agreed.

Dick assumed Dupree would be available for a seven- to ten-day stay in the United States, so he was stunned when he requested to be booked for a six-week tour. Quickly, he assembled dates extending from early May through June 1991.

"In those days booking was much different. I had been out of the music business for six or seven years, but I put together a really great tour. He landed in Memphis and played B. B. King's Club the night they opened. B. B. and Albert King were there, and it was really a festive day. He went to Jazz Fest in New Orleans and then recorded for Rounder. Then, we went out to the West Coast. I rented a car because it was just Jack, a guitarist, and me. We drove from San Diego to L.A. to Santa Barbara to Monterey to San Francisco, then across the bridge to Mill Valley and San Jose.

"While we were in L.A., I brought Champion Jack to Willie Dixon's house in Glendale. We sat around and ate chicken, and they talked about the old times. He had a little bungalow in the back where he had tape recorders and tapes. He began to tell Jack and me the projects that he was working on. He was putting together a soundtrack for Oliver Stone and a reissue of some Chicago sessions. He was going to get some East L.A. Chicano kids and fuse that sound with Chicago blues. His mind was great. He had many projects going at the same time.

"He was a really shrewd guy. He was several steps ahead of everybody. He was in the business of doing business. There were a lot of people who could ask for money, but he knew how to really capitalize on a more sophisticated level. Willie knew copyrighting and publishing. Willie worked for Willie."

Following their visit with Dixon, Dupree finished his dates on the West Coast. They headed east, with a few days of vacation scheduled after their arrival. "When we flew from San Francisco to St. Louis, we arrived on a Tuesday, and he had a gig on that Friday. He had a son there that he hadn't seen since he was a child. By this time, the son was in his thirties or forties, so he saw his son. I left them alone for a couple of days, then he played his gig on Friday. We got up the next morning and left. We're driving along from St. Louis down to Memphis and he turned to me and said, 'Don't ever do that again.' I said, 'Do what?' He said, 'Give me open days on the road. When I'm on the road I want to work every day.' I said, 'I thought since you hadn't seen your son in so many years you might want to have a couple days with him.' He said, 'Well, you thought wrong. Don't ever do that again.' I said, 'Okay.'

"He was a very tough guy. He was totally mentally in the moment. He had no sense of reverence or nostalgia about the past. I once tried to talk about people like Willie 'Lion' Smith, Fats Waller, and other great piano players. He just spat and said, 'Fuck 'em. They're dead. They ain't here, and I got a gig tonight. That's all I'm thinking about.'

"He said he was on a ship when it was torpedoed by the Japanese, and he was taken prisoner. They asked him, 'What do you do?' He thought fast and said, 'I'm a cook.' They said, 'Great. We can always use a cook.' They gave him a cell apartment next to the kitchen, so he wasn't kept prisoner like the others. He said, 'They beat the shit out of the white prisoners and the officers, but I didn't have it so bad, except I couldn't get any fucking cigars.' That was his complaint about being a prisoner of war! He didn't cook, and he couldn't cook, but he learned to cook because he knew that a cook would be treated better."

They flew to the East Coast for dates in Boston, Vienna (Virginia), Philadelphia, New York, and Canada. While in Boston, Dick drove to his parents' home in Plymouth to visit before his mother was to have a minor surgical procedure. His mother and father were now elderly, and his mother's bedroom had been moved to the first floor of the house to spare her the physical stress of climbing the stairs. Her surgery was scheduled for a few days later, the day Dupree was to perform at Wolf Trap in Vienna, Virginia.

After the surgery, Dick received an unexpected call from the hospital. The surgery had gone as expected, but she had suffered a major stroke while in recovery and had been placed on life support. He was advised to come immediately if he wished to see her.

Dupree's next performance was in Woodstock, so Dick dropped him and guitarist Ken Lending in Woodstock and sped toward Plymouth. "I went into the hospital and sat with my mother who was, at that point, comatose. I stayed with her for a long time, then I went and stayed overnight in a hotel. I called the hospital the next morning and said, 'Did Mrs. Waterman pass away during the night?' They said, 'Yes,' so I went to my parents' house. I walked in, and my father was sitting there alone in a chair. He looked up at me and said, 'I always thought I'd be first,' and put his head back down. That's all he said.

"Jack was still on tour, so I went back to take him to Rochester. Then I got a flight back to Boston and drove home for my mother's funeral. The day after the funeral, I flew to Windsor, Ontario, Canada, to be with Jack. Two weeks later, I had a conversation with him that was very long, slow, and arduous, but it gives a lot of insight into him. The guitar player is sleeping in the backseat, and Jack turned to me and said, 'I didn't tell you I was sorry your mother died.' I said, 'Thank you, Jack.' He said, 'I didn't tell you I was sorry your mother died.' I nodded. He said, 'If I had known what it was like to have a mother, but I didn't know what it was like to have a mother, then I would know what it was like to lose a mother. Since I never had a mother, I don't know what it was like to lose a mother. So, I can't tell you that I'm sorry you lost your mother. But, if I had had a mother and knew what it was like to lose a mother, *then* I would tell you that I was sorry you lost your mother.' I said, 'Thank you, Jack.'

"He was getting twenty-five hundred dollars per night. That's what he wanted. That was very good money then. The first night he said, 'Come to my room and count it out on the bed.' I went and counted it out in cash on the bed, and then he counted it. He said, 'Okay.' The next night, he said, 'Count it out on the bed.' I counted it out on the bed. The next night he said, 'Just give it to me in the car tomorrow.' So, I gave it to him in the car the next day. After a few more days he said, 'Why don't you just hold onto it, and give it to me at the end of the tour.' He had a little leather bag that hung around his neck, and he had filled it up to overflowing with hundred-dollar bills. He didn't have any more room. The point was, I had to prove I was trustworthy, and then I had to again prove I was trustworthy. Finally, once I had broken through, he was totally okay.

"I tried to describe percentages to him. I had created deals where he had made more, in some cases a lot more, in Mill Valley and St. Louis, but he said, 'I don't care about that. I don't give a shit. Give me my twenty-five hundred. You keep the rest.' I said, 'Jack, I got you a good deal. This is quite a bit of money.' He said, 'Just give me my money. If you make a good deal, you keep it. I just want my twenty-five hundred.' I said, 'Are you sure, Jack? This is a percentage thing.' He said, 'I don't care. You keep it.' So, I did. I made a deal in St. Louis at a club off Broadway which was near the Budweiser world headquarters. I protected them at the bottom with a smaller guarantee, but as it went up, it increased [exponentially]. As we made more money, his [Jack's] percentage went higher and higher. As the gross got bigger, he was getting 70 percent of everything. We reached the point where we were counting out more and more money, and I finally said to the guy, 'Okay, that's enough.' He said, 'We're not finished. You have more coming.' I said, 'That's okay. Leave it for the St. Louis Blues Society.' He said, 'Really? We could really use it.'

Sadly, it was Dupree's last tour in the United States. After returning to Germany, he succumbed to cancer on January 21, 1992. His old friend Willie Dixon died just a week later on January 29. "I got a letter from the guitarist. He said he was with Jack after the tour, and Jack said, 'I wonder how Dick Waterman's doing.' He said he was stunned because Jack had never referred to anything from the past."

In 1992, four years after Son House's death, Dick was surprised when Columbia decided to reissue House's 1965 Columbia recordings as a boxed set of two CDs including alternate takes of those on the original album. "I go looking for royalties, so Columbia says, 'Our contract with him gives us the option to do a second album.' I said, 'You're going to pick up this option twenty-five years later?! To pick up an option you have to send a registered letter within one year that says you invoke your right for an option album. What are you doing? You don't get [to release] a second album after twenty-five years.' They said, 'Yes, we do.'"

The original contract had allowed Columbia the option of releasing a second album within a year of the creation of House's first album. Dick was dismayed that they were acting on the option over two decades later without contacting him to even discuss the matter. "So, I was stuck. I didn't know what to do, so I mentioned it to Dave Marsh. Dave Marsh's wife, Barbara Carr, co-manages Springsteen with John Landau, and Dave is a heavyweight influence on his own."

Dick called Marsh and shared his plight. Marsh remembers, "He said, 'I've been able to get nowhere. I'll send you the correspondence.' I read the correspondence, which was pretty much all repetitious: [Dick would say] 'Please?' and [Columbia would say] 'No.' You could boil each side down to a word, and those were the words. So, I said, 'The thing is, you're not going to get reparations. That's not how the business works, but sometimes people can straighten things out going forward, and that might make a difference.'

"I wrote one of the top two or three people who dealt with such things at Columbia Records, and said, 'I'd love to be able to write a story about how it all worked out well and make you all look good. But, I can guarantee you I'm going to write the story if it's *not* going to turn out well.' It wasn't exactly a threat. It was like, 'Just do the right thing. It's not going to cost you a ton of money. Start paying them going forward.' They agreed to do that. Dick called me up one day with wonder in his voice. I didn't find it all that surprising for a bunch of reasons, including the fact that she [the contact at Columbia] and I are old friends, and it wasn't asking for anything very big. It was just asking for some justice for somebody.

"Here's the thing: Dick trusted me with that. I was very proud that happened. Not because it made me money, that's beside the point, but how many times do you get to help foster a little justice in the world and have it work out that well for the person you were trying to get justly treated. All I could think about was seeing Son at the Ann Arbor Blues Festival and seeing Muddy there with big, wet eyes and knowing I was seeing something that somebody had put there that would have been inconceivable just a few years before. It's already '69, and they found Son in '64, but I wasn't going to get to see him. Nobody was going to know who he was unless they had those 78s, and the whole thing came back to life. Dick did something for me as well as me doing something for him and the House family. It was a great thing, and it's a good example of how sometimes you can conspire with righteous people and get righteous results.

"A whole generation of blues musicians died poorer than they should have based on (A) the face value of their contracts, and (B) the huge amounts of money they made for somebody else. The important part of that story was that Dick, seeking an answer, was at least going to scour his phone book until he could get it done. That's the difference between him and somebody else, even somebody else who's goodhearted. He's very diligent."

Given the initial negative response he had received from Columbia, Dick was both stunned and relieved when they contacted him following Marsh's intervention. He had not received a royalty check in many years, and they proposed an offer to settle the issue. "Suddenly, they are in line and say, 'Okay, we're going to pay you back royalties. If you'll take two-thirds [of the amount owed], we'll write you a check now. If you want the full amount, we'll fuck around with lawyers for a couple of years.' I said, 'Give me the two-thirds now.' The artist royalties from 1965 to the early '90s came, but I didn't touch it. I endorsed the check and sent it to Evie House. Then, we set up a deal where every six months I'd get the royalties.

"A couple years later, I'm at Jazz Fest. I walked out past the Rayban Stage, turned left, walked down, and bumped into David Hirshland, president of

Bug Music. He said, 'Dick, I would really love to represent the Son House catalog.' I said, 'You're right, Dave. I'll think about it. I'll get back to you.'

"A year passes, and I'm at Jazz Fest. I walk out past the Rayban Stage, turn left, take a couple of steps and there is David Hirshland. He said, 'We'd really like to represent that Son House estate.' I said, 'Yeah, okay, let's do it. I'll get back to you.' He said, 'Okay.'

"A year later, I'm at Jazz Fest again. I walked out onto the track behind the Rayban Stage, I turn left, I look at David Hirshland, and I say, 'This is just freaky! Take the publishing. You're making me crazy.' Out of ninety thousand people, I walked into him three years in a row in the exact same place.

"Bug administers publishing and collects all the money. They take 10 percent off the top, but they look at publishing royalties not only from recording artists but TV, film, and everything else. Placing the catalog with Bug turned out to be a very good move. Son has a very small catalog, probably fifteen songs or so, and it's not the kind of material that just goes into popular television shows."

Dick's father, now advanced in age, was battling health issues, so the decision was made that he should move to an assisted living facility in Plymouth. "The older people there knew that he was Dr. Waterman and had been a most respected member of the community. He had been a doctor from 1928 to 1988. They gave him every respect and courtesy so that when one of the orderlies or nurses would come in to do some procedure or something and would refer to him as 'Mr. Waterman,' somebody would always say, 'It's *Dr.* Waterman.'

"My father was not a joking, backslapping guy. We played ball in the backyard a few times, but my father's job was to make sick people not sick, and that's what he did. He didn't go fishing or to ballgames and such. What he did was really serious. In the blues world, when people come to me for help or advice, I know that world. I learned from my father's example, and I don't shirk it.

"He was in a wheelchair, but his mind was all right. He used to take the newspaper, put his glasses up on his forehead, read the tiny print of the stock market, and then tell me which stocks he should have bought when he had the chance. He did that all the way until the very end.

"One day I visited him and we went out on the patio, which overlooked the town. It was a beautiful, sunny day. We talked about how much the town had changed and how much he missed my mother. I brought him into the day room where some of the residents were doing exercises. I knew he wasn't going to do that, so he nodded his head down. I went all the way to the door, and as the electric doors opened, I turned around and looked at him. I walked back to him, dropped down on one knee, and I put my hand on his wrist. He brought his head up and blinked a couple times to focus on me. I said, 'Dad, I just want you to know that I love you.' He nodded his head and said, 'I know that, Richard. I've always known that. I love you, too.' I turned around and left. That was the last time I saw him. When I think of the fifty-fifty chance that I might not have gone back, I'm always glad I did. I had my closure with my father. I did that right. I don't have any regrets about it. My father died March 21, 1993.

"He was a very hardworking, serious man, and he believed in education. I was never big on education, but he defended me against my mother's brother and sister. They had sons two days apart about twenty months younger than me. One went to Brandeis and Vanderbilt Medical and became a psychiatrist. The other went to Cornell and University of Pennsylvania Medical and became a dentist. They were both very successful. In the '60s and '70s when the family would gather for dinners and parties, they would always tell my parents how successful their sons were. They would always provide a little jab like, 'Richard—with his long, big hair, hanging around with hippies and colored people making music—what kind of future does he have?' My father finally reached a point where he said, 'You take care of your own and Hattie and I will take care of our own.' That was the end of it.

"I had a time period of rebellion when I lived in Cambridge, an hour away from them, and didn't see or talk to them for a long period of time—some years, actually. It was in the mid- to late 1960s. It was after I met Son. I was just doing other things. In hindsight, it was dumb because their love was unquestionable.

"Following his death, I got some inheritance, but not a lot, which I put into the stock market. I put it in tech stocks, and the tech market began to take off." The change in his financial status enabled him to begin traveling to performances and photographing them.

In April 1993, Dick attended Willie Nelson's sixtieth birthday celebration. It was being taped at KLRU-TV studios, home of the famous Austin City Limits show, on the campus of the University of Texas at Austin. While there, he had the opportunity to photograph many of the performers. "I'm not sure why I went. I think I knew I could get in because Bonnie was appearing. I didn't go with Bonnie. I just met her there.

"Willie Nelson is usually very laid back and low key, but they brought in a publicity firm to handle this event. There was a terrible woman who had a release form that limited your use of your negatives. It was like they virtually owned all your stuff. It was a horrible, confining release form. That was several years ago, and in those days it was really rare, especially around Willie, who's always been fairly loose with press arrangements. I didn't have any choice. I was there, so I signed it. I got more shots from that event than probably any other. I have a ton of photographs from shooting on that day. The performers were doing two or three songs, and then there was a set change. In the backstage area was Ray Charles, Bob Dylan, Paul Simon, and Willie. Backstage was awesome!"

Although he had worked with musicians for decades, he had never met one of his idols, Ray Charles. That evening, he finally had the opportunity to do so. "I had seen him many times. I'm not quite sure how you go backstage with a blind performer. You have to be ushered into his presence, and then somebody has to tell him who just came into the room. In the elevator is where I got my three words with Ray Charles. The elevator only goes from the second floor to the first at the Austin City Limits studio. I was on the second floor and was leaving. I went to the elevator, and as I pressed '1,' somebody said, 'Hold that elevator!' I held the elevator, and Ray Charles came in with two other people who were traveling with him. Ray was on my right, and as the doors closed, I pressed against his shoulder. I'm rubbing shoulders with Ray Charles! As we went down, I said, 'I saw you in Rome, Mr. Charles. You were wonderful.' We hit the ground floor, the doors opened, he took one step forward, and, like blind people sometimes do, he grabbed his [own] forearm. He turned in that Ray Charles manner and said, 'Rome. Nice town.' My three words from Ray Charles!"

In early 1994, Dick received a call from the office of producer/director Ken Burns. Burns was filming a documentary on baseball to be aired later that year and wanted to include a song recorded by Brownie McGhee. "They called and asked me how to get in touch with the Brownie McGhee estate. I said, 'Well, it's not his estate. He's still alive.' They said, 'Fabulous! We want to use a Brownie McGhee song about Jackie Robinson' ["Robbie-Dobie Boogie"]. I said, 'How much money have you got?' They said, 'How does five hundred dollars sound?' I said, 'Five hundred dollars gets you an area code, but it doesn't get you a number.' They said, 'Listen, we're so far over budget now it doesn't matter. How about a thousand dollars?' I said, 'Okay, I'll call him.'

"I called Brownie, and he was happy to hear from me. I said, 'Did you ever do a song about Jackie Robinson?' He said, 'Did I ever!' and started singing it to me. I said, 'Okay, I'm going to give somebody your phone number. When he calls, tell Bonnie [McGhee's daughter] to let him through to talk to you. They may use ten or fifteen seconds of the song, and they'll give you a thousand dollars.' He said, 'Okay. You get yours?' [asking if Dick received his commission] I said, 'No, that's okay. I'll pass. You can have it as a gift.' He said, 'Okay.' I called Ken Burns's guy back and told him 'Okay' and to call and work it out with Brownie. He said, 'Thanks a lot. I appreciate it.'"

Months later, another call came regarding McGhee from Barry Dolins, the deputy director at the Mayor's Office for Special Events in Chicago. Every year Dolins booked the artists for the Chicago Blues Festival, and he needed assistance in contacting McGhee. At the 1995 festival he planned to celebrate the eightieth anniversary of blues and jazz luminaries such as Muddy Waters, Billie Holiday, Hound Dog Taylor, Johnny Shines, Memphis Slim, and McGhee.

"Barry called and asked if I knew Brownie. He wanted to get Brownie [to perform], but he was having trouble getting Brownie on the telephone. I said, 'The first thing he's going to ask for is money. What have you got?' He said, 'If I *had to,* I could go seventy-five hundred dollars.' I said, 'With airfares?' He said, 'Airfares and hotel.' I said, 'Okay,' and called Brownie. I said, 'Look, Brownie, Chicago Blues Festival wants to have you there. I explained, as far as I know, you've no intentions of coming out of retirement . . .' Brownie immediately said, 'Don't use that word! Don't you use that word! I'm not retired. I never retired. They just stopped showing me the consideration.' I said, 'Okay, if they were going to have you there, what are you looking for with money?' He said, 'Well, I'm not going for what I was going for before. I gotta get real money.' I said, 'Tell me what real money is to you. Give me a figure.' He said, 'You think they got five thousand?' I said, 'Yeah, you're okay on this. When Barry Dolins calls from Chicago, tell Bonnie you want to take the call.'

"I called Barry back and said, 'Okay, he's good. Give him as much money as you can. Do this right. Give him the status he's earned. When he gets to the airport, meet him with a wheelchair—Brownie had a leg brace—and give somebody the luggage tags to get the baggage off the carousel. When he gets to the hotel, have him preregistered. Make it easy for him.' Barry says, 'I'd do that anyway.' *Yeah, right, I'm sure you would but here's a reminder.* Barry then said, 'Do you want a piece of this?' That is, did I want a percentage of what they were paying Brownie. Stupid me, in those days I had a whole ton of stock, so I said, 'No, that's okay. You can have it as a gift.' I go to the festival and visit with Brownie. Those were the last photographs I took of him. He played and sang brilliantly. He was mentally sharp and played with some old Chicago friends.

"The festival was in June, so a few months after it was over, Brownie called and said, 'That worked out okay. I'm not saying that I'd not come back to play, so if something like that comes around, you can put my name out there. I trust you. It could be a good thing.' I said, 'Okay.' I was living in Oxford, Mississippi, retired, and into photography. If a five- to seven-thousand-dollar act comes in and says, 'Do you want to book me?' yeah, you bet I do! This guy's been gone for ten or fifteen years. A whole generation of people had never heard him. He's a legend. They don't know he's alive."

In the spring of 1995, B. B. King and Bobby Bland played a concert in Oxford at Ole Miss, so Dick went to see his old friends. He was standing at the side of the stage enjoying the music when he was approached by Leo Allred, owner of the Beale Street establishment, *Tater Red's*.

"Leo came up and said, 'Luther Allison is over there. He just finished an album in Memphis and came down to see B. B. He wants to talk to you.' I said, 'I'm just a guy watching a show. I don't care who talks to me.' I was standing there, and I saw him out of the corner of my eye. He came over and stood next to me. He said, 'Look, man, I messed up. I know that I put you in a bad way. I don't expect you and me will ever be friends again, but I just want you to know that it's been on my mind all these years. I was listening to the wrong people, but that don't excuse what I done.' I nodded and said, 'You're right in saying that we'll never be friends again, but I hope your new album does well. I wish you a lot of success now that you're back in the country.' He walked away, and I never spoke to him again."

Luther's 1994 *Soul Fixin' Man* on Alligator Records was, indeed, a great success and numerous festival performances followed. His career was cut short less than three years later when he was diagnosed with inoperable brain cancer in July 1997 and died less than a month later. "He was a really talented guy, but he tried to be all over the place and all things to all people. He wanted everybody to like him, so he had ever-shifting loyalties. You can't do that. If I had worked with Fred McDowell and Robert Pete Williams and had loyalty from old, poor, black men who couldn't read and write, I was certainly going to hold that same standard to Luther Allison. He was disloyal to me."

Months later, Dick was embroiled in a legal battle to defend his reputation. Stephen Calt, author of various articles, liner notes, and books on the blues, had published a biography of Skip James in September 1994 titled *I'd Rather Be the Devil: Skip James and the Blues.* He had forged a friendship with James, and the book was largely drawn from Calt's communication with him. It contained a number of derogatory comments regarding others in the blues world, including Dick. Not having read the book, he was unaware of this until a friend brought it to his attention.

"Somebody said, 'Wow, man, he really trashed you.' I said, 'Really?' I got a copy of the book, and they were right. There was a line that said I was roundly accused of being a thief. Well, I couldn't let that go. It was published by Da Capo. They were a very famous reprint house. I got a lawyer, and we found that this was the first original manuscript that Da Capo had ever published.

"Calt had this correspondence with Skip. Skip was really always looking for sympathy, so Skip would write letters that said things like [paraphrasing],

'I'm sitting on the cracker barrel. I ain't got ne'er penny. Dick Waterman hadn't found me no work. I'm countin' on him, and here I am. I ain't got no money to pay for nothin.' Those days, 1966–1967, were really hard in the blues world, especially because Skip was so distant and aloof that he never really spoke to an audience. He didn't like autographs or shaking hands. He was never ingratiating in a way that got him invited back, and his records didn't sell. He was a very remote person. It was hard to find work for him, but I did my best.

"Calt had nothing to do with the music scene. He had met Skip at the 1964 Newport Festival in the 'blues house' where he hung around. Skip held Mississippi John Hurt, who was very popular, in contempt because John just did those 'play party songs.' John was a songster. He did songs that told a story, like 'John Henry' and 'Frankie and Johnny.' Skip regarded that as being the bottom of the barrel for music, and John's popularity just mystified him. Skip was complex and complicated. He was very vain. He wanted compliments. He wanted attention. Skip didn't like anybody but Skip. Calt picked up on this and basically just trashed everybody.

"I sued, and we met in a lawyer's office in New York. I couldn't remember having ever seen Calt before. My lawyer said, 'They're going to say you are a public figure, and because of that, the standard for libel is much higher and much different. If you're a public figure, the chances of winning are more difficult.' At that point, in the 1990s, I was not writing a column for the *Oxford Eagle*. I was just a guy living quietly in Oxford, Mississippi, with no connection to the public at all. What happened, though, is that a year or two before, Bonnie had her big breakthrough. She won four Grammies [three for *Nick of Time*, released in 1989, and a fourth for the duet "In the Mood" with John Lee Hooker on his album *The Healer*]. Bonnie then had an official biography written for her by Capitol Records. In it there was a line that mentioned that when she was in college in Cambridge, she came under the mentorship of Dick Waterman, noted blues manager.

"As Bonnie's fame increased, she started to tour extensively in the early 1990s. The promoters would get a publicity pack from her office, and this bio of her would be used to promote her tour dates. The lawyers did what they called a Nexis search, which would go through newspapers all over the world. When my name was entered, 'Bonnie Raitt, Dick Waterman, mentor, blues manager from Cambridge' popped up in various papers. This one line was enough to make them consider me a public figure. I lost the case. I appealed it to the sixth district federal court and lost the appeal. That meant the Calt biography went back for another printing because Da Capo had said if they won this they would reprint a second edition. And they did. I always know there are people who have read that and believe it. It was just ugly.

"The interesting thing was I had a line of people who were going to come into court, and they were all people I never managed and never booked: B. B., Taj Mahal, John Hammond, Koko Taylor, Brownie McGhee, and Robert Lockwood. I just never got it to trial."

Peter Guralnick comments, "In the book Calt uses partial quotes. Basically, what he does is if there's anything negative to say about anyone, he'll find it, and he'll use it. Over and over again you see that in his description of things like all the great paydays Dick missed for Skip. I went to see Skip every single time he came to town. I don't know how many times I saw him, but I saw him maybe three dozen times. Most nights when you would go to see him there could be as few as ten or twelve people, and a big crowd was thirty people. There just wasn't that much demand, and Dick was working his ass off for Skip."

Amid the distractions of the lawsuit, Dick worked to secure dates for Brownie McGhee to play blues festivals, but his efforts were in vain. "I get ready for the 1996 festival season, and in November/December he [Brownie] gets really sick. He was in bed and weakening, and he was not going to get better. He died February 16, 1996. I went to his funeral in Oakland, California. It was the only service I ever attended in which music of the deceased was played at the service. The graveyard was several miles away. On the way, the hearse got out on I-580, which was the interstate onto which pours all the traffic coming over the bridge from San Francisco and all the traffic out of Oakland. It's five or six lanes across, metal to metal, and we are hurtling at sixty to seventy miles per hour. I'm yelling, 'Follow that hearse! Follow that hearse!'"

The following month, Dick traveled to New York for the premiere of August Wilson's play *Seven Guitars.* Jack Viertel, his friend from Cambridge, who was working with theatrical company Jujamcyn, had contacted him months earlier about using some of his iconic photos to create a special piece of artwork. Viertel explains, "I co-produced six of August's ten plays, so he and I got quite close. I've known Dick as a photographer as well as a manager, and I know August has a deep, profound interest in the blues. There are quotes from prewar country blues in all of his plays. They're not announced as quotes, they're just stitched into the dialogue of the play. When *Seven Guitars* came along I thought it would be great fun to get an opening night gift, which would be close-ups of the guitars from pictures that Dick had taken. I contacted Dick, and he was happy to help. We worked together picking the images of which guitarists would look best and different from each other. I presented it to August as an opening night gift, and he was very touched by it."

Dick remembers, "My sister and I went to opening night on Broadway. I'm sitting in front of Al Hirshfeld, the caricaturist for the *New York Times*. This was a guy in his nineties who started to do caricatures of Broadway plays in like the 1920s and 1930s. He was sitting right behind me with a sketch pad. Wow! His work was so intricate, especially with beards, hair, fringes of curtains, and things like that. Just masterful!

"I turned around, introduced myself, and said, 'I'm a huge fan of your work and always have been.' He said, 'Thank you.' That was it. That was like my three words with Ray Charles in the elevator. I was thrilled."

The collage presented to Wilson was on display at the party immediately following the performance. "We went to the party afterward. Everybody was drinking. I looked at this man sitting alone at a table, and it was August Wilson. I went over and told him that I was Dick Waterman, and I had taken the pictures for the collage that had been given to him. He said, 'Did you meet all of those people?' I said, 'Yes, I did. Some I knew better than others, but I met all of them.' We talked about the people, and he asked me had I known Muddy and Wolf. I said that I had, and they were very nice people. He said, 'Thank you.' I had a nice conversation with him."

The photo collage for Wilson was a reminder to Dick of his vast archive of images and negatives dating back to the 1960s, largely unused and unseen, languishing in boxes at his house. A phone call from Chris Murray, the owner of the Govinda Gallery, in Washington, DC, in 1996 prompted Dick to delve into his archive.

A few months before Murray's call, Dick had walked into an art supply and framing shop in Oxford owned by his friend Jim Weems. He wanted to use his catalog of photo negatives to generate revenue, but was in need of ideas. As he and Weems conversed, he mentioned perhaps having the images printed onto mugs or t-shirts. Weems, who had seen some of his work, felt they needed to be presented in a more refined manner. He was acquainted with a printer in Jackson, Mississippi, and suggested Dick select a photograph and do a signed limited edition of a print. Dick immediately agreed. Weems chose a lovely cream paper and an image of Son House, Skip James, and Mississippi John Hurt.

Dick entrusted the negative to Weems, who put it in a safe deposit box and drove it to and from Jackson for printing. When the prints had been matted and signed, they placed an advertisement in *Living Blues* magazine and received a positive response. Eventually, more images were selected and printed for sale. The prints were featured in the window of Weems's shop.

Chris Murray's twelve-year-old son, David, was fascinated by the blues, so the two had come for a vacation to the Delta area and had driven to Oxford for a day of sightseeing. While strolling through the Oxford town square, they passed Weems's store and were captivated by photographs displayed in the window. Entering the store, Murray inquired about the photographs and was told they were the work of Dick Waterman. He requested Dick's phone number and telephoned him. Soon, they were discussing the possibility of creating a book and assembling a gallery show.

Although Dick was interested in generating income, it was not a necessity, as his wealth had increased substantially in the 1990s. "By 1997–98, I was genuinely rich: not comfortable or well off, I was really *rich.* It happened in about a year or two. From 1996 through about 2002, I had a tremendous amount of money and did nothing with it. I didn't put anything away. I put a down payment on my house and bought a red Mercedes, but nothing else. I had four thousand shares in Yahoo when it hit two hundred fifty dollars a share. That's a million dollars! I had Sun Microsystems and Worldcom. I had almost two million dollars, but did nothing. I should have put a quarter million in bonds and walked away from it."

Having amassed significant wealth, Dick could afford to travel to blues festivals around the country. "If I was going to go back on the road, I might as well take my camera back out. I started to go around and photograph a lot of blues festivals from 1995 to about 2003. That was a very big time for me in photography because I had the money to go to festivals, and there were a lot of festivals in that time period. I wasn't into live music as far as booking or managing, but I was probably doing more photography of higher quality, much of which has never been seen."

Although he had not regularly attended blues and folk festivals for some years, far more time had passed since he had taken photos. "I was taking photographs in the '60s and up to the Stones tour in 1970. I don't know why I never considered myself to be a photographer. I just had the camera around when I was at the festivals. I put my cameras down for over twenty years. It wasn't until about 1994–95, that I came back to photography. When I was working with Champion Jack Dupree, I took the camera along with me."

After he went on tour with the Stones in 1970, he put his camera away and it remained unused while he was living in California during most of the 1970s. "People say, 'Wow, how could you take so many great pictures and then abruptly put the camera down?' I don't know. It wasn't a big deal. I just had my camera.

"If only I had been a photographer with intent and purpose. The number of people I was with backstage was just awesome. The whole last fifty years of music! It never occurred to me the impact of the twenty years that I had lost. There really wasn't anybody famous in that time period that I didn't have access to. Buddy was doing shows with people like Clapton, the Who, and others. I could have had my camera in the stage area. It was really the fact that photography wasn't important to me because I had access to everybody."

Though Son House had earned few royalties during his lifetime, his estate received an unprecedented windfall in 1998 when one of his songs was used in a popular movie. The decision was prompted by his friend, Dave Marsh.

Blues Brothers 2000 was in production when Sam Moore, of famed duo Sam and Dave, mentioned to Marsh that he had a role in the movie and was searching for a song to perform. Marsh created a list of potential songs, including some of his favorite gospel music, and sent it to Moore for consideration. One of the pieces he included was Son House's "John the Revelator." Moore liked the piece, so it was included in the film.

Moore's wife, Joyce, contacted Marsh to inquire about ownership of the song because they were trying to determine who should receive credit for it. Marsh believed the lyrics to be public domain, but the recording he sent was Son House's, so he felt some royalties should go to House's estate. The first royalty check Dick received on behalf of the estate was far more than any of House's previous royalties. Dick immediately called Evie House to share the good news that she soon would be receiving a substantial sum of money.

In 2000, Dick received a call from the Blues Foundation informing him that he was to be inducted into the Blues Hall of Fame. "It was really no surprise, because they had told me that I was to be inducted the year before. I just don't like bringing attention to myself, so I had refused. The following year they said that there were twenty-one people voting, and I had gotten seventeen votes. It sort of mars the process if I had seventeen out of twenty-one votes and I refused it, so I said, 'Okay.'

"They asked who I wanted to induct me. Guralnick was willing, and I said, 'Okay.' Before the induction, I was backstage and said to him, 'Don't do anything to embarrass me.' He said, 'For what?' I said, 'You're inducting me.' He said, 'Oh yeah, that's right.' I thought to myself, *Something's not right here because he's not a forgetful person.* When it came to that point in the ceremony, Howard Stovall said, 'We have somebody here who knows Dick a lot better than I do who is going to speak on his behalf,' and then Jeffrey came out. I thought, *Wow—that's pretty great!*

"They did the ceremony in Washington, DC, on a Monday night. Bonnie was doing a benefit in California on the Saturday and Sunday prior. She also was a presenter at the Grammys on Tuesday, so I knew she wasn't going to be there. Jeffrey came out and spoke about our long friendship and working together. He said, 'But there's someone here who has known him longer and better,' and then Bonnie came out. It totally caught me by surprise. I knew she logistically couldn't do it, but she had flown in during the night to do it and then, after the ceremony, had gone to the airport to go back to L.A. for the Grammys. It was really very nice. She gave a really gracious speech.

"I did not have a speech. I spoke without notes. I basically talked about the different musicians and that I had been blessed with people of high integrity and honesty, which made it really easy to work with them. I mentioned Junior, who I think was probably the most ethical person, and I said, 'And Bonnie. And I would say that even if she wasn't here.'

"I concluded with my John Hurt story when he was at the Café Lena in Saratoga. He had finished and was in the dressing room when someone said to him, 'When will I see you again, John?' He said, 'Oh, you can see me anytime.' The guy said, 'Here? You're coming back?' John said, 'Oh, if you mean the booking thing, you've got to talk to Dick about that. As far as seeing me, you can see me anytime you want because now that I've met you, I have taken you into my heart to be my friend. I would hope that you have taken me into your heart to be your friend. Anytime you want to see me, you just think about me, and I'll come right up out of your heart. I'll be there with you anytime you want because good friends live forever in your heart.' That's where I ended my speech. I just said, 'That's how I feel tonight.'"

Along with accolades from the blues world, the new millennium also brought an unfortunate, dramatic shift in Dick's financial situation. The technology stocks he had purchased in the 1990s, which had soared to unprecedented levels, suddenly plummeted when the "dot com bubble" burst. He watched as the stocks that had made him a multimillionaire became virtually worthless.

"I had a stock investor who totally left me alone. Nobody said this might be a good time to take some out or put a quarter of a million away. Everything withered. Sun Microsystems went from ninety-seven dollars to three dollars a share. Yahoo went from two hundred fifty to eight dollars. It just melted. Every day I'd think it couldn't get any lower, that this was the bottom. When it had melted to one hundred twenty-five dollars a share, I remember thinking, *This can't be a one-hundred-dollar stock!* It turned out that if I had gotten out at a hundred, I'd have been blessed, because it went to eight dollars. I have all bad memories from that time period."

Although all of the early bluesmen with whom he worked were deceased, he had remained involved with some of their estates and occasionally received business calls on their behalf. In 2002, a representative from Fuel 2000, an independent record label founded less than a decade earlier, called him to discuss the re-release of some of Son House's live recordings.

House's 1965 performance at the Gaslight and 1966 Oberlin College concert had been recorded without consent. The Oberlin recording also featured John Hurt, and Vanguard had released the bootleg of Hurt's performance. When Dick learned of this, he was concerned and made some telephone calls.

"I knew whoever bootlegged John got Son because it was a double concert. I went to Maynard Solomon of Vanguard, who was a nice guy and a close friend, and he said, 'We're not at liberty to tell you, and we don't have to tell you where we get our tapes from.' I said, 'It's a bootleg.' He said, 'Well, we have this artist under contract, so we chose to buy this tape.' I said, 'You've got to tell me, because the guy who taped John got Son, too.' He just shrugged."

Decades later, the Son House Oberlin bootleg recording surfaced. It had been released, and the only contact information for the person or persons releasing was a post office box number. "So, then there were two bootlegs: Son House at the Gaslight and Son House at Oberlin. Fuel 2000 came to me and said, 'We want to put these out. We can go back to these originals, use them as masters, clean them up, and release them.' I said, 'Okay.' I wrote, 'These recordings are stolen from Son House at the Gaslight and Son House at Oberlin. If the people who recorded those concerts want to step forward and claim ownership, I admit that I have stolen what they stole. Let them come forward and speak up on their own behalf.' They never did. I threw the gauntlet down: if you can prove this is legal, you can sue me.

"*Live at the Gaslight* is from early 1965 when I was in the middle of negotiating Son House on Columbia Records. Why would I have *ever* authorized a Son House recording in a club to jeopardize my Columbia negotiations?! Insane! I never would have done that." Fuel 2000 released the recordings as a two-volume set later that same year.

Seven years after Chris Murray had called Dick to suggest he assemble some of his photos for a book and gallery showing, Dick's book, *Between Midnight and Day: The Last Unpublished Blues Archive*, was published in October 2003. A showing of some of the featured photographs was scheduled at Govinda Gallery to coincide with the release of the book.

The book was a fitting tribute to a host of legendary blues artists, presenting stories and photographs never before available to an audience of blues fans. Blues artist Hawkeye Herman comments, "If you mention the name of an older blues artist like Lightning Hopkins or Son House, Booker, Mance, Furry, the iconic picture that one has in one's mind of that artist was taken by Dick Waterman. We have a man who took pictures of blues icons whose photos have become iconic.

"There's something else about that book. Dick is very candid and honest. I think it's interesting to anyone who reads the text that accompanies those photos that Dick is as honest in words as he is in his photos. He does not hedge when it comes to talking about both the good and the bad in terms of his relationships with the artists. Some people would only share good experiences regarding their life tasks."

In early 2004, Dick received a call from the office of Folk Alliance International. Mississippi John Hurt was being honored with a posthumous Lifetime Achievement Award, and Dick was invited to share his memories of Hurt at the ceremony in February in San Diego, California. It was both an opportunity to honor a man who had been the catalyst for his initial work in blues music and a bittersweet reminder of the close friendship they had shared.

"I was getting ready to go to the microphone and someone said, 'We're going to have a brief video of John.' I said, 'Okay.' I go to the lectern with the microphone, I turn around, and a big screen is rising over me. The lights go down and John comes on the screen. He looks down at me [in my direction], and I heard the opening chord of 'My Creole Belle.' I thought, *Oh no!* I couldn't breathe. It just hit me. That was the song he always played for me. More than seeing him and more than hearing his speaking voice, when he hit the opening chord, it didn't wash over me, it just enveloped me. I staggered back with a catch in my throat. I thought, *Let me get through this!* And I turned away from the screen."

Shortly after returning to Oxford, he received an invitation to write another book. "B. B. [King] was turning eighty years old, so somebody wanted to release a book on his life. They went to B. B.' s management, and the manager said he would allow it but wouldn't participate. In other words, B. B. was not going to make himself available for any interviews. They asked his management who they could get to do it. The manager mentioned me and said, 'B. B.' s known him a long time and likes and trusts him.' They especially liked the fact that I knew all the players in the blues world, so I could get them all on the phone."

The company contacted Dick to inquire if he would be interested in the project, and he agreed. "I did about fifteen or twenty phone interviews. I'm a very bad interviewer. The reason is if I'm talking to Little Milton or Bobby Rush or somebody that I know, we're having a conversation between equals, so it's not an interview. The interviewer should ask a question and then shut up."

Given Dick's longstanding friendship with King, it was not surprising that King decided to be more involved in the creation of the book. On

Thanksgiving Day, Dick flew to Las Vegas to visit with his friend and interview him. "I had to get up at 6 A.M. They met me at the airport in Las Vegas and we took cars out to B. B.' s house. We actually filmed it. I did about an hour and a half to two hours with B. B., just winging it with notes."

The book was released on September 8, 2005, to great success. On September 20, Dick attended an event held in King's honor. Sam Haskell, an Ole Miss alumnus who had worked for the William Morris Agency, and his wife, Mary, hosted an eightieth birthday celebration for the blues singer at their home in Encino, California. The evening featured a concert and served as a fundraiser for the B. B. King Museum being built in Indianola, Mississippi. The occasion also afforded Dick the opportunity to reconnect with Jim Gianopulos.

Gianopulos remembers, "Dick called me and said, 'I'm coming to California.' I said, 'When?' He said, 'Well, B. B.' s having an eightieth birthday celebration out there at some guy's house.' I hadn't been invited, but Dick said, 'Do you want to come with me?' I said, 'Are you kidding?' So, we went to this party, and here is B. B. King and Buddy Guy, who came to honor B. B."

Dick was excited to see his old friend again. "That was the first time I'd seen Jimmy in a lot of years, and he looked great. We had so much fun just hanging out. When we had been sitting in my apartment in Cambridge, I wanted to be a big man in blues, and he wanted to be a major entertainment lawyer in Los Angeles. By the time we got to 2005, I was in the Blues Hall of Fame. We were going up the walkway and I said to him, 'I want to introduce you to B. B. and Buddy, so tell me exactly how to introduce you.' He looked at me and said, 'James N. Gianopulos, chairman of Twentieth Century Fox.' I looked at him, and he looked at me, and we started to laugh. Tears were streaming down our faces. We walked up to where the photographers were standing, and they said, 'What are you doing here, Mr. Gianopulos? Are you a blues fan?' Jimmy just said, 'I'm with him,' and looked at me. I introduced him to Buddy and B. B., and they hung out and had some pictures taken."

CHAPTER 15

He's the BEST EVER BEEN in This Town

"THERE'S ONE GUY I IDOLIZED AS MY ROLE MODEL. HIS NAME WAS Arnold 'Red' Auerbach. He lived in Washington. Boston got a basketball team called the Celtics, and they hired him. He worked there for decades. He was a magnificent coach.

"He knew when it was his time to step back and go from coach to general manager. He took his prize player, Bill Russell, and named him as coach, making him the first black man to coach a major sports team. Russell went on to coach champions. Auerbach eased into the role of general manager where his decisions brought many championships. He was brilliant because he thought ahead of the opposition. Then, in his later years, he became an elder statesman that people came to because he had seen the whole history of basketball pass in front of him. He proved he could do it as a coach, he proved he could do it as a general manager, and then he became a much-respected nonparticipating elder statesman.

"I patterned my life after him. I was a good agent, but when I became a promoter, and later, when I stopped being an agent, I took on kind of a senior status in blues and people come to me. I think that I was to blues music what Red Auerbach was to basketball: someone who could do it young, do it older, and when he got into his seventies, he was still a sage."

Dick credits Nat Weiss for offering advice that strongly influenced his career. "Nat was a lawyer and the partner of Brian Epstein, the Beatles' manager. He gave me the best piece of advice I ever had. He said, 'There's a lot of things in life that are good, and many things that are very good, and some things that are exceptional, but there are those few things that are shining superstars. Those few, few, firmaments of light are the true superstars. Life is short. There are only so many hours and years in your life. Discard everything else. Only pursue the tiniest number of superstars. Everything else wastes your time.'

"I look back on it, and the first musician I managed was Son House. The first band I had was Junior Wells. The first concert I ever produced was James Taylor. The first electric concert I ever produced was Bruce Springsteen. The first white person I ever managed was Bonnie Raitt. Nat was right.

"You've got to see a different horizon. People tend to look at this week, this month, 'right now.' You can't do that. You've got to say, 'What do I want this act to do in a year? In five years?' You've got to see a horizon and plan. You see something beyond the common. You just have to have that vision. I can still see the big picture and a vision of what is down the road."

Indeed, from a vantage point of more than a half century since Son House's rediscovery, it becomes clear Dick's vision was one of the things that set him apart from some others in the management business. Some had a vision of increasing their own wealth and status. Dick's vision was not one driven by self-aggrandizement, but rather an honest appreciation of the music. He had a desire to assist the careers of elder bluesmen, helping many to achieve unprecedented recognition and, in varying degrees, greater income, which benefited the lives of them and their families.

Certainly, there were those who sought to exploit musicians for personal gain to such an extent that it prompted questions for some as to whether the positive aspects of the rediscoveries always outweighed the negative. Phil Spiro, who played a role in the rediscovery of Son House and was witness to all that transpired as a result, harbored doubts for a time, but came to a more balanced view in later years. He acknowledges the missteps, some simply the product of youthful enthusiasm and inexperience, and the benefits experienced by the bluesmen and their families due to their rediscoveries. One thing is certain, the rediscoveries bequeathed an incomparable gift to both the blues lovers who experienced their music firsthand and future generations.

Reflecting on it, Spiro remarks, "Twenty years ago, I ranted in print about how some of the rediscoverers had not really seen the old guys as people. But that was twenty years ago, and both they and their rediscoveries are gone now, and so is any animosity I had about their attitude. People are what they are, and all we can do is accept that and get on with our own lives.

"There were just a small number of young white people involved, and generally none of us knew what we were doing at the time. Probably none of us looked beyond the challenge of finding one of the old guys. We were all pretty clueless about what the ramifications of a rediscovery might be. All of us did it out of a love of the music and out of curiosity.

"In spite of some screw-ups and isolated greed that emerged later on, in the end it was a good deal for the old guys, none of whom had any notion of a second musical career so late in life, and some had not had much of a first musical career to begin with. Those few who considered themselves professionals back in the '30s—Skip, for example—probably were best prepared for their second careers. Thanks to Dick's efforts, they earned money and had more worldwide fame and adulation than any of them had ever anticipated.

"When I was recruiting people to help look for Son, I could not have made a choice that was better for the music I loved than Dick Waterman. Dick has done a fantastic job of helping the old guys and deserves every bit of praise for what he has done. He has looked out for them when they needed it the most, and has unselfishly helped their families and heirs get the share of the royalty money to which they were entitled. In a music business where crooks are common enough to be considered the norm, Dick's integrity and competence remain unquestioned by anyone who has worked with him. If there was such a thing as a 'blues revival,' it was in no small part due to Dick Waterman's efforts.

"I started the ball rolling in finding Son House, but it was Dick who made Son the success that he became. I had neither the ability nor the patience to do what Dick did for Son, and later for the other old guys. Al Wilson helped Son remember music that he had forgotten, and his contribution was as necessary and as unselfish as Dick's, but in the end, it was Dick Waterman who did the heavy lifting."

Those whose lives have been touched by Dick and his work, personally and professionally, have their own unique perspective on his contributions and legacy. B. B. King acknowledged Dick's influence on the blues and the musicians by saying, "Dick Waterman was a big help to people that are in the blues, especially the kind that myself and a few others played. Somehow he seemed to know much more about this kind of music than many people, so he was able to contribute quite a bit.

"He had a good eye and a good ear for people. Like, how would you pick up on Bonnie Raitt among all the other greats? That's because he was paying attention—having that good ear and good eyes for appearance. He is a knowledgeable person. I always respect beauty and class. I think that he had class. I just say I respect him and think highly of him for things he did and how he did them."

Bobby Rush points out that Dick worked with honesty and integrity at a time when exploitation of black artists was not uncommon. "I think he was the best manager that anyone could have. He was more fair than anyone that I've ever known with the artists and with the money, and what he could or could not do. He didn't promise you something knowing he couldn't do it.

"I want people to know he's one white man who had the black man's work and interests at heart. That don't happen for everybody 'cause a lot of folks are just in it for the money, in it for themselves. A lot of things Dick did, there wasn't no money in it for him. He did it for the artist themselves."

Peter Guralnick eloquently summarizes the reasons Dick's relationships with others transcended race. "When you see him, when you talk with him, you're always struck by how much he is himself. What goes beyond that is his overall kindness, his genuine respect for others. It's a personal connection. He's not measuring people in terms of their status in the world. He has a genuine appreciation for the people that he loves as people. I don't think it has anything to do with either status or position, or even intellectuality, or anything but their underlying quality as a human being. I think that's what made him so successful. There couldn't be a hint of condescension in his dealings with Buddy Guy, Junior Wells, Skip James, or Son House, at least as I saw it, because condescension never entered into it with Dick. He would never have imagined himself above or beneath. He was just dealing with people as people. He could tell his performers if they were doing something wrong. He could tell them that as an equal."

Of Dick's work and their longstanding friendship Taj Mahal remarks, "He always left the dance with the party that he came with. For all that's gone down, for all the years, and for all that I've teased him and hustled him about what he was doing, he always took it in stride. I have no hesitation to give this man a clean bill of health as far as the music business and his handling of these great players: acknowledging who they were and looking out for them. He didn't have to do that. We've remained friends for almost fifty years now. I'm always glad to see him and hear what he's up to. I'm very serious when I say that this man was always a gentleman. I am very thrilled to have him as a friend and very happy to know that he carried out his work. A lot of people have their work cut out when they come to this planet and somehow fail the job. Well, Dick did not fail the job on any level and to this day is still maintaining a high level of integrity. I think that the music is that much better, sweeter, and richer as a result of the energy that he has put into it and these great artists."

Bonnie Raitt shares her thoughts on Dick's contributions to careers of the bluesmen and her own by saying, "He will always be known for the caretaking and shepherding of the careers and the personal lives of the blues artists with whom he worked. It will be his greatest legacy that he was able to get them the fees, treatment, recognition, and royalties they deserved. He handled the personal management of interfacing between their rural lives and going into the big time again: being suddenly at the Newport Festival, doing TV shows, or playing in Europe. He was able to humanize a business that could be just so brutal and so cutthroat. Dick was a wonderful, invaluable manager for bringing those people to us. He was able to bring them dignity, respect, comfort, and remuneration in a time when, if it wasn't for him, I don't think they would have had that kind of life and that kind of late-stage career resurgence and enjoyment in their lives. He has incredible integrity and respect, and he cared about whether they were treated fairly. There was no better booking agent than him. He was absolutely fantastic."

Indeed, due to both his work with the rediscovered bluesmen and his generosity, he left an indelible impression on later musicians. Hawkeye Herman credits Dick with having influenced his own career path. "Dick's intervention in the lives of those blues musicians whom he rediscovered, represented, and promoted gave visibility to an older generation of music that otherwise would have been lost to many people, not just musicians. His efforts on behalf of booking them opened up doors not only for those artists, but for those of us who followed. Dick's intervention changed the direction of many of our lives and made us realize the importance of the music and that we could viably follow that as a way of life. I'm not saying that I wouldn't be here and that John Hammond and Bonnie Raitt and all of us that came after wouldn't be here, but we certainly wouldn't have had access to the material and the artists that we had.

"Dick Waterman had a great deal to do with the direction of American music and American culture. It also affected world culture because it affected people like Eric Clapton, Mick Jagger, and the British blues rockers who also had benefited from Dick's efforts on behalf of these artists.

"I started doing in-school blues presentations in 1978 and, whether Dick realizes it or not, he's greatly responsible because he gave me entré into a deeper aspect of blues music, and the history and the people who made the music who were still alive. Those people freely shared information with me. I saw Lightning Hopkins, Mance Lipscomb, Booker White, Furry Lewis, and Sam Chatmon. It was a result of Dick sharing photos and information, and promoting and representing these artists that I gained access to these musicians. The information shared with me by these blues artists gave me a life's work."

Unquestionably, Dick touched many lives during his career. As an awkward stuttering boy he never imagined that one day he would stand before thousands and introduce musicians who influenced the course of American music. He was only searching for a good story on that trip in the summer of 1964, but what he found was his life's calling. He was befriended by blues musicians who lived a world away from his privileged New England upbringing. With the same sense of responsibility that made his father a respected physician, Dick managed and protected the interests of the musicians.

Through his work, he bequeathed to generations of blues enthusiasts the opportunity to see live performances and hear recordings that likely would never have existed. By ensuring their musical legacy, he created his own.

INTERVIEWS, CORRESPONDENCE, AND PERSONAL COMMUNICATIONS

Aldin, Mary Katherine. Personal interview with author and subsequent e-mail correspondence. Memphis, TN. February 18, 2011.

Charters, Samuel. Phone interview with author. March 22, 2011.

Clapton, Eric. Phone interview with author. August 15, 2013.

DiMucci, Dion. Phone interview with author. August 14, 2013.

Evans, David H. E-mail interview. July 8, 2014.

Fishel, Jim. Phone interview with author and subsequent e-mail correspondence. August 14, 2013.

Fishel, John. Phone interview with author and subsequent e-mail correspondence. August 6, 2013.

Flohil, Richard. Personal interview with author and subsequent e-mail correspondence. Memphis, TN. February 18, 2011.

Gianopulos, Jim. Phone interview with author. July 2, 2013.

Guralnick, Peter. Phone interview with author and subsequent e-mail correspondence. June 25, 2012.

Guy, Buddy. Personal interview with author. Chicago, IL. May 11, 2011.

Herman, Hawkeye. Phone interview with author. June 23, 2011.

Hersh, Jeffrey. E-mail interview and subsequent correspondence with author. August 10, 2012.

Iglauer, Bruce. Personal interview with author. Chicago, IL. May 10, 2011.

Jackson, Bruce. Phone interview with author. December 13, 2012.

Johnson, Dr. Patricia. Personal interview with author. Clarksdale, MS. May 30, 2011.

Kappus, Mike. Phone interview with author and subsequent e-mail correspondence. August 15, 2014.

King, B. B. Personal interview with author. Chicago, IL. January 15, 2011.

Krantz, Mark. Phone interview with author. February 23, 2012.

Leary, K. T. Phone interview with author and subsequent e-mail correspondence. July 13, 2011.

McFarlane, Will. Phone interview with author. December 19, 2013.

Mahal, Taj. Personal interview with author. Steele, MO. September 24, 2011.

Marsh, Dave. Phone interview with author. January 24, 2013.

Muldaur, Maria. Phone interview with author. August 14, 2013.

Petersen, Holger. Phone interview with author. August 17, 2012.

Pierson, Leroy. Phone interviews with author. July 23 and 24, 2013.

Raitt, Bonnie. Phone interview with author. September 22, 2011.

Reed, Carol. Phone interview with author and subsequent e-mail correspondence. July 15, 2012.

Rishell, Paul. Phone interview with author. May 22, 2013.
Rush, Bobby. Personal interview with author. Clarksdale, MS. August 10, 2012.
Russell, Tony. Phone interview with author. July 13, 2011.
Saal, Rollene. Phone interview with author. July 30, 2012.
Spiro, Phil. E-mail interview and subsequent correspondence with author. October 31, 2011.
Viertel, Jack. Phone interview with author. February 7, 2013.
Waterman, Dick. Personal interviews with author, e-mail correspondence, and telephone interviews. 2011–2018.
Weems, Jim. Personal interview with author. Oxford, MS. July 14, 2016.

INDEX

Studies in Naval History and Sea Power

Christopher M. Bell and James C. Bradford, editors

Studies in Naval History and Sea Power advances our understanding of sea power and its role in global security by publishing significant new scholarship on navies and naval affairs. The series presents specialists in naval history, as well as students of sea power, with works that cover the role of the world's naval powers, from the ancient world to the navies and coast guards of today. The works in Studies in Naval History and Sea Power examine all aspects of navies and conflict at sea, including naval operations, strategy, and tactics, as well as the intersections of sea power and diplomacy, navies and technology, sea services and civilian societies, and the financing and administration of seagoing military forces.

U-BOAT COMMANDER OSKAR KUSCH

Anatomy of a Nazi-Era Betrayal and Judicial Murder

ERIC C. RUST

NAVAL INSTITUTE PRESS
ANNAPOLIS, MARYLAND

Naval Institute Press
291 Wood Road
Annapolis, MD 21402

Library of Congress Cataloging-in-Publication Data
Names: Rust, Eric C., date, author.
Title: U-boat Commander Oskar Kusch : anatomy of a Nazi-era betrayal and judicial murder / Eric C. Rust.
Other titles: Anatomy of a Nazi-era betrayal and judicial murder
Description: Annapolis, Maryland : Naval Institute Press, [2020] | Series: Studies in naval history and sea power | Includes bibliographical references and index.
Identifiers: LCCN 2019056331 (print) | LCCN 2019056332 (ebook) | ISBN 9781682475140 (hardcover) | ISBN 9781682475157 (pdf) | ISBN 9781682475157 (epub)
Subjects: LCSH: Kusch, Oskar, 1918–1944. | World War, 1939–1945—Naval operations—Submarine. | World War, 1939–1945—Naval operations, German. | Kusch, Oskar, 1918–1944—Trials, litigation, etc. | Germany. Kriegsmarine—Officers—Biography. | Submarine captains—Germany—Biography. | Trials (Treason)—Germany.
Classification: LCC D781 .R87 2020 (print) | LCC D781 (ebook) | DDC 940.54/5943092 [B] —dc23
LC record available at https://lccn.loc.gov/2019056331
LC ebook record available at https://lccn.loc.gov/2019056332

♾ Print editions meet the requirements of ANSI/NISO z39.48-1992 (Permanence of Paper).
Printed in the United States of America.

28 27 26 25 24 23 22 21 20 9 8 7 6 5 4 3 2 1
First printing

CONTENTS

FOREWORD

FOR VERY SOUND REASONS, Nazi crimes against those who came under German control before and during World War II are among the best documented and most frequently treated subjects in historical works, fiction, and film. By contrast, public knowledge and discussion of Nazi crimes against non-Jewish German people remain at best uneven seventy years after the Third Reich collapsed. This book constitutes, in part, an attempt to address and redress this imbalance; but above all it is the story, the true and tragic story, of one remarkable individual—Oskar Kusch.

On May 12, 1944, Lieutenant Oskar Kusch, formerly skipper of the German submarine *U-154* on two patrols to South American waters, was executed for repeatedly having made remarks critical of the Nazi regime. In the opinion of the court-martial, Kusch's words and actions had undercut his crew's will and readiness to fight. The judges did dismiss an additional charge of cowardice in the face of the enemy that one of Kusch's subordinate officers had brought against his captain, while a navy expert testified that Kusch had acted at all times responsibly and in line with his military duties.

U-154's first patrol under Kusch in the spring of 1943 had been a successful one. He managed to sink one enemy ship and damage two others off Brazil. On his second patrol to the same waters later that summer and fall, increasingly sophisticated Allied countermeasures prevented Kusch from harming the enemy and inflicted serious damage to his boat. He did, however, bring his crew home safely at a time when German U-boat losses at sea were reaching catastrophic levels.

The denunciation of Kusch by fellow officers struck him like a bolt out of the blue. His has remained the only charge of "subverting the will and readiness to fight" ever directed against a prominent representative of the German U-boat service. After the verdict, Kusch's defense counsel repeatedly entreated his client to request clemency. Kusch always refused. While Grand Admiral Karl Dönitz, legendary founder and guiding spirit of the U-boat arm, would later state that, in this case, the navy needed "to put its foot down and set an example," Kusch's superiors, including Dönitz at the time, promised half-heartedly to do everything they could to save his life. In the end they did nothing. When put to the test, the acclaimed sense of camaraderie that supposedly pervaded the U-boat service turned out to be a hollow illusion. Neither his flotilla commander, nor the officer in charge of U-boat forces in France where Kusch was based, nor Grand Admiral Dönitz himself, felt compelled to visit Kusch in his prison cell, to talk or correspond with him, or otherwise to make his agony more bearable even while the march of injustice was pressing on without mercy.

By contrast, Kusch's true friends visited him in his cell in Kiel, wrote letters of encouragement, and kept in touch with his family and his fiancée. One of them even managed to put pressure on the judge in the case, only to be told vaguely that the whole matter was still under review and that mitigating circumstances were likely to come into play. Such statements—not unlike others made elsewhere in the naval hierarchy—show how, in the final analysis, no one wanted to be drawn into the case. Thus the real motives behind the indifference to Kusch's plight remained concealed.

Except for Kusch's mother and his fiancée, few of his friends were allowed to see him during his 106 days on death row. A navy staff judge determined who could and could not have access to Kusch, and under what conditions. This man also censored and often confiscated incoming and outgoing letters. On one occasion, he warned Kusch's prospective brother-in-law, an army officer, that no more letters sympathetic to a convicted criminal would be tolerated and would be duly reported to his superiors for punitive action. This is an example of how narrow-minded chicanery and other unwarranted intrusions made a mockery of an individual's basic human dignity in those days. Toward the end, even the already restricted visiting rights were curtailed. Only Kusch's mother was allowed to see her only child.

After the war, in 1949 and 1950, Kusch's judges were put on trial for crimes against humanity. However, West German courts deliberately downplayed the political character of Kusch's actions and the ideological reasons behind his conviction. Instead, they emphasized Kusch's supposedly grave military transgressions. This legal maneuver allowed those responsible for Kusch's death sentence to go free. Only in the 1990s, fifty years after his execution, did German authorities finally declare Kusch innocent and his sentence null and void.

While on a visit to his native Berlin months before his arrest, Kusch had a talk with his father who tried in vain to persuade his son to desert and seek refuge in neutral Switzerland. Kusch made it clear that he could not justify an act of desertion before the German people or before the brave men on his boat for whom he was responsible. He was, after all, a professional naval officer. For Kusch, service at sea with all its challenges was in a way an extension of the romantic perspective on life he had first encountered and absorbed as a follower of the *bündisch* youth movement while growing up in the 1920s and 1930s. Moreover, the patriotic yet liberal persuasion he had inherited from his parents continued to guide him after Hitler's totalitarian regime began to clip his options and when his conscience revealed itself in conversations with fellow officers.

The enlisted men under his command had come to appreciate Kusch's open and responsible way of exercising authority. They had no quarrel with him and indeed called their boat "U-Sunshine"—a telling compliment for their skipper who knew how to lead his men to success without endangering or terrorizing their lives unnecessarily.

During his apprenticeship in the U-boat service, Kusch had gained valuable experience as a watch officer under top-notch skippers. He knew what it meant to be ready for combat at a moment's notice. He had stood watch on the bridge when angry seas swept over him and drenched him in all their fury. He had been in the engine room when the noise reached almost unbearable levels and temperatures climbed above 130 degrees

Fahrenheit while diesel fumes seared his lungs and eyes. He knew how to get the most out of his men when it really counted, ready to take risks, yet, like a good gambler, alert to the need to calculate chances of both success and disaster realistically.

It is not easy to tread that line. Veering to one side means missing golden opportunities. No commanding officer likes to encounter or can ignore the questioning glances of his men who, after all, do want to soar home on wings of glory. Veering too far to the other side can mean a plunge into the abyss—and only the captain is to blame for such ultimate blunders. On no other type of vessel—such as cruisers, destroyers, or PT-boats—does a commanding officer exercise such undivided control and responsibility as on a submarine. Once the boat is submerged, he alone operates the periscope, relaying his instructions to the crew by way of his watch officer and the chief engineer in the central control room. No one counsels him in the moment of decision. This absolute dependence on a single person—their captain—creates the basis for the mutual trust that binds men aboard a submarine together, much like Horatio Nelson's proverbial "band of brothers."

Once again, as the defendant in his court-martial and especially after his conviction, Oskar Kusch faced a hostile world all by himself as he had done so often out in the Atlantic. No one was there to guide him in his decisions. A terrifying finality hovered over his situation as death cast its shadow over every day and every hour he languished in his cell. Kusch's thoughts inevitably returned to the vastness of the sea that he had learned to love, but also to fear as the threat of air attacks and depth charge pursuits could bring the end at any moment. The very isolation and solitude of his prison cell reinforced his yearning to be out there on his boat. Kusch somehow felt his men beside him as they gave him strength to meet his fate. This faith in having done the right thing carried him through all possible doubts into the twilight of his existence. Pausing briefly in awe over the vast chasm opening up below him, he continued on until the end of the night—*usque ad finem.*

—Erich Topp

Rear Admiral Erich Topp, a leading German World War II U-boat ace, died on December 26, 2005, some time after writing this foreword but before this work could be completed for publication.

PREFACE

I FIRST ENCOUNTERED bits and pieces of Lieutenant Oskar Kusch's fascinating story and heartbreaking fate in the early 1980s, when I interviewed a number of former U-boat captains and engineers for my book, *Naval Officers under Hitler*. One of them had befriended Kusch on a long patrol in the Atlantic when Kusch was a watch officer on *U-103* before advancing in 1943 to command a boat of his own, *U-154*. Another interviewee had sat in the audience at the January 1944 court-martial in Kiel that sentenced Kusch to death for "subverting the fighting spirit" of his boat. Almost four decades after the event, this individual remained profoundly shaken by his experience as a spectator at the trial. A third, the acclaimed U-boat ace and future rear admiral in the West German navy, Erich Topp, spearheaded efforts well into the 1990s to rehabilitate Kusch in the eyes of the law and to secure a place of honor and remembrance for him in German and international naval history.

Historiographical efforts in Germany to ascertain and assess what had really happened in the case of Oskar Kusch gathered momentum in the late 1980s and early 1990s through his inclusion in a 1987 autobiographical novel by a naval academy classmate, Baron Horst von Luttitz, writing under the pseudonym Walter Klenck; and most importantly, interest in Kusch's case received a boost thanks to the historian Heinrich Walle, whose carefully researched though occasionally controversial 510-page "documentation" (1995) on Kusch remains the standard treatment in German. Since 2005, there is also in circulation a work of semi-fiction by a certain Peter C. Hansen titled *Execution for Duty*, whose literary genre and factual basis remain elusive and suspect, just as its author's claims to have known Oskar Kusch personally and to have served with him in the Second U-Boat Flotilla out of Lorient in France have been proven to be patently implausible.

Most research for this first book-length historical study on Kusch for an English-language readership was completed between 2000 and 2005. An early synopsis of my findings appeared in the inaugural issue of the *International Journal of Naval History* in April 2002. Before his death in 2005, Rear Admiral (ret.) Erich Topp, whose memoirs I had translated into English, graciously contributed the foreword to this work, which remains unchanged from its original version. Then, regrettably, developments too complicated to relate here arrested progress on the manuscript for a dozen years. Not until the summer and fall of 2017 was I able to complete it without further disruptions.

In a central departure from Heinrich Walle's approach to the Kusch tragedy, I determined from the outset to limit my chronological focus to the lifespan of its protagonist, which ended at 0632 on May 12, 1944, on a military range adjacent to the Kiel Canal in northern Germany. Here, a firing squad carried out the sentence against Kusch assessed 106 days earlier and after clemency had been denied on all levels of the naval hierarchy. No one could bring Oskar Kusch back to life after that bright spring morning or undo what can only be characterized as a judicial murder. In 1949 and 1950, two trials were convened in Kiel against Karl-Heinrich Hagemann, the naval judge primarily responsible for the verdict, for having committed a crime against humanity. Testimony from those trials and other postwar evidence have been incorporated into the present study only to the extent that they help illuminate and clarify events and developments before Kusch's death. The next-to-last chapter, "Wakes," summarizes what happened eventually to all major dramatis personae.

Archival and other publicly available records on Kusch and many others involved in his case remain as complete and accessible as any historian could wish. Kusch's personnel file rests with the Wehrmacht Central Notification Office (WASt, or *Deutsche Dienststelle*) in Berlin. His complete court-martial records, before 2005 on deposit with the Central Depository for Court Martial Files (BA-ZNS) and housed inside a quaint medieval abbey in Kornelimünster near Aachen, have by now become a part of the Federal German Military Archives in Freiburg (BA-MA). Likewise on deposit at Freiburg are *U-103*'s and *U-154*'s complete war diaries along with documents detailing the naval career of Kusch's primary antagonist, Lieutenant Dr. Ulrich Abel, and pertinent *Kriegsmarine* records in general. Among personal papers kept at Freiburg, those of naval justice official Karl Helmut Sieber are particularly insightful in connection with the postwar Hagemann trials, as are, in turn, the official legal records of those trials on deposit in the Schleswig-Holstein state archives. Many letters to and from Kusch's parents, friends, and former shipmates have become a part of those court files, as have the testimony and recollections of classmates at the German naval academy and those of Kusch's civilian defense attorney, Gerhard Meyer-Grieben. Moreover, the U-Boat Archives at Cuxhaven-Altenbruch contain a large folder on *U-154*, an extensive photograph collection, and copies of Kusch's artwork, along with assorted memorabilia connected to the boat and its men. The authoritative website uboat.net can be consulted for historical and technical information on every German submarine and their patrols in both world wars.

To fathom and illuminate the human dimension of the Kusch tragedy, this study has also drawn on sources and records never consulted before. Claudia van Eyck, daughter of Oskar Kusch's fiancée, Inge von Foris, has graciously shared excerpts of her mother's personal correspondence from the war years and provided many additional insights into her mother's relationship with the man who could never become her husband. Dagmar Seemel of Humboldt University in Berlin made available von Foris's student file, including records pertaining to her upbringing and doctoral dissertation. Before her death in 2012, Herta Abel, wife and then for sixty-eight years widow of Lieutenant Dr. Ulrich Abel, answered patiently and in great detail the author's many questions about her husband, his civilian and military careers, and their family life together. Erhard Ohlhoff in Kiel, Dr. Wolfgang Beck in Berlin, and my late brother, Hans-Jürgen Rust of St. Peter-Ording, have supplied photographs of places pertinent to Kusch's life and legacy. I thank them all.

From personal experience and travels before, during, and since my own service in the (West) German navy, I am familiar with all European locations that figured in Kusch's life—from the German naval academy in Flensburg-Mürwik to the Breton coast of France, and from the cities of Kiel, Hamburg, and Berlin in northern Germany to the ski resort of Zürs in the Austrian Alps. The same holds true for the waters of the Baltic, the North Sea, and the eastern Atlantic. By a strange coincidence, when I took up my university studies at Kiel in 1971, I often chose to skip a dull lecture on a brilliant spring or summer day, gather my books and my lunch into my backpack, and bike the short distance to the Kiel Canal to watch the busy ship traffic passing there between the North Sea and the Baltic—all the while entirely unaware that only a few hundred meters away, beyond the northern bank of the canal, Oskar Kusch and so many other enemies and victims of the Nazi regime had been executed on a military range.

Inasmuch as my father, Horst Rust (1918–99), was three weeks younger than Kusch but had entered the *Kriegsmarine*'s officer corps a year earlier than Kusch as a member of Crew 36 rather than Kusch's Crew 37a, my three brothers and I grew up with reminiscences, stories, memorabilia, and occasionally visitors who connected us to a world very similar to the one Oskar Kusch must have encountered before and after his induction into the German navy. Moreover, my mother, whom my father met, courted, and married after the war following his release from long years in Canadian captivity, was the widow of *Kapitänleutnant* Hans-Jürgen Oldörp of Crew 35, who had gone down with all his men as commanding officer of *U-90* in a convoy battle off Newfoundland in July 1942. Oldörp's copy of the official *Marinewörterbuch Fünfsprachig* (Naval Dictionary, Five Languages) of 1940, which ended up in my possession, has proved a valuable companion in writing this study, notwithstanding the small eagle and swastika on its navy-blue cover.

Unless indicated otherwise, all translations in this book from German, French, Dutch, Spanish, and Latin into English are mine. German military ranks, where rendered into English, reflect equivalency to those of the U.S. Navy at the time. Instead of boring and confusing readers with the long and complicated titles of officials in the German naval legal system, I have uniformly called them naval justice officials while denoting their specific functions and indicating who ranked higher or lower in the bureaucracy.

Many institutions and individuals have contributed to this book over the years. Baylor University granted me two research leaves in 2000 and 2017, in addition to travel assistance to European archives. My colleague Dr. David Hendon and Claudia van Eyck critically read the manuscript and enriched it in terms of presentation, substance, and argument. It was a delight working with Paul Merzlak, editorial director at the Naval Institute Press, and his staff. Besides those already named, I am listing in alphabetical order others who were of assistance in a variety of ways: Brigitte Badelt, Stuttgart; Hendrik Beer, Berlin; Jana Brabant, Freiburg; Horst Bredow, Cuxhaven; Hans-Georg Dillgard, Kornelimünster; Helmut Döringhoff, Freiburg; Peter Fiedler, Berlin; Petra Grasse, Berlin; Dr. Michael L. Hadley, Victoria, Canada; Jörg Hagemann, Kiel; Jörg Hantelmann, Kiel; Gudmundur Helgason, Reykjavik, Iceland; Ulli Jochum, Lech, Austria; Emily Leavitt, Waco, Texas; Jak Mallmann-Showell, United Kingdom; Ronald Meentz, Kornelimünster; Clemens Meyer-Grieben, Kiel; Dr. Anke Mührenberg, Schwarzenbek; Dr. Timothy P. Mulligan, Washington, D.C.; Thies Oldörp, Flensburg; Dr. Dörte Pantenius, Heringsdorf; Dr. Jürgen Rohweder, Kiel; Rev. Thomas C. A. Rust, Glücksburg; Dr. Herbert Sauerwein, Lech, Austria; Joachim Scherneck-Czech, Mürwik; Heidi Schomann, Kiel; Elisabeth Schweizer, Lech, Austria; Dagmar Seemel, Berlin; Gerd Stolz, Kiel; Dr. Manfred Wegener, Berlin; Florian Weghorn, Berlin; and Frank Wunder, Kiel.

Lastly, I thank my wife, Karen, for her patience, assistance, and loving encouragement as she saw another of her husband's ideas mature from a vague project into a completed work.

—Eric C. Rust
July 2018

ABBREVIATIONS

I.W.O.	First Watch Officer (second-in-command): Erster Wachoffizier
II.W.O.	Second Watch Officer (third-in-command): Zweiter Wachoffizier
III.W.O.	Third Watch Officer (chief petty officer, also navigator): Dritter Wachoffizier
BA-MA	*Bundesarchiv-Militärachiv*: Federal German Military Archives in Freiburg
BA-ZNS	*Bundesarchiv-Zentralnachweisstelle in Aachen-Kornelimünster*: Central Depository for Court Martial Files, moved to Freiburg in 2005
BDM	*Bund Deutscher Mädel*: female equivalent of the Hitler Youth
BT	designation of convoys running between Bahia (Brazil) and Trinidad
cm	centimeter
C.O.	Commanding Officer
FdU West	Leader of U-Boats in the West, based at Angers, France
GMSA	postwar German Minesweeping Administration under British supervision
H.K.U.	Higher Command of U-Boat Training in Kiel; arranged Kusch trial
KSSVO	*Kriegssonderstrafrechtsverordnung*: Wartime Special Penal Code, decree specifying "subversion" crimes

L.I.	*Leitender Ingenieur*: chief engineer
Metox	German passive radar-wave receiver
MOV	German Naval Officers Association
MSM	*Marineschule Mürwik*: Germany's naval academy on Flensburg Bay
M.U.G.	*Marineuntersuchungsgefängnis*: Naval Detention Center
NARA	National Archives and Records Administration, Washington, D.C.
Naxos	German passive radar-wave receiver, later model
NKFD	*Nationalkommittee Freies Deutschland*: National Committee for a Free Germany
nm	nautical mile (1 nm = 1,852 meters)
NSFO	*Nationalsozialistischer Führungsoffizier*: National Socialist Guidance Officer
OKM	*Oberkommando der Marine*: Naval High Command
OKW	*Oberkommando der Wehrmacht*: Armed Forces Supreme Command
RAD	*Reichsarbeitsdienst*: Reich Labor Service
SA	*Sturmabteilung*: storm troopers
Sonar	Allied underwater listening and tracking device ("Asdic" in British terminology)
SPD	*Sozialdemokratische Partei Deutschlands*: Social Democratic Party of Germany
TJ	designation of convoys running between Trinidad and Rio de Janeiro
UACA	*U-Boot-Archiv*: U-Boat Archives in Cuxhaven-Altenbruch
WASt	Wehrmacht Central Notification Office, or *Deutsche Dienstelle*

DRAMATIS PERSONAE

Lieutenant Oskar Kusch, *U-154*'s commanding officer

Lieutenant (res.) Dr. Ulrich Abel, *U-154*'s First Watch Officer (I.W.O.), then C.O. *U-193*

Lieutenant Kurt Druschel, *U-154*'s chief engineer (L.I.)

Ensign Heinrich Meyer, *U-154*'s Second Watch Officer (II.W.O.), first patrol

Lieutenant (res.) Arno Funke, *U-154*'s Second Watch Officer (II.W.O), second patrol

Chief Petty Officer Heinrich Lüdmann, *U-154*'s navigator (III.W.O.), first patrol

Midshipman Horst Fröhlich, embarked as supernumerary on *U-154*, first patrol

Midshipman Hellmuth Kirchammer, embarked as supernumerary on *U-154*, first patrol

Army Staff Surgeon (res.) Dr. Hans Nothdurft, embarked on *U-154*, second patrol

Hans Janker, *U-154*'s chief radio operator, first patrol

Kurt Isensee, *U-154*'s chief radio operator, second patrol

Lieutenant Commander Werner Winter, Kusch's commanding officer on *U-103*

Lieutenant Gustav-Adolf Janssen, succeeded Winter as skipper of *U-103*

Lieutenant Siegfried Kietz, Kusch's classmate and commanding officer of *U-126*

Lieutenant Gerth Gemeiner, succeeded Kusch as *U-154*'s commanding officer

Commander Ernst Kals, in charge of Second U-Boat Flotilla in Lorient, France

Captain Hans-Rudolf Rösing, commanded all U-boats in France

Grand Admiral Karl Dönitz, Chief of U-Boat Command, later of Naval High Command

Admiral Hans-Georg von Friedeburg, Dönitz's successor at U-Boat Command

Rear Admiral Eberhard Godt, Chief of U-Boat Operations under Dönitz and Friedeburg

General Admiral Walter Warzecha, head of legal department at Naval High Command

Dr. Joachim Rudolphi, top legal official at Naval High Command

Naval justice official Karl-Heinrich Hagemann, presiding judge at Kusch's trial

Naval justice official Dr. Hans-Egon Breinig, investigator and prosecutor at Kusch's trial

Naval justice official Ernst Meinert, in charge of Kusch's incarceration and execution

Lieutenant Commander Wolfgang Dittmers, military juror at Kusch's trial

Lieutenant Otto Westphalen, military juror at Kusch's trial

Oskarheinz Kusch, Oskar's father, a disabled WWI veteran and insurance executive

ERNA KUSCH, Oskar Kusch's mother; after 1938 divorce married a Dr. Brockmann

INGE VON FORIS, Oskar Kusch's fiancée and student of art history in Berlin

ARMY LIEUTENANT HENNING VON FORIS, Inge's brother

ALMUTH KLUSEMANN VON FORIS, née Wilderink, Inge's mother

LIEUTENANT COMMANDER WALTER KLUSEMANN, Inge's stepfather

DR. RUDI PALLAS, leader of Kusch's youth group *Südlegion* in Berlin

LUFTWAFFE LIEUTENANT DIETER BERGER, Kusch's best friend, lost arm in Russia

KURT WIEMER, Organisation Todt official, Kusch's friend in France

GERHARD MEYER-GRIEBEN, Oskar Kusch's civilian defense counsel

BARON HORST VON LUTTITZ, Kusch's navy comrade and family friend

HERTA ABEL, Lieutenant Abel's wife and widow

CHAPTER 1

LORIENT

STRETCHING IN A GENEROUS arc from the western tip of Brittany to the littoral of ancient Aquitaine, Germany's submarine bases in World War II along the Atlantic's Bay of Biscay found themselves embedded in a country representing the finest French nature and culture had to offer. Its very names suggested romance and mystique, promising delightful adventures and endless summers by the sea: Brest, Lorient, Saint Nazaire, La Rochelle, La Pallice, Bordeaux. These ports had fallen to the Germans easily enough in the spring of 1940 when things had gone so terribly wrong for the Allies, when Hitler's armored columns and superior air force had wiped out France as a military power on the European continent in less than six short weeks and chased the British expeditionary forces back across the English Channel in humiliating flight.

Gaining the Atlantic bases, typically with their installations intact or quickly refitted to meet German needs, constituted arguably the most valuable windfall of the entire campaign against France. Along with the takeover of Denmark and Norway earlier that year, and the quick acquisition of the Low Countries synchronized with the attack on France, their capture meant nothing less than a quantum leap in strategic opportunities for Germany's submarines and to a lesser extent for its capital ships and aircraft. Before the summer of 1940, U-boats operating against the Allies had to traverse the shallow North Sea from their bases at Kiel or Wilhelmshaven and round the tip of Scotland before they could begin to prowl the waters west of the British Isles where most of the action was then taking place—a tiresome and dangerous detour of some five hundred nautical miles each way. This arrangement brought exposure to enemy countermeasures while the boats were in transit and reduced their presence in their areas of operation considerably. However, once Germany's U-boat flotillas had transferred to their new bases on the Bay of Biscay with their increasingly sophisticated repair and maintenance yards as well as their impregnable bombproof shelters, they could begin to challenge enemy shipping within days, sometimes within hours, of leaving port. No wonder that U-boat crews would fondly remember these first "Happy Times" from the middle of 1940 to the summer of 1941, when successes reached unprecedented levels while their own losses remained astonishingly light.

Among the units making the move from Germany to France was the Second U-Boat Flotilla, originally stationed at Wilhelmshaven on the North Sea and named the "*Saltzwedel*" Flotilla after a World War I ace who had undertaken no fewer than twenty-two combat missions and sunk a total of 111 ships before going down with his last boat, *UB-81*, when it struck a mine in the English Channel in December 1917.[1] The flotilla's new homeport would be Lorient in southwestern Brittany to the north and west of the ancient city of Vannes, not far from the mysterious "menhirs" (prehistoric stone monuments) of Carnac and the majestic Quiberon Peninsula, right where the rivers Blavet and Scorff merge to meet the Atlantic Ocean, an area that still strikes visitors as one of the most breathtakingly beautiful regions in Europe, if not the world.

Founded in 1664 under a charter from the "Sun King" Louis XIV in the mercantilist era, the city's unusual name derives from the circumstance that it once housed the headquarters of the French East India Company. But as France's fortunes in India and elsewhere in the East declined after the Seven Years' War (1756–63), so did the fame and prosperity of Lorient, reducing it to a sleepy backwater hugging the edge of the European continent. By the nineteenth century, commercial activity had revived somewhat around an expanding fishing industry and with the establishment of a small naval arsenal. Still, for yet another century little would change for this picturesque place along the rugged, tide-swept

Breton coast with its countless offshore islets, rocky cliffs and promontories, treacherous inlets, and sandy beaches that separate the open sea from the lush countryside of western France.[2]

When German army units occupied Lorient on June 21, 1940, advance navy teams were not far behind to assess the port's potential for accommodating as soon as possible a lair for Germany's gray wolves of the sea. What they found was highly encouraging: most facilities remained undamaged and in working order along the sprawling waterfront north of the suburbs of Kernevel and Port Louis in the inner harbor, with the sophisticated slipway and drydock for oceangoing fishing craft proving especially valuable. While the difference between high and low tide averages some ten feet at Lorient and can, with its reversing currents, make passage of the winding estuary a challenge, all navigational buoys and markers remained in place so that vessels could reach deep and open water with little delay. Even more promising, the protected Kéroman Peninsula at the southern tip of the city seemed well suited for a major U-boat base with state-of-the-art amenities and, above all, huge reinforced concrete pens, since Lorient lay within easy flying distance of British airfields and practically invited Allied bombardment of any German installations there.

While an improvised U-boat resupply facility began operating at Lorient as early as July 7, 1940, with *U-30* and *U-37* among the first boats to benefit from its services, just three months later a combined force of six hundred and fifty German and twenty-five hundred French dockyard personnel could repair and refit up to ten submarines simultaneously.[3] Before long, as in other ports along the Bay of Biscay such as Brest and Saint Nazaire, Germany's semiofficial general contractor "*Organisation Todt*" (O.T.) went to work on one of humankind's most colossal and complex building projects—creating bombproof U-boat bunkers on France's west coast, with nineteen fully serviceable and perfectly safe "wet" and "dry" berths for simultaneous use in Lorient alone, neatly arranged in three separate structures named K1, K2, and K3, respectively, for their location on the Kéroman Peninsula. From early 1941 well into 1944, some fifteen thousand workers conscripted from countries as distant as the Netherlands, Portugal, and Morocco, but also drawn from the local French population eager for employment in an otherwise depressed economy, labored around the clock, pouring concrete, stringing electrical wires, installing fuel and water lines, and designing workshops, ammunition depots, and torpedo-storage areas, in addition to setting up the huge array of machinery and equipment needed to overhaul tired U-boats after their missions. The reinforced concrete roofs of the pens, up to twenty-five feet thick, could withstand even the deadliest multiton bombs the Allies had at their disposal. In fact, they have withstood the teeth of time to this very day, servicing among other functions France's postwar nuclear submarine fleet. As one recent visitor mused, "six decades later, the enormous, monolithic structures still hulk over the town centers from which they were gouged—horrifying in their intent, incredible in their accomplishment, and still among the greatest construction feats of all time."[4]

In the meantime, the boats' weary crews recovered from their missions and prepared for their next one either with their families and friends back in Germany or, if service duties granted too little time for the train trip home, at nearby seaside resort areas lovingly dubbed "U-boat pastures." With typical German thoroughness, even the bordellos in Lorient's Rue de Sully were tightly regulated, distinguishing neatly between Wehrmacht and O.T. visitors and closing at 10:30 p.m. sharp. In addition, every female service provider was required to hand her customers printed cards bearing her name as well as the date and hour of the transaction. Soldiers and sailors had to keep these cards for at least a month in case the base's health staff needed to trace the source of medical complications resulting from such encounters.[5]

Given the very real menace the U-boats posed to Allied shipping, it remains somewhat implausible that the British and later the Americans as well failed to mount a heartier effort than they did to prevent or hinder construction of the bunkers, even in the face of concentrated German antiaircraft artillery and *Luftwaffe* fighter units stationed in the region. For, once completed, the shelters would be virtually unassailable bastions. Indeed, the U-boats' primary moments of exposure to mines or airborne attack came while they were approaching and moving up the estuaries to the ports, and during the hour or so it took at Lorient to lift them out of the water and into their berths by means of a sophisticated cradle mechanism. The same vulnerability existed of course when the boats put out to sea—a good reason why they usually left in groups of two or three with surface escorts and air cover before carefully dispersing once they had gained the open ocean and waters deep enough to dive. Over the course of the war, the Germans would record some three hundred air raids against the Lorient installations, yet not a single U-boat came to grief because of the raids, while the yard personnel serviced inbound boats and restored them to frontline readiness on no fewer than 492 occasions, more than at any other Atlantic base.[6] Meanwhile, Allied bombs reduced the once lovely city center and adjacent suburbs to dust and rubble. While the U-boat pens remained fully operational and additional bunkers protected the labor force in the yards from most harm, Allied bombs had destroyed fully 80 percent of the dwellings in Lorient by early 1943, whereupon both the French and the German authorities agreed to evacuate the rest of the population not employed at the base.[7] One may well wonder whether the hapless French civilians who called ports like Lorient their home grew to blame the Allies or the Germans more for their misfortune—provided they did not hold their own leaders accountable after the inglorious calamity of 1940 when France fell to German military might.

While individual German submarines entered the captured French ports as early as the summer of 1940 for improvised repairs, overhauls, and other services, the permanent transfer of entire squadrons and their staffs to France was not concluded until well into 1941 and 1942 as more and more bomb-proof bunkers became available. The first boat of the Second Flotilla to benefit from the protective cover of the pens at Lorient was *U-123* on August 25, 1941. Besides the Second, eventually another squadron, the Tenth, would be established at Lorient by early 1942. Typically, a newly commissioned boat would perform its shakedown and training exercises in the Baltic Sea before being sent out on its first combat patrol from Kiel, Wilhelmshaven, or Norway. At the end of the mission, assuming it had not been sunk, the boat would enter its designated French base and join its regular squadron mates there, usually never to ply home waters again.

The composition of the squadrons at any given instant was one of extreme fluidity. As boats were lost at sea, others would arrive to take their place. Only a third of the boats attached to a particular flotilla tended to be in port at any given moment while the remainder would be in transit to or from their assigned operational areas or actually engaging the enemy. Occasionally an older and exhausted boat, perhaps no longer fully seaworthy after extended and meritorious duty at the front, would be relocated to the Baltic to join the training commands there or would be decommissioned and cannibalized for parts. For example, while ninety-one different boats belonged to the Second U-Boat Flotilla at one time or another over the span of the war, it is doubtful if ever more than a dozen of them were in port together at the same moment under the watchful eye of their overall commander, Admiral Karl Dönitz, who temporarily transferred his headquarters to a chateau in the Lorient suburb of Kernevel from November 1940 to March 1942 before relocating to Paris and eventually back to Berlin because of the increased Allied air threat.[8]

The Second Flotilla amassed an outstanding record during World War II, particularly in the first three-and-a-half years of the conflict. In fact, Lorient became informally known as the "home of the aces" inasmuch as no fewer than seven of the top ten most successful German submarines of the war sported the stylized runic emblem of the squadron on their conning towers. Those seven boats alone sank a total of 298 enemy vessels between them, an almost unbelievable average of 42 ships per submarine, for a combined toll of 1.5 million tons of enemy shipping. They also damaged 22 additional vessels displacing some 150,000 tons.[9] Little wonder, there would be many ceremonies in Lorient after which proud skippers and crews could show off brand-new Iron and Knight's Crosses for everyone to admire.

Did all of this imply that the personnel of the Second U-Boat Flotilla possessed professional know-how, courage, a fighting spirit, and perhaps even luck to a degree that was missing or retarded in other units operating from French homeports? Hardly so. What distinguished the Second, and its sister squadron the Tenth, or for that matter the Twelfth Flotilla down the coast at Bordeaux, from other German squadrons? The difference had much less to do with the training of its officers and crews, or the leadership provided by their flotilla commanders, or the particular circumstances of their bases, than with the kinds of boats that made up the squadrons and the operational zones and tasks assigned to them.

Beginning in the 1930s, Germany designed, built, and commissioned in huge numbers essentially three different types of submarines, besides specialty boats for purposes of mine-laying and mid-ocean refueling and resupply, not to mention the revolutionary but never truly deployed "Electro-boats" of the Type XXI and XXIII designs late in the war. The smallest class of these mass-produced boats, designated Type II, consisted of forty-eight coastal boats with limited range, endurance, and weaponry. They participated in operations around the British Isles, in the Baltic Sea and, after transfer by way of the Danube, also in the Black Sea. Few were built after 1940, and most ended up in various training commands as the war grew old.

By far, the most numerous class of submarines Germany built and deployed in World War II, some 612 boats altogether, belonged to the Type VII design in its several variations, with its sleek lines and salient characteristics made famous in Wolfgang Petersen's motion picture *Das Boot* based on Lothar-Günther Buchheim's novel of the same title. Sometimes called "Atlantic boats" of about 850 tons displacement when submerged, these boats featured up to fourteen torpedoes along with ship-ship and antiaircraft artillery, a range of sixty-five hundred to ninety-five hundred nautical miles, a top surface speed of seventeen knots, and a crew of some forty-four officers and men.[10] They were the U-Boat Command's true workhorses: dependable, resilient, maneuverable, quick divers, and overall well suited for independent or wolfpack warfare west and north of the British Isles, along the great-circle convoy routes from the New World to the Old, in the Arctic Ocean, and in the Mediterranean. Refueled and reprovisioned at sea, or economically handled, they could and did even operate against shipping along the Eastern

Seaboard of the United States and Canada. Men such as Günther Prien, Otto Kretschmer, Jochen Schepke, and Erich Topp, besides dozens of other aces, grew to master this weapon to perfection. Their principal forward bases were Brest (First and Ninth Flotilla), La Pallice/La Rochelle (Third), and Saint Nazaire (Sixth and Seventh), all in France; Bergen (Eleventh), Trondheim (Thirteenth), and Narvik (Fourteenth), all in Norway; as well as Salamis (Twenty-Third) and La Spezia and Toulon (Twenty-Ninth) in the Mediterranean.

This leaves submarines of the Type IX class, the third group of mass-produced German boats and the ones exclusively allocated to the Second, Tenth, and Twelfth Flotillas in Lorient and Bordeaux. These vessels were conceived and designed from the outset for independent long-distance operations that called for endurance rather than the kind of agility and close teamwork so crucial in convoy battles. Considerably bigger and bulkier than their Type VII counterparts, they were the ones that would decimate American shipping along the Eastern Seaboard and in the Caribbean in 1942, threaten Allied ship traffic in the Central and South Atlantic throughout the war, and a handful of them even operated with remarkable success alongside Japanese submarines in the Indian and Pacific Oceans. Little surprise, then, that these boats often headed the statistics of enemy tonnage destroyed as they would encounter juicier targets and scantier enemy opposition in their theaters of operation compared with the fierce convoy struggles in the waters north and west of the British Isles or the altogether disappointing performance of Germany's sixty-four Type VII boats dispatched to the Mediterranean after the fall of 1941.

Depending on individual features in their four different design variations labeled IX-A through IX-D, Type IX boats were some 235 feet long, 20 feet wide, drew a little over 14 feet of water, and displaced between twelve hundred and eighteen hundred tons when submerged. They carried up to twenty-five torpedoes that could be launched from six separate tubes, four forward and two aft. A 10.5-centimeter (cm) gun just forward of the conning tower on the main deck could take on surface targets, while a 3.7-cm gun and up to four 2-cm automatic weapons arrayed on platforms on and behind the conning tower provided moderate protection against aircraft. Two 4,400-horsepower diesels allowed for up to nineteen knots on the surface while battery-powered electric motors could move the boat at speeds of up to eight knots when submerged. An extended range of some 10,000 nautical miles (up to 23,700 miles for Type IX-D boats operating in the Indian Ocean and the Far East) at an economical speed of ten to twelve knots allowed Type IX boats to roam the oceans for months at a time—a range that could be extended even farther by mid-ocean refueling and reprovisioning from German surface vessels early in the war, from specially designed U-boat tankers (Type XIV boats), or from captured Allied merchantmen.

While four officers and forty-four enlisted men made up the standard crew strength, typically additional personnel embarked on these extended missions, such as a medical officer, midshipmen-in-training, war correspondents, and so-called "confirmands"—officers slated to command a boat of their own but in need of acquiring additional hands-on experience. The boat's captain typically held the rank of Lieutenant Commander (*Korvettenkapitän*), Lieutenant (*Kapitänleutnant*) or Lieutenant (jg) (*Oberleutnant*),[11] with more junior officers functioning as the First Watch Officer (I.W.O.), Second Watch Officer (II.W.O.), and Chief Engineer (L.I.). During routine operations the watch personnel and lookouts on the bridge might also be entrusted to the most senior and therefore most experienced and respected petty officer of the nautical branch on board, invariably designated as the navigator and functioning as a Third Watch Officer. In German practice during World War II, an officer who had trained on a particular boat design, usually Type VII or Type IX, would remain assigned to that kind of boat throughout his career, with a few Type VII captains "upgrading" to become Type IX or Type XXI skippers late in the conflict.

The naming and numbering system of the *Kriegsmarine*'s U-boat program defies easy classification and remains baffling for anyone but experts in the field, for the numbers were allocated on the basis of the shipyards that constructed the boats in various subseries rather than in any chronological fashion or strictly according to design type. They also included boats that were ordered but never built, completed, delivered, or commissioned. For example, the Type IX boats Oskar Kusch served on carried the following numbers (builder in parentheses): U-37–44, 64–8, 103–11, 122–31, 153–60, 171–200, 841–81, 889 (AG Weser, Bremen); U-161–70, 801–6 (Deschimag, Bremen); and U-501–50 (Deutsche Werft AG, Hamburg). Any numbers before, between, or after these belonged to other designs, mostly Types II, VII, XXI, and XXIII, with boats coming from a total of nineteen different yards.[12]

Among the earliest boats attached to the Second U-Boat Flotilla first in Wilhelmshaven and then in Lorient was *U-103*. Placed on order by the *Kriegsmarine* in May 1938, construction began on September 6, 1939, at the AG Weser works at Bremen that specialized in larger boats. By the spring of 1940, just as France was being overrun by Hitler's armored and mechanized divisions, the core of *U-103*'s future crew found its way to Bremen to acquaint themselves with their new command while proud yard personnel put the finishing touches on the sleek, brand-new vessel. On July 5, 1940, the boat's first skipper, Lieutenant Commander Viktor Schütze, presided over the solemn commissioning ceremony and then took *U-103* through the Kiel Canal into the Baltic where he supervised the mandatory diving drills and tactical exercises that would transform a raw crew and an untested boat into an efficient fighting machine ready to engage the enemy.

Schütze, who had entered the navy in 1925 and been recruited by the head of the U-boat Command Karl Dönitz soon after the rebirth of the submarine service in 1935, had by this time become a virtual legend in the U-boat force on account of his leadership qualities and his outward appearance of a burly but kind and considerate sea-bear of a man. After peacetime experience in Type II coastal boats, Schütze assumed command of *U-25* at the outset of hostilities. Conceived as a slightly smaller precursor (Type IA) to the later Type IX series, *U-25* along with its sister *U-26* would operate to the west of the British Isles, in the Bay of Biscay, and off Portugal. There, on three patrols between late 1939 and May 1940, Schütze established himself as a competent, careful, and above all successful skipper, sinking seven enemy merchantmen of more than 33,000 tons.

By September 1940 Schütze's new boat, *U-103*, had completed its training routine in the Baltic and officially became a "front boat" in the Second Flotilla. Undoubtedly the flotilla leader, Lieutenant Commander Heinz Fischer, was more than pleased to see a fresh boat under such a distinguished skipper join his command. Schütze would not disappoint him: over the next ten months, from October 1940 until July 1941, on four patrols totaling 201 days at sea, Schütze and his men would challenge and surpass many a record. During these "Happy Times" in the history of the German U-boat campaign, with France out of the war, Italy a new ally, and the United States still on the sidelines, all circumstances favored the stealthy hunters as Britain and its few friends struggled to keep the Allied war effort alive. Out in the Atlantic this meant convoys plodding along with minimal cover from surface escorts or from the air, and many vessels simply sailed all by themselves from port to port with little more than a prayer for protection. *U-103* made the most of it by dispatching no fewer than twenty-seven vessels worth 142,000 tons of shipping to the bottom of the sea—an average of one vessel for every week at sea.[13] Viktor Schütze himself—his last name, appropriately, translates as "marksman" or "hunter" into English—received first the Knight's Cross and later the Oak Leaves for his brilliant exploits, with other suitable decorations going to the members of his crew.

When *U-103* returned to Lorient from its fourth mission in July 12, 1941, Schütze may have had a notion that his days as a U-boat skipper were numbered. Seven demanding patrols since the outbreak of the war, with additional service in peacetime prior to that, must have taken their toll even on someone as tough and resilient as he. Moreover, Dönitz may well have felt, after losing his top aces Otto Kretschmer, Günther Prien, and Jochen Schepke earlier that spring, and with the Russian campaign reducing prospects for an early cessation of hostilities, that good men of Schütze's caliber should be retained safely ashore to teach and inspire the next generation of U-boat officers. In Schütze's case, a special reward awaited him as he now assumed overall command of the squadron in which he had served since becoming skipper of *U-25* back in 1939. The Second U-Boat Flotilla could hardly have found a more competent leader.

Thus Schütze settled into his new role of squadron commander in the flotilla's comfortable quarters ashore in those heady days when the Atlantic campaign seemed virtually won and Operation Barbarossa against the Soviet Union, under way since June 22, promised to extend German hegemony deep into the Eurasian continent. About this time, two officers reported for duty aboard *U-103* to replace those moving on to other assignments. One of them was *Kapitänleutnant* Werner Winter, to whom Schütze handed over command of the now famous boat on July 15, 1941.[14] Winter, a handsome twenty-nine-year-old native of Hamburg with deeply set, expressive eyes that suggested a well of inner strength and determination along with a sense of human compassion, was no newcomer to Lorient. In fact, all he had to do on that day was to move from his staff position at U-Boat Command headquarters in the suburb of Kerneval to the bustling naval base on the Kéroman Peninsula. He had seen *U-103* depart for and return from its patrols on several occasions and closely followed its exploits at sea, perhaps wishing he were out there with it rather than being tied to his important but unspectacular responsibilities on Admiral Dönitz's operational staff. A member of Crew 30 and thus five years junior to Viktor Schütze in terms of his naval career, Winter, too, was a veteran of the U-boat service since its rebirth in 1935. By 1937 he had risen to command *U-22*, a Type II boat. In the opening weeks of the war he and his crew had twice surprised and attacked Allied submarines on the surface, only to be frustrated and dismayed when their torpedoes malfunctioned due to faulty fuses and detonated short of their intended targets.[15] Still, Dönitz knew a good man when he met one, and in November 1939 put Winter on his staff to help direct the ever-growing packs of "gray wolves" sailing against the enemy. Now the time had come for Winter to demonstrate anew his mettle as a leader in a frontline capacity. Dönitz was certainly justified in assuming that Winter and his men would make and remain a winning team.

The other officer reporting for duty aboard *U-103* in that pregnant summer of 1941 was its new second watch officer, a handsome, lanky, boyish-looking *Leutnant zur See* recently turned twenty-three, who had never been to Lorient before. His name was Oskar Kusch.

CHAPTER 2

LIEUTENANT KUSCH

One can only speculate about the range of thoughts, impressions, feelings, hopes, and apprehensions that pressed in on Oskar Kusch as he wrapped up his previous assignment as a company officer with the Second U-Boat Training Division at sleepy Gotenhafen on the Baltic Sea, today's Gdynia in Poland. From there he proceeded by train, with stops in his native Berlin and the French capital, through the lush, deceptively peaceful, sun-swept countryside of western Europe to his destination in southern Brittany. Since *U-103* was still at sea when Kusch received his transfer orders effective June 25, 1941, and would have to undergo an extended overhaul once safely returned to Lorient, Kusch was able to insert a brief stayover in Berlin. There were of course his mother and his father who, to their son's profound distress, had divorced three years before, with his mother remarrying, but who still lived in the upscale southwestern city sections of Schöneberg and Steglitz, respectively. He could link up with childhood friends, classmates from his school days, and others whom he had met as an active member and group leader in the youth movement. Some of them could be expected to be in Berlin or visiting family between frontline assignments as most of them, too, were now serving in various branches of Germany's armed forces. Kusch would also begin to devote no small attention to Inge von Foris, a young, bright, and stunningly attractive student of art history at Berlin's Friedrich-Wilhelms-Universität, today's Humboldt University, who would in due course agree to become his fiancée.[1]

Even though serious air raids against the German capital would not commence until two years later, Berlin in that summer of 1941 was anything but a calm and peaceful oasis compared to the busy but boring schedule Kusch had just escaped in provincial Gotenhafen. The campaign against the Soviet Union, so very recently unleashed and seemingly so promising with its initial triumphs for Germany's armies and air force, dominated the talk of the city everywhere and ruled activities at its hectic train stations, airfields, and turnpikes. While groups of individuals, soldiers, and entire units kept moving to the eastern front day and night, along with trainloads full of munitions, rations, and a thousand other items necessary for an army to fight what would become the fiercest land campaign ever waged in military combat, Kusch must have wondered and worried how the unprovoked onslaught on the Soviet Union would affect Germany's military fortunes, and especially the naval war against Britain, until then Germany's only, but uncompromisingly committed, adversary in the West.

All indications suggest that Kusch went through those midsummer weeks of 1941 in a state of deeply conflicting emotions and mental anguish. While undoubtedly cherishing and looking forward to the challenge of frontline duty in the glamorous U-boat service as a matter of personal ambition, professional fulfillment, and patriotic responsibility, he had also grown to loathe the ruling Nazi regime from the bottom of his heart, not least the imbecility of Nazi ideology, the mindless squashing of individual freedoms and liberties, the hateful anti-Jewish myths and measures, and the mediocrity of its leaders. Now the assault on the Soviet Union only confirmed for Kusch that Adolf Hitler was indeed an irresponsible madman beyond the reach of reason. Kusch had become convinced that, if history was any guide, far from assuring German leadership and hegemony over Europe, the newly unleashed "Crusade against Bolshevism" stood to envelop his country in the end in nothing but death, destruction, despair, and defeat.

Only his closest friends knew of Kusch's implacable aversion to the National Socialist regime. To most observers he seemed like any other young naval officer—bright, eager, and well qualified for any assignment ashore or afloat. Indeed, he fit in most respects the characteristics of the average German naval officer recruit in the 1930s: "born and raised in a sizable Prussian city not far from the sea; his parents Protestants and commoners, members of the middle class." In addition, the young cadet was "well educated, highly motivated, and physically fit; aware and supportive of the traditions of the naval officer corps; a supporter of Hitler's takeover on conservative grounds of order, normalcy and national revival, but with some misgivings over Nazi methods and the more radical aspects of the party program; and eager to serve the fatherland in a prestigious position that offered early responsibilities and adventures in a 'romantic' setting."[2] This composite picture appears remarkably applicable to the young man who moved into *U-103*'s officer quarters that summer, except that "misgivings" would have been an understatement when it came to Kusch's assessment of Nazi leadership, society, and ideological pretensions. How did Kusch arrive at this outlook on life?

Oskar-Heinz August Wilhelm Kusch was born on April 6, 1918, in Berlin, one month after Russia's withdrawal from World War I and just as the Kaiser's armies prepared to open their last offensives on the western front in a desperate gamble to gain the decisive victory that had eluded them since the debacle of the Schlieffen Plan four years before.[3] His father, somewhat confusingly listed in the records as Oskar Heinz Kusch, Oskarheinz Kusch, Heinz Kusch, or simply "Direktor" Kusch, was born on May 5, 1882, and provided well for the family as an insurance company executive.[4] His mother, Erna Auguste Kusch, née Kohls, was twelve years younger than her husband and apparently pursued no separate professional career of her own besides looking after their comfortable apartment at Berchtesgadener Strasse 26 in fashionable Berlin-Schöneberg.[5]

Oskar would remain an only child, a fact that might account for a certain aloofness vis-à-vis others later in life and a tendency to enjoy his own company, even though he did have numerous friends and never became overly shy or a loner. He grew up a handsome child and young adult, lanky and above medium height, with an athletic build. His face was even and friendly, with alert eyes, a well-proportioned nose, slightly fleshy lips, chubby cheeks, and somewhat large and protruding ears. He kept his full, blond hair neatly parted on the left side and longer than seems to have been the fashion in the 1930s and 1940s. In pictures snapped when he was a student in school he dressed with care, even wearing a tie on occasion, and later looked fit and smart in a naval officer's uniform. It was clear his parents loved and cared for him very much. He in turn did everything to reciprocate their affection and justify their expectations.[6]

Obviously Oskar would not remember personally and only learn later the bewildering circumstances under which World War I had come to a close in revolutionary Berlin and elsewhere, including the military defeat on the western front and the ignominious armistice that followed; the Kaiser's abdication and departure into Dutch exile; the tumultuous days in the capital as the Second Reich gave way to the Weimar Republic amid unfamiliar violence and intense anxiety over Germany's destiny; the fear that the "red" revolution might spill from Russia westward and grip the nation in a terrible civil war; the universally abhorred limitations and humiliations imposed by the Versailles Treaty; and the uprooting and dislocation of vast groups of people that accompany all great national catastrophes before normalcy and stability can return.

For the Kusch family, the transition from the conservative and in some respects even reactionary political, social, and cultural system under the Kaiser to the yet untried democratic and liberal republican arrangements after 1918 does not appear to have caused the kind of traumatic apprehensions so many other Germans expressed and endured at the time—and this despite the fact that Herr Kusch had been severely wounded in the war and would never fully recover his health. True, as good patriots they sensed their country had received a terrible blow and that it would take time and patience to repair the damage inflicted on its dignity and sovereignty. Common sense, if nothing else, required the restoration of the rule of law as soon as practicable, and no government in Germany after 1919 could expect popular support if it failed to express outrage over the amputation of so much territory, over the reduction of the German military to virtual impotence, and over the painful strain the reparations placed on economic recovery.

Still, for the Kusch family, few of these transformations were likely to translate into gloom and misery. The family would be able to enjoy their lives, their personal possessions and property, their social position, and the continued assurance of economic comfort. As members of the upper middle class they stood poised to play a formative role in the young republic now that the pillars of the old regime—the monarchy, the nobility, big business, and the military establishment—had come under a cloud. Above all, the new realities promised increased opportunities for personal growth, individual liberties, social elasticity, and exciting cultural experiments hardly imaginable under the old. Not least, as an active and ranking member of the Masonic movement in Berlin and as revealed in his postwar testimony, Herr Kusch greeted the new intellectual and cultural environment with relief and enthusiasm.[7] In short, the Kusches, by temperament and by persuasion, found themselves in harmony with the unaccustomed openness of Weimar society, welcomed its atmosphere of liberality, and resolved to raise their son in the newfound spirit of freedom, individualism, generosity, and toleration so pervasive in postwar Berlin, as long as such values did not conflict with basic human decency, dignity, or love of country. As his mother once stated, as parents they brought up their son "in a liberal and democratic sense because we ourselves embraced those values."[8]

When young Oskar entered his neighborhood elementary school in 1924, the Weimar Republic had just weathered the tough period of hyperinflation of the previous year and embarked on five years of economic expansion and relative political stability under its inspired leader, Gustav Stresemann. Extremism, both from the right and the left, seemed under control, and the future for the young boy and his family looked increasingly bright and heartening. For his part, Oskar displayed high intellectual and academic promise already in his first years at school, anticipating that mixture of curiosity, thirst for learning, pursuit of truth, and independence of judgment that would mark him for the remainder of his life. In addition, he began to lay the foundations for his excellence as an amateur artist, particularly in drawing and painting, no doubt encouraged by his parents who were unlikely to stifle their son's creative urges given the family's shared values and Berlin's stimulating ambiance as one the world's avant-garde cultural centers during the fifteen years of the Weimar Republic. Indeed, Oskar's sketches and drawings that have survived from his navy years, invariably powerful in their expression, inspiration, and attention to detail, imply an artistic talent and vision of remarkable sophistication.[9]

The nurturing Oskar received fed on a strong emotional component as well, particularly through the love and devotion his mother expended on her only child. Reading between the lines of subsequent letters, statements, and commentaries, it becomes clear that his mother was the one to whom Oskar could always turn for immediate comfort and understanding, the one whose love and commitment would remain patient, unconditional, and undivided to the end. By contrast, his father appears to have concerned himself more with Oskar's mental and intellectual development, providing a model of patriotic service and societal success, and encouraging Oskar to make learning, critical thinking, genuineness, and the search for truth and fulfillment his primary quests in life. If the Kusches, parents and son, professed nominal adherence to the Protestant faith in its Lutheran variety, their religious commitment does not appear to have extended beyond minimal social obligations, favoring instead the Masonic tradition of freely roaming inquiry, individualism, and open-ended spiritual pursuits. If, much later, a discernible estrangement and greater distance opened between Oskar and his parents, it did so not because of a shortage of parental love or filial respect, or over essential differences in their respective philosophies of life, but primarily over the strains the breakup of the Kusch marriage in March 1938 placed on filial-paternal relations.

After four years of elementary school, where he acquired basic skills, Oskar, like all German pupils prior to the 1970s, underwent a written examination as well as his teachers' assessment of past performance and future promise that determined Oskar's subsequent academic options of continuing to either a *Volksschule* (people's school), a somewhat more challenging *Mittelschule* or *Realschule*, or to an elite *Gymnasium*. Only about ten percent of all students made the transition to a *Gymnasium*, which was then and remains today comparable to a French *lycée* with its demanding curriculum centering on the humanities, mathematics, sciences, foreign languages, history, geography, music, and the arts. Given Oskar's solid achievements and even greater academic promise and expectations for the future, he switched in 1928 to the Hohenzollern-Gymnasium at the corner of Belziger and Eisenacher Strasse in Berlin-Schöneberg, less than seven blocks from his home and thus easily reachable for the boy on foot or by bicycle.

The all-male Hohenzollern-Gymnasium had opened its doors in 1900, its name honoring the ruling dynasty of Prussia and the Second Reich. For the next eight years, from 1928 until his graduation in the fall of 1936, it would become Oskar's second home and central intellectual and educational focus. While not a "humanistic" gymnasium with its primary dedication to classical languages, literature, and philosophy, Oskar's Reform-Gymnasium placed a profound emphasis on modern foreign languages as well as the natural and social sciences.[10] Still, as later evidence suggests, his instruction even in disciplines such as Latin, history, geography, literature, and the arts must have been thorough and intense, just as he acquired a solid proficiency in English. Indeed, numerous individuals would testify to Oskar Kusch's excellent education and analytical abilities, while no one, not even his detractors, ever characterized him as shallow or lacking in erudition. Graduation from a gymnasium, i.e., attaining the coveted *Abitur* or *Reifezeugnis* (literally: certificate of maturity), guaranteed Oskar access to any academic career at a university, in the free professions, in the higher civil service, or as a military officer.

Besides and beyond his family and school-related activities, participation in the German youth movement left a lasting and possibly profounder imprint on the boy than his other social and intellectual pursuits. In 1928, at age ten, Oskar joined the recently chartered *Deutsche Freischar*, a loose confederation of independent scout groups and survivors of the pre-1914 romantic *Wandervogel* movement with thousands of members primarily in the Berlin area and eastern Germany. Under the overall umbrella of the so-called *Bündische Jugend*, local organizations within the *Deutsche Freischar* tended to emphasize opportunities for adolescent children, mainly boys of middle-class background, to live their lives responsibly and fostered a conscious experience of nature and of community, of toleration and openness free from prejudices. Favorite activities included hiking, camping, singing, story-telling, experiencing the invigorating power of the countryside in fields and forests, and not least undertaking excursions and longer bicycle tours together, even abroad. Games, sailing, canoeing, and all kinds of athletic exercises emphasized fitness, teamwork, and promoted a sense of camaraderie. Before the Nazi takeover, *Freischar* members tended to keep their distance from the Hitler Youth, refusing to accept the latter's nationalistic, racist, sexist, chauvinist, violent, mindlessly conformist, and anti-intellectual bent, even while sharing a penchant for uniforms, physical fitness, hierarchical leadership arrangements, and deliberately or inadvertently drawing followers away from traditional attachments to family, school, and church.

In the end it was not Kusch's exposure to the German youth movement in general—an experience he had, after all, in common with hundreds of thousands of other middle-class boys his age—that would imprint such a deep and lasting mark on him, but his affiliation after 1931 with a small, exclusive, tightly knit circle of like-minded youths from Berlin who adopted the name *Südlegion* (Legion of the South). The group was founded and led by a young medical doctor named Rudolf (Rudi) Pallas (1907–52) who was then practicing at the Berlin University Hospital. In contrast to virtually every other subgroup of the *Bündische Jugend,* and especially opposed to the despised Hitler Youth, the *Südlegion* dedicated itself not to paramilitary pursuits and physical toughness, but to "humanistic literature, the arts and philosophy," with ancient Greece serving as a reference model and with the study of the poetry and folk music of other countries becoming an especially cherished pursuit.[11] Pallas and his followers saw Germany's past and future "embedded in a transnational Europe and believed that those who did not dare open themselves to the world only exemplified the poverty and limitations of German culture."[12] Pallas cultivated connections to literary figures such as Hans Carossa and Ernst Wiechert at home as well as André Gide in France, all of whom, after the Nazis rose to power, would suffer persecution or denigration on account of their philosophical ideals or sexual orientation. As early as 1929 at the international scout jamboree convened in connection with the World Fair in Barcelona, Pallas had infuriated other members of the German delegation by his overly cordial attitude toward the French.[13] The mutual friendship, understanding, respect, and admiration that developed over the next decade between Rudi Pallas and Oskar Kusch were destined to become ingredients in the tragic events of 1944 and beyond.

What did the *Südlegion* stand for, and what attracted and inspired its members? Besides the group's obvious contradistinction to the Nordic orientation of Nazi ideology, mythology, and racialist nonsense, references to "the South" in Germany often express a hankering for simpler and happier places far away—sunny, warm, lush, and exotic locales, home to a free, easy, and unhurried life with plenty of leisure to fathom the meaning of our existence without being encumbered by the stale social and cultural conventions of highly developed modern societies like Germany's.[14] Such romantic yearnings and escape fantasies imply and promote an atmosphere of liberality, individual fulfillment, toleration of others, and a generous cosmopolitanism, while also elevating the community of like-minded seekers for truth, meaning, and happiness over those trapped in the banalities or false rewards of everyday existence. The search for such places of the imagination, this flight from the depressing and mundane normality of the world of the 1920s and 1930s, would predictably lead members of the *Südlegion* to an idealized Mediterranean antiquity where, in particular, Greece's perceived quest for open-ended inquiries into the purpose of life, along with protections for individual freedoms and alternative standards of behavior, could act upon youthful minds and spirits as powerful magnets. Curd Lähn, Rudi Pallas' friend, once quoted Nietzsche who himself had once longed "to rediscover the South in oneself, to look up to a bright, shining, mysterious southern sky high above, to stretch one's horizons and become transnational, more European, more in touch with the Levant, more Greek."[15] Even when the *Südlegion* became outlawed after 1934 and its members were officially folded into the Hitler Youth, Dr. Pallas and his core followers continued to undertake secret meetings and group trips by bicycle and train south to Switzerland, France, the Balkans, Italy, and Spain, with the obvious and presumably enthusiastic support and encouragement of the children's parents.[16]

Other aspects and routines of the *Südlegion* remain decidedly murkier, from the exact implications of the word "legion," to the rituals at campfire get-togethers deep in the woods surrounding Berlin, to the organization's cryptic motto taken from a favorite song, "You know it—the signs did not err." This song, first published in 1902 by the Jewish poet Karl Wolfskehl in Stefan George's famous *Blätter für die Kunst*, appears to invoke and celebrate a group's eternal, unbreakable bond against the backdrop of nature's seasonal wonders in language ranging from the gloomy and foreboding to the overbearing and bombastic.[17] The elitist nature of the *Südlegion*'s program, its celebration of hazy group sentimentality, its nature-based myths of self-expression and self-renewal, but also its cosmopolitan reach, are revealed potently in its songbook (*Liederbuch*) of 1932, which would quickly be banned under the Nazis. The collection's twenty-one entries are divided into subsections, each headed by Latin phrases such as *Legionis signa* (The Legion's Banner), *Litora peregrina* (Shores Far Away), *Lacrimae solitudinis* (Tears of Loneliness), *Voces noctis* (Voices of the Night), and *Exitus mundi* (As We Leave This World). No fewer than eight of the songs are foreign in origin or set in places far away, including "Embaterion" (Greek); "Kosakenlied" and "Platoff" (Russian); "Haul Away, Joe," "Loch Lomond," and "The Night Has a Thousand Eyes" (British); "Sont trois jeunes garcons" (French); and "Ou elé" (origin not clear).[18] The actual "Song of the Legion" was based on a French melody.[19] Other youth groups who were then also drifting into silent opposition to the totalitarian ideology of the day, including Christian groupings and the "White Rose" student movement in Munich, would draw inspiration from the *Liederbuch* and spread the popularity of its songs in some cases well into World War II and beyond.[20]

Rudi Pallas has summarized the mesmerizing atmosphere and almost transcendental intensity of those gatherings in the woods in a 1949 tribute to his murdered friend, Oskar Kusch:

> We were products of the *bündisch* youth movement. In a thousand nights spent around the campfires by our tents we conjured up the vision of a wondrous world. Removed from reality and

> beyond clear definition, it was a yearning born in the ecstatic friendships of our youthful days; it was the rapturous reverie our songs instilled in us as they filled the air above our secluded and remote campgrounds; it was the dreamlike and intimate conversations among friends on our trips to distant destinations such as Sicily, Spain, Albania, and elsewhere. However blissful and unforgettable it may have been, all in all here were adolescents daydreaming and escaping from reality into a romanticized land of everlasting youth. Whoever had become rooted in this idealized world, as had happened to us young people in those days, and if we were true to ourselves, would sooner or later find himself in a conflict with how things really stood, especially between 1933 and 1945. This contradiction was resolved behind the barbed wire of the concentration camps or, in the case of Oskar Kusch, by means of a firing squad. . . . Their opposition was based on an aesthetic resistance against a regime they would never be able to embrace because of the enduring experiences in the land of their youth.[21]

Kusch himself used remarkably similar language in a wartime letter to Pallas around the time he was posted to *U-103* to express the overpowering and yet insatiable longing he felt for those bygone days in the *Südlegion*:

> Those autumnal nights, blue and windy, when we moved closer to our blazing campfire and were dreaming and talking of the South, when the stars twinkled above and the woods rose up in deep and somber silence all around us—when I recall those autumnal hours by the fires, then I know that in those moments we realized, as if a lightning flash had suddenly illuminated the night, that our eternal longing had become reality for a short time and rushed like an all-consuming current through a broken dam carrying us along on its crest. . . . There and then we drank in life, our life, out of the soil, out of the woods, from each other,

> from everything around us; there and then we sensed what it means to grasp the hand of a friend and to say, "Come, let us go on." And in these present days [1941] when all our dreaming leads to nothing, in a time when the world impresses itself harshly and noisily upon us and challenges us hour after hour, we want to fortify ourselves with the memory of those times and those hours. We want to lock them away, just as we would do with a precious chalice in its shrine. And in deep stillness, far from the prying eyes of the uninitiated, far from any business and noise, it shall shine and sparkle for us.[22]

These lines suggest a sensibility and sentimentality in the youngster and later in the more mature naval officer whose reach and intensity kept him suspended between the imagined dreamland of his youth and the discordant realities of a world at war.

By all appearances, the close friendship between Pallas, who was homosexual, and Kusch also suggests at least a latent homoerotic dimension as the language of the previous and other communications bears out, as revealed in the *Südlegion*'s admiration for the aesthetics and practices of ancient Greece, and as noted in the songs, rituals, and ethos of this secretive all-male group. "He was fourteen years old when we first met," Pallas recalled. "The first thing I noticed was his unusually firm and hearty handshake, so firm indeed that others not expecting it would have considered it almost painful." Later Pallas, eleven years older than Kusch, would bemoan the long physical "separation" occasioned by his own prewar persecution by the Nazis and Kusch's assignment to faraway Lorient. One can well imagine how Pallas found the frequent communications from his friend, even in times of ubiquitous censorship, "totally different from the countless letters I received from my other friends and companions." To him, "every sentence conveyed an unquenchable yearning for the lost land of our youth."[23]

There exists a black-and-white photograph of 1935, by which time the group was officially disbanded and could only assemble clandestinely, that nevertheless captures the spirit of the group. The picture shows Pallas' charges arranged in a circle in a clearing somewhere in the woods surrounded by tall grass, with Oskar Kusch, then seventeen years old, facing the camera directly. They are wearing open-necked white shirts with their sleeves rolled up, short dark pants, lighter-colored stockings, and have their arms folded over their knees. Their hair is carefully parted and well groomed, their faces somber and concentrated, some heads even turned down in contemplation or meditation. The picture shows the young men in the midst of singing a song, presumably one from their favorite collection, in a moment full of fervor and devotion.[24]

After the Nazi takeover in January 1933, the days of youth groups outside the Hitler Youth were numbered. The adult mentors of the *Südlegion* determined to meet the new situation with a dual strategy to rescue at least some of their independence and immediate control over their followers into the new era. As a result, later that year the *Südlegion* was folded into the Hitler Youth as a so-called *Spielschar*, that is, as a subordinate detachment with a special focus, just as others specialized in sports or music. As Kusch's close friend Dieter Berger recalled after the war, for a brief period these former *bündisch* groups exercised a considerable influence on Hitler Youth organizations as the latter began to lose their formerly militant character after 1933: "They sang the songs of the *bündisch* youth movement, the *Jungvolk* [boys aged 10 to 14] adopted our uniforms, and publications often reflected the spirit of the *bündisch* tradition more than those of the Hitler Youth."[25] In fact, Oskar Kusch acted as its *Scharführer* until 1935, after which the Hitler Youth was systematically purged of all remaining *bündisch* ballast. With his group officially disbanded, Kusch ended his enforced, temporary, and altogether repulsive membership in the Hitler Youth, a step made easier by the approach of his eighteenth birthday, his focus on earning his *Abitur* at school, and his longtime determination to join the German naval officer corps upon graduation.[26]

The other alternative, both more courageous and more dangerous, was to continue the *Südlegion*'s activities in the underground. For some time Kusch appears to have lived a double life as both an official Hitler Youth *Scharführer* and as a prominent member and sometimes leader of an illegal youth group congregating quietly in the woods and around the lakes and rivers of greater Berlin, all the while continuing to undertake during school vacations those cherished group trips to destinations in southern Europe with perhaps uneasy but always loving parental support. For a while the group even renamed itself "Group Oskar," apparently to help minimize notice and notoriety. Still, sooner or later, such secret defiance of official directives was likely to draw the attention of the authorities. As records from 1944 reveal, Kusch had been under Gestapo surveillance for some time as an adolescent and must have continued his now illegal association with the remnants of the *Südlegion* into early 1937, with only his acceptance into the navy shielding him from arrest and prosecution for continued *bündisch* subversive activities.[27]

Joining the navy had been Oskar's dream ever since he was a little boy. In court testimony in 1949, his mother recalled Kusch's early fascination with maritime and naval literature, how happy he later was in his chosen profession, and how proud he felt upon becoming the commanding officer of a U-boat.[28] Healthy and strong, and no doubt familiar with Juvenal's ancient exhortation to cultivate a *mens sana in corpore sano*, he enjoyed athletic challenges such as swimming, diving, rowing, canoeing, sailing, and similar aquatic sports for which his school, his scouting activities, as well as his travels provided multiple outlets. By the time he applied to become an officer cadet and easily passed the required mental and physical examinations in 1936, his motivation may have been strengthened by the narrowing occupational options under the Nazi regime and resembled a classic push-pull scenario. With university curricula ideologically colored and membership in Nazi-dominated student organizations mandatory, an academic career had lost its former attraction, as it probably required full party membership as well. For Kusch and so many other bright young men critical and wary of the political situation, the German navy, recently renamed *Kriegsmarine* from the previous *Reichsmarine*, "offered an escape into a world presumably untouched and untouchable by the brown hordes, a life that combined adventure, social respectability, professionalism, and patriotic service to the fatherland rather than to the mediocre men who had usurped the state."[29] Not only were all professional German officers forbidden to join political parties, to vote, or become politically active, but in contrast to the more aristocratic army and the tradition-poor air force, the navy also promised frequent travel to faraway places, close and more democratic shipboard camaraderie, exposure to cutting-edge technology on modern warships, and quick promotion in a rapidly expanding military establishment. Clearly, too, Kusch's apprenticeship as a group leader in the youth movement made him confident in assuming positions of leadership later in his career. For most applicants to the navy in the mid-1930s the likelihood of another devastating war seemed remote.

After the excitement of the Summer Olympic Games in Berlin (August 1–16), which opened the opportunity to meet scout troops and other visitors from around the world, in the fall of 1936 Kusch passed his last academic exams with ease and graduated from his gymnasium with excellent grades and the coveted *Abitur*. At about the same time he received notice of his acceptance as a naval officer candidate effective April 1937. Still, a hated and mindless exercise loomed that would cost him half a year of his life and further embitter him vis-à-vis the regime—a compulsory six-month stint in the *Reichsarbeitsdienst* (RAD), or Reich Labor Service. Originally adopted in 1931 as a measure to combat unemployment in the Great Depression, the RAD was continued and expanded gladly by Hitler in the Third Reich to indoctrinate young men and women ideologically and to pre-militarize sections of the population in what amounted to another violation of the despised Versailles Treaty. Housed in barracks under military-like discipline, wearing uniforms with Nazi insignia, and equipped with a bicycle and a spade for each, RAD workers provided over seventy hours a week of labor on an assortment of military and civilian construction and preservation projects. While the exact location and nature of his assignments are no longer ascertainable, it requires little imagination to see how and why Oskar Kusch came to dread those awful winter months between October 1936 and the end of March 1937. As the Gestapo noted in its file on Kusch after it had intercepted and read several letters he had written to Rudi Pallas, he "minced no words" as he reported to his friend the insults and absurdities of his experience in the RAD.[30]

On Saturday, April 3, 1937, three days before his nineteenth birthday, Oskar Kusch boarded a train north from Berlin to the Pomeranian city of Stralsund on the Baltic Sea. There he reported for basic training to the *II. Schiffsstammabteilung*, traditionally the "boot camp" unit for German naval officer recruits. The facilities were located on the Dänholm, a small islet in the Strela Sound between the city itself and the adjoining large island of Rügen. Kusch joined some 490 fellow officer recruits who would forever after be known as Crew 37a or, more rarely, Crew IV/37. In German practice ever since the days of the Imperial Navy, a "Crew" is "the aggregate of all officer recruits who enter the German navy in a given year, plus any officers attached at a later point and in turn accepted as equals by the original members," with the entry year attached as a two-digit number.[31] For example, Crew 07 would comprise naval officers who began their service in 1907, while Crew 33 began theirs in 1933, typically in early April. The year 1937 introduced an anomaly, however, since the expected officer crunch in a rapidly expanding *Kriegsmarine* prompted authorities to accept and train not one but two entire Crews that year, one beginning its service in April—Kusch's Crew 37a—and the other in October, the latter known as Crew 37b or sometimes as Crew X/37. Despite limited space on training vessels and at the German naval academy, the *Marineschule Mürwik* on the Baltic Sea near Flensburg on the German-Danish border, the next full-size recruiting class followed in April 1938, with a more erratic schedule taking over in and after 1939 during the war. Since Crew 37a received their commissions as ensigns on August 1, 1939, American readers may find it convenient in general terms to think of them as the equivalent of the U.S. Naval Academy's Class of 1939. The individual and collective bonds among Crew comrades would last a lifetime through periods of peace or war.

Each Crew was subdivided according to specialization. Most prestigious and envied of all were *Seeoffiziere,* that is, line or executive officers like Kusch, who eventually could command ships and fleets. They made up the largest contingent. Ranking below them were the various "specialists," including engineers, weapons officers (artillery, torpedoes, mine warfare), administrative officers (the former paymaster branch), naval architects, and medical officers. According to the official *Rangliste* of the *Kriegsmarine* published in November 1938, after eighteen months of service Crew 37a consisted of 341 future *Seeoffiziere*, 44 engineers, 36 administrative officers, 36 weapons experts, 16 construction officials, and 15 naval surgeons, or 488 officer candidates altogether.[32] Total numbers may have originally been slightly higher, as Crew records by 1939 list three deaths through accidents alone and one can assume a few additional departures on academic, psychological, or physical grounds.[33] Earlier classes like Crew 34 also lost members because of their Jewish background, but by 1937 all German naval officer candidates required satisfactory documentation of their own and their family's "Aryan" purity (*Ariernachweis*) as part of their applications.

Compared to Crews of the 1920s and early 1930s, Crew 37a was considerably larger than its predecessors and its training schedule would be substantially shortened and tightened to feed the voracious personnel hunger of a growing surface fleet, a nascent submarine component, and a fleet air arm nominally under the supervision of the air force. Kusch's own experience with fellow officers aboard *U-154* would demonstrate how much the quality of junior officers had eroded by 1943, but on the whole prewar Crews maintained the elevated professional standards that had marked the German naval officer corps since the days of the Kaiser. Much of this had to do with the deep and broad education their gymnasia had provided and with the relatively limited ideological indoctrination they had suffered compared to those who came after them.

The various stations in the making of German naval officers in the 1930s have been described and analyzed in other publications, including the author's collective biography of Crew 34, so a summary of Oskar Kusch's specific experiences may suffice.[34] While his "boot camp" on Dänholm Island was undoubtedly rough and demanding, and may have pushed some of his comrades to the limits of their physical and mental endurance, Oskar's athletic fitness and recent exposure to the chicaneries of the Reich Labor Service allowed him to survive it, as other recruits in his situation, with a smile on his face and contempt in his heart for his drill sergeants whom he would outrank in very short order and likely never encounter again in his career.[35] Gratefully, basic training only lasted for ten weeks until June 14, 1937, when a far more delightful sight replaced the dull environment of barracks, shooting ranges, and parade grounds at Stralsund—namely, the beautiful, tall, three-masted sailing bark *Gorch Fock*, lovingly known as the "Swan of the Baltic," taking its name from a popular naval poet who had drowned at the Battle of Jutland in 1916.

The German navies enjoy a long tradition of teaching officer recruits hands-on nautical expertise on a genuine windjammer, considering this part of their education more crucial and beneficial in view of later assignments than additional time in basic training, weapons courses, or at the naval academy. Indeed, nothing can rival or replace the immediacy of sense perceptions about the effects of winds, currents, steerage, drift, trimming, and other features of a ship moving through water than time spent on a sailing vessel. After a previous training bark, the *Niobe*, had capsized and sunk in a ferocious thunderstorm, sadly taking down with it a third of Crew 32's cadets, a generous public subscription paid for an immediate replacement in 1933. The *Gorch Fock* would be joined by a sister ship, the *Horst Wessel* (commissioned in 1936), and still later by the *Albert Leo Schlageter* (1938), the latter two named after political martyrs dear to the Nazi movement.[36] Crew 37a was divided evenly between the *Gorch Fock* and the *Horst Wessel*, with Kusch embarking on a voyage under Commander Bernhard Rogge of later raider *Atlantis* fame that took him into the North Sea to the Netherlands and Norway and parts of the North Atlantic as far west as the Faroe Islands between Scotland and Iceland. On this occasion, and even more so on his subsequent midshipman cruise on the cruiser *Emden*, Kusch's youthful yearnings for romantic adventures in faraway places gained generous if sometimes bittersweet fulfillment.

For at some point in the late summer of 1937, when posted either to the *Gorch Fock* or to the *Emden*, Kusch received devastating news: upon returning to Berlin from one of his illegal group trips to France with what was left of the *Südlegion*, Rudi Pallas had been arrested on August 3 on dual accusations of subversive *bündisch* activities and homosexual acts under the notorious paragraph 175 of the German criminal code. On December 23, 1937, a special court sentenced him to ten months in jail on the political charge, with the Gestapo having him immediately transferred to the Sachsenhausen concentration camp north of Berlin on the second charge upon completion of his prison sentence. Here Pallas had to wear the notorious pink triangle that identified him as a gay prisoner.[37] Once World War II had begun, Pallas was released in 1940 and offered the opportunity to "prove himself" on the Russian front as a staff surgeon eventually attached to the ill-fated Sixth Army under Field Marshall Friedrich Paulus at Stalingrad. One can only wonder how often Pallas touched here the limits of human endurance and human depravity in those horrific winter months of late 1942 and early 1943. Whether he eventually defected to the enemy or became a regular prisoner of war in early 1943 when Paulus surrendered the ragged remnants of his command to the Soviets, can no longer be ascertained. It happened literally within days of Kusch's taking command of *U-154*. Except for Pallas' time in jail and at Sachsenhausen, and then again from 1940 to the catastrophe at Stalingrad, Kusch kept up a busy but carefully self-censored correspondence with his mentor. There is no indication that the revelation or confirmation of Pallas' homosexuality upset Kusch in an essential way or that he thought less of Pallas because of it. If anything, much of Kusch's later criticism of the Nazi leadership, as well as of its lies and ideological imbecilities, must have stemmed from information and assessments Pallas and like-minded friends provided to him, be it in the form of letters or during visits home from the front.

Midshipmen cruises in all navies constitute a crucial and invariably enjoyable segment of a naval cadet's education. Because of its size, Crew 37a had to split into three groups, two of them embarking on the ancient pre-dreadnoughts *Schlesien* and *Schleswig-Holstein*, respectively, and one on the light cruiser *Emden* commissioned in the 1920s as the first new ship allowed under the terms of the Treaty of Versailles. While his comrades on the old coal-firing dinosaurs with their crammed quarters and frightfully inefficient ventilator systems rounded all of South America (*Schlesien*) and even circumnavigated the globe (*Schleswig-Holstein*), the *Emden* undertook a leisurely 22,000-mile cruise from October 1937 to April 1938 through the Suez Canal to the Far East where it visited India,

Ceylon (now Sri Lanka), Malaya, and the Dutch East Indies (modern Indonesia), among many other stops along the way coming and going. The cruiser sailed under the command of Captain Leopold Bürkner, who later worked under and was in 1944 to succeed the legendary anti-Hitler conspirator Admiral Wilhelm Canaris as head of the *Abwehr*, Germany's counterespionage organization. Besides encountering many different cultures under late imperial European rule, as well as stunning natural wonders in tropical and subtropical settings, Kusch and his companions acquainted themselves with seamanship, navigation, communications, weaponry, propulsion, and administration of a modern warship as they took turns serving in those shipboard departments whenever the cruiser was at sea.

Kusch's emotional state at this time must be imagined as a mixture of competing sentiments. On the one hand he felt profoundly satisfied and elated over his career choice, while simultaneously growing numb and sad over developments in his personal sphere and in the darkening political world. The incarceration and denigration of Rudi Pallas by the Nazi authorities certainly remained on his mind throughout this time, and just before the conclusion of the cruise he learned of his parents' formal divorce. Whatever the causes for their separation and the dissolution of their marriage, both his father and his mother remained proud and supportive of their only son. Oskar's relationship to his mother continued to be close and loving, whereas the one to his father cooled somewhat.[38] His father continued to live at the familiar address in Schöneberg, while his mother soon married a Dr. Brockmann and settled in the nearby suburb of Steglitz. How Oskar reacted to Germany's annexation of Austria that same month is not recorded. Given his positive experiences there as a scout in the preceding years when it was still a free country, however, he likely harbored grave misgivings over the *Anschluss* and the additional power and clout it brought Hitler and his columns.

As soon as the *Emden* and the other training ships reached home waters again, Crew 37a became reunited for its last and longest time at the *Marineschule Mürwik*, Germany's naval academy near Flensburg on the Baltic Sea. Reshuffled into four companies and further broken up into smaller groups, the cadets deepened and strengthened their academic and professional expertise in the school-like atmosphere at the "Red Castle by the Sea" from late April until their graduation on November 15, 1938. Kusch belonged to Group 15 of the 4th Company and continued to solidify his standing in the Crew, officially ranking in the top quintile of all cadets in the *Seeoffizier* branch as No. 72 of 344 in 1938 upon graduation, as No. 54 out of 306 a year later, and as No. 41 of 296 by 1941, when the Crew already bemoaned a number of fallen comrades.[39] Such fine performance would not go unnoticed in the navy's personnel office and undoubtedly played a role in Kusch's future service assignments.

What impressions did Oskar Kusch make on his fellow cadets? One would remember him as an "intelligent, very sensitive young man who seemed to prefer his own company, but never acted in an unpleasant or offensive way. I had the feeling he enjoyed being a naval officer and that he had ambitions. He was a fine comrade." Another recalled him as "a blond Germanic type, strongly built and a very good athlete. He came across as rather reserved and serious-minded, in contrast to most of the rest of us who looked upon the world in general, and upon our superiors and the atmosphere at the naval academy in particular, in a more relaxed way and with a strong sense of humor." Yet a third cadet knew him as "a very quiet comrade who rarely initiated a conversation, but once he got involved in a discussion, he presented his arguments clearly and persuasively. His opinions carried weight with us. He was studious, quick-witted, and also could react in a split second, something I often came to experience on the losing end when we were boxing—but I enjoyed our bouts very much."[40]

Ten years later, Gerhard Meyer-Grieben, who had been Kusch's civilian defense lawyer at his court-martial, added this:

> He was a very handsome, distinguished-looking man who left you with the impression of being friendly and amiable from the moment you met him. He did not correspond to the stereotypical image of an officer. He reminded you more of an artist instead.

> Also, the way he wore his hair, long and blond, seemed incompatible with the profession of an officer. He spoke with a Berlin accent, sometimes in a slightly condescending manner. I actually had minor disagreements with him. He fancied he had to take on the air of a celebrated U-boat hero, that was his goal. His voice and intonation were not always suitable for the occasion. On the other hand, he was extremely kind, extremely interested. [During his time in jail] I supplied him with literature; he read very profound books, Rilke, serious novels, etc.[41]

In the meantime and all along Kusch had been promoted in rank on the same schedule as his comrades, provided they had not been held back or expelled because of physical, mental, or behavioral shortfalls. Thus Kusch became a *Fähnrich zur See* (midshipman) on May 1, 1938, an *Oberfähnrich zur See* (passed midshipman) on July 1, 1939, and eventually a *Leutnant zur See* (Ensign) effective August 1, 1939, just before the outbreak of war. Comparisons between *Kriegsmarine* officer ranks and those of the U.S. Navy or Britain's Royal Navy should be undertaken with caution, however, as they did not necessarily imply perfect equivalency despite similar or identical nomenclature. As an illustration, and clearly indicative of Germany's excellent preservice educational system and its worsening naval personnel crunch in the 1930s and beyond, Kusch could call himself a commissioned officer after only twenty-eight months of active service, whereas a graduate of the U.S. Naval Academy would have to wait forty-eight months for that distinction. For purposes of consistency, in this study ranks have been rendered either in their German original or as their American equivalents at the time.

From September 1938 through March 1939, just as his fellow midshipmen did on a rotational basis, Kusch attended a succession of courses focused on weapons systems and other areas of responsibilities a future officer might face at sea. The courses were taught at Flensburg, Kiel, and Stralsund on the Baltic Sea and built on the men's initial experiences during their midshipman cruise and on their classes at the naval academy. They covered the fields of coastal and shipboard artillery, communications, advanced infantry training, torpedoes, and mine warfare.[42] In the meantime their comrades in branches other than *Seeoffiziere*, such as the engineers, were off to specialized schools and practical experiences in their respective fields of expertise and rarely saw their colleagues in the line officer branch again unless posted to the same command or to the same base.

Effective April 3, 1939, having completed his theoretical and practical schooling with distinction, Kusch took up his regular service with the fleet. He may have hoped to see duty on a torpedo boat or a destroyer,[43] or even on a battleship or battle cruiser, but to his great surprise he found himself reassigned to the cruiser *Emden* along with three other Crew 37a comrades. In a way Kusch was fortunate not to have been picked for duty with the *Seeluftwaffe*, as every crop of freshly minted ensigns was obligated to detach several dozens of its members for as long as four years to the German naval air arm under the overall auspices of Hermann Göring and the regular *Luftwaffe*. Such service, during which the officers kept their navy ranks, uniforms, and insignia and flew as observers or actual pilots with a mixed *Kriegsmarine/Luftwaffe* flight crew, was generally hated and in practice quite dangerous. For one thing, the young officers had signed up in the first place, not to fly, but to serve on battleships, cruisers, destroyers, fast torpedo boats, and perhaps in the newly revived U-boat branch. For another, their antiquated, slow, accident-prone Dornier and Heinkel flying boats and floatplanes became easy prey for enemy fighters. Subsequent participation in the Battle of Britain in somewhat more modern aircraft did little to enhance their life expectancy. A typical example is Kusch's friend and group-mate at the naval academy, Paul Otto, whose sojourn with the *Seeluftwaffe* would last from April 1939 until February 1942 when he returned to full-time duty in the blue navy and subsequently commanded the submarine *U-285* from May 1943 until Germany's surrender in 1945.[44]

Even while being caught up in his busy responsibilities aboard the *Emden*, Kusch likely continued to follow the political developments at home and the darkening international situation. Two weeks before Kusch rejoined his old cruiser, Hitler had invaded and destroyed the remnants of Czechoslovakia, thereby signaling to the world that no mere revocation of the Versailles Treaty was his goal; indeed, Hitler desired nothing less than hegemony over the continent. *Kriegsmarine* officers may have entertained for a while the illusion that the Anglo-German Naval Agreement of 1935 might shield them against a conflict with Britain. But when France and the United Kingdom guaranteed the inviolability of Poland later that spring, the possibility of armed conflict in the near future became palpable. War grew virtually inevitable when Hitler, in one of history's most unexpected turnarounds, teamed up with his old nemesis Joseph Stalin to destroy hated Poland through what was euphemistically proclaimed as the Nazi-Soviet Non-Aggression Pact of August 23, 1939. Within a week, on September 1, 1939, the Nazi invasion of Poland began and, with the Allied declaration of war against Germany two days later, the world was at war again.

Except for one harrowing incident at the very outset of the war, Kusch's days on the *Emden* turned out to be relatively uneventful. At last withdrawn from the training of midshipmen, the light cruiser for much of the spring and summer of 1939 engaged in the not overly glorious task of protecting German fisheries in international waters until the approach of war induced the Naval High Command to recall the *Emden* to its home port of Wilhelmshaven on the North Sea where it witnessed the outbreak of hostilities. Reminiscent of initial moves in World War I, the ship's first wartime mission on September 3 was to help lay a defensive minefield in the North Sea. The next day, having returned to Wilhelmshaven for more mines, the cruiser and the base came under attack from a flight of British Wellington bombers. One of them, fatally hit by antiaircraft fire, crashed between the jetty and the *Emden*, its bomb load exploding and causing considerable damage to the vessel's bow section, killing two officers and eight enlisted men, and injuring many others in the process.[45] Kusch survived unhurt. The *Emden*, following repairs, transferred to the Baltic to hunt for much of the winter of 1939–40 for merchant ships carrying contraband. Just days before the cruiser got ready for Operation *Weserübung*, the clandestinely prepared German occupation of Denmark and Norway in early April 1940, orders arrived for Kusch to report to the navy's U-Boat Training Command.

When exactly Oskar Kusch sought reassignment to Germany's U-boat arm remains uncertain, but he definitely volunteered. He could have done so as early as at the naval academy, during the subsequent weapons courses, or at any time while aboard the *Emden*. The reasons for his move are not difficult to detect. The glamor and glory of the German submarine service in World War I must have been the subject of many of the books Kusch consumed as a boy, with its daring and dedicated crews under youthful commanders performing feats of remarkable courage and success. Similar to the daring raids of the Zeppelin airships against England and its capital, U-boat exploits between 1914 and 1918, despite wretched shipboard conditions and a technology not fully matured, dominated the German naval effort at sea and achieved an acclaim that took off straight into the realm of myth and legend.[46] Since the restoration of Germany's U-boat service in 1935 under the inspired supervision of Karl Dönitz, then a naval captain before rising to overall command of the *Kriegsmarine* in 1943 as a grand admiral, both the popularity and the size of Germany's submarine fleet had vastly increased. This trend was likely to continue inasmuch as submarines constituted the ideal weapon of a naval underdog like Germany—unable to dominate the oceans, but perfectly suited to deny maritime hegemony to the enemy and capable of dealing deadly blows to its merchant fleet.

Two additional considerations likely motivated Kusch in his request. Every naval officer dreams of commanding as soon as possible a vessel of his own, and here the U-boat arm offered opportunities rarely encountered in the surface navy. Except for Germany's fast torpedo boats, so-called *Schnellboote* or *S-Boote*, and minesweepers, only submarines granted a young officer early responsibility for a powerful fighting unit and its complement of up to fifty men in a frontline capacity.[47] Lastly, the crew of a submarine forms a tight, close, and mutually dependent group of men for weeks and months on end. A boat's very survival and any success in combat rely on its men's highly specialized training, on their knowledgeable and responsible conduct, on a level of camaraderie unknown in other branches of the service, on selfless dedication to one's duties, and on absolute trust in the capabilities, courage, character, and overall comportment of its captain. Having provided exactly this kind of leadership for his former comrades in "Group Oskar" of the *Südlegion* less than three years before and on other occasions after, Kusch must have felt assured he and the U-boat arm constituted a perfect match.

Given his athletic prowess and intellectual agility, qualifying physically and mentally for the strenuous conditions on a submarine was clearly not a problem for Kusch. He would spend the next six months in various locations along the Baltic coast, including on boats belonging to the Twenty-First U-Boat Flotilla based in Pillau in East Prussia, a collection of smaller and older units earmarked for the practical training of future frontline personnel. As in World War I, these facilities in places like Flensburg, Eckernförde, Kiel, Neustadt, Gotenhafen (Gdingen or Gdynia) near Danzig, and Pillau, all in the southern and generally peaceful reaches of the Baltic Sea, were perfectly suited for shakedown exercises of newly built submarines and the thorough training of U-boat crews in general. For all countries bordering the Baltic were either allies of Germany or officially neutral, and until 1944 these largely rural and remote areas stayed beyond the reach or target priorities of Allied bombers. Even when the Soviet Union joined the Allies in 1941, its Baltic Fleet remained bottled up in the Gulf of Finland until the very last phase of the war.

For Kusch, this period meant the same mandatory and thorough basic training all new U-boat personnel had to undergo, followed by specialized courses with fellow future watch officers in such fields as torpedo technology and attacks, target practice with the deck gun, antiaircraft automatic weaponry, communications, and lots of diving, diving, diving. As one analyst summarized, besides noting that boats had to run no fewer than sixty-six attacks on a moving target before being permitted to fire a live torpedo, "the exercises ran day and night: diving to periscope depth, emergency dives, deep dives, firing the deck artillery, diving at night. The sequence of every activity was preset in every detail. It was crucial to be both quick and accurate. Once on duty, every officer and sailor was held to the strictest standards of discipline."[48] Karl Dönitz himself insisted on this tough and thorough schedule, at times even endangering the safety of his own boats and men while simulating combat situations out in the

Atlantic as realistically as possible, even moving around a twenty-ship mock convoy with German escorts in all seasons to practice individual attacks and wolfpack tactics with dummy torpedoes, while planes of a *Luftwaffe* squadron patrolled overhead in their assumed role as Allied antisubmarine chasers.[49]

Kusch concluded his formal U-boat officer training at the end of September 1940, again with high marks and no doubt expecting to be posted without delay to a fighting submarine as a junior watch officer. But that was not be, at least not yet. Disappointed and impatient, Kusch would spend the next nine months as a company officer with the Second U-Boat Training Division at Gotenhafen. The most likely explanation for Kusch's delayed deployment to a frontline boat was a temporary glut of watch officers—obviously a good problem to have from the *Kriegsmarine*'s point of view. In other words, while relatively few boats were being sunk by the enemy, only a trickle of new boats was arriving from Germany's shipyards at this time to join the combat flotillas, so that temporarily there were simply not enough berths available for men of Kusch's qualifications. Both situations would change shortly and indeed completely reverse themselves by 1942 and 1943, but for the time being Kusch remained stuck in Gotenhafen.

This formerly Polish city and resort on the Baltic west of Danzig had recently been renamed by the Nazis after the pagan Germanic tribe who had settled there before going on to wreak all sorts of havoc as Ostrogoths and Visigoths in the late Roman Empire. Now, with its Polish population removed, the port, its depot ships, its shore-based facilities, and its staff of naval and civilian instructors were pressed into service to teach as many as four thousand green trainees at a time how to become submariners. Kusch's duties were primarily shore-based in a supervisory and administrative capacity for between 90 and 250 enlisted men, while hands-on exercises at sea were left to the various units of the Twenty-Second U-Boat Flotilla.[50]

Those cold and miserable nine months in Gotenhafen, during which he continued to carry out his duties with competence and praise, placed a first damper on Kusch's enthusiasm for his career choice and coincided with ominous political and military developments. By the first half of

1941 Germany had lost the Battle of Britain, and it grew plain, despite lukewarm and eventually aborted preparations for a seaborne invasion (Operation Sealion), that Britain and its former colonies Canada, South Africa, Australia, and New Zealand would stay in the war indefinitely. This meant an ever-growing emphasis on the German U-boat campaign in the Atlantic and also in the Mediterranean, to where Germany would dispatch no fewer than sixty-four Type VII U-boats from 1941 onward to make up for the lackluster contributions of the Italians. Furthermore, the spring of 1941 brought the unexpected death or capture of four of Germany's top U-boat aces—Günther Prien, Jochen Schepke, Julius Lemp, and Otto Kretschmer—and, of course, the destruction of the battleship *Bismarck* on its first and only foray into the open Atlantic. Perhaps most troubling of all, in view of what had transpired in World War I, the United States with President Franklin Roosevelt in the lead showed signs of tilting its political sympathies and material support once more toward Britain by adopting the Lend-Lease program; by extending the Pan-American Security Zone twenty-three hundred nautical miles eastward to a point just west of Iceland in April 1941; and by ordering the U.S. Navy to escort convoys bound for the United Kingdom all the way to this mid-ocean point where the Royal Navy then took over protection for the remainder of their voyages.

One advantage Kusch enjoyed at Gotenhafen was the city's relative proximity to Berlin. With a change in Stettin he could make the trip by train in about seven or eight hours. In addition, the winter of 1940–41 was one of the harshest ever, with the Baltic freezing over early and the U-boat training flotillas becoming icebound and stuck in port for months.[51] This situation allowed Kusch to travel to Berlin with some regularity to meet family and friends. While letters were always subject to censorship, such personal visits with their confidential conversations among trusted friends allowed for frank assessments of Germany's declining military fortunes and of the ever-tightening dictatorship at home. Besides Rudi Pallas, released from the Sachsenhausen concentration camp the previous year for frontline duty, one of Kusch's best friends was Hans-Dietrich (Dieter) Berger. Two years younger than Kusch,

Berger had been in his youth group in the early 1930s and shared his anti-Nazi convictions entirely. In 1936, when he was only sixteen, Berger had been arrested by the Gestapo for continued *bündisch* activities and managed to flee to Switzerland for a while under a clever pretext. Now a *Luftwaffe* officer, he and Kusch renewed and deepened their old friendship. Another close confidant was the slightly older Kurt Wiemer who saw Kusch several times in France where he was posted as an employee of the Todt construction organization and who, along with Berger, would later be instrumental in finding a civilian defense lawyer for Kusch at his court-martial.

Exactly when and under what circumstances Kusch first met his future fiancée, Ingeborg von Foris, remains uncertain.[52] It could have happened as early as those fateful summer days of 1941 in Berlin, but definitely no later than Christmas 1942.[53] Miss von Foris—she preferred to be called Inge and always signed her name that way—was two years younger than Kusch, the daughter of Colonel Bernhard von Foris and his wife, Almuth, and had grown up in Hamburg. Her Huguenot forebears had belonged to the upper French nobility before fleeing to Prussia after the Bartholomew's Day Massacre of August 1572. Had she so chosen, Inge could have called herself the Marquise de Foris et Foris-Valois. Mindful of her family history, and just as her father, she adhered to the reformed, Calvinist faith of the Huguenots rather than to Lutheranism as her relatives on her maternal side preferred.[54] Not unlike Oskar Kusch, she had belonged to the *bündisch* youth movement and became for a while a compulsory member of the BDM, the female equivalent of the Hitler Youth, from which she extricated herself by going on a hunger strike.[55] She also had to spend a brief stint in the dreadful RAD following her graduation from an all-female *Gymnasium* in Wandsbek, a fashionable middle-class section of Hamburg. In the summer of 1940, at age twenty, she relocated to Berlin to study art history and archaeology at Friedrich-Wilhelms-Universität, today's Humboldt University, with the goal of obtaining a doctorate and becoming a museum assistant upon graduation. As her major professor, she chose Wilhelm Pinder, a widely acclaimed expert on German art and architecture from the Middle Ages to the Baroque period. Highly popular with his students, Pinder was also known to embrace some of the murkier aspects of Nazi culture and aesthetics. Given Oskar's and Inge's mutual and profound passion for the arts, their first encounter may well have occurred at a museum or an art exhibit. Since the young art student's rejection of the Nazis and their program was possibly even fiercer than that of the budding naval officer, they also could have met through mutual friends who shared their political views and concerns.

From the beginning a strong physical attraction sprang up between the handsome, highly gifted but also remarkably sensitive officer who could look forward to a shining professional career, and this charming, smart, vivacious young woman from such a distinguished background—very probably a case of infatuation at first sight. A later admirer, Henry C. Alter, who met Inge a year after Kusch's death, has left this account of his first encounter with her:

> The door was opened and there I stood, completely stunned, as if struck by lightning: an enchanting creature appeared before me who subsequently introduced herself as Inge von Foris. The ideal of a female, one hundred percent North German, slender, tall, blonde, with sparkling blue eyes, who later revealed herself as even more precious, namely, as free and easy, completely natural, neither too aggressive nor too guarded, a princess in a pullover, an angel who could curse without coming across as offensive.[56]

Kusch may have found more poetic language to characterize the woman he came to love, or even preferred to express his feelings in a drawing, painting, or other piece of art, but it is clear enough that Inge von Foris exerted a mesmerizing effect on him and all who met her in those days.

Still, if Oskar's courtship of Inge and her attachment to him were relatively slow to blossom over the next year and a half, there was a plausible impediment besides his long and frequent absences at sea, namely, her continuing bond to a competing suitor. For some time, Inge had been close to a young man named Heinrich P., a smart, warm-hearted, extremely sensitive but also reserved, often irresolute, and overall somewhat colorless student of German literature. Heinrich was then serving as an ordinary soldier in Russia and had become, like her, an implacable foe of National Socialism. They remained in a deep and mutually affectionate relationship and continued to correspond even after her official engagement to Oskar in the summer of 1943. The nature, tone, and substance of their letters and postcards make quite certain that Oskar never knew of his fiancée's secret and that she did not want him to. Without revealing a name or details to Heinrich, she in turn would later characterize her involvement with Kusch obliquely as "a flirt, a real flirt," never once mentioning that she had actually become engaged to Kusch with the intention of marrying him.[57] Whether her odd and secretive behavior sprang from a sense of responsibility for someone who loved her passionately and had grown emotionally dependent on her, from needing more time to sort out her true feelings and options, or from yet other sources, remains difficult to gauge. At any rate, as her postwar marital choice would suggest, and others confirmed at the time, Oskar Kusch resembled her ideal of a male companion far more closely than his highly intellectual and introverted competitor.[58]

But much of this lay clouded in a yet uncertain future. For Kusch, the more immediate challenge became to prove his mettle as a watch officer to his skipper Werner Winter, to his fellow officers and men on a famous frontline boat, and to U-Boat Command; he also had to prove whether he was fit to take on even higher responsibilities in the future, including command of a boat of his own. Upon arriving in Lorient and reporting to the flotilla staff, Kusch and Winter met for the first time and immediately knew they could trust each other, indeed that they were likely to become close friends. Both were on hand when Viktor Schütze brought *U-103* in from its fourth patrol on July 12, 1941, after 103 days at sea and with the astounding total of thirteen ships sunk, mainly off the West African coast, with a combined tonnage of 65,172 tons.[59]

U-103's most recent exploit was especially remarkable as it occurred just when the German U-boat campaign was entering a slump at the end of the "First Happy Times." The reasons for this decline in enemy tonnage destroyed, while mysterious to Admiral Dönitz and his staff, are not difficult to fathom in retrospect. With American and Canadian help in the western Atlantic, the British operated at last a well-functioning convoy system in the waters most threatened by German submarines, thereby vastly reducing the number of vessels sailing without escort. Solid advances in radar and sonar technology, the more sophisticated use of depth charges, radio high-frequency direction finding, and antisubmarine tactics generally—especially the spectacular breaking of the German Enigma cipher by Alan Turing and his team at Bletchley Park—began to erase the advantages the hunters had so far held over the hunted. Moreover, the number and range of Allied aircraft available for patrols over ever-wider stretches of the Atlantic and the coastal waters of France and Norway steadily increased. This included prominently surveillance of the Bay of Biscay through which all departing and returning U-boats had to pass en route to and from bases like Lorient. To be sure, once Dönitz's wolfpacks had spotted a convoy, the ensuing battle could be fierce and Allied losses of ships, men, and cargo most grievous. But just as more and more boats were being funneled from German shipyards and the U-Boat Training Command in the Baltic to the frontline flotillas in France and Norway, so did quickly built corvettes, frigates, destroyers, and long-range aircraft bolster Allied defenses. Moreover, the Allies improved their strategic position by occupying Iceland in 1940 and later operating from Bermuda and the Portuguese Azores as well, thus reducing the spaces at sea where German submarines could hide without the threat of being detected from the air.

Perhaps Germany's greatest handicap strategically and technologically remained that its present submarine campaign had hardly evolved beyond its arrangements and experiences in World War I. Just as in and after 1917, Germany had waged an unrestricted tonnage war predicated on the notion that Germany would inevitably win the conflict if its submarines could destroy merchant ships faster than the enemy could replace them, thus Dönitz now stayed wedded to the idea of a relentless *Tonnagekrieg* against an island nation desperately dependent on seaborne imports. The slightest decline in the destruction of enemy shipping by his U-boats meant a setback in a vast global struggle whose goal was the isolation and starvation into surrender of Great Britain, the only major country still at war with the Third Reich at that time.

Even more fatally, U-boat technology and weaponry had either stagnated or only incrementally progressed from the state they had reached by 1918. In terms of size, speed, range, weaponry, diving depth, sensors, communications, propulsion on and below the surface, or comfort levels for officers and crew for that matter, a boat like *U-103* in 1941 was in no essential feature different from its predecessors a generation before. Without active radar, and in the absence of any sustained or reliable German airborne reconnaissance over the Atlantic, the boats were also blind. Any perception of enemy activities remained restricted to a radius of a few nautical miles visible from the top of their conning towers or, when submerged, by the ears of the hydrophone operator. To remedy this situation in part, U-Boat Command had taken over long-range control of the movements of the boats from its headquarters ashore, requiring two-way radio contact to ascertain their whereabouts and to direct them to reported targets, a practice which in turn endangered communications security and frequently gave away the boats' locations to a network of high-frequency direction-finding stations the Allies had set up around the Atlantic and the Mediterranean. The only significant advance occurred in torpedo technology, allowing commanding officers sometimes the choice between traditionally aimed "eels" running in a straight line toward their targets, those that reacted to a ship's propeller noises, and even some that ran a preprogrammed search pattern through a convoy and essentially self-selected their victims. The real revolution in submarine technology and capabilities, however, came far too late in the war to influence its outcome. This was the arrival of Type XXI and Type XXIII boats with massive batteries and high and sustained underwater speed, making them both extremely dangerous and virtually undetectable. None of them saw actual combat.

In view of subsequent developments, it seems useful to describe briefly the layout of a Type IX boat. Immediately below the bridge with its attack and panorama periscopes and other navigational and torpedo-aiming devices, and connected to it by vertical steel ladders down the conning tower, was the central control room, or *Zentrale*. Both during regular operations and during combat situations, especially when submerged, all decisions affecting the boat's movements and other activities were made from here by the commanding officer and carried out by various specialists whose work and battle stations were arranged along and to both sides of a narrow passageway that ran fore and aft over the length of the boat. These highly trained petty officers and enlisted men ranged from the navigator and helmsman in the *Zentrale* itself to the torpedo "mixers" in the bow and stern compartments, to the radio operators just forward and to starboard of the central control room, to the diesel mechanics and the operators of the electrical motors in the rear. Almost all members of the crew had dual or even triple functions, with the radio personnel also being trained as hydrophone operators, the cooks doubling as a medics if necessary, and many men with other basic responsibilities manning the antiaircraft automatic weaponry just aft of the bridge when the boat was under the threat of an attack from the air or actually under fire. Most men slept at or near their work and battle stations on narrow bunks or in hammocks, often on a rotational basis depending on whether they were on watch or off.

Immediately forward of the *Zentrale*, on the port side across the passageway from the radio room and the space for the hydrophone operator, were the skipper's cabin and the tiny officers mess with another bunk behind it on the outer wall. Lacking doors, these areas were equipped with curtains that could be pulled shut for a modicum of privacy. A mess attendant, or *Backschafter*, would bring the food from the galley and keep the area tidy between meals. It was in this confined space—within earshot of the radio operators on duty, surrounded by and on top of fuel bunkers, food and ammunition storage areas, diving cells, and the massive, rechargeable batteries that allowed the craft to move under water—that most of the conversations between the boat's officers would take place, even though it would be rare for all four of them to be present at the same time once the boat got under way.

The thorough overhaul of *U-103* inside the bomb-proof facilities at Lorient would not be completed until early September 1941, by which time Kusch could celebrate his promotion right on schedule to the rank of *Oberleutnant zur See*, or Lieutenant (jg), and had become familiar with the duties of a second watch officer (II.W.O.). The latter included, of course, standing watch with his lookouts on the bridge for four hours at a time and directing the movements of the boat during that span; supervising the crew of the 10.5-cm gun on the main deck and the antiaircraft artillery behind the bridge when needed; and overseeing the radio department. Along with the executive officer, or I.W.O., and the chief engineer (L.I.), Kusch would also be expected to help ready the boat for departure.

Kusch would remain *U-103*'s II.W.O. for three successful patrols under Werner Winter until the summer of 1942 and to nobody's shock distinguished himself as a highly competent and popular officer. On June 26, 1942, Winter placed the following evaluation into Kusch's personnel file:

> Between June 25, 1941, and June 26, 1942, *Oberleutnant zur See* Kusch (Oskar) served as II.W.O. on board of *U-103* of the Second U-Boat Flotilla and participated in three long patrols. Kusch has become an excellent young officer. The war has matured him, and with his irreproachable character, his vast intelligence, and his quick grasp of all things he became a valued assistant to the commanding officer. As a superior he shows much heart and cheerfulness but also a steady hand towards his subordinates. He is gifted artistically and highly educated. In combat situations he demonstrated tenacity, vigorous but never irresponsible courage, as well as great reliability and responsibility. His knowledge level is very high and he masters his tasks and duties under all circumstances. As weapons officer he was precise, circumspect, and invariably dependable. He has been decorated with the Iron Cross, First Class. After his next patrol as an I.W.O. he will be very well qualified to command a U-boat himself.[60]

Winter's assessment was mirrored almost perfectly by the recollections of an enlisted sailor from Austria, Peter Marl, who served on Kusch's watch as a lookout:

> Kusch was one of the finest officers and men I met in the German Navy, a great leader of his bridge watch. It was a pity there were not more of Kusch's type as officers in the German Navy. Kusch inspired his men and never pulled rank or acted the conceited big shot. Kusch convinced his men, had a sunny disposition and cared deeply about the people serving under him. In tight situations Kusch kept his calm and sense of humor.[61]

Not surprisingly, *U-103* continued to fare well with such a capable and dedicated officer on board, especially as it continued to expand its operational reach into waters previously unpatrolled or rarely visited by German submarines. Kusch's first outing into the Atlantic since his days as a cadet, and the boat's fifth, lasted sixty-one days from September 10 to November 9, 1941. Besides Werner Winter of Crew 30, Kusch's officer colleagues were I.W.O. Friedrich Markworth and L.I. Gerhard Bielig, both of Crew 34 and eventually decorated with the Knight's Cross for outstanding accomplishments. Winter was not too happy with the job the shipyard workers in Lorient had done, describing the state of his boat on September 12 as "unsatisfactory" after eight weeks of repairs and bemoaning specifically problems with the starboard diesel, leaky valves that required activating the pumps every thirty minutes, and the boat trailing an oily film emanating from supposedly watertight fuel bunkers. In the end the experienced chief engineer and his petty officers fixed or alleviated the most urgent problems and Winter decided to continue his patrol after dodging a surprise air attack in the Bay of Biscay with an emergency dive. His lookouts had been late in spotting the Consolidated PBY flying boat's approach.[62]

With yields along the North Atlantic convoy lanes drying up, and given the boat's long range and endurance, *U-103* was again dispatched to the bulge of West Africa where Allied ship traffic on its great-circle routes from South America and South Africa to Britain converged and where *U-103* had done so well on its last mission. But after torpedoing two British freighters of about 5,000 tons each west of the Canary

Islands, the boat's lookouts only encountered an empty ocean for weeks on end. Even a three-day attachment to a wolfpack group named "Störtebecker" on the way home did not change *U-103*'s poor luck on this patrol. But, as the chief engineer Bielig would later remember, it gave the officers plenty of opportunity to get to know each other and to engage in animated discussions and speculations within the confines of their tiny mess room. "[Kusch] and I became friends. For entire nights we discussed every possible topic under the sun. In those days I was still a firm believer in Nazism whereas he rejected it, already persuaded of the regime's diabolical character. But this never affected in any way his commitment to his duties as a soldier."[63]

Lieutenant Bielig's comment is the first recorded indication of Kusch sharing his political convictions outside his small circle of friends in Berlin, unless a fellow officer's reported friendly advice to Kusch during a training course in Pillau to "watch your tongue" can be dated to the year 1940 or earlier in 1941.[64] It is significant that the political discussions aboard *U-103* occurred under a commanding officer who himself was critical of Nazi ideology; also, such practices were carried out, not in a public place or for a general audience, but among trusted fellow officers in a confidential setting. Here the proud, somewhat elitist, and often invoked comradely spirit that pervaded the U-boat service merged with the unwritten code and ethos of the naval officer corps, namely, to continue its cherished traditions, to respect each member's individual views unless they reflected or encouraged cowardice, desertion, or treason, and to stand up for each other and to shield others from harm. These very values Kusch knew perfectly well from his days in the *Südlegion* and at the naval academy, and he confidently and logically extended them now to his new surroundings—trust for trust.

While *U-103* readied itself in Lorient for its next mission and its men looked forward to spending Christmas with their families at home, an event halfway around the globe changed the character of the war forever like a lightning bolt out of a clear sky—the attack on Pearl Harbor on December 7 and the entry of the United States into the war on the side of the Allies three days later when Hitler declared war on America in sympathy with his Japanese Axis partner. While Britain and the Soviet Union welcomed this development with elation and relief, the wiser analysts on the German side recognized the move immediately as either guaranteeing a war without end or, more likely, as marking the beginning of the end itself. For someone like Oskar Kusch who knew his history and had been taken aback by the folly of the attack on Russia six months earlier, December 1941 must have brought, not a season of joy, but the terrifying realization that all he, his friends, his boat, his navy, indeed Germany as a nation, could hope and fight for from then on was a peace without victory, without punishment, without another Versailles treaty or worse. This also meant a reassessment and rearrangement of Germany's political and military leadership before too many more human beings had to die and too much more damage was done in this latest European orgy of self-destruction. Yes, Kusch would do his duty as always, for he could never become a traitor, a turncoat, or a deserter. But his thoughts shifted inevitably from any notion of a military victory to the hope for an early settlement of the conflict under the best terms Germany could attain, even if it meant a continuation of the struggle to force such a solution on the enemy.

Paradoxically, these distant signs of gloom and defeat brought German submarines in the short term their most lucrative hunting season yet. For while the United States, with its overwhelming resources in manpower, wealth, science and technology, industrial production, and military establishment, would surely be indefatigable in any protracted conflict, it had a short-term vulnerability of sizable and perhaps unexpected proportions—its maritime traffic along the Eastern Seaboard, in the Gulf of Mexico, and in the Caribbean. Here merchantmen of all kinds and sizes had plied their trade unprotected and unmolested since the beginning of the war because Hitler, for fear of America openly joining the Allied cause, had not dared to penetrate President Franklin Roosevelt's Pan-American Security Zone that stretched halfway across the Atlantic. Likewise, the U.S. Navy had largely failed to devise contingency plans to protect this dense ship traffic in case America became a belligerent. The events of December 1941 changed all that, and Admiral Dönitz was not going to waste the opportunity to decimate American shipping by allowing this quasi-Edenic state of innocence, unpreparedness, and naiveté to continue until the United States had organized its coastal defenses, instituted a functioning convoy system, and set up competent aerial surveillance of the threatened shipping lanes. The result was Operation Drumbeat (*Paukenschlag*), the six-month-long U-boat onslaught on Allied merchant traffic in American waters, often labeled the "Second Happy Times."[65] Oskar Kusch would be in on this feast from the beginning, as indeed every one of his remaining five patrols in *U-103* and *U-154* would take him to the Western Hemisphere or close to it.

With a new I.W.O. and a new chief engineer on board, Winter and Kusch left Lorient for New World waters on January 3, 1942, just three weeks after the United States had joined the Allies. Both outward bound and on their way home they sailed on a southerly route just north of the Azores to reach America's mid-Atlantic coast to minimize detection and to avoid fierce winter storms along the otherwise more economical great-circle trajectory farther north. Given the distance to their area of operations, their stay there would be limited to a few weeks, but *U-103* made the most of it. Within a spate of three days in early February, and with minimal interference from the U.S. Navy, the boat sank three large American tankers and a Panamanian freighter off the shores of New Jersey and Delaware while other German boats, including a few Type VII ones, extended the carnage all along the coast from Canada to Florida.[66] On the way back, on February 24 and in the middle of the Atlantic, *U-103*'s aft hydroplane suddenly jammed, and it was athletic and fearless Kusch to the rescue despite the frigid waters. That night, with the boat's engines stopped, Kusch put on his *tauchretter*, a breathing device for work or escapes under water, and tried for forty-five minutes to ascertain the nature of the problem. After four separate dives, however, as *U-103*'s war diary recorded, "the effort has to be abandoned because the ocean swell is too severe for him to stay close to the boat and it is not possible for him to reach the required depth."[67] Fortunately the problem disappeared soon afterward.

Once returned to Lorient without further incident on March 1, and since there was little combat damage to repair except the usual wear and tear, the boat was quickly turned around in just six weeks. Refueled, reprovisioned, with a fresh supply of torpedoes and an exciting new assignment in the Caribbean and Gulf of Mexico, *U-103* was back at sea and westward bound on April 15, 1942. Joined by Lieutenant Hellmuth Pich of Crew 34 as a supernumerary watch officer (with a remarkable career ahead of him in the Far East as commanding officer of *U-168*), Winter and his men encountered and sank northeast of Bermuda a freighter carrying war materiel for the British Eighth Army fighting in the North African desert. They then steered straight for the Windward Passage between Cuba and Hispaniola and entered the Caribbean undetected, in the process traversing the very waters Christopher Columbus had sailed 450 years before on his first voyage to a bewildering New World. If the famous Genoese captain often compared these rich, lush, and unspoiled parts to an earthly paradise in his letters and diaries, the same notion, in a slightly modified sense, must have occurred to Winter, Kusch, and the rest of *U-103*'s men when considering the Caribbean's balmy climate and bountiful hunting grounds. Sailing singly, with minimal air cover, and still without naval escorts, these Allied tankers and steamers carrying oil, nitrate, coffee, bananas, and general cargo moved freely from port to port, occasionally zigzagging as their only precaution against U-boat attack. Using its torpedoes and the deck gun supervised by Kusch, *U-103* sank no fewer than eight vessels in just eleven days between May 17 and May 28 in the northwest Caribbean, with the Yucatán Channel and the waters around the Cayman Islands yielding especially rich results. Winter's kindness to the survivors on their rafts and lifeboats and the relative proximity to land allowed all but 36 of the 318 men on these vessels to survive. He could not, of course, take any of the shipwrecked sailors onto his already crammed boat. Having used up all its torpedoes and escaping the Caribbean once more through the Windward Passage, *U-103* had a relatively uneventful voyage home to Lorient where it arrived on June 22 after sixty-nine days at sea and with credit for having destroyed 42,169 tons of enemy shipping on this patrol alone—an achievement high enough to earn Winter a Knight's Cross and Kusch an Iron Cross, First Class.[68]

Just as Viktor Schütze had been replaced by Werner Winter as *U-103*'s commanding officer the year before and put in charge of the entire flotilla, now Winter was making room for a new skipper, Lieutenant Gustav-Adolf Janssen of Crew 36, and was himself rewarded by taking over the First U-Boat Flotilla of Type VII boats at Brest up the Breton coast from Lorient. Kusch in the meantime was promoted to First Watch Officer of *U-103* with the expectation of taking over a boat of his own after the next patrol and upon passing the required additional courses for submarine commanders conducted at the U-boat training facilities on the Baltic Sea. If a solid friendship had developed between Werner Winter and Oskar Kusch, the latter's relations with Janssen would become even more cordial, perhaps because they were only one year apart in age, both ranked high in their respective Crews, and the mutual reliance and trust between a commanding officer and his No. 2 and deputy on board were usually more intimate than interactions with other officers. Janssen, like Winter a native of Hamburg, had most recently been in charge of *U-37*, an early Type IX boat that had been retired to the U-Boat Training Command in the Baltic in 1941 after eleven successful patrols in the Atlantic. *U-103*'s new skipper continued to allow open-ended discussions about Germany's military situation and general fortunes in the confines of the boat's officer quarters and was quite aware that Kusch opposed the then-prevailing political arrangements in Germany.[69] Janssen's postwar assessment of his former I.W.O. could not have been more positive:

> Kusch was a young naval officer of excellent manners, superior intelligence, superb education, and very solid expertise in his field. In combat situations as a watch officer under my direction on *U-103*, he demonstrated courage, determination, and vigor. In dealings with superior officers and comrades he was somewhat reserved, but never a loner. Motivated by a thirst for knowledge and a deep sense of responsibility he thoroughly enjoyed tackling all sorts of problems and to discuss them with others. . . . He treated his subordinates in a correct but always comradely way and was well respected and popular as a result. I know that he

> continued this kind of relationship with his men when he took over his own boat.[70]

Clearly, no one who knew him well entertained the slightest doubt about Kusch's leadership qualifications as a future U-boat commander or about the way he interacted with those entrusted to his care and responsibility. Above all, his political persuasions, whether known or suspected, did not in the least interfere with his sense of duty or with the respect and esteem fellow officers or enlisted men extended to him. In this context, Kusch's friend Kurt Wiemer recalled the following in 1950: "Kusch was foremost of all a soldier and an officer. That was his ideal. I do not know how far his artistic tendencies came into play. . . . It was a profession to which he was dedicated body and soul."[71] Earlier Wiemer had described a series of meetings he had with Kusch that summer in France: "In August 1942, I saw him in Lorient where we talked almost daily before his boat was due to leave on patrol again, except when he went home on leave. It became very clear from our talks that under Lieutenant Janssen it was possible to discuss Germany's military and political situation without anyone involved entertaining the slightest notion of reporting such conversations to a higher naval command or to Nazi Party officials."[72]

After three extended patrols in rapid succession, an achy *U-103* and its tired men deserved a longer respite before venturing out again on October 21, 1942. Kusch managed to get away to Berlin on leave and, in anticipation of receiving soon a boat of his own, spent five weeks in Memel on the Baltic with a U-boat training flotilla from July 16 to August 16 to perfect his skills in firing torpedoes, especially at night and when the boat was at periscope depth. Such expertise would be in high demand in the future as the days when U-boats could spend the majority of their time safely on the surface, even during attacks on enemy shipping, were rapidly drawing to a close. Indeed, the careers and war diaries of *U-103* and Kusch's later boat *U-154* mirror the changing nature of the war in 1942–43 perfectly. Through June 1942, except in the Bay of Biscay, they and other Atlantic boats had little to fear from aerial or surface attacks in the open stretches of the ocean. If they still dived from time to time they did so to test the skills of the crew and the mechanical strength and stability of the boat, to give the lookouts and radio operators a break, or to escape stormy weather on the surface for a while, rather than due to any imminent detection by the enemy. They sailed to their designated areas of operation swiftly and unmolested, using their diesels to trek along and simultaneously to recharge the batteries that drove the electrical motors that were required to move the boat when submerged. It was the need for oxygen and the generation of lethal exhaust fumes inside the boat that prohibited running the powerful diesels under water—a major limitation not much relieved later in the war by the introduction of so-called snorkels. With the boat running at periscope depth, these devices under ideal conditions sucked in fresh air from the outside for the diesel engines and expelled the deadly fumes, but in practice the snorkel heads often cut under the water surface and exposed those inside the boat to horrific and painful changes in air pressure, if not leaving them on the brink of suffocation. Staying on the surface for a while also allowed the men to refresh the hot, humid, and fetid air inside and to take a turn on the conning tower for a cigarette break or to work on their tans.

After June 1942 all this changed. The "Second Happy Times" off the American Eastern Seaboard came rapidly to a close by midyear never to be revived as Canada and the United States organized an effective aerial surveillance system hundreds of miles out to sea, herded merchant ships into well-guarded convoys, and required nightly blackouts in coastal communities. Meanwhile, their increasingly experienced naval and Coast Guard submarine chasers began to exert an ever-fiercer toll on their unwanted intruders from Europe. Admiral Dönitz had little choice but to pull back his precious boats from American coastal waters into the bloody convoy lanes of the North Atlantic or into the Mediterranean, and to dispatch his long-distance Type IX boats to the peripheral reaches of the Central and South Atlantic with only occasional visitors continuing to menace the weakly defended Caribbean and Gulf of Mexico. Never again would German Atlantic U-boats equal or exceed their sinking of 635,126 tons of enemy shipping in the month of June 1942, while only losing two boats of their own. Whereas Germany's monthly losses in Atlantic waters had averaged between two and three U-boats since the beginning of the war, they now rose quickly to over eight per month for the rest of 1942 and to over twenty per month for all of 1943.[73] To be sure, more boats were operational now than ever, but the yield per boat per day at sea plummeted from over 350 tons when *U-103* was active in the Caribbean to well below 50 tons by the time Kusch took *U-154* out on his first patrol in the spring of 1943—a precipitous and disastrous decline.[74] This was the crisis of the U-boat war, and the Allies were triumphing thanks to superior resources, organization, and intelligence.

Little wonder, then, that Gustav-Adolf Janssen's orders for *U-103* did not include a return trip to the Caribbean but an assignment to stalk the West African coast and the Central Atlantic in the general vicinity of the Azores instead. It would be a long affair of seventy days, facilitated in part by taking on at sea some seventy tons of fuel and assorted provisions from *U-509*, which was returning to base after using up all its torpedoes in a successful mission under Werner Witte of Crew 34.[75] But while *U-509* had been able to sink seven enemy vessels in those same waters, Janssen was not as lucky. After firing a coup de grâce at the *Tasmania*, a British merchantman previously damaged by *U-659* north of Madeira on the last day of October, he and Kusch cruised up and down and back and forth in the balmy northeast trade winds for the entire month of November without the slightest reward for their exertions. Amazingly, they missed completely the Allied armada carrying American and British troops to their landing sites around Safi, Casablanca, Oran, and Algiers on November 8, 1942, as part of Operation Torch. Only on December 6, by then well northwest of the Azores, did they manage to sink the British freighter *Henry Stanley* that had originally belonged to Convoy ON-149. This time, they took the vessel's master on board for questioning and brought him back to Lorient from where he was moved to an internment camp in Germany. The rest of the ship's crew took to its lifeboats with Janssen providing them with emergency supplies and the compass direction to the nearest land, but sadly none of the sixty-three men were ever seen alive again.[76]

U-103's last chance to harm the enemy on this mission came on December 13 when it encountered in those same waters the large, brand-new, fast, and unescorted British freighter *Hororata* of 13,945 tons en route from Auckland in New Zealand to Liverpool, England, by way of Cape Town. After a prolonged surface chase at full speed and in poor visibility, Janssen fired one torpedo at dusk that hit the merchantman but did not cripple it enough to prevent it from escaping in the gathering gloom to Santa Cruz in the Azores. Following an emergency repair there and additional attention in nearby Horta, the ship moved on to Britain for permanent repairs. No lives were lost.[77] Having refueled one more time in midocean from the Type XIV U-tanker *U-463* on December 23, *U-103* reached Lorient safely on December 29, 1942. Kusch now took leave of his friend Gustav-Adolf Janssen and the good men on *U-103* with whom he had shared so many adventures in so many distant places on four lengthy patrols over the past year and a half. Once back in Berlin for a well-deserved break from his daily duties and drudgery at sea, he learned in a telephone call from staff headquarters that he was to take command of *U-154*, another boat belonging to the Second U-Boat Flotilla, once it had come back to Lorient from its latest mission under Lieutenant Commander Heinrich Schuch.[78] Those bulky bunkers in Lorient would remain Kusch's home away from home.

The mood among Kusch's family and friends in Berlin in early 1943, and of course his own, were substantially more depressed than a year before following the declaration of war on the United States. Not only were matters going mightily wrong in the Atlantic, as Kusch knew from personal experience with many of his comrades already dead, in captivity, or on the shelf. But also the news from North Africa and Russia was becoming ever more alarming. While official Nazi propaganda tried to camouflage or belittle the imminent catastrophes on the eastern front and in the Tunisian desert, letters and postcards from the frontlines, soldiers and sailors on leave, enemy broadcasts, the many death notices to parents and spouses, and the fearful air campaign against Germany's cities, industrial facilities, and infrastructure—all of these factors left little doubt about Germany's worsening predicaments and eventual fate.

Indeed, what was left of Field Marshal Paulus' Sixth Army in the Stalingrad pocket—some 90,000 of its original strength of over 300,000 men—surrendered to the Soviets on February 2, 1943, and an even larger force of Germans and Italians laid down its arms and entered Allied captivity when the Africa Corps gave up its last positions on African soil by early May.

Kusch must have been profoundly concerned about the well-being and fate of his old mentor Rudi Pallas, by then a German staff surgeon in the wintry hell at Stalingrad. It is not known whether Kusch ever learned that Pallas survived as a prisoner of war and, while in Russian captivity, would join Field Marshal Paulus and other German prisoners of war in the *Bund Deutscher Offiziere* (League of German Officers) who later merged with the anti-fascist and pro-communist *Nationalkommitee Freies Deutschland* (National Committee for a Free Germany, or NKFD). The latter called for strict opposition to Hitler and helped Russian propaganda undermine the German military offensive against the Soviet Union.

Then there was his old friend Dieter Berger, like Pallas an implacable opponent of everything the Nazis represented. Berger would remember seeing Kusch in Berlin in those days:

> After I had lost my right arm on the Eastern Front as a lieutenant in the *Luftwaffe*, I met my friend Kusch again after a long interval late in 1942 or early in 1943. We knew each other from our days together in Dr. Pallas's youth group. We talked at length about the military and political situation and agreed that Germany could only survive if National Socialism were destroyed. Both his girlfriend in those days and later fiancée, Inge von Foris, and I encouraged Kusch in these views directed against National Socialism and the war. Inge von Foris was an especially passionate opponent of National Socialism.[79]

Another good friend from his school days, Wolfgang Kühns-Bernsau, whom he visited every time he happened to be in Berlin, urged Kusch to be more careful and circumspect, especially in his remarks to fellow officers, for "there are many people who disagree with you and may want to do you in." Kusch reportedly replied, "I don't care. They are educated people of whom I demand that they think for themselves and reach their own individual conclusions" rather than repeat and believe blindly the fare dished up by Nazi propaganda.[80] It thus must have been with a mixture of gloom, bitterness, and apprehension, but also invigorated in his hatred of the regime and perhaps emboldened to act on his convictions, that Kusch took leave of his friends and boarded the train back to France.

As always, he passed through Paris, to where U-Boat Command headquarters had been pulled back the previous March from its quaint chateau outside Lorient and from where it would retreat all the way to Berlin two months later, thus symbolizing Germany's increasingly defensive posture. In addition, on January 30, 1943, the U-boat arm's founder and leader, Admiral Karl Dönitz, was promoted to grand admiral and replaced Erich Raeder as commander in chief of the entire *Kriegsmarine* in a move that rewarded Dönitz's steadfast loyalty to the regime and signaled, as in World War I, the ascendency of the submarine branch over the surface fleet as Germany's most potent weapon at sea. Nominally Admiral Hans-Georg von Friedeburg now assumed control over all U-boat operations, but inasmuch as the submarine force essentially equaled what remained of Germany's offensive naval strength, Dönitz's promotion did not remove him far from his former responsibilities. In another change in command with future consequences for Kusch, Commander Ernst Kals of Crew 24 replaced Viktor Schütze as chief of the Second U-Boat Flotilla that January.

In the meantime, *U-154* had returned from its latest patrol on January 7, 1943, and begun a lengthy overhaul in the safety of its concrete pen on the Kéroman Peninsula in Lorient. There, on a cold day in early February and apparently without the old or the new skipper actually being physically present, the official change-of-command occurred in which Kusch assumed responsibility over his boat from Heinrich Schuch who moved on to a series of staff positions after a distinguished career at sea. Among the other officers headed to Lorient in those days was

Kusch's future I.W.O. and second-in-command, *Oberleutnant zur See* Ulrich Abel, a thirty-year-old reserve officer with a doctorate in law and a membership card of the Nazi Party. Abel had never served on a frontline U-boat before.

CHAPTER 3

LIEUTENANT ABEL

U*-154*'s NEW FIRST WATCH OFFICER, Ulrich Abel, was born in Leipzig on March 3, 1912, the son of Gustav Abel, who worked as an editor in the publishing trade, and his wife, Gudrun, née Steinbrück, a schoolteacher.[1] He had an older and a younger brother. During Ulrich's elementary school years, which coincided with the turbulent aftermath of World War I, the Abel family changed its place of residency four times, including stays in Berlin and in Frankfurt on the Oder River, before settling in northern Pomerania near the Baltic Sea. Here, between 1923 and 1929, Abel completed his secondary education at the humanistic gymnasium at Greifenberg, earning the coveted *Abitur*, then as today key to advanced professional and academic careers in Germany. Ulrich was barely seventeen when he graduated from his school on Easter 1929, suggesting a young man of uncommon scholastic ability and promise.

Relatively little is known about Abel's childhood and adolescent years. He did enjoy a close relationship with his father who offered a respected role model for his children in terms of integrity, hard work, and shouldering responsibility for his family in trying times. Gustav Abel was fond of taking his boys on hiking and biking excursions and instilled in them a profound love of nature. While it is uncertain whether Ulrich belonged to a *völkisch* or *bündisch* youth group in those years, the likelihood that he did seems high, given the experience of other boys of his educational and social background. Ulrich's mother rarely participated in family outings, however, as she was plagued by recurring health problems whose precise nature she and her husband concealed from their children, but which severely limited the range of her physical activities. As a consequence, Mrs. Abel had to suspend her employment as a schoolteacher from time to time and instead took to giving private lessons to help out with family finances. In short, against the backdrop of the challenging years of the Weimar Republic, Ulrich Abel grew up in a caring middle-class family for whom respectability, professional integrity, hard work, as well as a fondness for learning, nature, and culture appear to have been central values.

At some point in the late 1920s, Ulrich Abel informed his family of his desire to become an officer in Germany's merchant marine instead of pursuing studies at a university, as was perhaps expected of him. Ulrich's envisioned career goal may well have stemmed from his closeness to nature, from the ever-alluring romance of the sea, and from the same acute yearning to encounter faraway places and people that motivated Oskar Kusch to join the youth movement and later the *Kriegsmarine*. While an *Abitur* was not an absolute prerequisite for a future merchant marine officer, it certainly gave Ulrich Abel an advantage over competitors who often had terminated their formal schooling prematurely. At any rate, Gustav Abel backed his son's decision enthusiastically.

Ulrich underwent a prescribed two-year apprenticeship "before the mast" on German commercial sailing vessels that would allow him to learn the art, craft, and science of navigation and seamanship literally from the bottom up, besides satisfying a prerequisite for enrolling in a nautical school and obtaining an officer's patent later. His endeavors under sail took him to the West Indies on the square-rigger *Grossherzogin Elisabeth* and around Cape Horn to Chile on the barque *Bremen* of the North German Lloyd Shipping Line. By 1931 Abel switched to steam-propelled freighters of the same line, completing five additional transatlantic voyages, two to Brazil and three to the East and Gulf Coasts of the United States, primarily to earn enough money to attend one of Germany's prestigious and demanding nautical schools.[2]

By August 1932, when Ulrich Abel was twenty years old, the deepening worldwide depression began to overwhelm the German merchant marine as countless vessels were tied up in ports everywhere because of a lack of business. This meant instant unemployment for their crews, with those last hired and without family to support usually becoming the first ones to be let go. Abel was not spared: three years after embracing his youthful vision of one day captaining merchant ships and passenger liners across the seven seas, he discovered himself out of work, without prospects of being rehired in the foreseeable future, and facing the urgent need for a new beginning, even though his superiors testified that his character and performance as an officer recruit had been praiseworthy in every respect.[3]

Worse, Abel's father had succumbed to a sudden illness two years before, an emotional blow that hit Ulrich so hard and unexpectedly that for years afterward it pained him even to mention the loss of the one individual to whom he owed all and who had been at the center of his life for so long.[4] Still, Abel did have his *Abitur* and with it the opportunity to attend a university in preparation for a respectable academic or professional career. Not without causing additional financial hardship for his family—his mother tried desperately and ultimately unsuccessfully to eke out a position in the publishing or the book-selling trade—but undoubtedly with their encouragement, on November 2, 1932, Abel enrolled at the nearby University of Greifswald to study law. Here, toward the end of his first semester, he witnessed the Nazi seizure of power and Adolf Hitler's installation as Germany's chancellor on January 30, 1933.

Abel, a handsome young man of medium height and a somewhat compact appearance that suggested strength and endurance, turned out to be a dedicated and diligent student despite distracting demands on his time and attention. In Greifswald he shared with his mother a two-room apartment for which he paid in part through a meager government student loan, by working extra hours in the university dining hall, and by tutoring gymnasium students in various subjects. During his fourth semester, from December 1934 through September 1935, he took time out for a ten-month reserve training course in the *Reichsmarine* (soon to be renamed *Kriegsmarine*), presumably for patriotic reasons, certainly to satisfy his undiminished love of the sea, but also to keep open the option of renewing his nautical career in case he did not pass his legal and civil service exams or found the legal profession too dull in the long run.[5]

In 1935 Abel also met for the first time the woman whom he would marry three years later. Herta Freese, like many young women in her situation, had been forced to abandon her schooling at the gymnasium in Greifswald when her father's textile business went under in the continuing economic downturn. As an interim measure, in order not to burden her parents financially, she accepted the position of an au pair on the rural estate of Wampen near Greifswald. It so happened that a scion of this family fell seriously ill and had to miss school for many months. To make up, the family chose to engage a university student as a house teacher on weekday afternoons to keep the boy from falling behind in his scholastic duties. Abel, eager to steady his financial situation, jumped at the opportunity, even though it entailed a daily commute by bicycle from Greifswald out into the countryside.

The inevitable encounters between the tutor and the au pair, although discouraged by the estate's owners, eventually blossomed into a full romantic relationship. By the next year the couple became engaged and Miss Freese decided to abandon her poorly paying job on the estate so she could move back to Greifswald and enroll in a trade school for professional training as an accountant. Again, money was a problem because neither her parents nor Abel's mother could contribute financially to the six-month course that required tuition payments of some RM 700 at the private school. Just when all hopes seemed to have evaporated that the endeavor might ever come off, Miss Freese's old host family on the Wampen estate offered to advance her the money, to be paid back at her convenience once she held down a steady job of her own. Overjoyed, she enrolled in October 1936 and by April 1937 found work as a bookkeeper at the busy Arado Aircraft Manufacturing Company in Anklam, some fifty kilometers southeast of Greifswald on the rail line to Stettin. This arrangement meant that Abel and his fiancée would be able to see each other for the foreseeable future only on Sundays and holidays.

In the meantime, Ulrich Abel pushed ahead with his legal studies, passing his first state exam in May 1936 before the superior state court in Stettin. This accomplishment allowed him to join the Greifswald district and lower state courts on July 1, 1936, as a junior staff member. In this position Abel could presumably have concentrated his attention on his daily routine and on preparing himself for the crucial second and final state exam that was to follow three years later, with the prospect of securing a permanent legal career in either the public or private sector. Instead, in addition to taking care of his regular duties and assignments as a *Gerichtsreferendar* in Greifswald, he not only remained active at the University's law school as an unpaid research and teaching assistant, but also took on the extra burden of completing a doctoral dissertation.[6] He successfully defended the latter, titled "The Basic Structure and Historical Foundations of Germany's Maritime Labor Laws," on April 13, 1938. His doctoral focus covered primarily the historical development of labor relations in the German merchant marine and even suggested how such relations might evolve further in the future.[7]

With just over a year left before his second state exam, Abel began to send out feelers about future employment opportunities. Not surprisingly—given his former service in the merchant marine, his reserve status in the *Kriegsmarine*, and the topic he had chosen for his dissertation—he was especially interested in a position, governmental or corporate, that would continue to connect him to matters maritime or allow him to practice law in a port city. Remembering his stint with the North German Lloyd Shipping Line in Bremen, he now inquired whether the company foresaw job openings in its higher administration for men of Abel's background. The response could not have been more encouraging: "We are not only highly interested in offering you employment but will facilitate in every way your relocation [from Greifswald to Bremen] when the time comes, including assistance in finding you a place to live."[8]

The important professional milestone of completing his dissertation, along with the assurance of a reasonably secure and exciting career ahead, became the signal for Abel and his fiancée to tie the knot after their long engagement in a civil ceremony at the Greifswald city hall on December 28, 1938. Abel was twenty-six at the time, his bride five years younger. There would be no formal church ceremony inasmuch as Abel had renounced his affiliation with the Christian church, describing himself instead as "*gottgläubig*" ("believing in God")—a blurry and deliberately imprecise term popular among adherents of National Socialism who had broken with traditional Christianity but tried to avoid being called atheists.[9] For the newlyweds there was neither time nor money for a honeymoon. It would have to wait until the following summer.

Indeed, throughout their five-and-a-half years of marriage, and despite the arrival of two sons and a daughter, Ulrich and Herta Abel would see very little of one another and never quite experienced that unconditional intimacy of married life, that open and open-ended sharing of one's deepest thoughts, feelings, and apprehensions, which would very likely have become the norm in a longer-lasting marital union in less chaotic times. Their difference in professional pursuits may also have inhibited their emotional closeness and the frank exchange of views. Mrs. Abel noticed how her husband sometimes avoided talking about unpleasant or controversial subjects and instead sought to reassure his young wife by coming across as deliberately "straightforward, uncomplicated and relaxed," besides being an ideal family man, "helpful, friendly and perfectly decent."[10] Abel knew, for instance, that his wife had traveled little while he had been to many faraway places. As his widow would recall, "he enjoyed sharing stories and encounters from his days in the merchant marine to engage my imagination and to allow me to become a part of his world."[11] Once, during the war, when Abel had returned from a mission and spent a few days with his family, he avoided his wife's direct questions about his time at sea and instead tried to direct her thoughts toward other matters: "Why should I tell you that our patrols are no walks in the park? You know that already and I am perfectly aware that you worry about me all the time. On top of that, you suffer far too much from the war here at home without us out there being able to shield you from it. Let's talk about the future and the times when waking up together in the morning will not be restricted to my precious days on leave."[12]

In the end, the sheer force of circumstances appears to have been decisive in shaping Abel's relationship with his wife and hers with him.

"Friends who knew both of us later said that our honeymoon could not possibly ever have come to an end," Mrs. Abel remembers. "We wanted to start a life together but were never given a real chance. We never even faced the stress of everyday life together, the kind which can often strain a marriage to the point of separation."[13] Not surprisingly, Mrs. Abel shows little but scorn for those who claim to have known her husband intimately and consequently feel competent to judge his actions and his character more accurately than she, who had observed Ulrich Abel as closely as anyone through nine years of acquaintance, engagement, and marriage. Her picture of him remained forever after that of a thoroughly decent human being, of a dedicated father and loving husband, and of a hardworking professional, whether at sea or in the legal service, whose energy was absorbed in caring for his family and in worrying, once the war had been unleashed, about the fate and survival of his country.

The evolution of Abel's political views, in particular the origins of his association with the National Socialist Party and its ideology, continues to pose a curious enigma, not least to his widow. It is not possible in retrospect to reconstruct the political persuasions that characterized the Abel family during the 1920s. The father's profession in the publishing business presumably encouraged political discussion and engagement, but it remains a matter of speculation whether this activity tended to favor the political left or the right. Abel's two brothers do not appear to have exercised a profound formative influence on him inasmuch as his contact with them became sporadic and virtually ceased with the onset of the war.[14] It seems more plausible that Ulrich Abel's affinity with Hitler's party date from his apprenticeship in the merchant marine between 1929 and 1932, before he took up his legal studies. His widow implied as much when she stated, "I would suspect that my husband decided in favor of the [National Socialist] party while he was an ordinary seaman trying to earn money to attend nautical school. With growing unemployment nobody on board could be sure whether there would be another job waiting when they got home from their voyages. People who were smarter than I in those days have told me later that Hitler's promises raised genuine hopes among those who were about to lose their jobs."[15]

Germany's merchant marine was indeed a ripe target for Nazi advances and propaganda. Few branches of the Weimar Republic's economy had been hit as hard and as often as its *Handelsmarine*. First, it suffered from the long-term effects of the reparations imposed under the Versailles Treaty, which required the surrender of every German merchant vessel larger than sixteen hundred tons to the winners of the war to compensate for Allied tonnage sunk by German U-boats.[16] Gone, too, were the days when the Kaiser's *Weltpolitik* created a virtual trade monopoly with German colonies and other German interests around the globe. The regular Weimar *Reichsmarine* was a pitiful shadow of its former powerful presence with little new construction or crossover job opportunities that might have acted as a stimulus for the merchant sector. Competition for cargo and passengers was fierce on the transatlantic routes, with Britain claiming the lion's share of the business and the profits. Finally, the Great Depression after 1929 literally emptied the seas of German ships as the worldwide recession dried up the global market for the better part of a decade and sent German merchant marine officers and men to the unemployment office or in search of alternative careers.

In this milieu Abel, then in his late teens or just turned twenty, may very well have taken to National Socialism and joined the party, either as a promising solution to his immediate woes or as the most likely avenue to renewed national greatness and international prestige for Germany, or both. He spent three long years almost entirely either aboard ships or in sailors' dormitories ashore between voyages.[17] With few distractions to occupy his mind otherwise, he may have had time to ponder the future of Germany and the fate of the merchant marine, especially in the company of fellow sailors who had already come around to embrace Hitler's worldview. Several young merchant marine officers who managed a career switch to the regular navy in the early 1930s, have testified to the intensity of National Socialist, especially SA (storm troopers), activity aboard passenger liners and regular merchantmen. Special shipboard party organizations (*SA-Bordgruppen*) sprang up on many German vessels "and peer pressure often made membership a social necessity." Party functionaries would claim control over a good portion of their fellow members' private lives, and sometimes "lowly stewards and stokers with senior party membership tried to bully superior officers who had signed up more recently."[18] Not surprisingly, German shipyard owners and shipping industry magnates welcomed Hitler's takeover enthusiastically in the not unreasonable anticipation that naval rearmament would mean busy construction activity and economic revival at home and bring the resumption of trade and commerce on a global scale.[19] Their expectations were not disappointed.

Abel joined the Nazi Party formally on June 1, 1932, as member No. 996967, eight months before Hitler's accession to power.[20] He was then twenty years old, single, and listed his occupation as ordinary seaman. His local affiliation was originally with the subgroup "Seafaring Members" in the Pomerania District before being switched to "Greifswald-North" when he entered law school. Abel's party membership remained dormant briefly after December 1934 during the longest of several stints on active military duty, but resumed when he received an honorable discharge on September 30, 1935. It would be suspended again, but never cancelled, when he was called up for active duty in 1939.

In light of future developments, just how deeply did Abel identify with official Nazi ideology in the 1930s, and did any such commitment translate into specific activities or party offices and responsibilities for him? His widow recalled that in her first encounter with Abel in 1935, he wore a swastika pin on the lapel of his jacket. She did not remember asking him about its meaning at the time and insisted that between the beginning of his courtship in 1935 and the onset of the war in 1939, indeed until his death in 1944, her husband's relationship to Nazi ideology and the Nazi Party must have been essentially perfunctory and passive. True, he renounced his church membership presumably for ideological reasons, but "did he really have any time to get involved in politics?" "Until 1939," his widow stated, "I usually did not see him for six out of the seven days of the week, but when we were together at last we did talk about our activities and experiences. Why should he have kept from me any possible participation in political meetings, demonstrations, and the like? . . . Surely, he would have told me without me prompting him what he knew about National Socialism at the time and whether he regarded himself as a fighter for its cause."[21] In particular, Mrs. Abel rejected as preposterous and chronologically utterly implausible a suggestion by one of *U-154*'s officers that Abel held for a while the position of a local group leader (*Ortsgruppenführer*) of the Nazi Party in Hamburg.[22]

Ulrich Abel's busy schedule, filled with strenuous legal studies, taking on odd jobs to make ends meet, writing a dissertation, looking for permanent employment as a trained lawyer, and spending every free minute on weekends with his future bride, all appear to rule out anything beyond a superficial involvement with the Nazi Party organization while not excluding a deeper agreement with its ideology. The roots of this affinity were evidently planted in his days as a teenager in the merchant marine. Presumably Abel also felt vindicated and confirmed in his political instinct by the remarkable economic recovery, triumphs in foreign policy, and successful military rearmament his country enjoyed under Hitler between 1933 and 1939. In addition, the latter experience seems to have induced Abel to change his mind about seeking a job with a private company and instead to enter the civil service permanently. In February 1939 he withdrew his application to work as a corporate lawyer for the North German Lloyd Shipping Line and moved from Greifswald to his favorite city of Hamburg to accept a judicial position there. Later that year, on September 15, 1939, while on temporary leave from his wartime command, Abel passed his second state exam with the overall assessment of "good" and was elevated to the permanent civil service rank of *Gerichtsreferendar*.[23] In 1943, while serving under Kusch on *U-154*, he was promoted in absentia to *Gerichtsassessor* at the Superior District Court (*Oberlandesgerichtsbezirk*) in Hamburg.[24] Abel never actively exercised these formal judicial positions in the German civil service because of his wartime duties.

If the young couple had hoped the move to Hamburg would introduce stability and normalcy to their married life, they were soon disappointed. Within months of their relocation, harbingers of impending war multiplied, and already on July 17, 1939, some six weeks before the actual outbreak of hostilities, Abel received orders to report for duty with the staff of the Seventeenth Minesweeper Flotilla at the rank of reserve *Bootsmann* (Petty Officer First Class). This particular squadron, to be formed from eight converted high-seas fishing trawlers numbered *M-1701* through *M-1708*, existed as yet on paper only and would not be officially constituted until September 22, 1939.[25] While the old coal-firing boats underwent their refit from civilian to military purposes in various shipyards with the installation of minesweeping gear and assorted weaponry, Abel participated in an additional training course at the *Kriegsmarine*'s Navigation School in Flensburg-Mürwik. Upon his graduation on August 25, he proudly received his commission as a reserve *Leutnant zur See* (Ensign) and could sport from then on one solid stripe on the sleeves of his uniform jacket. This did not mean, however, that he would be attached to a regular Crew of naval officers the way Kusch belonged to Crew 37a. To celebrate the occasion, and since the trawlers were still being converted into auxiliary minesweepers, the Abels decided on a belated two-week honeymoon on the island of Rügen in the Baltic. On their second morning there, on their way to the beach, they learned that "since the early morning hours [German forces] are returning fire" against Polish aggressors.[26] By noon Abel received a telegram ordering him to return immediately to his squadron. It was Friday, September 1, 1939, and the world was at war once more. One can imagine the profound distress of the newlyweds over this ominous turn of events as, instead of embarking on a safe and sound legal career in one of Germany's most cosmopolitan cities, Abel from that moment on would become no more than an occasional visitor for his wife and their infant children in their apartment in Hamburg-Wandsbek.

Under its squadron leader Lieutenant Commander Hermann Rehder, also a reservist, the Seventeenth Minesweeper Flotilla took up its wartime duties in October 1939 and participated in operations in the western Baltic Sea as well as in the occupation of Denmark and Norway in the spring of 1940. Abel served as the executive officer, that is, second in command, of *M-1705*.[27] This position placed him in charge of a myriad of responsibilities for the vessel and its crew of approximately fifty men, both in routine maneuvers and in encounters with the enemy. Auxiliary minesweepers were conceived as multipurpose vessels whose activities went far beyond clearing waterways of mines and other obstacles to ensure safe navigation. They also functioned as convoy escorts, antiaircraft artillery platforms against enemy air attacks, submarine chasers, improvised transports for personnel and cargo, vessels used for supply, survey, and salvage, and even as minelayers if the situation so demanded. In contrast to the regular minesweeper squadrons whose boats were constructed from the outset for mine detection and removal and were considered a part of the active fleet, auxiliary minesweepers consisted of converted civilian craft of many designs, typically fishing vessels. Both their officers and enlisted crews tended to be reservists and simply kept over from their civilian jobs. After all, there were many similarities between a trawler catching fish and searching for mines. Mrs. Abel recalled that many of her husband's sailors had been fishermen before the war and lived in the Hamburg area, sometimes visiting her at the Abels' apartment when they were on leave to pass along greetings from the front.[28]

In September 1940 Abel, now as commanding officer of a boat of his own, switched to the Fifteenth Minesweeper Flotilla under Commander Friedrich Uebe then operating along the Dutch, Belgian, and French North Sea and Channel coasts, with Rotterdam as its main base.[29] Abel's *M-1503*, with the prewar name of *Holstein*, was another of those old coal-firing vessels, having to take on as many as 230 tons of the black and bulky fuel at a time. On the morning of October 10, just three weeks after Abel had taken it over and while protecting a German coastal convoy, *M-1503* hit a mine off the Dutch coast that caused extensive damage but no fatalities. Besides engine failure and a major water leak, several sea valves had been broken by the explosion. Fortunately, a nearby tug helped pump out the water and *M-1503* managed to limp into Rotterdam for repairs. Abel received much praise from his superiors for his handling of the situation and for saving his boat when, in less capable hands, it could have easily been lost. No doubt his experience in the merchant marine had much to do with his competent performance.

Two months later, *M-1503* rejoined its squadron after major repairs, just as the bitterly cold winter of 1940–41 brought early ice formation even in waters normally too warm for ice buildup. The minesweeper continued routine escort runs from Den Helder in the northern Netherlands to Boulogne in France beyond the Straits of Dover, providing antiaircraft cover and other services for German shipping in those waters. Then, in May 1941, orders arrived to transfer the entire flotilla via the Kiel Canal to Pillau in East Prussia on the Baltic, an operation completed by June 4. Having already received the Iron Cross Second Class in April 1940 when with the Seventeenth Flotilla, Abel could add an Iron Cross First Class to his decorations after arriving in Pillau in recognition of his courage and competence since joining the squadron.

The relocation to the Baltic was not by accident. Within three weeks Hitler would unleash Operation Barbarossa against the Soviet Union. Using Gotenhafen, Pillau, and Memel as bases, the boats of the squadron made their accustomed escort runs, often transporting German soldiers and their equipment to advanced positions along the coastline of the Baltic Provinces and sometimes carrying Russian prisoners of war in the opposite direction. The Soviet response was virtually negligible, as marine hazards and aging machinery became far greater headaches for Abel and his men than any enemy resistance. With winter lurking once more, on November 15 the flotilla received orders to shift to yet another theater of the war after a refit in Kiel, this time to northern Norway. Here Operation Barbarossa had likewise opened a new front against the Soviet Union while other units were already busy there fending off British interference with German naval operations.

Abel's *M-1503* continued to distinguish itself, for instance when it set a new squadron coaling record by averaging sixty tons an hour on November 30 after guiding a convoy from Kristiansand to Egernsund. Late in December, by now well north of the Arctic Circle, it opened fire on an enemy submarine one thousand meters away that had launched two torpedoes against the minesweeper while in the process of diving. In the pursuit Abel dropped seven depth charges, but to his dismay they failed to detonate for unknown reasons. Darkness, fog, snow, ice, cold, and fierce storms, as well as the frequent refusal of Norwegian pilots to assist the invaders in navigating the treacherous fjords, rendered the boat's daily tasks absolutely miserable and exceedingly dangerous. In his year-end summary, the German admiral commanding in those waters found these words of praise for the officers and men aboard the hard-working minesweepers: "Carrying out convoy duties under arctic and difficult navigational conditions, in severe snowstorms, with malfunctioning magnetic compasses, and often without the benefit of local pilots, represents an accomplishment deserving of the highest recognition."[30]

For the old minesweeper and its crew of about fifty, the new year of 1942 offered familiar fare as well as new challenges. In the continuing terrible weather, Abel and his I.W.O., a reserve officer with World War I experience on a U-boat, had to be at their best nautically and on constant lookout for dangers on and under the surface as well as from the air. The following brief excerpts from *M-1503*'s war diary in early 1942 illustrate the constant vigilance required:

> January 4: M-1503 destroys a drifting mine with artillery fire.—January 11: While escorting a convoy from Kirkenes to Tromsö, two steamers run aground and need to be towed free. Hard work. They were at fault.—January 20–27: Convoy Tromsö to Kongfjord. Periscope sighted. Alarm! We drop 19 depth charges on submerged submarine that is visible in the clear water. Later stand down. Many aircraft alerts, mainly our own planes.—February 2: Convoy runs aground, including us. Manage to get everyone off. Later battle stations sound again due to sighting of a submarine and aircraft.—Flotilla commander is full of praise for our boat.[31]

But it would be on February 18, 1942, that Abel and his men had reason to celebrate their most remarkable feat yet in a nine-minute encounter with the Soviet 600-ton submarine *ShCh-403*.

Shortly before midnight, at 2323 in thick fog and while escorting yet another convoy from Billefjord to Kirkenes in the company of the large German minelayer *Brummer*, lookouts spotted a Soviet submarine close by on the surface of the Porsanger Fjord and opened fire immediately. *Brummer*, having scored hits on the submarine with its artillery, then attempted to ram the enemy craft but missed. This allowed the more agile *M-1503* to try the same maneuver at 2328. This time the minesweeper's bow drilled itself into the lower rear section of the Russian submarine's conning tower. In the confusion, with *M-1503* "badly shaken," the Russian boat's severely injured commanding officer, Lieutenant Commander Semyon I. Kovalenko, ended up falling onto the deck of the minesweeper where he was immediately detained, then treated for his leg wounds, and transferred to the *Brummer* the next day. At 2332, *ShCh-403* slipped beneath the surface again and for good measure Abel dropped a couple of depth charges on the spot where the Russian boat had gone under. Neither its commanding officer nor any Germans on the scene ever imagined the submarine could have possibly survived its multiple wounds. But somehow its crew, minus its skipper, managed to close the tower hatch, stabilize the flooding, and get the boat into a controlled dive, eventually to reach their base at Polarny near Murmansk and fight another day after summary repairs. Following numerous abortive attacks on German shipping in Norwegian and Arctic waters, *ShCh-403* disappeared on October 2, 1943, with all hands, most likely the victim of a mine. Kovalenko died under mysterious circumstances in a German POW camp.[32]

Naturally Abel's feat was celebrated within his flotilla and beyond. Commander Uebe's official assessment could not have been more gratifying:

> Nautically as well as militarily the destruction of the Russian U-boat represents a truly superior accomplishment of M-1503's commanding officer. Lieutenant (res.) Abel carried out the attack without a second's hesitation, without wondering whether the enemy's fighting power might be superior to his, with a willingness to take risks, and with full use of his boat's capabilities. The commanding officer and the entire crew of the boat deserve the highest recognition.[33]

The German Admiral of the Norwegian Arctic Coast added that Abel had "exploited his opportunity systematically and with determination," thereby "making a unique contribution to securing and protecting the ship traffic along the Arctic coast."[34] Inasmuch as Abel had added the second stripe of an *Oberleutnant zur See der Reserve* on his sleeves earlier that month and already displayed the Iron Cross First Class on his uniform jacket, his superiors were likely looking for additional ways to reward the bravery and exceptional performance of *M-1503*'s skipper. On June 18, 1942, they awarded Abel the German Cross in Gold, an honor broadly considered to rank just below the Knight's Cross. Even at a time of decoration inflation, and particularly for someone commanding a lowly auxiliary minesweeper, this was something to cherish and by all evidence fully deserved.

The next month brought a respite as *M-1503* underwent repairs at a Norwegian shipyard to fix its mangled bow from the collision with Kovalenko's submarine and to refurbish its tired boilers. The day after rejoining its squadron on March 15, a fire broke out in a storage shed, with the minesweeper's crew earning praise "for helping put out the flames and salvaging the goods stored at the facility." More convoy duty followed and finally the welcome news that the Fifteenth Flotilla would be relieved and replaced in Norwegian waters by the Fifth Flotilla of regular fleet minesweepers that had seen service in the Baltic until then. By April 25, *M-1503* had turned in its polar equipment at the naval arsenal in Kiel and two weeks later began a lengthy overhaul at a shipyard in Antwerp in Belgium. Ulrich Abel, however, would not be around to witness the remaining episodes of his boat's odyssey, which ended with the flotilla's formal breakup early in 1943 after additional service in the English Channel. On July 16, 1942, he formally handed his command over to Ensign Tuleweit and prepared to begin the next and final chapter of his career—and his life—in the German U-boat service.

Whether Abel's move was voluntary may be subject to speculation. Indeed, its modalities could help deflate the widespread myth that everyone who served on U-boats in World War II did so without compulsion. "My husband told me in 1942 that he had received orders to detach four members of his [*M-1503*'s] crew for service on submarines," Mrs. Abel recalled after the war. "When he shared this message with his men, he indicated that he himself would volunteer to be one of the four." She did not know who had issued the order, but "it does not surprise me in the least that my husband wanted to be one of the four. That was in line with his character. I understood and accepted his decision with heightened concern for his wellbeing."[35]

From August 1, 1942, until January 4, 1943, Ulrich Abel received a somewhat abbreviated version of the training routine Oskar Kusch had undergone before assuming his duties as a watch officer on *U-103*. This included two months at the First U-Boat Training Division (1. U.L.D.) at Pillau in East Prussia, then most of October and November at the Torpedo School in Flensburg-Mürwik adjacent to Germany's naval academy, and finally a brief stint over Christmas and New Year's at the Naval Communications School, then as today located on those same premises. Generally, this schedule made sense inasmuch as Abel required no refresher courses in navigation, artillery, or antiaircraft weaponry. Still, what remains surprising and significant in view of future developments is the extremely brief time Abel actually spent on submarines in basic surface and diving exercises at Pillau and in firing torpedoes under simulated frontline conditions. None of his outings on a U-boat in the Baltic prior to his duties on *U-154* could have lasted longer than a day or two, on occasion perhaps just a few hours, and none involved actual combat. In other words, Abel's experience level in handling a submarine under normal circumstances, let alone in helping guide it in an attack or when under attack, was essentially nil, or at the very least vastly inferior to that of Oskar Kusch, a veteran of four long patrols in the Atlantic on a highly successful boat.

CHAPTER 4

FIRST PATROL

A YEAR YOUNGER THAN *U-103* and not quite as experienced or famous by early 1943, *U-154* belonged to the slightly larger Type IX-C version of that remarkably successful class of German long-range submarines. Like *U-103*, it had been built in Bremen and commissioned there on August 2, 1941, by its first skipper Lieutenant Commander Walther Kölle of Crew 26. After obligatory shakedown exercises in the Baltic and subsequent transfer around the British Isles to Lorient, Kölle had taken it out on two patrols to the New World during which he had destroyed seven vessels in the Caribbean and southern Gulf of Mexico. Upon returning prematurely to France in August 1942, Kölle had to be replaced because of serious medical problems.[1] His successor was Lieutenant Commander Heinrich Schuch of Crew 25, a veteran captain with prior distinguished performance on *U-37*, *U-38*, and *U-105*. After only one mission in *U-154* to the Windward Islands and destroying three Allied ships there, Schuch also had to be replaced due to ill health.[2] Thus when Oskar Kusch took over command on February 8, 1943, at age twenty-four, he was by far the youngest skipper the boat had ever had, and Kusch was fortunate and elated to inherit a seasoned crew of petty officers and enlisted men who knew their business and were thoroughly familiar with their boat and its idiosyncrasies.

The same could not be said of Kusch's officer colleagues. One must wonder what prompted the *Kriegsmarine*'s personnel department to mix up the new leadership arrangements aboard *U-154* after Schuch's departure, and why the Second U-Boat Flotilla's staff went along with them. For, except for the second watch officer, twenty-one-year-old Ensign Heinrich Meyer of Crew XII/39, every single officer was new on board, and two of them had never served on a frontline boat. Besides thrity-year-old I.W.O. Dr. Ulrich Abel, who of course had commanded a vessel before and had accumulated much nautical expertise but knew virtually nothing about handling a U-boat, the incoming chief engineer, twenty-one-year-old Ensign (Ing.) Kurt Druschel of Crew X/38, had likewise transferred straight from his training courses at the U-boat engineering school. From the beginning, the patent inexperience of these two officers generated among the crew a distinct "feeling of insecurity"[3] and led to a remarkable act of preventive self-preservation on part of the seasoned petty officers in charge of the boat's technical departments. When learning of Druschel's appointment, and while Kusch was still on leave, a delegation of these veteran petty officers requested a meeting with flotilla commander Ernst Kals. They asked him to keep the boat's departing chief engineer, the experienced and popular Lieutenant (Ing.) Fritz Reinicke, on board for at least the beginning of the next patrol to teach Druschel the ropes. And so it was arranged.[4]

On any submarine, no matter its type, size, or nationality, a competent chief engineer was then and remains today key to the boat's safety, survival, and any successes in combat. Simply understanding and handling the complex technical equipment could be a daunting task. The engineer's know-how and calm self-control was especially in demand when the boat was diving or surfacing and in keeping its desired trim under all circumstances by manipulating the boat's fuel tanks, diving cells, and hydroplanes. Given the ever-lurking danger of a sudden attack from the air, U-boats had to dive frequently and fast. For a Type IX boat like *U-154*, from the moment of the order to dive until the boat was completely under water, ideally no more than 35 seconds were to elapse.[5] Every crewmember had to carry out his pre-assigned duties fast and with absolute precision: clearing all personnel from the bridge and the antiaircraft weaponry platforms; flooding the diving cells; lowering the angle of the hydroplanes; turning off the diesels and switching to the battery-powered electrical motors for underwater propulsion; shutting airtight all hatch covers and valves through which water might otherwise enter the boat; and rushing as many men as possible through the long passageway to the forward torpedo compartment to accelerate the momentum of the dive. Depending on the circumstances, the boat might level out at periscope depth so the skipper could keep surveying the action on the surface or in the air above him, or the boat might descend to its maximum safe diving depth or any level in between. Observing absolute silence when enemy vessels hovered in the vicinity was another must. The entire process would be reversed whenever the boat surfaced, with the engineer ordering the diving cells blown out with compressed air, raising the angle of the hydroplanes, switching the electrical motors over to the diesels while opening the exhaust valves, and having the skipper and the bridge watch reoccupy their lookout and battle stations on top of the conning tower. Little wonder, then, that *U-154*'s long-serving crewmembers should have felt leery about Druschel's youth and inexperience on the job. As one of them put it, "among us 'old hands' he did not enjoy a particularly stellar reputation."[6]

Kurt Druschel, born in 1921, grew up in wooded and hilly Upper Hesse northeast of Frankfurt, where his relatives still operate a picturesque restaurant and hotel today.[7] He entered the Hitler Youth early and rose to a high leadership position, an accomplishment of which he was fond to boast loudly and frequently when posted to *U-154*.[8] Only seventeen at the time, he joined Crew X/38 as an officer cadet and underwent the usual abbreviated training routines. By 1941 he ranked No. 22 out of the 75 ensigns in the engineering branch of his class who were still alive at that time.[9] Clearly the men on *U-154* were in concert and correct in assuming he lacked frontline experience. Druschel also liked to remind others of the stellar career and achievements of his older brother Alfred, one of the most successful, rapidly promoted, and highly decorated aces in the *Luftwaffe*. Reportedly, Alfred Druschel enjoyed special privileges when visiting Hitler's headquarters, including ways of ascertaining his younger brother's position at sea and his likely return date.[10] Interestingly, the boat's navigator and senior petty officer, Heinrich Lüdmann, who only shared the first patrol with Druschel on *U-154*, came away with a more positive impression, characterizing his relationship to him as "very friendly" and even spending three days with Druschel's family in Wiesbaden when on leave.[11]

Besides the boat's held-over engineer Lieutenant Reinicke, Kusch would embark two other supernumeraries on this patrol, the barely nineteen-year-old midshipmen Horst Fröhlich and Hellmuth Kirchammer. Their presence reflected the intensifying officer shortage in the *Kriegsmarine* and the inability to train cadets any longer on sailing vessels or on lazy peacetime cruises to exotic locales. Much of their professional know-how was now acquired on the job and every new class graduating from the naval academy found itself quickly distributed throughout the fleet. The two young men would be useful as additional lookouts on *U-154*'s bridge and in various other capacities as they apprenticed themselves in the boat's weaponry, propulsion, communications, and navigation departments in preparation for more independent assignments later. They would also witness the fallout between Kusch on one side and Abel and Druschel on the other.

By early March, *U-154*'s men, mainly old hands but also some on only their first or second patrol, reassembled in Lorient in anticipation of moving back on board from their temporary quarters ashore and of the boat's imminent departure.[12] Kusch, as one of the last to arrive from his leave in Berlin, organized a "meet-and-greet" evening to introduce himself. Chief radio operator Hans Janker has left this account of the occasion:

> I remember perfectly well how he [Kusch] stood in front of us in his unassuming way and pointed out that, while he was still young in years, he had the heart of an old submariner and was fully aware of the responsibility he would now have to shoulder for his boat and its crew. We were all in agreement that if our "Old Man" was and stayed the way he presented himself we would be fortunate indeed. As they always say, your first impression is the best. Abel and Druschel, too, attracted our scrutiny because they were not only new on board, but also new to the

> U-boat service. Druschel was too young and inexperienced to be chief engineer on a U-boat. . . . Abel adjusted himself to the situation by feigning to be a good buddy. After all he was much too old and too experienced in life not to know how to ingratiate himself with us younger soldiers. A careful observer with a psychological antenna and experience, however, knew immediately that Kusch was the born comrade and Abel and Druschel only pretended to fit that image. Had our skipper conformed to the mold of the typical German naval officer, i.e., been arrogant, vain and unmilitary, the two would have adjusted themselves to such a man accordingly. . . . I should add that from that evening forward I had a tense relationship to Abel and Druschel and later was virtually at loggerheads with them.[13]

Druschel would testify that Kusch closed his address with the observation, "Ideally a commanding officer should be given a little extra push by his men when going into action."[14] He and Abel would later interpret this remark as a sign of Kusch's general reluctance to seek out the enemy, whereas the historian Heinrich Walle—quite to the contrary—has seen it "as the invitation of a military leader apprenticed in the *bündisch* youth movement for his men to line up behind him while displaying initiative, teamwork, and informed obedience and discipline."[15]

Janker's characterizations match remarkably well the impressions and recollections of other witnesses among the boat's petty officers and enlisted personnel. For example, the boat's other radioman, Kurt Isensee, who undertook two patrols under him, found Kusch popular from the beginning "because he did not shout people down. He treated every man as an individual . . . and was evenly kind to everyone."[16]

On or around the same day as Kusch's introductory speech, the following episode occurred, according to the report Ulrich Abel submitted to naval authorities on January 12, 1944:

> When Kusch came on board shortly before our departure in March 1943, he ordered one of our stokers to remove from the

> officers' mess the one and only Führer portrait we had on board and to replace it with a curious picture of a sailing vessel he himself had painted. He did so with the comment, "Take that away, we don't practice idolatry here." We other officers remained silent, but it was clear to us that serving under Kusch in some ways would become a difficult challenge.[17]

Neither Kusch's action and comment, nor Abel's and Druschel's reaction, appear out of character given the men's political persuasions and loyalties. They represented the opening round in a recurring clash of views and personalities destined to end, in just over a year's time, in an early dawn execution for one man and in watery graves for the others. For the record, no standard orders or procedures governed the presence or placement of Hitler likenesses on German warships. Some U-boats carried none; others, such as *U-103*, kept one in the central control room; the one on *U-154* may have originally been a gift of the building shipyard or routinely supplied by the flotilla staff. Kusch later testified that the picture ended up either in his boat's *Zentrale* or in a less conspicuous spot near the officers' wardroom.[18] This was confirmed by his II.W.O. at the time, Lieutenant Arno Funke, who spotted it on the side of a locker pointing away from the mess and restored it to its original location once Kusch had been removed from command.[19] As one historian has commented in a different context, "On a U-boat you did not discuss politics and rarely hung up a Hitler portrait. . . . Instead—and it certainly yielded a more attractive sight—you pinned up pictures of pretty girls."[20]

Having been restored to full combat readiness by the busy German and French shipyard workers in Lorient's U-boat bunkers, and having taken on board its full supply of torpedoes, ammunition, fuel, provisions, and assorted other equipment, *U-154* cast off from its wharf at 1645 on March 20, 1943, and headed out to sea. Kusch and his men must have had the distinct and haunting feeling that things out in the Atlantic were taking a very serious turn for the worse as Allied superiority in ships and aircraft, sensor technology, antisubmarine weaponry, intelligence gathering, training and tactics, operational research, and just plain momentum were becoming palpable. Clearly the "Happy Times" of 1940 and 1942 were gone once and for all. Actually, the men were fortunate to be shielded from realizing the true extent and horror of the catastrophe that was beginning to decimate the German U-boat arm. During the five months from March through July 1943, when *U-154* was on its first mission under Kusch, Germany had available an average of 225 front-line boats in the Atlantic and Arctic Oceans. During that span and in those waters no fewer than 112 U-boats vanished due to various Allied countermeasures, as well as accidents, most of them total losses without survivors.[21] Indeed, in "Black May" 1943 alone, a record total of 41 German submarines went to the bottom.[22] And the most lethal U-boat graveyard of them all lay straight ahead for Kusch and his boat—the Bay of Biscay.

If one draws a line on a map from the tip of the Breton Peninsula to Cape Finisterre (Cabo Fisterra) in Spain, the westernmost point of the continent of Europe, all waters eastward back to the coasts of France and Spain are known as the Bay of Biscay. Often lashed by fierce storms, the bay had to be traversed by any U-boat attempting to gain the open Atlantic or returning to its bases in France. Since early in the war Britain had concentrated many of its antisubmarine measures on this bottleneck. What helped from their perspective was the bay's relative proximity to naval installations and airfields in southwestern England and in Northern Ireland, since the even closer Republic of Ireland as well as Spain and Portugal chose to remain neutral. In addition, the British knew that the German boats had to run a fair amount of time on the surface using their diesel engines to replenish the batteries of their electrical motors and to air out their boats. To take advantage of these technical limitations on the German side, Britain had added mathematicians to its operational research teams not only to figure out the most economical size, sequence, and tracks of its transatlantic convoys and the number and movements of their escorts, but also to optimize the hunt for enemy submarines in the Bay of Biscay. These clever minds had determined that, instead of covering the entire bay all the time, it sufficed to patrol thoroughly a relatively narrow strip of ocean running north to south. In this fashion the British could be virtually assured to catch German outbound and inbound boats on the surface day or night with their destroyers and corvettes and especially with radar-equipped patrol aircraft, because the U-boats had no choice but to pass through this narrow strip of ocean. Moreover, this heavily patrolled cordon could be moved east or west to keep the Germans off guard. Another technological breakthrough for the Allies was the so-called Leigh Light, a powerful searchlight mounted underneath the wings of bombers and patrol planes that could illuminate a U-boat on the surface at night after it had been located by radar. Flying low and only switching the light on at the last moment before an attack, British aircraft caught many a German boat off guard with little or no resistance—and with often lethal consequences.

By April 1943 these methods had become so effective and irksome that Admiral Dönitz and U-Boat Command instructed the boats to transit the bay as quickly as possible on the surface, where their speed was several times higher than when traveling submerged, and to rely on their antiaircraft weaponry for protection instead of diving for cover. He even suggested for a while, but then thought better of it, that boats form small groups of three or five to combine their defensive firepower against single attackers from the air in those threatened waters.[23] Besides these tactical improvisations, German scientists also developed a passive radar-wave receiver, the so-called Metox set. It could alert U-boats that they were under enemy radar surveillance, particularly from aircraft. In theory Metox was a useful device and concept, but it had several flaws that vastly impaired its effectiveness. Like all radio receivers, it emitted weak signals of its own and could give away the boat's bearing and even location to the enemy. Moreover, it worked best when the Allies used radar frequencies in the one-meter wavelength range and lost much of its usefulness when Allied radar transmissions moved to higher frequencies later in the war. A third handicap of the Metox would actually play a fateful role toward the end of Kusch's patrol, namely, its clumsy antenna with its vertical and horizontal wires affixed to a wooden frame, typically called a "Biscay Cross," including thick, long feed lines that barely fit down the tower hatch in case the boat had to make an emergency dive.

For the first three hours of *U-154*'s emergence into this hostile environment, the boat enjoyed the usual escort of minesweepers, mine-destroyers (*Sperrbrecher*), and coastal patrol craft with their dual purpose of clearing a safe passage out to sea through suspected enemy minefields and warding off any lurking hostile aircraft.[24] After this last act of friendly protection, *U-154* would be on its own as the coastline receded and dusk settled in over the boat with high cirrus clouds shielding the setting sun to the west. The sea was almost calm and low haze limited visibility to ten nautical miles. After midnight, upon leaving the shallower stretches of the continental shelf, Kusch ordered a deep dive forty meters beyond the usual safe limit to test the boat's tightness and stability under maximal water pressure. This must have been a first major competency test for Kurt Druschel as the boat's new engineer. Apparently the yard at Lorient had done a solid job and only minor problems were noted at this time in the form of leaky valves or poorly welded fuel tanks, some of which were located outside the boat's pressure hull, just as the boat carried several spare torpedoes in special containers on the upper deck.

The next days brought any number of anxious moments as *U-154* sailed straight through the most dangerous section of the outer Bay of Biscay where the Allies had concentrated their antisubmarine defenses away from likely encounters with German aircraft or surface craft. Progress was slow as the boat had to travel submerged much of the time. Again and again its Metox receiver indicated enemy radar searches in the vicinity and forced Kusch to dive, sometimes very quickly. Instead of covering about two hundred nautical miles (nm) a day, as would have been normal in the open ocean without enemy interference, *U-154* only managed a little over half that distance on a good day, and sometimes, as on March 23, only thirty-eight nm on the surface and twenty-six submerged. That day the boat flirted with instant destruction when a land-based twin-engine bomber caught *U-154* in the act of surfacing and dropped four bombs. They missed the boat by a mere twenty-five meters. Kusch ordered an immediate crash dive. The next morning, lookouts detected on their port quarter an inbound German U-boat on an easterly course. On several occasions they saw enemy aircraft and the hydrophone operator heard bomb explosions astern, while the bright, moonlit nights likewise kept anxiety levels high. "Those were always wild and woolly days," recalls one crewmember with respect to crossing the Bay of Biscay. "They required strong nerves. When we were through the worst of it we were reassured that our new commanding officer knew exactly what he was doing and secretly we respected him greatly—never panicky, always friendly, and fully aware of his responsibilities."[25]

Gradually *U-154* gained the open ocean and signs of nearby enemy activities abated. Kusch could be proud of his men. They had performed more or less like veterans, including Abel, who predictably did well in all matters nautical and navigational, and even Druschel. As the boat's radio operator confided to his diary, the young engineer had presided over a number of "deep and rather hair-raising dives," but apparently Kusch and Lieutenant Reinicke had encouraged him or at least seen no reason to intervene. The rest of the crew, except the technical personnel, judged these maneuvers as evidence that Druschel was gaining experience and was beginning to master at least routine tasks and standard situations competently.[26]

Late on March 26, then some four hundred nm northeast of the Azores, Kusch broke radio silence and let U-Boat Command know his position in a short signal. Just before noon the following day, *U-154* received instructions regarding its operational area. Together with *U-126*, another Type IX boat of his flotilla and commanded by his friend and fellow Crew 37a comrade Siegfried Kietz, Kusch was to proceed to a point off Sierra Leone on Africa's west coast and attempt to intercept Allied ship traffic there, in a similar fashion as he done on *U-103*. Meanwhile on March 28, apparently satisfied with Druschel's learning curve and performance so far, Kusch requested that a homeward-bound boat pick up Lieutenant (Ing.) Fritz Reinicke so he might join the command for which he had been originally slated. Subsequently, U-Boat Command arranged a noon rendezvous with Carl Emmermann's *U-172* on April 1 in naval grid square DG 9932 west of the Canary Islands, on which occasion Reinicke was transferred without incident by rubber dinghy to the sister boat. Two hours later Kusch resumed his march south. On April 7 a radio message brought the good news that Druschel had been promoted to the rank of a lieutenant (*Oberleutnant*) in the engineering branch.

As the days of heightened anxiety receded and *U-154* rode the steady northeast trades to its tropical destination, a sense of normalcy and calm marked the boat's daily activities. When not attending to the many demands on a captain's time and attention, Kusch liked to retire to his little cabin, stretch out on his bunk and read "good books," as was noted admiringly among the crew who also appreciated his artistic pursuits.[27] When not by himself in his cabin, Kusch would sometimes spend hours on the bridge, chatting in a kindly manner with the men on duty there, doing so in a most natural way without coming across in the least as condescending or inquisitive.[28] Thus, from the outset, Kusch engendered in his men respect for his experience, professionalism, and leadership style, coupled with a popularity stemming from his easygoing manner, genuineness, and obvious "people skills." There must have been moments, had it not been the midst of this relentless war, when Kusch found a good many of his adolescent longings fulfilled as he surveyed the wide expanse of the ocean under a southern sun all around him and thought of the many good and loyal men entrusted to his care and leadership.

We may never know whether it was his memory of the open, ever comradely, and self-contained atmosphere in *U-103*'s wardroom, his newly acquired authority over fellow officers and men, his growing despair over the looming crisis of the U-boat war, or simply his personality and erudition that could not leave unchallenged or uncommented upon the expression of persuasions that ran counter to his own and to common experience. But, quite apart from the episode over the Hitler portrait, the men of *U-154*, and particularly its officers, soon discovered that their captain strongly rejected the Nazi leadership, ideology, practices, and propaganda. Again Hans Janker, whose radio room adjoined the officers' mess and who could overhear many of the conversations in question, has furnished perhaps the most insightful account of Kusch's efforts to broaden his men's perspectives on history and politics and the deepening alienation vis-à-vis Abel and Druschel, whose persuasions in such matters predictably ran in the opposite direction:

> Whenever a conversation was underway and its focus turned to politics, the war or to history, it often reached a point at which the commanding officer really warmed up to the subject and everyone allowed him to speak without interruption. This happened, not because he was in charge, but because he enjoyed truly superior rhetorical skills that one would not otherwise have associated with him, and also because he spoke with the power of conviction as he only offered views that had been thought through, made sense and were entirely his own rather than reflective of what the masses believed. These extended discussions were held mainly in the officers' mess with Abel, Druschel, and Ensign Meyer usually present. In addition, the petty officers in the neighboring compartment and the radio operators on watch could listen in unless their duties called them away. Kusch never used incendiary language in these speeches, nor did he make remarks openly hostile to the Nazi party, except for lashing out against disgusting behavior in the private life of certain prominent party individuals as it harmed the reputation of everyone, and in that we all agreed with him.

Janker also quickly noticed and appreciated how Kusch applied his ideals from his *Südlegion* days to the shipboard situation:

> He judged everything from the viewpoint of human rights and human dignity. When the conversation turned to men like Hitler, he not only examined the commonly held views about him that we all had been told to embrace, but he expressed sympathy for those who had a different opinion, as in life everything has its two sides. One only had to think of Frederick the Great's reign that brought such misery to millions of people in his time but today is thought of as brilliant and glorious. That was so typical of Kusch: he never considered just one perspective on a matter, and if someone only looked at one side of a coin, he showed him that there was another. And when someone predicted how fabulously

> history would celebrate the achievements of the Third Reich, he would reply that the misery it was creating would be lamented to the same degree. Not surprisingly no one contradicted him because his argumentation was untouchable. He never brought into play the fact that he was our commanding officer, and if someone had spoken up, Kusch would have accepted that but also challenged him by asking in a friendly way, "what's your evidence?" He only judged people on the basis of their character and intellect. It would never have occurred to an Abel or a Druschel to make these rich and rewarding conversations the basis of a denunciation if those two had not developed personal grievances against Kusch later. But any judge, especially given the psychological acumen ascribed to the legal profession, should have noticed that this was a case of wounded pride and vanity and had nothing to do with undermining anyone's fighting spirit.[29]

The boat's senior petty officer and third watch officer at the time, Heinrich Lüdmann, likewise cherished a personal relationship with Kusch based on trust and friendship and on countless conversations with him on the bridge, in the control room, and even in Kusch's private cabin. Yes, Kusch may have "teased" others from time to time, but never made explicit "negative comments about the regime or Hitler." By contrast Lüdmann, who in the line of his duties also had many dealings with Ulrich Abel, characterized the latter as a "fanatical National Socialist."[30] Lüdmann would remember:

> Regarding morale at that time I can only say the crew of our "U-Sunshine" acted like a band of brothers. On the first patrol the enlisted men had no idea of the political differences between the commanding officer and the I.W.O. The skipper made his comments only in the wardroom with all officers present there, especially when I was on watch. He never said anything of the kind in the central control room.[31]

In a similar way, Kurt Isensee, Janker's subordinate on the first patrol and later successor as chief radio operator, could pick up fragments of conversations that often began as personal disagreements and later took on political overtones. But Kusch's statements and comments "in no way affected the crew's combat spirit or combat readiness."[32]

Yet another enlisted man, Hans Kuhlmann from the engine department, has commented on the tensions between Kusch and Abel and the skipper's constant concern for the well-being of his men:

> From my perspective Kusch was a very good commanding officer. He really cared about his men. I was on duty in the diesel room and he [Kusch] often came by to see how we were doing under the tough conditions there. He always had an encouraging word for us. By contrast Lieutenant Abel often made provocative comments to us. For him we were mere "bilge crawlers," which was not exactly meant as a compliment. When Kusch and Abel toured the boat together, I sometimes picked up pieces of conversations between them that indicated they were not true comrades living together on our cramped boat. One had the impression as if Abel did not accept or respect Kusch because of his own professional training [as a jurist] and that he was envious of Kusch's successes as a U-boat officer. After all, we managed to sink five ships [actually far fewer] on that first patrol and received a special radio message from Dönitz congratulating Kusch and the crew. Considering that we were the only one out of ten boats of the 2nd U-Boat Flotilla that actually returned from its patrol at that time, who can argue with that?[33]

Even the two midshipmen Horst Fröhlich and Hellmuth Kirchammer noticed the tensions between the boat's skipper and his subordinate officers, whereas II.W.O. Heinrich Meyer appears to have preferred not to involve himself in political discussions while performing his duties with competence and circumspection. For Kusch, Nazi propaganda remained a major point of contention and a source of irritation. Kirchammer, Fröhlich, and even Druschel would testify that at one point Kusch encouraged the midshipmen in their capacity as future officers to form their own opinions, to seek and speak the truth at all times, and not to allow their views to be influenced by manipulated propaganda trash. "Later the I.W.O. [Abel] took us aside and told us not to pay too much attention to what the commanding officer had said."[34] While certainly critical of Germany's political arrangements and eventually also of the tone and substance of some of Grand Admiral Dönitz's military directives, Kusch never undercut with his comments his boat's fighting spirit, or worse, encouraged or tolerated subversive activities along the lines of treason, desertion, or cowardice.

In the meantime, *U-154* passed Cape Verde and proceeded toward the Gulf of Guinea where it had a brief rendezvous with *U-126* on April 10 some three hundred nm southwest of Freetown. Four days later, forty men on *U-154* underwent the always hilarious and teasingly embarrassing "baptismal ceremonies" every navy in the world has in store for sailors who cross the equator for the first time. Kusch (since his cruise on the *Emden*) and Abel (thanks to his days in the merchant marine) no longer had reason to fear the mythical Triton's visit, while Druschel, Meyer, the midshipmen, and all but the most senior enlisted personnel must have undergone and somehow survived the elaborate initiation rites. On a more serious and maddening note, *U-154*'s search for enemy shipping yielded absolutely no results except occasional encounters with neutral Spanish and Portuguese vessels en route to or from South America. Even more frustrating were several aircraft sightings and an unexpected attack on April 18 that forced the boat to crash dive while the plane's bombs plowed into the ocean nearby without causing damage. Incidentally, and contrary to widespread claims in the U-boat literature in print and on the Internet, *U-154* was not involved in the transfer and repatriation of the crew of *U-167*, which had scuttled itself off Gran Canaria on April 6 after sustaining lethal damage in a British air attack. The boats involved in the daring and successful rescue two weeks later were *U-455*, *U-159*, and *U-518*. On the day in question Kusch had almost reached the equator well south of the Canary Islands.[35]

As instructed by U-Boat Command, in the following days *U-154* sidled gradually to the west into that part of the Central Atlantic where Africa and South America come closest to each other northwest of Ascension Island. While the lookouts continued to scan the open sea above without results, Druschel and his engineering team discovered a fuel leak from a starboard tank that caused the boat to trail some oil on the surface, a problem likely caused by poor welding or the shock waves of near misses. By April 27 the boat had lost three tons of oil in this manner and Kusch decided to stop the diesels at night to conserve fuel and simply drift in the gentle southeast trades whenever there was little danger of being detected. Two days later *U-154*, along with two other boats in the vicinity, were ordered to complete the Atlantic crossing and make for the coastal traffic south of Brazil's Cabo Sao Roque, the country's easternmost promontory. Kusch acknowledged his new instructions adding that he still had all twenty-two of his torpedoes and one hundred and forty tons of fuel.

On May 5, *U-154* gingerly approached the Brazilian port of Maceió south of Recife to see if any ships happened to be anchored in its roadstead. Detecting none after closing to within five thousand meters in poor visibility while the city in the background was brilliantly illuminated, Kusch resumed his move up the coast, often bringing the boat up to periscope depth once an hour during the day to have a look around. At night he remained on the surface for better observations and to recharge the batteries. Then, shortly before local dawn on May 8, lookouts reported a shadow on the port quarter. Upon further investigation it turned out to be a tanker of an estimated seven thousand tons zigzagging irregularly and running at a speed of about ten knots. One can imagine the crew's excitement as it deemed itself on the verge of bagging its first victim after such a long time at sea. Kusch decided immediately to attack at close range with two torpedoes from the bow tubes. Since this was a surface attack, Abel was in charge of all calculations, including the aiming and actual firing. From the very short distance of four hundred meters, just twenty-seven minutes after the first sighting, Abel launched the two torpedoes—and missed. Radio operator Hans Janker noted laconically in his diary, "I.W.O. wastes two eels."[36]

Assuming there had been problems either with the detonator or because of the minimal distance, Kusch quickly ordered a second attack before daybreak from a little farther out and before the tanker realized it was in trouble. This time the torpedoes were to be fired singly and from approximately fifteen hundred meters away. After a runtime of ninety-eight seconds the men on *U-154* could hear the metallic sound of a torpedo apparently striking the tanker's hull without exploding. Within minutes the vessel—it turned out to be the German-built 8,798-ton *Motocarline* of Panamanian registry on its way to Montevideo—sent out distress signals in open language and tried to evade further danger by steering erratic courses and speeding up to twelve knots. After three hours and a half an explosion occurred on the tanker, inducing the men on *U-154* to surmise that one of their torpedoes had lodged in the *Motocarline*'s hull and detonated at last. But the ship continued its southward escape without reducing speed. Kusch followed from a distance for several more hours hoping to get another chance at sinking his prey, but when a Catalina PBY flying boat of the Brazilian air force appeared overhead, he took his boat down. After an extended cat-and-mouse game with the aircraft and once being shaken by eight depth charges going off close by, Kusch decided to look for opportunities farther north, rounding Cabo Sao Roque to the northwest while continuing to hug the coast. Over the next couple of days *U-154* frequently had to dive after sighting aircraft or picking up enemy radar transmissions on its Metox receiver on wavelengths between 164 and 228 centimeters. At one point, Abel on his watch spotted an attacking aircraft much too late, earning him the comment of "gross failure" in Hans Janker's diary.[37]

On May 14, *U-154* was instructed to make a quick run to the northeast to refuel from *U-460* under the command of Lieutenant Ebe Schnoor. This was one of Germany's Type XIV U-tankers acting as floating gas stations, repair shops, grocery stores, and makeshift hospitals if necessary. At 1850 on May 20, in naval grid square ES 8888 just north of the equator halfway between the Old World and the New, *U-154* began taking on seventy tons of fuel oil, two tons of lubricating oil, some spare parts, and over a ton of provisions good for twenty days from its "dairy cow," as these supply U-boats were lovingly dubbed by German submariners. At the same time, *U-460*'s shipboard surgeon came over to Kusch's boat to treat a sailor for an unspecified illness or injury. Apparently, the case was serious enough for the doctor and his patient to be taken back to the U-tanker for more intensive treatment overnight. In the meantime, *U-154* turned off its engines and drifted. The next morning the patient returned to Kusch's boat in a rubber dinghy while Kurt Druschel and his men attempted to weld a damaged ballast tank some twenty cm below the waterline on the port side. Not succeeding at first, work continued for the rest of the day and into the next as Druschel received help from *U-460*'s team of specialists and their more sophisticated equipment.

Early on May 22 a third boat arrived on the scene for refueling. This was *U-515* under legendary Lieutenant Commander Werner Henke of the Tenth U-Boat Flotilla likewise stationed in Lorient. Unable to fix more than half of the tear in the ballast tank because of the swell, Kusch had no choice but to leave the repair work unfinished, though he noted in his war diary that the problem was not as bad as before. By 2010 that evening, *U-460* and *U-515* disappeared below the horizon as Kusch hurried back for more adventures off Brazil. To this day the file "*U-154*" at the U-Boat Archives in Cuxhaven holds an elaborate "thank you" note signed by Kusch and all his officers in gratitude for all the goods and services received from the U-tanker. A drawing by Kusch shows the silhouette of *U-154* before a radiant sunrise along with the four-pointed star that Commander Kölle had once chosen as the boat's distinct identifying emblem painted on its conning tower. On the reverse side of the note, the men of *U-154* thank their "noble donor" for his generosity and wish him "perfect U-boat weather at all times, a thousand juicy steamers, and always positive buoyancy." The document miraculously survived when *U-460* was sunk on October 4, 1943, by American carrier-based aircraft. Most of the *Kriegsmarine*'s herd of "dairy cows" was lost that year as enemy code-breakers routinely read their radio traffic and ever better aerial coverage turned the Atlantic into a deadly place for any German vessel on its surface.

At 0033 on May 28, shortly after it had resumed its lurking position about one hundred nautical miles northwest of Cabo Sao Roque,

U-154 spotted a convoy heading up the coast. Convoy BT-14 was traveling between Bahia in Brazil and Trinidad in the Windward Islands and consisted of twelve merchant ships in three columns guarded by five American destroyers. Most of the vessels rode high in ballast and the escorts were positioned ahead and astern to both sides of the merchantmen. Despite picking up strong radar emissions on his Metox set, Kusch decided on a surface attack on the starboard column. At flank speed he managed to break through the destroyer screen and between 0443 and 0446 launched four torpedoes from his bow tubes before turning the boat around and firing two more "eels" from the stern tubes at ranges between six hundred and two thousand meters. Interestingly, this time Kusch himself carried out the aiming and firing, even though standard procedure would have entrusted that task to his I.W.O. Ulrich Abel. While speeding away from the convoy out to sea to reload, and as the destroyers fired star shells to illuminate the scene and locate the culprit, the men on *U-154* heard and observed visually several distinct explosions.

Bothered by the bright moonlight, Kusch waited a while before returning to the scene of his attack "to look for survivors or damaged ships." Remaining on the surface in those pre-dawn conditions he noticed in the distance a drifting tanker that was obviously disabled with two destroyers circling it for protection. Kusch ordered the boat to dive and continued his careful approach. Eventually one of the destroyers steamed off to rejoin the convoy. Kusch had the stern tubes V and VI readied and was about to fire a coup de grâce at the tanker when a Catalina PBY flying boat overhead forced him to take the boat down from periscope depth to eighty meters. Fifteen minutes later he had another look around through his periscope when he suddenly noticed that the remaining destroyer was heading toward him at high speed only three thousand meters away. Without hesitation he told Druschel to take the boat down again as quickly as possible, but this time it leveled out at "A + 80," which meant at one hundred and sixty meters, or eighty meters below the boat's safe diving limit (A = 80m) as guaranteed by the building shipyard.[38] *U-154*'s war diary is unclear whether this deep and precipitous dive was intentional or whether Druschel had simply lost control. It is quite likely that this was one of those "dangerous moments when Druschel became dysfunctional and the commanding officer had to take over the responsibilities of a chief engineer as well," according to radio mate Janker.[39] Predictably, the enormous and unaccustomed water pressure damaged valuable equipment that protruded outward through the pressure hull such as pumps, valves, vents, and the hydrophone gear whose "repair will be necessary at a later point."[40]

Several more times Kusch would take *U-154* up to periscope depth to see if he could finish off the tanker for good, but each time he observed enemy planes circling overhead and around the stricken vessel. He also noticed that the tanker appeared to be settling deeper and deeper by the stern. When he finally dared to surface after sunset, the sea was empty and he assumed, as it turned out mistakenly, that his victim had gone to the bottom. *U-154* then headed off to the north to find a quiet spot to move its spare torpedoes from their containers on the upper deck carefully into the interior of the boat and load them into the waiting tubes. This was also a time to do repair work on the damaged equipment, especially the bilge pumps, and to catch up on radio traffic with U-Boat Command. Not until early on May 30 was Kusch able send a longer message describing the attack in some detail, claiming "two hits on a tanker type *British Zeal*, one hit each on a tanker type *Empire Oil*, on another six-thousand-ton tanker, on a freighter type *Prome*, and on another six-thousand-ton freighter." Kusch added that he still had one hundred and twenty-seven tons of fuel, twelve torpedoes, and that it was raining.[41] Dönitz responded promptly with an encouraging "Well done!" and would eventually credit Kusch with having destroyed two tankers and one freighter of 20,000 tons combined and having damaged two more tankers and a freighter displacing an additional 24,400 tons, including the attack on the *Motocarline*, whose name and specifications were of course known from the distress signals it had transmitted in the clear under its international call sign HPGM.

Reality was rather more sobering. According to uncontestable postwar assessments, Kusch's torpedoes only damaged three vessels in Convoy BT-14, of which one, the 8,166-ton Standard Oil tanker *John Worthington* whom Kusch had stalked, managed to rejoin the convoy the next day and made it via Port-of-Spain, Trinidad, to Galveston, Texas. There it was determined that the damage sustained was not worth the cost and trouble of a lengthy repair and the ship thus became a total loss. Two other American vessels, the 7,191-ton freighter *Cardinal Gibbons* and the 8,580-ton Texaco tanker *Florida*, suffered serious hits but returned to service after refits. No Allied sailors perished in the attack.[42] Kusch should not be blamed for overstating his accomplishments as he and his men had to rely on their sense perceptions in a tense and chaotic situation. By 1943 it had become quite common for German U-boat commanders, even for the best, to claim double or even triple the actual enemy tonnage destroyed. While hopeful thinking may have been a factor as the fortunes of war grew bleaker and spectacular feats increasingly rare, most inflated assessments resulted from the inability to observe without obstruction or punishment the results of an attack.

By May 1943, one year after the end of the "Second Happy Times," Grand Admiral Dönitz seemed to blame his boats' declining successes not on the ever-expanding triumphs of Allied countermeasures, but on the lack of an aggressive spirit on the part of his skippers. Many of Dönitz's subsequent exhortations to be hard-hitting and ready to take much greater risks, were transmitted as radio messages under the code word "Rose" and meant for officers only. A pertinent example is one he had transmitted to U-boats comprising the wolfpack "Mosel" on May 21, 1943, and which *U-154* may have picked up as well:

> Those who believe it is no longer possible to attack a convoy successfully is a weakling and no true U-boat commander. The Battle of the Atlantic is getting tougher, but that cannot be helped because that is how we will win the war. Be aware of the high responsibility you carry and that you will have to justify your actions. Give your very best in striking at this convoy. We must destroy it. If you encounter aircraft and conditions are favorable, do not dive but shoot back and defend yourselves. Try to outrun destroyers on the surface. Be tough, press forward and attack. I believe in you. Commander-in-Chief.[43]

Dönitz's message revealed not only how desperate the convoy battles had become by mid-1943, but betrayed as well the admiral's ideologically based and unprofessional conviction that mere willpower and madcap risk-taking could overcome Allied dominance at sea.

For the first half of June, by this time well over seventy-five days out on patrol, *U-154* shifted its focus to the waters east of the Windward Islands. The troubles with the boat's pumping system continued, even though they were not of the fatal variety, and early on June 7 Kusch informed U-Boat Command that his Metox receiver had given up its ghost in addition to the hydrophone system. In return he was instructed to steer generally to the northeast and that, with about one hundred tons of fuel left, no further resupply at sea was intended. A fast steamer sighted that same day and run down after a daylong chase turned out to be of neutral Spanish registry. On June 18, with sixty-one tons of fuel oil left, *U-154* began its long trip home. Kusch suggested a meeting with Kietz's *U-126* in waters northeast of the Azores to coordinate their remaining voyage and to obtain a spare Metox set from his friend who in turn planned to pick it up from *U-487* before the rendezvous. The radar detector would be useful to have for the transit through the Bay of Biscay. In the meantime, *U-154* had to let pass another Spanish freighter and a Swedish tanker.

Chief radio operator Hans Janker's relationship with Abel deteriorated further in those days as the latter kept interfering with Janker's activities at his radio station. After all, the boat's radio department was within Ensign Meyer's divisional responsibilities, not Abel's. Perhaps the friction had also to do with Kusch's tendency to have Janker and Isensee tune quietly to foreign radio broadcasts, particularly English-language ones, when those stations were within receiving range. True, Nazi laws prohibited and punished such monitoring of enemy "propaganda," but for Kusch it must have been a valuable source of information and commentary on the course of the war. Besides, listening to shore-based radio stations could provide useful weather forecasts and help to fine-tune the boat's radio direction-finding gear and test its reliability on various frequencies. In the end, matters grew so annoying that Kusch had to "take

Abel to task. Kusch was clearly not fully satisfied with Abel's performance and Druschel always backed up his friend."[44]

It is also possible that Abel's run-in with Janker had to do with a political joke Kusch had contributed to the boat's periodically distributed information sheet. For these sheets the radio personnel collected and summarized news from home and spiced it up with jokes and anecdotes supplied by the boat's crew to maintain and boost morale. The joke ran as follows: "Question: What do the German people and a tapeworm have in common? Answer: Both are surrounded by a brown mass and are in constant danger of being killed."[45] Again, what for Kusch must have been a minor matter, another "tease" with a good laugh-line as Lüdmann and the vast majority of the men would have interpreted it, became for Abel an unacceptable smear on Germany's political leadership and further proof of Kusch's unfitness for command.

At 1720 on June 28, the two boats met as scheduled and *U-126* came alongside *U-154* so the two skippers could confer about their next moves. In a midnight meeting after transferring the Metox gear, Kusch and Kietz agreed to stay in sight of one another for the remainder of their patrols for better protection against air attacks. In the likely event that they should be forced to dive, they would try to stay in touch by means of their underwater telephones and anticipate where the other would likely be when they surfaced again to resume their march home, even returning to the location of the initial dive if necessary. At 1255 the next day, Kusch detected in the distance through the midday haze a westbound American passenger liner of the *Mariposa* class, most likely the *Malolo,* that had been converted into a troopship and was steaming along at an estimated speed of twenty knots, zigzagging from time to time.[46] The boats dived four minutes apart hoping to gain a better attack angle and to close the distance to their target, but the two torpedoes Kusch eventually fired at 1330 from thirty-five hundred meters away missed, apparently unnoticed by the Americans, even though one of the torpedoes self-destructed as planned at 1345 at the end of its run in a loud explosion distinctly audible on *U-154*. After some difficulty locating *U-126* again because of malfunctioning underwater telephones and hydrophone equipment, and with the speedy liner having disappeared below the western horizon, Kietz and Kusch resumed their trek northeastward into the Bay of Biscay.

Things remained relatively uneventful for both boats until they reached a position two hundred nautical miles northwest of Spain's Cape Finisterre (Cabo Fisterra). At 0244 on July 3, while the boats were on the surface and racing in tandem for the French coast, Kusch's Metox suddenly picked up a scratching sound on a wavelength of one hundred and thirty cm, while simultaneously the bright searchlight of a low-flying plane about one thousand meters away pierced the darkness and homed in on *U-126* as the apparently more promising target. With *U-154*'s automatic guns jamming for unexplained reasons and *U-126* defenseless in the act of diving, the enemy plane, a twin-engine Wellington XII bomber of the RAF's No. 172 Squadron equipped with a Leigh Light, dropped a series of four bombs that hit the water about thirty to forty meters short of Kietz's boat on the starboard side, by all indications causing no damage. Midshipman Hellmuth Kirchammer, who was on *U-154*'s bridge at that time would distinctly remember that the bombs fell short and that *U-126*'s watch personnel made it into the interior of the diving boat, but had difficulty getting the bulky Metox antenna and its feed lines into the boat through the tower hatch.[47] Since the boat was never to surface again, the most plausible explanation for *U-126*'s tragic loss is a catastrophic inrush of water through the tower hatch that could not be closed properly because of the Metox cables and rendered the boat quickly out of control and beyond recovery. Inasmuch as the British pilot, Flight Sergeant A. Combis, dropped a total of eight depth charges, it is also possible that he made a second run and fatally damaged the boat when it was already well underwater.[48] Kietz and all fifty-four men of his crew perished.

When Kusch himself dived moments later to avoid a second attack by the plane during its next pass, a last glance from *U-154*'s bridge at the spot where *U-126* had disappeared showed a blinking light and some smoke, most likely from a marker the British plane had dropped to identify the spot for itself or for other aircraft and vessels in the vicinity. Once Kusch had reached safety at a depth of forty meters, he immediately tried to contact Kietz by underwater telephone but received no answer. Since the range of underwater telephony is limited and depends in part on the temperature and salinity of the water, Kusch assumed that Kietz was too far away to hear him. More ominous was a series of six to eight explosive or crackling sounds that resembled the firing of a distant 3.7-cm gun. It crossed Kusch's mind that *U-126* might have resurfaced for some reason and was fighting it out with the plane above, but then he dismissed this idea as highly unlikely and simply noted in his boat's war diary, "situation confusing." In all likelihood, the sounds he and the other men on *U-154* heard came from Kietz's boat cracking up and imploding when the outside water pressure became overwhelming for the doomed vessel.

At this odd and curious moment, the long-simmering tension between Kusch and Abel boiled over into open and implacable conflict. It seems that Abel, too, had a friend on *U-126*, possibly one of its watch officers, both of whom were reservists, and he and Druschel now repeatedly and furiously berated Kusch in front of everyone in the central control room to surface immediately and search for survivors. Kusch held his ground stubbornly with the obvious observation that surfacing at that instant was much too dangerous for *U-154* with at least one enemy plane in the vicinity and with chances of locating any survivors, if there were any at all, virtually nil in the middle of the night and in the rough seas above. This was all in addition to the considerable marine phosphorescence that night that might have given a surfaced U-boat away to any aircraft present. Radio operator Kurt Isensee totally agreed with his skipper: "Abel demanded that we surface and look for survivors. We would have been located immediately. Therefore, Kusch refused because we would have been unable to rescue anyone and would have been lost ourselves."[49] And midshipman Hellmuth Kirchammer recalled long after the war, "From that moment on Abel was practically enflamed with hatred [toward Kusch] and any understanding among the three officers, who after all had behaved until then more or less as a team professionally and as comrades despite their diametrically opposed political views, was forever destroyed."[50] Thus what everyone else on board of *U-154* regarded as perfectly justified caution, common sense, and self-preservation on the part of their experienced skipper, the newcomers Abel and Druschel in their deepening and blinding opposition to Kusch came to interpret as cowardice. Considering Kusch's daring attack on Convoy BT-14, the care and concern he had expressed for stricken sailors then and for his own men on many other occasions, and having personally seen *U-126* dive without apparent difficulties, it would be absurd to assume he would not have done everything in his power to assist his Crew 37a comrade Siegfried Kietz and his men if he had grounds to believe they were in trouble.

In what may have been a compromise on Kusch's part, he did take his boat back up to periscope depth at 0305, twenty-one minutes after the air attack, for a look around, but nothing could be seen. Since he and Kietz had arranged to continue submerged if they became separated and eventually surface when it was safe to do so, Kusch left the scene of the attack at 0400 and surfaced at 0707 some four nautical miles from the original spot. With good visibility of twelve nm under a blue sky and neither foe nor friend in sight anywhere, *U-154* dispatched a brief message to U-Boat Command describing the "unsuccessful" attack on Kietz and sharing *U-154*'s intention of continuing on alone. The next two days in the Bay of Biscay brought the familiar and exhausting routine of diving and resurfacing upon the detection of enemy radar emissions on wavelengths between 120 and 164 cm or the actual sighting of enemy aircraft, all the time worrying about *U-126*'s fate. At 2112 on July 5, both Kusch and Kietz were instructed to meet their surface escorts of minesweepers and patrol craft at 1300 the next day at a predetermined point off Lorient. Sadly, only *U-154* acknowledged the message, picked up its escort on schedule, and at 1700 the next day tied up at its base after a hundred and nine days at sea.

Kusch could be well satisfied with his first mission as the skipper of a fighting submarine, even though to a friend he characterized it as "very long, very hard and very demanding."[51] He had inflicted damage on the enemy in his attack on Convoy BT-14 off Brazil, demonstrated courage, coolness, and solid judgment in guiding the boat through dangerous situations, led his men with a sure hand and a human touch, and brought the boat home when so many others just then perished in the wastes of the oceans. Rear Admiral Eberhard Godt, chief of operations at U-Boat Command, saw it the same way when he added this comment to the boat's war diary:

> First mission with a seasoned crew (Schuch), operating by himself in South Atlantic waters. The attack on May 8 [*Motocarline*] was unfortunately unsuccessful because of the near miss and the failure of the torpedo's detonator. Subsequent tenacious efforts on part of the commanding officer stymied by enemy air cover. The attack on July 3 [against BT-14] was well planned and skillfully carried out. Success very pleasing! Regarding events on July 3 [attack on Kietz]: Commanding officer acted correctly during the air attack; an energetic search for *U-126* would have been appropriate. In addition to valuable experience, the commanding officer's first patrol brought him a nice initial success.[52]

Kusch's immediate superior, flotilla commander Ernst Kals, likewise praised his "remarkable expertise and aggressive spirit" while always remaining "calm and mindful of the circumstances. . . . Cool and never rash, he can pounce when an opportunity beckons."[53] This assessment was shared and approved by Captain Hans Rudolf Rösing a little farther inland at Angers where he headed the staff overseeing the administrative and operational needs of all German U-boat flotillas in France.[54]

Before departing Lorient for a well-deserved leave in Berlin, and after he and Druschel had conferred with the technical staff of the facility as to his boat's repair needs during its forthcoming overhaul, Kusch attended a debriefing with his flotilla commander. No record of his meeting with Kals remains, but it is highly likely that Lieutenant Dr. Ulrich Abel's performance as *U-154*'s first watch officer and second-in-command was a central topic of the conversation.

It had been everyone's understanding, and certainly his own, that Abel had undertaken his just completed tour as Kusch's I.W.O. as a so-called confirmand, that is, as a skipper-in-training who simply needed a little more hands-on experience on a frontline U-boat before becoming fully qualified to command one himself.[55] When Abel left for Lorient for the first time, he calmed his wife's worries by emphasizing that he would make one patrol under an experienced U-boat captain as second-in command before taking over his own boat.[56] After all, Abel was already thirty-one years old with an admirable career in the legal profession and with experience in the merchant marine and in the naval reserve. He had commanded a minesweeper with distinction and been decorated highly for bravery. He was undoubtedly ambitious. Now he had a lengthy patrol behind him looking over the shoulder of a man who truly knew his business as a U-boat officer and commander. Kusch must have known that a recommendation containing serious reservations would likely doom Abel's prospects of commanding a boat right away and might even induce the personnel department to pull Abel out of the U-boat arm altogether and return him to the surface fleet. On the other hand, could Kusch, with a clear conscience and knowing Abel's limitations, advise his superiors to entrust a frontline boat to him, even one with a seasoned crew?

To gain an idea of how he viewed Abel then and subsequently, it may be instructive to cite from the assessment Kusch wrote about his second-in-command later that year:

1. Outward appearance and impression: Short, straight, compact. Strong and physically tough. Polite manners, kindly disposition, sometimes too laid-back.
2. Mental abilities: Holds a doctorate in law and is a county judge in his civilian life. His thoughts and actions betray a certain immobility, rigidity, and one-sidedness. . . .
4. Service expertise, performance, resourcefulness: Excellent nautical knowledge and capabilities due to long time spent in the merchant marine. He applied them in all situations without fail. Approaches every task calmly, sometimes almost too slowly. In many ways he has grown out of the position of an I.W.O. and as a result acts not energetically and enthusiastically enough.

5. General attitudes and character: Simple, uncomplicated, very calm, at times rather sluggish, with an excellent attitude regarding service expectations and duties . . .
7. Overall assessment:
(a) Personality: Straightforward, calm, staid personality, focused and reliable under fire.
(b) Strong points: Calm, determined, uncomplicated, self-assured.
(c) Weak points: Sluggish, could display more energy and initiative.
(d) Overall impression: A good officer with average abilities.[57]

So much for Kusch's assessment, whose essence he likely shared with his flotilla commander, perhaps also mentioning Abel's poor performance when firing torpedoes, his quarrels with the boat's radio staff, his almost obsequious servility toward his commanding officer in routine situations, and his lack of professionalism and quasi-emotional breakdown when he and Druschel demanded from Kusch against all reasonable judgment *U-154*'s immediate return to the surface during the air attack on *U-126*.

Ulrich Abel's widow, who read Kusch's evaluation of her husband for the first time more than half a century later, remembered Abel differently, both physically and mentally. To her, Abel's tenacity in advancing and adjusting his career, and particularly his constant and profound worry over the well-being of his family, remained to her incompatible with the rigidity and lack of mental mobility Kusch claimed to have observed in her husband.[58] "He would have chosen the wrong line of academic studies," she commented, "if his thinking could in any way be characterized as 'immobile, rigid, and one-sided.' . . . I know that my husband stated his well-considered views in a simple, uncomplicated and calm manner, and that he was caring, kindly and honest." There was nothing "sluggish" about him.[59] Herta Abel expressed regret that her husband did not reveal his disappointment over Kusch to the flotilla commander after this first patrol. "It must have been unacceptable to him that a German officer proclaimed his opposition to the regime so loudly and openly, especially on a submarine. Surely Kusch's behavior was incompatible with the great admiration and respect [Abel] had always had for U-boat commanders."[60]

Ernst Kals, as flotilla commander, could have known neither the existence nor the nature and intensity of the profound political dissonances that were poisoning and tearing apart the professional and personal relationship between *U-154*'s commanding officer and his subordinates Abel and Druschel. But after Kusch's report, he could not have been blind to the "fundamental differences in temperament and mentality that distinguished the slow-moving and often pedantic jurist from his commanding officer. In this sense the academically trained Dr. Abel must have felt intellectually inferior to the mentally agile, highly intelligent and rhetorically gifted Kusch."[61] In the end Kals had to weigh and choose from three alternatives: (1) he could recommend that Abel be given a boat of his own right away despite's Kusch reservations; (2) he could transfer him to another boat in his or the Tenth Flotilla for one more patrol as a "confirmand" under a different skipper; or (3) he could keep Abel as *U-154*'s I.W.O. with the understanding that he would take command of his own boat after that mission. In all this Kusch seemed less concerned about Druschel, regarding him primarily as an arrogant loudmouth and immature extension and sycophant of Abel who entertained few original ideas outside the party line, even though he carried out his duties as *U-154*'s chief engineer with increasing competence. Given the complexity of the case, for the time being Kals would keep the matter under advisement and not announce his decision until the men of *U-154* reassembled for their next mission two months later.

For the period between July 7 and September 23, 1943, while the boat lay protected in its massive concrete lair in Lorient and the yard's technical personnel scrambled to restore it to full combat readiness, *U-154*'s war diary states laconically, "Leave and further training for the crew."[62] For Kusch this meant primarily administrative paperwork and meetings with the flotilla staff, brief midsummer excursions to the lovely seashores and countryside around Lorient despite the ruins and rubble of the city itself, and longer time on leave in Berlin. While his boat had been at sea,

Germany's military fortunes had suffered significant additional setbacks. The fighting in North Africa was over, with the German-Italian forces wiped out and the Allies set to invade Sicily and the Italian mainland within the next two months. The news from the Russian front was even grimmer following the Stalingrad disaster as Soviet tank armies pushed German units ever farther to the west in permanent and costly retreat. Kusch himself knew better than most the beating the *Kriegsmarine* was taking in the Atlantic and its adjacent waters. But perhaps most noticeable in that summer of 1943 was the impact of the Allied air war and the inability of the *Luftwaffe* to prevent massive raids on German shipyards, factories, infrastructure and, increasingly, its civilian population.

Signs of this destruction multiplied as Kusch's train crossed the French-German border on his way to Berlin. Railway stations, switchyards, tunnels, and bridges were coming increasingly under bombardment, as were highways, airports, and power plants. The German capital itself remained largely shielded from this assault until late in 1943 due to its considerable flying distance from British bases and its formidable air defenses, even though the suburb of Steglitz where his mother now lived had seen some bombs fall.[63] Thus, physically, the Berlin Kusch saw on his leave was not vastly changed from the one he remembered from his previous visit, but the atmosphere was unquestionably gloomier and more foreboding than ever before. Hitler himself hardly spent time in the German capital anymore, preferring his heavily fortified military headquarters in East Prussia or his private retreat in the Bavarian Alps. This did not mean, of course, that he and his followers had loosened their grip on Germany's political life and institutions. If anything, absolute loyalty and allegiance to the regime and the man who had created it became ever more expected and enforced as dissidents in academic, artistic, and religious circles, along with any remaining Jews, if they were not being eliminated outright, now populated the growing number of concentration camps to and beyond their capacities.

Unquestionably, Oskar Kusch's rejection of everything National Socialist grew deeper and fiercer during this visit to Berlin and was reinforced by numerous confidential conversations with longtime and like-minded friends such as Dieter Berger and Wolfgang Kühns-Bernsau, and by speculations as to what might have happened to Rudi Pallas at Stalingrad. But his visit was also driven by another, much more immediate and personal motive—clarifying and regularizing his relationship with Inge von Foris. The two had become very good friends during his last visit, sharing their fascination with art and architecture, their disdain for the Nazis, and their attraction to one another. Now was as good a time as any for Kusch to press her into making the kind of loving commitment that would bind the two of them together for good. Inge was by then in her seventh semester at Berlin University and about to start research on a doctoral dissertation on the life and work of the Bavarian Baroque architect Johann Dientzenhofer (1663–1726) under the guidance of Professor Wilhelm Pinder.[64] Over the preceding months she had allowed her attachment to her friend Heinrich on the Russian front to cool off, even though the two continued an intermittent correspondence. This development did not go unnoticed by a common friend who lamented her change in preferences but refrained from alerting Heinrich to the existence of a rival for Inge's favors.[65]

Oskar and Inge made the most of their weeks together and by the end of the summer became engaged. Presumably Kusch had occasion to introduce his future bride to both of his parents while Inge took him to meet her grandmother Amalie ("Mala") von Foris, with whom she was staying during her studies in Berlin, as well as to her mother and stepfather, also a naval officer.[66] Her father, Colonel Bernhard von Foris, was commandant of the prisoner-of-war camp Stalag X-B at Sandbostel in Lower Saxony at the time. Kusch also began or resumed a close friendship with Inge's only brother, Henning von Foris, then serving as a lieutenant in the Wehrmacht and like his sister an implacable opponent of the Hitler regime.

On September 15, one week before setting out on his second patrol on *U-154*, Kusch formally filed for permission from U-Boat Command to get married. This awkward requirement dated back to the Imperial Navy under the Kaiser when officers wishing to marry had to be at least twenty-five years old, free of debt, had attained the rank of *Oberleutnant*, were earning enough to support a family in appropriate circumstances, and could prove that the social status of their bride and her family was compatible with that of a German officer. Under Hitler the *Kriegsmarine* had added proof of "Aryan" ancestry to these criteria. After the beginning of World War II, these rules were eased somewhat, especially the age requirement.[67] Since both Oskar and Inge had already submitted documentation of their Jewish-free lineage to the *Kriegsmarine* and to Berlin University, respectively, they had no reason to expect impediments in that regard.[68] Both his bride and his future mother-in-law admonished Kusch to exercise great care and watch his language when it came to criticizing the Nazi regime.[69]

Kusch's excitement about his pending marriage and his guarded optimism regarding the situation out in the Atlantic are expressed well in a letter to a friend named Roland written on the eve of his second mission on September 22, 1943:

> I just completed a wonderful vacation. . . . In Berlin I was out sailing almost every day. Now I am ready for my next patrol. We will get under way in a few days. Overall, I think the situation is improving somewhat, especially for us. I am more optimistic than I have been before. Expect to be back around Christmas. That's when I will get married. You cannot believe it? You better! My bride is the daughter of a lieutenant colonel and is studying art history in Berlin. You see, my dear Roland, you are not the only one who has hit on that splendid idea. . . . Let us hope the ever-fickle fortunes of war will continue to favor us. Kind regards to your fiancée, your parents and siblings. And for us especially let us hope for a happy reunion.[70]

As one observer has commented, this was the letter of a "proud, young U-boat commander, eager for additional successes, betraying not the slightest trace of defeatism."[71]

If Kusch's life seemed to come together in that summer of 1943 with a successful first U-boat mission behind him as commanding officer and the prospect of marital bliss stretching out before him into a yet unfathomable future, Ulrich Abel's world and that of his family were about to fall apart. Before his first patrol under Kusch, Abel had made his wife Herta promise him to accept a friend's invitation and relocate with their two toddlers, a boy and a girl, from their apartment in Hamburg-Wandsbek to the safety of rural Strippow, a small village southeast of Greifswald near the Baltic Sea. The British air attacks on Hamburg were intensifying every month and targeted no longer just the port and shipyard facilities of the huge city, but also increasingly its residential neighborhoods, Hamburg being within a much shorter flying distance from British bases than Berlin.[72] One of the Abel boys had actually been born in a Hamburg air raid shelter in 1941. Now, eager for a reunion with his family, Abel instructed his wife by telephone to await him at her parents' home in Greifswald from where all four of them would return to Hamburg and spend his leave there as usual, for he did not want to sacrifice even one day of their precious time together. In retrospect, it occurred to Mrs. Abel that her husband's haste to return to their cozy little place in Hamburg might also have grown from a desire on his part "to discuss in private a matter weighing heavily on his soul."

Then came news over the radio of very severe air attacks on Hamburg. Trying to buy tickets at the Greifswald train station for the ride to Hamburg, Abel soon returned without them and seemed perplexed. He had met at the station a number of Hamburg residents who had just left their city because they could not stand it any longer. Many sections were without water and electricity, and even the air raid sirens had stopped functioning. After a night discussing their options, Ulrich and Herta Abel decided to return their children to the friend in Strippow for three days and to make a dash for Hamburg to try at least to save their personal belongings, along with household items and furniture.

When they reached Hamburg's central train station at last, a chaotic mess greeted them. All the platforms were overflowing with people trying to escape with more belongings than they could possibly carry. After some delay, the Abels were able to catch a local train to Wandsbek:

> Our street looked eerie, with just a few people scurrying from house to house. None of our neighbors could be seen anywhere. Probably they had all left. Our apartment had been burglarized, many of the windows broken, the torn curtains blowing in the breeze. Our radio had been stolen. We quickly filled a few suitcases and boxes with our children's belongings, our own clothes, a few items from the writing desk, and then we simply stood there worrying about the night. We had neither water nor electricity.[73]

Commandeering an abandoned wheelbarrow, the Abels managed to drag their assorted containers to a post office in the outskirts of the city and dispatch them to Greifswald, never expecting to see any of them again. Kindly people offered to share the night with them in a truck garden as it had become too dangerous to stay in houses. That night Hamburg experienced its worst air raids yet. "We saw and heard it and feared for our lives."

When the Abels tried to take the commuter train back to Wandsbek the next morning, people told them that it would be useless because Wandsbek had just been wiped out the previous night. But Ulrich and Herta Abel would not be deterred:

> Using various means of transportation underneath darkly menacing clouds of smoke, we managed to make our way back into the burning city. It took hours to reach our street, our house. Yesterday it had still been our cozy little nest. Now it was in flames, but our ground-floor apartment was still mostly spared. We simply stopped thinking and started dragging our living-room furniture out into the street. Suddenly the ceiling collapsed as the apartment above us was burning fiercely. Fortunately, we were unhurt, but we now realized how futile our actions were, as there was no way of moving our furniture away from the street. There was also no way of helping those people around us who were screaming for help from their collapsed basements. For a few days afterwards, we stayed in the lower parts of Hamburg's central train station

> until we could leave in a cattle car for Greifswald. Fortunately, the air attacks had abated somewhat. It took us two days to reach our destination because the train kept stopping for hours at a time.[74]

Reunited with their children at last, and enlisting the services of the local county administration, Abel succeeded in having three furnished rooms requisitioned for his family in the largely abandoned seaside resort of Lubmin on the Baltic. The owners were not terribly excited about their new renters, as in better days they had become used to charging wealthy vacationers much higher rates.

What the Abels had just experienced, and survived, has gone down in history darkly as the "Hamburg Firestorm," or "Operation Gomorrah," as Bomber Command of the RAF labeled the five-day, around-the-clock bombing of Hamburg between July 24 and 28, 1943, that took 42,600 civilian lives, injured 37,000 more, and brought utter destruction to entire sections of the city. Ulrich Abel would make one more trip by truck from Greifswald into the ruined city of Hamburg, seeking to salvage what was left of the worldly possessions of one of his wife's aunts from an otherwise destroyed apartment building in a southern suburb. Casting a last look at the burned-out shell of the building that used to be Abel's home and surveying the destruction all around them, the aunt asked Abel whether he still believed Germany could win the war. "We should be glad to have escaped by the skin of our teeth this time," he replied. "That did not sound too optimistic," his widow would later comment, "but it also tells us little about how he imagined the end."[75]

Certainly, Abel's foresight in evacuating his family from Hamburg in good time was a smart decision, but it also may have robbed him of the only opportunity to discuss confidentially with his wife his unhappy months on *U-154*, Kusch's annoying and constant criticism of Hitler and the Nazi Party of which Abel was a proud member, as well as whether he and Druschel should perhaps request a meeting to discuss the whole situation with the flotilla commander. Mrs. Abel would never know of these tensions and apprehensions and the inner turmoil that tormented her husband. She later speculated he kept them to himself not only to not bother her in troubled times, but also on the outside chance that the moment he arrived back in Lorient there might yet be a boat waiting for him to take over.

Abel himself could not have been so optimistic. After all, he was on leave specifically as *U-154*'s I.W.O. and not as someone already earmarked to attend the additional training courses required to command a boat. Not only bitter from the traumatic loss of his home in Hamburg to the British air raids and worried over how his family would fare while he was away, he must have returned to Lorient with cheerless premonitions about what lay ahead. When no change was announced regarding his duties aboard *U-154* during its upcoming patrol, Abel knew Kusch's evaluation had not been an altogether positive one. With no time left to talk the situation over with the flotilla staff, and silently "gritting his teeth," as his widow suspected, Abel braced himself for three more months of political and personal conflict with Kusch in the cramped confines of a fighting submarine.[76] Unwittingly, flotilla commander Ernst Kals—to Kusch's regret and Abel's deepest disappointment, resentment, and mortification—was thus prolonging and intensifying a drama he could have defused and ended in that summer of 1943 with a modicum of imagination and without serious consequences for anyone involved.

CHAPTER 5

SECOND PATROL

While Ulrich Abel and Kurt Druschel remained *U-154*'s first watch officer and chief engineer, respectively, on their second mission under Kusch, there would be several personnel changes. Reliable Ensign Heinrich Meyer, the quiet and competent II.W.O., moved on to commission the Type VII boat *U-287* in Bremen that same September and saw subsequent service mainly with the Twenty-Fourth Training Flotilla in the Baltic. He and all his men survived the war. In his place, thirty-eight-year-old Lieutenant Arno Funke came on board, a reserve officer like Abel with whom he would establish a close friendship largely grounded in overlapping political persuasions and common merchant marine background. Funke was reportedly a Nazi party member since before the war and, again like Abel, did not subscribe to the Christian faith, professing instead to be *gottgläubig*, a common code word for a vaguely deistic spirituality popular among Hitler's followers.[1]

Among other departures were the two midshipmen, Horst Fröhlich and Hellmuth Kirchammer of Crew X/41. They had learned much under Kusch. After a brief stint aboard the cruiser *Köln*, Fröhlich would become a watch officer on *U-541*, a Type IX boat that surrendered at war's end at Gibraltar after a last patrol from a Norwegian base in April and May 1945. Kirchammer likewise stayed with the U-boat arm and at the end of the war served as a watch officer on *U-3501* and *U-3517*, both brand-new boats of the revolutionary Type XXI class that were commissioned too late to see action.[2]

Kusch would moreover lose two close confidants among the boat's enlisted men—his III.W.O. and most senior petty officer, *Obersteuermann* Heinrich Lüdmann, along with chief radio operator Hans Janker. Lüdmann had been on board ever since *U-154*'s commissioning, had participated in every one of its patrols under three different skippers for a total of 361 days at sea, and had earned the undivided respect and admiration of the crew. His replacement was Karl Hoffmann. Three years older than Kusch, Hoffmann would fulfill his duties with solid professionalism even though his relationship with his commanding officer appears to have been less intimate than that of his predecessor. Janker, who had to leave for unspecified health reasons, turned his radio department over to his No. 2 Kurt Isensee, whom Kusch already knew well and trusted fully.

U-154 also welcomed an unexpected and unusual participant on its second patrol under Kusch—Army Staff Surgeon Dr. med. habil. Hans Nothdurft. As a trained medical doctor, Nothdurft held the rank of a reserve army captain and in his civilian capacity worked as a research scientist for Heidelberg University specializing in hydrogen and carbonic acid measurements and the design of scientific equipment in that field. He was now on special assignment for the U-Boat Command to extend earlier work he had done aboard German submarines in the Baltic. In particular Nothdurft was to investigate "how to prevent hydrogen explosions on U-boats operating under tropical conditions and to measure the amount and distribution of hydrogen in the battery compartments and in the boat as a whole."[3] While it was neither his assignment nor a part of his medical specialization, Nothdurft would also compose a lengthy and fascinating report on the physical environment under which U-boat crews had to live and fight in tropical climates.[4]

While his scientific credentials and research work aboard *U-154* must be judged as outstanding, Nothdurft would come to play a central and to this day oddly oscillating role as a participant, observer, manipulator, witness, chronicler, commentator, arbitrator, and even amateur psychologist and psychiatrist, in terms of the continually unfolding drama between Kusch and his other officers. These were Nothdurft's initial impressions upon arriving in Lorient:

> Since the commanding officer returned from his leave only a few hours before we sailed, I spent several days in the company of just the boat's officers. Abel and Druschel had already undertaken one mission under Kusch. Funke was new. I immediately noticed with how little respect they spoke of their skipper. In their eyes he was completely unqualified to lead the boat. They told me he was an artist, not an officer. He only showed up two minutes before departure, never paid attention to routine matters, his successes were really theirs, and they typically had to push him into action, which he then avoided or broke off prematurely. It became immediately obvious that Abel and Druschel were close friends and stood in fierce opposition to Kusch.[5]

Clearly, Nothdurft was preparing himself for a most terrible experience even before he learned of the political chasm that separated Kusch from his officers. In all this, one must bear in mind that Nothdurft, despite all apparent attention to detail in his writings and oral testimony, by his own admission had no experience whatsoever when it came to command arrangements on a frontline submarine, especially when in action, and that consequently his descriptions and judgments represent the impressions of an outsider and amateur rather than those of a knowledgeable expert.

During its lengthy overhaul, *U-154* had been fitted with additional antiaircraft weaponry and a more advanced version of radar-wave detecting equipment, in addition to having its hydrophones put back in order. Everyone understood that the main threat to the boat emanated from enemy aircraft whose ubiquity was further enhanced at this time by so-called hunter-killer groups built around U.S. Navy escort carriers and their destroyer escorts. In this manner, the Allies managed to close the remaining gaps in aerial coverage over those portions of the Atlantic not previously reachable by land-based planes. In short, even when not in combat situations, sheer survival required and demanded permanent and painstaking monitoring of the surrounding airspace, the surface of the sea, and the depths below it. And no one aboard *U-154* needed a reminder that the Bay of Biscay represented a special circle of hell for any U-boat in transit.

At 1800 on September 23, 1943, Kusch gave the order to cast off and directed the boat out to sea, this time in the company of *U-211* and *U-306* and the customary mine-clearing and aircraft-deterring escorts. The two accompanying smaller Type VII boats had been in Lorient just for repairs and were now returning to their home base up the Breton peninsula in Brest in preparation for their next extended patrols—from which neither of them was destined to come back. As before, Kusch put *U-154* into a deep dive once he had reached waters safe to do so to test whether the pressure hull was tight, no fuel tanks or diving cells were leaking, and all pumps were working properly. The results were far from satisfactory this time, and Kusch quickly decided to follow his two companions up to Brest for necessary repairs. It took the yard there an entire week to fix the problems and so it was only at 1530 on October 2 that *U-154* could begin its sixth patrol of the war in earnest.

Crossing the Bay of Biscay turned out to be a relatively uneventful passage in October, given its much shorter daylight hours than on previous occasions closer to the summer solstice. By day, the boat proceeded economically under water and then surfaced after dark to run westward at high speed while Druschel's dynamos recharged the batteries and lookouts kept their eyes peeled for enemy vessels and aircraft. In fact, autumn storms represented a fiercer menace than any Allied measures. On October 7 the boat's diary recorded that all lashings securing the quadruple flak behind the bridge had parted and required fixing.

On his way into the South Atlantic, Kusch spent several days reconnoitering the waters off Ponta Delgada in the neutral Portuguese Azores without detecting a suitable target. After a brief mid-ocean encounter on October 14 with the legendary *U-123*, likewise of the Second U-Boat Flotilla, and a chat with its skipper Horst von Schroeter of Crew 37b, Kusch was assigned once again an operational area off the Brazilian coast covering 10 degrees of latitude on both sides of the Equator, or roughly the offshore waters north and south of the mouth of the Amazon River. U-Boat Command added significantly: "Be always prepared for a surprise and make sure the lookouts are completely focused despite the heat; aircraft usually show up one at a time, but once they have spotted a U-boat they are tenacious and try to call in reinforcements."[6] Not everyone on board looked forward to spending the next eight weeks in the tropics.

Dr. Nothdurft's medical report conveys a fairly stark picture of what it meant physically for submariners to live and fight under tropical conditions, particularly when the boat had to remain submerged for an average of over twelve hours a day.[7] Skin diseases were widespread, largely because of poor hygiene, exposure to salt water, and the rationing of fresh water to one liter per man per day. With only two toilets for fifty men and tightly regulated schedules as to when they could be used and for what business, along with limited bodily movement when under water, intestinal problems and constipation were not uncommon. Removing human waste in coverless buckets up the conning tower to the bridge and from there out into the sea amounted always to a messy chore and inevitably distracted the officer and lookouts on watch. During longer dives without outside ventilation, the air quality deteriorated rapidly as its carbonic acid content rose and oxygen levels fell so that crewmembers began feeling a tightening in their chests along with numbness and dizziness. In tropical latitudes, the inside temperature ranged from 30 to 36 degrees Celsius with humidity readings at or near the saturation point after a twelve-hour dive. Under such conditions the body can no longer sweat properly and overheating and exhaustion become serious concerns, particularly for the engine personnel laboring under the most unfavorable conditions of all. "It is not possible to expose the crew to an underwater march lasting more than 20 days," Nothdurft observed. "After that the boat *must* leave its operational area, if only to rest the men." He advised that "any improvement in conditions on boats operating in the tropics has to begin with drying out the inside air" and rearranging the ventilation systems to optimize air circulation within the boat.

On the other hand, Nothdurft found the quality, quantity, variety, and preparation of the food excellent. Also, the general health of the crew amazed him, noting that no surgery was required and no accidents occurred during the patrol. The most common ailment was *otitis media*, an infection of the ear canal, presumably caused by the fetid air and frequent changes in air pressure. Nothdurft likewise praised the boat's medical equipment, noting in a humorous aside that he considered syringes for injections against gonorrhea "unnecessary ballast." Interestingly, he did not comment on the psychological dimensions of a submariner's plight, even though he subjected Kusch later to an extensive albeit improvised psychological analysis.

Then, on November 3, about one hundred nautical miles northwest of Cabo Sao Roque, a situation developed whose outcome would generate yet a further and deeper estrangement between Kusch and his other officers. At 1004 in the morning, while the boat was moving along submerged at slow speed, the hydrophone operator registered propeller noises some distance away to the southwest (253 degrees true) in the direction of the Brazilian coast. Kusch brought the boat up to periscope depth and saw at an estimated distance of nine thousand to ten thousand meters a convoy consisting of twelve to fifteen merchant vessels, including tankers, in a rather loose formation. This was Convoy TJ-12 running between Trinidad, where it had left on October 23, and Rio de Janeiro, where it arrived on November 10.[8] According to Kusch's observations, the ships were guarded at a minimum by a frigate, a corvette, and a blimp flying at low altitude just ahead of the convoy. They moved at about eight knots on a southeasterly course away from *U-154*'s present position.

Upon assessing the situation in the seclusion of his little cabin for about a quarter of an hour, and especially taking into account the considerable distance and increasingly unfavorable angle to the enemy, Kusch announced it would be best for *U-154* to stay submerged until the afternoon.[9] He would then seek to overtake the convoy well out to sea at top speed and to attack on the surface from its port side after moonset around 0230 the following morning. The boat was too far away for an immediate attack at periscope depth, and a dash on the surface to within torpedo-firing range would have been far too risky and alerted the escorts without delay, even though Druschel claimed later that he informed Kusch of the boat's ability of running at top speed under water when the convoy was first reported and that Kusch deliberately opted for a slower speed.[10]

Kusch denied ever hearing Druschel offering such a suggestion.[11] True, *U-154*'s batteries were nearly fully charged at this time as the boat had just dived an hour earlier after an entire night on the surface, and Kusch must have known this without Druschel's reminder. But was it wise to undertake a full-speed underwater race with quickly diminishing battery capacity against a target that was moving away at an unfavorable angle at about the same speed as the submarine's? This was highly risky business.

Remaining undetected and opting for a better chance to pounce later at night became clearly preferable to a quasi-suicidal dash straight into the arms of the enemy and not knowing whether enough battery power remained if a strike brought on a day-long depth-charge response. In addition, Kusch had to be mindful of the warning from U-Boat Command not to expose his boat unnecessarily to a sighting by enemy aircraft. After all, the situation was vastly different from the attack on Convoy BT-14 in almost exactly the same waters several months earlier. Instead of spotting the enemy at night and being able to strike almost immediately, Kusch this time came upon a distant convoy in the morning hours and in bright daylight. The accompanying blimp with its superior observation radius was bound to spot any U-boat in the vicinity that was running on the surface. While the convoy was pulling away at eight or more knots to the southeast toward Cabo Sao Roque, for the moment *U-154* could only follow at an economical underwater speed of at best three to four knots in order not to exhaust its batteries prematurely and to keep a reserve for additional dives if necessary. With every hour that passed under these speeds, the boat's distance to the convoy inevitably widened by four or five nautical miles. Even after Kusch surfaced at 1530 and picked up the chase at flank speed of about fourteen knots under the prevailing ocean and wind conditions at the time, it would be a long afternoon, evening, and night, provided there were no further complications or delays.

It was not to be. Late that afternoon, at 1757, as *U-154* was following the convoy on a parallel course well over ten miles out to sea, a PBY Catalina flying boat was spotted just one hundred meters above the waves making straight for the boat from astern. It apparently had seen the submarine from a higher altitude and approached undetected by human eyes or electronic sensors, cleverly using a series of billowing cumulus clouds and a favorable angle of the sun for cover. Kusch's instinctive reaction was to order a crash dive as the Catalina at that point was still about four thousand meters away. At a presumed airspeed of 250 km/h, it would take the lumbering plane about a minute to reach the submarine. But with extra personnel on the bridge and on the platforms manning the flak, the boat's usual emergency diving time of thirty-five to forty seconds now would have to be stretched and became a recipe for disaster because the Catalina would reach the boat's diving spot just as *U-154* slipped below the waves and find it in its most vulnerable and defenseless state.

Abel, who was in charge of the bridge watch at that moment, quickly and loudly overruled his commanding officer and ordered the machine-gun operators to remain at their stations and to open fire when the distance to the plane had shrunk to between twenty-five hundred and three thousand meters. While the fire was initially aimed low, the barrage from *U-154*'s eight flak barrels must have irritated the plane's pilot enough for him to change direction about a thousand meters from his target. He now flew about twenty to thirty meters parallel to the boat's course on its port side at an altitude of just fifteen or twenty meters above the water. Dr. Nothdurft, who happened to be on the bridge, later wrote that Kusch at the last moment ordered the boat to veer sharply to starboard and through this maneuver may have further confused the flying boat's bombardier and prevented direct hits.[12] At any rate, the Catalina, still under fire, dropped four five-hundred-kg bombs of which three exploded twenty meters from the boat at a water depth of ten meters, sending terrific shock waves throughout the hull and huge water columns into the air. The fourth bomb, released too late, detonated harmlessly two hundred meters farther on. After the attack the Catalina pulled up into a steep bank to the left.[13]

Immediately after the explosions, Kusch at 1800 ordered *U-154* to dive carefully. He and Abel and everyone else on board were relieved to learn the boat had sustained no serious injuries besides minor leaks and some damaged equipment. In a tribute to Abel, Kusch later wrote in his war diary: "The timely activation of our anti-aircraft weaponry prevented the plane from aiming its bombs accurately and thus saved the boat." An hour later, *U-154* rose to periscope depth for a quick sweep but descended again to a safe depth upon realizing that the original Catalina or a relief plane was still circling above the boat. Over the next hour, as *U-154* slowly followed the convoy under water, Kusch reassessed his chances of ever catching up to it. Now that his presence was no longer a secret, it would have been highly imprudent to surface again before actual nightfall, which would occur several hours later at 2215. In the meantime, the convoy would have continued to speed away, rounding Cabo Sao Roque and changing course from SE to SSW on its likely route to Rio de Janeiro. Kusch figured that, even if *U-154* were to run at top speed the entire night, it could not catch up with its target until 1015 on the morning of November 4 in full daylight and it would still be standing behind the convoy rather than on a course parallel to it. In other words, even a supreme effort would only restore the situation he had found himself in earlier that day, with the additional impediment that the enemy now knew of his presence and was looking for him. Weighing all factors and noting in his war diary, "The area around Cape Roque is contaminated," Kusch decided at 2000 on November 3 to break off the chase and try his luck in waters farther north instead as a further pursuit of the convoy seemed pointless and would have also carried him too far south of his assigned operational area. After all, TJ convoys sailed from Trinidad in his direction once a week and the corresponding reverse JT convoys from Rio could likewise be expected in seven-day intervals. Presuming aerial surveillance to remain tight over Brazil's coastal waters, Kusch did not surface to recharge his batteries until the moon set at 0300 the next morning.

Many witnesses would remember how this encounter with TJ-12 and the highly lucky outcome of the Catalina attack lodged yet another wedge between Kusch und his disaffected officers. One of them was Hans Kuhlmann in the boat's engine room:

> During the second patrol under Kusch it was very difficult to sink any ships at all. Our main problem was aircraft that damaged the

> boat severely. I very well remember a conversation between Abel and Kusch. It was very animated, and Kusch said verbatim: "Abel, would you continue to press on with all the damage we have sustained and run the risk that we never make it, or should I make sure to bring boat and crew home safely?"[14]

Chief radio operator Kurt Isensee, who also acted as hydrophone operator when the boat was submerged and had been the first to detect the convoy, has left these recollections:

> One day I heard a convoy through my hydrophones. During our approach we were bombed severely by a flying boat. Because we had been detected and the enemy's aerial surveillance was well organized, it became impossible to keep pressing our attack during daylight hours. The commanding officer saw the possibility of another attack on the convoy the next night but decided to remain passive for the time being. Everyone [of the enlisted men] applauded his decision because surfacing again would have surely meant the destruction of the boat and its crew and would have inflicted no damage on the enemy. In a most unreasonable manner Abel and Druschel tried to persuade Kusch to resurface immediately, whereby they were most likely driven more by their officers' etiquette than by common sense. In conformity with his responsibility for all of us the skipper did not cave in to their demands. From that moment forward the hostile attitude of those two officers toward their commanding officer was plain to see. Whenever Kusch gave instructions from then on, especially Druschel would criticize them openly.[15]

Isensee also commented that, except for two or three "loathsome characters" out to ingratiate themselves with the I.W.O., the entire crew, consisting as it did of seasoned mariners perfectly capable of forming their own opinions, was on Kusch's side. For them it was Abel's and Druschel's constant criticizing and later semi-sabotage when carrying out orders, rather than any of Kusch's words or actions, that should have been investigated by a court-martial for undercutting the fighting spirit and diminishing the combat readiness of the boat.[16] In a similar vein, Werner Jahn of the boat's engine personnel has left behind testimony that he regarded Abel, Druschel, and Funke as "characterless and incompetent officers who only created trouble and dismay for the commanding officer and who in their vanity as superiors showed not the slightest concern for ordinary members of the crew."[17]

Lieutenant Arno Funke, the boat's second watch officer, would later support Abel and Druschel in testifying that Kusch apparently exhibited a lack of aggressiveness and was also overly cautious during the entire episode, even though Funke stopped short of implying cowardice. Upon spotting the convoy for the first time through the periscope, Kusch had estimated its distance at nine to ten km based on how fast, or in this case how slowly, the ships moved across the crosshairs of the optical device. Funke's personal observations—Kusch allowed all his officers, including Nothdurft, to take a quick look through the periscope—placed the convoy somewhat closer to the boat:

> If the distance was indeed less than assumed, we could have easily approached the convoy at maximum underwater speed and attacked within the hour. I cannot but conclude that [Kusch] wanted to gain time so that we would eventually lose touch with the convoy upon its next change of course. As soon as the commanding officer announced his observations to us, Lieutenant Abel and I agreed that an immediate approach toward the convoy was both possible and promising. The commanding officer did not share his intentions with us. We were surprised when during that afternoon he gave the order to surface, as we had not expected such a maneuver until the evening. In my view, despite the delay due to the air attack, we could and should have tried to catch up with the convoy that night. Abel was of the same opinion.[18]

Others agreed, including the senior petty officer of the nautical branch, Konstantin Wagner, who is reported to have stated upon being asked for his assessment, "It surely would look awkward if we simply ran away from a convoy that has been sighted."[19]

In its review of the war diary upon *U-154*'s return to Lorient, U-Boat Command complimented Kusch on the way he handled the morning situation and the Catalina attack, but noted he might have had a second chance to attack the convoy the next night if he had followed TJ-12 much farther out to sea after the encounter with the flying boat.[20] A careful reconstruction of the movements of *U-154* and that of the convoy, including calculations that assume a continued convoy speed at eight knots and a sustained top speed of fourteen knots for *U-154* under the prevailing sea conditions after presumably surfacing at 2200 hours on November 3, and even discounting the enemy's advantage of rounding Cabo Sao Roque first, suggests that Kusch's decision to break off the chase was sound. By 0600 on November 4 the convoy would have traveled an additional 160 nautical miles from the spot at which Kusch had originally encountered it, whereas a pursuit at flank speed would have placed *U-154* still 40 nautical miles behind it at that point, not taking into account the additional miles sacrificed by staying way out to seaward to avoid detection while the convoy enjoyed the benefit of an inside track around the cape.

Besides his oral testimony at Kusch's trial, Dr. Nothdurft has left two rather lengthy accounts of his experiences on *U-154*. The first is an affidavit from the year 1946 prepared for British occupation authorities in Germany who were seeking to indict Kusch's court-martial judges on charges of crimes against humanity. The second dates from the year 1993, written fifty years after the events. In the latter, Nothdurft added substantially more details and speculated about Kusch's mental condition and other matters. A copy of this document rests today in the U-Boat Archives at Cuxhaven-Altenbruch. Here is how Nothdurft covered the events of November 3 in his first testimony in 1946:

> As we approached the convoy [TJ-12], Abel and Druschel forced Kusch to undertake a daytime surface attack. At first the

> commanding officer equated this to a senseless sacrifice of the boat. When we sustained damage in an air attack half an hour after surfacing, Kusch openly mocked his officers. In our defense, Abel and the bridge personnel fired at the plane while Kusch gave orders for the boat to dive. In this way the rift between the officers endangered the boat on many occasions. Nothing worked and nothing could work. As a medical doctor and the most senior officer, but also as a one-time, uninvolved visitor on board, I saw it as my duty to play the role of an arbitrator so that we might at least return home safely.[21]

Despite obvious factual inaccuracies, Nothdurft captured the overall situation fairly well, in particular the brief instance of confusion after the flying boat was spotted. Not surprisingly Abel as a former minesweeper commander would rely foremost on an active antiaircraft defense, whereas Kusch, who initially may not have been on the bridge when lookouts spotted the plane astern, opted for a dive as the safer countermeasure. As it turned out, far from confirming a disastrous professional disagreement between Kusch and his second-in-command, the two officers complemented each other perfectly under the given circumstances and with their respective decisions prevented looming harm to the boat.

Nothdurft's more extensive document of 1993, considerably more critical and accusatory of Kusch than the first one and composed when its author was over eighty years old, adds a number of noteworthy observations about the TJ-12 incident along with passages for which absolutely no historical corroboration exists and which cannot possibly have happened the way Nothdurft described them. For example, Nothdurft reports a lengthy artillery and depth-charge attack by the convoy's escorts that is pure fabrication. Still, Nothdurft makes the remarkable claim that Abel, Druschel, Funke, and Wagner collectively had to push Kusch that morning into pursuing the convoy at all after he had allegedly proposed to leave this one alone because of the strong air defenses and to wait instead for the next one somewhere closer to the Brazilian coast since a convoy was bound to appear sooner or later either from the northwest or the southeast. After a dramatic clash of views, during which Abel is described as "shaking with agitation" and turning "white as a sheet" while Kusch was "likewise extremely agitated and quite pale" and speaking with a "hectic and unsure voice," the officers are said to have succeeded in changing Kusch's mind. Nothdurft continued:

> Even though the word "cowardice" never fell during the confrontation, it became patently obvious that all three officers, as well as the navigator [III.W.O. Karl Hoffmann] and I, regarded Kusch's behavior as such. Kusch had lost all followership [among the boat's officers] because of his defeatist "sermons." Now everyone saw his decision as an attempt to avoid facing the enemy. No one wanted to have a part in that. That was the main reason why the I.W.O. rose in opposition and why the II.W.O., the chief engineer, and the navigator agreed with him [Abel]. If Kusch had proposed what common sense suggested in this particular military situation, not a single officer would have chosen to disobey him. The military chaos aboard *U-154* was exclusively the result of Kusch's failure as the commanding officer of a fighting submarine.[22]

No other witness ever testified that Kusch desired to abandon the pursuit of TJ-12 altogether at this time; his plan was to delay an attack until the following night when it could be carried out under far safer and far more promising circumstances.

Curiously, in all their deliberations and disagreements over when, how, or perhaps even whether to attack TJ-12, none of the officers aboard *U-154* apparently took into consideration the extent to which this convoy operated differently from the ones crossing the North Atlantic to and from Europe. On the transatlantic routes, all merchantmen congregated at a single point of departure, typically in eastern Canada or western England, picked up their screen of naval vessels, and then stayed together during the entire crossing until dispersing at their final destination. By contrast, TJ-12 was a coastal convoy. As it sailed from Trinidad along the northern littoral of the South American continent, it would dispatch individual vessels from time to time to ports such as Paramaribo, Belém, Recife, and Bahia, while also picking up ships from those places and integrating them into the convoy. That may have been the reason why Kusch found the convoy in a rather loose formation. In addition, no fewer than six ships departed from TJ-12 along the route or after reaching Rio de Janeiro to sail independently without escorts to ports like Santos or Montevideo in South America or Durban, Cape Town, and Freetown in Africa. In fact, a total of twenty-three merchantmen belonged to the convoy at one time or another, ranging in size from 1,386 to 8,917 tons and obviously far more than Kusch was able to detect through his periscope on the morning of November 3.[23] The mongrel nature of the convoy should have been an argument for a closer and longer pursuit as TJ-12 had to slow down and open itself up when it sent merchantmen away or added new vessels to its columns, and there must have been increasing chances to catch vessels sailing singly as or after the convoy rounded Cabo Sao Roque. Conceivably, U-Boat Command had these possibilities in mind when it later disagreed with Kusch for breaking off the chase so soon.

The composite picture that emerges of the events of November 3 shows Kusch as a generally prudent and circumspect commander who, mindful of his experiences on *U-103* under Winter and Janssen, elevated the safety of his boat above rash and irresponsible heroics, in particular avoiding reckless exposure to strikes from the air. One will never know if an immediate submerged run at the convoy at maximum underwater speed would have brought *U-154* within torpedo striking range on the morning of November 3. Certainly the majority of Kusch's officers thought he should at least have attempted such a move while the presence of the boat remained concealed to the enemy.[24] His idea to deliver his attack on TJ-12 in the early morning hours of November 4 was sound enough, but had to be abandoned based on sheer mathematical calculations after the enemy had located and almost destroyed his boat late in the afternoon. Abel's decision to overrule his commander and fire back at the Catalina rather than to dive earned Kusch's subsequent approval as the wiser and luckier move under the circumstances. If Kusch was guilty of anything, it was his reluctance to communicate his plans and his decisions clearly and in good time to his officers and to supply satisfactory justifications and explanations for rejecting Abel's and Druschel's passionately advocated, high-risk alternatives. Prudence and occasionally indecision had marked Kusch's actions, not cowardice.

No one on *U-154* could have anticipated that its run-in with Convoy TJ-12 was destined to remain its only significant encounter with the enemy on the entire patrol, even though the boat would linger and lurk off the coasts of Brazil, the three Guianas, and Venezuela for the better part of another month. Given the proximity of Allied airbases, Kusch stayed mainly submerged during the day, relying on his hydrophone operators and intermittent sweeps of the periscope to make sure he did not miss any enemy ship traffic. At night he would bring *U-154* to the surface, recharge the batteries, air out the boat, and depend on his lookouts and the Metox receiver to alert him to both opportunities and dangers. It was also during these long intervals marked by boredom, ennui, and weariness in the hot and fetid interior of the boat that the discussions among the officers on political, military, and personal subjects reached levels of intensity and animosity far beyond anything that had taken place on the first patrol.

To gauge the nature and extent of Oskar Kusch's eventual legal troubles regarding utterances and actions ascribed to him aboard *U-154* by Ulrich Abel and other officers, it seems useful to cast a brief glance at six laws, regulations, and decrees that had some bearing on his situation. All German military personnel regardless of service branch were subject to the *Militärstrafgesetz* (Military Penal Code), which had first been promulgated in 1872 and been updated in stages by the Nazi regime, most recently in 1940. In the process, the number of violations punishable by the death penalty had increased from three to no fewer than forty-four. As one postwar analyst has observed, it gave prosecutors and judges "practically unlimited possibilities of proceeding against 'internal and external' enemies" of the state.[25]

Next was the *Kriegssonderstrafrechtsverordnung* (KSSVO), or Wartime Special Penal Code, of August 17, 1938. Sections 1 and 2 of Paragraph 5 specified that the death penalty for eroding the fighting spirit of the military was to be assessed against anyone

> (1) who openly encourages or incites others to refuse to fulfill their military duties in the German armed forces or those of their allies, or who otherwise openly tries to cripple or erode the will of the German people or its allies to self-assert themselves militarily;
> (2) who induces a soldier . . . to disobey orders, to oppose or physically attack a superior, to desert, to go absent without leave, or otherwise to undermine the discipline in the German or allied military forces.

In less severe cases a jail sentence could be substituted.[26] The key word in German is *Wehrkraftzersetzung*, which translates into "subverting one's country's military strength or potential,"[27] with its imagery conjuring up the process of chemical degradation or decomposition.

The third restriction was the prohibition after September 1, 1939, to listen intentionally to foreign radio broadcasts, including those of neutral and allied countries. Doing so could be punished with jail sentences, and the distribution of information obtained in this manner could even draw the death penalty, as it supposedly eroded "the will of the German people to resist." Every radio set sold in Germany carried the warning, "Always remember: Listening to foreign radio stations constitutes a crime against the national security of the German people. As ordered by the Führer, it will be punished with severe jail sentences."[28]

Of even older provenance was the so-called Treachery Act of December 20, 1934, or "Law against Treacherous Attacks on the State and Party and for the Protection of Party Uniforms." It punished with jail up to two years anyone who openly made disparaging remarks detrimental to the welfare of the Third Reich, its leading personalities, the prestige of the Nazi Party, or the Nazi government. The term "openly" was interpreted to apply even to cases "where one must assume that the utterance in question will reach the public."[29] This law was formulated in such vague language that "even the mildest criticism directed at prominent representatives of the state, the party or its directives became punishable."[30]

While the Nazis never formally adopted a "failure to report" decree threatening to punish those who neglected to turn in others deemed in violation of the "Treachery Act" and related laws, they came close to doing so in the shape of the "Directive for the Protection of the German People" ("*Verordnung zum Schutz des Deutschen Volkes*") of February 2, 1933, and especially in a draft regulation titled "*Verordnung über den Volksmeldedienst*" ("Directive Regulating the People's Duty to Report") of October 4, 1939.[31] Even in the absence of specific laws or government orders, the thrust and spirit of the intended decree were ubiquitously understood in a totalitarian regime. Dr. Abel as a trained jurist clearly felt uneasy about his failure to report Kusch's activities earlier than he did, and Dr. Nothdurft is quite specific about this perceived dilemma in his 1946 affidavit and in his document of 1993. Certainly, the vague legal situation encouraged denunciations not only from ideological and malicious motives, but also as a form of self-protection and forward defense.

Last, mention must be made of Grand Admiral Karl Dönitz's decree of September 9, 1943, addressed to the entire *Kriegsmarine* and titled "Directive against Habitual Criticizers, Whiners, and Complainers" ("*Erlass gegen Kritiksucht und Meckerei*"). The central passage of its first paragraph reads: "Complainers who openly transfer their own pitiful attitudes onto their comrades and onto other fellow Germans, and thereby paralyze the will to military self-assertion, are to be court-martialed without mercy for undermining the fighting spirit of the military."[32] Dönitz continued: "Ideological conviction and engagement are obligatory for military officers. It is therefore necessary for a soldier to carry out his duty with his soul and all his spiritual strength and willpower committed. And this includes his overall view of the world. For it is utter nonsense to say a soldier or officer must be nonpolitical. The soldier embodies the state in which he lives. He is the representative, the outspoken advocate of the state. Therefore, he has to stand behind this state with all his strength."[33] Whether any of *U-154*'s officers knew of this directive to assert ruthlessly military and political conformity, perhaps especially in the U-boat service, is not certain because the boat sailed so soon afterward. It would play a central role, however, in an address Ernst Kals delivered to the officers of his Second U-Boat Flotilla on December 23, 1943, which Abel and Kusch attended after their boat's return to Lorient.

Whereas Abel, Druschel, and Funke focused their eventual reports and testimonies on the substance of Kusch's actions and remarks, Dr. Nothdurft was given to lengthier descriptions of the circumstances and contexts in which they allegedly occurred. Given his status as an outsider, his unfamiliarity with naval practices and traditions, and a tendency to exaggerate, dramatize, distort, and even to invent so as to emphasize and celebrate his own role as an arbitrator and peacemaker, it is impossible to read his affidavit of 1946 and especially his report of 1993 without major reservations. Some of his observations ring true, add color, and enjoy corroboration from separate sources; many others do not at all.

Lodging close to Kusch's little cabin and the officers' mess just forward of *U-154*'s central control room, and not being involved in the rotation of watches on the bridge and elsewhere, Nothdurft saw and observed Kusch often and at close range:

> Kusch enjoyed great artistic talent and was deeply interested in philosophy. He spent his entire time on his bunk writing poetry, drawing sketches and reading books. He completely delegated control over his boat to his officers, not caring about routine matters at all. Even veteran crew members he did not know by name. If someone asked him a question or made a report, Kusch seemed to regard it as an act of impudence and interference. He did not take his meals with his fellow officers. He was awake when others slept and vice versa. His occasional orders were disregarded by his officers and he did not insist on them being carried out.

It is difficult, if not outright impossible, to reconcile the medical doctor's assertions about Kusch's quirks with the recollections of *U-154*'s enlisted personnel, and especially with the specific allegations advanced by Kusch's subordinate officers before and at his court-martial. At any rate, Nothdurft continued:

> After days of self-centered withdrawal, he [Kusch] had phases when he felt the urge to communicate with others. He would then sit in the wardroom for hours and talk, usually without eating a meal himself. He brought his drawings and his poems and told us about the books he had read. He admired everything English with abandon and hated Hitler and the whole Third Reich with a vengeance. For days he would only speak English. The enlisted men ridiculed this eccentricity by speaking English themselves. His favorite activity was to give accusatory speeches against Hitler and the Third Reich. In this he demonstrated an almost suicidal frankness. He did not try to restrict his audience to the officers. He shouted through the entire boat, called Hitler a criminal, an idiot, an out-of-control maniac, and so on. The cook and the radioman heard this kind of talk all the time, as did those who happened to walk by. He repeated these speeches on the bridge to those who were on duty there. He considered the war a criminal act and already lost, and the U-boat branch laughable and done for. He tried to impose his views on everyone, even though many were afraid to listen to him. Once, after he had read over the address system an admonition from Dönitz not to slacken off in the pursuit of winning the war, Kusch added, "Comment from your commanding officer: of course, this is just made-up Nazi balderdash." If someone dared to contradict him, he became even more specific in his argumentation. The enlisted personnel were afraid to be drawn into such discussions, but some of them courageously stood their ground. I am reporting all this in such detail to show that Kusch shared his highly dangerous views with all and sundry on board.
>
> By contrast, Abel and Druschel, gradually joined by Funke, were typical officers who believed in Germany's victory and called themselves often and proudly "followers of the Führer."[34]

Lieutenant Oskar Kusch in front of a U-boat bunker in Lorient. *U-Boat Archives Cuxhaven*

Oskar Kusch as a boy paddling a canoe. *Steiner Verlag*

Oskar Kusch (*looking into camera*) and his *Südlegion* scout group meeting secretly near Berlin in 1935. *Verlag der Jugendbewegung*

Dr. Rudi Pallas, leader of Kusch's youth group *Südlegion*, from a 1947 identification card. *Verlag der Jugendbewegung*

Midshipman Oskar Kusch at the German naval academy. *U-Boat Archives Cuxhaven*

Oskar Kusch (*foreground*) in *U-103*'s wardroom. Arrangements on *U-154* would have looked very similar. *U-Boat Archives Cuxhaven*

Dr. Ulrich Abel commanded minesweeper *M-1503* before transferring to *U-154* in early 1943. *U-Boat Archives Cuxhaven*

Kurt Druschel, *U-154*'s chief engineer. *U-Boat Archives Cuxhaven*

Grand Admiral Karl Dönitz. *Wikimedia, Bundesarchiv 146-1976-127-06A*

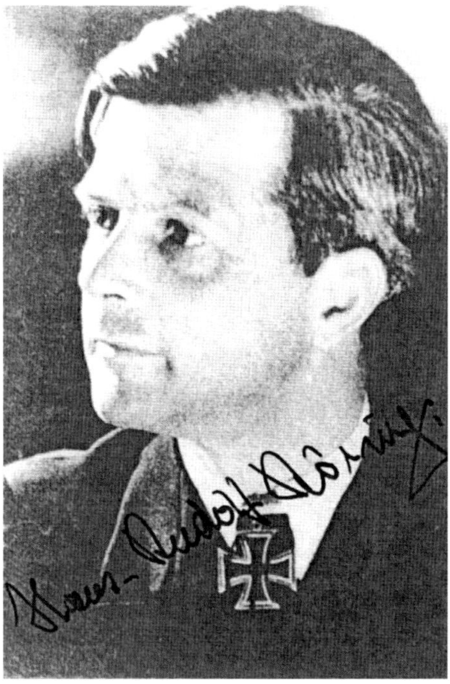

Captain Hans-Rudolf Rösing, in charge of all German U-boats based in France. *U-Boat Archives Cuxhaven*

Commander Ernst Kals, Kusch's immediate superior as chief of the Second U-Boat Flotilla. *U-Boat Archives Cuxhaven*

Oskar Kusch and Ulrich Abel salute from *U-154*'s bridge as the boat returns to Lorient in July 1943. *U-Boat Archives Cuxhaven*

Kusch (*right*) and Second U-Boat Flotilla commander Ernst Kals discuss *U-154*'s just-completed patrol in July 1943 outside the Kéroman bunkers in Lorient. *U-Boat Archives Cuxhaven*

Inge von Foris, Kusch's fiancée. *Claudia van Eyck*

Lieutenant Commander Werner Winter, Oskar Kusch's friend and former commanding officer of *U-103. U-Boat Archives Cuxhaven*

Lieutenant Gustav-Adolf Janssen, Oskar Kusch's friend and Winter's successor as commanding officer of *U-103. U-Boat Archives Cuxhaven*

Villa Forsteck in Kiel, site of Oskar Kusch's court-martial. The building was destroyed in the summer of 1944 in an Allied air raid. *Jörg Hagemann*

Lieutenant Otto Westphalen, one of two military jurors at Kusch's trial. *U-Boat Archives Cuxhaven*

Naval Detention Center in Kiel where Kusch spent the last 106 days before his execution. Picture taken in 2000.
Erhard Ohlhoff

Basement windows at Naval Detention Center in Kiel-Wik. Compare to lower right segment of Kusch's sketch, "The Merry-Go-Round." *Erhard Ohlhoff*

Oskar Kusch's sketch "The Merry-Go-Round," April 4, 1944. It blends reminiscences of Zürs with apocalyptic visions from his prison cell. *U-Boat Archives Cuxhaven*

"Judas." A sketch Kusch completed in his prison cell on March 8, 1944. *U-Boat Archives Cuxhaven*

"Fire!" Kusch's sketch anticipating the moment of his own execution. *U-Boat Archives Cuxhaven*

The street named after Oskar Kusch in 1998 running underneath the Kiel Canal bridge and adjacent to the shooting range where he died. *Hans-Jürgen Rust*

Kusch Memorial in Kiel-Holtenau.
Julia Backen/Wikimedia Commons

Clearly a good number of Nothdurft's observations must have been exaggerated or entirely off the mark because no frontline boat could possibly have functioned with someone of Kusch's alleged obsessions at the helm. There is no supporting evidence that he ever lost control over, or was denied full respect from, the men serving under him, or that the relationship to his officers deteriorated to a level where anarchy and chaos prevailed. Otherwise, *U-154* would have never made it back to Lorient. To the contrary, Kusch's popularity among the enlisted men suffered no measurable harm from his unconventional behavior and discipline and professionalism among his officers, including Abel and Druschel, remained intact, however grudgingly granted, despite all personal and political disagreements.

Kusch's fondness for English, incidentally, and particularly the fact that his men liked to ape him in good humor, are no indications whatever of any loss of esteem for their skipper. To the contrary, they should be seen as an indication of a close personal identification with him. Both the historian Heinrich Walle and this author have witnessed similar behavior in Germany's postwar navy, just as twisted English expressions—"Wahrschau" for "Watch out," for example, or "Reise, Reise, Aufstehen" for "Rise, Rise," the morning call to duty—remain prevalent in German naval and maritime lingo to this day and indicative of the central role the Royal Navy played as a model in the formation of the German navy in the nineteenth century.[35] Even radio operator Janker in his diary referred to Druschel's "enorme tauchings" (tremendous dives) in an odd mixing of the two languages.[36]

In his memoirs of 1993, half a century after the events, then retired Professor Dr. Nothdurft was even blunter in characterizing Kusch's peculiarities and his obsession with teaching his officers critical thinking and political insights:

> In regular intervals and with a certain solemnity, Kusch assembled us officers around the little table in the wardroom and imparted to us political lessons. He called this the "education for my officers" and considered it a part of his responsibilities

as commanding officer. He claimed he acted in accordance with the navy's duty "to educate officers to know and tell the truth." To make sure the chief engineer could participate as often and as long as possible, the two of them coordinated their schedules. Once, when Kusch appeared and I wanted to leave, he ordered me to stay with the words: "You are on duty!" Typically, Kusch wanted to discuss topics he had picked up from a foreign radio broadcast. Invariably they contained insults to Hitler and/or the Nazi Party or indictments of their warmongering political moves.

It would be impossible to imagine an even fiercer rejection of Hitler than Kusch's. Everything the military tribunal brought up against him . . . was true and not exaggerated. Kusch's verbal insults were not necessarily very original but they included every abuse ever hurled at Hitler. For Kusch, Hitler was an idiot, a criminal, the greatest disaster that had ever been visited upon Germany, an uncontrollable maniac, etc. Hitler alone was responsible for starting the war. It was the duty of all reasonably intelligent Germans to remove Hitler and to make peace immediately. Short of Hitler's removal, no peace was possible. In a similar way he made negative remarks about Mussolini. But as far as criminal traits went, Hitler clearly outranked him.

All of this Kusch sought to force upon his officers to "teach them the truth," among them two ardent admirers of Hitler, one a local Nazi Party official and the other a prominent Hitler Youth leader before they joined the navy. Kusch repeated his hostile comments about Hitler at almost every meal, i.e., several times a day. On our march south they took on the form of "education to see the truth" every two or three days. . . .

Through the I.W.O. and the chief engineer I had been prepared for Kusch's rejection of Hitler. But in its intensity and doggedness his hostility surpassed anything I had deemed possible. I found his dogmatism and missionary intentions beyond comprehension. . . . But ultimately, they only put a concrete face on something that the vain young man exuded at every turn and

> revealed to everyone who met him, namely, how unfinished he was and how unfit for his position.[37]

Nothdurft warned Kusch on several occasions that his behavior would inevitably bring about denunciations given the sheer number of people who were aware of his views and activities:

> I beseeched him to desist from continuing to make his disparaging remarks. If he could not do so on his own behalf, at least he should do so for my sake as someone who had no stake in his quarrels with his officers. I also tried to cure him of the notion that as an experienced and irreplaceable U-boat commander he enjoyed immunity in all matters political. It was his central delusion to believe that in a worst-case scenario he would simply be removed as the boat's commander, something that would actually have conformed to his wishes. I also raised the possibility that one of his officers might report him, not just one of the enlisted men. It was impossible for me to overcome his conviction that in such a case not he but the reporting officer would be cashiered. On the other hand, I told the other officers that Kusch suffered from a nervous imbalance and should not be taken seriously. They often accused me of sympathizing with Kusch's anti-Nazi views and of not contradicting him more forcefully. On one occasion when he declared both Hitler and Mussolini to be mentally deranged, warmongers and the main obstacles to an immediate peace, I withdrew from the debate without contributing an opinion. Afterwards they reproached me severely and demanded that I as the most senior officer on board should have hit Kusch in the face, etc. It took a real effort to calm them down. In the wake of this incident the officers developed a plan to submit a joint report about Kusch the moment we returned home. I rejected the idea with every argument I could muster, and it was thanks to my intervention that no such report was filed, at least not immediately.[38]

Nothdurft often reminded Kusch that Abel was likely his most implacable enemy as he had been a local party official (*Ortsgruppenführer*) in Hamburg before the war. While no evidence has emerged of Abel actually holding such an office, and his widow has always regarded the very idea as preposterous,[39] Nothdurft tried to employ it as a tool to tame his commanding officer:

> I wanted to make Kusch see how it was both a futile and an extremely dangerous undertaking to attempt to transform a Nazi *Ortsgruppenführer* into an enemy of Hitler. I emphasized that any adult German in his daily affairs must have had a run-in with an *Ortsgruppenführer* at one point or another, with a man who had the power to get you sent to a concentration camp or placed before some tribunal.
>
> But Kusch knew everything better. He only saw that I as an army officer knew nothing about his navy. He told me that denunciations in the navy against enemies of Hitler had absolutely no chance of success. Upon receiving such a report any superior officer would throw it without hesitation into the trash where it belonged and then subject the reporting officer to a thorough dressing-down. Thus, my remark that the I.W.O. and the chief engineer were keeping a diary in preparation of an official report against him, made no impression on Kusch. He completely rejected any notion that he might be in danger.
>
> I brought up Kusch's life-threatening misconceptions on several more occasions with him, always with a slightly different emphasis. My comments only bored him. He would not listen to reason. As far as he was concerned, I had to be in error because I knew nothing about the navy. When the I.W.O. indeed denounced him later in an official report, half a dozen naval officers could have suppressed it before it made its way to a military tribunal. No one intervened because they did not dare deliver themselves up to possible prosecution.
>
> In a second matter that I had occasion to discuss with Kusch he came across as just as dangerously prejudiced and unreasonable.

> He embraced the fixed idea that as a U-boat commander he was simply indispensable for Hitler until the end of the war and that nothing could happen to him personally no matter what he did. Should it ever come to a disciplinary reprimand, the worst punishment he could imagine was being reassigned to the Baltic Sea to one of the U-boat training flotillas.[40]

Kusch's efforts to enlighten his officers' political and ideological world may on occasion have made him sound and act like a preacher on a mission, and even if in an attack of vanity he liked to take on the air and tone of a celebrated and cocky U-boat captain, the vast majority of witnesses and observers among Kusch's enlisted men took such behavior as just another of several eccentricities which coexisted and could easily be tolerated in combination with his thorough professional and "people" skills. The U-boat arm was notoriously forgiving and generous in tolerating idiosyncrasies among its officers and men as long as these did not diminish the combat eagerness and readiness of their boats or, worse, involved cowardice, treason, or desertion. As Kusch certainly knew, the most notorious such episode occurred when Lieutenant Commander Reinhard Suhren in *U-564*, upon returning to his base after one of his patrols, approached the pier and inquired through his megaphone of the assembled welcoming crowd, "Are the Nazis still at the helm?" Receiving an affirmative answer, Suhren jokingly issued the order, "Both engines full speed astern."[41] His flotilla commander and Grand Admiral Dönitz knew Suhren as a good man and successful U-boat captain and nothing happened to him. The very idea of turning in a fellow officer for embracing divergent political persuasions seemed absolutely preposterous to Kusch and virtually all others in Germany's naval officer corps.

By late 1943, to keep on fighting a losing war with poor equipment and ever-diminishing returns had become a difficult and often fatal experience; but to contemplate desertion, to act cowardly, or somehow to pull their boats out of the war was never a realistic or morally acceptable option for Kusch and so many others in his situation.

Through daily and scary reminders, and warily noticing that ever more of their friends and comrades failed to return from their patrols, Kusch and his men were keenly aware that the U-boat, even a Type IX model like *U-154*, was increasingly outmoded as a weapon in this war. Bulky German Metox antennas on their wooden frames were no match for sophisticated Allied shipboard and airborne radar; depending on Isensee's good ears to detect a convoy a few miles away through his hydrophones clearly represented not the same level of reconnaissance as the British and the Americans spanning the Atlantic with an efficient aerial surveillance system; and, as the pursuit of convoy TJ-12 had just manifested, the inability of U-boats to keep up under water and during daylight hours with an enemy ship formation, left the other side with immense advantages and opportunities for countermeasures. The hunters had become the hunted for good.

Kusch would not have been Kusch had he not brought up such obvious deficiencies in his wardroom discussions with Abel, Druschel, Funke, and Nothdurft. Such analyses did not represent defeatism, as Abel and Druschel would later charge, but a sober assessment of Germany's military equipment, leadership, and the increasing paucity or total absence of tactical as well as strategic alternatives short of Japanese-style kamikaze sacrifices. For Kusch, it was self-evident that Germany's war effort was failing spectacularly, be it the almost hopeless struggle at sea, the inability to protect the homeland against frightful bombardments from the air, or the wholesale retreat of German armies in every theater of the war. None of the "miracle weapons" promised by the Nazi propaganda machine had ever materialized or made any noticeable difference when put to the test. The lesson Kusch drew from all this was to demand and support an immediate reassessment and rearrangement of Germany's political and military leadership. In his conviction, men like Adolf Hitler, but also Grand Admiral Karl Dönitz, amounted not only to warmongers but irresponsible war prolongers, exposing Germany, Europe, and much of the rest of the world to unnecessary and inexcusable death, suffering, and destruction. Kusch may have been unable to affect any grand developments directly, but at least he could seek to bring the officers and men under his care and command around to his view of the war and the world.

On one point of contention Abel was right and Kusch was wrong. In his Anglophile sympathies, and with few visits to German cities other than well-protected Berlin, it would not occur to Kusch that the British and Americans might deliberately target civilian populations in their strategic air campaign along with justifiable military targets. To Kusch's line of thinking, if, from time to time, some civilians died, this was surely not the result of a deliberate plan or policy but the accidental result of a few bombs falling astray. Abel, of course, knew better from his harrowing experience in the Hamburg firestorm, the total loss of his property, and the painful relocation of his family to the relative safety of a small town in Pomerania on the Baltic Sea. For Abel, no profound moral difference or gradient existed between the enemy in the west and the enemy in the east; the war was simply a relentless struggle until the end, and if a German U-boat captain had doubts about a victorious outcome for his side and tried to infect others with such premonitions, perhaps the time had come to have him removed from command.

The fact seems incontestable that Kusch frequently asked his radio operators to tune to foreign broadcasts, allowed others to listen in, and drew from such transmissions some of his evidence and arguments against the Nazi regime and the shortfalls of Germany's military leadership. This desire to obtain information from as many sources as possible conforms entirely to the impression chief radio operator Janker had gained of his skipper during the first patrol and mirrors Kusch's reservations about the evils of one-sided, manipulated propaganda. Favorite stations were those transmitting from Mexico City and New York.[42] Interestingly Abel, who must have known about this and may have kept notes or a diary recording Kusch's actions and utterances, did not make illicit radio receptions and the dissemination of their substance a major part of his report on January 12, 1944. Possibly Abel himself found the broadcasts interesting or did not see in them a major violation, because tuning to enemy radio stations with their known locations helped calibrate the boat's direction-finding devices and radio receivers, ensured accurate timekeeping, supplied weather reports and forecasts, and generated similar benefits when reception of home stations was poor or impossible due to distance, static, unsuitable transmission frequencies, or the fact the seven-year sunspot cycle so crucial for shortwave propagation had reached a minimum in 1943–44.[43] Picking up foreign radio broadcasts was a practice so widespread aboard *U-154* and other German submarines in World War II that Dr. Nothdurft mistakenly believed U-boat personnel to be exempt from the legal restrictions imposed on foreign broadcast reception at home. He also observed how Kusch ordered the helmsman, apparently with Abel's and Druschel's full approval, to keep close to the water surface when running submerged so as to facilitate radio reception.[44] Inasmuch as low-frequency signals in the range of fifteen to twenty-five kHz from U-Boat Command's powerful transmitting stations "Nauen" and "Goliath" were audible up to thirty meters below the surface and could be picked up all across the Atlantic with the boat's receiving antennas running from the bridge to the stern, Kusch's instructions made much sense.[45] Reception on frequencies in the medium- and shortwave range, however, where public and commercial radio stations would be transmitting, is impossible under water, as is the sending of outgoing signals.

At some time during *U-154*'s long sojourn off the South American coast or subsequently on the homebound voyage, Abel and Druschel, with Funke in tow, asked Dr. Nothdurft to be the one to take the lead in reporting Kusch to the authorities. After all, a staff surgeon was the equivalent of an army captain and as such he was the ranking officer on board even though subject to Kusch's directives. Moreover, as someone attached to the army he could not be accused of benefitting personally from Kusch's removal if it should come to that. A report by Nothdurft would also carry more credibility as it came from an independent and presumably unprejudiced observer outside the formal chain of command and without prior service on a frontline submarine.[46]

Nothdurft rejected the proposal out of hand as preposterous, unprecedented, unnecessary, and ultimately harmful to all involved. Besides showing remarkable foresight, the medical expert displayed at that instant a far finer grasp of what it meant to be a member of the German naval officer corps than Kusch's principal subordinates and embodied far more authentically the unspoken imperatives arising from the U-boat spirit. Whether soon thereafter or after some contemplation of his uncomfortable dilemma that thrust upon him the role of a reluctant co-conspirator, Nothdurft arrived at a triple strategy that combined the elements of delay, separation, and reconciliation. First, he asked for and received a solemn commitment from all three officers not to report Kusch to the flotilla commander the moment the boat arrived back at Lorient. Second, without telling Abel, Druschel, and Funke, he would request as soon as practicable a talk with the flotilla's chief medical officer, Dr. Ernst Frenzel, himself a former shipboard surgeon aboard the Type IX boat *U-516*. He would tell Frenzel of the tense political dissonances on board *U-154* and urge him to do everything in his power "to effect a separation between Kusch and his officers."[47] Third, hailing as he did from southern Germany and this being the winter season, but not yet revealing this particular project to anyone, Nothdurft would propose that all four officers and he himself, along with their wives, fiancées, and other family members, undertake a ski vacation at picturesque Zürs in the Austrian Alps as soon as they could get away from their obligations upon arrival at Lorient. He knew the *Kriegsmarine* maintained a hotel at the resort for the recreation of its officers and he would see to it that the chief administrative officer of the flotilla made all necessary reservations and travel arrangements and that the navy picked up the tab.[48] Nothdurft's hope, if not necessarily his expectation, was that the radical change of environment and the presence of their families would exercise a soothing effect on excited temperaments and inaugurate a reconciliation, particularly with Abel, who was now moving on to command at last a boat of his own.

After stalking the waters between the mouth of the Amazon River and the island of Trinidad for the better part of a month and not encountering a single additional Allied vessel or convoy, a frustrated Kusch noted in his war diary on November 29 that he was turning around and heading home with seventy-six tons remaining in his boat's fuel tanks. "Sadly, and despite all favorable prospects, our operational area did not yield any successes," he added. "Let us hope we get a last chance to score a hit on our march home."[49] It was not to be. Retracing its outbound route first to the waters off the Azores and then through the dreaded Bay of Biscay, *U-154*'s voyage remained remarkably uneventful; the sighting of a neutral steamer on December 5 and a cautionary dive before a high-flying plane ten days later were the only diversions from the men's accustomed routine as the seas churned around them in the miserably stormy winter weather. One can well imagine the somber mood on board when the boat passed the waters where Kietz and *U-126* had disappeared during their last mission. At 0900 on December 20, Kusch picked up his minesweeper escorts outside Lorient and *U-154* was safely moored at its wharf by 1150. Not a single one of the boat's twenty-two torpedoes had been fired.

Hectic days ensued. Kusch met with flotilla commander Ernst Kals and the shipyard staff to discuss details of the patrol just completed and his boat's repair needs after eighty days at sea. Several days later, Kusch turned in his formal evaluation of Ulrich Abel, this time favorable enough to gain him command of a boat of his own after completing the obligatory commander training courses at a facility on the Baltic. Before leaving for Germany, Abel sought and had a last talk with his commanding officer concerning their differences, but nothing could be resolved as Kusch was not about to be intimidated or turn Nazi in his sentiments, and Abel remained more convinced than ever that his soon-former skipper was unfit for command because he would not equate service to his country with undying loyalty to the Führer.[50]

There were other personnel changes and farewells. Some of the enlisted men and petty officers, including chief radio operator Kurt Isensee, were bound either for another boat, for additional specialized training, or simply hit the trains for a well-deserved reunion with their families, spouses, brides, and girlfriends. *U-154* itself would have a quicker turnaround than at its last overhaul in Lorient and was scheduled to sail out again under Kusch before the end of January 1944 with a yet-to-be-appointed new first watch officer to replace Abel—certainly a sign of how desperate things were becoming in terms of material and personnel and of turning the fortunes of war around.

Three days after *U-154*'s arrival, on December 23, 1943, Commander Ernst Kals delivered an address to the officers of his Second U-Boat Flotilla. Besides conveying holiday greetings from U-Boat Command, his speech consisted of a reading of and subsequent exposition on the "Directive against Habitual Criticizers, Whiners, and Complainers" as issued by Dönitz three months earlier. While one can imagine Kusch's amused reaction when listening to his flotilla chief's tortured endorsement of the grand admiral's exhortation to line up unconditionally behind the Führer and to expose malcontents as obvious defeatists and enemies of the German people, Abel would later claim the speech pumped fresh enthusiasm into his plan to report Kusch to the authorities, even though for the time being he remained conflicted as to when and how to go about it, perhaps even if it should be done at all. Commanding officers in attendance were supposed to call their crews together and share Dönitz's message with them. It seems unlikely Kusch made this request a prime priority.

In another matter there was encouraging news. Dr. Nothdurft's intervention and proposal to have the boat's officers spend a joint ski vacation in the Alps had borne fruit. The flotilla's administrative officer agreed to make all necessary travel arrangements and hotel reservations in Zürs at the *Kriegsmarine*'s expense and for good measure included close family members and brides in the deal. Kusch, Druschel, and Funke agreed to accept the generous invitation, provided they could first travel home to spend a few days with just their families. They all would meet again in Zürs on New Year's Eve.

Abel was already off to spend Christmas with his wife, Herta, and their children on the icy Baltic Sea and then on January 2 took up his remaining courses at the Third U-Boat Training Division in Neustadt located likewise on the Baltic near Lübeck. At the same time, Kusch finished up his leftover business in Lorient and then headed to Berlin to see his fiancée, his and her parents, and any friends who happened to be in town over the holidays. With Berlin having been under serious Allied bombardment since the previous month, the devastation he saw along the route and in his native city must have filled him with deep grief and convinced him more than ever that this war had to come to an end as soon as feasible.

By every indication Oskar and Inge had planned to get married during his leave, at the very least in a civil ceremony for the time being, and now had to share their consternation about some missing or delayed paperwork with respect to her Aryan bloodline. Their bewilderment must have grown all the more perplexing inasmuch as each of them had submitted the appropriate records years before when he applied to become an officer and she was a student at the university. Timing could not have been worse because, even in the midst of a world war, bureaucrats tend to take time off between Christmas and New Year's and will not answer their telephones or expedite files. After a visit with his father during which he rejected any notion of sitting out the rest of the war in Switzerland, Kusch had an opportunity to see his mother and complained to her about the difficulties he had with his officers. "The two officers Abel and Druschel," his mother recalled after the war, "just talked a lot and were clearly pro-Nazi whereas he [Kusch] had to do all the work for them, including giving orders, as they failed at their tasks. . . . As a result, the relationship between my son and his two officers was very strained."[51] Then, with little else to do, Kusch packed his suitcase and looked forward to a wonderful getaway vacation in the Alps. When he, Inge, her mother, Almuth, and Inge's stepfather, *Korvettenkapitän* Walter Klusemann of Crew 25, boarded their train for the journey south, he had no idea he would never see Berlin again.

Then as today, and no matter in what season of the year, Zürs is a lovely place to visit.[52] Rising over 1,700 meters above sea level in the Austrian Alps of Vorarlberg, a little more than midway between Innsbruck and the Swiss border, it features everything a ski fanatic or even a casual winter vacationer may desire: lots of snow; some easy and some more challenging slopes, readily reachable by lifts; smart hotels; fine restaurants, bars, and nightclubs; and a spectacular alpine world to behold, enjoy, and explore. Even in 1943 the town's reputation was well on the make. Little wonder then that the *Kriegsmarine* had selected the place as one of its favorite spots where weary U-boat crews, and especially officers, could exchange the hardships and drudgery of their service at sea for days of unspoiled recreation with their families and brides. Not only as a medical doctor, Nothdurft knew what he was doing when he proposed Zürs as an ideal antidote to the crowded, hot, steamy, smelly, and mind-constricting confines of *U-154*. It requires little imagination to picture the group as Nothdurft must have in their glittering, unfamiliar, and snowy environment: four men, deeply tanned from their many weeks under a tropical sun, amazingly surrounded by majestic mountains rather than surveying the endless ocean, relaxed and free from immediate worries, and intensely savoring the reunion with their families and loves.

Almost immediately this idyllic scenario with its wholesome promises would go sour. Complicating Nothdurft's effort at meaningful reconciliation, II.W.O. Arno Funke along with his wife and their several small children had to cancel at the last moment for family reasons. Already thirty-eight years old, this reserve officer, wiser in his ways than Druschel and apparently somewhat less imbued with the spirit of Nazism than the excitable chief engineer, would have had a soothing and moderating influence on Druschel and the party as a whole. Now there were only eight of them: Dr. Hans Nothdurft and his wife; Kusch's prospective mother-in-law with her second husband; Oskar Kusch and Inge von Foris; and Kurt Druschel with his fiancée. Nothdurft has left a detailed and convincing account of what happened next:

> From the very first day Kusch and Druschel quarreled bitterly. Kusch was supposed to arrive in Zürs already married and be on his honeymoon, but the marriage had not taken place for bureaucratic reasons. Therefore, the room reserved for him and his wife was no longer suitable [and they were given a single room each]. By contrast, Druschel shared a room with his fiancée. Kusch now accused Druschel of behavior improper for an officer and arranged for Druschel and his fiancée to be given separate rooms. Druschel in turn countermanded the new arrangement and continued to cohabitate with his fiancée to the vehement protest of Kusch, who was backed by Miss von Foris and her parents in this matter. Once again, I had to assume the role of mediator, not only with regard to the room debacle, but also because Druschel

> now threatened to report Kusch immediately and declared he would never again serve under Kusch under any circumstances. Together with my wife I succeeded in dissuading Druschel from taking action, particularly with the argument of how suspicious it would look to denounce someone in the wake of a dispute over a room during a joint vacation. In addition, I pointed out that a report would likely result in Kusch's death. Deep down Druschel only desired a separation from Kusch. In the end, he desisted from reporting Kusch and he promised me also not to submit a report when he returned to Lorient.[53]

Thus Druschel, despite another agitated run-in with Kusch and deeply angry that his captain could and would not mind his own business even on a vacation, kept honoring and extending the pledge he had given Nothdurft out in the Atlantic weeks before. Nothdurft's hunch that Druschel simply had enough of Kusch and wanted nothing better than to get away from him was likely correct. Whether Nothdurft confided to Druschel that he was working behind the scenes through Dr. Frenzel to have either Kusch or Druschel reassigned to a different boat within the flotilla, is not certain, but it would have provided a powerful additional argument to keep Druschel under control. Also, Druschel as a regular naval officer on active duty may have felt greater ethical restraints when it came to turning in a fellow officer than Abel and Funke, who were reservists. Finally, given the political dimension the report was likely to assume and the legal complications it would generate, a denunciation might backfire on those making it for not submitting the report earlier. After all, some of the allegations dated back to the previous winter.

The uneasy standoff in Zürs would last for more than two weeks until January 16, 1944. On that day, a Sunday, Kusch received a telephone call from his flotilla in France ordering him to return to Lorient. No reasons were given. Perhaps the boat was ready for its next patrol earlier than expected, as indeed it had left the dock six days before.[54] With his tendency to delay his appearance on board until as close to the boat's sailing as possible, Kusch decided to linger a few more days in Zürs with Inge, her parents, and the Nothdurfts. After Druschel had departed the next day as scheduled, Kusch inquired from Nothdurft whether the engineer might have reported him. Nothdurft could assure him that this was definitely not the case, even though Inge and her family remained convinced at the time that it must have been Druschel because of the hotel room flap.[55] If his recall was unconnected to his next patrol, having heard nothing about a possible reassignment, and remembering his last talk with his former second-in-command, Kusch's suspicions must have quickly turned to Abel.

After taking leave of his fiancée, her family, and the Nothdurfts, Kusch left for Lorient on January 19. On her trip back to Berlin later that week, Inge von Foris shared a train compartment with the Nothdurfts for part of the way. Nothdurft would write after the war:

> I remember perfectly well my conversation with Kusch's bride on the train. I made clear to her that Kusch's expectation to be merely reassigned was much too optimistic. Deep down she agreed with me. She broke down in tears and complained that not even she and her stepfather, who was also a naval captain, had been able to rein in Kusch's careless remarks. . . . I promised to do my utmost on Kusch's behalf, but also reminded her how serious the whole situation had become. When I predicted as a minimal sentence a reduction in rank, Miss von Foris replied that in such a case Kusch would kill himself.[56]

Without telling Inge von Foris, by this time Nothdurft already carried a telegram in his pocket ordering him to appear on January 26 as a witness in a criminal case against Lieutenant Oskar Kusch before the military court of the Higher Command for U-Boat Training in Kiel.

CHAPTER 6

THE REPORT

DEEP INTO THE FIFTH winter of the war, without further consultation or coordination with his friends Kurt Druschel and Arno Funke, ignoring the assurance he had given Dr. Nothdurft, and never once discussing the matter with his wife, on Wednesday, January 12, 1944, Lieutenant Dr. Ulrich Abel submitted a three-page report to his immediate superior officer at the time, Captain (Ing.) Heinrich Schmidt of the Third U-Boat Training Division at Neustadt in Holstein on the Baltic Sea, where Abel was attending the remaining technical, tactical, and practical exercises and instructional courses prior to qualifying as a U-boat captain himself. The report read:

> *Report*
>
> Having weighed carefully the possible consequences of my decision, I hereby respectfully request permission to submit the following report about my former commanding officer on *U-154*, Lieutenant Oskar Kusch:
>
> In the course of two war patrols, which lasted a total of 189 days in 1943, I witnessed how Kusch offered repeated and unmistakable indications of being strongly opposed to Germany's political and military leadership. I therefore consider him unfit to serve as a U-boat commander.
>
> 1. When Kusch arrived on board in March 1943 shortly before we were about to sail, he ordered one of our stokers to remove

from the officers' mess a picture of the Führer, the only one we had, and to replace it with an awkward-looking picture of a ship he himself had painted. He justified his action with the words, "Take that away; we are not practicing idolatry here!" We officers kept our silence over this incident, but it was clear to us that serving under Kusch would be no small challenge in some respects.

2. Countless subsequent conversations revealed that our apprehensions were more than justified. Kusch's attitude was not only directed against National Socialism but it was quite unpatriotic and unworthy of a soldier. On one occasion he said verbatim, "Only the fall of Hitler and his party can assure peace for the German people and bring about a cultural renewal. Once the German people have the strength and courage to overthrow the regime, then the enemy will be ready to make peace with us. The people are suffering dreadfully under the burden of the regime and only its removal can set free their true strengths."
3. Our radio personnel circulated every few days a shipboard newspaper consisting of press reports from home and occurrences on our boat as reported by various members of the crew. One day Kusch supplied a joke for our newspaper—a very bad joke that clearly reflected his own political views: "Question: What do the German people and tapeworms have in common? Answer: Both are surrounded by a brown mass and live in constant fear for their lives." When our chief engineer told the senior radio operator that such a joke should not be circulated officially among the crew under any circumstances, the radio operator stated that the commanding officer himself had requested that the joke be included.
4. Kusch let it be known that he had never belonged to the Hitler Youth but instead had been a member of the *bündisch* movement that resented intrusions by the Hitler Youth into its affairs. According to Kusch, on one occasion his

involvement in such acrimonies almost led to his arrest just as some of his friends had been arrested, but his subsequent acceptance into the navy took care of the matter.

5. Kusch tried to influence in a political sense the two midshipmen who were on board for training purposes. Following a particularly lively discussion in our wardroom he told them, using these or similar words, "Pronouncements or instructions from our leaders should not be taken at face value. Smart people and future officers like you must form their own opinions about our present regime." Later I had a little talk with the midshipmen and reminded them in no uncertain words that—no matter what the captain said—both of them were bound by their oath of loyalty to the present military leaders and to the Führer himself to be brave soldiers under all circumstances, even if they harbored personal doubts or reservations in some or indeed in many matters.
6. Kusch called the Führer a "mad utopian, a megalomaniac, and pathologically ambitious." He claims he knows from reliable sources that "the Führer is prone to bouts of rage during which he tears down window curtains and rolls around on the floor." Once, when I was on watch on the bridge, the chief engineer clambered up all agitated and with his fists clenched. When I asked him what was the matter, he told me in a low voice that he had just had another of those discussions with Kusch where the latter had made his customary wild accusations against the Führer and that he, the engineer, had barely been able to restrain himself from attacking Kusch physically.
7. When in the spring and early summer of 1943 we received, for the eyes of officers only, a number of radio messages under the codename "Rose," Kusch compared these messages to "whips fit for slaves" and characterized our military superiors who had sent them as "slave drivers."

8. Kusch has few doubts that Germany will lose the war. He makes a great fuss about German defeats while vastly playing down our own successes or assuming that our propaganda makes them appear greater than they really are. Even after we stabilized the situation in Italy he predicted that by Christmas 1943 British and American forces would reach the Brenner Pass in the Alps. Kusch is convinced that Germany's impending defeat will end the war before 1944 is over. For him such a defeat is by no means a misfortune since the Western powers have no intention of destroying us and will protect us against Russian intrusions.
9. When asked why he views a German defeat as imminent, Kusch refers to Germany's lack of raw materials and manpower while our enemies suffer no such shortfalls. This also applies to submarine technology. He believes that the boats now in service, because they are hopelessly outdated, have no longer a real chance of success.
10. Moreover, Kusch claims that the idea of a worldwide Jewish conspiracy bent on Germany's destruction is sheer nonsense and merely the invention of our propaganda, just as any other talk about global conspiracies. When listening to foreign radio broadcasts, as he does on a regular basis, he takes as the truth whatever those stations report while claiming that our own propaganda is spreading nothing but lies.
11. In the same vein Kusch regards the terror attacks against German cities as being greatly exaggerated by our propaganda. As far as he is concerned, enemy attacks are exclusively aimed at military targets, such as weapons plants. If from time to time some bombs fall into residential areas nearby, no one should be blamed. After all, our German pilots are prone to making the same mistake.

I am particularly concerned that, for all practical purposes, Kusch has forced his opinions upon us officers much against our own desire, and has done so always in a way that enlisted personnel, such as the radioman at the hydrophones or the cook or the steward, could easily overhear him. He even talked about the conduct of the war and similar subjects in front of everybody in the central control room.

Kusch's inner critical attitude is complemented by a lack of aggressive spirit against the enemy, which I observed on at least three occasions and which I will prove with the help of the boat's war diary.

I ask for your indulgence if I did not submit this report to my flotilla commander immediately upon returning from our most recent patrol on December 20, 1943. The flotilla commander seemed extremely busy, and I was still undecided about taking this step during the three days that I remained stationed at the U-boat base. I only made up my mind on December 23 when the flotilla commander warned all of us officers under his command about the seriousness of our present situation. By the way, I did have one more talk with Kusch, but it settled nothing.

The following individuals can testify to the truthfulness of my statements:

1. Lieutenant (Ing.) Druschel, chief engineer, U-154;
2. Lieutenant Funke, first watch officer, U-154;
3. Lieutenant Meyer (Heinrich), formerly second watch officer, U-154;
4. Midshipman Kirchammer, formerly of U-154;
5. Midshipman Fröhlich, formerly of U-154;
6. Staff surgeon Dr. Nothdurft, Dantestr. 15, Heidelberg.

Inasmuch as the boat is scheduled to sail on its next patrol before the end of January, I humbly request that the two first-mentioned witnesses be deposed in Lorient as soon as possible at the headquarters of the 2nd U-Boat Flotilla.

[signed] Abel[1]

On January 25, 1944, while temporarily posted to the Twenty-Third U-Boat Training Flotilla at Eckernförde on the Baltic that was part of the Third U-Boat Training Division, Lieutenant Abel submitted a lengthy and detailed addendum to his original report. Its three central points were: (1) that Kusch had failed to alter course toward a distant enemy convoy [SL-126] sighted by German aircraft when *U-154* was exiting the Bay of Biscay into the open Atlantic on his first patrol and that he had done so out of "personal fear"; (2) that Kusch had shown little enthusiasm to reengage the enemy after his successful pre-dawn attack on Convoy BT-14 on May 28, instead preferring to stand out to sea because, in his words, "we need to get away from here and will be lucky not to get hurt"; and (3) that in its encounter with Convoy TJ-12 on November 3, Kusch had broken off the pursuit of the enemy much too soon after the Catalina attack and thus intentionally wasted a chance to catch up with the enemy the next morning.[2] All three incidents have been discussed in chapters 4 and 5 above in detail and demonstrate how Kusch, with his enlisted men's full concurrence, sought to avoid unreasonable dangers to his boat in contrast to Abel, Druschel, and sometimes Funke who, in each case, advocated rash, risky, and unrealistic alternatives.

Besides pointing to the nature and substance of his report as entirely unprecedented in the history of the German navies and their officer corps, analysts have wondered and pondered why Abel did not submit his complaint to the Chief of the Second U-Boat Flotilla in Lorient, since that remained Kusch's command and had been Abel's own when the alleged incidents occurred. Was Abel afraid his report might be suppressed or cashiered by Kals or by the Leader of all U-Boats in the West, Captain Hans-Rudolf Rösing, with his headquarters in Angers not far from Lorient, in short, in circles and units where Kusch was known and respected? Was he hoping Captain Schmidt, who probably knew neither Kusch nor Abel, would be a safer conduit to make sure the report found its way into the naval judicial system without delay? Why did Abel insist on going ahead with the report when his goal of commanding a boat of his own was about to be fulfilled and he probably would never have to see Kusch again? Was it after all a bruised ego and wounded vanity that drove Abel to take his step because of Kusch's lukewarm evaluation following the first patrol and the humiliation for Abel of serving on a second mission under him? Or worse, had it become a case of intense hatred and calculated revenge with the desire to eliminate a personal and political enemy?

Then there is the riddle of timing and whether Abel gauged the full implications of his action. Why did Abel wait until after the second patrol to submit his report when the essence of his complaints and two of his three "cowardice" accusations against Kusch dated to the initial mission? Why did he break the pledge he had given Nothdurft, however reluctantly, not to file a report until further consultations with *U-154*'s other officers upon returning to Lorient? At least Druschel was caught completely off guard by Abel's report so that he could not assure Nothdurft until January 23 that it had indeed been Abel who "got the whole thing rolling."[3] Was Abel aware that, by naming Druschel, Funke, Meyer, Nothdurft, and the two midshipmen as witnesses, he exposed them to the charge of having known about and tolerated potentially punishable transgressions on Kusch's part and not reported them up the military chain of command themselves? Did he ever think of Kusch's family, his fiancée and parents, and his friends, who would fall under the automatic suspicion of associating with and presumably supporting a bitter opponent of the Nazi regime? Had he contemplated what might happen to his own reputation in the service if he denounced his commanding officer to his superiors?

Abel, according to his widow, "in his judicial training did not have the opportunity to acquire expertise about the jurisprudence and jurisdiction specific to the *Kriegsmarine*, not even when he was called up from the reserves."[4] If so, this might in part explain why Abel's report does not specify which particular legal boundaries Kusch had allegedly violated. She further believed her husband was quite aware a report against Kusch would hurt his own reputation in the navy generally and among his officer comrades, and that he weighed this risk carefully for a long time against the guilt that would be unloaded upon *U-154*'s second-in-command if the boat somehow fell under suspicion of sabotage and desertion and he had done nothing to prevent it. She pointed out that Dr. Nothdurft experienced a similar dilemma of knowing too much and searching desperately for ways to defuse an escalating situation. In her estimation, a talk with the flotilla commander behind Kusch's back during those three days before Christmas 1943 would "definitely not have been" in her husband's nature and was no longer feasible once he was posted back to Germany.

Mrs. Abel was not certain whether her husband had an opportunity to visit her and the children before taking up his commander training courses in early January 1944. "It would have been our last Christmas together and would have stayed in my memory as we had celebrated so few together."[5] Had Abel ever brought up the subject of his differences with his commanding officer, she believed she would have agreed with her husband "after weighing carefully whether reporting Kusch or keeping silent would have been the less dangerous option. After all the most important thing for me was to have him home safely at the end of the war."[6]

While Abel's ultimate motives for submitting his report will likely remain clouded in eternal mystery, his own testimony and that of others point to late December 1943 as the most likely time when he made up his mind to turn Kusch in. Clearly, he had been collecting evidence on his commanding officer all along and may have kept a formal diary, even though no such document has ever been produced and would have been somewhat difficult to maintain in the cramped physical space of a submarine with virtually no privacy. He knew his friends Druschel and Funke would back him up, possibly even Nothdurft, particularly when testifying under oath. His last attempt at reaching an understanding with Kusch had been a disaster. In his mind, he had done what he could. Then came Kals' speech. Did Kusch not fit perfectly the image of the perpetual criticizer, whiner, and complainer whom Dönitz had identified and ostracized so forcefully in his September decree as an internal enemy deserving death? At this crucial moment of the war when Germany's fate hung in the balance and any dissonant voices needed to be silenced, should individuals like Kusch, with their uncertain loyalties, their ridicule for the genial Führer, and their odious pro-Allied sympathies, not be removed from power and prominence? Finally, a major naval disaster was playing itself out in the icy wastes of the Barents Sea north of Norway in waters Abel knew well from his minesweeper days. The Battle of the North Cape on December 26, 1943, would lead to the destruction by superior British forces of the German battle cruiser *Scharnhorst* with frightful losses (only thirty-six survivors), essentially sealing the fate of Germany's surface fleet. From Abel's increasingly grim perspective, the war must have reached a point where only absolute solidarity, loyalty, and determination focused on final victory could now save Germany from disaster and defeat.

Several sources suggest there may have been efforts to dissuade Abel from submitting his report, either to withdraw it before it had reached a circulation beyond recall or at least to tone it down. Captain Schmidt must have grasped the seriousness of Abel's accusations and likely invited him to rethink the matter before proceeding.[7] Reportedly "several of Kusch's superiors," possibly including Admiral Hans-Georg von Friedeburg himself, Dönitz's successor at U-Boat Command, got wind of the report early on and may have tried to dissuade Abel from pursuing it or perhaps allowing the legal chain to set it aside.[8] As a complicating factor, Rösing as commander of all U-boats based in France (FdU West) was on vacation and unable to prevent or otherwise influence the formal initiation of legal proceedings against Kusch even had he wished to do so.[9]

At this point, several clarifications about the German naval justice system during World War II are in order.[10] Naval military courts, called *Bordgerichte* or *Kriegsgerichte*, were created by and operated under the authority of a so-called *Gerichtsherr*, a regular military commander into whose purview it fell to decide, typically upon receipt of a report, if a violation had likely occurred and who then tasked an official in the naval judicial service with investigating the case. This official would be drawn from a pool of some three hundred individuals with university law degrees, both career public servants and reservists, who collectively made up the corps of naval judges, or *Marinekriegsgerichtsräte*. They enjoyed civil service status, wore uniforms with silver insignia, and could be members of the Nazi Party. The *Kriegsmarine* system was somewhat odd in the sense that the respective roles of investigator, prosecutor, defense counsel, judge, expert consultant, and executor of sentences rendered were freely interchangeable within this group of officials. It could very well happen that in a specific case Official A served as investigator, Official B as prosecutor,

Official C as presiding judge, Official D as defense counsel, and Official E as the individual making sure that any judgment rendered was duly applied. The next day, in a different case, Official C might be the investigator, Official A the defense counsel, Official E the presiding judge, and so on. All judgments were rendered by a panel of three individuals consisting of the presiding judge and two non-expert *Schöffen* or "jurors," one of whom had to be an officer and the other a member of the military equal in rank to the accused. It was also the privilege of the *Gerichtsherr* to determine the place and date of any trial. In cases where the death penalty might be applied, the accused was automatically entitled to a military defense counsel. He also might engage instead a civilian lawyer for that role if he so preferred, regardless of the potential sentence level.

After 1939 Germany's naval justice arrangements knew no provision for appeals once a sentence had been rendered, only an automatic hierarchical system of review, comment, and confirmation, as well as the possibility of commutation and clemency at the highest levels, usually upon petition by the accused. Legal review simply followed the chain of command. In Kusch's case, any verdict was liable to review by Commander Ernst Kals, Commander of the Second U-Boat Flotilla and deputy *Gerichtsherr*; by Captain Hans-Rudolf Rösing, leader of all U-boats in France and *Gerichtsherr* in Kusch's case; by Admiral Hans-Georg von Friedeburg at U-Boat Command; by Grand Admiral Dönitz as commander in chief of the *Kriegsmarine*; and finally, by Adolf Hitler himself in his role as Germany's highest military authority. In case Hitler had been a target of the offense in question, Reich Marshal Hermann Göring would substitute for him to avoid the appearance of a conflict of interest. In cases where the death penalty or a jail sentence of one year or more had been assessed at the trial, the *Gerichtsherr* and all reviewers at a higher level were obligated to obtain a legal assessment from a naval justice official not involved in the trial. Significantly, however, the *Gerichtsherr* was not bound by this opinion, retained the right to confirm or set aside a verdict, and, while unable to influence the course of a trial or the decision of a presiding judge, could issue directives to prosecutors and enforcement officials.[11]

While this system gave the appearance of being set up and operating in such a way as to guard the independence of the courts and its judges, and of guaranteeing the grounding of all decisions in existing law, in reality the potential for manipulation, corruption, misuse, and abuse was considerable. As in any other totalitarian regime, the judicial apparatus of the Third Reich ultimately functioned as an extension of the state, which, in turn, had been conquered and absorbed by the ruling party and inundated with its ideology. Especially after the start of World War II, the naval courts became not only instruments for the legitimate goal of maintaining military discipline, but enforcement tools for ideological conformity subject to instructions and directives from Berlin, sometimes subtle but often quite specific. In the case of the *Kriegsmarine* this was usually done through *Admiralstabsrichter* Dr. Joachim Rudolphi, who served as the highest naval legal official on Grand Admiral Dönitz's staff. Thus, besides the possibility that the totalitarian nature and premise of a particular law might render it suspect or invalid by the yardstick of global humanitarian and legal standards, there was always the possibility and indeed likelihood that the application of such laws would be handled by compromised officials who knew and covered for each other and whose prime loyalty might not be to the sanctity and majesty of the law, but to the protection and preservation of the state and the regime, provided they did not act more basely from sheer self-interest and self-preservation.

While the *Kriegsmarine* carried this unacknowledged problem of collusion and corruption in its legal system, it also suffered from what is often termed the "Trauma of 1918." World War I had ended with Germany's defeat on the battlefields of the western front in France and Belgium, which in turn had caused widespread mutinies in the German surface fleet, brought down the Kaiser's government in Berlin, and eventually led to the armistice with the Allied powers. Ever after the memory of these mutinies, this stain on the honor of the navy, this singular act of supposed treachery and betrayal, had haunted and traumatized Germany's naval leadership and its officer corps and elicited the silent pledge that the events of 1918 would never, ever recur. In particular under Dönitz, any sign of disloyalty or defiance against the state, its representatives and institutions, would bring on an iron-fisted response. His legal representatives knew this and would act accordingly. No one has expressed this attitude more forcefully or honestly than Ernst Meinert, the naval justice official eventually tasked with overseeing Kusch's incarceration and execution and thus someone who could very well have presided over his trial: "I eliminate revolutionary types. I make sure there will no more 1918s. When I decide the severity of a sentence I keep in mind whether the accused has the potential of being a revolutionary type or not."[12] In a similar vein, Captain Rösing stated: "Our whole education in the navy after 1918 was predicated on the notion that those things [political dissent] had not been sufficiently suppressed at the time and a repetition had to be avoided at all costs." No cases of weakening of military discipline or questionable loyalty would be tolerated.[13]

In an apt summary, the historian Heinrich Walle has branded the subversion decree as an "instrument to destroy not only political enemies but already those who merely deviated in their thinking" from the officially sanctioned line. "Its character as an instrument of a system of injustice manifested itself in the fact that it did not only limit fundamental human rights such as freedom of conscience and free speech under the impact of war, but negated such rights on principle." Paragraph 5 of the decree "was worded in such an elastic manner as to practically invite arbitrary interpretations."[14]

The command arrangements in early 1944 required that not Ernst Kals—as Kusch's immediate superior in Lorient—acted as *Gerichtsherr* in his case, but instead Captain Hans-Rudolf Rösing in his capacity as leader of all U-boats in the West, who resided with his staff in nearby Angers. Kals and Rösing had much in common. Both belonged to Crew 24 and thus knew each other extremely well after two decades of common service in an ever-expanding naval establishment. Both were seasoned, very successful U-boat commanders in their own right and had earned the coveted Knight's Cross for their accomplishments. While Kals as Kusch's immediate superior had dealt with him on many occasions and Rösing had met Kusch in social settings, it was unfortunate in the long run that neither had personally experienced how much the war in the Atlantic had changed since their heydays and therefore might have found it difficult to imagine and comprehend the difference between commanding a boat during the "Happy Times" of 1940 and under the much more challenging and lethal circumstances of 1943. In addition, both owed their positions to Dönitz, and while likely disposed to judge Kusch's situation with sympathy and with as much understanding as possible, would ultimately follow the lead of their commander in chief. Kals was extremely critical of the way Abel had submitted his report and would have much preferred for Abel to have discussed the matter at flotilla headquarters in December so that it could have been resolved without formal proceedings.[15]

Since Abel had submitted his report in a different jurisdiction, and to make travel more convenient for any witnesses, it was arranged that not Rösing in Angers but the court of the Higher Command for U-Boat Training (H.K.U.) in Kiel would officially handle the case, even though the initial investigation would be carried out in France. Eventually Rösing would be asked to review any verdict. H.K.U.'s commanding officer was Captain Albrecht Schmidt, paradoxically with Captain Viktor Schütze, the former skipper of *U-103*, former chief of the Second U-Boat Flotilla, and Kals' immediate predecessor, in command of the training flotillas under him. Their involvement in the case would remain entirely pro forma. With Rösing still on leave, it was actually Kals as his most senior subordinate in France who on Sunday, January 16, initiated the proceedings against Kusch for "undermining the fighting spirit of the military, insulting the Reich, and spreading so-called horror propaganda." Also on that day, he issued a warrant for Kusch's arrest for "subverting the military discipline," "endangering the reputation and security of the German people," and "publicly insulting the Reich and the Wehrmacht in a premeditated and mean-spirited fashion." Soon thereafter a telephone rang in Zürs.[16]

In what could and should have resulted in a decided break for Kusch and his case, the justice official designated to investigate the charges against him, to prepare a detailed indictment, and later to serve as prosecutor at his trial, was Dr. Hans-Egon Breinig, who was at that time attached to Rösing's command. Born in 1909 in Lübeck and following his *Abitur* there in 1929, Breinig had studied law in Vienna, Berlin, and Göttingen. When all law students in Göttingen after 1933 were required to become members of the Nazi *Sturmabteilung* (SA), Breinig also joined the party, apparently for the entirely opportunistic and utilitarian reason of ensuring future employment in the legal profession, and particularly since his father as a former deputy of the German People's Party remained "politically suspect" to the Nazis. Breinig would testify after the war: "I was then still very young and my father had advised me to be careful politically. I have always rejected the Nazi Party and especially its methods. In addition, I regarded the leadership and the Nazi elite, but also the lower officials, as professionally incompetent."[17] Upon receiving his doctorate in law and having served in the military as a reservist, Breinig was assigned to the naval justice service and had since been posted to a series of commands, including ones in the Netherlands and Italy. He had assumed his position on Rösing's staff in March 1943.[18]

At this juncture it should be permissible to interject briefly a "what-might-have-been-if" scenario—counterfactual, of course, but still infinitely intriguing three-quarters of a century later. What if Dr. Hans-Egon Breinig had been designated to serve as the presiding judge at Oskar Kusch's trial rather than Karl-Heinrich Hagemann, his colleague in the naval judicial service? To gauge the resulting possibilities, one needs to go no further than to contemplate Breinig's own sworn testimony after the war:

> As a naval judge I was involved in a number of cases having to do with "subverting the fighting spirit." I always rejected the severe punishments recommended by the law and have always tried to help the accused in such cases. As I recall with certainty, I never assessed the death penalty in such situations. When possible, I even tried to avoid convictions in such political matters altogether. As far as I remember I served as presiding judge in 7 to 9 "subversion" cases, and all my verdicts were later overruled because they were deemed too lenient. Whenever I was the prosecutor in such political trials, I have always sought to change the accusation of "subverting the spirit" judicially into something less

severe, for instance into "creating military mischief," in order to shield the accused from severe punishments.[19]

Breinig added that for recommending a sentence considered too light in a "subversion" case, he once received both an oral and a written reprimand from his superiors. Breinig also believed Abel had reported Kusch for personal reasons as evident in his attempts to accuse the latter of cowardice.[20]

On the morning of Thursday, January 20, while Kusch was still riding the trains back from Zürs and Druschel would not arrive until later in the day, Breinig traveled from Angers to Lorient to depose Lieutenant Arno Funke, who had assumed Abel's former position as *U-154*'s first watch officer. In doing so, Breinig received clerical assistance from the administrative staff of the flotilla. Under oath, Funke declared he had been presented with a copy of Abel's report and that its submission "was in conformity with the consensus among us officers to file a report about our experiences with our captain through the most senior officer among us."[21] Breinig then asked him to comment on each of the eleven points in Abel's report. Inasmuch as Funke had only been on board during the second patrol, he was no witness to Kusch's removal of the Hitler portrait (Item 1) but stated he himself restored the picture later to a more appropriate location, presumably after Kusch had gone on leave. Nor could Funke provide direct testimony regarding the tapeworm joke (Item 3), Kusch's membership in the *bündisch* youth movement (Item 4), the midshipmen controversy (Item 5), radio messages received under the code word "Rose" (Item 7), or discussions about Allied terror attacks (Item 11).

In all other respects Funke fully confirmed Abel's version of events, adding that he judged Kusch's comments and remarks, "because he made them repeatedly," as reflecting his commander's "innermost convictions which he tried to impose on us." Fortunately, older and more experienced officers (presumably, Funke had Abel, Nothdurft, and himself in mind) were not as impressionable as younger ones. Even the youthful chief engineer Druschel held his ground, "joining us in our rejection of the person of our commanding officer." In particular, Funke confirmed Kusch's characterizations of Hitler as a utopian madman, and so on. Prompted by Breinig, Funke also revealed Kusch's monitoring of foreign radio stations with the audio volume turned low. In discussions afterward, Kusch would repeat what he had heard to the other officers, for instance details about the number of victims in "terror attacks." Lastly Funke provided observations and calculations why he believed Kusch had "showed a lack of aggressive spirit" when engaging convoy TJ-12 on November 3, 1943, both before and after the Catalina attack. The other two cases of alleged cowardice preceded his service aboard *U-154*.

Whereas Funke added virtually no serious new charges against Kusch, remained factual and measured in tone, and merely supported several of the accusations against Kusch already contained in Abel's report, Kurt Druschel's deposition later that Sunday afternoon went considerably further.[22] Having been present for both of Kusch's patrols, Druschel endorsed Abel's entire report except for a minor point regarding Kusch's membership in the *bündisch* youth movement and the Hitler Youth. He continued:

> In addition, the accused stated in case of a lost war and a likely change in government, he would march on Berlin and help shoot the representatives of the current regime, all of whom he characterized as war criminals. He also said the Führer had planned this war for years and started it. On another occasion he declared, "Germany can only reach acceptable peace arrangements once the current regime has been toppled and replaced by a military dictatorship." Furthermore, I have overheard how he told our men in the central control room that the U-boat arm is outmoded and incapable of achieving any more successes. By doing so he extinguished the men's will to fight and their faith in their own weaponry.
>
> I have further observed that the accused continuously listened to foreign radio stations. He also frequently said complimentary things about the English. He once said the English are physically in better shape than we and have better weapons. Should a German submarine ever run into a British one, we would be on the losing end of such an encounter.

After reiterating the charges about Kusch's supposed lack of aggressiveness on November 3, Druschel signed the typed copy of his sworn testimony and stood by for further developments. Since Abel had identified only him and Funke as individuals to be deposed as soon as possible, Breinig apparently felt no urge or need to extend his inquiries to the boat's enlisted personnel who were gathering in Lorient for their next patrol. Had Breinig done so, he would have taken away from these enlisted sailors a very different impression of Oskar Kusch and the incidents aboard *U-154*.

While Breinig began collecting evidence in the case against him, Kusch on his way back from Austria and never in a hurry to rejoin his command after a leave, had stopped that day in Paris to visit his friend Kurt Wiemer at his office there. According to Wiemer, Kusch at this point still did not know the reason for his recall and assumed *U-154* had completed its refit earlier than predicted.[23] Thus when Kusch arrived in Lorient and was arrested at the Hennebont train station on the outskirts of the city late that afternoon, he knew his apprehensions had been fully justified after all. Having been made familiar with the substance of the warrant, Kusch was allowed for a brief time to move freely around "Camp Lemp," a facility located a safe distance away from the U-boat bunkers and named after Fritz-Julius Lemp, the fallen commander of *U-110*. This is where the crews stayed when not embarked on their boats. Here Kusch met and took leave of three of his enlisted men, including Horst Kuhlmann, a petty officer serving in *U-154*'s engine department, and chief radio operator Kurt Isensee. Kuhlmann would later be appalled by Kusch's fate and declare that "the entire crew, with the exception of the officers, considered him an outstanding captain, both as a military superior and as a human being."[24] Isensee has left this account of the last time he or any other enlisted man of *U-154* would see their captain alive:

> When we reached Lorient after our patrol, the commanding officer went immediately on leave. Several days later Abel [Isensee confused Abel with Funke] and Druschel spread the news among the boat's crew that the commanding officer had fallen ill and

> would not return. When our captain did come back from his leave, he was immediately arrested at the train station but was allowed to walk freely around the camp. Since two of my comrades and I had orders to disembark and attend petty officer school, we went up to our commanding officer to say good-bye. He informed us that Abel, Druschel, and Nothdurft had denounced him because of defeatist remarks he allegedly had made and that he would have to appear before a court-martial. We three were so stunned and outraged over this colossal callousness on part of the three denouncers that we were speechless.
>
> To let the crew know what was really going on we repeated to them word for word what Kusch had told us and everyone was infuriated over this fake story about the captain's illness. . . . Later Druschel tried to make us reveal what our conversation with the commanding officer had been all about. Instinctively we suspected Kusch was not supposed to have talked to anyone about his case and we told Druschel nothing in order not to make life more difficult for our commanding officer than it already was. . . .
>
> Some time later I happened to run into Ensign Kirchammer who had been on board when he was a midshipman. He told me about the death sentence. Just like he the entire crew was outraged in the highest degree. Unfortunately, we were not in a position to come to the defense of our commanding officer, whom everyone liked immensely, because none of us knew about the accusation and the course of the trial. It would have never come to this verdict if the crew had been allowed to testify.[25]

Toward evening Kusch left Lorient for good as he was driven to the military prison in Angers that the *Kriegsmarine* shared with the Wehrmacht in that ancient French city and longtime capital of the province of Anjou in the lower Loire valley. He was booked into the facility at 2035 hours and would spend the next three days there.[26] Breinig stayed the night in Lorient but returned to his command in Angers to interrogate Kusch the next morning.

Friday, January 21, brought a number of developments crucial for Kusch and the handling of his case, beginning with his questioning by Breinig.[27] As with Funke and Druschel, Breinig asked Kusch to comment on the various accusations contained in Abel's report. Kusch began with a general declaration:

> In the broadest terms I would like to say that the facts and conversations to which Dr. Abel refers in his report do correspond to certain occurrences and talks we had on our boat. But in their general thrust they have been presented in such a one-sided manner as to obscure what really happened. I will not deny that considerable differences of opinion divided me from both Dr. Abel and the chief engineer. I can only assume the report is grounded in a completely opposite way of looking at the world, and thus many of my statements have been utterly misunderstood as far as their true meaning is concerned.
>
> Allow me to address the specific accusations:
>
> 1. It is true that I had the Führer picture removed, but only so that it could be placed in the central control room where more people could see it, just as it had been the case on the boat [*U-103*] I had served on previously. To the best of my recollection the Hitler picture eventually ended up in another spot in the officers' wardroom. I cannot recall the specific utterance attributed to me, but if I said anything on that occasion I cannot imagine I used those words.
> 2. I cannot believe that I made all those statements concerning the fall of the Führer and the possible consequences of a change of regime. I must deny having said those things because they do not reflect my innermost convictions. It may be true that we played a kind of mental game in which we imagined as objectively as possible what might happen if the Führer were removed. But I have never said in any sense that toppling the Führer would be a desirable step. Possibly, in the course of our speculations, we may have touched on

questions concerning the continuation or conclusion of the war. Obviously, as with all speculations however objective they may be, the mentioned outcome could only have been one of many possible scenarios.

3. The joke was one of many the radio personnel shared with me and with the crew. This was the only political joke that I remember. I selected it along with many other harmless ones that came to my mind without the slightest intention of making a political commentary with this one.
4. It is not true that I never belonged to the Hitler Youth. Until 1933, I was a member of the *bündisch* youth movement, specifically the *Deutsche Freischar* and the *Deutscher Pfadfinder-Bund*. In 1933, I was incorporated into the Hitler Youth's *Junkvolk* section and later into the Hitler Youth proper. I even belonged to the honor guard of our local detachment in Berlin-Charlottenburg. I rose to the rank of squad leader before leaving the Hitler Youth in 1935 because my favorite group, the *Spielschar* with its close ties to the former *bündisch* youth, was being disbanded. In this sense the statements in the report are clearly misinformed and misleading. It is correct, however, that I did speak out against certain excesses and what I perceived as mistakes that occurred in our local group, but this did not, of course, amount to an overall criticism of the Hitler Youth.
5. My suggestions to the midshipmen have been reported in a biased manner. I especially reject the notion that I implied they should distance themselves from the current regime. Instead I encouraged the midshipmen more generally to ground their opinions in as many different experiences as possible as well as in critical reflection. My suggestions to the midshipmen may have been in connection with item 8 below in the sense that I warned them against the kind of one-sided reporting that is typical of propaganda efforts and of which men in leadership positions need to be aware.

6. I deny ever having characterized the Führer as a mad utopian. What I probably did was to share with my officers some rumors I had heard to the effect that the Führer was prone to suffer such attacks from time to time. I always made sure to depict these statements as rumors, not facts. I always indicated my information came from friends and acquaintances who may or may not have been in a position to know about such matters.
7. Regarding the "Rose" messages I cannot recall that I ever used the expressions "whips worthy of slaves" or "slave driver." I do remember saying that the messages were primarily intended to boost our morale.
8. Again this point is misconstrued. What I said was that if we continued to suffer losses on the scale we had incurred on Pantelleria, Lampedusa, and with the landings on Sicily, then the enemy was likely to reach the Brenner Pass in short order. I never claimed that it was more than a possible scenario, let alone a desirable one. In fact, as with similar points raised in the report, I was speculating, I was projecting past developments into the future, I was weighing possibilities. I was not so much talking about probabilities and definitely not about certainties. This is what I mean by one-sided and biased allegations, as if I ever wanted an unfavorable outcome of the war.

9. and 10. Basically my previous comments apply here as well. I think it likely that in the course of our discussions I brought up the fact that the enemy enjoys better access to raw materials than we do. I am also fairly sure I said our propaganda tends to show matters in a rosier light than would be justified by the plain facts. I did this not to belittle our own accomplishments but to encourage a more sober and realistic assessment of the situation. Here as in other instances, such as my alleged comments about the Jews, I am the victim of biased accusations based on statements taken out of context.

11. Our conversations about air raids came primarily in the wake of the attacks on Hamburg. I took the stand that the enemy went primarily after military targets. Only as a secondary priority did the enemy go after civilian targets such as residential areas. My comments did specifically address the situation in Hamburg and to some extent in Berlin. I never denied that raids on other cities could have been sheer terror attacks.

Kusch added his suspicion that the report was ultimately grounded in personal dissonances and distorted deliberately what he had actually said:

> I fear that a deep animosity against me personally lies at the root of these misinterpretations of remarks I made in the course of our conversations on board. In addition, during our recent vacation in Zürs I had differences of opinion with my chief engineer about his lifestyle, particularly about the fact that he was openly living together with his fiancée. This matter even bothered people who were not directly involved.
>
> Moreover, I must categorically reject the allegation that my behavior or attitudes were at any time unmilitary, unpatriotic or somehow contrary to the National Socialist worldview. As proof I could name any number of witnesses who know me much better than my accuser. In particular I would like to name the following individuals as character witnesses: Lieutenant Commander Werner Winter, 1st U-Boat Flotilla; Lieutenant Gustav-Adolf Janssen, commanding officer of *U-103*; and Lieutenant (Ing.) Otto Strelow (probably 2nd U-Boat Training Division).[28]

Kusch went on to refute the three instances of "lack of aggressive spirit" alleged in Abel's addendum. He explained his behavior and decisions in each of the three instances and characterized the accusations as deliberately misconstrued and without merit. After all, "no one at U-Boat Command later criticized the decisions I made." Kusch concluded his comments as follows:

> Allow me to conclude by refuting Druschel's allegation that I described our present U-boats as being essentially worthless, and did so in front of everyone in the central control room. Very deliberately I never shared information with the crew about our U-boat losses or the causes behind them. What I did say was that better times were bound to follow the disappointing ones we were experiencing at the time. Even in front of my officers I merely said that our present types of submarines needed to be upgraded to assure again the kind of successes we had enjoyed earlier in the war. In short, I did not criticize as such the submarine as a useful weapon in naval warfare; I merely pointed out that future successes depended on modernizing and perhaps revolutionizing the types of boats in our arsenal.
>
> [signed] Oskar Kusch

Here was a first glimpse at how Kusch planned to defend himself. He would only admit what could not be denied, and maintain his actions and words had been misunderstood, misinterpreted, twisted, taken out of context, or that they involved hypothetical speculations rather than his actual views or intentions. Most of Abel's charges were entirely political in nature, some were of the *lèse-majesté* variety, and only the claims of defeatism and cowardice carried any military implications. But had Kusch in fact "undermined the fighting spirit" of *U-154*? Where was the evidence? Had his boat in some sense pulled out of the war under him because of some enduring chaos on board? Even during their worst quarrels with their commanding officer, Abel, Druschel, and Funke had carried out their duties and Kusch's orders, not to mention the rest of the crew, many of them service veterans, who saw in Kusch a seasoned, competent, caring, and kind commanding officer whose political persuasions and behavioral idiosyncrasies in no way diminished the fighting spirit and combat readiness of the boat.

It remains a mystery, if not a costly omission of the highest order, why Kusch did not request or insist in his first questioning by Breinig that enlisted men aboard *U-154* be deposed or otherwise be heard in his defense. If Lüdmann, Wagner, Kuhlmann, Janker, Isensee, Jahn, and others had stated under oath in January 1944 what they would testify unanimously after the war, the prosecution would have been hard-pressed to maintain the "subversion" charge and would have seen the entire case reduced to a matter of petty political disagreements and injured pride—unless political dissonances by themselves had become an indictable offense and punishable crime. The problem with calling up only Winter and Janssen as character witnesses was that they had not been on *U-154* when the alleged infractions occurred. On the other hand, the enlisted men remained available for depositions on or after January 21 for another ten days because *U-154* would not sail again until January 31, 1944. Whether it was lack of foresight, the rushed nature of the entire proceedings, or perhaps the apprehension that especially the radio operators would have had to confirm the acrimonious political discussions and the monitoring of foreign radio broadcasts, one can no longer tell. But omitting the voices of the enlisted personnel left central charges unchallenged and Kusch in a much weaker position than he should have been.

Also on that Friday, January 21, it was decided to conduct Kusch's trial in Kiel the following Wednesday, January 26, 1944, beginning at 0900. It would be held at the Villa Forsteck at Niemannsweg 178, a spacious and imposing structure in a park overlooking Kiel Bay that the *Kriegsmarine* had leased for such and similar purposes just to the south of its naval facilities and administrative buildings in the suburb of Kiel-Wik on the western side of the city. Dr. Breinig, already familiar with the issues and individuals involved in the case, would be traveling from Angers to Kiel to serve as prosecutor at the trial, whereas Karl-Heinrich Hagemann, a naval justice official on the staff of the H.K.U., would act as presiding judge. The court designated Lieutenant Commander Wolfgang Dittmers of Crew 29 and Lieutenant Otto Westphalen of Crew X/38 as the two lay jurors.[29] Dittmers had commanded a minesweeper early in the war and at the time of Kusch's court-martial was in charge of a company in the Second U-Boat Training Division. He suffered from increasingly poor health and was no longer fit for a shipboard assignment.[30] Westphalen, at the time commanding officer of *U-968* of the Fifth U-Boat Flotilla based in Kiel, happened to be at U-Boat Command headquarters on unrelated business when he was asked to serve as the juror equal in rank to the accused. He had been educated for a while at a Nazi cadre school, or *Napola*. Kusch's former commanding officer on *U-103*, Werner Winter, who saw Westphalen again in a prisoner of war camp in 1947, described him even then as an "overgrown poster boy for the Hitler Youth."[31] For whatever it may be worth, Kusch's file contains the curious note that originally Lieutenant Commander Herbert Schultze of Werner Winter's Crew 30 had been scheduled to serve in place of Dittmers.[32] Schultze, a Kiel native known throughout the U-boat branch as "Daddy Schultze," was a bona fide U-boat ace decorated with the Oak Leaves in addition to the Knight's Cross, a one-time skipper of legendary *U-48*, the most successful boat of the war, and subsequently commander of the Third U-Boat Flotilla at La Rochelle, south of Lorient. As one of many imponderables in Kusch's case, it seems appropriate to speculate whether the verdict would have been different had someone of Schultze's stature and personality rather than Dittmers' been entrusted with helping to decide Kusch's fate.

The designated presiding judge, Karl-Heinrich Hagemann, was born on April 4, 1908, the son of a shipbuilding engineer in Blexen-Nordenham in the former north German state of Oldenburg across the Weser River from Bremerhaven, but grew up in Kiel and completed both his secondary education and his early law studies there. He later transferred to universities in Jena and Berlin where he barely passed his state law exams in 1935 on the second try with the minimal academic mark of "sufficient." In 1936 he joined the naval justice system and by early 1944 had seen service in a number of commands and capacities, most recently on the staff of the U-Boat Command under Admiral von Friedeburg. Hagemann never became a formal member of the Nazi Party, but as a reservist during his student days had joined the naval branch of the storm troopers (Marine-SA). According to postwar testimony, he welcomed the nationalistic and expansionist program of the Nazis and had joined a student fraternity known for its anti-Jewish sentiments and practices.[33] Regarding his wartime legal performance, colleagues, superiors, and other observers have described Hagemann as "a diligent and conscientious official, a good jurist with a talent for organization," and as someone whose verdicts were not necessarily always on the severe side. But in a number of cases they had not been "sufficiently and convincingly justified."[34]

On that Friday, January 21, Kusch was officially relieved as commander of *U-154* and replaced by Lieutenant Gerth Gemeiner of Crew 37b. Gemeiner, a native of Dresden, had seen service on the smaller Type II coastal boats *U-146* and *U-137* in the Baltic earlier in the war and more recently been attached to the Second U-Boat Flotilla in Lorient in a standby capacity in case a need arose for a replacement watch officer or a skipper. With Arno Funke moving up to I.W.O. and reserve Lieutenants Hermann Bartelsen and Erwin Peter sliding into Funke's former spot on the roster, chief engineer Kurt Druschel, so youthful and inexperienced just ten months before, suddenly found himself *U-154*'s longest-serving officer on board.[35] A recent suggestion that Rösing also blocked at this time an imminent promotion for Kusch to the rank of *Kapitänleutnant*, or full lieutenant, seems unconvincing since even the most deserving members of Crew 37a were not elevated to that rank until April 1, 1944.[36] Certainly no written record relative to Rösing's supposed move can be found in the archives.

Upon his arrest, Kusch's treatment by men such as Kals and Breinig was correct and even generous, allowing him to move around on the grounds of the flotilla headquarters, to take leave of some members of his crew, and to place a number of telephone calls from Lorient and Angers to let family and friends know of his situation. One must assume Kusch at once informed Inge von Foris of his predicament and certainly called Wiemer, with whom he had spent his last hours as a free man in Paris. It would be the last contact between the two friends.[37] Most importantly in view of future developments, he contacted his one-armed old-time friend *Luftwaffe* Lieutenant Dieter Berger in Berlin with the request to engage a civilian defense counsel for the trial that was a mere five days away at that point. Berger moreover got in touch with Kusch's former commanding officers on *U-103*, Winter and Janssen, to alert them to their need to testify in Kiel as witnesses on Kusch's behalf. He even made a call to Lieutenant

Commander Walter Klusemann, Kusch's prospective stepfather-in-law, who then served in Ancona in Italy but indicated he would be unable to attend the trial over half a continent and only days away.[38]

Kusch had made it clear to Dieter Berger that the matter was extremely serious and that he could lose his head over the affair. Consequently, Berger lost no time trying to locate in Berlin a suitable defense counsel who could take on the case in Kiel, but his efforts ended in frustration and growing despair. When contacted in person, two promising and prominent lawyers and their firms, one of whom was Kurt Gollnick, either demanded a horrendous fee beyond anyone's financial reserves (20,000 Reichsmarks), declared themselves generally unfamiliar with the naval justice system, or pointed to the extraordinarily short span in which they would have to prepare the case for the defense.[39] Moreover, it was difficult to get responses on a winter weekend. Never slackening in his commitment to his friend, Berger then decided to travel to Kiel to try his luck there on Kusch's behalf. It must have been on Monday, January 24, that he stepped into the offices of Dr. Hans Beyersdorff, a former Imperial naval officer who had turned to practicing law in the 1920s. While Beyersdorff himself was unable to take the case, he could point Berger to his son-in-law, Gerhard Meyer-Grieben, likewise a lawyer and a veteran defense counsel with experience in almost two hundred legal cases since 1941 involving naval and military personnel. Meyer-Grieben agreed to take the case despite having less than forty-eight hours to prepare his defense and never having met his client.[40]

Meyer-Grieben turned out an ideal choice under challenging circumstances. Born in 1902, he had joined the socialist movement when he was eighteen, become a Social Democratic Party of Germany (SPD) party member, and been politically active after 1928 as a student and young lawyer in Kiel. He knew Hagemann quite well from those days and did not like him at all. Meyer-Grieben stated in 1946:

> I have known Hagemann for a long time since our days together in Kiel. He is a committed National Socialist, anti-Semite, and member of the Teutonia fraternity, which, as all fraternities, has

> anti-Semitic tendencies. I know for a fact that Hagemann as a student participated in National Socialist demonstrations against the Weimar Republic even before 1933.[41]

Meyer-Grieben's sympathies for Kusch and his plight undoubtedly grew in good measure from their mutual resentment of the Nazi regime. In addition, it took a special kind of courage for him to get involved in political cases because defense lawyers were routinely suspected of not only pleading their clients' cases, but of sharing their persuasions, especially if they had a history of opposing the regime.[42] In the person of Meyer-Grieben, Berger had found a man who combined professional competence and extensive experience with the naval justice system, and would demonstrate a caring and compassionate disposition when Kusch was abandoned to his fate by almost everyone else.

By that Monday, January 24, while Kusch was still on his way from Angers and Berger began to familiarize Meyer-Grieben with the background and legal troubles of his friend, Dr. Breinig as chief investigator and later prosecutor of the case had arrived in Kiel. He and Hagemann both occupied office space and enjoyed clerical assistance from the H.K.U. staff aboard the *Erwin Wassner*, a former freighter and submarine tender then moored along the waterfront on the west side of the bay not far from where Kusch would be held in a prison, close to the villa where the trial was to take place, and where the state government of Schleswig-Holstein has its seat today. Breinig that day sent an inquiry to the Berlin security police requesting any information they might have in their files on Kusch and his family. Then, at 1500 hours on the *Erwin Wassner*, Breinig came face-to-face for the first time with the man whose report had touched off the case against Kusch. Abel had been asked to cover the short distance to Kiel from Eckernförde, where he was temporarily stationed, for a pre-trial deposition and oral testimony at the main proceedings themselves two days later.[43] This time, Breinig asked Abel not only for clarifications about the original report, but also for his response to comments and statements contained in Kusch's deposition of January 21 in Angers.[44]

Abel now reinforced his initial charges against Kusch and added details not contained in the original report. He placed great emphasis on the notion that he had not written the report from a motive of hatred, malice, or vindictiveness against Kusch. Instead, it had taken him a long time and much soul-searching to reach his decision and he had definitely not coordinated it with Druschel. He simply had arrived at the conviction Kusch was no longer tenable as a U-boat captain based on his remarks and actions. According to Abel, his personal feelings toward his former commander did not come into play at all.

Expanding on the details of his original report, Abel specified that Kusch regarded a military dictatorship under a proven general the ideal replacement for the Hitler regime. Such a change would also spawn a cultural revival. Kusch spoke up often against the Hitler Youth and against the RAD (Reich Labor Service), arguing that both organizations forced members to mingle with too many unworthy people in contrast to the more exclusive membership of his *bündisch* club. Regarding the "Rose" messages from Dönitz, Kusch had denied that the exhortations of their commander in chief toward greater sacrifice could realistically lead to increased successes against the enemy. Considering Germany's limited raw materials, Kusch had declared them an insoluble problem. The idea of a worldwide Jewish conspiracy was rejected by Kusch as nonsense. "He also opposed the extermination of the Jews in Europe. He characterized Jews as valuable people." Abel further dwelled on Kusch's denial or belittling of Allied "terror attacks" against German cities. Lastly, Kusch reportedly had complained in front of others in the central control room how frustrating it was to be fighting a war with poorly designed boats like his.[45]

Around noon on Tuesday, January 25, less than twenty-four hours before his trial was to begin, Kusch finally reached Kiel in the company and custody of Lieutenant Dormeier of his flotilla's administrative staff, and at 1220 was checked into the Naval Detention Center (*Marineuntersuchungsgefängnis*, or M.U.G.) at the corner of Rostocker Strasse and Weimarer Strasse in the sprawling naval complex at Kiel-Wik.[46] He was assigned Cell No. 107 in the lower part of the four-story building. Later that afternoon, he granted Meyer-Grieben official authority to defend him at the trial the following morning.[47] The lawyer then hastened to see Breinig to take a look at Kusch's legal file, primarily Abel's report, the depositions by Funke and Druschel, and Abel's addendum charging Kusch with lack of aggressive spirit. Breinig had not yet completed the written indictment, in part because he was still waiting for an expert opinion on Abel's added charge before deciding whether to include cowardice or avoidance of the enemy as part of the indictment. As Meyer-Grieben later testified, he had barely enough time to thumb through the documents, let alone to give them a thorough study in preparation for his defense, as he shuttled between Kusch in the prison and the prosecutor's office.[48]

In the course of his hurried errands, Meyer-Grieben may well have run into Dieter Berger who decided that day to visit Hagemann aboard the *Erwin Wassner* to sound out the man who would preside over the court-martial and primarily determine his friend's fate. For Berger as a *Luftwaffe* lieutenant, getting access to Hagemann posed no problem. He later remembered:

> He [Hagemann] and I talked about questions related to the defense. He suggested Kusch should hire a civilian defense counsel inasmuch as that lawyer would be more effective and engaged than someone appointed by the court. In providing this advice Hagemann was entirely correct. In the further course of our conversation I tried to influence Hagemann in favor of my friend. But Hagemann ignored my efforts while coming across as professionally correct, matter-of-fact, and distant. Upon my request as an officer severely wounded in the war, he granted me a pass to attend the proceedings the next day.[49]

Whether Berger also tried to see Kusch at the nearby jail is not known but seems unlikely, as he knew his friend and the lawyer had not a minute to spare in preparing for the trial.

The man designated to offer an expert opinion on the "lack of aggressive spirit" charge was Lieutenant Wilhelm Franken of Crew 35, former commander of *U-565* in the Mediterranean where he had sunk four and damaged two other ships on eleven patrols and been decorated with the Knight's Cross. He now served on Admiral von Friedeburg's staff at U-Boat Command and was quite critical of the nature of Abel's report and the manner in which it had been submitted.[50] The day before, on January 24, Franken had received copies of *U-154*'s war diaries and now briefed Breinig on the three supposedly suspicious incidents specified in Abel's supplementary report.[51] In retracing Kusch's moves against Convoys TJ-12 and BT-14, Franken detected moments of some inexperience and "indecisiveness" on Kusch's part, but no indications of personal cowardice. In other respects he found the evidence inconclusive.

Franken did chide Kusch, however, for failing to record in the war diary and to comment on the message of 1500 on March 26, 1943, in which U-Boat Command had informed boats in the area that an enemy convoy had been sighted in naval grid square CF 6669 moving north at eight knots. Other boats, for instance *U-662*, did record the message as required, and *U-154*'s radio operators must have picked it up because otherwise Abel would not have known about it. Still, as Franken must have calculated, at precisely that moment Kusch stood in grid square BE 8555, some 358 nautical miles to the north-northwest and moving away from the convoy in a westerly direction toward his designated operational area.[52] Even on converging courses it would have taken Kusch some three days to intercept the convoy in waters polluted with enemy air surveillance and always assuming the convoy maintained the reported course, which seemed unlikely. Abel's calculations must have appeared plausible to an I.W.O. on the sixth day of his first patrol, but made no sense under realistic conditions to experienced skippers like Kusch or Franken. Again Franken could detect no sign of cowardice in Kusch's decision and praised him for his successes off Brazil. How Abel knew of the radio message in the first place, whether he recorded its time and text in his personal journal, or whether Kusch omitted it deliberately or unintentionally from the boat's war diary, remain unanswerable questions. Curiously, on January 30, 1944, four days after the verdict, Hagemann made a note in Kusch's file that the prosecution against Kusch regarding "dereliction of duty because of fear" had merely been postponed because it would require more time to investigate.[53]

Franken's explanations prompted Breinig to drop the charge of "lack of aggressive spirit" and he finalized his written indictment shortly before 1900 later that evening before sharing it by telephone with Kals in Lorient as deputy *Gerichtsherr* and providing copies to Hagemann, Kusch, and Meyer-Grieben. Thus, the defendant and his counsel only learned some twelve hours before the beginning of the trial the exact nature of the charges and a summarized version of the supporting evidence. Kusch was accused of "continuously and publicly paralyzing or eroding the will of the German people to self-assert themselves militarily and undermining the discipline of the German military." In addition, Kusch was charged with listening to enemy broadcasts during his patrols "even when it was not required in his line of duty."[54]

As Wednesday, January 26, 1944, dawned over Kiel Bay exactly two weeks had elapsed since Abel had submitted his report and fewer than six days had passed since Kusch had been arrested and first learned of the accusations against him.

CHAPTER 7

THE TRIAL

When the sun rose over Kiel at 0818 on January 26, 1944, its intermittent rays came to rest upon a city and a bay deeply marked both by their function as Germany's primary naval base on the Baltic Sea since the days of the Kaiser and by Allied efforts to destroy the vessels, shipyards, administrative buildings, and training facilities that helped keep the *Kriegsmarine*'s war effort alive. Between 1940 and 1944, British planes delivered no fewer than one hundred major air raids on Kiel and by war's end 80 percent of the city's public structures and private houses lay in ruins, along with much of the city's infrastructure.[1] Arrayed around the bay from its western sections to its head near the central train station and up its eastern shoreline to the suburbs of Gaarden, Heikendorf, and Laboe, the targets were obvious: the locks and bridges of the Kiel Canal at Holtenau, eastern terminal of the strategic waterway that connects the North Sea with the Baltic; the main naval base at Wik with sprawling installations ashore, including the jail where Oskar Kusch was being held; several huge shipyards across the bay in Gaarden capable of building and repairing warships ranging in size from battleships to submarines; the adjacent naval arsenal; and a sizable underground munitions depot. Not surprisingly, the Germans had concentrated much anti-aircraft weaponry and searchlight positions in and around Kiel along with fighter squadrons on bases nearby. The ferocity of the attacks and the stubbornness of the defenders remain visible to this day. For example, visitors who nowadays cross by train the high bridges spanning the Kiel Canal at Levensau, Rendsburg, or Hochdonn, can detect numerous round ponds filled with frogs and ducks in the lush green fields below them; but few of these visitors will realize that those peaceful pools of water were once craters from near-misses of Allied bombs aimed at those very bridges. For six decades another reminder was the massive U-boat bunker and former antiaircraft gun emplacement "Kilian," whose dynamited remains disfigured the eastern shoreline of the bay until they were removed at last in 2001.

Villa Forsteck, site of Kusch's trial and literally translating as "the villa at the edge of the forest," had been built in 1866 by the wealthy Hamburg merchant Heinrich Adolph Meyer on land he had acquired to both sides of the Niemannsweg just to the south of Wik, with spectacular views north and east across Kiel Bay.[2] He turned the imposing three-story building into a first-class cultural meeting place for visiting celebrities, including the physician and physicist Hermann von Helmholtz, the pianist Clara Schumann, the poet and novelist Theodor Fontane, and the German-American statesman Carl Schurz who had married Meyer's youngest sister Margarethe. Four years after Meyer's death in 1889 his widow sold the entire estate to the prominent Kiel merchant and shipyard owner Heinrich Diederichsen, who continued Meyer's tradition of sponsoring major scientific and cultural activities. He renovated parts of the villa, adding a covered terrace and a winter garden. When Diederichsen died in 1942, the city of Kiel acquired the property amidst a prolonged legal and political quarrel with local Nazi Party representatives and eventually leased it to the *Kriegsmarine*.[3]

The month of January regularly delivers fierce storms and icy weather to Germany's coasts, but the day of Oskar Kusch's trial turned out to be relatively mild with no freeze overnight and a high temperature of 6 degrees Celsius by early afternoon under largely cloudy skies.[4] Soon after 0800 that morning, Kusch was driven the short distance from his cell at the Wik naval compound to Villa Forsteck as the members of the court, the witnesses, and an audience of about fifty naval personnel, primarily officers from local naval commands, and of course Kusch's *Luftwaffe* friend Dieter Berger, gathered to attend the proceedings. Kusch's defense counsel Gerhard Meyer-Grieben appears to have been the only non-uniformed person in the room. There is speculation that a good part of the audience may have been under orders to attend the trial in order to magnify the "deterrence effect" of a harsh sentence. Meyer-Grieben would remember several cases later in 1944 when up to five hundred soldiers were in attendance and that their very presence in those "show trials" guaranteed much harsher sentences than in trials in more intimate surroundings—a situation naval justice officials freely admitted.[5]

Meyer-Grieben knew his options were limited and that the naval justice system suffered at the very least from three major impediments: (1) procedural and sentencing instructions imposed from above that sought to guarantee conformity with the wishes of the political and military leadership; (2) collusion among justice officials who knew and covered for each other while maintaining outwardly the appearance of an independent judicial system; and (3) ideological affinity to the Nazi regime as expressed in the party membership of many officials and a tendency to equate, as in Kusch's case, criticism of the party and its leaders with disloyalty to state and country.

The nature and extent of these corrupting influences and practices have been thoroughly illuminated since World War II and are competently covered by Heinrich Walle in his work on Kusch.[6] Besides Dr. Rudolphi, and also serving on Dönitz's staff, a major originator and transmitter of such political directives to the middle and lower ranks of naval justice officials, was Vice Admiral Walter Warzecha in his capacity as head of the General Naval Main Office (AMA) within the Naval High Command in Berlin. For instance, in February 1942 he reminded an assembly of naval justice officials of their requirement to follow instructions by the military leadership when it came to prosecutorial and sentencing decisions in "voluntary cooperation" with the political and military leaders, thus clearly exposing the illusion of an independent judicial apparatus.[7] After 1942, as the historian Lothar Gruchmann has argued, conformity-inducing directives grew measurably more conspicuous as Germany's chances of winning the war receded:

> In this manner the heads of the naval justice administration transmitted the pressure downward that they themselves felt from their superiors regarding Hitler and the political leadership. The navy had to fulfill its role of boosting morale and discouraging defeatism. This development played itself out against the backdrop of the Trauma of 1918 when, as defeat loomed, the navy had become the first service branch to show signs of subversion of its will to fight. This time around any possible decline in discipline had to be met head-on from the very beginning.[8]

Meyer-Grieben had seen it himself in many trials and knew how limited his prospects were to protect Kusch from politically motivated harm.

By 1944, the language, interpretations, and application guidelines of the notorious "Subversion of the Military Strength and Spirit" Decree (*Wehrkraftzersetzung*) of August 17, 1938, had undergone several evolutions.[9] As of March 31, 1943, the wording of the added Article 1, Paragraph 5a, Sections 1 and 2, served to tighten sentencing guidelines and weaken evidence requirements, reading as follows:

> (1) Persons subject to military law who commit punishable acts by subverting military discipline or failing to display military courage will be assessed an augmented limited or lifelong jail sentence or the death penalty, if the maintenance of discipline or the safety of the armed forces so require.
> (2) The same applies to punishable acts by which the perpetrator has caused an especially severe harm for the conduct of the war or diminished the security of the Reich, if the regular sentencing guidelines according to the sound judgment of the German people are considered insufficient in expiating the committed act.[10]

The prominent Nazi legal commentator and postwar apologist Erich Schwinge at the time defined subversion of the military fighting spirit or combat readiness simply as the "disruption or diminishment of the total mobilization of the people in pursuit of final victory in this war,"[11] thereby opening the floodgates for tens of thousands of accusations and prosecutions under the provisions of the decree, especially in the later phases of the conflict. Most prominent among the expanded interpretations was the notion that now the mere *intent* or the existence of a *motive* to commit subversion, rather than any *provable act* or measurable *consequences,* sufficed to render the accused guilty. Moreover, the earlier requirement that the subversive utterances or acts had to have been made "in public" was watered down and essentially eliminated. As Schwinge wrote in 1943 and again in 1944, "the term 'public' for the purposes of this decree is to be understood in the broadest terms" and should not be subject to any specific definition of the number or kind of people in the audience. "That would be too narrow and would render impossible a robust intervention by the state against subversive utterances within the population."[12]

To set the tone for moral considerations dictating the proper punishment frame, as early as December 29, 1939, the German Naval High Command had declared, "when the best soldiers at the front sacrifice their lives for the fatherland, no one will understand or tolerate that at the same time cowards and saboteurs are able to sit out the war in our jails."[13] No doubt, Karl-Heinrich Hagemann, Hans-Egon Breinig, and the other naval justice officials connected to Kusch's trial were thoroughly aware of the legal cosmos in which they moved and of which they had become a part.

Regarding the extent of collusion among justice officials and the widespread practice of fixing trials ahead of any proceedings, Meyer-Grieben could not harbor the slightest illusions. He testified after the war:

> Based on my experience with members of the naval justice system it is quite clear that prior consultation among officials was rampant. It went so far that once a prosecutor and a presiding judge agreed as to what sentence to propose and what sentence to assess, they even brought the defense counsel into their discussion. I regularly knew ahead of time what sentence the prosecution would seek. Once, when I expected a jail sentence for the accused, the prosecutor pulled me aside shortly before the trial and told me:

"The presiding judge wants to sentence him to death, therefore I also have to demand the death penalty because otherwise my superiors will go after me." In short, prosecutors felt badly whenever a judge went beyond their proposal for a sentence. He would try to avoid such a situation so as not to be seen as a poor team player by those above him. Therefore, I had the strong feeling that Mr. Breinig [in the Kusch case] would not want to leave himself open to a reprimand from above if he advocated a sentence at variance with what the presiding judge had in mind. I felt sure the matter had been coordinated beforehand. . . .

[Justice officials] rotated their function in the system so blatantly that in a single session with four or five separate cases, the prosecutor and the presiding judge might quite literally get up and change places. I could not help but surmise that if a prosecutor received certain instructions and guidelines for his investigative work, such instructions would have consequences the next time he functioned as a judge. It is hard to believe that a human being can compartmentalize himself so as to say, "I am the judge today and therefore will apply very different standards tomorrow when I am the prosecutor."[14]

Meyer-Grieben did credit Breinig with having undertaken a reasonably objective investigation of the case and to have shown no indication he might go for the death penalty. Indeed, the prosecutor had left the lawyer with the distinct impression he did not think Kusch's actions were so severe as to necessitate his death.[15] In all likelihood Meyer-Grieben would have classified Breinig as one of the more acceptable representatives of the naval justice system:

I knew a good number of naval justice officials who did not represent the [Nazi] perspective and therefore in political cases were eager to help the accused as much as they could without alerting their superiors to what they were doing. Based on my experiences, those judges welcomed any possible argument to ease the

> burden on the defendant and thus to avoid the death penalty, whereas those judges who had bought fully into the regime generally pursued every possible argument to increase the number of death sentences they assessed.[16]

Precious little time remained for Kusch and Meyer-Grieben to discuss and coordinate their defense strategy. The deposition Kusch had given Breinig on January 21 in Angers—without being able to consult legal counsel or having him present—clearly restricted Kusch's maneuvering room, while Meyer-Grieben knew from bitter experience what to expect once the court convened:

> It was usually the case that the defendant had made certain utterances in front of witnesses and the court had to accept them as evidence. The defense then had no real option but to admit that the utterances had occurred, but that they constituted merely a one-time hiccup or "failure." . . . Next, one called character witnesses to establish that the accused had no record of taking a political stand . . . and could be seen as a loyal follower of the Hitler regime. In order to be successful the defense counsel also had to emphasize the defendant's accomplishments for his country and how praiseworthy his conduct had been in the past. Nothing else made sense under the circumstances.[17]

In Kusch's case, of course, it would have been implausible to sell him as a loyal follower of the Führer given the nature and weight of the evidence against him. His lawyer's efforts had to concentrate instead on trivializing what Kusch had said, raising the possibility of misunderstandings and misinterpretations, and pointing out that Kusch had never acted on any of his political persuasions and demonstrably no actual erosion of his boat's fighting spirit or combat readiness had ever occurred. Given the impossibility of transporting any of *U-154*'s enlisted personnel from France to Kiel on one day's notice, Meyer-Grieben also did not seek to add loyalty statements from men like Lüdmann, Janker, or Isensee, who might also have been forced to admit to overhearing Kusch's anti-Nazi remarks. However subtly, Meyer-Grieben might even attempt to suggest or sow doubts about the accusers' true motives. At the same time, Kusch's educational accomplishments and outstanding military record could act as a counterweight to the political accusations, reinforced by Winter's and Janssen's character testimony and their outstanding written assessments of their former watch officer. While not present at the trial in person, even Commander Kals as flotilla chief and Captain Rösing in their evaluations of *U-154*'s patrols would cast a positive light on an exemplary officer who had served his country successfully and courageously, and who stood ready to continue to do so as his fatherland sorely needed him at this crucial juncture of the war. Perhaps a reassignment within the navy or some form of probation would be more appropriate than applying the full sanctions contemplated by the "subversion" decree.

To the very end Kusch considered himself innocent of the charges, something his lawyer knew, respected, and admired, but also found awkward to reconcile with a defense plan aimed at ensuring a lenient verdict rather than one of "not guilty." As Meyer-Grieben stated several years later, Kusch's claims of being innocent put him as a lawyer into a potentially "embarrassing situation" where the judge might insinuate, "Counsel, what you are trying to tell the court, you cannot possibly believe yourself."[18] In short, Kusch's native quest for truth and honesty and his loathing for manipulation and obfuscation as practiced by Nazi propaganda, for example, clashed with his lawyer's desire to shield his client from as much harm as possible. Certainly, Kusch knew that any idea of throwing himself on the mercy of the court and of currying favor with the three judges by submitting a full but false "confession" to alleged crimes he knew in his heart he had not committed, was no option. At the same time Kusch never fully denied his opposition to the regime but instead maintained, correctly, that his words and actions were aimed at educating and enlightening his officers, never to harm the war effort.

The trial lasted from 0900 in the morning until 1800 in the evening with a break for lunch and another between the end of the evidence phase and the announcement of the sentence. All witnesses stayed in a separate room until called and after their testimony were allowed to remain in the courtroom. By all accounts the proceedings took place in an outwardly dignified atmosphere with proper courtroom decorum, and observers have described Kusch as calm and composed throughout, neither visibly nervous nor concerned.[19] No exact word-for-word transcript of the trial exists, but the official protocol as prepared by Inspector Koops is detailed enough to gain a solid impression of how the trial went.[20] Additionally, numerous participants and attendees have left first-hand accounts in letters and postwar personal and legal testimonies.

Hagemann followed standard procedure by first introducing the members of the court, reacquainting Kusch with the provisions of Paragraph 5 of the "subversion" decree and placing the two military jurors under oath. He reminded the witnesses, before dismissing them for the time being, to tell the truth in accordance with the oath they too would take upon delivering their testimonies. Since Arno Funke as *U-154*'s new I.W.O. was unable to make the trip from Lorient to Kiel, his deposition of January 20 would be entered into the record instead.

Kusch would be the first to be questioned. Upon confirming his personal and career data, he listened as his service evaluations were being read out loud and Breinig presented the indictment he had completed the night before. Kusch was then asked to comment on the charges. For the most part, he reiterated the comments, diminutions, deflections, and denials he had already employed in his deposition in Angers, typically claiming that he could not remember certain remarks or particular word choices, that most allegations ran counter to his innermost persuasions or that had been distorted or misunderstood, with the witnesses simply "concentrating on everything negative in our discussions" and therefore "getting everything wrong." As for calling Hitler a mad megalomaniac who occasionally pulled down curtains and rolled around on the floor, that must have been based on something Kusch had heard from someone else, a mere rumor repeated in "a general discussion over the borderline between madness and genius." He had never declared Germany's defeat or Hitler's fall a desirable certainty. To the contrary, he "always hoped it would not come to pass" and "never used [his] position as the commanding officer to impose my views on others." The following excerpt captures Kusch's defense approach well:

> Regarding the global Jewish conspiracy, I never made the remarks attributed to me. I only said the Jews are not our only enemy, that other forces are also involved, for example the Catholic Church. I further stated that it was an exaggeration of our propaganda. I did notice that my officers did not share my view. I simply wanted to talk about it. Our conversation about the terror attacks was a result of the air attacks on Hamburg. I stated that the enemy was only aiming at our industries. I do not know Hamburg from personal experience.
>
> As for "Rose," we received messages that were meant to boost our morale in those days when things were not going well for us. I cannot imagine having said what I am accused of. I may have said something about "whipping up enthusiasm," but that is all. I only listened to foreign radio stations when reception of ours was poor. I wanted to hear something about Berlin. For the most part I only listened to music. If there happened to be news items, I discussed them with my officers. That was done for their information. I am familiar with the regulations regarding foreign broadcasts.

As for neglecting to mention or failing to try to engage the reported convoy when *U-154* was heading west out of the Bay of Biscay the previous March, Kusch stated the convoy was 240 nautical miles away according to his calculations, that he would have had to turn around and away from his designated destination, so that nothing could have been accomplished. "Something like that does not belong in a war diary."

While Kusch remained in the courtroom and was occasionally asked to respond to their testimony, the witnesses made their appearance one after another, Ulrich Abel first. It remains difficult to assess whether the fact that Kusch's second-in-command held a doctorate in law and had drawn up the original report made his charges more believable or weighty in the eyes of Hagemann and the two lay judges than the often equally damning statements of Druschel and others. Again, little additional information emerged compared to what had already been set down in the depositions, be it with regard to the Führer portrait, Kusch's characterizations of Hitler and his entourage, Nazi propaganda, or Dönitz's messages at the time of the Stalingrad disaster to spur his U-boat crews to take unreasonable risks. Abel added a few details not previously revealed, for instance Kusch's alleged claim that a British and American victory would keep communism from engulfing Europe and that transnational forces such as a global Jewish plot or Free Masonry simply did not exist and were mere products of propaganda.

Since Arno Funke could not be present in Kiel but had been properly placed under oath at the time, his deposition of January 20 in Lorient was read aloud and entered into evidence instead. Kusch declined to comment. Then the court adjourned until 1400 for lunch. Apparently, there was a dining facility at the Villa Forsteck sufficiently equipped to feed the court and the spectators with everyone but the witnesses mingling freely. When Hagemann reconvened the court, Druschel was next to take the stand. He fully backed Abel's testimony, emphasizing Kusch's expressed desire to have Hitler and the party replaced by a military dictatorship and that, according to Kusch, Grand Admiral Dönitz "is chasing us out into the Atlantic without giving us adequate means to defend ourselves." As for propaganda efforts, Druschel said Kusch rejected them and believed instead the German people wanted facts, not lies, to know what was going on. After overhearing from his bunk a conversation between Kusch and Nothdurft during which Kusch had made disparaging remarks about the regime, Druschel became so agitated that he had got up and climbed up to the bridge to tell Abel about it. He told the I.W.O. that he "was almost ready to punch Kusch in the face."

Lieutenant Heinrich Meyer, who had been *U-154*'s II.W.O. during the first patrol, was personally appalled over Abel's report and evidently attempted in his recollections to minimize harm to his former commanding officer: "We talked a few times about the political situation. The accused always had an opinion different from everyone else's." Otherwise

Meyer confirmed that "there used to hang a Führer picture above the wash basin. It was later gone and now there was one with a sailing ship."

The official record of the proceedings falls considerably short of capturing the impression Dr. Hans Nothdurft left on the court as the next witness and the more differentiated picture he tried to paint of Kusch on the second patrol. Given his persistent but ultimately futile labors to keep Abel and Druschel from filing a report, Nothdurft now had to maneuver between a desire to shield Kusch from further trouble and apprehension over not having reported the situation aboard *U-154* himself. Dieter Berger remembered how the staff surgeon "wiggled like a worm on a hook because Nothdurft himself had often taken Kusch's side in his criticism of National Socialism, as Kusch told me himself. He must have been afraid of self-incrimination."[21] Nothdurft himself left this account in his 1946 affidavit:

> Initially I restricted my testimony to the military state of affairs on board and the tensions that existed between Kusch and his officers. Then I was asked whether I thought Kusch was opposed to National Socialism. In response I chose these or similar words: "Yes, I could not help but come to that conclusion." . . . I did not dare characterize Kusch as a loyal National Socialist—something he himself chose not to do. The prosecution could draw on such an overwhelming amount of incriminating testimony—easily augmentable by deposing enlisted personnel—that no declaration of mine was going to rescue Kusch in that respect. My very cautious remarks drew a reprimand from the presiding judge. He said verbatim: "You appear to want to tell us as little as possible." . . . I also dropped Kusch a hint on how best to defend himself. I assumed, as was customary under such circumstances, that he would claim to have suffered some form of a nervous breakdown, some illness, etc., to account for his behavior. Therefore, I stated that I believed his remarks grew from having been exposed to the tropics for too long and that his nerves must have taken a beating. This suggestion resulted from having contemplated my

> own situation at some length, as I would have defended myself exactly like that if I had been accused of not reporting the incidents myself. But Kusch did not take me up on my suggestion. He did not deny his anti-Nazi sentiments and tried to explain and defend them exclusively on the basis of his family's values and his experiences when growing up.[22]

One may well wonder what Kusch and Meyer-Grieben thought of Nothdurft's timidity and patronizing attitude when it came to their defense strategy. Meyer-Grieben has commented at some length on this point:

> Dr. Nothdurft was quite hesitant to testify. When confronted with the central questions, he seemed embarrassed and highly uncomfortable. One saw clearly how he struggled over whether or not to incriminate the defendant by telling the truth. Not only did I notice his embarrassment, but also Hagemann, the presiding judge. Hagemann reminded him that as an officer and German man . . . he had to tell the truth and would be placed under oath later on. Only as a result of this mental pressure was Nothdurft willing to share his knowledge of the subversive utterances the accused had made. I had the feeling he was engaged in a gigantic inner battle.[23]

Meyer-Grieben obviously appreciated Nothdurft's dilemma and characterized it in a different context as a "conflict between his sympathy for the accused and his antipathy for the regime on the one hand, and his obligations when testifying under oath on the other."[24] The official summary of Nothdurft's testimony runs as follows:

> The accused is a pessimist when it comes to the end of the war and the role of the U-boat service. He opposes National Socialism. He believed the U-boat war was lost and the war as well. For him establishing a military dictatorship appears to be a solution. The other officers disagreed strongly with their commanding officer's

> views. The accused rejected the Führer. He once said we are only at war because a megalomaniac wants to gobble up Europe. I know the defendant listened to English news. I was personally present in the radio room when he did so. He also opposed the persecution of the Jews. He left no doubt that a military dictatorship must eliminate the party.

For once Kusch agreed he may have expressed himself in the manner Nothdurft indicated, probably realizing what an effort it was for the medical doctor to make his statements against someone with whose political persuasions he largely agreed.

The last two witnesses for the prosecution were the two Passed Midshipmen Hellmuth Kirchammer and Horst Fröhlich, who had been on board during Kusch's first mission. Even now only nineteen years old, they had a keen understanding of what was at stake for their former commanding officer and only confirmed the one incident Kusch had urged them to form their own opinions and not to rely blindly on Nazi propaganda. Abel had then admonished them to pay no attention to what Kusch had said. Fröhlich in particular found a smart way to avoid further complications for Kusch:

> I did not overhear any conversations where the commanding officer mentioned the Führer. On one occasion when I was the helmsman I heard the commanding officer having an argument with the chief engineer. I cannot remember what it was all about because I had to pay attention to my duties as helmsman.

By general agreement both young men were not required to be placed under oath and were dismissed from the proceedings.

Before the witnesses for the defense could take the stand, Hagemann permitted the prosecutor to read to the court a telegram that had arrived at 1120 that day at the Kiel office of the state police and been rushed to Villa Forsteck. It came from the Berlin state police and was the answer to Breinig's inquiry of the day before about Kusch's police record in Berlin and that of his parents. It had been delayed because Breinig had forgotten to include Kusch's date of birth. While the document showed nothing negative or noteworthy about his parents, it demonstrated Kusch's criticism of the regime and its institutions went back many years:

> Based on our records Kusch was a member of the *bündisch* youth movement in 1937. On several occasions he acted as the leader of a group named "Oskar." The regular group leader was the medical doctor Rudi Pallas, born on November 3, 1907, in Posen, who was then attached to the Wehrmacht. While a member of the RAD [Reich Labor Service] Kusch wrote several letters to Pallas in which he criticized the RAD in the strongest terms. No further political or criminal activities are on record here.[25]

If nothing else, the telegram proved Kusch had not acted on the spur of the moment, that there was a pattern of activities and utterances against the regime reaching back many years, and thus added an element of credibility to Abel's charges. Had it been delivered just a few hours later, it would not have found its way into the evidence against Kusch.

Next and last came the only two witnesses for the defense, since the former chief engineer of *U-103*, Otto Strelow, was unable to attend the trial for undisclosed reasons. Lieutenant Commander Werner Winter had been Kusch's first captain on *U-103* and remained a genuine and trusted friend. Perhaps more than anyone, Winter as chief of the First U-Boat Flotilla in Brest was incensed that Abel had circumvented the usual chain of command by submitting his report not to Commander Kals in Lorient but instead to Captain Schmidt, who was in charge of a unit to which Abel had been only loosely and temporarily attached. As a result, the case gained a momentum of its own before Kals and Rösing in France knew of the report and before they could have intervened to stop its march into the naval justice bureaucracy. In addition, as he stated after the war, Winter knew of no precedent in the history of the U-boat service in which subordinate officers had stabbed their own captain in the back in such a "perfidious and impudent manner" and "surrendered an impeccable frontline officer to the death machinery of the wartime naval justice system."[26] Now on the witness stand and not familiar with what had transpired on *U-154*, all Winter could do was to accord Kusch "in every way the highest praise. [On *U-103*] we also talked about political topics. Kusch always maintained a positive attitude just as everyone else." No doubt Winter also expected Lieutenant Commander Wolfgang Dittmers as one of the three judges determining Kusch's fate to be impressed by the defendant's outstanding credentials, especially when verified by a member of Crew 30 and thus by someone only one year junior to Dittmers himself, and to prevent the worst. Lieutenant Gustav-Adolf Janssen, Winter's successor as skipper of *U-103*, likewise characterized his former second-in-command as "excellent. I can only report good things about him."

After the war, Dr. Nothdurft would criticize Winter and Janssen for not having done enough for Kusch, especially in failing to weaken the politically based charges:

> Winter really said little that provided relief for Kusch. He could have characterized Kusch's utterances as not to be taken seriously or due to some illness, as I had tried to do. When Winter suggested the boat's officers should have warned Kusch in good time, I raised my hand and told the court that I had warned Kusch on several occasions. These warnings later became part of the prosecutor's argumentation. I thought it was necessary for me to mention them because as an outsider in the *Kriegsmarine* I wanted it to be known that I had done everything that could be expected of me as a good comrade.[27]

By contrast, Gerhard Meyer-Grieben thought Winter and Jannsen supplied an "excellent portrait of the character and abilities of the accused and thereby tried everything possible to bring about a more favorable and lenient verdict."[28] They conveyed the impression that Kusch was simply not capable of having made the remarks ascribed to him because they stood in such a stark contrast to his character and personality:

> Winter's and Janssen's statements were very impressive and showed great sympathy for the accused as a human being. It would be appropriate to say they spoke as true comrades. One also noticed how they went through all sorts of contortions and had to be very careful as both were opposed to the regime themselves. That was always the same story with character witnesses for the defense: you emphasized again and again that the whole thing had to be a misunderstanding.[29]

From his perspective as a spectator, Dieter Berger was less impressed than Meyer-Grieben with what he had seen and heard, including his friend's own defense. To him the defense counsel had acted in too "timid" a fashion and Kusch's own statements had come across as "awkward and clumsy." Of course, the ones most responsible for aiming at the death penalty were Hagemann, Abel, and Druschel. "All other witnesses for the prosecution were insignificant and acted in a cowardly manner by trying to protect themselves, especially staff surgeon Dr. Nothdurft."[30] Berger would add later:

> The proceedings were conducted in a one-sided way inasmuch as the incriminating evidence was strongly emphasized while the witnesses for the defense, Winter and Janssen, and also the defense counsel, were urged to keep their remarks short. Whenever the defense lawyer wanted to interject or make a point, he was told to save his comments for his concluding remarks. As I remember, the defense counsel tried to cross-examine the witnesses. But almost immediately the presiding judge would cut him off. After the evidence phase was over I had a chance to talk to Janssen and Winter and both indicated they planned to complain about the way their testimony had been cut short. . . . My impression of Abel and Druschel as witnesses was that they only testified bad things about Kusch and hated him with a vengeance.[31]

The testimony of Kusch's former commanding officers ended the evidence-gathering part of the trial. Hagemann placed all witnesses under oath except Druschel who had already sworn to tell the truth in his deposition in Lorient on January 20 and remained covered. Meyer-Grieben had been given the opportunity to cross-examine each witness very briefly, just as Kusch on several occasions had denied, deflected, or belittled specific accusations. Still, even Meyer-Grieben thought his client could have left a stronger mark on the court:

> I don't know how to put it best, but [Kusch] sometimes chose very unfortunate expressions in his defense. After all, so much hinges on making a good impression. This impression suffers greatly if the word choice is poor or seemingly insecure because then the judge will not be convinced that the defendant is telling the truth. Testimony should always be such that the personal impression does not suffer. If it does, it becomes an embarrassment, also for the defense counsel.[32]

There was little Meyer-Grieben could have done about this and now had to see what the prosecution was up to:

> I was handicapped by still having to acquaint myself with the case as the trial unfolded. One had to be on one's guard. In a way one had to feel one's way into the case.... From a defense counsel's point of view, it looks like this: the evidence-presenting phase is over, you try to sort in your mind what has been placed on the table. Professionally speaking, then comes the moment of greatest suspense: what will the prosecutor make of it all? Perhaps one has a notion that it might be the death penalty, but you never know until the prosecutor makes his recommendation. From then on, the defense's strategy is predicated on what the prosecutor has requested.[33]

Late that afternoon came the first of two crucial moments for Kusch as Dr. Hans-Egon Breinig rose to announce what sentence the prosecution would seek. As silence settled over the court, Breinig requested for Kusch ten years in a penitentiary for subverting the fighting strength of the military, exclusion from future service in the armed forces, loss of basic civil and political rights, plus one additional year in a penitentiary for unauthorized monitoring of foreign radio stations. In combination the proposed sentence would run for ten years and six months.

Kusch, Berger, and the two defense witnesses must have felt the same sense of "relief and optimism" that Meyer-Grieben embraced over this midrange recommendation, knowing full well that a "not guilty" would have been illusory on the radio-monitoring charge alone and that the assumed pretrial arrangements between judge and prosecutor apparently contemplated a sentence for Kusch short of life in prison or the death penalty.[34] Then it was Meyer-Grieben's turn to offer concluding arguments for the defense. Picking up where Winter and Janssen had left off, he presented Kusch as an exemplary officer of the highest professional and moral qualities with an outstanding and unblemished military record as acknowledged by all evaluators from his former commanding officers, to his flotilla commander in Lorient, to Rear Admiral Eberhard Godt on Dönitz's staff at the Naval High Command in Berlin. Kusch's comments on the regime, if true as alleged, must have emanated from his upbringing in a liberal and democratic family and from his experiences in his youth groups whose thrust may have been different from that of the Hitler Youth. On no occasion had his attitude and actions been unpatriotic or detrimental to his boat's combat readiness or combat performance, just as his acknowledgment of the enemy's superior resources had not in the least hampered his willingness to continue to fight for his country or his desire to win the war.

With some of the weightiest accusations against Kusch growing out of conversations and discussions conducted in the boat's wardroom with only fellow officers present, Meyer-Grieben questioned whether the decree against "subverting the military strength" was even applicable to Kusch's situation inasmuch as any incriminating remarks had to have been made "in public." After all, none of the remarks in question had been deliberately directed at enlisted personnel on board even if some of the men may have overheard them on occasion. In fact, a published legal opinion of 1943 by Dr. Bernhard Leverenz—himself since 1942 an official in the German naval justice system, a future defense counsel for his colleague Karl-Heinrich Hagemann in postwar trials, and attorney general of the state of Schleswig-Holstein after 1954—had provided a useful hint on how to play down and trivialize "subversion" charges:

> How many of us can claim never to have made occasional utterances of a negative nature as a result of feeling temporarily distraught in the present war? No law can possibly forbid people to engage in thoughts about the ups and downs in our lives. Whenever one is at one's wits end, when one's thoughts circle around and around without a way out, is it not so that a frank discussion with one's spouse or a friend offers a reasonable way to resolve this inner conflict?

Leverenz had further argued that too narrow an interpretation of the term "public" stood to encourage denunciations and would actually "undermine and destroy comradely solidarity among soldiers."[35] While in theory Leverenz's suggestions might have given helpful guidance for the defense, the very frequency and persistency of Kusch's remarks, their unquestionable sincerity, and the proven circumstance that he had opposed and resisted the regime at least since 1936 when he led an illegal underground youth group as a teenager, induced Meyer-Grieben not to pursue this line of argument. Probably even Kusch would have agreed it would have presented him as someone he was not.

That left the question of what sentence to propose, if any, as an alternative to the prosecutor's recommended ten-and-a-half years in a penitentiary. Here, too, Meyer-Grieben could fall back on legal commentary and precedent, even though his experience in "subversion" cases may have served him as a better and more practical guide. So-called less severe cases presumed that no actual intent to do harm had existed or that the remarks had not been grounded in a mindset principally opposed to the military or the state. In short, they may have been expressed in the context of someone being angry, in a bad mood or temper, boastful, pretentious, obstinate, disputatious, or prone to impulsive gossip. A milder case could even be assumed when the "inflammatory remarks had bounced off their recipients because of the latter's national steadfastness and no actual injury had been inflicted." In such circumstances the utterances could have been meant as serious, but may not have been taken as such by those on the receiving end.[36]

Meyer-Grieben could have found some fodder for an argument here, as Kusch from time to time had indeed come across as pushy and confrontational, and all his political remarks had ricocheted off Abel and Druschel as if they had hit an armored turret. But any such concessions and admissions in pursuit of a lenient sentence would also have served to reinforce the testimony for the prosecution and weakened the defense's case built upon and around Kusch's upbringing, moral character, professional excellence, and military successes. Moreover, the prosecutor likely had already embraced such factors when he went for a sentence in the medium range. In the end, Meyer-Grieben decided not to scare up the presumed pretrial arrangements between Breinig and Hagemann and entered no plea or suggested sentence for his client. Kusch likewise chose to remain silent when offered the chance for a final statement. Hagemann then retreated with Dittmers and Westphalen to his chambers to deliberate and to settle on a verdict.

By this time the sun had set over the city of Kiel. Dieter Berger had a chance to exchange a few words with Kusch before the judges returned from their deliberations some three-quarters of an hour later:

> I felt quite reassured and Kusch also was very calm because the prosecutor had only requested a long jail sentence and we were sure the court would not exceed the recommended sentence except under the rarest of circumstances. We both agreed the length of the sentence did not matter because it would be lifted at the end of the war anyway. I, and most likely Kusch as well, considered Germany's defeat inevitable. I personally had expected it since 1939.[37]

Meyer-Grieben, Winter, Janssen, and others on the side of the defense felt equally confident that the worst-case scenario had been averted. Thus, when the judges returned and Hagemann declared the court had unanimously assessed the death sentence for Kusch for "continuously subverting the military strength," plus one year of penitentiary for violating the radio broadcast act, the announcement hit most observers like lightning from a blue sky. Kusch's immediate reaction is not recorded, but his friend Berger was "completely surprised." Winter's "inner turmoil" resulted in a major jaundice attack the next day, and a court orderly with experience in hundreds of cases was dumbfounded and unable to explain how the proceedings could have possibly ended with the maximally applicable sanction. Naturally, prosecutor Breinig was also taken aback having proposed and expected a much more limited sentence.[38] It helped little when Hagemann informed Kusch the verdict would not take effect until the Führer had confirmed it.

There can be no doubt that Karl-Heinrich Hagemann as presiding judge, from whatever legal persuasions, personal motives and prejudices, and possible instructions or suggestions from his judicial and military superiors, was principally responsible for the verdict. It would be he who drew up the formal reasons for the decision three days later on January 29, 1944, in a document that will be discussed below. Still, two active-duty naval officers sitting next to him on the bench had agreed with him and consented to condemn a comrade and worthy fellow human being to die when they could have easily prevented such a fate. Why did they do it?

Both Lieutenant Commander Wolfgang Dittmers and Lieutenant Otto Westphalen survived the conflict and testified in legal depositions and as witnesses at two postwar trials against Hagemann in which the latter was accused of having committed crimes against humanity in the Kusch case and with regard to another wartime verdict. They themselves were never charged as accessories to a judicial murder, but of course they had a decided self-interest in upholding and defending the legality of their wartime actions. From their statements it becomes quite clear they never grasped the fundamental character of the "subversion" decree as an instrument of totalitarian injustice to be wielded against critics of the regime. Instead they became convinced or allowed themselves to become persuaded in a way reminiscent of Ulrich Abel's argumentation in his report that opposition to the Nazi regime and verbal criticism of questionable military directives automatically and in themselves constituted an endangerment of military discipline and patriotic loyalty no matter whether a specific breach of discipline or manifestation of disloyalty had actually occurred. Moreover, while Kusch's initial conviction rested entirely on supposed transgressions of a political nature, in the Hagemann trial the focus shifted markedly to alleged military failures and misdeeds on Kusch's part, not least driven at the time by a series of irresponsible, exaggerated, unverifiable, and largely disproved statements by staff surgeon Dr. Hans Nothdurft.

Korvettenkapitän Wolfgang Dittmers' conclusion on the day of the court-martial appears to have been that Kusch's mere utterances had endangered the combat readiness of his boat and thus placed the lives of his men in danger:

> At the time of the trial I was profoundly impressed by the fact that such a weighty accusation could have been leveled against an officer, especially because he had by his action stabbed his fighting men in the back. In my view, if such a thing were tolerated, it then made not the least sense for others to contribute the slightest sacrifice in this war.

Having decided that Kusch's political remarks simply must have undercut military discipline and were a punishable transgression under the terms of the subversion act, it then became for Dittmers a mere question of how severe a sentence to impose. For him, based on the evidence produced by the witnesses, the intentional, determined, and persistent nature of Kusch's criticism of the regime made the crucial difference between proposing time in jail and a death sentence: "On the one hand I believed it was my military duty to vote for the death penalty on the basis of the law, on the other hand I trusted in order to ease my human conscience that the case would be judged in a more lenient manner in the course of the review process." This awkward reasoning finds confirmation in the written statement Dittmers had to produce as part of the subsequent military and legal review of the case. In it he expressed his hope that the sentence be commuted.[39]

In his testimony in 1948 and 1949, Dittmers veered away from defending his participation in an almost exclusively politically justified verdict to one in which Kusch's allegedly military misdeeds had loomed large as inherently detrimental to patriotic solidarity and the demands of total war:

> I concluded that it was less a political matter than one with undoubted military consequences. The war had reached a point where the harshness of daily experiences brought one logically to the conclusion that only the full and unconditional use of all our strength could bring a solution. To me it seemed outrageous and criminal to undermine the striking power of the military by such behavior. I had to think of the hundreds of thousands of soldiers who daily put their lives on the line in this spirit, and here along comes an officer who lacks this willingness to fight. . . . I regarded Kusch as a very open-minded human being who nevertheless tended to think like an amateur. At the same time his character and way of thinking lacked a strong sense of moral and ethical responsibility.

When asked further whether only Kusch's death could have atoned for his severe legal transgressions, Dittmers did not hesitate: "Yes. It was not supposed to be a kind of deterrence. The weight of his guilt was such that no other punishment would have been sufficient."[40]

A year later, in an almost complete reversal of the justification for the original verdict, Dittmers went even further in stressing Kusch's military culpability:

> Kusch carried the full responsibility for the boat and its crew and he acted entirely irresponsibly. . . . The fact that Kusch's remarks

> were of a political nature played absolutely no role in the court's considerations and decision. Whether the name of the head of state happened to be Hitler, Hindenburg or Ebert [the latter two held the office of Reich President before Hitler] was entirely immaterial in our deliberations. I would have voted for the death penalty even if the Weimar Republic had conducted the war. From a human standpoint it was not easy to assess the death penalty, but based on my convictions I had no other choice.[41]

Listening to Dittmers' testimony, Werner Winter must have felt terribly let down when he saw his efforts to save Oskar Kusch sadly betrayed. It may be noteworthy that no one could have accused Dittmers of failing to fight to the very end for his head of state, no matter what his name. Just four days before Hitler blew his brains out in the Führer Bunker in Berlin on April 30, 1945, Dittmers and the rest of his 445 green recruits of Crews I/45 and IV/45 of the First Naval Instruction Battalion he commanded at that time in Stralsund on the Baltic, were ordered by Dönitz to be flown into beleaguered Berlin to participate in the capital's and the Führer's personal defense in what were dubbed "Operation Berlin" and "Operation Reich Chancellery." Flying in at night and landing at Gatow air base under heavy Soviet artillery fire, only a few of the Junkers Ju-52 transport planes made it through with at most one hundred poorly equipped officers and sailors on board. Dittmers and all officers survived, except one navy lieutenant who was killed by a mortar grenade in the garden of the Reich Chancellery.[42]

Otto Westphalen's postwar testimony resembled that of Dittmers in most respects. Prior to the trial, presumably on that Wednesday morning, Westphalen tried to speak to Abel, but Hagemann stopped him from doing so as he feared the juror might compromise himself.[43] He stated after the war, "An officer and U-boat commander, no matter his qualities as a human being and his political views, cannot tolerate such actions from a military standpoint, let alone commit them himself." Kusch should have exercised restraint because otherwise "he ran the risk the discipline on his boat might suffer and that the boat became endangered in a military sense as a result." After all, "a frontline U-boat is no political debate club where everyone can do and say what he wants." The men need to have trust in their commander on whom they rely for everything. "When such a man makes deprecating political remarks, how can his men follow him into combat when they do not know if he will order them the next day to make for the nearest enemy port under a white flag?"[44]

In defending his endorsement of the death sentence for Kusch, Westphalen now believed that "from a strictly military standpoint a mere jail sentence did not do justice" to what Kusch had done as his was clearly "not a case of diminished seriousness." Still, claiming to feel sorry for Kusch, he "hoped the death sentence would be changed in the review process and Kusch be given the chance to serve as a simple enlisted man without responsibilities toward others and without endangering subordinates as a result of his political persuasions." Interestingly he considered "Abel's actions as a comrade irresponsible; after the matter had taken on momentum, its outcome was essentially pre-programmed."[45] The historian Heinrich Walle has pointed out the inherent fallacy in Westphalen's argument here: If Kusch had indeed been guilty of committing a capital crime, no one should have felt pity for him. At the same time Westphalen castigated Abel's actions as irresponsible. "Would the laws of logic not suggest that Abel did the right thing by delivering a criminal to face his deserved punishment?"[46]

There remains a further intriguing possibility when it comes to explaining the court's decision to deal Kusch the toughest allowable sentence: Grand Admiral Karl Dönitz's programmatic speech to young officer recruits the day before at the Naval Academy in Mürwik, the gist of which must have quickly reached Kiel just seventy kilometers to the south. Here are key passages from Dönitz's address of January 25, 1944:

> How would Germany look today without National Socialism now that we are in the fifth year of the war? It would be full of warring parties, full of Jews, who would use every opportunity to criticize, to cause damage, to widen divisions, to pull us down, to spread weakness, and to interfere with the authorities.

> It would be interesting to learn how Germany would function without National Socialism in the face of enemy air raids. For everything it has the German people must be grateful to the Führer and to National Socialism. It would be dreadful to think what might have happened if we had had to cope without the Führer. Therefore every soldier must stand behind the Führer and our National Socialism with full and unshakeable dedication, and with unquestionable commitment. Any deviation from this principle means a diminishment of our strength and weakens the power, the immense power, we have as a people if we stand united.[47]

Could Hagemann, Dittmers, and Westphalen have found themselves inspired, encouraged, and justified and reinforced in their action by Dönitz's remarks?

News of the verdict against Kusch spread quickly through the navy's grapevine. One U-boat officer felt "stunned that a fellow U-boat man could have been charged with something like that. . . . Who could have possibly benefited from it?" Another commented, "the 'crime' with which he [Kusch] was charged we more or less were all guilty of: listening to foreign broadcasts and making fun of our political leadership. I recall vividly a discussion at the Mürwik naval academy in 1944 . . . during which we company and group officers absolutely refused to believe our new commandant, Captain Wolfgang Lüth, when he tried to convince us that [SS Leader] Heinrich Himmler was a decent and capable man."[48]

While Dittmers and Westphalen made their comments many years after the events of January 1944 in an atmosphere of aggressive self-defense, Karl-Heinrich Hagemann as presiding judge at the court-martial composed the required explanation and justification of the verdict within three days of the proceedings. This ten-page document remains impressive and incontrovertible proof that Kusch's political convictions and the resulting dissonances with his fellow officers doomed him and not any military shortfalls of his that might have diminished *U-154*'s effectiveness as an instrument of war.[49] After reiterating and acknowledging Kusch's outstanding career record, Hagemann picked up item after item of Abel's report. Declaring the testimony of the witnesses fully trustworthy and Kusch's criticism of the regime, its leaders, and its propaganda "unmistakable and beyond misunderstandings," Hagemann made a special point of stressing Kusch's pessimism and defeatism when it came to winning the war:

> All witnesses gained the impression that the accused no longer believed in a German military victory and that he opposed the current form of government. For example, at one point the accused stated he intended to emigrate after a lost war. Without exception the witnesses tried again and again to change the defendant's opinion. This was not possible, in part because he quickly cut off any criticism with such words as "nonsense" or "rubbish." When the witness Nothdurft once asked the accused what inspired him to continue to command a U-boat despite his defeatist convictions, he replied more or less verbatim, "A certain sense of duty."

Hagemann then rejected as "in error and incompatible with military concerns" Meyer-Grieben's suggestion that Kusch had committed no punishable act under the "subversion" decree because his remarks had not been made "in public":

> The premise that a submarine due to its nature and purpose is automatically removed from constituting a public place is wrong. Most utterances of the accused were made in the officers' mess where they were meant for officers only. The mess is not identical with the boat in terms of defining what is public and what is not. The remarks made in the mess were audible to the cook, the steward, and the radio and hydrophone operators whose room extends partially into the officers' mess, as well as other sailors who had to pass through the passageway. These facts suffice to prove the public nature of his remarks without a need to expand

> the definition of what constitutes "the public" as previously laid down in peacetime regulations.

Apparently, the court had a difficult time reconciling Kusch's personality and military record with the gravity of the offense he allegedly committed:

> Based on how the accused conducted himself at the proceedings and on other evidence, the court is convinced he did not intend to subvert the military strength and spirit of the German people when he disparaged the Führer and spoke out against the political and military leadership. The defendant is a proven U-boat officer who as a watch officer under several captains has demonstrated excellent leadership and exemplary military performance. As a commanding officer on two patrols he has achieved good successes and has been decorated with the Iron Cross, first class. His superiors describe him as an intellectual with an aesthetic bent who likes to retire when possible to read a good book and to expand his mind. Based on his character and personality it is difficult to believe the accused had it in him to act subversively in a deliberate manner. For this reason, the court struggled to reconstruct the developments that led to the defendant's deed, especially since he did not say much about this at the trial.
>
> The defendant's suggestion he made his remarks solely to animate the discussions with his officers and to offer an opposing viewpoint for rhetorical purposes, is to be rejected out of hand. Rather the court believes the accused lost his faith in a final victory early in 1943 due to the military setbacks in several theatres of the war. Under the impact of Stalingrad and the events in North Africa he grew faint-hearted and weak. His liberal tendencies, which already had led him to withdraw from the Hitler Youth in 1935 when his *bündisch* youth group was dissolved, regained the upper hand. In this emotionally challenging situation, and given the opposition of his officers, he allowed his rejection of National Socialism, its institutions and its leader

> to grow more pronounced and in its form more confrontational than it really was. Given the nature of the reported utterances, and considering the defendant's intelligence and education, the court could not doubt the accused was fully aware his statements had a potentially subverting effect. This in itself is sufficient to find the accused guilty under the current interpretation of the law. For, as the Reich Supreme Court has established, not only are those deeds punishable that are directly undercutting the fighting spirit of the military and were undertaken for that very end. The law applies no less to actions where the perpetrators do not intend to bring about such subversion through their behavior but realize clearly that their actions have such an effect and do not desist from continuing their activities. On this basis it is established that the accused acted with the necessary and required premeditation to be in violation of the law.[50]

In addition to this twisted application and interpretation of the "subversion" decree, Hagemann found Kusch guilty of monitoring foreign broadcasts "beyond operational needs." In particular, Kusch's intentional juxtaposition of enemy news and German propaganda in front of his officers was deemed to subvert Germany's will to resist, the more so since Kusch routinely granted more credence to the veracity of enemy broadcasts than to products of Nazi propaganda.

Lastly, Hagemann defended the court's assessment of the death penalty in place of a more lenient one on three separate grounds. First, Kusch had committed his "subversive" activities in a repeated, sometimes daily pattern over months and years. Therefore, his crime was not excusable as a one-time derailment, but constituted a habitual, deliberate, and premeditated activity. Second, his subversive utterances had not even stopped short of the person of the Führer and carried in part connotations of high treason. Third, subversive activities were deemed particularly dangerous and harmful when perpetrated by popular individuals who had good evaluations and were otherwise judged competent and responsible.

Hagemann's tortured explanations reveal in remarkable clarity and chilling starkness the extent to which the naval justice system had succumbed to the entirely political and ideological mandate of creating a monolithic "people's community" and of lining it up to boost and prolong a failing war effort while at the same time doing everything possible to eliminate its critics and opponents. He followed in spirit and deed the head of the Wehrmacht's central legal department, Rudolf Lehmann, who had advised high military officials as early as 1939:

> It is not the court's responsibility to search for the truth as such, as it may be elusive or even non-existent. Rather, it is the court's task to use the means of the law to protect and maintain this community, of which it itself is a central part. Those who violate the spirit of this community and rise up against it as individuals are to be punished especially severely.[51]

Accordingly, Hagemann never questioned Abel's or Druschel's motives, never inquired into what really went on aboard *U-154*, never saw in Kusch much more than someone who failed to elevate the community over the individual and whose pessimism over the outcome of the war and insults to the Führer had to be silenced. The most Hagemann and the chief witnesses were willing to grant Kusch was that he displayed "a certain sense of duty."

CHAPTER 8

AGONY

After his conviction on the evening of January 26, 1944, and a brief farewell to Dieter Berger and his former commanding officers on *U-103*, Oskar Kusch was driven back to the Naval Detention Center at the Wik naval compound where he would be held in Cell No. 107 for the next 106 days. The prison had a total of 104 cells of which four were in the basement. Most of the inmates were kept in solitary confinement awaiting final disposition of their cases.[1]

While his file made its way slowly through the prescribed review process, and after Karl-Heinrich Hagemann's formal explanation and justification of the verdict had been added to it on January 31, Kusch quickly learned that his daily activities from then on would be tightly controlled by *Marineoberstabsrichter* Ernst Meinert. He was the official charged with making sure Kusch's sentence was properly carried out in conformity with military regulations. To assert that Meinert became Kusch's prime nemesis in those final days and may have contributed to blocking a possible commutation of his prisoner's sentence, would be a vast understatement.

Ernst Meinert, as so many men in the naval justice system, was a North German born in 1909 near the city of Elmshorn northwest of Hamburg. After his *Abitur* in 1929 he studied law at universities as far away as Geneva in Switzerland and Grenoble in France. In 1935 he passed his first and in 1939 his second state exam. As a *Kriegsmarine* reservist, he was incorporated into the naval justice administration in 1940, with assignments primarily in Norway and after March 1943 at the H.K.U.'s military court in Kiel.[2] As a member of the Nazi storm troopers, he was incorporated into the party itself on May 1, 1937. He claimed after the war his membership grew from purely utilitarian considerations because an ascent into the judicial hierarchy "without a touch of brown varnish" seemed difficult. He also freely admitted to having taken over the Nazi propaganda line on the causes, nature, and goals of the war, something quite evident in his record when acting as a prosecutor and judge. He thought it his obligation "to contribute [his] part to the positive outcome of the war" and hoped, despite doubts after the fall of Stalingrad, for a final victory:

> I believed despite the challenging military situation that everyone should continue to carry out his duty and that it was crucial to suppress any manifestations of subversion by all appropriate means.... Even though the military situation continued to deteriorate over the years, I kept up my faith until the enemy crossed the River Rhine and I remained convinced every soldier should do his duty and shut his mouth.[3]

For example, when presiding over a case against a passed midshipman accused of desertion and absence without leave that eventually, and perhaps unexpectedly, resulted in a "not guilty" verdict, Meinert leaned into one of his two military jurors with the words, "If you dare find in favor of the defendant, I will make sure you will not rise above the rank of passed midshipman yourself."[4]

Still, despite undisguised endorsements of the political and ideological mission of the naval justice system such as these, Meinert felt genuine sympathy for the former U-boat commander now under his care:

> Kusch pursued many intellectual interests and had extraordinary gifts as an artist. During his detention he completed many drawings, including one showing his whole life in a sequence of scenes.[5] These drawings were very moving. For these reasons I have often

> mentioned among comrades that it was really a shame that it should have come to this. I had sincere human feelings for him.

Meinert liked to emphasize that he was not responsible for Kusch's death sentence and had only been tasked with supervising its implementation. When it came to his censoring letters to and from Kusch, to limiting access for visitors, and to committing several related chicaneries, he asserted he was simply enforcing standard regulations. Moreover, not he but guidelines from Hitler and the Naval High Command had been responsible for the harshness of the verdict.[6] Fortunately, Kusch's lawyer Gerhard Meyer-Grieben enjoyed relatively unfettered access to his client and supplied Kusch with reading and drawing materials along with news about family, friends, and the status of his case.

A certain element of Meinert's meanness to Kusch and presumably other inmates must have sprung from personal frustration over the damage British bombs had done very recently to his home and property. In a letter to the chief naval judge of the Baltic Command on January 24, 1944, just two days before the trial and while Kusch was already in his custody, Meinert wrote:

> I hereby reiterate the oral report of January 5, 1944, that I had given to district magistrate Hoje at the time. My townhouse at Niebuhrstrasse 18 has been severely damaged by bombs. The greater part of our furniture has been torn apart by the blast, doors and windows are blown out, walls have caved in, and the plaster has come down from the ceilings, so that we cannot live there anymore. The other half of the house has collapsed down to the ground level. I presently live at the Villa "Forsteck" (above the offices) at Niemannsweg 178. I have managed to find housing for my family in Bad Segeberg.[7]

Both the tender *Erwin Wassner* with its floating offices for naval justice officials as well as Meinert's temporary refuge at Villa Forsteck would be gone within months of Kusch's trial, both victims of Allied aerial attacks.[8] The *Wassner* sank on July 24 and Villa Forsteck was bombed and destroyed on August 26, 1944, exactly seven months after the trial.[9] Today merely the villa's foundations remain in what became Diederichsen Park in 1958, its generous promenade and benches inviting visitors to linger and enjoy the same majestic view across the bay that had attracted Heinrich Adolph Meyer's fancy so long ago.[10] Bombing attacks on Kiel grew so fierce by July 1944 that the entire court made plans to evacuate to the town of Plön in more rural surroundings east of Kiel.[11]

Even though his prison eluded Allied bombs, in some of his drawings, for example "Cell No. 107, Naval Detention Center, with Inmate" of March 15, 1944, Kusch himself has left a hauntingly depressing picture of what his room looked like. The walls were thick, and the only natural light entered through one small window high up near the ceiling with vertical and horizontal metal bars through which there could be no escape. Three-quarters of a century later, those very windows at or just below ground level, with the same bars and in danger of being overgrown by bushes and weeds, remain visible from the outside of the four-story structure that was converted into a government office building after the war and functioned as such until recently. Narrow, numbered doors with the warning "Watch your step!" lead down into the former cells from an equally narrow and poorly lighted corridor—the same one Kusch must have walked down on the way to his execution.[12] The furniture in his cell consisted of a metal bunk, a wardrobe, a wooden desk with a drawer, a chair, a stool, a small closet for personal sanitary items, a water jug, a bucket, and a broom. It is not known how Kusch received his meals, whether he could shower, and whether he was allowed access to fresh air and recreation or much contact with other prisoners. When not sleeping or contemplating his fate, Kusch spent most of his hours reading, writing letters, and working on his sketches. He signed all his works with the letter "K" inside a capital "O."[13]

On February 5, 1944, Kusch's file reached for review the *Gerichtsherr*, that is, the Leader of U-Boats in the West, Captain Hans-Rudolf Rösing in Angers in France, with the request "to inform the Naval High Command by teletype of his opinion regarding clemency" for Kusch.[14]

By then the folder contained also a sealed envelope in which Kusch's three judges—Hagemann, Dittmers, and Westphalen—had indicated their views regarding possible clemency for Kusch. Postwar testimony has revealed that both Dittmers and Westphalen recommended commutation of the death sentence to service in a penal company at the front as an ordinary soldier. The envelope carried the instruction "Only to be opened by the Naval High Command" and, unsealed but empty, remains today in Kusch's file.[15]

Whether Rösing conferred for his assessment of the case with Kusch's flotilla commander Ernst Kals in nearby Lorient, or with Werner Winter as Kusch's former commanding officer and then chief of the First U-Boat Flotilla up in Brest, or anyone else on his staff besides Breinig, is not recorded. Rösing's decision, coming as it did from a close associate and confidant of Grand Admiral Karl Dönitz, would mark a crucial fork in the path that could lead either to a reprieve and a chance for Kusch to live, or to his execution. Considering the matter for less than a day, Rösing chose the latter option without a single word of explanation. He had Breinig inform the Naval High Command in Berlin on January 6 that he was "not in favor of any form of clemency."[16] The German naval historian Heinrich Walle must have had Rösing prominently in mind when he wrote fifty years later:

> In considering the [postwar] testimony of all those who shared responsibility for Kusch's death, it strikes one as noteworthy that none of them exhibited the slightest sign of feeling guilty for what had happened. At most one encountered a kind of indifferent regret, as if with a shrug of the shoulders, that they had to send this previously so exemplary and irreproachable U-boat commander to his death. It is furthermore remarkable that everyone responsible for the death penalty or for the refusal to grant clemency conveniently attempted to place blame on those higher up in the chain of command, on unfortunate but immutable circumstances, on the need to maintain and boost discipline, or on the prevailing laws that had to be strictly enforced. No one ever examined the

> actual impact of Kusch's utterances on the behavior of his men on *U-154* or asked what actually happened aboard the boat. . . . Rösing declared in his testimony in May 1949 that Abel's way of filing his report had been inappropriate. "Had he chosen a different way, who knows what might have happened?" Apart from the fact that [Rösing, Dittmers, and Westphalen] tried to justify their decisions as predetermined by circumstances beyond their control, their comments also contain a curious contradiction. If Kusch had indeed been guilty of a major military transgression, it would have been Abel's absolute duty and responsibility to report it.[17]

With Rösing's refusal to do anything in Kusch's defense, the file moved to the Naval High Command in Berlin, placing the matter squarely into the lap of Grand Admiral Karl Dönitz and his legal team. In anticipation of this event, Kusch's defense counsel Gerhard Meyer-Grieben had already indicated upon receipt of the written justification of the verdict that he would continue to represent Kusch and submit his own required response to Berlin as soon as possible.[18] He knew by then that Kusch would not make a formal plea for clemency himself as a matter of honor, principle, and out of the conviction that he had done nothing wrong. As Victor Nonn, Kusch's former roommate at the naval academy, has stated, "The way I knew Kusch, I do not believe he would have asked for clemency."[19] Thus the seven-page document Meyer-Grieben drew up immediately, either on February 2 or 3, and apparently with Kusch's knowledge and approval, served as a kind of substitute plea for review and leniency, a semiformal legal appeal in a system that knew no longer an independent appeal process, pointing out doubts about the correctness of the verdict and the appropriateness of the sentence.

Aware how much was at stake for his client in this literal life-and-death matter, Meyer-Grieben took special care that his objections to the way the proceedings had been conducted, the verdict that had been reached, and how Hagemann's justification had been worded, were impeccably phrased and argued. As an extra precaution and assurance against mistakes or missing pertinent legal points in favor of his client, however minor, Meyer-Grieben asked Lieutenant Dieter Berger in Berlin to contact Kurt Gollnick, the prominent lawyer in the capital who had refused to take Kusch's case two weeks before, for a second opinion on the wording. This time Gollnick cooperated and transmitted the edited pages to Kusch's lawyer in Kiel forthwith. Then Meyer-Grieben took another extraordinary step. Not trusting the postal system to deliver his appeal safely in the midst of Allied aerial attacks on both Kiel and Berlin, and to make sure it reached Dönitz's legal department before the weekend, he employed his wife as a personal courier. On Friday, February 4, Frau Meyer-Grieben boarded the first train from Kiel to Berlin long before sunrise, hand-delivered the envelope to the Naval High Command, obtained a receipt, met briefly with Dieter Berger's family, and was back in Kiel after nightfall that evening.[20] Clearly Kusch had no reason to fear his lawyer was slowing down or had given up on efforts to save his life.

Unfortunately, the document in question no longer exists. Meyer-Grieben's copy was lost in a bomb attack on Kiel that burned his office down later in 1944. It never became a part of Kusch's official file or was removed from it at some point. Nor is it available among the surviving records of the Naval High Command (OKM) at Germany's military archives in Freiburg or in the holdings of Gollnick's law firm in Berlin.[21] Thus it remains difficult to reconstruct the formal legal objections to the nature, course, and outcome of the case put forth by Kusch's defense lawyer for consideration by the legal staff at OKM, including ultimately Dönitz himself.

In the meantime, while rumors of Abel's report and Kusch's conviction and death sentence spread by word of mouth among stunned fellow submarine commanders and the wider naval officer corps, his former skippers on *U-103* once again took the lead in fighting for Kusch's cause and did so without delay. Both Werner Winter and Gustav-Adolf Janssen knew Dönitz very well, were not reluctant to go straight to the top outside regular channels, and had a sense that urgent intervention was of the essence to prevent the worst. About two weeks after the trial, probably on the weekend of February 12, Lieutenant Janssen and Kusch's old friend Kurt Wiemer had a talk in the lobby of the Claridge Hotel in the rue

François Premier near the Champs-Élysées in Paris. The following are Wiemer's recollections of their meeting as put to paper two years later:

> Herr Janssen related to me in great detail what had happened at the trial and the course of a conversation he had had with Dönitz about it a few days later. I can remember our talk as if it had taken place just a few weeks ago, except for the names of a few cities that I can no longer recall. . . .
>
> This is what Lieutenant Janssen told me: "After the trial and the announcement of the death sentence it became clear to me that I had to undertake everything in my power to save Oskar Kusch. I at once tried to ascertain Dönitz's whereabouts and learned that he was staying at one of our bases on the Atlantic. There [in Lorient] I indeed met up with him, and since I had been his former aide-de-camp it was not difficult to get an appointment to see him. Dönitz asked me if I was in a great hurry because otherwise I might accompany him in his car on the trip back to Berlin. . . . On this ride I described to him the course of the trial. Unfortunately, as a junior officer it was not possible for me to criticize the manner in which the proceedings had been conducted because in that case I would have thrown doubt on the objectivity and fairness of the court. As a result, I had to restrict my remarks in defense of my former I.W.O. and friend . . . to efforts to convince Dönitz of Kusch's soldierly and personal qualities as I had come to know them during many months together on board of our submarine. I did suggest that the court had been unfamiliar with these personal traits and strengths of the defendant and as a result had reached the harsh verdict.
>
> "At first Dönitz reacted in a decidedly negative and even angry manner. But I kept pressing my point relentlessly and in the end when we parted Dönitz told me: 'Janssen, I find it awfully decent of you to speak up on the boy's behalf. I will arrange for him to see me so I can have a good look into his heart. We will then take matters from there.'

"I was very happy about the outcome of my talk with Dönitz. The way I knew him, I could now be assured that he would do everything to push for clemency and leniency in Oskar Kusch's case."

Janssen was so convinced that Dönitz would keep his word that he succeeded in the end even to dispel my [Wiemer's] doubts about promises of such a kind. These statements are true to the best of my knowledge and conscience, and I will gladly swear an oath to that effect.[22]

Erwin Rau, a Crew 37a comrade of Oskar Kusch, reported a slightly different version of this conversation in 1984:

> Many years ago I mentioned the Kusch case to the late Gustav-Adolf Janssen. . . . He told me he had asked Dönitz to allow him to share a car ride from Lorient to Berlin with him and that he tried during the entire trip to dissuade Dönitz from enforcing the death penalty on Kusch. Dönitz, however, rejected the idea out of hand and stated he had to set down an example as a warning to others.[23]

Commander Werner Winter was no less eager than Janssen to express to the Grand Admiral his displeasure about the course of the trial and his horror over the sentence. Immediately upon the conclusion of the trial he wrote a letter to Dönitz imploring him to do everything in his power to allow clemency to prevail:

> Later Dönitz sent me back a personal reply to the effect that under the prevailing circumstances he was simply unable to do anything for Kusch. I believe I can infer from the letter that Dönitz did regret the verdict. Personally, I was shocked by the sentence. I believe Dönitz, whom I know personally very well, would have done more if his hands had not been tied, if the verdict had been different.[24]

According to Winter, fellow officers regarded Abel's and Druschel's actions as "uncomradely and despicable," while a staff officer at U-Boat

Command noted in his memoirs, "we were sad about the denunciation and the verdict, but our losses at the front and the air attacks on Kiel overshadowed the case; the public was not aware of it at all."[25] Significantly Ulrich Abel, whose sole stated goal in filing his report had been to remove Kusch from command of a U-boat, never contacted the court or Dönitz with a request to spare his former commander's life. Neither did Kurt Druschel or Arno Funke.

Kusch's family and friends were no less active and determined to save him than his naval comrades. While little is known about the reaction of Kusch's father to Oskar's predicament at the time, his fierce postwar determination to bring Hagemann, Dittmers, Westphalen, and their surviving superiors to justice for having committed or abetted a judicial murder based on purely political motives, and to rehabilitate his son's name, honor, and legacy, strongly suggest that he used his presence in Berlin to influence the review of the case at Naval Command. Kusch's mother traveled twice to Kiel to speak with her son, and Inge von Foris was later allowed to visit her fiancé once despite Meinert's usual objections and interference. Oskar Kusch had no further relatives on his father's side of the family and only a distant niece on his mother's.

Not surprisingly the ubiquitous Dieter Berger spearheaded efforts to raise Kusch's spirits through regular letters and exerted pressure on Dönitz and his legal department to let fairness and leniency prevail:

> After the verdict against Kusch his friends went into action to obtain a reprieve to save his life. In the course of these efforts Lieutenant Janssen spoke with Dönitz and received the assurance that he would review the file in Kusch's favor and have the case tried again based on the statements by Lieutenant Commander Winter and Lieutenant Janssen that the original proceedings had been biased and one-sided. On the very day of Kusch's execution Admiral Godt [Rear Admiral Eberhard Godt of the U-Boat Command's operational division] assured me that the verdict would not be enforced without a new trial. Shortly thereafter the sentence was carried out.[26]

Another close friend from their days in the *bündisch* youth ten years before, Wolfgang Kühns-Bernsau, traveled to Kiel to see what could be done:

> After the death penalty had been announced, I went to Kiel with Frau Brockmann, my friend's divorced mother, to see Oskar and to gain a personal impression of the circumstances there. The sentence seemed unaccountably harsh and went far beyond what the prosecutor had asked for. . . . None of the experts whom I queried about the naval justice system could understand or explain how the verdict had come about. I then spoke to Hagemann . . . aboard a warship [*Erwin Wassner*] in the port of Kiel and came away with this impression: In the course of our conversation which lasted maybe thirty minutes he appeared extremely cautious, evasive, and negative. His comments—for example that the case would be carefully reviewed "as a matter of routine" and that all mitigating circumstances would naturally be taken into consideration—were obviously meant to belittle his involvement in the matter and to obscure to interested parties the true motives behind the verdict. As it turned out, nobody offered any satisfactory explanations until we heard from the attorney Mr. Meyer-Grieben in Kiel that the sentence had been carried out. In my opinion [Abel] must have had a personal motive to get rid of a difficult comrade. Hagemann himself was known in naval circles as an unpleasant superior and fanatical National Socialist. As the verdict proves, his legal interpretations and decisions and his take on what constitutes the duties of the state were driven by his identification with Nazi ideology. There was nothing humane about his understanding of justice.[27]

Much the same could be said about Ernst Meinert, Kusch's warden and daily nemesis at the Naval Detention Center, who apparently saw in his prisoner little more than a hardened criminal and opponent of the regime awaiting just punishment.

Kusch expressed his mood, hopes, and anxieties during his incarceration primarily in the form of artistic sketches and dozens of handwritten letters, many of which have survived either as part of his file or remain in the hands of their recipients and their descendants. In his bureaucratic overreach, Meinert compiled a list of thirty-eight letters Kusch either wrote or received between March 8 and May 7, 1944, meticulously recording the names and addresses of senders and recipients.[28] No such list exists for the first six weeks of his detention or for the days immediately preceding his execution. In total Kusch may have composed or received more than sixty letters, all of them censored by Meinert and many confiscated if their contents revealed too much sympathy for the prisoner and his cause. For Meinert the very notion that someone would want to communicate with the dangerous criminal in Cell No. 107 appears to have been ipso facto proof of that person's critical and potentially harmful view of the regime.

A quantitative analysis of Kusch's known correspondence reveals an interesting pattern. Fifteen letters involved family members, including his fiancée Inge von Foris (4) his mother (4), his father (4), as well as Inge's brother Lieutenant Henning von Foris (2), her father Colonel Bernhard von Foris (1), and her favorite grandmother Mala (1). Thirteen letters came from or went out to friends from his youth movement days, among them 3 each to or from Dieter Berger and Kurt Wiemer. Another 9 involved either fellow naval officers or crewmembers of *U-154.* In 7 cases the exact relationship between Kusch and the correspondent could not be ascertained and may have included the widows or parents of friends from his *Südlegion* days who had been killed during the war or had been captured by the enemy. Only in his very last letters does it appear as if Kusch had resigned himself to his fate. Until then he expressed regret about his situation but never remorse and maintained hope for a modification of his sentence. As he wrote to his father a week after his trial, "Now we have to wait and see what course fate has in store. Let us hope it is a favorable one."[29]

Kusch often pondered the discrepancy between Abel's and Druschel's charges and what had actually happened aboard his boat in terms of a diminished fighting spirit or impaired combat readiness. A month after his conviction, he addressed two similarly worded letters to former members of *U-154*'s crew, one each to his navigator and III.W.O. on the first patrol, Heinrich Lüdmann, and to his chief radio operator at the time, Hans Janker. Both letters remain in Kusch's file to this day because Meinert considered them subversive and never allowed them to reach their addressees. Here are Kusch's lines to his former navigator:

> Dear Lüdmann—first of all many thanks for your letter of January 14 that only reached me a few days ago. . . . Perhaps you have heard in the meantime about the events involving our good old "U-Sunshine." If not, here is a short summary. When I returned from my leave on January 20, I was arrested in Lorient. While I was gone, and without my knowledge, Lieutenants Abel, Druschel and the new II.W.O. [Funke] had filed a report against me containing the harshest of accusations of a political nature. They had to do with remarks I had allegedly made on board, listening to foreign broadcasts, and similar matters. On January 26, I was put on trial in Kiel for subverting the military spirit. Based on witness testimony, etc., that I was unable to refute completely, the court regarded the charges as proven and imposed the death penalty on me for "undermining the fighting spirit and discipline" without considering mitigating circumstances. As you can see, Lüdmann, one can descend very quickly from the status of a U-boat commander to being a delinquent, or at least a prison inmate. From your experiences on our patrol together you can judge for yourself how badly I ruined the fighting spirit of our boat and undercut the discipline on board. I am sure if one were to ask the crewmembers about this matter, a very different picture would emerge compared to the one presented by Abel and Druschel. Well, one can do nothing about that at the moment. I have been here at the Naval Detention Center since January 27 and am waiting for either the confirmation of the verdict or a pardon. Right now the matter rests with the Naval High Command and

> it will take a few more weeks before they reach a decision. You can probably imagine my situation here in prison. An old mariner and U-boat commander like me in jail—incredible! And all that based on a verdict for something so ridiculous and ignominious. Yes, it is bitter and hard even to think about it. Should you happen to be in Kiel, I would very much appreciate if you could see me or write to me. A visitor permit can be obtained on the *Erwin Wassner.* Nothing much positive to report about the most recent patrol—plenty of enemy aircraft, long stretches of time spent submerged, etc. Still, let us hope the whole thing will have a favorable outcome. . . . Kindly accept the best wishes for yourself and your wife from your former commanding officer. Oskar Kusch.[30]

Kusch repeated his characterization of *U-154* as "U-Sunshine" in his note to Janker and added at the end, "I had planned to get married, but that is now out of the question."[31]

Several days later Ernst Meinert was at it again, this time confiscating an incoming letter from Dieter Berger dated March 1. In fact, Meinert had a copy made of the letter with the intention of reporting Berger to his superiors on the charge that a German *Luftwaffe* lieutenant should not express sympathy for a criminal convicted of eroding his men's fighting spirit and discipline. Berger, who had lost one of his arms in combat against the Soviet Union, had typed the letter with one finger:

> Dear Oskar! So far I have been unable to write to you for reasons I cannot specify here, but I also was reluctant to do so because my inner bond to you is so strong that a letter written in the knowledge that a third person will peruse it is hardly worth writing.
>
> But just now you have spoken to me in your strongest language—your pictures—and I have to respond.
>
> Inge [von Foris] just left, it is late, and I am sitting in my pajamas on the edge of my bed after I had walked Inge to the [metro station]. . . . I had taken out the large folder with your sketches, looked through them once more, and then turned out the light.

But as I lay awake in the darkness I heard you speak to me, and so I am sitting up again and am typing this first letter to you since I last saw you in Kiel.

Those pictures, Oskar! You have such an immense power of expression and your soul speaks from them with such purity and clarity—my God, others must understand it just as easily.

Until now I thought that in our age we cannot produce genuine art anymore because real art grows from our subconscious, from the depths of one's soul. Art today is mostly the product of a deliberate process and is intentionally created. But your pictures have taught me differently and I now know that you still have much to say to others when you project your personality outward upon a sheet of paper.

Always remember what I told you before each of your patrols: that nothing can harm you because you still have to fulfill a mission in life and no one dies before he has done so. Just as Rembrandt simply could not have been born without arms, so you will follow down your path despite all seemingly insurmountable obstacles.

I believe in you and your destiny and you should do so as well. God is only a word to remind us that life is ultimately incomprehensible, but to believe in God means there is a purpose to our life even if we are incapable of understanding it. His ways are not our ways.

Alas, Oskar, my words do not have the power of expression that your sketches have, but I am sure you will understand what I am trying to say, just as you did so long ago in the Pompeji Bar [in Berlin-Schöneberg] where we first spoke to each other.

It is almost midnight. In a few days I will visit you again. I just do not know when exactly I can get away from here. I will then tell you what is so difficult to put down in a letter, since a letter can be no more than a brief extract of what one really means to say. I am looking forward to seeing you again despite all the miserable circumstances. Heartfelt regards. Dieter.[32]

Kusch's growing gloom, the first signs of becoming resigned to his fate, and certainly his longing for happier times past, speak strongly from these lines he sent to his Crew 37a comrade Karl Otto (Karlo) Flindt and another friend on March 8, 1944:

> The irrevocable decision is coming closer and closer. Its deadly seriousness and its significance cast their shadows over every day and every hour. I am trying hard to prepare myself for the moment when there can be no more doubt about the outcome. It is bitter and hard, especially when I imagine such a wretched and shameful end. That is the worst. How often did we have to face death out at sea through air attacks, depth charges, and all the other challenges of U-boat warfare, but it is quite a different thing to suffer death in such a miserable manner. How happy I would be if I could be back out there on my boat. Given the crammed confines and loneliness of my prison cell such longings are particularly agonizing and painful. You know only too well that being an officer meant everything for me. But that is all over now. It is so bitter that I wish my thoughts would not come back to it all the time. Never again taking your men out to sea, never to be in charge of a submarine again! If they only could give me a boat now! What all could I accomplish now with all my experience and expertise, as I demonstrate to them that the picture they have of me is completely wrong. I believe and know that everyone would be better off that way than if the sentence were to be carried out, above all the U-boat service and the state. But that is out of the question now; it is too late. So I am confined to do the only thing left to me—to gather the strength to face my fate with dignity and composure. I very much hope I can display those traits when it counts. But one never knows ahead of time. One can only hope and beg that it will be so.[33]

Of all the officers aboard *U-154*, the only one who ever made an attempt to contact Kusch during his incarceration was Dr. Nothdurft. From distant

Heidelberg he inquired on March 17 whether Meinert could forward a letter to Kusch on his behalf since he was not sure of the proper address or procedure.[34] Whether Meinert did as asked—Nothdurft, after all, had signed the request with "Heil Hitler!"—or whether he withheld the letter, is not recorded. Certainly, Kusch never responded to the man who tried to help him but, in the process, created so much more harm than good.

On April 1, 1944, Ernst Meinert's unkindness and spitefulness reached a new low point when he returned to Inge von Foris' brother Henning a letter the army lieutenant had written to his prospective brother-in-law a week before from Wetzlar:

> We are herewith returning to you the letter you had written to Lieutenant Kusch. If it is true that you are familiar with the reasons why he has been charged and sentenced, it is to be expected from you as a German officer that you distance yourself from him as soon as possible and discontinue any contacts you might have had with him. . . . It seems more than curious that a German officer with any sense of honor should have written such a letter to someone who has received the death penalty and has been stripped of every right to wear a military uniform. Should you make a second attempt to get in touch with K., we will report you to your superiors to enable them to take additional measures against you. In the present case no further action will be taken for special reasons.[35]

After the war, Gerhard Meyer-Grieben criticized Meinert's attitudes and behavior sharply, citing the revealing comment on Meinert's part that "Kusch's friends apparently viewed his deed as a trivial matter," and that "no government could tolerate such an interpretation because otherwise 'we would cut off the very branch on which we are sitting.'"[36] Around the same time, in 1946, Meyer-Grieben wrote the following in a letter to prosecutor Robert W. M. Kempner at the International Military Tribunal in Nuremberg:

> Mr. Meinert was a convinced National Socialist who created great difficulties when it came to Kusch's communications with friends and family. He complained about the letters that went back and forth, confiscated some of these and sent them on to the Naval High Command in Berlin in order to influence the review process of Kusch's case in a negative way. In the end he ordered all visits by Kusch's friends and family to cease, except for those of his mother. On several occasions I complained about his actions. He told me he could not tolerate that a defendant who had been convicted for political reasons was allowed to maintain amicable relations with his chums who were likewise opposed to the political system. Failing to prevent such contacts would bring about the end of the regime.[37]

Two months into his detention Kusch himself had become so annoyed and enraged over the pesky justice official that on March 29 he lodged an official complaint over Meinert's arbitrary and narrow-minded censorship practices:

> At the end of February I wrote three letters from the naval detention center that the court has taken exception to. Since I believe the objections are based on misunderstandings of what I was trying to express in those letters, allow me to offer an explanation. Since no specific objectionable passages were pointed out to me . . . I can only assure the court that none of my letters had a subversive purpose. Any poorly chosen phrases can be traced to the depressive state in which I found myself after the verdict and that may have colored the letters here and there in a minor way as they were overwhelmingly of an informational nature.[38]

Kusch goes on to explain a particular passage in a confiscated letter to a Miss Bischoff in Lübeck in which he had stated he hoped to resume creating "beautiful" drawings after completing his time in the penitentiary:

> I did not write the phrase in question to indicate that I expected to spend a few years in the penitentiary and then resume doing my sketches. Rather, using self-irony and bitterness while fully aware of my circumstances, I meant to point out the exact opposite, namely, my impossibility of ever creating something "beautiful" again. The court concluded from this passage that I am not aware of the seriousness of my situation. I would like to assure the court that the serious nature of my situation has always been perfectly clear to me and that I never meant to misrepresent that fact or my prospects. . . . At the same time, and especially since I am expecting the confirmation of my sentence in the very near future, I am asking the court's permission for my fiancée, Ms. von Foris, to visit me. I would like to discuss and arrange with her a number of personal and practical matters before the sentence is carried out. I am asking for this favor exactly because I am aware how serious and urgent my situation is.[39]

Meinert noted at the bottom of the letter, "Defendant's counsel Meyer-Grieben has been notified that a one-time permission to visit will be granted." Whether Kusch desired to delay this last encounter with Inge for as long as possible before facing the inevitable, whether Meinert placed additional bureaucratic obstacles in his path, or whether he perhaps needed more time to sort out in his mind what to tell Inge, is no longer ascertainable. At any rate, not until three weeks later on April 18 did Meyer-Grieben formally request and obtain this permit for Inge to speak to her fiancé for the last time on the morning of Thursday, April 20, 1944.[40] It would not have escaped the young couple that this final meeting—their first since parting in Zürs three months before—fell on Hitler's fifty-fifth birthday.

No account of their last meeting exists either in ink or in charcoal. Given the cold and depressing surroundings at the detention center, it must have lacked any sense of privacy or intimacy. At least Kusch was allowed to wear civilian clothes rather than prison garb since his sentence was still awaiting confirmation. How far ahead their thoughts and plans extended into the future, if at all, can only be guessed. It is quite likely that Oskar gave Inge on this occasion additional items for safekeeping, including some of his artwork and his correspondence. A letter from Gerhard Meyer-Grieben to Ernst Meinert on June 26, 1944, some six weeks after Kusch's death, throws some light on the issue:

> The award certificates for his decorations can no longer be located. His relatives (mother) do not have them. As far as the mother recalls the certificates were transferred to his fiancée when Kusch was on leave in Berlin in 1943. The apartment at the Heydtstrasse where she lived at the time belonged to Lieutenant Commander von Foris [correct: Lt. Cdr. Walter Klusemann, Inge's stepfather] and has been destroyed by the enemy. On that occasion the certificates were likely destroyed as well, along with the other papers of the deceased (his commission as an officer, his correspondence, his library, etc.).[41]

Even earlier Kusch had notified his flotilla commander and the navy's personnel office that he had lost his pay book during his vacation in Zürs.[42]

Kusch's surviving drawings from this time confirm how frequently and how profoundly Inge and recollections of their weeks together in the Austrian Alps occupied his mind. At the same time, they reflect notions of deep despair and impending doom. Between March 15 and April 7, just as he requested a last meeting with Inge, he created a sequence of three sketches he collectively labeled "Zürser Bilderbogen," or "picture memories of Zürs," and dedicated them to a mysterious recipient identified only as "das Mariechen."[43] Whether this was an intimate nickname for Inge only the two of them could have known, or was someone else altogether, remains unclear, but it obviously was a female who had been with them in Austria or whom they had met there. At any rate, the first and most positive and optimistic of the sketches shows four scenes: Oskar and Inge on their skis being pulled uphill by a lift as he holds her close to him; Oskar standing in Inge's hotel room door and gently waking her up in the morning after what must have been a long but happy night out; both of them dancing exuberantly to "swing" music, presumably at a bar or club; and a concerned Inge trying to cheer Oskar up as he pensively embraces a miniature merry-go-round with the inscription, "It goes around and around and around."

His vision of life and of his relationship with Inge as a merry-go-round also dominates his sketch of April 2 titled "Das Karussel." Except for a ragged body swinging from one of three gallows while vultures lurk in the distance, the upper section of the drawing, above the busy and crowded merry-go-round and a pavilion in the center, is all happiness: a warm sun shining on Inge and Oskar as they enjoy a lover's kiss; another dance scene with Inge in high heels and a fashionable dress showing off her legs to the audience and to her admiring beau all spiffy in a coat and tie; and, slightly smaller and less distinct, Inge and Oskar emerging through a portal after their wedding, she all in white and he in a formal coat, tie, and a silk hat. The lower third of the drawing stands in total contrast to the other scenes and is hauntingly disturbing. It is dominated by the "Grim Reaper" in the form a hovering skeleton illuminated by two flickering candles to his right. An adjacent scene to the left shows Kusch, his head lowered in shame and steadying himself with a cane or ski pole, being escorted into a waiting horse-drawn carriage by a man in a dark coat and otherwise unidentifiable as his body is turned away from the viewer—an allusion to how his sojourn in Zürs ended for him. Lastly, in the right-hand lower corner of the sketch a face, all pale and its eyes wide with horror, peers through a barred window at the dead body of a man outside lying prostrate with a dagger stuck in his chest. The window with its bars and surrounding brickwork is a perfect replica of the basement windows, eerily unchanged to this day, of the naval detention center in Kiel.

The third panel of this triptych of sorts is titled "The Wanderer between Both Worlds" and is a further testament to Kusch's literary and artistic erudition as well as his enduring rootedness in the cosmos and traditions of the *bündisch* youth movement. Inspired both by Caspar David Friedrich's romantic painting "Wanderer above a Sea of Fog" of 1818 and by Walter Flex's World War I novel of 1916 so popular in the 1920s and

1930s when he grew up, Kusch depicts himself as meditative and bareheaded in his naval uniform gazing into the distance before the vastness of an Alpine landscape while below him he and Inge and another couple are shown dancing away the night in oblivion and abandonment. This quasi out-of-body experience, neither here nor there, somewhere between life and death, between heaven and earth, between now and forever, must have been symptomatic for Kusch's condition as he pondered the stations of his life and the abyss that had opened before him.

For the two weeks after March 6, Kusch must have undergone a particularly morose mental spell, as his sketches from this period reveal with terrifying clarity and intensity. Drawing inspiration from Greek mythology, the Old and New Testaments, Dante's *Inferno*, and other, more elusive sources, Kusch's imagination projects him into the midst of a cosmic struggle between the forces of light and dark, good and evil, from which there is neither rescue nor escape. Words cannot match the artistic power of his stark and apocalyptic projections. Some of the sketches replicate aspects or effects of well-known masterpieces. For example, a self-portrait of March 7 depicts Kusch, his empty eyes wide open, his hair falling wildly onto his forehead, his mouth ajar in impotent protest, and with his hands fiercely grasping the bars of his cell door, eerily similar to the central figure in Edvard Munch's *The Scream*. The next day Kusch completed "Judas," a grim rendition of the eternally secretive, scheming, plotting, calculating, slanted-eyed enemy of all that is good, decent, and true. The fact that Ernst Meinert allowed this work to pass his censorship and leave the prison along with the rest of Kusch's drawings indicates how well Kusch was able to disguise any outward similarities to the Judases in his life. On March 19, an infernal "Moloch" devours a huge assembly of terrified children in his vast orifice, his huge and menacingly sharp teeth spearing them mercilessly as they try to get away, including a hapless and hopeless Kusch impaled on one of the monster's lower eyeteeth, his eyes gaping wide and his arms stretched down in desperation for a relief that never arrives. And on the very next day, March 20, the first day of his last, abbreviated spring on earth, Kusch transplants the forever damned from Canto III in Dante's *Inferno* to the *Kriegsmarine*'s detention center in Kiel, as a large collection of faceless male prisoners, in striped garb and wearing their cell number on their backs, crosses a street into the welcoming gates of the facility. The last in the group, No. 107 of course, looks up and reads on the welcoming sign beneath the barbed-wire security fence the Italian poet's famous line, "Abandon all hope ye who enter here."

In his deep and frequent preoccupation with Dante's *Inferno* in those dark days of despair, Kusch was likely guided by a desire to sort into their appropriate circles of hell those who had harmed him through fraud and malice. Dante's three major traitors (Judas, Brutus, and Cassius) may well have turned into Abel, Hagemann, and Dönitz as a slobbering Lucifer makes a meal of them at the lowest level in Canto XXXIV. Not far above, in the *Malebolge* of Lower Hell, one would have encountered their scheming accomplices among the flatterers, deceivers, hypocrites, sowers of discord, and other falsifiers. In Kusch's estimation this might well have been the proper eternal place of damnation for Druschel, Funke, Nothdurft, Dittmers, Westphalen, Kals, Rösing, and Meinert, as they allowed through acts both of commission and omission a great tragedy to take its course.

By early April 1944, Kusch had every reason to begin to abandon hope for a merciful outcome of his case. By this time his file had been in the hands of the Naval High Command for nearly two months and a decision had to be imminent. Any death penalty against a *Kriegsmarine* officer had to be reviewed by Grand Admiral Karl Dönitz and confirmed by Hitler—the latter step typically a mere formality. Dönitz in turn relied in his decisions heavily on the advice of the top legal official on his staff, Dr. Joachim Rudolphi, while the head of Dönitz's administrative department, and Rudolphi's immediate superior, General Admiral Walter Warzecha, also signed off on major decisions. Kusch's lawyer Gerhard Meyer-Grieben later remembered and stressed the centrality of Rudolphi's role in the review of the verdict:

> Dr. Rudolphi inserted himself regularly into the process. He either signed or co-signed the pertinent documents. Dr. Rudolphi's name was well known among defense counsels and throughout the naval justice system. We were often advised that "Dr. Rudolphi

> wants the matter handled this way or that way," or "Dr. Rudolphi disagrees with this arrangement," etc. He was the decisive official when it came to reviewing death penalty cases.[44]

Interestingly, Rudolphi would testify after the war that he had not been involved in the Kusch case at all as he had been on sick leave at the time and often away from Berlin on official business. According to him, he only cosigned the document confirming Kusch's death sentence on direct orders from Dönitz because Warzecha was just then surveying bomb damage to his home and unavailable for a signature.[45] Rudolphi's postwar sworn statement would be exposed as patently false and misleading by none other than Dönitz himself, even though the jurist never suffered prosecution for perjury as a result.

Still, Dönitz must shoulder ultimate responsibility for making the decision at the Naval High Command that sent Kusch to his death. He had been aware of the case almost from the moment Abel made his report, had conferred with Captain Rösing in France as well as Admirals von Friedeburg and Godt at U-Boat Command, and heard on Kusch's behalf from Werner Winter and especially from Lieutenant Janssen during their long car ride through France in early February. Now the file, forwarded after initial scrutiny and recommendations by Rudolphi and Warzecha, lay on his desk. While or just before serving his ten-year sentence at Spandau after the war, and apparently worried that the Kusch case might yet catch up with him in some fashion, Dönitz addressed the following undated note, probably composed in 1946 or 1947, to the former naval justice official Karl Helmut Sieber, who had taken it upon himself to help fellow naval judges weather the ongoing denazification hearings:

> My *recollection* is as follows: Received the list of charges from the Leader of U-Boats in the West, Captain Rösing, containing the report of the officers of the boat and also of enlisted men (mate in charge of the central control room?). Trial at the court of the Higher Command for U-Boat Training. Death sentence

for subverting the fighting spirit. Verdict endorsed by *Gerichtsherr* [Rösing] and U-Boat Command, Admiral von Friedeburg. Case file came to me. It showed Kusch, on one long patrol (or perhaps 2), had made again and again very disparaging remarks in front of his crew about the Führer, the military leadership and the prospects for winning the war. Negative effect on the boat regarding combat spirit and military discipline.

I was very impressed by the case. Simply unbelievable that something like this could have happened under the auspices of one of my own U-boat commanders! How was it possible that neither fellow submarine commanders nor the flotilla commander noticed anything and did something about it? Further discussions about the case with Godt and also with Rösing.

I kept the file in my office for a long time—about 8 to 10 days—because the case really caused me anguish and I wished I could find a way out that would have made it possible for me to modify the sentence. Held additional consultations with Admiral Warzecha and Admiralty Staff Judge Rudolphi in their capacity as the responsible officials at Naval High Command. Their unequivocal position was that the gravity of the case—subversive speeches in front of the crew while in the presence of the enemy—rendered any form of clemency out of the question. We simply could not make an exception in favor of U-boat commander Lieutenant Kusch since we had always imposed the death penalty before in similar cases, usually on enlisted personnel. Both [Warzecha and Rudolphi] were correct. The military situation in that hard last phase of the war required such a sentence. I endorsed the verdict. The Führer agreed. It was carried out.[46]

Notwithstanding such self-righteous justifications, the case of Oskar Kusch must have given the Grand Admiral recurring nightmares and weighed on his conscience. As late as November 30, 1968, at age seventy-seven and more than ten years after his release from prison, and without any specific occasion to worry about renewed prosecution, Dönitz addressed the following inquiry to Otto Kranzbühler, his former defense counsel at the International Military Tribunal in Nuremberg and himself a high-ranking official in the *Kriegsmarine*'s naval justice apparatus before 1945:

> Concerning the death sentence for Kusch, I was of the opinion in those days that we could not maintain a moral double standard. It was my duty to prevent that someone who had weakened the strength of the U-boat service ended up in the safe protection of a prison cell through a show of clemency. Especially so, if at the same time in that hardest phase of the war I demanded from our brave U-boat commanders and their crews that they gave their very best and continued to fight in order to bind vast enemy resources that would otherwise have been turned directly against our homeland, against Germany. I am thinking of the hundreds of large aircraft that otherwise would have dropped bombs on our civilian population. And these U-boat crews continued to perform their duty courageously and with great sacrifice.
>
> Therefore, allow me to ask: Is there a legal way for the present state authorities to roll the Kusch case back out? Clearly, if *I* confirmed the sentence, I never did so with the intention of murdering anyone. Instead, as I have pointed out, I did so while fulfilling a difficult but necessary duty in an extraordinarily trying phase of the U-boat war when everything had to be concentrated on maintaining our strength to fight. There can be no doubt that I had the full backing and concurrence of Dr. Rudolphi and Warzecha. Should there be any question about that, I would know about it.[47]

Besides portraying more than twenty years after the war a vastly skewed picture of Allied resources and the actual effect of his submarines against the enemy after 1943, here Dönitz makes quite clear that no one in the official review chain—namely, Kals, Rösing, Godt, von Friedeburg, Rudolphi, Warzecha, or among those he may have consulted informally—

ever lifted one finger for Kusch. He also implies he paid little or no attention to those who knew Kusch best—Winter and Janssen—or to the suggestion by Dittmers and Westphalen that the sentence be commuted to some rehabilitative service at the front. He and Rudolphi may also have been influenced by the letters Meinert forwarded to the Naval High Command to demonstrate that in detention Kusch showed no sign of changing his political views or revealed any kind of contrition for his terrible deeds. Far from wishing to grant Kusch another chance through a new trial or a lighter sentence, Dönitz had decided by then that by having Kusch executed he would set down an example as a warning to others, presumably in the sense Voltaire commented on British Admiral John Byng's execution in 1757 by his own side as an act designed "*pour encourager les autres*" (to encourage the others). Not what Kusch had or had not done became the central criterion in Dönitz's mind, but the need to keep up the will to victory in line with the Nazi spirit. By this reckoning, Kusch executed became more valuable than Kusch incarcerated. Dönitz never kept his promise to see Kusch and listen to his version of events. He never called him or corresponded with him, nor did any other individual involved in the review process ever seek to meet with the lonely inmate of Cell No. 107 at Kiel's naval detention center. Naively or deliberately taking the trial record for a complete and unbiased account of what had happened on *U-154*, Dönitz and his subordinates allowed the myth to take root that the boat had somehow pulled out of the war under Kusch's direction.

As a further clue to Dönitz's thinking and hardening mindset in that spring and summer of 1944, there exists a speech he delivered a month after the failed coup attempt against Hitler on July 20, 1944—some three months after refusing clemency for Kusch. A typewritten version of Dönitz's address to high-ranking naval brass was widely distributed at the time, even though the copy once appended to the war diary of the Naval High Command was removed at some juncture before the end of the war. In Section IX of this programmatic address, Dönitz reiterated what fate awaited soldiers who had lost faith in the Führer and in a final victory:

> The German armed forces must stick fanatically to the man to whom they have sworn allegiance for otherwise this Wehrmacht will go under. . . . Who is there besides the Führer whom we can serve unconditionally with all our soul? The [July 20] conspirators in the General Staff in the end failed precisely because they had not dedicated themselves with all their soul to the Führer. It is therefore necessary to become fully aware of these circumstances and the fact that in the midst of our current life-and-death struggle nothing can replace our fanatical loyalty to this man and to this state. Any deviation would amount to a loosening of commitment and a crime. I would rather eat dirt than to see my grandchildren being educated in this Jewish spirit and filth and to become poisoned by it. . . . We therefore demand from the officer corps that it stands unconditionally behind this state and that it educates its men to absolute fanaticism. This education will and must find its fulfillment not in well-sounding speeches but in a fanatical readiness to die. Whoever does not have the wish or the will to do this, cannot rise to higher leadership positions and must be removed.[48]

Clearly, Kusch could not expect one ounce of understanding or mercy from a man who thought in these categories and was fully prepared to act on them.

On Monday, April 10, 1944, having received the file from Dönitz, Reich Marshal Hermann Göring, head of the *Luftwaffe* and Hitler's official deputy as head of the German armed forces, signed Kusch's death warrant. Göring had the last word in the matter, technically and symbolically substituting for Hitler who had been a subject of Kusch's comments and therefore was recused. In this further act of purely legalistic conformity to the letter of the law in a substantially lawless system, it must be doubted whether Göring ever read Kusch's file, let alone raise questions about him and his case. Certainly none are recorded. After Göring's signature had been affixed, the documents were passed back down the chain of command. On May 8, 1944, ironically exactly one year before

Germany's surrender, a bureaucrat at Naval High Command (OKM) simply notified Captain Rösing in Angers as the *Gerichtsherr* in the matter that "the verdict of January 26, 1944, has been confirmed, the execution of the sentence ordered, and clemency denied."[49] At this point any additional petitions for leniency were automatically doomed. As the legal department of the Naval High Command decreed on February 26, 1944, "futile requests submitted immediately upon receipt of an execution order or the denial of clemency, unless they contain new information, are not to be considered and should be returned to the petitioner."[50]

Following standard protocol, three days later, on Thursday, May 11, Ernst Meinert in Kiel issued this directive:

1. The sentence shall be carried out at 06:30 on Friday, May 12, 1944.
2. The detention center has been notified accordingly and is in charge of the preparations. Lieutenant Gerdes [name added in longhand] is in charge of the execution.
3. Naval chaplain Lucht has likewise been notified.
4. Since the case file has not yet been returned, it would be useless to convene for the night before the execution a panel of naval justice officials to deliberate in case an order is received to take up the case again. In the unlikely event that such a request should be received, the execution may have to be postponed.
5. The prisoner shall be informed at 21:30 on May 11, 1944, of the confirmation of the sentence and the time of its execution.
6. Defense counsel Meyer-Grieben has been notified in the usual manner.[51]

While for Meinert and others in Germany's naval justice bureaucracy "the usual manner" may have been all too familiar, Oskar Kusch must have listened with utmost apprehension to the sound of footsteps approaching his cell door that evening. After being taken up to the main prison office, Kusch listened as Meinert informed him that the Reich Marshal, acting on behalf of the Führer, had confirmed his sentence, that no clemency would be granted, and that the execution would be carried out at 0630 in the morning. Kusch was then asked whether he had anything to declare. He answered "Nothing," and signed the document in the prescribed place.[52] He had nine more hours to live.

CHAPTER 9

EL DOCE DE MAYO

MADRID'S MUSEO NACIONAL DEL PRADO houses countless masterpieces, but few evoke feelings and associations as powerful as the large twin paintings by Francisco Goya in Room 64, *El Dos de Mayo* and *El Tres de Mayo*. Created in 1814, they commemorate the failed uprising by Spanish patriots on May 2, 1808, against the French who had invaded the country, occupied its capital, driven away the legitimate Bourbon ruler, and were about to place Napoleon Bonaparte's brother Joseph on the throne instead. The spontaneous revolt in Madrid's Calle de Alcalá shown in *El Dos de Mayo*, carried out by courageous but poorly armed Madrilenians, was no match for the French cavalry and quickly suppressed. Revenge and retribution followed swiftly. The very next morning, as depicted in a powerful appeal to Spanish nationalism, sacrifice, and martyrdom in *El Tres de Mayo*, the French had the captured rebels lined up and executed one by one by a firing squad.

The emotive thrust and tension of the painting derive centrally from the juxtaposition of the cold, heartless, anonymous French infantrymen on the right aiming the steely barrels of their weapons at the unarmed, huddled, desperate men on the left, some of them already dead in their blood, others awaiting their certain fate. The central figure, his light brown trousers, white shirt and horrified face illuminated by a lantern on the ground, has his arms raised in a posture reminiscent of Christ on the Cross in anticipation of the bullets that will tear through his body, turn his shirt crimson, and snuff out his life the very next instant. Here brave, decent, innocent fighters for freedom and country pay the ultimate price for daring to oppose those who have usurped the state, placed might over right, and deprived the Spanish people of the right to determine their own destiny in liberty.

Very likely Oskar Kusch had seen and studied *El Tres de Mayo* in the Prado on one of his group trips with Rudi Pallas to Mediterranean countries when he was in his teens, which was before Spain erupted into Civil War in July 1936. If not, Kusch must have come across this most famous artistic rendering of a modern execution scene through his extensive knowledge of European art, possibly even in conversations with his fiancée Inge von Foris, who was then an advanced student of art history in Berlin. At any rate, among the items found in his prison cell in the hours following his own execution by a firing squad on May 12, 1944, is his last drawing in which Kusch anticipates the moment and manner of his own death in a scene eerily and hauntingly reminiscent of Goya's masterpiece.

Kusch must have been thinking about creating the drawing for some time inasmuch as a preliminary, still incomplete outline of it exists on page 136 of his sketchbook.[1] In this as well as in the final version, Kusch has rotated Goya's perspective angle by ninety degrees and depicts the actual moment of fire from a position behind the victim as he faces directly and without a blindfold the ten men lined up five paces in front of him against the backdrop of a bright, slightly transfigured eastern sky soon after sunrise. The soldiers are faceless just as Goya's, their steel helmets, greatcoats, belts, and black boots obscuring any individual features. The earlier sketch has both of Kusch's arms elevated slightly above shoulder level as if in a crucifixion, whereas in the completed drawing his left arm and hand are raised toward the sky as he falls backward, his legs and body giving way under the impact of the salvo. His entirely black hands with their fingers spread wide apart seem to take his soul heavenward like birds of death. A broken rifle with fixed bayonet immediately to the right of the victim captures Kusch's antiwar sentiments.

Actually, Kusch knew quite well he would not be facing the firing squad standing free, but instead would be bound to a wooden post and blindfolded. That is how he had portrayed his likely end in his earlier curriculum vitae sketch in six panels of March 17, the one that Ernst Meinert had so admired. The guidelines for military executions were very explicit and showed how efficient the navy's judicial death machinery had grown by 1944. Here are excerpts:

> II.1. As the death sentence has to be carried out immediately after the confirmation of the verdict and the rejection of clemency, the execution has to be prepared down to the smallest detail to avoid complications. The firing squad needs to be thoroughly familiar with the place of the execution. Emphasis on where to hit—the heart—. . .
>
> 2. Under no circumstances may the condemned become aware of the preparations. Otherwise there is the danger that he might act in an unpredictable way. Moreover, it is in the interest of the condemned not to be aware of the preparations. . . .
>
> III.3. The condemned will be notified no earlier than on the morning of his execution. Example: Execution at 08:00. At 06:00 the officer on duty wakes the condemned and tells him a military judge will come at 06:30 to inform him of a very serious matter.
>
> 4. The condemned should wear canvas work clothes and be driven to the place of execution in a covered truck—no car because of the need to take the coffin back.
>
> 5. All access roads are to be blocked by double sentries. Erect a wooden post 2 meters high in front of the backstop for bullets. Keep a rope ready. The coffin should be nearby, but not within sight of the condemned.
>
> 7. The firing squad consists of 10 men—only older and non-excitable soldiers, preferably petty officers, who shoot well—and takes up its position in front of the post.
>
> 8. The officer in charge shall communicate to the firing squad the commands "Cock!" and "Aim!" by flag and the order

> "Fire!" by spoken word or whistle. . . . The medical officer orders the medical detail to place the body into the coffin—lined with straw to absorb the blood—and to load the coffin onto the truck. If the condemned is wearing shoes owned by the Reich, they are to be taken off and reused.[2]

Additional guidelines covered funeral arrangements and notification of next-of-kin under a general policy of *damnatio memoriae* (condemnation of memory). Under no circumstances were family members to place a death notice or an obituary in a newspaper, observe religious rites or funeral services for the deceased, or wear signs of mourning. Only in rare cases did the victim's relatives receive the corpse in a closed coffin. Since the families had to bear all expenses for funeral arrangements incurred at the place where the execution had taken place, many preferred to avoid the financial burden of a cremation or interment and instead donated the body for research purposes to a civilian or military medical school. If these institutions had no use for the body, it often ended up in a remote section of some public cemetery in a grave marked by a simple wooden cross. It showed only the name as well as the birth and death of the condemned. That way no visitor would know it was the last resting place of an executed soldier.[3]

Besides putting the final touches on the drawing in which he pleaded so movingly and powerfully that his impending execution be placed into a wider political, historical, and philosophical context, Oskar Kusch completed in his last hours a brief note to Gustav-Adolf Janssen and a farewell letter to his father. The lines to his former commanding officer on *U-103*, still dated May 11, ran as follows:

> Dear Gustav—Fate has turned against me after all. Accept my gratitude, my best wishes for your future, and my last regards. Remember me fondly. You know I am going to my death an innocent man. But it cannot be helped. I grasp your hand once more and remain forever your true friend. Oskar

Predictably and reliably Ernst Meinert also confiscated this note. Lieutenant Janssen never received it and it remains in Kusch's case file to this day still bearing Meinert's handwritten assessment, "Contents questionable."[4]

At 0130 on the morning of May 12, five hours before his death, Kusch sat down at his desk and wrote to his father:

> My dear Dad,
> All hopes have come to nothing. The sentence will be carried out at 06:30. I am barely able to write these lines in the knowledge and under the impact of what lies ahead. I regret that we could not speak with one another one more time, but what is there to say when death is so near. It could have been so beautiful—my life—but a senseless fate has destroyed and torn apart everything. Therefore, at this moment when my thoughts are with you I can only thank you for all you have done for me and for your love and to wish somehow for a better future. It is all so difficult and hopeless for me in these last hours—I am thinking only of you, your terrible pain—and the future that I will never know. All of that is now gone and over forever. —My dear, good father—it is so sad that it had to come to this. So please accept from me my best wishes and deepest gratitude—I shall be yours forever until, somehow and somewhere, we will perhaps be together again. Fare well, Daddy—and forgive me if I ever caused you anguish. You always had, have now, and always will have the place in my heart that you wanted and deserved. It was the restlessness of youth that drove me on. There is no time now to make up for what was missed along the way. Accept it as something we can no longer change.
>
> I embrace you, grasp your hands—and will remain for all eternity your faithful
> Oskar
> Give my best to Mrs. Teger.[5]

Even in these moments of deepest existential despair Kusch does not appear to have embraced any notion of a Christian afterlife. Instead he must have imagined himself becoming reabsorbed into that vast and eternal cosmic order of which he had obtained a fleeting glimpse in those ecstatic hours by the autumnal campfires in the woods around Berlin a decade earlier.

The last friendly face Oskar Kusch encountered that night belonged to his faithful lawyer Gerhard Meyer-Grieben. The latter had received a telephone call from Meinert at his private residence shortly after 2200 the previous evening "in the usual manner" alerting him to Kusch's impending execution.[6] The lawyer's visit must have filled the final hours between Kusch composing the letter to his father and the arrival of the detail that would take him away. Meyer-Grieben would remember:

> I was with him the night before the execution. He was holding up admirably. After all, his thoughts and general attitudes were not so very different from my own. We had talked often and he knew he could confide in me completely. Yes, he somehow sensed he perhaps had gone too far and should have pulled back in time. But there was no moment of despondency where he would say, "I should never have done what I did." He must have hoped to the last moment that his life would be spared.[7]

That morning Meyer-Grieben must have gone home with a feeling of profound pain over the personal catastrophe he had been unable to avert from a man who had by then become so much more than just another client to him.

Dawn arrives early and lasts long in Kiel's high geographical latitude six weeks before the summer solstice. As an old U-boat hand, Kusch would have known to distinguish between *nautical twilight*, which sets in when the sun is still 12 degrees below the horizon, and *civil dawn*, when light has become bright enough to distinguish the horizon and the shapes of objects in the vicinity. That morning nautical dawn arrived in Kiel at 0331 and the sun rose at 0520 in the northeastern sky over the bay beyond the naval compound at Kiel-Wik.[8] It promised to be a gorgeous spring day. An area of high pressure over Ukraine was spreading its influence northwestward, sending southerly breezes, balmy temperatures and clear skies to the city on the Baltic.[9]

Kusch's ride to the place of his execution was a short one and thoroughly familiar to the men of the local guard detachment who had been detailed to serve as firing squad. All they had to do on this Friday morning was to drive straight north for less than two kilometers, cross the Kiel Canal to the suburb of Holtenau by way of the Prinz Heinrich Bridge, and immediately thereafter curve back. From the bridge high above the canal Kusch would have been able to see to starboard in the low rays of the morning sun the Holtenau locks through which he had passed so many times in his naval career and the wide expanse of the bay and the open Baltic beyond it. Here, between the north bank of the canal and the Holtenau airfield, and partially on the territory of the neighboring community of Altenholz, there still exists today a military shooting range originally built before World War I and expanded several times later.[10] The entire drive from the detention center should have taken no longer than about a quarter of an hour. When he arrived at the range, Kusch asked the officer in charge not to blindfold him.[11] Just as the hapless victims in Goya's painting had been without choice, Kusch wanted to look his killers directly in the eye.

The range at Holtenau served as the central location within the territory of Schleswig-Holstein between the North Sea and the Baltic where the *Kriegsmarine* and the Hitler regime carried out military death sentences in World War II, primarily during the later phases of the conflict. One analyst has characterized its role thus:

> Oskar Kusch was only one of most likely hundreds of naval personnel who became victims of Hitler's naval justice system in Kiel and whose blood would soak the soil at Holtenau. Almost every morning after 1943 the salvoes of the firing squads echoed across the Holtenau range near the airfield. . . . The soldiers had become quite adept at their job and knew perfectly well how to dispatch their comrades from the here to the hereafter in the "cleanest" manner. . . . The executions ordered by the military

> courts had become so frequent that the bureaucrats in charge had developed a pre-printed form in which only the name of the condemned, the supervising official, and the exact times of the execution as well as the confirmation of the death by the attending medical officer had to be entered.[12]

Indeed, Oskar Kusch's case folder contains exactly this form, neatly marked as document R.H.J.II 90/44 and dated "Shooting Range Holtenau, May 12, 1944." It reads as follows:

> Protocol of the execution of Lieutenant Oskar Kusch of the 2nd U-Boat Flotilla
> Present:
> 1. Lieutenant Gerdes [inserted by hand] as officer in charge
> 2. Naval justice official Meinert as judge
> 3. Assistant Naval Surgeon Dr. Bloebaum [inserted by hand] as medical officer
> 4. Naval chaplain Lucht
>
> Further present: a platoon of the guard company.
>
> The condemned had taken up his position at 06:30 [inserted by hand]. The platoon stood at attention with rifles shouldered. The judge read aloud the verdict and its confirmation. He then asked the condemned if he had any declaration to make. He answered "None" [inserted by hand]. The chaplain had opportunity to address the condemned one last time.
>
> The firing squad took up its position 5 paces in front of the condemned. The order "Fire!" was given at 06:32 [inserted by hand]. The medical officer confirmed the death at 06:34 [inserted by hand]. The corpse was immediately placed in a coffin and removed from the premises.

Lieutenant Gerdes, Dr. Bloebaum, and Ernst Meinert then affixed their signatures to the document and the case against Oskar Kusch was closed.[13]

CHAPTER 10

WAKES

Although Oskar Kusch could not have known it, by the time ten bullets ripped into his chest on May 12, 1944, his former second-in-command on *U-154* and chief accuser at his court-martial, Lieutenant Dr. Ulrich Abel, had been dead for three weeks. Upon completing the required training courses for new commanding officers, he had transferred back to Lorient and on March 31 taken charge of *U-193*. This boat, also of the Type IX design, had been shifted recently from the Second to the Tenth U-Boat Flotilla likewise stationed at that base. In its brief life since being commissioned in Bremen in December 1942, it had accumulated a rather dismal record. Under its first skipper, Lieutenant Commander Hans Pauckstadt of Crew 26, the boat had undertaken two extended patrols into the Central Atlantic without sinking a single vessel. During an air attack at the end of its second mission in February 1944, *U-193* had accidentally or inadvertently dived into the ocean floor off the Iberian Peninsula and received such severe damage that it had to seek refuge in the neutral Spanish port of El Ferrol for emergency repairs. Overstaying his internationally sanctioned stay of twenty-four hours by ten days thanks to a Spanish regime friendly to Hitler's, Pauckstadt finally managed to get his boat out to sea again, made it to the German base at La Pallice in France, and from there up the coast to Lorient by February 24. The boat underwent a major two-month refit thereafter.[1]

By the time Abel reached Lorient, accounts and rumors of his role in the Kusch case were circulating widely. If he showed up in the officer's quarters of the base, he could be certain of encountering his comrades' silent scorn, while his men on *U-193* likewise felt apprehensive about serving under a skipper with a tainted reputation. On April 23, 1944, Abel took his boat out into the Bay of Biscay off the mouth of the Loire River, his first patrol as commanding officer and with orders to head for the Central and South Atlantic. By the next day all radio and other contacts were lost. The boat, with its entire crew of fifty-nine officers and men, has been missing ever since. For a long time, it was thought *U-193* had become the victim of Allied aircraft. But painstaking research by noted U-boat historian Dr. Axel Niestlé and others has determined that a reported air attack in the area at the time was actually directed against a different boat, *U-802*.[2] Whether Abel's boat went down as a result of a diving accident, structural failure, an internal explosion, hitting a mine, or some other cause remains speculation.

For Abel's wife Herta weeks and months of uncertainty followed. There was always the possibility that the mishap had not been lethal, that there had been survivors, that the International Red Cross might report her husband to be safe and sound in an Allied POW camp. Perhaps the time had not yet come to bury all their plans for the future:

> Naturally my husband and I had talked about our life together after the war.... As soon as we could afford it, we desired to have a house of our own. My husband wanted it to be in [the fashionable Hamburg suburb of] Blankenese along the Elbe River. We also wanted to be more mobile than had been possible on our bicycles, and the children would come with us wherever we went. I had a car in mind, my husband a boat—of course. We spun out our dreams and allowed them to take off, and the war was never a part of them. I think that was our way of trying to forget it....[3]

It was not to be. Abel's widow never remarried or moved far from the coastal region on the Baltic Sea to where her husband had evacuated her and the children from burning Hamburg in 1943. There, in what became the German Democratic Republic of East Germany during the Cold War before German reunification in 1990, she brought up their three children, two sons and a daughter, all of whom would earn doctorates in their respective fields just as their father had. For half a century they remembered Ulrich Abel only as a loving husband, a devoted family man, an accomplished jurist, and as a brave U-boat commander who had sacrificed his life for his country. They thus reacted with absolute shock, disbelief, and anger when they learned for the first time from Dr. Heinrich Walle's 1995 publication about Oskar Kusch that their beloved husband and father had been viewed in naval circles for the past fifty years not as a highly decorated war hero, but as a doctrinaire Nazi and heartless denouncer responsible for delivering a worthy and innocent man to the death machinery of the *Kriegsmarine*'s naval justice system. The resulting correspondence and other exchanges between the Abels and Walle, who in a major shortfall in his research efforts had never bothered to inquire whether Abel was married and had a family, has been acrimonious and hardly flattering for the historian from both a professional and humane point of view.[4]

A widow for more than sixty-eight years, Herta Abel died on May 13, 2012, in Heringsdorf on the island of Usedom on the Baltic Sea, just nine days short of her ninety-fifth birthday, leaving behind her three children, six grandchildren, and fifteen great-grandchildren. Her ashes were entrusted to the sea. In the obituary her children also honored "the memory of our father Dr. Ulrich Abel whom we lost already in 1944 as a U-boat commander in the war."[5]

✠ ✠ ✠

Under its new skipper, Lieutenant Gerth Gemeiner, *U-154* undertook a long but fruitless patrol to the Caribbean and the Nicaraguan coast lasting from January 31 to April 28, 1944. Arno Funke served as I.W.O. and Kurt Druschel as chief engineer. Following a two-month refit in Lorient and Funke's departure for another command, Kusch's former boat set out again on June 20, still under Gemeiner and with Druschel continuing to supervise the engine department and diving maneuvers. This time their intended operational area was the Eastern Seaboard of the United States after a swing through the Central Atlantic. By then the Normandy Invasion of June 6, 1944, had rendered future German operations from French bases highly problematic, and Dönitz had begun recalling his remaining boats from France to safer havens in Norway and home waters.

After passing through the Bay of Biscay undetected despite the long daylight hours, *U-154* had reached a position about halfway between Madeira and the Azores when its previously charmed life ended abruptly. Already alerted to its presence by radio intercepts, on July 3 a sonar search of the destroyer escort USS *Inch* (DE 144) located the German boat. *Inch* belonged to the hunter-killer Task Group 22.5 built around the escort carrier USS *Croatan* (CVE 25) that had recently left Casablanca after refueling there. While the carrier's planes were of no help because of a malfunctioning catapult, *Inch* received valuable assistance from USS *Frost* (DE 146). Gemeiner must have lurked at periscope depth because he managed to launch two torpedoes that narrowly missed his American pursuers before ordering Druschel to take the boat deep. *Inch* and *Frost* delivered a series of attacks with depth charges until "a single explosion was heard. Almost immediately a stream of oil and debris rose to the surface. Among this debris were found German uniforms, pieces of wood, and human body parts. This stream of oil, one hundred and forty miles northwest of Funchal, marked *U-154*'s final resting place."[6] All fifty-seven officers and sailors in the submarine perished, presumably instantly, including Kurt Druschel and so many others who had once sailed under Oskar Kusch.

All other individuals prominently connected to the Kusch drama survived World War II. The further fates of Kusch's parents, friends, and other personae dramatis are summarized below, mostly in connection with the two postwar trials against Karl-Heinrich Hagemann and efforts to rehabilitate Oskar Kusch's name and secure his legacy.

+ + +

In the wake of Kusch's execution, his fiancée Inge von Foris, only twenty-three years old at the time, struggled to pick up the shattered pieces of her life just when the Allied invasions of continental Europe and Soviet advances in the East sealed Germany's military defeat. Berlin became ever more a city in ruins as British and American bombs kept raining down on its hapless citizens. Emotionally drained and desperate to stabilize her life, Inge sought to renew and deepen her relationship with her old friend Heinrich on the eastern front in a long, from-the-heart letter on June 11, 1944. Only hinting at her time with Kusch and couching it in terms of a superficial episode, "a flirt," she now offered Heinrich the key "to the secret lock that protects the innermost recesses of one's soul and that can only be opened by one, very special hand."[7]

Heinrich's encouraging response allowed Inge to regain her bearings and concentrate on her studies. In what must have been a titanic effort, she managed to finish enough of her dissertation on the baroque architect Johann Dientzenhofer to have it accepted on April 10, 1945, under the eerie conditions prevailing in Berlin at the end of the war. The work's oral defense and Inge's comprehensive exams in her major fields of art history and archaeology, with a minor in history, were then scheduled for April 18, and the formal granting of the degree occurred two days later on April 20, exactly one year after her final meeting with Oskar Kusch and as Adolf Hitler celebrated his last birthday in his underground bunker a few blocks away. Both of her major professors, Wilhelm Pinder and Gerhart Rodenwaldt, rated her work summa cum laude, with Pinder commenting, "In my forty years in academia no female student has ever demonstrated such a remarkable aptitude for the history of architecture."[8] In retrospect it seems astonishing and almost implausible that academic activities at Friedrich-Wilhelms-Universität should have continued uninterrupted until and even beyond the end of the war on May 8, even as Soviet forces shelled the core of the city with artillery and infantry overran the last pockets of German resistance. Sadly, Professor Rodenwaldt and his wife committed suicide when Russian soldiers reached their home in Berlin-Lichterfelde on April 27, a mere week after Dr. von Foris had been granted her degree.[9]

The siege and later the first weeks and months after the fall of the German capital to the Russians must have been horrific for its surviving citizens. Only gradually would a semblance of order replace chaos, especially when troops of the western Allies reached the city and ended the brief Soviet monopoly on power in the soon to be divided city. Apparently, Inge von Foris and her family escaped bodily harm in those days of extreme confusion, lawlessness, and anxiety. The same could not be said about her friend Heinrich:

> Heinrich, his brother Klaus, and their mutual friend Wolfgang had returned to Berlin from the war in 1945 and were arrested there by Russian soldiers who tied their arms behind their backs and ordered them to climb onto the bed of a truck. As the truck left the city, Wolfgang had a notion that they were about to be executed and whispered to his two companions, "Let's jump off as soon as we pass a stretch of road with bushes and trees around to hide in." When they found themselves on a rural road headed toward Brandenburg, Wolfgang suddenly shouted, "Now! Jump!" He and Klaus jumped, but Heinrich could not muster the courage to join them. The truck stopped. There was a brief search for Klaus and Wolfgang, but they were well hidden and got away. The Russians shot Heinrich to death right then and there before the truck moved on.[10]

Thus, Inge von Foris received the second bitter blow in her young life—senseless and arbitrary and entirely devastating—just when matters promised to improve.

Both her long opposition to the Hitler regime and her background in art history brought her soon thereafter into contact with Allied control officers. Their task was to denazify and revitalize Berlin's formerly so brilliant cultural scene, ranging from museums, concerts, and the opera to theater and film. Supervising such efforts were typically German émigré writers, composers, musicians, actors, and film directors who had moved to the New World after 1933, had acquired American citizenship, and now served in the military occupation forces. Inge developed a particularly close friendship with one of them, Austrian-American Henry C.

Alter, during his days in Berlin until he was posted to Salzburg to revive that city's vast musical tradition. Before Alter left Berlin, he introduced Inge to the German-American film actor Peter van Eyck, a good friend of his and fellow control officer for film, with specific instructions for him to look after Inge in those dangerous and uncertain times.[11]

Tall, blond, handsome, and accomplished, a North German like her, and also belonging to the German nobility—he had been born as Götz von Eick in Pomerania in 1911 before emigrating in 1931—Peter van Eyck exercised an immediate hold on Inge, no doubt reminiscent of the way Oskar Kusch had swept her off her feet a few years before. It was soon abundantly evident that the attraction was mutual, and Alter had to admit he had lost her to his friend, although he and Inge remained on friendly terms, with her chiding Henry years later in good humor possibly mixed with a touch of regret, "Why didn't you put up more of a fight for me?" Their age difference was no major obstacle, but the fact that van Eyck had married the American model and actress Ruth Ford in 1940 and had a daughter from that union, clearly was an issue.[12] However, a divorce settlement was reached before the end of the decade and Ms. Ford remarried in 1952 the American actor Zachary Scott, who also adopted her daughter Shelley from her first marriage.[13]

Peter and Inge married in 1951. As Peter's acting carrier gathered further momentum and acclaim, the couple lived in California, Paris, and Switzerland, with Inge devoting much of her time to the upbringing of their two daughters Kristina and Claudia, while remaining interested but no longer very active in the field of art history. Kristina van Eyck has followed her father into the entertainment field and is today a well-known German actress in film, television, and on the stage. Her sister Claudia, having been brought up fluent in multiple languages, works as a certified translator and interpreter.

Inge van Eyck never once brought up the subject of Oskar Kusch with her daughters, her memories of him and of Heinrich remaining hidden in a secret compartment of her soul. Her surviving correspondence with Heinrich and others provides the sole clue to two passionate attachments cruelly extinguished before their time, first by Hitler's henchmen and then by Stalin's. Only from their uncle, Dr. Henning von Foris, who had come to know Kusch during the war and went on to practice law in Munich before his death in 2014, would the daughters learn of the events of 1944 and 1945 in which their mother had become so heartbreakingly entangled.[14]

Inge's string of misfortunes would not abate. After only eighteen years of marriage, Peter van Eyck died in 1969 at the height of his career from complications of a misdiagnosed sepsis. Inge survived him by fourteen years in their lovely Swiss retreat overlooking Lake Constance and died in 1983, no doubt pondering to the end the long string of might-have-beens in her life.

+ + +

On February 12, 1946, Mrs. Ingeborg Lämmchen, a distant niece of Oskar Kusch's mother and acting in her name, addressed a letter to Gerhard Meyer-Grieben. She requested Kusch's former defense attorney to "take up the case again to punish the traitors," specifically referring to Abel, Druschel, and Hagemann.[15] Her letter set in motion a complex, almost five-year-long process that would result in two trials in 1949 and 1950 against Karl-Heinrich Hagemann, the presiding judge at Kusch's court-martial. This process would also reveal in stunning clarity several issues: the wartime-to-postwar continuity in terms of judicial personnel and attitudes in Germany; the corrupt collusion among former colleagues on the bench to avoid post-1945 prosecution; the continued failure to grasp the totalitarian character of core Nazi legislation; the efforts to destroy incriminating files and records; and, above all, a profound breakdown of denazification efforts resulting frequently in the practical or symbolic re-conviction of victims who had already been punished unjustly under the Nazi regime. This entire phenomenon, especially in Germany's northernmost state of Schleswig-Holstein, has been exhaustively studied by a younger generation of historians and is competently presented by Kusch's first biographer, Heinrich Walle, in 1995.[16] Therefore, a summary will suffice.

Gerhard Meyer-Grieben deserves much credit for doing the right things quickly, thoroughly, and with circumspection. On March 20, 1946, he managed to locate and copy Kusch's extensive case file in a rural depository in Schleswig-Holstein with the help of the British military government before Hagemann, Dr. Breinig, or other former naval justice officials could get ahold of it and possibly make it disappear. He thus preserved crucial evidence without which any future legal action on Kusch's behalf would have been difficult or outright impossible to initiate.[17] While Kusch's mother thus opened one avenue to try to achieve belated justice for her son, Kusch's father pursued another lead with almost fanatical commitment both in the courts and in the press. Knowing that Karl Dönitz was under indictment at the International Military Tribunal in Nuremberg, Oskarheinz Kusch alerted one of the chief prosecutors there, Robert Kempner, to the case against his son and to Dönitz's failure to exercise clemency despite his promise to Gustav-Adolf Janssen to do so. Kempner requested from Meyer-Grieben a full summary of the case, including the names and addresses of key participants and witnesses, and even encouraged Kusch's father to file murder charges in the district court in Kiel against Hagemann, Dr. Breinig, Meinert, Dittmers, Westphalen, Dr. Abel, Druschel, Dr. Nothdurft, and Dönitz. Kusch's father did so on May 9, 1946, on the basis of the Allied Control Council Directive No. 10, which allowed prosecution for "crimes against humanity," among others. His justification contains a father's moving and impassioned plea to reverse the injustice done to his son:

> Not my son has subverted the Wehrmacht, but rather all those criminals who today sit accused before the International Tribunal in Nuremberg, and those Hitler-crazy judges, officials and denouncers who in their courtroom in Kiel on January 26, 1944, sentenced to death a completely innocent and morally far superior young man for having discerned and told the truth, even though they knew at the time he had done nothing wrong.[18]

Besides not knowing that Abel and Druschel were dead, Dittmers and Westphalen in captivity, and Dönitz tied up in the Nuremberg proceedings, several other impediments quickly combined to slow down and in due course arrest the momentum of these parental initiatives. Germany's division into four occupation zones rendered the movement of persons and mail still difficult at the very time that the western Allies increasingly preferred that German authorities and courts adjudicate crimes committed by Germans against Germans during the Hitler era, rather than impose their own authority and procedures. Moreover, the impatience of Kusch's parents and their inability to grasp the complexity of the legal situation led to an unpleasant rift between them and Meyer-Grieben. In the meantime, Hagemann's wartime colleagues, who again held secure and prominent positions in Schleswig-Holstein's judicial apparatus while he himself found employment for a while as a judge in the postwar German Minesweeping Administration (GMSA), were beginning to put together a defense strategy for him, just in case.

The former *Kriegsmarine* justice official Karl Helmut Sieber, with others in the background, took the lead because he feared any indictment and conviction of Hagemann for sentencing Kusch to death might create an undesirable precedent for other wartime cases where the verdict and sentence assessment had been grounded in political and ideological rather than in strictly military criteria and had differed markedly from the prosecutor's recommendation. As early as July 6, 1946, Hagemann had complained in a letter to Sieber that "it looks as if they are trying to place a noose around my neck [regarding the Kusch decision]. . . . As you can imagine, I am worried." Sieber confirmed ten days later that Meyer-Grieben, who had been tasked by the British occupation authorities with helping denazify the judicial system in Schleswig-Holstein, was indeed "active on behalf of Kusch's relatives by painting him as a victim of fascism. . . . To put anything more in writing at this point may not be advisable."[19] Four days later, ignoring his own suggestion, Sieber wrote to Hagemann again and directly criticized the latter's decision of 1944: "Regarding your justification for your verdict [against Kusch], opinions may very well vary. Given the excellent evaluations the condemned had received, one would have imagined you would have rather chosen the more lenient alternative."[20]

Not until November 21, 1946, did Directive No. 10 of the Allied Control Council with its provision about crimes against humanity take effect in the British occupation zone of which Schleswig-Holstein and the city of Kiel were a part; and not until February 3, 1947, did the public prosecutor in Kiel request indictments against Hagemann and Abel on its basis. Four days later, the district court did issue an arrest warrant for Abel, whose death in April 1944 remained unconfirmed, for his politically and personally motivated denunciation of Kusch, but refused to do so for Hagemann on the grounds that he had committed no provable or intentional perversion of justice. Chief prosecutor Dr. Paul Thamm twice appealed this assessment to the state court, on February 10 and again on March 9, 1947, arguing Hagemann had "deliberately distorted justice to follow the wishes of the state leadership" and had "interpreted the law not under legal but under political aspects." Furthermore, the court had failed to grasp that the "subversion" decree was part of the totalitarian system of injustice and that its very application to Kusch's situation constituted a distortion of justice. Five days later, the state court again rejected Thamm's arguments, holding that Hagemann had acted within the bounds of discretion as allowable under the law and no intentional bending of justice had been committed.[21] For the same reasons, a charge of murder was deemed inapplicable.

Further objections and appeals, twice in December 1947 and once in January 1948, were all rejected. Thamm tried to keep the court's focus on the political dimension of Hagemann's decision and thereby counteract a gradual tendency of the judges to stress the military nature of Kusch's alleged transgressions, namely, those undermining the discipline and lowering the combat readiness of his boat. Here are also visible the first outlines of how Hagemann might structure his defense should the case ever come to trial. In the meantime, all charges against Dr. Abel (dead), Druschel (dead), Dr. Nothdurft (only witness), Dr. Breinig (lenient sentence recommendation), and Meinert (not involved in decision) had been dropped; however, Dittmers and Westphalen, co-responsible jurors and recently released from captivity, remained for another period of time in the prosecutors' crosshairs as possible accessories to a judicial murder.

By late 1947 and early 1948, it looked as if Hagemann was off the hook. His former friends and colleagues on the bench had prevented his arrest and fended off all efforts to place the case on the docket. They remained wary, however, that the matter might not go away completely and, if ever tried in a court, might have Germany-wide implications for every former military judge who had sentenced a soldier to death during the Hitler regime. Siebert's papers contain a revealing letter to Hagemann with almost fatherly advice from Kay Nieschling, one of Dr. Rudolphi's former subordinates in the Navy High Command's legal division. Nieschling wrote on December 22, 1947:

> Colleagues in Kiel sometimes feel you are underestimating the seriousness of the matter and take it too lightly, as was noticed recently when you dared apply for a position in our present judicial system. Preventing an arrest warrant against you is about as far as they can go in terms of doing you a favor at this time. Be aware that the father of the condemned keeps pestering the authorities and in his seemingly unquenchable hatred seeks to expose the allegedly guilty parties. . . . In a legal sense it is important and it speaks against you that the prosecutor at the trial only requested a prison sentence. One cannot but gain the impression—notwithstanding the seriousness of [Kusch's] transgression—that in the last analysis the verdict may have been influenced by ideological considerations. It is difficult to understand why the court showed itself more inhumane than the prosecution, especially since the naval justice system as a rule followed the letter of the law rather than totalitarian principles.[22]

Even before this note reached Hagemann, Gerhard Meyer-Grieben had had enough of the constant interference and occasional insulting remarks by Kusch's father about his professional competency and resigned as the legal counsel of Kusch's parents, pointing out that it was not up to him anymore but to the prosecutors in Kiel to bring a case against Hagemann.[23] He would, of course, be available as a witness to what happened before, during, and after Oskar's court-martial.

If Meyer-Grieben had done his very best to preserve crucial evidence and help initiate postwar proceedings against Hagemann, Dr. Rudolf Katz

(1895–1961) must be credited with providing the decisive push. Like Meyer-Grieben he was trained in law and an early member of the Social Democratic Party. Katz had been chased out of Germany by the Nazis, first to France and later the United States. Stripped of his German citizenship by his own country, he became an American citizen in 1941. Katz returned to Germany in 1946, regained his citizenship, became attorney general for the state of Schleswig-Holstein from 1947 to 1950, and then vice-chair of the West German Constitutional Court from 1951 until his death in 1961.[24]

On March 23, 1948, Katz instructed Schleswig-Holstein's chief prosecutor to prepare an indictment against Hagemann for having committed a crime against humanity out of political motives. The renewed preparation of the case took time and the actual indictment based on Directive No. 10 of the Allied Control Council was delayed for almost another year until March 14, 1949. Hagemann by then no longer worked for the German Minesweeping Administration (GMSA), whose important service of clearing Europe's waters and waterways of wartime mines had ended two years earlier. Unable to undergo proper denazification procedures because of the pending case, let alone find employment in the legal field, he had worked as a day laborer for some time. Almost destitute, Hagemann was grateful for financial assistance from former colleagues, complaining to Sieber that "it is hard to take that I had to wait three years for a case finally to be heard whose origins go back to May 1946 (!). In all those years I could not work on a new career for lack of denazification papers and feel already punished in a matter in which I do not feel culpable in the least."[25] His former comrades did come through as Mrs. Hagemann gratefully acknowledged the receipt of 120 deutsche marks in West Germany's new currency.[26]

After Hagemann's defense counsel, Dr. Bernhard Leverenz, had attempted in vain to prevent the case from coming to trial by filing a number of pretrial motions, the court convened at last in Kiel for ten days between May 2 and May 23, 1949, with *Landgerichtsdirektor* Wilhelm von Starck presiding, *Landsgerichtsräte* Grunert and Panteleit as associate judges, and six lay jurors.[27] Dr. Paul Thamm was chief prosecutor, assisted by Dr. Traugott Albrecht. Every single court official had been a member of the Nazi Party and had served in either the military or civilian justice system under Hitler. Dr. Thamm built his case not primarily around the inherent inapplicability of the subversion decree to Kusch's situation because of the decree's totalitarian nature, but on Hagemann's perversion of justice when he used the decree to eliminate a political opponent and by his complete dismissal of mitigating circumstances at Kusch's trial, since Breinig had only requested ten years in jail and that no subversion of *U-154*'s combat spirit or readiness had actually occurred. "The attack on Kusch was meant to hit all who dared utter the same thoughts as he did."[28] Thamm also argued Hagemann's "rejection of a less severe case can only be understood out of an exaggerated fear of a recurrence of the events of November 1918. The court only considered the objectively dangerous actions of the defendant and placed the idea of deterrence far more into the foreground than was justified by the evidence."[29]

Because of the ongoing Berlin Blockade, a number of witnesses were deposed there on May 7, including Kusch's father who had not been admitted to the trial as a co-plaintiff. The trial began with the reading of the indictment and Hagemann's response to the various points raised in it. Hagemann was supported and encouraged by a phalanx of former naval justice officials in attendance, who included Joachim Rudolphi and Otto Kranzbühler, Karl Dönitz's defense attorney at Nuremberg. Hagemann denied any political dimension to his decision or its deterrent intention, emphasized the supposed military impact of Kusch's actions, insisted the captain's remarks had been made "in public," and believed the death penalty had been fully appropriate given the severity of the infractions. Moreover, Dittmers and Westphalen had voted for it and even proposed it in the first place. There had been no pressure from superiors to follow any politically inspired or motivated guidelines.[30] Over long stretches of the proceedings, it seemed as if the true defendant was Oskar Kusch rather than Hagemann. The latter's defense became a posthumous onslaught on and renewed vilification of the former.

Dr. Hans Nothdurft's testimony played into the hands of the defense in a major and perhaps decisive way. Nothdurft had been worried in the immediate postwar period about his role in the January 1944 court martial and also about obtaining a clean denazification record so he could resume his career at Heidelberg University. In 1946 he had submitted an affidavit to Allied officials in which he went far beyond his 1944 testimony in terms of condemning Kusch's actions. Now, in 1949 and 1950, he repeated and enhanced these statements, and as late as 1993 he deposited in the U-Boat Archives a lengthy document on his "fateful encounter" with Oskar Kusch.[31] Nothdurft caused the prosecution great harm by continuing to submit Kusch to his amateurish psychiatric analyses and by spreading entirely irresponsible myths about Kusch's alleged intention of deserting to the enemy. According to Nothdurft, Kusch

> invited the question whether he suffered from a pathological inability to detect and assess dangerous threats. As symptoms one could cite the intensity and stubbornness with which he displayed a missionary or savior complex when it came to the re-education of his officers in a patently hopeless situation as there was no chance they would change their minds. Especially in private conversations his imagined missionary role as a teacher and educator of others took on the form of a delusional obsession.... Without any doubt the "re-education lessons" Kusch imparted to us officers implied the possibility of going over to the enemy with the entire boat. Kusch never proposed any concrete steps in this direction. He never used words like "desertion," "surrender" or "joining the other side," or anything like it. But did he think of it?
>
> [Druschel and Abel] were convinced Kusch was planning outright desertion with his boat. I spoke with the chief engineer several times about this subject. From him I know that we had a good number of handguns on board that were supposed to be distributed in crisis situations. There was an actual list as to who was to be armed in this manner. The chief engineer manipulated this list in such a way that among our enlisted men only those would receive a gun who like himself had been leaders in the Hitler Youth and would have followed Druschel's orders rather

> than Kusch's in a desertion scenario. In reality the guns were never distributed.[32]

For reasons never explained and unfathomable even today, Nothdurft also volunteered his appraisal of Kusch's sexual preferences in a phase of the trial during which the public and the press were excluded. The only written allusion to this episode can be found in a letter the presiding judge Wilhelm von Starck wrote months after the trial to the president of the state court to justify his choices as to who had been allowed to testify and who had not:

> References to the so-called "legends" of the witness Dr. Nothdurft apparently center on the statements this witness made at the trial in his capacity as a medical doctor about the character and the sexual orientation of Lieutenant Kusch. For this part of the testimony I arranged for the public to be excluded for reasons of protecting public morality. I did not ask other crewmembers about this matter because they were medical laymen. As far as I remember, other crewmembers as witnesses did not make contradictory but rather complementary observations when it came to describing the conditions on the submarine.[33]

Hagemann's take on Nothdurft's theories and other suggestions about Kusch's physical and psychological makeup will be discussed below.

In all their written statements, depositions, and oral testimony of 1944, Abel, Druschel, and Funke, and also Captain Rösing in 1949, never once brought up the subject of Kusch's possible desertion or plans to entrust the boat's small arms to Druschel loyalists, even though such observations, if true, would have been absolutely central to their report. Nor did they ever hint at problems with Kusch's mental state.[34] Once again Nothdurft's recollections suggest an overactive imagination on part of the medical doctor, genuine confusion, falsely remembered or improperly interpreted events and conversations, or worse. For example, Nothdurft believed Kusch's mere Anglophile disposition and fondness for the English language were in themselves harbingers of his impending desertion to the United Kingdom.[35]

Regarding desertion, there exists to the contrary a remarkable statement from Oskar Kusch's father in which he recounted the last meeting he ever had with his son between Christmas and New Year 1943:

> At Christmas 1943/44 my son visited me during his leave and we had a long conversation in my parlor about the hopelessly messed-up political situation in Germany. We agreed it was pointless for Germany to continue the war. Oskar thought it made no sense to keep sending human beings and materiel to the bottom of the sea. I thereupon advised him to drop everything, take his passport, and move across the border to Switzerland to wait out the end of this accursed war. I could have easily arranged for him to stay with friends of mine there. My son rejected my proposal with these words: "Dad, I could not possibly do such a thing to my men, my boat, my people, or to myself."[36]

Still, Nothdurft's outrageous and unverifiable suggestions no doubt allowed the judges at Hagemann's trial to assume that Kusch's military transgressions had been far greater than previously suspected and to consider them prominently when justifying their eventual verdict.

After Dr. Thamm had requested a jail sentence of two years for Hagemann for abusing his discretion as a judge by imposing a politically motivated sentence disguised as military necessity, and heard Dr. Leverenz's plea that the defendant should go free because the "crimes against humanity" directive of the Allied Control Council was too vague and ran counter to the German legal tradition of *nulla poena sine lege* ("no penalty without a law"), the court announced its decision on May 23, 1949, to an overflow crowd—"not guilty." The subsequent written justification of the verdict ran to some forty-four pages and culminated in the following statement:

> The court did not absolve the defendant of wrongdoing because it agrees with his verdict [against Kusch] or because it regards

> as just what the defendant has done. Rather the court believes that in assessing the death sentence the defendant exceeded the sentencing standard that would have been appropriate based on the available evidence. As is evident in his poorly argued justification for his verdict, the defendant failed to weigh carefully all circumstances of the case, as one would expect from a true and impartial judge. Still, and even after the lengthy proceedings just concluded, the court does not see as sufficiently fulfilled the evidence requirement for a crime against humanity committed by a duly installed and qualified judge. For that reason, the court had to find the accused not guilty.[37]

And thus, for all practical purposes, pending a possible appeal by the prosecution, Karl-Heinrich Hagemann walked out of the courtroom in Kiel a free man, while those who had hoped to see Oskar Kusch avenged and rehabilitated found him, in effect, convicted for a second time.

Reactions to the course of the trial and to the verdict differed markedly. One witness, a teacher from Bremen named Karl-Hans Seemann who had been a prisoner alongside Kusch at the naval detention center and knew Hagemann, Meinert, and other former naval officials well, sent this note to Kusch's father immediately after the trial:

> Whenever there was a break in the proceedings, I was profoundly disturbed to discover how matter-of-factly and with complete assurance Hagemann circulated among the countless fellow jurists who had come to support him and chatted with them as if the whole matter was hardly worthy of his attention. Meinert—he was only present as a witness—strutted about as if he had made the court his home. He is now—believe it or not—a county judge in Elmshorn near Hamburg!! While this sorry crowd formed the bulk of those present, Hagemann at his height of 1.90 meters . . . towered over everyone, all the while grinning cynically. Mr. Isensee from Munich [*U-154*'s chief radio operator on the second patrol] and I were put on the defensive from the beginning. It

was extraordinarily unfortunate that you could not come to Kiel or engage a lawyer as an observer. Only after we had testified did we learn that two other gentlemen (an art historian and a former leader in the *bündisch* youth movement) [Wolfgang Kühns-Bernsau and Kurt Wiemer] had likewise testified in favor of your son [as did Werner Winter and a few others]. . . . Others told me afterwards that Nothdurft had leveled very serious accusations against your son and again claimed that the combat readiness of the crew had suffered and that handguns had been distributed to prevent any desertion. . . . Since no one told us, we of course did not know about Nothdurft's charges. Isensee described your son as a superb and popular commanding officer but had no idea he was supposed to refute that legend about the handguns. No one even asked him about it!! In any appeal it will be crucial to have Isensee testify again. He is the only survivor of the crew and only he can know what happened. . . . Our testimony . . . was the only one during all the days of the trial that addressed your son as a U-boat commander, as a human being, as a soldier, and specified what had happened at the court martial. . . . Hagemann is triumphant today—the luck of the devil—and pretty soon we may have to store away our ideals again. As a teacher I find the experience more than bitter.[38]

By contrast, Karl-Heinrich Hagemann could barely conceal his glee when he wrote confidentially to his former colleague Karl Helmut Sieber four days after the "not guilty" verdict:

> Now that the battle has been fought and won, allow me to thank you once more for your assistance from the bottom of my heart. . . . Rudolphi provided very good insights into how the naval justice system had torpedoed any efforts by the state to exert political influence on our decisions. That made a big impression on the court, even though he [Rudolphi] painted himself as a poor, uninformed underling. When he claimed he had nothing to do

> with the confirmation of the [Kusch] verdict in Berlin, even I was mightily surprised, to say the least. During the war we had a very different impression of the role he played. The poor guy even stated he had never seen the assessment of the case by his own subordinates. As you can imagine, he was sweating bullets the entire time he testified during my trial. It was clearly not easy for him to pretend to be innocent. . . . The prosecution's witnesses for Kusch were very much spineless softies [*ganz müde Knaben*] whose closeness to homosexual circles [known as the *175ers*] we could establish during the proceedings. . . . By the way, we never shared the "Red Folder" with anyone. Leverenz will return it to you.[39]

Besides revealing the extent of Rudolphi's perjury and the almost conspiratorial manner in which former naval judges closed ranks to support any comrade in trouble over controversial verdicts rendered before 1945, Hagemann's letter inadvertently shines a spotlight on two issues not previously much discussed but potentially of considerable significance. The "Red Folder"—or "Red Donkey" [*Roter Esel*] as it was usually disguised in the nomenclature of former naval justice officials with reference to its cover color and to a similar work of instructions for general staff officers[40]—referred to a set of internal, confidential, procedural, and sentencing guidelines that the *Kriegsmarine*'s legal department in Berlin had distributed to naval judges during the war and that was not to be shared with anyone outside that circle. No copy of it has ever surfaced in public, but the gist of its instructions must have been to ensure the alignment of legal decisions with the political and ideological agenda of the state, especially in a country at war. Just how revealing the existence of these guidelines could have helped Hagemann in his defense remains unclear, inasmuch as they would have undermined any pretense that judges acted independently in accordance with the letter of the law and made their decisions without guidance from legal, military, or political superiors.

A second issue was Hagemann's blatant homophobia and disparaging reference to homosexuals in Oskar Kusch's social and intellectual circle—the term "175er" refers derisively to persons in violation of Section 175 of the German penal code that outlawed homosexual acts between adult males until 1994. Hagemann's display of homophobia illuminates a dimension of his character and worldview that may well have played a role in his original verdict, just as much as it colored the former judge's perception five years later of witnesses testifying on Kusch's behalf. Hagemann—who grew up in Nazi party organizations thoroughly opposed to the ideas and ideals of the *bündisch* youth movement such as the *Südlegion* with its emphasis on individualism, tolerance, dignity, cosmopolitanism, and aesthetics in artistic and literary pursuits—had clearly not abandoned by 1944 or by 1949 his preference for "manly" conformity and uniformity under an authoritarian figure. Kusch's friendship and intercepted correspondence with Dr. Rudi Pallas, who had spent time in the Sachsenhausen concentration camp because of his sexual orientation and had espoused decidedly left-wing sympathies since his release from Soviet captivity, could not have been a mystery to Hagemann in either January 1944 or in May 1949. In a similar fashion Hagemann must have viewed witnesses for the prosecution, such as Kusch's father, a prominent and hated Free Mason, or the future art historian and collector Wolfgang Kühns-Bernsau as representing that soft but pretentious aesthetic elitism Kusch himself had sported on *U-154*. Could Hagemann have chosen the death penalty for Oskar Kusch to eliminate in him not only a dangerous political opponent but also an intellectual and cultural deviant guilty by association with a group of people inherently suspicious and un-German?

To no one's surprise, Kusch's father insisted, only one day after the verdict, in a sharply worded telegram to Dr. Thamm, on an immediate appeal, this time to the Supreme Court for the British Occupation Zone in Cologne whose top judges were known to be less tainted with Nazi ideological ballast. After consultation with the justice minister of Schleswig-Holstein, Dr. Katz, this was done on July 6, 1949.[41] At the same time, Oskarheinz Kusch informed Dr. Thamm that Oskar's mother, Erna Brockmann, had died suddenly of a heart attack on June 26, 1949, just weeks after Hagemann's trial. He attributed this further tragic development "not least to the grief and bitterness about the injustice posthumously inflicted upon her son."[42]

On October 18, 1949, the court in Cologne did indeed throw out the existing verdict and ordered a retrial of Hagemann before the same state court in Kiel that had found him "not guilty" on May 23. Besides chastising the jurists in Kiel for having interpreted applicable laws too narrowly, for having neither found nor demanded military justifications for Kusch's condemnation, and pointing out the obvious discrepancy between the alleged crime and its punishment, the Cologne court justified a renewed trial as follows:

> That which the Allied Control Council's Directive No. 10 places under punishment as a crime against humanity was already a punishable crime in the eyes of all decent human beings at the time of the [Kusch trial]. It remained unpunished, however, because the National Socialist state itself committed crimes through its institutions and followers. Even then punishing such injustices was the duty of any legally constituted state. To rectify such a dereliction of duty ex post facto therefore must be a principle of justice and part of a state's legal foundations. A German judge is in line with these principles whenever he applies the provisions of the Directive No. 10 of the Allied Control Council.[43]

Hagemann, though invited to Cologne to attend the hearing over the appeal, had decided not to travel there or to send a legal representative because he "had absolutely no funds to spare for such extravagant excursions," placing his hopes instead on an amnesty rumored to be on the agenda of the newly constituted federal government in Bonn.[44]

It would take almost another year, until September 1950, for the case to be retried in Kiel. In the meantime, a bitter, discouraged, but always defiant Karl-Heinrich Hagemann reported to his friend Sieber in May 1950:

> Currently I am eking out a living as a local reporter for the *Husumer Nachrichten*, as a continuing education teacher (2 hours

> a week), as a supervisor of bankruptcy settlements, and from time to time as a paralegal inasmuch as the justice ministry in Kiel has not dared certify me as a full legal counsel in cases where the regular lawyer had some conflict and could not show up. Well, we are really looking forward to the statewide elections in July and hope the Social Democratic regime will be fully swept away. If that were the case, things would look up for me, for Attorney-General Katz is clearly the driving force behind all this. Would anyone be surprised?![45]

Insofar as Dr. Rudolf Katz was of Jewish extraction, and given Hagemann's political and ideological provenance, it would indeed not be in the least surprising that the stymied jurist should have attributed his continuing misfortunes to a Jewish-Socialist plot.

The elections did indeed bring a conservative government into power in Schleswig-Holstein and Dr. Katz was gone, or rather promoted to the German Constitutional Court, by the time Hagemann's second trial began on September 18, 1950. Personnel changes compared to the previous year were minimal: Dr. Paul Thamm was replaced by Dr. Trautgott Albrecht as chief prosecutor in the case and Albrecht's seat as associate prosecutor taken by a Dr. Wolff. Dr. Wilhelm von Starck still presided and Dr. Bernhard Leverenz repeated as Hagemann's defense counsel. During only three days of actual proceedings, a total of thirty-six witnesses testified in person or by way of depositions. This time Kusch's sixty-eight-year-old father was allowed to take the witness stand and impressed observers both with his impassioned plea for justice for his son and with a less than perfect grasp of what had transpired on *U-154*, at Oskar's court-martial, and at the first Hagemann trial.[46] Despite Mr. Seemann's urgent demand of the year before, neither of the two surviving radio operators of the boat, Hans Janker and Kurt Isensee, were present to rebuke Dr. Nothdurft's wild claims. Thus, the court remained convinced Kusch's actions indeed had grave military implications and consequences, and that he must have labored under any number of mental and physical afflictions and perversions. After all invited witnesses had testified, the prosecutor in his final arguments proposed a jail sentence of eighteen months for Hagemann, whereas Leverenz suggested his client should go free due to his proven innocence.

On September 25, 1950, the court rendered its verdict—"not guilty for lack of evidence." "In the final analyses," the court argued, "it was impossible to prove that there was a connection between the verdict rendered by the accused and the violent and arbitrary nature of National Socialist rule. At the same time, the court found itself unable to acquit the accused based on 'proven innocence' because the possibility of such a connection could not be dismissed entirely." The court again reprimanded Hagemann for his sloppy justification of the death sentence against Kusch, including the use of "National Socialist diction" in the document, and noted "the logic that led to the assessed sentence rather than to a more lenient one remains not entirely clear."[47]

Initially the prosecutor did file another appeal, but on November 28, 1950, Dr. Thamm informed Kusch's father he had decided to withdraw it because "it does not offer a reasonable chance of success," just as any plans to go after Wolfgang Dittmers and Otto Westphalen, the two military jurors at Kusch's trial, had now to be abandoned. And thus ended the long postwar struggle to bring Kusch's judges to justice.

A free man at last, Karl-Heinrich Hagemann was readmitted to the bar and opened a private practice in Lauenburg on the Elbe River east of Hamburg, a short distance from Aumühle where Grand Admiral Karl Dönitz would choose to spend the last years of his life after his release from Spandau Prison in 1956. Hagemann died in Lauenburg on March 15, 1998, at age eighty-nine.[48]

Both Dr. Hans-Egon Breinig and Ernst Meinert found immediate employment in the Schleswig-Holstein justice system after the war, the latter returning to his hometown of Elmshorn as a county judge. Dr. med. habil. Hans Nothdurft, whose compulsion for self-justification in the Kusch drama never abated for the rest of his life, resumed his scientific research at Heidelberg University where he eventually rose to the rank of Professor of Physiology and discovered the so-called Nothdurft Effect in his field of specialization. He died on November 25, 1997, at age eighty-six.[49]

Commander Ernst Kals, Kusch's flotilla commander at Lorient, who was so gravely upset about the irregularity of Abel's report, ended the war as a full captain and suffered severe injuries when Allied forces surrounded the German Atlantic bases in France. He was set free after three years in French prisoner-of-war camps and died in 1979 at age seventy-four.

Hans-Rudolf Rösing, himself the son of an admiral and in charge of all German submarines in France, rejoined the West German navy after World War II and rose to the rank of rear admiral before retiring in 1965. Throughout his lifetime, he steadfastly refused to initiate or support efforts to rehabilitate the good name and legacy of Oskar Kusch. Rösing died in 2004 at age ninety-nine in Kiel, ironically in the very city whose courts had by then wiped Kusch's legal record clean and whose political and civic leaders had erected a memorial in his memory and honor.[50]

+ + +

As for Kusch's friends and comrades, his Crew 37a classmates have regularly honored his memory at postwar reunions and in their newsletters. Werner Winter rejoined the West German navy after the war and retired as a full captain in 1970. He died two years later in Kiel at age sixty.[51] Gustav-Adolf Janssen, who had likewise joined the *Bundesmarine* and served for a while—entirely appropriately, given his Scandinavian name—as naval attaché to Denmark and Sweden, survived Winter by eight years.[52] Dieter Berger, Wolfgang Kühns-Bernsau, Kurt Wiemer, and others from Kusch's school days and *Südlegion* experience rose to prominent civilian positions in postwar society, more often than not in the arts, the media, and education. Gerhard Meyer-Grieben continued his successful law practice until his death in 1972. His son Clemens then followed the family tradition in Kiel beyond his own retirement, generously allowing historians access to his father's records and even assisting a class of gymnasium students in nearby Altenholz recently to recreate Kusch's life and legacy in the form of an extended blog and "diary."[53]

Upon his release from Russian captivity, and after posting his impassioned essay on his friend Oskar Kusch in the *Aachener Nachrichten* on October 29, 1949,[54] Dr. Rudi Pallas chose to make a living as a radio journalist in East Berlin, although he never fully identified with the Communist regime and made frequent trips back and forth across the Iron Curtain. As one observer commented, "In the West he was under suspicion because of his contacts to the East, while both East and West Germany ostracized him because of his homosexuality." In 1952, Pallas committed suicide when West German police were about to arrest him for maintaining improper sexual relations with a minor.[55]

When Kusch's father died, his son's papers and remaining artwork became the possession of Oskar's Crew 37a comrade, Baron Horst von Luttitz, in the absence of any surviving relatives. Writing under the pseudonym Walter Klenck, Luttitz in 1987 published the autobiographical novel *Wer das Schwert nimmt . . .* [*All Who Take the Sword*], in which he reserves long passages and much of the dialogue for the plight and death of his friend, "Lieutenant Oskar Burk."[56] While many supposed scenes are clearly and deliberately the product of the author's imagination, as Kusch never served in Germany's naval air force, for instance, or offered a lengthy tirade against the Nazi regime at his court-martial, Luttitz captures Kusch's character, personality, and philosophical persuasions extremely well. He also became one of the first to publish in his book some of the artwork Kusch had created in his prison cell in Kiel.

+ + +

Over the quarter century that followed Karl-Heinrich Hagemann's final acquittal, the case of Oskar Kusch moved rapidly from front-page news to virtual oblivion. Much happened in Germany and the world during that time as economic recovery and the Cold War dominated priorities and experiences west and east of the Iron Curtain. After 1955, the two German states rearmed as members of their respective alliances, including the formation of the *Bundesmarine* and *Volksmarine*. With the widening distance to the events between 1933 and 1945, there also grew, however gradually and reluctantly, a self-critical reassessment of the German military's role in Hitler's rise and rule as a sub-aspect of overall *Vergangenheitsbewältigung*, or efforts to come to grips with Germany's Nazi past. Not least importantly, the question arose what stand the

Kriegsmarine had taken between complicity and resistance during the Nazi years.

East German historiography was quick to align the *Kriegsmarine* and its officers with the fascist state and purged its own top cadres of men with Nazi connections.[57] Not surprisingly, for example, only a single one of the 167 survivors of naval officer Crew 34 made his home in the communist state after the war.[58] By contrast, West German portrayals of the *Kriegsmarine* well into the 1960s followed the lines of defense adopted by Grand Admirals Raeder and Dönitz at Nuremberg. In this blinkered and sanitized version, links between the brown state and its navy had been minimal and strictly along professional lines; the Naval High Command had gone to great lengths to resist ideological infiltration by maintaining an independent judicial system and by stymying efforts to plant National Socialist Guidance Officers aboard its vessels; the war at sea, forced upon Germany by an unkind fate, had been hard but always fair and clean; especially the submarine arm, even though doomed after 1943, had fought with exemplary valor and unassailable patriotic commitment until the end; and the indelible "Trauma of 1918" allowed for nothing short of absolute loyalty to the government that happened to be in place no matter what its policies—or crimes. In addition, Dönitz's courageous intervention in 1945 allowed millions of German soldiers and civilians to reach the West before being overrun by Soviet savages. These convenient myths and self-serving simplifications, along with a massive outbreak of collective amnesia, found their expression in a flood of romanticizing and apologetic memoirs compiled by former war correspondents, U-boat captains, and eventually the two grand admirals themselves upon their release from prison in 1956.[59] The slow return to Germany of the *Kriegsmarine*'s archives from Allied custody further impeded efforts to create a realistic and evidence-based picture of what had actually happened and to place the life and legacy of men like Oskar Kusch into their proper context.

Access to pertinent documents, the gradual passing from social and political prominence of the wartime generation, and a genuine passion to dig deep for the truth no matter what the findings, combined at last to move historians to revise and reverse the accustomed whitewash of

Hitler's *Kriegsmarine* and its personnel. The publication of Michael Salewski's "Self-Image and Historical Consciousness of the German *Kriegsmarine*" (1970) and particularly Lothar Gruchmann's "Selected Documents on German Naval Justice in World War II" (1978) in prominent historical journals, along with subsequent work by Manfred Messerschmidt, Lothar Walmrath, Wolfgang Wette, and many others, may be regarded in retrospect as the starting point for a historiographical revolution and re-education of the public in terms of the *Kriegsmarine*'s long-denied affinity to Nazi practices and ideology. The ensuing research, impassioned debates, and even novels and films such as *Das Boot,* have animated excellent scholarship on both sides of the Atlantic and continue to correct deeply rooted misconceptions. One prominent victim of these investigations was Hans Filbinger, the governor of the state of Baden-Württemberg, who as a former judge in the *Kriegsmarine*'s judicial branch had been involved in controversial capital punishment decisions late in World War II.[60] Filbinger had to resign in disgrace in 1978, and one may be forgiven for wondering what Karl-Heinrich Hagemann's thoughts and comments may have been at the time. Dönitz's death in late 1980 allowed younger officers and academics to offer more freely a sophisticated picture and analysis of the *Kriegsmarine*'s entanglements with the regime and to appreciate anew the lives and sacrifices of men like Kusch. For instance, Keith Bird's and Dieter Hartwig's recent critical biographies of Erich Raeder and Karl Dönitz, respectively, strike readers as ranging light years ahead of and beyond any historiographical productions in the more immediate postwar era.[61]

Dieter Hartwig in particular deserves credit for exposing long-held myths and distortions about Karl Dönitz and his place in history.[62] The picture that has emerged from his inquiries reveals Dönitz as a cold and calculating opportunist, a strategic dilettante with a limited grasp of modern technology, and above all as a man exercising a slavish subservience to Hitler and his ideology. Any admiration for Dönitz's "people skills" vis-à-vis his U-boat men must be balanced against the grand admiral's perfect willingness to sacrifice them after 1943 to an overpowering Allied supremacy at sea when his earlier concept of a "tonnage war" had lost every meaning or prospect for success—something Kusch's experience richly confirmed at the time. That same disdain for human life and human suffering governed Dönitz's directives to abandon shipwrecked enemy sailors to their fate as a desirable measure to weaken Allied manpower resources. Hartwig's careful research stands out as particularly damning when it comes to Dönitz's speeches—several of them formerly unknown or misplaced. The admiral's shrill anti-Semitic rhetoric, his self-abasement with regard to the person and "genial" faculties of Adolf Hitler, and his drivel about death being preferable to honorable surrender, not only make for painful reading but belie Dönitz's postwar assertions that he had no clue about the regime's darker goals and practices. Were Werner Winter and Gustav-Adolf Janssen still alive, they would be stunned to realize how miserably futile and doomed their courageous interventions with Dönitz on Kusch's behalf had been from the outset.

While the name of Oskar Kusch occasionally came up in postwar histories of the *Kriegsmarine* and its personnel, genuine familiarity with the details and background of his case remained limited and elusive. For example, as recently as 1997 U-boat historian Jordan Vause claimed Kusch had been "a devout Christian," that his service in the RAD had lasted an entire year, that he had served under three different commanding officers on *U-103*, that he "blithely dumped the Führer's portrait into the trash" upon taking charge of *U-154*, and that Abel had submitted his report to Ernst Kals rather than to Captain Schmidt.[63] Even a researcher as meticulous as Timothy Mulligan has described Kusch as a "devout Catholic" and claimed his trial lasted three days.[64] *U-154*'s navigator Heinrich Lüdmann is likely responsible for this transformation of Kusch from a lapsed Lutheran into a devout Catholic when he likely confused Kusch's supposed religious beliefs and practices with those of an earlier captain of the boat.[65]

The first analyst to subject Oskar Kusch and his case to a renewed investigation and appraisal in the 1980s was retired rear admiral Karl H. Peter of Crew X/38, one-time commandant of Germany's naval academy in Mürwik. Working from some of Kusch's trial records, newspaper coverage of the Hagemann trials, and a few additional sources, in

1986 Peter authored a twenty-six-page typed manuscript titled, "Wider besseres Wissen zum Tode verurteilt. Stimmt das? Ein Bericht von Karl Peter" [Sentenced to death despite evidence to the contrary? Is that what happened? A Report by Karl Peter]. Peter's central concern appears to have been to provide facts and context about Kusch in place of rumors and erroneous assumptions that had made their way into parts of the naval literature over the years, even though Peter himself inadvertently misrepresented some facts in the process.[66] His paper was not widely distributed.

By the time Admiral Peter "rediscovered" Oskar Kusch and Baron von Luttitz (a.k.a. Walter Klenck) created the figure of Lieutenant Oskar Burk in his autobiographical novel in 1987, a far more ambitious project had gotten under way thanks to Dr. Heinrich Walle. An active-duty officer in the *Bundesmarine* (Crew 63) until his retirement in 1994, Walle earned a doctorate in 1979 under noted naval historian Michael Salewski and then worked at the Research Office for Military History in Freiburg. There he set out to tell Kusch's story in a 510-page documentation, eventually published in 1995. It remains the standard work on Oskar Kusch and the postwar trials against Hagemann in the German language; and this writer has relied on Walle's research in major ways, especially when covering the trials against Hagemann. In addition, one of Walle's goals was to achieve a full legal, public, and historical rehabilitation for *U-154*'s former captain.

Even before Walle's work reached a wider readership, he featured his findings in a series of lectures, exhibitions, and articles that started a spirited debate between 1992 and 1996 in the *Marineforum*, the periodical publication of the German Naval Officers Association (MOV). In letters to the editor and in several online blogs ever since, Oskar Kusch's life, actions, and legacy have remained a frequently discussed topic. Even Dr. Nothdurft became involved in these exchanges as he felt his views had been at first largely omitted and later misrepresented in Walle' documentation. Far from bringing closure to the memory of Kusch's sacrifice and civil courage, Walle's book, and especially his readiness to lift Kusch into the ranks of active resistance fighters, has fueled a bitter debate whose full resolution remains elusive. One side, mainly veteran officers, believes Kusch was essentially guilty of the accusations against him; that U-boat commanders in the midst of a war should not turn their wardrooms into political debate clubs even if they spoke out against an evil regime; and that Abel did the proper thing in reporting his superior if Kusch's opposition to Hitler seemed to him to endanger harmony and discipline among his officers and had the potential of diminishing the combat readiness of his boat, no matter what the consequences might entail for his captain. For adherents of this camp, questions of honor, duty, loyalty, patriotism, and military discipline remain central when judging Oskar Kusch.

His supporters, mostly younger officers and historians, insist that Kusch, as an exemplary and patriotic soldier, was the target of a personal vendetta by his disaffected officers and victim of an unprecedented breakdown in U-boat camaraderie; that his activities, far from criminal, aimed at the enlightenment of his officers rather than at treason, desertion, or sedition; that his superiors abandoned him even though they knew he was being offered up to an ideologically corrupt legal system; and that quiet removal from command and inconspicuous reassignment should have been the appropriate way of resolving the matter once it had been reported. The only thing both sides seem to agree on is that Kusch should never have lost his life.[67]

As the surviving German naval officers of Kusch's generation first retired and then gradually went to their graves, the tone and acrimony of the debate over Walle's work have softened and its thrust redirected to what Kusch's proper legacy should become in German naval and general history. An indicator of this shifting emphasis can be found in the more than one hundred entries in the online blog of the *Marine-Archiv* marking the seventieth anniversary of Kusch's execution in 2014.[68] Virtually gone are references to his supposedly unpatriotic, endangering, traitorous, elitist, naïve, and self-destructive behavior. Instead, contributors are wondering how best to remember Kusch, to what extent he can serve as a model for young officers in the armed forces of a free and democratic society, if the German navy should perhaps name a vessel after him, whether the now empty naval detention center in Kiel should be turned into some kind of museum, and how appropriate it is that the military range at Holtenau continues to be used for target practice by Germans in uniform.[69]

Indeed, some Germans even raise the question how and to what extent the memory even of deserters and saboteurs might be incorporated into a fair-minded assessment of their military past.[70]

Most recently, since February 2017, a portrait of Oskar Kusch painted by Rolf Osker Michelmann greets visitors to the fireplace lounge of the officers' mess at the German naval academy in Mürwik.[71] Perhaps the feelings Kusch stirred in his admirers and in his detractors are giving way at last to a more measured appreciation of the man who would not allow his conscience, his common sense, and his commitment to human dignity and individualism to atrophy while remaining true to his patriotic and professional duties as an officer.

+ + +

A primary purpose of Walle's documentation had been to bring about the legal rehabilitation of Oskar Kusch through renewed publicity of his case. Within a year of the publication of his book, an envelope was added to Kusch's case folder. Carrying the file number 591 AR 217/96 and duly signed by District Attorney Thomas-Michael Hoffmann, on September 16, 1996, the document issued by the District Court at Kiel formally rescinded and made void the court-martial decision against Oskar Kusch of January 26, 1944. It did so based on legal authority first granted by the British occupation administration on June 3, 1947, and extended by the German parliament in its "Law Annulling Verdicts Based on National Socialist Injustice" of May 25, 1990.[72] It had thus taken more than half a century to wipe out Hagemann's verdict and to restore Kusch's legal status as an innocent and exemplary officer from that of a convicted and executed felon.

+ + +

One of the unresolved mysteries surrounding Oskar Kusch concerns his final resting place. Once his bloodied and lifeless body had been placed into a coffin at the range in Holtenau and taken back across the canal bridge into Kiel, all inquiries into verifiable vestiges of what happened to his corpse have run into a void. As the two most likely places, neither the sizable North Cemetery (*Nordfriedhof*) on the Westring in Kiel, where indeed many victims of *Kriegsmarine* executions were laid to rest in those days, nor the Old and New Urn Cemeteries down the road, possess any record of Kusch's body or ashes ever being delivered to them, even temporarily, or of him being buried on their premises. In this sense, Peter C. Hansen's contention in his novel on Kusch that the urn with the U-boat commander's cremated remains was buried in Field 14, Plot 631, of the Old Urn Cemetery, is exactly that—pure fiction. Field 14 demonstrably has only 149 plots and Kusch's is not one of them.[73]

It is known that Gerhard Meyer-Grieben communicated with Kusch's parents about the disposition of their son's body, but unfortunately his copies of that correspondence fell victim to one of the many bombing raids on Kiel in 1944 and the parents' inquiries were lost to the attacks on Berlin. It seems logical and likely that Kusch's parents should have wanted the remains of their only child in a place close to them, but again despite numerous inquiries no trace of a transfer of Kusch's urn to the capital or its interment in one of Berlin's many cemeteries could be ascertained, particularly not in the city sections of Steglitz, Dahlem, and Schöneberg where the parents lived at the time.[74]

Still, there exists today a quiet place where mourners will find Oskar Kusch appropriately commemorated. On May 12, 1998, the fifty-fourth anniversary of Kusch's execution, the City of Kiel and the community of Altenholz renamed a street adjacent to the shooting range in Holtenau, just north of the Kiel Canal, the Oskar-Kusch-Strasse.[75] At the same time, officials unveiled at this site a large granite boulder with a bronze plaque that reads:

OSKAR KUSCH
*6. 4. 1918 +12. 5. 1944
His name stands for the many victims of the National Socialist
system of injustice who died here and in other places.
Their death is our legacy.
Community of Altenholz—City of Kiel
12 May 1998

CHAPTER 11

A SUMMING UP

Oskar Kusch joined approximately 33,000 other German soldiers and sailors who were executed by their own side out of about 50,000 men condemned to die by formal and informal German military courts—a stark and frightful measure of the totalitarian character and ideological infiltration of Germany's military justice system in World War II. While many were sent to their death for "subverting the military spirit," others had been found guilty of desertion, treason, cowardice, and an assortment of other infractions. Only the Soviet regime in its Great Patriotic War trumped this German brutality, with about 158,000 executions of its own men for desertion alone.[1] By contrast, the United States executed 146 of its soldiers in World War II, France 102, and Great Britain 40. The corresponding numbers for World War I are especially startling: Germany executed 48 of its military personnel between 1914 and 1918, the United States 35, Britain 346, and France about 650. As the compiler of these statistics notes, "rather than representing an enclave of resistance, the German military justice system . . . functioned as a willing and cooperative partner of the regime, demonstrating its loyalty by adopting Nazi views and imposing the death penalty with a relentless vigor fully in line with Hitler's draconian strictures."[2]

Kusch became a tragic victim of this system. His family background, his schooling, his intellectual quests and artistic inclinations, his formative experiences in the *bündisch* youth movement, as well as his character, temperament and sense of humanity, his integrity and conscience, placed him on a predictable collision course with the Nazi regime. He would maintain this dedication to the ideals of his adolescent years unwaveringly into the last hours of his life. Well into World War II, the inherited ethos of the *Kriegsmarine*'s officer corps, and especially the camaraderie among U-boat men regardless of rank, offered a safe refuge and haven for political dissidents like Kusch and shielded them against the ever-expanding grasp of the regime in its drive for absolute totalitarian domination. It would have been inconceivable for a Werner Winter, a Gerhard Bielig, an Erich Topp, a Gustav-Adolf Janssen, a Wilhelm Franken, or even the two young midshipmen on *U-154*'s first patrol under Kusch, let alone any of his enlisted men, to turn a worthy human being and exemplary U-boat officer over to the authorities for embracing persuasions that ran counter to official ideology.

Sadly, Kusch failed to realize that this protective cocoon of service traditions, plain human decency, and forgiveness for minor signs of ideological differences as long as they did not affect the basic bonds of camaraderie or the military effort, kept thinning out by the fourth and fifth years of the war. The caliber, educational breadth, and value-forming opportunities of junior naval officers decreased due to Germany's political and cultural isolation while their politicization and ideological indoctrination grew. They missed the moderating palliative of travel abroad, contact with and appreciation for other cultures, and guidance by pre-Hitlerian role models the way Kusch and naval officers of older Crews had enjoyed them. Kurt Druschel, as a former Hitler Youth leader, is just as typical an example in this regard as Ulrich Abel and Arno Funke are as longtime Nazi party members. Indeed, the case of Oskar Kusch suggests that the greater use and therefore heightened presence and influence of reserve officers in the later phases of the conflict deserve more scholarly attention than has been the case in the past when the focus had been almost exclusively on regular active-duty officers.

Several analysts have characterized Kusch primarily as an artist, an aesthete, a reality-defying dreamer stuck in youthful fantasies and ideals, a naïve romantic equally blind to the demands of a career as a professional naval officer as to the dangers of political dissent in a wartime and totalitarian context. Therefore, such critics would claim, his experiences added up to a special and solitary case and cannot lend themselves, pars pro toto, to any broad generalizations about Germany's naval officer corps under Hitler. From the perspective of these critics, Kusch should never have become an officer in the first place. The present study has proved otherwise, or at the very least has shown that Kusch personified a vision of a better, richly cosmopolitan, free, and tolerant German society and culture, while simultaneously performing his duties as a naval officer and U-boat commander with exemplary competence, circumspection, and enviable leadership abilities. It was exactly this extraordinary mental and professional skill set, which Kusch already demonstrated as a watch officer under Winter and Janssen and was highly valued by them, and which was later praised by men like Janker, Isensee, and Lüdmann on *U-154*, that placed Kusch above and beyond the automatons in uniform who populated so many ranks of the *Kriegsmarine* at the time. The latter served Germany bravely enough as typical soldiers, but lacked Kusch's imagination, erudition, honesty, and civil courage.

Robert F. Kennedy likely never heard of Oskar Kusch, but he must have had nonconformists like him in mind when he declared in 1966: "Few men are willing to brave the disapproval of their fellows, the censure of their colleagues, the wrath of their society. Moral courage is a rarer commodity than bravery in battle or great intelligence. Yet it is the one essential, vital quality for those who seek to change a world which yields most painfully to change."[3] Kusch, too, wished to enlighten his bleak and darkening world one convert at a time, even if Abel, Druschel, and Funke proved predictably immune and vengefully hostile to his advances. For them, any criticism of the Nazi regime, attacks on Hitler's person and decisions, and doubt about a miraculous final victory of German arms and German ways, amounted to defeatism rather than a triumph of common sense. In their eyes, only would-be traitors and cowards would dwell on Allied superiority in numbers, equipment, and leadership—daily and scary reminders to the contrary out at sea and in the skies above them notwithstanding. For these soldiers, honor, duty, patriotic fervor, and strict military discipline remained central demands and included prominently the equation of defense of country with loyalty to the regime.

Kusch performed his military duties conscientiously even though he had lost all faith in a German victory and had never embraced Hitler's war aims. When he returned to Lorient from Zürs in January 1944, he was fully prepared to take *U-154* out to sea again in the face of forbidding odds. As many other Germans did, Kusch imagined, hoped for, and would have joyfully joined a coup d'état carried out by the Wehrmacht's top military leaders to topple and remove Hitler and his brown columns, to terminate Europe's latest orgy of self-destruction, to rescue German honor by ending atrocities committed against Jews and others based on racial hubris, and to help create a postwar European and world order predicated on the values of his youthful convictions and experiences. In all this he could not count on the least assistance and inspiration from Germany's top naval leaders. Traumatized by the memory of the World War I naval mutinies, Grand Admiral Karl Dönitz and his closest subordinates and associates had sold their souls to the Nazis unconditionally, saw their own fate and future linked to the survival of the regime, and while generally not implicated in outright crimes against non-Germans, became willing accomplices in keeping the Nazi authorities in control by eliminating dissenters such as Kusch. Following the inner logic and questionable rewards of this variety of *Nibelungen* loyalty, Hitler chose Dönitz as his successor as Germany's head of state and government so that the latter could finally surrender what little remained of Germany's forces—a step the dictator had cowardly postponed beyond all military reason to add a few more days to his wretched life.

Many contributed to Oskar Kusch's tragic death through deliberate actions or by failing to act when they could have, and they did so for a range of reasons, considerations, and excuses. No one can deny that Ulrich Abel triggered his commanding officer's plunge into the abyss. Without Abel's cleverly launched and carefully timed report—whether it grew from personal enmity, envy, humiliation, revenge, ideological ardor, or any number of other motives or a combination of them, is ultimately immaterial—Kusch would at the very least have taken *U-154* out on another patrol. His survival chances would have been grim, as Abel's own fate and that of Kurt Druschel would demonstrate. In fact, of some

42,000 sailors who served at one time or another on German submarines between 1939 and 1945, at least 28,748 perished, more than half in and after 1943, and another 5,000 were captured, amounting to a casualty rate unequalled in any other service branch.[4] Abel has been rightly singled out for knowingly turning Kusch over to a politically corrupt and ideologically obsequious naval justice apparatus. In doing so he violated cherished traditions of the German naval officer corps and betrayed comradely trust. Still, it must be remembered in fairness to Abel that his report called only for Kusch's removal as commanding officer, not for his incarceration or death, and it was not certain the report would indeed bring on an elaborate trial rather than quiet and inconspicuous reassignment for Kusch. On the other hand, once Kusch had been assigned the death penalty, Abel chose not to approach the court or anyone else in the naval or judicial hierarchy to plead for clemency for his former skipper on the grounds that Kusch's execution had never been his goal or intention. Thus, the suspicion lingers that personal and political considerations, as well as Abel's grave and pessimistic apprehensions about Germany's military misfortunes, were foremost on his mind when he composed and submitted his report.

Kurt Druschel's culpability is somewhat more challenging to assess. As the junior-most member of the officer group opposed to Kusch, the engineer took his cue from the considerably older, less excitable, and more experienced Abel. Druschel's was a wilder and more easily piqued temperament, as shown in his willingness to employ physical force against his commanding officer if necessary and in his preparedness to drive the hotel room episode in Zürs to an irresponsible climax. As a prominent product of the Hitler Youth, Druschel held a worldview and had experiences as a child and adolescent that could not have been further apart from Kusch's. The engineer had matured professionally by the time of the second mission, but his ideological convictions and his faith in final victory remained as set as they had been when he first came on board. His initial deposition and subsequent court testimony revealed not one gram of sympathy for his commanding officer and instead showed outright contempt for a man so openly and often abrasively critical of Druschel's idol. Indeed, Kusch's removal of the Hitler picture and his accompanying comments must have filled Druschel with fierce rage. To his credit, Druschel did honor the promises he had given Dr. Nothdurft out in the Atlantic and again at Zürs not to report his captain, and he seemed genuinely surprised, but far from bitter or concerned, when he learned of Abel's action. The fact that Druschel was a regular officer with at least some immersion into corps traditions at the naval academy and subsequently, and not a reservist such as Abel or Funke, appears to have acted as a further brake on extreme measures on his part.

Reserve Lieutenant Arno Funke's culpability in the Kusch tragedy appears lighter than Abel's and Druschel's. He only came on board for the second patrol and did not initiate any direct action against his commanding officer. His disagreement with Kusch as to when and how to attack the TJ convoy appears to have reflected genuine nautical alternatives rather than an ideologically or personality-driven confrontation. Funke, in his pretrial deposition to Dr. Breinig, did verify many of Abel's allegations, but was careful to distinguish between what he had witnessed himself and what had reached him as hearsay. Not personally present at the court-martial at Kiel or at the postwar Hagemann trials, but clearly a card-carrying member of the Nazi Party, Funke has remained a shadowy figure in the background, driven more by notions of self-preservation than by a desire or temptation to thrust another knife into Kusch's back.

A highly controversial and elusive figure in the Kusch drama was Dr. Hans Nothdurft, primarily because he acted inconsistently and changed his numerous accounts as a nonexpert witness on *U-154* several times over the span of fifty years. Moreover, most of his obviously exaggerated and at least in part self-serving contentions lost any chance of being verified, corroborated, corrected, or dismissed by other witnesses on board once Abel and Druschel and so many other men who had served on *U-154* under Kusch had died. In the end, Nothdurft's oscillation between "good cop" and "bad cop" fell far short of shielding Kusch from his fate and contributed vastly to Hagemann's acquittal after the war in allowing the naval justice official's lawyers to invent a whole range of military shortfalls on Kusch's part that had played not the slightest role in the justification for the initial verdict. Hagemann could not have found a more fortuitous and elaborate witness accusing Kusch of all sorts of mental afflictions and plans for desertion, sabotage, and worse military crimes and thus vindicating the original sentence. Further, Nothdurft's contentions also cast belated doubt on the entirely political nature of the proceedings in Kiel, thereby assuring Hagemann's acquittal for "lack of evidence" for having acted inhumanely and delaying Kusch's rehabilitation for fifty years after the war. Why the medical doctor did so, and who besides himself could have benefitted from his shifting testimony, remain mysterious and troubling questions to this day.

Judge Karl-Heinrich Hagemann foremost, but also the two military jurors Wolfgang Dittmers and Otto Westphalen at his trial, bear the most immediate responsibility for Kusch's death. Exceeding by far the prosecution's recommendation of ten years in jail, interpreting without factual basis Kusch's opposition to the regime as a severe military transgression on the dubious basis of an inhumane totalitarian decree, allowing major logical gaps in the formal justification for the verdict to persist unexamined, unexplained, and uncorrected, and, above all, by making a mockery of the supposedly ideological independence of the naval justice system, these three men headed a procession of fellow conspirators and colluders, spineless naval brass, assorted opportunistic underlings, and a coterie of cowardly hangers-on down the path to a judicial murder. While Hagemann's motive for Kusch's removal appears to have been primarily ideological and secondarily grounded in an antipathy to the social and intellectual circles in which Kusch and his friends moved and to the fashionable lifestyles attributed to them, Dittmers and Westphalen deliberately harmed and betrayed a fellow officer and comrade. They did so, not based on his having committed a specific military misdeed, but on the vague and unproven suspicion that his political outspokenness simply must have created chaos on his boat when, *in actuality*, no such conditions materialized. The behavior and utterances of both officers also betrayed at least a latent subscription to National Socialist ideas and ideals. Once Hagemann had been acquitted, legal proceedings against Dittmers and Westphalen lost any prospect of success.

Kusch's immediate superiors, Ernst Kals and Hans-Rudolf Rösing, had two opportunities to prevent the worst but chose not to grasp them. Together, they could have delayed, deflected, or even cancelled Dr. Breinig's investigation in France by pointing to the irregular nature and submission of Abel's report. As *Gerichtsherr*, Rösing clearly had the power to call off court-martial proceedings against one of his better U-boat captains, but to do so was not within the range of his courage or imagination. Then, when the file containing Kusch's death sentence recommendation reached Rösing's desk for review two weeks later, he threw away his chance to speak up for leniency and instead endorsed the court's decision after a most cursory review, in the process chiding Breinig implicitly for the latter's recommendation of a "mere" jail sentence. Had Kals and Rösing expressed reservations about the appropriateness of the verdict and how it had materialized, and characterized Kusch as the popular and successful skipper that he was, Grand Admiral Dönitz and his legal advisers might have likewise viewed Kusch less as a supposedly war-weary defeatist with anti-Nazi persuasions and more as the victim of a conspiracy among his officers grown from personal and political animosities.

Even though Ernst Meinert only oversaw Kusch's incarceration and eventual execution, through his countless chicaneries against Kusch, his relatives, and friends he tipped and tilted the scales further against the U-boat captain by forwarding to Dönitz and his staff in Berlin copies of Kusch's private correspondence. For Meinert, the simple act of communicating with someone sentenced to death for subversion suggested complicity in the same crime, revealed the same opposition to the regime, and deserved to be exposed and punished. By the same logic, receiving a letter, any kind of letter, from Kusch out of his jail cell in Kiel placed the recipient in jeopardy of being identified as someone in sympathy with Kusch's views and actions. Clearly Meinert wished to convey to Berlin that Kusch had not changed his attitudes, that he was indeed politically guilty as charged, and that any thought of leniency or clemency was woefully misplaced. Guilt by association, after all, had always been a popular instrument in the Nazi arsenal of terror.

That leaves Karl Dönitz and his legal staff in Berlin as the ultimate arbiter and decider of Kusch's fate, since everyone knew Reich Marshal Göring's confirmation of the sentence, whether left unchanged or modified, would amount to a mere formality. Despite Dr. Rudolphi's later denial or equivocation, all available evidence indicates that he, Dönitz, and Admiral Warzecha did indeed weigh the matter for some time and with deliberation. Kusch's friends Werner Winter and Gustav-Adolf Janssen had sensed from the moment they learned of Hagemann's verdict that ultimately only Dönitz was in a position to reverse it. Bypassing the timid Kals and hostile Rösing, they knew instinctively that the grand admiral was their only hope. They became immediately active, in Janssen's case spectacularly so, and were well placed for success: Winter had been one of Dönitz's original converts for service in the revived U-boat arm and Janssen had been the grand admiral's aide-de-camp before taking command of *U-103*. In short, the proven, battle-tested active officers who knew Kusch best and appreciated him for who he was tried everything to save their comrade's life. At the same time, Rudolphi felt he had to defend Hagemann's verdict to save face and demonstrate the "integrity" and "independence" of the naval justice system, besides demonstrating loyalty to the political regime. It is not unimaginable that Dönitz did indeed ponder these conflicting influences and perspectives during the ten days or so that Kusch's file was in his hands. But why did he, in the end, side with the bureaucrats and not with "his" U-boat men despite his promise to Janssen to hear from Kusch personally in the matter?

Dönitz's postwar argument that he had to set down an example in Kusch's case to maintain discipline and uphold the will to fight in the U-boat arm carries all the persuasive power of an ex post facto made-up excuse for an irreversible personal mistake or misdeed. The grand admiral visited his U-boats and their crews with regularity and knew first-hand that discipline, in the French bases as elsewhere, remained extremely solid, if not exemplary, to the very end—just as had been the case in World War I. There was no fear that the events of 1918 in the Kaiser's surface fleet could somehow play themselves out again in 1944 or 1945 in the submarine service. Lack of discipline had not been a problem aboard

U-154 and constituted the rarest of grievances throughout the U-boat force. How Kusch's execution could have resolved a nonexistent breakdown in discipline remains a question and mystery Dönitz would take to his grave. Moreover, to have any deterrent effect at all, it seems logical that reports of Kusch's execution should have been distributed widely throughout the navy. But nothing of the kind was done. Most surviving former *Kriegsmarine* and U-boat personnel learned of Kusch's fate only in the 1990s.

Essentially the same argument applies to Dönitz's claim that Kusch had to die because he was a defeatist and might infect those around him. It was true enough that Kusch no longer believed in a German victory by 1943, or in a stalemate, but in this conviction he was neither alone nor different from those who sat in judgment over him. Given Dönitz's grim "will-to-victory" messages under the code word "Rose," for example, and the frank admission of men like Hagemann, Breinig, and Meinert that they had lost faith in a German military triumph after the catastrophe at Stalingrad, it remains one of the more perfidious dimensions of the Kusch tragedy that he was condemned to die by men who themselves considered a victorious outcome of the war illusory by 1944, Dönitz included. Indeed, Kusch had never displayed and always consciously rejected any of the typical and traditional symptoms of defeatism such as sabotage, disengagement from the enemy, desertion, collaboration with the enemy, and treason. For Kusch, fulfilling his military obligations to the end had grown from a far stronger commitment to his men, his country, and his profession than that "certain sense of duty" Dr. Nothdurft had detected in *U-154*'s commanding officer in their animated conversations out in the Atlantic. Instead of publicizing Kusch's fate throughout the *Kriegsmarine* as the just punishment for someone who had lost faith in the cause, Dönitz and his staff must rather have "feared" that news of Kusch's execution would not occasion applause and approval within Germany's naval officer corps, but would instead evoke incredulity, resentment, and the very erosion of the fighting spirit with which they had charged him. So much for Dönitz's pious fable that getting rid of Oskar Kusch had amounted to a "difficult but necessary duty." Kusch died as a consequence of his political convictions, not because of any military shortfalls or misdeeds.

The case of Oskar Kusch remains unique in the annals of German naval history, not least because of Abel's role in the affair. Having three ardent and vengeful Nazis as subordinate officers amounted to an unlikely constellation even on a German submarine, just as the selection of Hagemann instead of Breinig as presiding judge and of Dittmers and Westphalen as jurors at the trial constituted imponderables impossible to foresee. Few officers anywhere in the German armed forces equaled Kusch's moral courage of frankly speaking up and standing up for truth, integrity, and higher ideals in the face of ideological idiocy, obstinacy, and blind obedience to an evil regime.

And yet, Kusch was not atypical when it came to his societal background, education, sense of patriotism, and overall career experience. German naval officer Crews at least through 1937, including those of Gerhard Bielig or Gustav-Adolf Janssen for instance, drew their members from a highly educated segment of society that saw service in the navy at least in part as an escape from and an alternative to academic pursuits in an ideologically corrupted system of higher education in Germany. Later Crews, such as those of Kurt Druschel and Otto Westphalen, demonstrated a much higher affinity to Nazi concepts and behavioral norms in part because of their extended exposure to the Hitler Youth and a corresponding lack of experiences in more liberal and cosmopolitan organizations. The dire officer crunch by 1942 washed many reservists such as Abel and Funke into positions previously occupied exclusively by regular active-duty officers with their more independent and traditional sets of ethical norms. These newcomers often had roots in the Nazi-leaning merchant marine, held party membership, and resented the superior reputation and prestige of men like Kusch who had made the navy their career from the start. They often viewed themselves as guardians of ideological conformity and in that sense anticipated the use of NSFOs (National Socialist Guidance Officers) in the last phase of the war.

As a proud and highly competent U-boat officer and captain even after the "Happy Times" had ended in mid-1942, Kusch exemplified both the esprit de corps and some of the elitist exclusivity of that service branch. On pictures taken at the time he wore his cap with its distinctive white cover proudly at a rakish angle, sported the ubiquitous beard popular among submariners returning from their missions, and could very well have convinced himself that frank political talk and criticism of the regime would necessarily be protected by time-honored shipboard camraderie and confidentiality or, if somehow reported to superiors, weighed little in comparison to his professional accomplishments and the personnel needs of the U-boat arm.

Kusch's trust in such traditions was fully justified when it came to the enlisted men serving under him. They understood their captain instinctively, chuckled about his eccentricities, applauded his leadership and concern for them, and rewarded him with excellent performance, loyalty, and support to the end and beyond. It was other officers—heavily politicized ones like Abel, Druschel, Funke, and Westphalen, but also more seasoned and presumably more sympathetic men such as Dittmers, Kals, Rösing, von Friedeburg, and Dönitz—who dropped their support, colluded with the ideologically tainted naval justice bureaucracy, and sacrificed a worthy man even though Winter and Janssen told them in no uncertain terms they were making a terrible mistake. Some of them must have found Abel's case persuasive, even if the death penalty seemed inappropriate. Some, perhaps unduly bothered and embarrassed, withdrew behind a screen of indifference and opportunism. Others feared a similar fate as Kusch and elevated self-preservation over comradely responsibility. Dr. Nothdurft, even though only on loan to the *Kriegsmarine*, would be fairly representative of this category.

Collectively, the behavior and decisions of these men stand in stark contrast to the still widespread myth that the U-boat service constituted a Nelsonian band of brothers, forever loyal to each other, to their leader, and to their mission. If not yet in the beginning, by 1943 and 1944 this mythical community, if it ever really existed, showed serious cracks, limitations, and growing incoherence. The ever-deepening totalitarian character and pressure of the regime, along with the quickly deteriorating military situation, were dissolving old bonds of trust, honor, and dignity and replacing them with the false notion that responsible patriotic service required loyalty to the Nazi regime even if it had its brutal and indecent sides. Dönitz fell for this false equation easily and willingly enough, as did Abel, Druschel, and their friends. For Kusch it always constituted a pact with the devil that no decent, thinking, feeling human being could possibly honor.

In remarkable detail, Kusch's case and tragic fate have also laid to rest the widely circulating notion that the naval justice system under Hitler was somehow independent in its decisions and immune to political guidance from above, that blue and brown could never mix. No such integrity ever existed or could possibly prevail in a system lacking an independent process of appeal and review, or in its adherence to laws and decrees whose inhumane and totalitarian nature should have been plain to any practitioner of the legal profession at the time. The very possibility and sometimes outright demand for party membership among justice officials in a one-party state rips apart the veneer and illusion of an independently operating judicial branch. In reality, collusion among officials, ideological instructions from Berlin, and draconian sentencing guidelines—to isolate just three major problems—transformed the naval judicial service into a convenient tool to silence or remove political opponents, quite apart from its massive and unsavory postwar coverup. Karl-Heinrich Hagemann's proceedings at the Villa Forsteck in Kiel may have employed subtler means of injustice and observed more traditional decorum than Roland Freisler's notorious People's Tribunal where the accused suffered outright insults along with other psychological and physical indignities; still, in the end Oskar Kusch was just as dead as the victims of Freisler's special court in Berlin.

A particularly troubling dimension of the case is how long it took to rehabilitate Kusch after 1945. In this regard, the collective obstructionism of former naval justice officials, the eagerness of the Allies to return to German courts as soon as possible the responsibility for handling transgressions of Germans against Germans, the early end to denazification after a rather perfunctory effort, and the reluctance of large segments of German society to engage in meaningful *Vergangenheitsbewältigung* before the 1960s and 1970s, account for much of the delay. Even the remilitarization of the two German states in the context of the Cold War, with its vetting of candidates applying for reenlistment, did little to revisit and confront problematic decisions and traditions of the past. The novel concept of the "citizen in uniform," so applicable to Kusch's life and legacy, seemed difficult to teach and even more challenging to live out in a society with shallow democratic experiences and reluctantly embraced liberal values. Only a generational change and a set of uncommonly courageous and conscientious historians at last brought relief.

Some analysts, Heinrich Walle in particular, have raised the issue of whether, how, and to what extent Oskar Kusch could and should be classified as part of the broader resistance movement against Hitler and the Nazis. Certainly, his persuasions, utterances, and to some degree even his actions, such as removing the Hitler portrait, constituted a deliberate, tangible, and courageous turning against the Nazi state, its ideology, and its symbols, even if Kusch never formally joined an identifiable group of individuals planning a violent overthrow of the Third Reich. Kusch's opposition stopped short of outright resistance, sabotage, and counteractions and thus must be located somewhere between passive rejection of the regime and a proactive willingness to start an open rebellion to bring about its demise, just as his circle of friends around Rudi Pallas, Dieter Berger, Kurt Wiemer, as well as Inge von Foris and her family, seemed ready to support a coup by the top military leadership but hesitated to initiate an uprising for a variety of plausible concerns and considerations. As far as is known, no contacts or communications linked Kusch's cluster of friends to the men behind the July 20, 1944, conspiracy to kill Hitler.

A perhaps more meaningful way of weighing and assessing Kusch's legacy would be to ask: What can the postwar world in general and today's German officer corps in particular take away from Kusch's example and the details and knowledge of his fate? How does one balance patriotic duty as a soldier in a democratic state with the demand that carrying out orders and engaging in military actions should be accompanied and tempered by an ever-active and well-trained conscience? Does Oskar Kusch's legacy not invite every soldier for all times to come to ask: Are my actions ethical and right? Am I a good comrade? Is my behavior in line with the highest principles of a free and tolerant society? Are the orders I am carrying out just and compatible with the lessons learned from that terrible struggle against totalitarian regimes in the 1930s, 1940s, and others since?

Germany would sorely miss men of Oskar Kusch's character and caliber, along with other victims of German-on-German violence and brutality, as the country rebuilt its state and society after the war and sought to step away from its bouts of national hubris and entanglements with inhumane, criminal totalitarianism. Had Kusch survived, one pictures him with Inge von Foris and their friends cleaning up and reconstituting Berlin's cultural scene. Perhaps Oskar Kusch would have become an artist, a writer, an academic, a social critic, or even a politician. He had it all in him. Or he might have ended up more like Rudi Pallas, never really recovering his bearings after the horrors of the war experience and long incarceration, full of frustration that so little could be changed, that so many former followers of the brown regime remained in office and good standing, and that fundamentally the ideals of their youth remained as elusive as ever. These and other thoughts tease our imagination a full century after Kusch's birth.

NOTES

Chapter 1. Lorient

1. For the history and exploits of this squadron, see Lawrence Paterson, *Second U-Boat Flotilla* (Barnsley, UK: Leo Cooper, 2003). By far the best internet source on German U-boats remains http://uboat.net (accessed July 6, 2017).
2. Information on Lorient and other French U-boat bases in Lars Hellwinkel, *Hitler's Gateway to the Atlantic: German Naval Bases in France, 1940–1945* (Barnsley, UK: Seaworth, 2014). For Lorient's history, see http://www.christopherunger.de/lorient/history.htm (accessed July 17, 2001).
3. Hellwinkel, 24–25, 51.
4. Jerome M. O'Connor, "Into the Gray Wolves' Den," *Naval History Magazine* (June 2000), at http://www.usni.org/NavalHistory/Articles00/NHoconnor.htm (accessed July 18, 2001). Details on the pens at Lorient at http://www.uboat-bases.com/ang/index.php (accessed July 18, 2001).
5. Bundesarchiv-Militärarchiv (BA-MA), Federal Military Archives in Freiburg, RM 91/18, 2. U-Flottille, "Ständige Befehle: Heft I: Wichtige Befehle für U-Bootsbesatzungen," sheets 18–19, items 6a and 6b.
6. "The U-Boat Bases," Lorient history page. See also "U-boat Bases, Lorient, France" at http://uboat.net/flotillas/bases/lorient.htm (both accessed July 18, 2001).
7. Hellwinkel, *Hitler's Gateway to the Atlantic*, 68.
8. For a list of boats belonging to the Second U-Boat Flotilla, see Bodo Herzog, *U-Boote im Einsatz 1939–1945* (Podzun-Verlag: 1970), 20.
9. See http://uboat.net/ops/successful_boats.htm (accessed July 23, 2001).
10. Information based on Erich Gröner, *Die Schiffe der Deutschen Kriegsmarine und Luftwaffe, 1939–45* (Munich: Lehmanns, 1972).
11. German naval ranks, if translated, will appear as their equivalent in the U.S. Navy at that time. For a fuller discussion of this issue see chapter 2 below.
12. Data from http://www.uboat.net/technical/shipyards/ (accessed Aug. 8, 2017).
13. Jürgen Rohwer, *Axis Submarine Successes, 1939–1945* (Annapolis, MD: Naval Institute Press, 1983), 31–32, 36–38, 42–43, 50–53, 55, and 58. See divergent figures in Heinrich Walle, *Die Tragödie des Oberleutnants zur See Oscar Kusch* (Stuttgart: Steiner, 1995), 33.

Walle confuses the award dates for Viktor Schütze with those of Herbert Schultze. Correct data at http://uboat.net/men/decorations/ritter_oak.htm (accessed Oct. 11, 2001).

14. BA-MA, RM 98/106, "KTB U-103."
15. Rohwer, *Axis Submarine Successes*, 3, 214.

Chapter 2. Lieutenant Kusch

1. Email from Claudia van Eyck, Inge von Foris' daughter, to author on July 30, 2017, as well as her mother's student records at Humboldt University, Berlin.
2. Eric C. Rust, *Naval Officers under Hitler: The Story of Crew 34* (Westport, CT: Praeger, 1991), 36.
3. Bundesarchiv-Zentralnachweisstelle (BA-ZNS) in Aachen-Kornelimünster, RM 123/K 3140, "Verkürzter Auszug aus dem Personalnachweis für den Oblt. z. S. Oskar Kusch," Untersuchungsakten (investigation file), sheet 1. Most documents central to Kusch's life, naval career and trial are included in his court-martial file, hereafter cited as BA-ZNS, RM 123/K 3140. The BA-ZNS files were transferred from Kornelimünster to the German Military Archives (BA-MA) in Freiburg in 2005.
4. Kusch's father consistently signed his correspondence as Oskarheinz Kusch.
5. BA-ZNS, RM123/K 3140, Staatspolizeileitstelle Berlin an Staatspolizeistelle Kiel, Jan. 26, 1944, Kusch Untersuchungsakten, sheet 9.
6. All existing photographs of Kusch are in black and white, except a large portrait in the Fireplace Chamber at Germany's naval academy at Mürwik, painted by Rolf Osker Michelmann and exhibited since early 2017. See http://www.marine.de/portal/a/marine (accessed July 19, 2017).
7. Heinrich Walle, *Die Tragödie des Oberleutnants zur See Oskar Kusch* (Stuttgart: Steiner, 1995), 27.
8. Walle, *Tragödie*, 27.
9. Copies of most of these drawings and sketches are in the possession of the author, courtesy of the U-Boot Archiv Cuxhaven-Altenbruch (UACA).
10. Under the Nazis, the Hohenzollern-Gymnasium was renamed in 1938 the "Scharnhorstschule." In 1956 the school received its current name, the "Riesengebirgsschule." See "Schöneberg: Schule feiert ihren 100. Geburtstag" *Berliner Zeitung*, Apr. 11, 2010.
11. "Rudi Pallas," at https://www.scout_o_wiki.de/index.php/Rudi_Pallas (accessed July 13, 2017). See also Klönne, "Du weisst es," 7. Further information on "Schliess Aug und 'Ohr für eine Weil,'" in the blog "Der Erde treu" of Aug. 6, 2012, at https://gastonfebus.wordpress.com/2012/08/06/schliess-aug-und-ohr-fuer-eine-weil/ (accessed July 19, 2017) and at http://www.pbhorizonte.de/bund/geschichte.html (accessed May 4, 2004). Rudolf Kneip, *Jugend der Weimarer Zeit*, 42–44, offers an excellent overview of *bündisch* opposition.
12. Klönne, "Du weisst es," 7.
13. "Rudi Pallas," at https://www.scout-o-wiki.de/index.php/Rudi_Pallas.
14. On the *Südlegion's* ideological origins, see Thun, "Hellas ewig unsere Liebe," 97–100.
15. Klönne, "Du weisst es," 7.
16. "Rudi Pallas," at https://www.scout-o-wiki.de/index.php/Rudi_Pallas.

17. "Du weisst es—keine Zeichen irrten." Full text in Stefan George (Karl August Klein, ed.), *Blätter für die Kunst*, Vol. 6 (1902), 32. For the titles of all 21 *Südlegion* songs in its Liederbuch of 1932, see https://www.scout-o-wiki.de/index.php?title=Lieder_der_S%C3%BCd-Legion_(Liederbuch) (accessed July 17, 2017).
18. "Lieder der Südlegion."
19. Klönne, "Du weisst es," 14.
20. "Schliess Aug' und Ohr für eine Weil," in blog "Der Erde treu" of Aug. 6, 2012, at https://gastonfebus.wordpress.com/2012/08/06/schliess-aug-und-ohr-fuer-eine-weil/ (accessed July 19, 2017).
21. Rudolf Pallas, "Der Ast, auf dem sie sassen . . . ," *Aachener Nachrichten*, Oct. 29, 1949.
22. Pallas.
23. Pallas.
24. Photo reproduced in Klönne, "Du weisst es," 3.
25. Testimony on May 7, 1949, in Hagemann trial, quoted in Walle, *Tragödie*, 23.
26. Kusch's initial interrogation on January 21, 1944, in BA-ZNS, RM 123/K 3140, Ersatzakte, sheet 9.
27. Telegram from Gestapo Berlin, dated Jan. 26, 1944, in BA-ZNS, RM 123/K 3140, Untersuchungsakten, sheet 39.
28. Cited in Walle, *Tragödie*, 25.
29. Rust, "The Case of Oskar Kusch," 1.
30. BA-ZNS, RM 123/K 3140, Untersuchungsakten, sheet 39.
31. Rust, *Naval Officers under Hitler*, 4.
32. Oberkommando der Kriegsmarine (Marinepersonalamt), *Rangliste.*
33. "Crewbuch der Crew 37 A," cited in Walle, *Tragödie*, 28, n28.
34. Rust, *Naval Officers under Hitler*, esp. 4–76.
35. For example, testimony by Friedrich Guggenberger of Crew 34 in interview with author on July 26, 1982. Other veterans of the Dänholm have expressed similar experiences.
36. All three survived. The *Gorch Fock* was claimed by the Soviet Union, sailed for the Red Navy as the *Tovarish*, was later returned to Germany, renamed the *Gorch Fock*, and is now a museum ship in Stralsund. The *Horst Wessel* became the USCGS *Eagle* and still trains U.S. Coast Guard personnel. The *Schlageter* continues to sail as the *Sagres II* for Portugal's navy.
37. Information on Pallas from Pretzel, *NS-Opfer*, 214–15.
38. Janssen testimony on Mar. 7, 1950, in trial against Karl-Heinrich Hagemann. See 1993 memoirs of Dr. Hans Nothdurft, also quoted in Walle, *Tragödie,* 35–36, 75.
39. See *Ranglisten,* 1938 and 1941.
40. Testimony by Heinz Wolff, Paul Otto, and Victor Nonn in Crewbrief Crew 37A No. 2, 1983, 9–12, reproduced in part by Walle, *Tragödie*, 29–31; and Peter (1986), 4.
41. Cited in Walle, *Tragödie*, 86–87.
42. For the equivalent experience of Crew 34, see Rust, *Naval Officers under Hitler*, 64.
43. Hansen, *Execution for Duty*, 11. No source provided.
44. Otto obituary at http://uk-muenchen.de/pdf/otto.pdf (accessed Aug. 2, 2017).
45. Bekker, *Hitler's Naval War*, 35–36.
46. For each service's enduring myths, see Robinson, *The Zeppelin in Combat*; and Hadley, *Count Not the Dead.*
47. English-language literature often refers to *S-Boote* as E-boats or PT-boats.

48. Peillard, *Histoire Generale*, cited at http://www.kbismarck.com/u-boot/ausbild.htm (accessed Aug. 3, 2017).
49. Werner, *Iron Coffins*, 86.
50. For a description and analysis of activities at a ULD, see Mulligan, *Neither Sharks nor Wolves*, 140–44.
51. Meteorological data and analysis by Paul Schlaak, "Das Wetter in Berlin 1933–1945," available at http://www.luise-berlin.de/bms/bmstxt00/0009gesd.htm (accessed Aug. 3, 2017). Both Copenhagen and Stockholm in 1940–41 registered the coldest winter in over a century; see http://www.seatraining.net/image/r/_5_DE.pdf (accessed Aug. 3, 2017).
52. Biographical and academic data based on information supplied by Dagmar Seemel of Humboldt University in Berlin on July 28, 2017, on Foris' student records, on emails from her daughter Claudia van Eyck to author on July 30, Aug. 4 and Oct. 1, 2017, and on contemporary correspondence to and from Inge von Foris transcribed by van Eyck.
53. Letter from Inge von Foris to Heinrich P., June 11, 1944. Copy courtesy of Claudia van Eyck.
54. "Ahnennachweis" of Aug. 23, 1940, in Ms. Foris' student records.
55. Email from Claudia van Eyck to author, dated Oct. 1, 2017.
56. Henry C. Alter, as quoted in Häussermann, *Mein Freund Henry*, 113.
57. Letter from Inge von Foris to Heinrich P., June 11, 1944, quoted above.
58. This notion was expressed by Heinrich P.'s friend Wolfgang H., as quoted by Claudia van Eyck in email to author, July 30, 2017.
59. http://www.uboat.net/boats/patrols/u103.html (accessed Aug. 9, 2017).
60. BA-ZNS, RM 123/K 3140, Untersuchungsakten, sheet 3 (typed copy of the original).
61. Quoted in Hansen, *Execution for Duty*, 15.
62. BA-MA, RM 98/106, *U-103* War Diary, entries for Sept. 12 and 13, 1941.
63. Gerhard Bielig, letter to the editor, *Marineforum* Vol. 1 (No. 2, 1993), 4.
64. "Halt bloss die Klappe!" Information from The Rev. Thomas C. A. Rust in Glücksburg, Germany, on Jan. 9, 2000, referencing a comment from one of his parishioners. The exact date and context of the admonition can no longer be pinpointed.
65. One of the best books on this subject is Gannon, *Black May*.
66. Based on BA-MA, RM 98/106, *U-103* War Diary, and http://www.uboat.net/boats/patrols/patrol_3695.html (accessed Aug. 14, 2017).
67. *U-103* war diary, entry for Feb. 24, 1942. The incident happened in grid square BE 4950, or near 46N, 21W. Readers may use http://www.navalgrid.com/find (accessed Aug. 17, 2017) for German naval grid square conversions to/from latitude/longitude.
68. Data on this mission from BA-MA, RM 98/106, *U-103* War Diary, and http://www.uboat.net/boats/patrols/patrol_3696.html (accessed Aug. 14, 2017).
69. Janssen's testimony on Mar. 7, 1950, in Kiel. Cited in Walle, *Tragödie*, 35–36.
70. Janssen's testimony on Mar. 7, 1950.
71. Wiemer testimony on May 3, 1949, in Kiel. Cited in Walle, *Tragödie*, 37.
72. Wiemer, deposition of Aug. 7, 1948, for use at Hagemann trial.
73. Data from Rohwer, *Axis Submarine Successes;* Niestlé, *German U-Boat Losses*; and http://www.uboat.net/fates/losses/1942/htm (accessed Aug. 15, 2017).
74. Author's calculations from data available on uboat.net.

75. BA-MA, RM 98/106, *U-103* War Diary, entry for Nov. 6, 1942.
76. See http://www.uboat.net/allies/merchants/ships/2492.html (accessed Aug. 15, 2017).
77. http://www.uboat.net/allies/merchants/ships/2509.html (accessed Aug. 15, 2017).
78. Phone call reported in Hansen, *Execution for Duty*, 49–50, without identifying source.
79. Statement of 1949, deposited in U-Boat Archives files.
80. Testimony at trial of Kusch's judge in Kiel, May 3, 1949. Cited in Walle, *Tragödie*, 38.

Chapter 3. Lieutenant Abel

1. Biographical information on Ulrich Abel is based on his widow's responses to author's questionnaire (dated July 14, 2000) and attached documents, including Abel's curriculum vitae of 1937, titled "Lebenslauf," which he submitted in connection with his application for a doctorate in law at the University of Greifswald. Copies in author's files.
2. Herta Abel response to questionnaire, including "Lebenslauf."
3. Letter to Abel from the nautical-technical division of the Norddeutscher Lloyd [1932], quoted in Herta Abel response to questionnaire, item 1, p. 2.
4. Herta Abel response to questionnaire, item 1.
5. When Abel proposed marriage to his future wife in 1936, he immediately cautioned her he might decide to resume his seafaring career if he failed his bar exams. Herta Abel response to questionnaire, item 2, p. 3.
6. In contrast to Anglo-American legal and social practice, in Germany a doctorate in law based on a strenuous dissertation allows its holder to be officially called "Dr." or "Dr. jur.," just as those who complete a dissertation in the humanities can add "Dr." or "Dr. phil." or "Ph.D." to their names. All service records invariably refer to Lieutenant Dr. Ulrich Abel.
7. See "Gutachten" of Abel's supervising professor, quoted in Herta Abel response to questionnaire, item 4, p. 9.
8. Letter quoted in Herta Abel response to questionnaire, item 1, p. 4.
9. For Abel's religious classification see BA-ZNS, RM 123/K 3140, Untersuchungsakten, sheets 2a and 32.
10. Herta Abel response to questionnaire, item 2, p. 5; item 3, p. 8.
11. Herta Abel, item 3, p. 7.
12. Herta Abel, item 6, p. 11.
13. Herta Abel, item 2, p. 5.
14. Herta Abel, item 2, p. 6.
15. Herta Abel, item 3, p. 7.
16. Treaty of Versailles, Article 236, Annex III.
17. Herta Abel response to questionnaire, item 3, p. 7.
18. Rust, *Naval Officers under Hitler*, 54.
19. For the reaction of the shipping industry to the Nazi seizure of power, consult Peter Müller, "Seebeckwerft 1933–1945" at http://werften.fischtown.de/ssw5.html (accessed July 11, 2002).
20. Nazi Party (NSDAP) records pertaining to Ulrich Abel can be accessed on NARA Accessioned Microfilms A3340-MFOK-roll A0001, frame 1742, and A3340-PK-roll V002, frames 0524–0536, at the National Archives and Records Administration in

Washington, DC, and Suitland, MD. The author is grateful to Dr. Timothy Mulligan, since retired from NARA, for supplying the information in a communication on Apr. 25, 2007.

21. Herta Abel response to questionnaire, item 3, pp. 7–8.
22. Dr. med. habil. Hans Nothdurft, Documents and Recollections, U-Boat Archives (1993), 22; and Hansen, *Execution for Duty*, 49–50, repeat this claim without supporting evidence. For Mrs. Abel's view, see her response to questionnaire, item 3, p. 7.
23. Certificate of the Reichs-Justizprüfkammer, cited in Herta Abel response to questionnaire, item 4, p. 9.
24. Herta Abel response to questionnaire, item 13, p. 24; and postcard from her to author on July 15, 2000. Abel's position equaled that of a district judge in the United States.
25. For the operations of the flotilla see BA-MA RM 69/128, K.T.B. der 17. Minensuch-Flottille vom 22.9.39—31.12.1940, and subsequent volumes.
26. Herta Abel response to questionnaire, item 1, p. 4.
27. BA-MA, RM 17/84, "Offizierbestandsnachweisung 17. Minensuchflottille."
28. Herta Abel response to questionnaire, item 2, p. 6.
29. All references to the flotilla's and Abel's activities are based on its war diaries, especially BA-MA, RM 69/396 through RM 69/399.
30. BA-MA, RM 69/398, "Stellungnahme des Admiral Nordmeer zum K.T.B. der 15. M.S. Fl. für die Zeit v. 15.—31.12.1941."
31. BA-MA, RM 69/399, War Diary, 15th Minesweeper Flotilla, Jan. 1 to Sept. 30, 1942.
32. Details from War Diary Fifteenth Minesweeper Flotilla, including Abel's "Gefechtsbericht M 1503 über die Vernichtung eines feindlichen U-Bootes am 18.2.1942 im Porsangerfjord." Supplemental information on *ShCh-403* from http://uboat.net/allies/warships/ship/5074.html (accessed Aug. 22, 2017). See also Paterson (2016), chapter 4.
33. "Stellungnahme, Flo. Chef," attached to BA-MA, RM 69/399, K.T.B. 15. M.S. Fl.
34. Stellungnahme.
35. Herta Abel response to questionnaire, item 5, p. 10.

Chapter 4. First Patrol

1. See BA-MA, RM 98/358, *U-154* war diary, esp. entry for July 19, 1942.
2. Data from http://www.ubootarchiv.de/ubootwiki/index.php/U_154 and http://www.uboat.net/boats/u154.htm (accessed Aug. 25, 2017).
3. Letter of Hans Janker, *U-154*'s chief radio operator on Kusch's first patrol, to Kusch's father, dated Aug. 15, 1946. Cited in Heinrich Walle, *Die Tragödie des Oberleutnants zur See Oskar Kusch* (Stuttgart: Steiner, 1995), 46–49.
4. Episode related in Hansen, *Execution for Duty*, 50–51. No source provided.
5. Data from http://www.ww2technik.de/dsub_booteII.htm (accessed Aug. 25, 2017).
6. Janker letter to Kusch's father.
7. http://www.landgasthof-druschel.de/ (accessed Aug. 25, 2017).
8. Nothdurft comment in his UACA file.
9. *Rangliste 1941*, 134.
10. Hellmuth Kirchammer, cited in Walle, *Tragödie*, 53.
11. Lüdmann letter to the editor of the *Marineforum*, No. 12/1996, 27.

12. Complete list of every crewmember assigned to *U-154* available at http://historisches-marinearchiv.de/projekte/crewlisten/ww2/eingabe.php (accessed Aug. 28, 2017).
13. Janker letter to Kusch's father.
14. BA-ZNS, RM 123/K 3140, Untersuchungsakten, sheet 8.
15. Walle, *Tragödie,* 82–83.
16. Isensee testimony of May 3, 1949. Cited in Walle, *Tragödie*, 50.
17. BA-ZNS, RM 123/K 3140, Untersuchungsakten, sheet 1.
18. BA-ZNS, RM 123/K 3140, Untersuchungsakten, sheets 12–13.
19. BA-ZNS, RM 123/K 3140, Untersuchungsakten, sheet 7.
20. Léonce Peillard, *Histoire Generale de la Guerre Sous-Marine 1939–1945*, cited at http://www.kbismarck.com/u-boot/uausbild.htm (accessed Aug. 28, 2017).
21. Author's calculations based on information available on Uboat.net.
22. See Gannon, *Black May*.
23. McCue, *U-Boats in the Bay of Biscay*, 25–27.
24. For a complete (though amateurish) translation into English of *U-154*'s war diary on this patrol, see http://uboatarchive.net/U-154/KTB154-5.htm (accessed Aug. 29, 2017). The German original is BA-MA, RM 98/358. Unless indicated otherwise, the latter has been used to retrace Kusch's patrol.
25. Janker letter to Kusch's father.
26. Janker letter to Kusch's father.
27. Isensee testimony, cited in Walle, *Tragödie*, 50.
28. Janker letter to Kusch's father.
29. Walle, *Tragödie,* 48.
30. Peter, appendix A.
31. Lüdmann letter to the editor of the *Marineforum,* no. 12 (1996), 26–27.
32. Isensee testimony quoted in Walle, *Tragödie*, 50–51.
33. Kuhlmann statement in *Marineforum,* no. 10 (1996), 34.
34. BA-ZNS, RM 123/K 3140, Untersuchungsakten, sheets 33–34.
35. Correct version at http://www.ubootarchiv.de/ubootwiki/index.php/U_455 (accessed Sept. 13, 2017).
36. Janker letter to Kusch's father.
37. Janker letter to Kusch's father.
38. For a discussion of maximal diving depths, see http://www.forum-marinearchiv.de/smf/index.php/topic,18889.0.html (accessed Sept. 2, 2017). The theoretical or calculated depth at which a boat stood to implode because of the external water pressure was assumed to be near 2A + 50m for a Type IX boat, but no skipper or engineer would be so foolish or suicidal as to test this assumption.
39. Janker letter to Kusch's father.
40. *U-154* war diary, entry for 1405 on May 28, 1943.
41. *U-154* war diary, entry for 0056 on May 30, 1943.
42. Data from http://www.uboat.net/allies/merchants (accessed Sept. 2, 2017).
43. Rahn, *Deutsche Marinen im Wandel*, 366.
44. Janker letter to Kusch's father.
45. BA-ZNS, RM 123/K 3140, Untersuchungsakten, sheets 1–2, item 3.
46. See http://ww2troopships.com/crossings/1943.htm (accessed Sept. 3, 2017).

47. Walle, *Tragödie*, 61.
48. http://www.ubootarchiv.de/ubootwiki/index.php/U_126 (accessed Sept. 5, 2017).
49. Isensee testimony in Walle, *Tragödie*, 61.
50. Isensee.
51. Letter dated Sept. 22, 1943, cited in Walle, *Tragödie*, 300–301.
52. BA-MA RM 98/358, *U-154* War Diary.
53. BA-ZNS RM 123/K 3140, Untersuchungsakten, sheet 3, dated Sept. 25, 1943.
54. Hansen, *Execution for Duty*, 62.
55. See Janker's letter and Isensee's testimony, cited in Walle, *Tragödie*, 49–50.
56. Herta Abel response to author questionnaire, item 7, p. 12.
57. BA-ZNS, RM 123/K 3140, Untersuchungsakten, sheet 2a.
58. Herta Abel response to author questionnaire, pp. 25–26.
59. Herta Abel, pp. 25–26.
60. Herta Abel, p. 6.
61. Walle, *Tragödie*, 62.
62. BA-MA, RM 98/358.
63. Letter to Roland.
64. See Inge von Foris' student file at Humboldt University, Berlin.
65. Correspondence cited in email Claudia van Eyck to author, Aug. 4, 2017.
66. Email, Claudia van Eyck to author, July 30, 2017.
67. See Rust, *Naval Officers under Hitler*, 73–74.
68. Inge von Foris' "Ahnennachweis," dated Aug. 23, 1940, in her student file.
69. Nothdurft affidavit of June 12, 1946, cited in Walle, *Tragödie*, 337.
70. Letter to Roland.
71. Letter to Roland; Walle's commentary.
72. Description based on Herta Abel response to questionnaire, item 7, pp. 13–15.
73. Herta Abel, pp. 13–14.
74. Herta Abel, p. 14.
75. Herta Abel, p. 15.
76. Herta Abel, p. 15.

Chapter 5. Second Patrol

1. Funke testimony of January 20, 1944, in BA-ZNS, RM 123/K 3140, Untersuchungsakten, sheets 7–10. See also Hansen, *Execution for Duty*, 136.
2. Data from historisches-marinearchiv.de/projekte/crewlisten/ww2/eingabe.php and http://uk-muenchen.de/pdf/kirchammer.pdf (both accessed Sept. 14, 2017).
3. Nothdurft affidavit, dated June 12, 1946, at UACA; also quoted in Heinrich Walle, *Die Tragödie des Oberleutnants zur See Oskar Kusch* (Stuttgart: Steiner, 1985), 333.
4. This report is attached to *U-154*'s war diary at BA-MA, RM 98/358, and reproduced in its entirety and with an addendum in Walle, *Tragödie*, 312–32.
5. Nothdurft affidavit; also quoted in Walle, *Tragödie*, 333.
6. *U-154* war diary, entry for Oct. 22, 1943.
7. Information from Dr. Nothdurft's medical report.
8. See http://www.convoyweb.org.uk/tj/index.html (accessed Sept. 18, 2017).

9. Nothdurft, "Mein schicksalhaftes," also quoted in Walle, *Tragödie*, 77–78.
10. BA-ZNS, RM 123/K 3140, Untersuchungsakten, sheets 7–10.
11. BA-ZNS, RM 123/K 3140, Untersuchungsakten, sheet 13.
12. Nothdurft, "Mein schicksalhaftes," also quoted in Walle, *Tragödie*, 80.
13. *U-154* war diary, entries for Nov. 3, 1943.
14. Kuhlmann statement in *Marineforum* 10 (1996), 34.
15. Letter, Kurt Isensee to Kusch's father of Sept. 16, 1946, quoted in Walle, *Tragödie,* 69–70.
16. Letter, Kurt Isensee.
17. Description contained in a letter Jahn wrote to his father who, in turn, shared it with Kusch's father after the war, who in turn included it in a letter to the Prosecutor's Office at the District Court in Kiel on Dec. 12, 1946. Here cited from Walle, *Tragödie*, 70.
18. BA-ZNS, RM 123/K 3140, Untersuchungsakten, sheets 7–10.
19. Nothdurft, also quoted in Walle, *Tragödie*, 79.
20. Attached to war diary, BA-MA, RM 98/358.
21. Nothdurft, 1946 affidavit at UACA, also cited in Walle, *Tragödie*, 71–72.
22. Nothdurft (1993), also cited in Walle, *Tragödie*, 78–79.
23. http://www.convoyweb.org.uk/tj/index.html (accessed Sept. 21, 2017).
24. Nothdurft (1993), also quoted in Walle, *Tragödie*, 79.
25. Baumann and Koch, "Was damals Recht war," 145.
26. *Reichsgesetzblatt, I*, 1455–57. Author's translation.
27. *Cassell's German Dictionary* (New York: Macmillan, 1972), 712, 742.
28. Author's translation. See also Hensle (2003), *passim.*
29. Paragraph 2. Author's translation.
30. Böske, *Denunziationen in der Zeit*, 59.
31. Böske, 57. Walle, *Tragödie,* 91, is mistaken when he implies the draft decree actually became law. It did not.
32. BA-MA, RM 26/73, OKM, "Erlass gegen die Kritiksucht und Meckerei," Sept. 9, 1943.
33. Translation partially adapted from Hansen, *Execution for Duty*, 78.
34. Nothdurft (1946); also quoted in Walle, *Tragödie*, 333–34.
35. Compare with Walle, *Tragödie*, 82.
36. Cited in Walle, *Tragödie*, 48.
37. Nothdurft (1993), also cited in Walle, *Tragödie*, 73–74.
38. Nothdurft (1946); also cited in Walle, *Tragödie*, 334–35.
39. See chapter 3.
40. Nothdurft (1993); also in Walle, *Tragödie*, 75–76.
41. Episode cited from Teddy Suhren, *Teddy Suhren, Ace of Aces*, 162–64. Compare with Peter (1986), appendix B.
42. See BA-ZNS, RM 123/K 3140, Bordurteil, in Untersuchungsakten, sheets 40–49.
43. See http://iopscience.iop.org/article/10.1086/125539/pdf (accessed Sept. 25, 2017).
44. Nothdurft (1993), quoted in Walle, *Tragödie*, 73.
45. See http://uboat.net/articles/35.html (accessed Sept. 26, 2017).
46. Nothdurft (1993); also in Walle, *Tragödie*, 72.
47. Nothdurft (1946); also in Walle, *Tragödie*, 335.
48. Hansen, *Execution for Duty*, 79.
49. BA-MA, RM 98/358, entry for Nov. 29, 1943.

50. Abel's official report at BA-ZNS, RM 123/K 3140, Ersatzakte, sheets 1–2.
51. Erna Brockmann's testimony of May 7, 1949. Cited in Walle, *Tragödie*, 84.
52. Elisabeth Schweizer and Ulli Jochum of its tourism office, as well as Dr. Herbert Sauerwein of Lech, Austria, provided detailed information about Zürs and its history.
53. Nothdurft (1946); also in Walle, *Tragödie*, 336.
54. *U-154* war diary, entry for Jan. 10, 1944.
55. Nothdurft (1946); also in Walle, *Tragödie*, 336.
56. Walle, *Tragödie*, 337.

Chapter 6. The Report

1. BA-ZNS, RM 123/K 3140, Untersuchungsakten, sheets 1–2.
2. BA-ZNS, RM 123/K 3140, Untersuchungsakten, sheet 28.
3. Cited in Nothdurft (1946); also reproduced in Heinrich Walle, *Die Tragödie des Oberleutnants zur See* (Stuttgart: Steiner, 1995), 336–37.
4. Herta Abel response to author questionnaire, item 4, p. 9.
5. Herta Abel, item 11, pp. 20–21.
6. Herta Abel, item 11, p. 22.
7. Peter C. Hansen, *Execution for Duty: The Life, Trial and Murder of a U-boat Captain* (Barnsley, UK: Pen & Sword Books, 2005), 96.
8. Peter, "Wider besseres Wissen," 11.
9. Rösing testimony at Hagemann trial in May 1949, cited in Walle, *Tragödie*, 95.
10. For a further discussion of this system and its potential for ideological corruption, consult Walle, *Tragödie*, 95–98; and Hansen, *Execution for Duty*, 96–99. Historical context in Manfred Messerschmidt, *Die Wehrmachtjustiz 1933–1945* (Paderborn: Schöningh, 2005) and Gerhard Paul, *Landunter: Schleswig-Holstein und das Hakenkreuz* (Münster: Westfälisches Dampfboot, 2001).
11. Walle, *Tragödie*, 97.
12. Meinert testimony on Oct. 11, 1946. Cited in Walle, *Tragödie*, 243.
13. Rösing testimony at Hagemann trial on May 12, 1949; cited in Walle, 243. See also RM 31/3345, Marinechefrichter Ostsee, Generalakten betr. Beiträge zur Auslegung des Para 5 KSSVO, Band 1.
14. Walle, *Tragödie*, 121.
15. Dr. Hans-Egon Breinig's testimony at Hagemann trial, cited in Walle, 103.
16. BA-ZNS, RM 123/K 3140, Untersuchungsakten, "Haftbefehl," sheet 5.
17. Undated testimony at the trial of Kusch's judge; cited in Walle, *Tragödie*, 102.
18. Breinig's career information from Peter, "Wider besseres Wissen," 9.
19. Breinig testimony as above; see Walle, *Tragödie*, 102.
20. Breinig testimony, 103.
21. Funke's deposition in BA-ZNS, RM 123/K 3140, Untersuchungsakten, sheets 7–9.
22. Funke's deposition, sheets 9–10.
23. Wiemer testimony on Aug. 7, 1948, in Hagemann trial, cited in Walle, *Tragödie*, 104.
24. Kuhlmann statement reproduced by "M-54842" on May 13, 2014, in blog contribution No. 8 under "Re: 70. Todestag von Oblt. z. S. Oskar Kusch" under http://forum-marine-archiv.de/smf/index.php?topic=21798.0 (accessed Oct. 30, 2017).

25. Letter from Isensee to Kusch's father of Sept. 16, 1946. Cited in Walle, *Tragödie*, 94.
26. BA-ZNS, RM 123/K 3140, Handakten, sheet 6.
27. BA-ZNS, RM 123/K 3140, entire deposition available in Untersuchungsakten, sheets 12–13.
28. Otto Strelow had been chief engineer when Kusch served as II.W.O. on *U-103*.
29. BA-ZNS, RM 123/K 3140, Untersuchungsakten, sheet 20. Both Peter (1986), 8, and Walle, *Tragödie*, 103, list Dittmers incorrectly as a member of Crew 30. Compare with *Rangliste* 1941.
30. Letter Werner Winter to Rear Admiral Bernhard Rogge, dated Dec. 14, 1965, cited at http://www.apt-holtenau.de/holtenau-info/history/kusch-oskar.htm (accessed Oct. 19, 2017).
31. Letter Winter to Rogge.
32. BA-ZNS, RM 123/K 3140, Untersuchungsakten, sheet 24.
33. Biographical data from Peter, "Wider besseres Wissen," 8; and Hagemann's deposition before the district court in Kiel on Sept. 24, 1946, cited in Walle, *Tragödie*, 100–101.
34. Testimony of Paul Becker, Hans-Boie Kröger, and Otto Kranzbühler cited or summarized in Walle, *Tragödie*, 101, from postwar trials against Hagemann.
35. Personnel data from http://www.uboat.net and http://historisches-marinearchiv.de/projekte/crewlisten (accessed Oct. 10, 2017).
36. Hansen, *Execution for Duty*, 101, claims the promotion "was due and already in the pipeline." No source provided.
37. Wiemer testimony of Aug. 7, 1948, in Hagemann trial; cited in Walle, *Tragödie*, 104.
38. Berger testimony at Hagemann trial, May 7, 1946; see Walle, *Tragödie*, 104.
39. Berger testimony and testimony by Gerhard Meyer-Grieben recorded as stenographic copy taken on Sept. 20, 1950, in trial against Hagemann; cited in Walle, *Tragödie*, 105.
40. Berger and Meyer-Grieben testimony, reproduced in Walle, *Tragödie*, 104–5. For a history of Meyer-Grieben's law firm, see his son's website at http://www.m-g-vh.de/ (accessed Oct. 10, 2017).
41. Gerhard Meyer-Grieben to Robert W. Kempner, Apr. 4, 1946. See Walle, *Tragödie*, 100.
42. For a further discussion of this point, see Walle, 105.
43. BA-ZNS, RM 123/K 3140, Untersuchungsakten, sheet 16.
44. BA-ZNS, RM 123/K 3140, sheet 25.
45. BA-ZNS, RM 123/K 3140.
46. BA-ZNS, RM 123/K 3140, sheet 21, and Handakten, Akte 085, "Einlieferungsbestätingung."
47. BA-ZNS, RM 123/K 3140, Untersuchungsakten, sheet 37.
48. Meyer-Grieben testimony at Hagemann trial, Sept. 20, 1950, in Walle, *Tragödie*, 105–6.
49. Berger testimony at Hagemann trial, May 7, 1949, cited in Walle, 106.
50. Nothdurft affidavit of June 12, 1946.
51. Franken's brief, dated Jan. 25, 1944, is contained in BA-ZNS, RM 123/K 3140, Untersuchungsakten, sheet 30.
52. Positions, distances, and bearings calculated from http://uboatarchive.net/U-154/KTB154-5.htm (entry for 1200 on March 26, 1943); http://www.navalgrid.com/ and https://www1.baylor.edu/Navigator (all accessed Oct. 12, 2017).
53. BA-ZNS, RM 123/K 3140, Untersuchungsakten, "Aktenvermerk," sheet 51.
54. BA-ZNS, RM 123/K 3140, Untersuchungsakten, "Anklageverfügung," sheet 30.

Chapter 7. The Trial

1. http://www.historynet.com/time-travel-kiel.htm (accessed Oct. 16, 2017).
2. Data from Sievert, *Kiel einst und jetzt*, 10.
3. Lehmann, "Der Streit um Forsteck," 127–44.
4. Climate data courtesy of Petra Grasse of the Institute for Meteorology of the Free University of Berlin in fax to author on Mar. 2, 2001.
5. Shorthand copy of Meyer-Grieben's testimony at Hagemann trials on May 12, 1949, and Sept. 20, 1950, as cited in Walle, *Die Tragödie des Oberleutnants zur See Oskar Kusch* (Stuttgart: Steiner, 1995), 117.
6. On this point see especially Walle, *Tragödie*, 114–25.
7. Walle, *Tragödie*, 115.
8. Gruchmann, "Ausgewählte Dokumente," 448.
9. For one such reinterpretation, see BA-MA, RM 31/3345, Marinechefrichter Ostsee, Generalakten betr. Beiträge zur Auslegung des Para 5 KSSVO, Band I, sheets 20–21, dated Mar. 16, 1940.
10. "Vierte Verordnung zur Ergänzung der Kriegssonderstrafrechtsverordung vom 31. März 1943," *Reichsgerichtsblatt* 1943, I, 74. Author's translation.
11. Wüllner, *Die NS-Militärjustiz*, 513.
12. Wüllner, 543.
13. Gruchmann, "Ausgewählte Dokumente," 458.
14. Meyer-Grieben at Hagemann trial, May 3, 1949; cited in Walle, *Tragödie,* 116.
15. Meyer-Grieben testimony of Aug. 9, 1946, cited in Walle, *Tragödie*, 116.
16. Testimony in denazification proceedings involving Ernst Meinert, dated Aug. 5, 1946. Cited in Walle, *Tragödie*, 115.
17. Meyer-Grieben testimony of Sept. 20, 1950, as cited in Walle, *Tragödie*, 121.
18. Walle, *Tragödie*, 123.
19. Comments by Harald Jeppener-Haltenhoff (Crew 31) and Rüdiger Burchards (Crew 34) who attended the trial. Cited in Walle, *Tragödie*, 107.
20. Unless indicated otherwise, all references to the trial are based on its official minutes in BA-ZNS, RM 123/K 3140, Untersuchungsakten, sheets 31–39.
21. Berger testimony at Hagemann trial on May 7, 1949, in Walle, *Tragödie*, 113.
22. Nothdurft affidavit of June 12, 1946, cited in Walle, *Tragödie*, 338–39.
23. Meyer-Grieben affidavit of Aug. 9, 1946, before the prosecutor of the Kiel District Court, cited in Walle, *Tragödie*, 109.
24. Meyer-Grieben letter to the public prosecutor at Heidelberg dated May 27, 1947. Cited in Walle, *Tragödie*, 110.
25. BA-ZNS, RM 123/K 3140, Untersuchungsakten, sheet 39.
26. Statement quoted at http://www.apt-holtenau.de/holtenau-info/history/kusch-oskar.htm (accessed Oct. 19, 2017).
27. Nothdurft affidavit of June 6, 1946, also cited in Walle, *Tragödie*, 111.
28. Meyer-Grieben to R.W. Kemper, Apr. 11, 1946. Cited in Walle, *Tragödie*, 111.
29. Meyer-Grieben testimony of May 3, 1949. Cited in Walle, *Tragödie*, 112.
30. Berger testimony of May 12, 1948; reproduced in Walle, *Tragödie*, 136.
31. Berger testimony of May 5, 1949. Cited in Walle, *Tragödie*, 112.

32. Meyer-Grieben testimony, Sept. 20, 1950. Cited in Walle, *Tragödie*, 123.
33. Meyer-Grieben testimony of May 3, 1949. Cited in Walle, *Tragödie*, 122.
34. Walle, *Tragödie*, 124.
35. Leverenz, "Der Begriff der Öffentlichkeit," 411, 432–33.
36. Leverenz, 432.
37. Berger at Hagemann trial, May 7, 1949, cited by Walle, *Tragödie,* 112–13.
38. Werner Winter's letter to Kusch's father, dated Aug. 8, 1946; and Breinig testimony in Hagemann trial, undated, cited in Walle, *Tragödie*, 125.
39. Dittmers' testimony before state prosecutor Dr. Paul Thamm in Kiel, Oct. 24, 1946, cited in Walle, *Tragödie*, 129.
40. Walle, *Tragödie*, 129–30.
41. District Court Kiel, explanation of verdict against Hagemann on Sept. 25, 1950; cited by Walle, *Tragödie*, 130.
42. Details at http://kriegsmarinemsw.blogspot.com/2015/06/sailors-in-berlin.html (accessed Oct. 25, 2017). See also Kieschnick, *Stralsund 1945*, entries for Apr. 25 and 26, 1945. Further commentary in Graul and Kämpf, eds., *Dieter Hartwig*, 89–90.
43. Westphalen's notes, referenced in Peter, "Wider besseres Wissen," 13.
44. Excerpts from Westphalen's testimony in Hagemann case of Apr. 21, 1948, and May 3, 1949, respectively, and explanation of verdict on Sept. 25, 1950. Cited in Walle, *Tragödie*, 130–32.
45. Walle, *Tragödie*.
46. Walle, *Tragödie*, 132.
47. Cited from Hartwig, *Grossadmiral Karl Dönitz*, 404–7. In his critical Dönitz biography Hartwig reprints and analyzes most of the grand admiral's wartime speeches and directives in detail, emphasizing their fiercely ideological and loyalist diction, their constant glorification of Hitler's person, their anti-Semitic character, and their cold and mindless "honor-above-life" thrust, especially in Chapter XI and the appendices.
48. Harald Jeppener-Haltenhoff and Eberhard Wallrodt in Peter, "Wider besseres Wissen," 13.
49. Based on BA-ZNS, RM 123/K 3140, Untersuchungsakten, sheets 40–49.
50. Verdict justification, dated Jan. 29, 1944, in Kusch's trial file.
51. Cited in Messerschmidt and Wüllner, *Die Wehrmachtjustiz 1933–1945*, 527.

Chapter 8. Agony

1. BA-MA, RM 31/3354, Marineoberkriegsgerichtsrat für den Ostseebereich, General-Akten: Gerichtsgebäude und Ausstattung, begonnen 1. Januar 1941, sheet 45: Belegung des M.U.G. Kiel Wik, Tirpitzstr.
2. Heinrich Walle, *Die Tragödie des Oberleutnants zur See Oskar Kusch* (Stuttgart: Steiner, 1995), 145.
3. Meinert testimony on Oct. 11, 1946, in Kiel District Court, in Walle, *Tragödie*, 145.
4. Karl-Heinz Wiemer's testimony before Bremen Investigative Police on Aug. 25, 1947. Cited in Walle, *Tragödie*, 144–45.
5. Kusch's drawing, dated Mar. 17, 1944, is titled "Lebenslauf in Figurinen."
6. Meinert testimony in Kiel District Court, Aug. 8, 1946; cited in Walle, *Tragödie*, 146–47.

7. BA-MA, RM 31/3358, Marinestation der Ostsee, "Fliegerschäden durch Bombenangriffe, März 1943–April 1945," sheet 28.
8. http://www.balsi.de/Weltkrieg/Waffen/Schiffe/ubootbegleitschiffwassner.htm (accessed Oct. 16, 2017).
9. Information from Mr. Gerd Stolz, Kiel, in email message of Jan. 2, 2006.
10. Hedwig Sievert, *Kiel einst und jetzt* (Kiel: Mühlau, 1964), 1.
11. BA-MA, RM 31/3358, "Fliegerschäden," sheet 32.
12. Pictures taken in 2000 by Erhard Ohlhoff, Kiel. Copies in author's files.
13. The drawings that show his cell best are "Zelle 107, M.U.G. mit Insasse" of Mar. 15, 1944, and "M.U.G. Kiel, Skizze meiner Zelle" of Apr. 4, 1944.
14. BA-ZNS, RM 123/K 3140, Zusatzakten, "Aktenvermerk," sheet 67 (penciled sheet number partially illegible), dated Jan. 30, 1944, and signed by Hagemann on board the *Erwin Wassner*.
15. BA-ZNS, RM 123/K 3140, Untersuchungsakten, sheet 50.
16. BA-ZNS, RM 123/K 3140, Handakten, "Verfügung," sheet 13 (red), dated Jan. 6, 1944, and initialed by Breinig in Angers.
17. Walle, *Tragödie*, 243.
18. BA-ZNS, RM 123/K 3140, Handakten, "Verfügung," sheet 13 (red), dated Jan. 6, 1944, second section.
19. Peter, "Wider besseres Wissen," 13.
20. Meyer-Grieben testimony in Hagemann trial, Sept. 9, 1950. Reproduced in Walle, *Tragödie*, 134–35.
21. Letter of Gollnitz's partner Günther Adler to Meyer-Grieben of Jan. 8, 1947, referenced in Walle, *Tragödie*, 135.
22. Wiemer to Kusch's father, Apr. 14, 1946, cited in Walle, *Tragödie*, 136–37.
23. Erwin Rau to Robert Hering, Jan. 4, 1984; cited in Peter, "Wider besseres Wissen," 11.
24. Winter testimony in Kiel District Court, Dec. 2, 1947. See Walle, *Tragödie*, 135.
25. See Rolf Steinhaus, *Soldat, Diplomat* (Herford: Köhler, 1983), 63.
26. Berger testimony on Dec. 15, 1947, in Kiel District Court; cited in Walle, *Tragödie*, 136.
27. Kühns-Bernsau testimony in Kiel District Court, Dec. 15, 1947. Cited by Walle, *Tragödie*, 139–40.
28. BA-ZNS, RM 123/K 3140, Handakten, sheets 2–3 (documents 064–065), "Liste der Personen, die mit dem Oblt. z. See Kusch schriftlich in Verbindung getreten sind."
29. Oskar Kusch to his father, dated Feb. 2, 1944, cited in Walle, *Tragödie*, 382.
30. BA-ZNS, RM 123/K 3140, Handakten, document 27.
31. BA-ZNS, RM 123/K 3140, document 25.
32. BA-ZNS, RM 123/K 3140, document 26.
33. BA-ZNS, RM 123/K 3140, document 18.
34. BA-ZNS, RM 123/K 3140, Handakten, sheet 19 (red), document No. 110.
35. BA-ZNS, RM 123/K 3140, document 29 and sheet 20 (red), numbered as document No. 111.
36. Meyer-Grieben testimony on Apr. 11, 1946. Cited in Walle, *Tragödie*, 144.
37. Letter dated Apr. 4, 1946. Quoted in Walle, *Tragödie*, 143–44.
38. BA-ZNS, RM 123/K 3140, Handakten, sheet 22.
39. BA-ZNS, RM 123/K 3140, Handakten, sheet 29.
40. BA-ZNS, RM 123/K 3140, Handakten, sheet 32, document No. 119.

41. BA-ZNS, RM 123/K 3140, sheet 43, document 137.
42. BA-ZNS, RM 123/K 3140, Untersuchungsakten, sheet 59.
43. Since 1993 copies of the sketches have been deposited in Folder "*U-154*" at the U-Boat Archives in Cuxhaven-Altenbruch.
44. Meyer-Grieben at Hagemann trial, May 12, 1949. Also cited in Walle, *Tragödie*, 133.
45. Rudolphi testimony at Hagemann trial, May 12, 1949.
46. BA-MA, N 623/v. 6, Sieber papers, "Notiz Dönitz."
47. Dönitz to Kranzbühler, cited in Walle, *Tragödie*, 138; and Hartwig, *Grossadmiral Karl Dönitz*, 145.
48. Cited from Graul and Kämpf, 88. Author's translation.
49. See BA-ZNS, RM 123/K 3140, Handakten, sheet 35.
50. BA-MA, K12–1/136, OKM-MR/AMA 2/II No. 02818, also in Walle, *Tragödie*, 147–48.
51. BA-ZNS, RM 123/K 3140, Untersuchungsakten, "Verfügung," sheet 54.
52. BA-ZNS, RM 123/K 3140, sheet 55.

Chapter 9. El Doce de Mayo

1. Copy in Folder "U-154" at U-Boat Archives at Cuxhaven and in author's files.
2. "Merkblatt für die Unterbringung zum Tode Verurteilter und die Vollstreckung von Todesstrafen" (1941), cited in http://www.apt-holtenau.de/holtenau-info/history/marineschiessplatz.htm and http://docplayer.org/54551186-Reichseigenes-schuhwerk-ist-dem-verurteilten-vorher-auszuziehen-die-schiessanlage-in-alten-holz-bei-kiel-als-hinrichtungsstaette.html (both accessed Nov. 13, 2017).
3. Further details in Marco Dräger, *Deserteur-Denkmäler in der Geschichtskultur der Bundesrepublik Deutschland,* rev. ed. (Frankfurt/Main: Lang, 2017), 5–6.
4. BA-ZNS, RM 123/K 3140, Handakten, sheet 28.
5. Letter contained in Oskarheinz Kusch's papers, quoted in Heinrich Walle, *Die Tragödie des Oberleutnants zur See Oskar Kusch* (Stuttgart: Steiner, 1995), 390–91. "Mrs. Teger's" identity and relation to the Kusch family could not be ascertained.
6. BA-ZNS, RM 123/K 3140, Untersuchungakten, sheet 55.
7. Meyer-Grieben testimony in Hagemann trial on May 3, 1949. See Walle, *Tragödie*, 122.
8. https://www.timeanddate.com/sun/germany/kiel?month=5&year=1944 (accessed Nov. 14, 2017).
9. Meteorological information based on "Täglicher Wetterbericht des Deutschen Reichswetterdienstes, Herausgegeben von der Deutschen Seewetterwarte Hamburg," Jahrgang 69, Nr. 113, Freitag, 12. Mai 1944, 1–3. Charts and data tables courtesy of Ms. Petra Grasse and Mr. Manfred Wegener, Institut für Meteorologie, Free University Berlin, Mar. 21, 2001.
10. Further details in Bert Morio, "Der Marineschiessplatz Holtenau" at www.apt-holtenau.de/holtenau-info/history/marineschiessplatz.htm (accessed Nov. 14, 2017).
11. Gerhard Paul, *Landunter: Schleswig-Holstein und das Hakenkreuz* (Münster: Westfälisches Dampfboot, 2001), 269, 273.
12. Paul, 269, 273.

13. BA-ZNS, RM 123/K 3140, Untersuchungsakten, sheet 56. Both Walle (1995) and Hansen (2005) specify that Bloebaum pronounced Kusch dead at 06:37, but a close inspection of the handwritten insertion on the document appears to indicate "06:34."

Chapter 10. Wakes

1. https://uboat.net/boats/u193.htm (accessed. Nov. 16, 2017).
2. Axel Niestlé, *German U-Boat Losses During World War II: Details of Destruction* (Annapolis, MD: Naval Institute Press, 1998), 128, 237.
3. Herta Abel's response to author questionnaire, item 13, p. 24.
4. A complete copy of this correspondence is in the author's files.
5. *Ostsee-Zeitung*, June 16, 2012.
6. Y'Blood, *Hunter-Killer*, 162–63.
7. Letter in author's files courtesy of Claudia van Eyck.
8. Foris' student records. Pinder quotation from "Bericht Pinder," dated Apr. 11, 1945.
9. https://www.archaeologie.hu-berlin.de/de/lehrbereich_klarcho/winckelmann/institut/institutsgeschichte (accessed Nov. 18, 2017).
10. Email Claudia van Eyck to author, July 30, 2017.
11. Information based on Ernst Häussermann, *Mein Freund Henry: Dokumentarroman* (Vienna: Zsolnay, 1983), 106–17.
12. http://www.imdb.com/name/nm0886870/bio (accessed Nov. 19, 2017).
13. http://www.imdb.com/name/nm0285864/bio?ref_=nm_ov_bio_sm (accessed Nov. 20, 2017).
14. Email Claudia van Eyck to author, July 30, 2017.
15. Meyer-Grieben papers, cited in Heinrich Walle, *Die Tragödie des Oberleutnants zur See Oskar Kusch* (Stuttgart: Steiner, 1995), 181.
16. Walle, *Tragödie*, 157–239.
17. BA-MA, N 623/v.8, Sieber papers, letter Sieber to Hagemann, July 16, 1946, and N 623/v.9, letter Sieber to Breinig, Nov. 12, 1947.
18. *Neue Zeitung* (Stuttgart), July 8, 1946. Clipping in BA-MA, N623/v.6, Sieber papers.
19. BA-MA 623/v.8, Sieber papers, letters of July 6 and 16, 1946, respectively.
20. BA-MA 623/v.8, Sieber papers, Sieber to Hagemann, July 7, 1946.
21. BA-MA 623/v.8, Sieber papers, 200–201.
22. BA-MA, N 623/v.9, Siebert papers, Vol. II.
23. Meyer-Grieben to Erna Brockmann, Oct. 14, 1947, cited by Walle, *Tragödie,* 206.
24. Obituary at http://www.spiegel.de/spiegel/print/d-43365287.html (accessed Nov. 24, 2017).
25. BA-MA, N 623/v.11, Sieber papers, Vol. IV, Hagemann to Sieber, Apr. 20, 1949.
26. BA-MA, N 623/v.11, Sieber papers, Ilse Hagemann to Sieber, Oct. 12, 1949.
27. First names of associate judges not specified in court records or newspapers.
28. Summary of prosecution arguments, also quoted in BA-MA, N 623/v.11; Walle, *Tragödie,* 216–18.
29. Walle, *Tragödie*, 219, item 19.
30. Summary based on newspaper coverage in *Kieler Nachrichten*, *Schleswig-Holsteinische Volkszeitung*, and *Neue Zeitung* (Stuttgart) between May 3 and June 22, 1949. Newspaper clippings in BA-MA, N623, v.6, Sieber papers.

31. Nothdurft 1993 report in *U-154* file at U-Boat Archives Cuxhaven-Altenbruch.
32. Cited in Walle, *Tragödie*, 76–77.
33. Letter of Feb. 28, 1950, included in trial record, also quoted by Walle, *Tragödie*, 85.
34. For summaries of Rösing's testimony see *Kieler Nachrichten* and *Schleswig-Holsteinische Volkszeitung* of May 12, 1949.
35. Nothdurft, "Mein schicksalhaftes Zusammentreffen;" also in Walle, *Tragödie*, 73.
36. Kusch's father to state prosecutor's office, Dec. 28, 1949. See Walle, *Tragödie*, 86.
37. *Schleswig-Holsteinische Volkszeitung*, May 24, 1949.
38. Letter Seemann to Oskarheinz Kusch of June 19, 1949, forwarded to chief prosecutor of Kiel district court on Dec. 28, 1949. Cited in Walle, *Tragödie*, 221–22.
39. BA-MA, N623/v.6, Sieber papers, letter Hagemann to Sieber, May 27, 1949.
40. *Handbuch für den Generalstabsdienst im Kriege*, issued Aug. 1, 1939; see http://www.ifz-muenchen.de/heftarchiv/2001_3.pdf (accessed Nov. 29, 2017).
41. Oskarheinz Kusch to Prosecutor in Kiel, Dec. 28, 1949. See Walle, *Tragödie*, 220–21.
42. Walle, *Tragödie*, Oskarheinz Kusch to Prosecutor in Kiel.
43. "Urteilsbegründung" of Oct. 10, 1949. Quoted in Walle, *Tragödie*, 225.
44. BA-MA, N623/v.11, Vol. IV, Sieber papers, Hagemann to Siebert, Oct. 20, 1949.
45. BA-MA, N623/v.11, Vol. IV, Hagemann to Sieber, May 29, 1950.
46. *Kieler Nachrichten* and *Schleswig-Holsteinische Volkszeitung*, Sept. 22, 1950, editions.
47. "Urteilsbegründung," partially cited in Walle, Oskarheinz Kusch to Prosecutor in Kiel, 229–30.
48. http://www.henckert.com/family/henckert/106.htm (accessed Dec. 1, 2017).
49. https://www.aerzteblatt.de/archiv/9299/Gestorben (accessed Dec. 1, 2017).
50. https://uboat.net/men/roesing.htm (accessed Nov. 1, 2017). For Rösing's refusal to help rehabilitate Kusch after the war, see Blair, *Der U-Boot-Krieg*.
51. https://uboat.net/men/winter.htm (accessed Dec. 1, 2017).
52. http://www.geschichtsthemen.de/u-bootkommandanten.htm (accessed Dec. 1, 2017).
53. Email, Clemens Meyer-Grieben to author, Nov. 7, 2017. See also http://oskarheinzkusch.blogspot.com/p/blog-page.html (accessed Dec. 1, 2017).
54. Pallas, "Der Ast, auf dem sie sassen," *Aachener Nachrichten*.
55. Pretzel, *NS-Opfer unter Vorbehalt*, 215.
56. Klenck (1987). Bible reference: Matthew 26, 52.
57. On the history of the German navies after 1945, see Douglas C. Peifer, *The Three German Navies: Dissolution, Transition, and New Beginnings, 1945-1960* (Gainesville: University Press of Florida, 2002).
58. Eric C. Rust, *Naval Officers under Hitler: The Story of Crew 34* (Westport, CT: Praeger, 1991), 140.
59. Erich Raeder, *Mein Leben*, 2 vols. (Tübingen, 1956–57); Karl Dönitz, *Zehn Jahre und Zwanzig Tage* (Bonn: Athenäum, 1958). On literature, see Bird, *Erich Raeder*.
60. For details and context of the Filbinger Affair, see Wolfram Wette, *Ehre, wem Ehre gebührt: Täter, Widerständler und Retter, 1939–1945* (Bremen: Donat, 2015).
61. Keith W. Bird, *Erich Raeder: Admiral of the Third Reich* (Annapolis, MD: Naval Institute Press, 2013); and Dieter Hartwig, *Grossadmiral Karl Dönitz: Legende und Wirklichkeit* (Paderborn: Schöningh, 2010). For a fine summary of changing historiographical perspectives in postwar Germany, see Douglas C. Peifer, "Selfless Saviours or Diehard Fanatics?" *War & Society*, Vol. 26, No. 2 (Oct. 2007).

62. The following observations draw on Hartwig, *Grossadmiral Karl Dönitz*, chapters X and XI.
63. Jordan Vause, *Wolf: U-Boat Commanders in World War II* (Annapolis, MD: Naval Institute Press), 188–89.
64. Timothy P. Mulligan, *Neither Sharks nor Wolves: The Men of Nazi Germany's U-Boat Arm, 1939–1945* (Annapolis, MD: Naval Institute Press, 1999), 232.
65. Letter of Lüdmann to Rear Admiral Karl Peter of Apr. 24, 1985, referenced in Walle, *Tragödie*, 49–50.
66. For example, Peter claimed Hagemann had died by 1986 when in fact he was living in retirement in Lauenburg at the time. Peter, "Wider besseres Wissen," 8.
67. Summary adapted in part from Eric C. Rust, "The Case of Oskar Kusch and the Limits of U-Boat Camaraderie in World War II: Reflections on a German Tragedy," *International Journal of Naval History*, Vol. 1, No. 1 (Apr. 2002).
68. http://www.forum-marinearchiv.de/ (accessed Dec. 5, 2017).
69. See, for example, Jens Rönne, "Marine-Untersuchungsgefängnis: 2. Weltkrieg in Kiel: Die Geheimakte Kusch," at https://www.shz.de/regionales/schleswig-holstein/panorama/2-weltkrieg-in-kiel-die-geheimakte-kusch-id7542706.html (accessed Mar. 23, 2017); Karina Dreyer, "Marine-Untersuchungsgefängnis in der Wik: Unbekannter Ort des Grauens," at http://www.kn-online.de/News/Nachrichten-aus-Kiel/Marine-Untersuchungsgefaengnis-in-der-Wik-Unbekannter-Ort-des-Grauens (accessed Dec. 8, 2017); Heiko K.L. Schulze, "Reichseigenes Schuhwerk ist dem Verurteilten vorher auszuziehen: Die Schiessanlage in Altenholz bei Kiel als Hinrichtungsstätte," at http://docplayer.org/54551186-Reichseigenes-schuhwerk-ist-dem-verurteilten-vorher-auszuziehen-die-schiessanlage-in-altenholz-bei-kiel-als-hinrichtungsstaette.html (accessed Mar. 23, 2017).
70. On this question see Norbert Haase and Fietje Ausländer, *Die anderen Soldaten* (Frankfurt/Main: Fischer, 1995); Ulrich Bröckling and Michael Sikora, *Armeen und ihre Deserteure* (Göttingen: Vandenhoeg, Ruprecht, 1998); Detlef Vogel and Wolfram Wette, eds., *Das letze Tabu* (Berlin: Aufbau, 2007); as well as Marco Dräger, *Deserteur-Denkmäler,* rev. ed. (Frankfurt/Main: Lang, 2007).
71. See Tim Gabrys, "Oskar Kusch an der Marineschule" (2017), available at http://www.marine.de/portal/a/marine/start/ueberuns/markdo/schulen/msm/.
72. BA-ZNS, RM 123/K 4130, last, unnumbered document in open envelope.
73. Hansen, *Execution for Duty*, 134. The author thanks Frank Wunder of the North Cemetery and Jörg Hantelmann of the Old and New Urn Cemeteries in Kiel for their invaluable and continuing assistance in trying to help solve the riddle of Kusch's burial site.
74. Email Hendrik Beer to author, Nov. 2, 2017.
75. See http://www.kiel.de/presse/9833154537.html (accessed July 12, 2001). See also Hartwig, *Grossadmiral Karl Dönitz*, 357–61.

Chapter 11. A Summing Up

1. http://www.smh.com.au/news/opinion/patriots-ignore-greatest-brutality/2007/08/12/1186857342382.html?page=2 (accessed Dec. 22, 2017). No separate data on women were consulted.

2. Stephen R. Welch, "Harsh but Just? German Military Justice in the Second World War," *German History*, Vol. 17, No. 3 (1999), 369–99.
3. https://www.goodreads.com/author/quotes/98221.Robert_F_Kennedy (accessed Dec. 28, 2017).
4. Timothy P. Mulligan, *Neither Sharks nor Wolves: The Men of Nazi Germany's U-Boat Arm, 1939–1945* (Annapolis, MD: Naval Institute Press, 1999), 72.

BIBLIOGRAPHY

Primary Sources

Bundesarchiv-Militärarchiv (BA-MA), Freiburg, Germany

N 237/v. 21, Nachlass Marinedekan der Nordseestation Friedrich Ronneberger, Gnadengesuche.

N 623/v. 6, Nachlass Helmut Sieber; includes

(1) Clipping, *Neue Deutsche Zeitung*, July 8, 1946, "Der Fall des Oberleutnants zur See Kusch."

(2) Handwritten note, undated, "Fall Kusch," "Notiz Dönitz."

(3) Clipping, *Der Tagesspiegel* (Berlin), Dec. 5, 1946, Demokratisches Forum, Lesezuschrift von O. Kusch, Berlin-Steglitz.

(4) Letters between Sieber and O. Kusch regarding possible trial against Hagemann.

(5) Letter, Dr. Bernhard Leverenz (Kiel) to Helmut Sieber (Köln), April 4, 1949.

(6) Numerous clippings from *Kieler Nachrichten*, *Schleswig-Holsteinische Volkszeitung*, and *Die Neue Zeitung* (Stuttgart), May/June 1949.

(7) Letter, Helmut Sieber to Heinrich Hagemann, Dec. 22, 1949.

N 623/v. 8, Nachlass Helmut Sieber; includes

(1) Letters, Heinrich Hagemann to Helmut Sieber, July 6, 1946, Sieber to Hagemann, July 16, 1946; Sieber to Hagemann, July 20, 1946.

(2) Letter, Helmut Sieber to unknown recipient, dated July 20, 1946.

N 623/v. 11, Nachlass Helmut Sieber; includes

(1) Letter, Otto Kranzbühler to Helmut Sieber, Feb. 23, 1949.

(2) Letter, Ilse Hagemann to Helmut Sieber, Oct. 12, 1949.

RM 17/84, Offizierbestandnachweisung, 15. und 17. Minensuchflottille.

RM 17/96, Offizierbestandnachweisung 2. Unterseebootsflottille.

RM 26/65, Trauerfeiern, Beerdigungen: Schriftverkehr und Erlasse, 1921–45.

RM 26/73, OKM, "Erlass gegen die Kritiksucht und Meckerei," Sept. 9, 1943.

RM 31, Ostseestationstagesbefehle, bzw. Geheime O.T.B, 1937–44.

RM 31, Nordseestationstagesbefehle, bzw. Geheime N.T.B, 1937–44.

RM 31/2243, Marinestation der Ostsee, "Todesermittlungen, Sept. 1925–Apr. 1945."

RM 31/3258, Marinestation der Ostsee, "Fliegerschäden durch Bombenangriffe, März 1943–April 1945."

RM 31/3301, General-Akten betr. Allgemeine Verfügungen des Oberkommandos der Kriegsmarine, Band 2, 1939–.

RM 31/3345, Marinechefrichter Ostsee, Generalakten betr. Beiträge zur Auslegung des Para 5 KSSVO, Band 1.

RM 31/3349, Vortrag Korv. Kapt. Lüth, "Menschenführung auf einem U-Boot."

RM 31/3354, Marineoberkriegsgerichtsrat für den Ostseebereich, General-Akten: Gerichtsgebäude und Ausstattung, begonnen 1. Januar 1941.

RM 31/3358, Marinestation der Ostsee, "Fliegerschäden durch Bombenangriffe, März 1943–April 1945."

RM 69/128, Kriegstagebuch 17. Minensuchflottille.

RM 69/396–399, Kriegstagebuch 15. Minensuchflottille; includes "Gefechtsbericht M 1503 über die Vernichtung eines feindlichen U-Bootes am 18.2.1942 im Porsangerfjord."

RM 91/18, 2. U-Flottille, "Ständige Befehle, Heft I: Wichtige Befehle für U-Bootbesatzungen."

RM 91/18, 2. U-Flottille, Fotoalbum Lorient 1941.

RM 91/19, Geheime Flottillenbefehle, 2. U-Fl.

RM 91/22, Fotomappe, 2. U-Fl.

RM 96/1160, Kriegstagebuch u. Unterlagen Minensuchboot "M 1503."

RM 96/913–919, Logbücher/Kladden Minensuchboot "M 1701."

RM 98/106, Kriegstagebuch *U-103*.

RM 98/358, Kriegstagebuch *U-154* vom 2. Aug. 1941 bis 28. April 1944.

RM 98/397, Kriegstagebuch *U-193*.

RMD 10, Marineverordnungsblatt, 1920–45.

RMD 12, Ranglisten der Deutschen Kriegsmarine, 1937–45.

Bundesarchiv-Zentralnachweisstelle (BA-ZNS), Kornelimünster, Germany

RM 123/K 3140 (old file name RM 123/78071), Oblt. z. S. Oskar Kusch, Folder "Untersuchungsakten;" includes Kusch's personnel file (short version); Abel's report, with addendum; Kusch's arrest warrant; pretrial depositions and related papers; protocol of the court-martial; Kusch's sentence as well as its judicial justification; records related to review of the verdict by higher naval authorities and Hermann Göring; list of letters Kusch wrote from prison or received; protocol of execution.

U-Boot-Archiv, Cuxhaven-Altenbruch (UACA), Germany

Photographs (5) of Oskar Kusch and *U-154*, including Ref. No. MAR 74/1/4, 74/2/1, 74/2/2, 404/6/1.

Photographs (2) of Dr. Ulrich Abel.

Photographs (2) of Kurt Druschel, Ref. Nos. MAR 54/2/5, 54/4/4.

Photograph of ERWIN WASSNER, Ref. No. Rauschenberg 898/2-6.

Folder "U 103."

Folder "U 154," includes:

(a) copies of sketches Oskar Kusch drew in his jail cell in Kiel between the verdict and his execution. Donated by Helmut Jäger, Eschborn, Oct. 7, 1993.

(b) Letter, Herta Abel to Horst Bredow, Apr. 4, 1995.

(c) Copies of questionnaires, Hellmuth Kirchammer and Heinrich Lüdmann (survey conducted by Dr. Timothy P. Mulligan).
(d) Peter, Karl (Rear Adm., ret.). "Wider besseres Wissen zum Tode verurteilt. Stimmt das? Ein Bericht von Karl Peter." Typed manuscript (22 pp., plus appendices), 1986.
(e) Sketch and remarks composed for *U-460* guestbook on occasion of mid-ocean refueling of *U-154* from *U-460* on May 20, 1943, off Brazilian coast.
(f) Photographs of Kusch and Druschel, partial crew list of *U-154*, and comments on Kusch's court-martial by Heinrich Lüdmann (from his "Album").
(g) Nothdurft, Dr. habil. Hans. "Mein schicksalhaftes Zusammentreffen mit dem Oberleutnant zur See Oskar Kusch" (1993). Documents and recollections of Dr. Hans Nothdurft, shipboard surgeon on Kusch's last mission.
(h) Letter, Wolfgang Benzino to Volkmar König, Mar. 9, 1997.

Printed Sources Containing or Reproducing Primary Source Material

Deutscher Reichswetterdienst, Seewarte Hamburg, "Täglicher Wetterbericht und Wetterübersichten des Deutschen Reichswetterdienstes," Jan. 26–27 and May 12, 1944.

Hansen, Peter C. *Execution for Duty: The Life, Trial and Murder of a U-boat Captain.* Barnsley, UK: Pen & Sword Books, 2005.

Hering, Robert. *Chronik der Crew 37A, 1937–1987.* Gärtringen: Selbstverlag, 1987.

Klenck, Walter, *Wer das Schwert nimmt . . . Erleben im Luft-und Seekrieg 1940–1945: Bericht und Mahnung.* Munich: Universitas, 1987.

Marine-Offizier-Vereinigung. *MarineForum.* Articles and letters to the editor pertaining to the case of Oskar Kusch appeared in the following issues of this journal: Heft 7–8, 1992, pp. 234–38; Heft 9, 1992, pp. 308–9; Heft 10, 1992, p. 358; Heft 11, 1992, pp. 400–401; Heft 12, 1992, pp. 442–44; Heft 1–2, 1993, pp. 33–34, 39; Heft 3, 1993, pp. 86–87; Heft 5, 1993, p. 181; Heft 10, 1994, pp. 345–46; Heft 10, 1996, pp. 33–35; Heft 12, 1996, pp. 26–28.

Oberkommando der Kriegsmarine (Marinepersonalamt). *Rangliste der Deutschen Kriegsmarine nach dem Stande vom 1. November 1938.* Berlin: Mittler, 1938.

Oberkommando der Kriegsmarine (Marinepersonalamt). *Rangliste der Deutschen Kriegsmarine nach dem Stande vom 1. Oktober 1939.* M. Dv. 293.

Oberkommando der Kriegsmarine (Marinepersonalamt). *Rangliste der Deutschen Kriegsmarine nach dem Stande vom 1. Juni 1941.* M. Dv. Nr 293.

Ostsee-Zeitung. Obituary for Herta Abel, June 16, 2012.

Pallas, Rudolf. "Der Ast, auf dem sie sassen: Zu dem Fall des Geschwaderrichters Hagemann, der den U-Boot-Kommandanten Oskar Kusch zum Tode verurteilte." *Aachener Nachrichten*, Oct. 29, 1949.

Walle, Heinrich. *Die Tragödie des Oberleutnants zur See Oskar Kusch.* Stuttgart: Steiner, 1995.

Internet Sources Containing or Reproducing Primary Source Material

Historisches MarineArchiv, Crewlisten. Results for U-154: 3 pp. Available at: http://historisches-marinearchiv.de/projekte/crewlisten/ww2/eingabe.php. Accessed Mar. 23, 2017.

Uboat.net.

Mail and/or Email Correspondence (Originals or Copies in Author's Possession)

Herta Abel to Dr. Heinrich Walle, Aug. 31, 1997; Herta Abel to Heinrich Walle, Oct. 10, 1997; Herta Abel to Deutsches Marine Institut, Oct. 24, 1997; Deutsches Marine Institut (represented by Retired Captain Gunter Guseck) to Herta Abel, Dec. 22, 1997; Herta Abel to Captain (ret.) Gunter Guseck, December 31, 1997; Dr. Jürgen Abel to Deutsches Marine Institut, c/o Captain (ret.) Gunter Guseck, Jan. 13, 1998; Drs. Jürgen Abel, Dörte Pantenius (née Abel), and Peter Ulrich Abel to Heinrich Walle, Jan. 21, 1989 [1998]; Dörte Pantenius to Heinrich Walle, Feb. 2, 1998; Heinrich Walle to Dörte Pantenius, March 30, 1998; Captain (ret.) Gunter Guseck to Jürgen Abel, July 15, 1998; Herta Abel to Heinrich Lüdmann, Sept. 14, 1998; Heinrich Lüdmann to Herta Abel, Oct. 8, 1998.

Rear Admiral (ret.) Erich Topp to author, May 27, 1999; Aug. 9, 1999; Aug. 13, 1999; Aug. 15, 1999; Aug. 21, 1999; Sept. 11, 1999; Feb. 2, 2000; Dec. 19, 2000.

Jörg Hagemann to Ursula Rust, March 6, 2000.

Claudia van Eyck to author, March 24, 2000, *et passim* since July 2017.

Herta Abel to author, April 24, 2000; May 29, 2000; July 14, 2000 (includes copy of Ulrich Abel's curriculum vitae and responses to author's questionnaire); July 15, 2000; July 27, 2000; Dec. 15, 2000; Dec. 2003; Feb. 27, 2006.

Additional communications of author with Dr. Michael L. Hadley, Sept. 6, 2000; Peter Fiedler (WASt Berlin), Apr. 28, 2003; Dr. Dörte Pantenius, Nov. 11, 2005; Gerd Stolz, Jan. 2, 2006; Peter C. Hansen, Aug. 26, 2006; Dagmar Seemel, Aug. 4, 2017; Frank Wunder, Oct. 23, 2017; Jörg Hantelmann, Oct. 27, 2017; Hendrik Beer, Nov. 2, 2017; Clemens Meyer-Grieben, Nov. 7, 2017.

Secondary Sources

Books and Dissertations

Bald, Detlef, and Wolfram Wette. *Zivilcourage: Empörte, Helfer und Retter aus Wehrmacht, Polizei und SS.* Frankfurt/Main: Fischer, 2004.

Baumann, Ulrich, and Magnus Koch. *"Was damals Recht war . . ."—Soldaten und Zivilisten vor Gerichten der Wehrmacht.* Berlin: Bebra, 2008.

Bekker, Cajus. *Hitler's Naval War.* New York: Kensington, 1977.

Bird, Keith W. *Erich Raeder: Admiral of the Third Reich.* Annapolis, MD: Naval Institute Press, 2013.

———. *German Naval History: A Guide to the Literature.* New York: Garland, 1985.

Blair, Clay. *Der U-Boot-Krieg, Band 2: Die Gejagten, 1942–1945* (Munich: Heyne, 1999).

Böske, Stefan Christian. *Denunziationen in der Zeit des Nationalsozialismus und die zivilrechtliche Aufarbeitung in der Nachkriegszeit.* Dr. jur. dissertation. Bielefeld University, 2008.

Bröckling, Ulrich, and Michael Sikora. *Armeen und ihre Deserteure: Vernachlässigte Kapitel einer Militärgeschichte der Neuzeit.* Göttingen: Vandenhoeg, Ruprecht, 1998.

Buchheim, Lothar-Günther. *The Boat.* New York: Knopf, 1975.

Dönitz, Karl. *Zehn Jahre und Zwanzig Tage.* Bonn: Athenäum, 1958.

Dräger, Marco. *Deserteur-Denkmäler in der Geschichtskultur der Bundesrepublik Deutschland.* Rev. ed. Frankfurt/Main: Lang, 2017.

Duppler, Jörg, ed. *Festschrift: 80 Jahre Marine-Offizier-Vereinigung 1918–1998.* Wilhelmshaven: MOV-Selbstverlag, 1998.
Ehlert, Hans, ed. *Deutsche Militärhistoriker von Hans Delbrück bis Andreas Hillgruber.* Potsdam: MGFA, 2010.
Förster, Jürgen. *Die Wehrmacht im NS-Staat: Eine strukturgeschichtliche Analyse.* Munich: Oldenbourg, 2007.
Frei, Norbert, et al. *Karrieren im Zwielicht: Hitlers Eliten nach 1945.* Frankfurt: Campus, 2001.
Gannon, Michael. *Black May.* New York: HarperCollins, 1998.
———. *Operation Drumbeat.* New York: HarperCollins, 1990.
Graul, Jens, and Michael Kämpf, eds. *Dieter Hartwig—Marinegeschichte und Sicherheitspolitik. Vorträge und Texte aus drei Jahrzehnten. Festschrift zum 60. Geburtstag.* Bochum: Winkler, 2003.
Gröner, Erich. *Die Schiffe der Deutschen Kriegsmarine und Luftwaffe 1939–45 und ihr Verbleib.* 7th rev. ed. Munich: Lehmanns, 1972.
Gruchmann, Lothar. *Die Justiz im Dritten Reich, 1933–1940: Anpassung und Unterwerfung in der Ära Gürtner.* Munich: Oldenbourg, 1988.
Haase, Norbert, and Fietje Ausländer. *Die anderen Soldaten: Wehrkraftzersetzung, Gehorsamsverweigerung und Fahnenflucht im Zweiten Weltkrieg.* Frankfurt/Main: Fischer, 1995.
Hadley, Michael L. *Count Not the Dead: The Popular Image of the German Submarine.* Annapolis, MD: Naval Institute Press, 1995.
Hannemann, Ludwig. *Die Justiz der Kriegsmarine 1939–1945 im Spiegel ihrer Rechtsprechung.* Regensburg: Roderer, 1993.
Hartwig, Dieter. *Grossadmiral Karl Dönitz: Legende und Wirklichkeit.* Paderborn: Schöningh, 2010.
Häussermann, Ernst. *Mein Freund Henry: Dokumentarroman.* Vienna: Zsolnay, 1983.
Hellwinkel, Lars. *Hitler's Gateway to the Atlantic: German Naval Bases in France 1940–1945.* Barnsley, UK: Seaworth, 2014.
Hensle, Michael P. *Rundfunkverbrechen: Das Hören von "Feindsendern" im Nationalsozialismus.* Berlin: Metropol, 2003.
Herzog, Bodo. *U-Boote im Einsatz 1939–1945.* Podzun-Verlag, 1970.
Hildebrand, Hans H., et al. *Die deutschen Kriegsschiffe—Biographien—ein Spiegel der Marinegeschichte von 1815 bis zur Gegenwart,* 8 vols. Koehler, 1982–1995.
Hillmann, Jörg. *Der 20. Juli und die Marine: Ein Beitrag zu Ereignis und Rezeption.* Bochum: Winkler, 2004.
Huck, Stephan, ed. *Die Kriegsmarine: Eine Bestandsaufnahme.* Bochum: Winkler, 2014.
Kieschnick, Peter. *Stralsund 1945: Ein unvollständiges, nie geschriebenes Tagebuch.* Tredition, 2015.
Klausch, Hans-Peter. *Endstation Hela? Die Sonderabteilungen der deutschen Kriegsmarine (1936–1945).* Bochum: Winkler, 2017.
Klönne, Arno. *Gegen den Strom: Bericht über den Jugendwiderstand im Dritten Reich.* Hannover: Goedel, 1957.
Kneip, Rudolf. *Jugend der Weimarer Zeit: Handbuch der Jugendverbände 1919–1938.* Frankfurt/Main: Dipa, 1974.
Kühne, Thomas. *Belonging and Genocide: Hitler's Community, 1918–1945.* New Haven: Yale University Press, 2010.
Kunz, Andreas. *Wehrmacht und Niederlage: Die bewaffnete Macht in der Endphase der nationalsozialistischen Herrschaft 1944 bis 1945.* Munich: Oldenbourg, 2005.

Lohmann, Walter, and Hans H. Hildebrand. *Die Deutsche Kriegsmarine 1939 bis 1945: Gliederung, Einsatz, Stellenbesetzung*. Bad Nauheim: Podzun, 1956–1964.
McCue, Brian. *U-Boats in the Bay of Biscay: An Essay in Operations Analysis.* Washington, DC: National Defense University Press, 1990.
Messerschmidt, Manfred. *Die Wehrmachtjustiz 1933–1945*. Paderborn: Schöningh, 2005.
Messerschmidt, Manfred, and Fritz Wüllner. *Die Wehrmacht im Dienste des Nationalsozialismus—Zerstörung einer Legende*. Baden-Baden: Nomos, 1987.
Mulligan, Timothy P. *Neither Sharks nor Wolves: The Men of Nazi Germany's U-Boat Arm, 1939–1945*. Annapolis, MD: Naval Institute Press, 1999.
Nicosia, Francis R., and Lawrence D. Stokes, eds. *Germans Against Nazism: Nonconformity, Opposition, and Resistance in the Third Reich*. Oxford: Oxford University Press, 1990.
Niestlé, Axel. *German U-Boat Losses During World War II: Details of Destruction*. Annapolis, MD: Naval Institute Press, 1998.
Ostendorf, Heribert, and Uwe Danker, eds. *Die NS-Strafjustiz und ihre Nachwirkungen*. Baden-Baden: Nomos, 2003.
Padfield, Peter. *Dönitz: The Last Führer. Portrait of a Nazi War Leader*. New York: Harper, Row, 1984.
Paterson, Lawrence. *Second U-Boat Flotilla*. Barnsley, UK: Leo Cooper, 2003.
———. *Steel and Ice: The U-Boat Battle in the Arctic and Black Sea, 1941–1945*. UK: History, 2016.
Paul, Gerhard. *Landunter: Schleswig-Holstein und das Hakenkreuz*. Münster: Westfälisches Dampfboot, 2001.
Peifer, Douglas C. *The Three German Navies: Dissolution, Transition, and New Beginnings, 1945–1960*. Gainesville: University Press of Florida, 2002.
Peillard, Léonce. *Histoire Générale de la Guerre Sous-Marine 1939–1945* (Paris: Laffont, 1970).
Pretzel, Andreas. *NS-Opfer unter Vorbehalt: Homosexuelle Männer in Berlin nach 1945*. Münster: LIT, 2002.
Pretzel, Andreas, and Gabriele Rossbach. *"Wegen der zu erwartenden hohen Strafe . . .": Homosexuellenverfolgung in Berlin 1933–1945*. Berlin: Rosa Winkel, 2000.
Priemel, Kim Christian. *The Betrayal: The Nuremberg Trials and German Divergence*. Oxford: Oxford University Press, 2016.
Raeder, Erich. *Mein Leben*. 2 vols. Tübingen, 1956–1957.
Rahn, Werner, ed. *Deutsche Marinen im Wandel: Vom Symbol nationaler Einheit zum Instrument internationaler Sicherheit. Beiträge zur Militärgeschichte*. Vol. 63. Munich: Oldenbourg, 2005.
Reichel, Peter. *Vergangenheitsbewältigung in Deutschland: Auseinandersetzung mit der NS-Diktatur in Politik und Justiz*. Munich: Beck, 2007.
Robinson, Douglas H. *The Zeppelin in Combat: A History of the German Naval Airship Division 1912–1918*. London: Foulis, 1962.
Rohwer, Jürgen. *Axis Submarine Successes, 1939–1945*. Annapolis, MD: Naval Institute Press, 1983.
Rohwer, Jürgen, and Gerhard Hümmelchen, *Chronology of the War at Sea, 1939–1945*. Annapolis, MD: Naval Institute Press, 1999.
Rust, Eric C. *Naval Officers under Hitler: The Story of Crew 34*. Westport, CT: Praeger, 1991.
Salewski, Michael. *Deutschland und der Zweite Weltkrieg*. Paderborn: Schöningh, 2005.
Sievert, Hedwig. *Kiel einst und jetzt*. Kiel: Mühlau, 1964.
Steinhaus, Rolf. *Soldat, Diplomat*. Herford: Köhler, 1983.

Stolz, Gerd. *Heinrich Adolph Meyer und sein "Haus Forsteck" in Kiel.* Husum: Verlag, 2004.
Suhren, Teddy, and Fritz Brustat-Naval. *Teddy Suhren, Ace of Aces: Memoirs of a U-Boat Rebel.* Annapolis, MD: Naval Institute Press, 2006.
Thiessen, Harro. *Der Schiessstand Holtenau in der Gemeinde Altenholz.* Altenholz: Gemeinde Altenholz, 1999.
Thomas, Charles S. *The German Navy in the Nazi Era.* Annapolis, MD: Naval Institute Press, 1990.
Ueberschär, Gerd R. *Für ein anderes Deutschland: Der Deutsche Widerstand gegen den NS-Staat 1933–1945.* Frankfurt: Fischer, 2006.
Vause, Jordan. *Wolf: U-Boat Commanders in World War II.* Annapolis, MD: Naval Institute Press, 1997.
Vogel, Detlef, and Wolfram Wette, eds. *Das letzte Tabu: NS-Militärjustiz und Kriegsverrat.* Berlin: Aufbau, 2007.
Walle, Heinrich. *Die Tragödie des Oberleutnants zur See Oskar Kusch.* Stuttgart: Steiner, 1995.
Walmrath, Lothar. *"Iustitia et disciplina": Strafgerichtsbarkeit in der deutschen Kriegsmarine 1933–1945.* Frankfurt: Lang, 1998.
Werner, Herbert A. *Iron Coffins.* New York: Rinehart, 1969.
Wette, Wolfram. *Ehre, wem Ehre gebührt: Täter, Widerständler und Retter, 1939–1945.* Bremen: Donat, 2015.
———. *Filbinger: Eine deutsche Karriere.* Springe: zu Klampen, 2006.
———. *Zivilcourage: Empörte, Helfer und Retter aus Wehrmacht, Polizei und SS.* Frankfurt: Fischer, 2003.
Wette, Wolfram, and Joachim Pereils, eds. *Mit reinem Gewissen: Wehrmachtrichter in der Bundesrepublik und ihre Opfer.* Berlin: Aufbau, 2010.
Wiggins, Melanie. *U-Boat Adventures: Firsthand Accounts from World War II.* Annapolis, MD: Naval Institute Press, 1999.
Wüllner, Fritz. *Die NS-Militärjustiz und das Elend der Geschichtsschreibung.* Baden-Baden: Nomos, 1996.
Y'Blood, William T. *Hunter-Killer: U.S. Escort Carriers in the Battle of the Atlantic.* Annapolis, MD: Naval Institute Press, 2012.

Selected Articles in Print and Information Accessible on the Internet

Anonymous. "Lost Places DJI Phantom 3|Marineschiessplatz Kiel-Holtenau." Video of German shooting range at Holtenau, including drone footage. Published Sept. 18, 2016. Available at https://www.youtube.com/watch?v=B7-d3YMwV_U. Accessed Apr. 4, 2017.
Arp, Jochen. "Ein neues Marinevorbild." *Das Ostpreussenblatt*, Apr. 5, 1997, 4.
Bolwig, Gunther. "Aufbau eines Stadtteils durch die Marine in den Jahren 1900–1915." Article on naval buildup in Kiel Wik, dated 1993, includes photographs and maps. Copy courtesy of Mr. Erhard Ohlhoff, Kiel.
Bruneau, Jean-Baptiste. "Les sous-mariniers allemands: genèse et développement d'un mythe héroïque." In *Histoire et littérature de l'Europe du Nord-Ouest* 52 (2012. Available at http://hleno.revues.org/249. Accessed Apr. 4, 2017.
"Der Fall des Oberleutnants zur See Oskar Kusch." *Briefe an die Führerschaft der Europapfadfinder St. Michael.* Part I, 03/2001, 19–22.

Deutsches Ärzteblatt, Vol. 95, No. 5. Obituary for Prof. Dr. med. habil. Hans Nothdurft. Available at: http://www.deutschesaerzteblatt.de/v4/archiv/artikeldruck.asp?id=9299. Accessed Aug. 25, 2006.

Dreyer, Karina. "Marine-Untersuchungsgefängnis in der Wik: Unbekannter Ort des Grauens." *Kieler Nachrichten-Online*, July 14, 2014. Available at: http://www.kn-online.de/News/Nachrichten-aus-Kiel/Marine-Untersuchungsgefaengnis-in-der-Wik-Unbekannter-Ort-des-Grauens. Accessed March 23, 2017.

Dülffer, Jost. "Politische Geschichtsschreibung der '45er-Generation': Von der Militärgeschichte des Zweiten Weltkriegs zur kritischen Zeitgeschichte (1950–1970)," in Christoph Cornelissen, ed., *Geschichtswissenschaft im Geist der Demokratie: Wolfgang J. Mommsen und seine Generation*. Berlin: Akademie, 2010, 45–60.

Fischer, Vera. "Hoffnung auf Gerechtigkeit: Der Fall Kusch und die NS-Justiz." *Berliner Morgenpost*, Sept. 15, 1996 (copy in U-Boot-Archiv, Folder "*U 154*").

Förster, Jürgen. "Weltanschauung als Waffe: Vom 'Vaterländischen Unterricht' zur 'Nationalsozialistischen Führung.'" In Bruno Thoss and Hans-Erich Volkmann, eds., *Erster Weltkrieg—Zweiter Weltkrieg: Ein Vergleich. Krieg, Kriegserlebnis, Kriegserfahrung in Deutschland*. Paderborn: Schöningh, 2002, 287–300.

Gabrys, Tim. "Oskar Kusch an der Marineschule." Article about unveiling of Kusch portrait painted by Rolf Osker Michelmann at the German Naval Academy. Published Feb. 22, 2017. Available at: http://www.marine.de/portal/a/marine/start/ueberuns/markdo/schulen/msm/. Accessed Apr. 4, 2017.

Gruchmann, Lothar. "Ausgewählte Dokumente zur deutschen Marinejustiz im Zweiten Weltkrieg." *Vierteljahreshefte für Zeitgeschichte* 26, no. 3 (1978): 433–98.

Gymnasium Altenholz. "Oskar Heinz Kusch: Ein Beitrag zum Geschichtswettbewerb Anders sein." Published March 18, 2015. Available at oskarheinzkusch.blogspot.com. Accessed Apr. 4, 2017.

Hartwig, Dieter. "Benennung einer Strasse in Altenholz und Kiel nach dem Oberleutnant zur See Oskar Kusch." In Jens Graul and Michael Kämpf, eds. *Dieter Hartwig—Marinegeschichte und Sicherheitspolitik. Vorträge und Texte aus drei Jahrzehnten. Festschrift zum 60. Geburtstag*. Bochum: Winkler, 2003: 357–61.

———. "Karl Dönitz—Versuch einer kritischen Würdigung." *Deutsches Schiffsarchiv* 12 (1989), 133–52.

———. "Persönlichkeiten als Gestalter und Opfer der Geschichte—Kapitänleutnant Heinz Wilhelm Eck und Oberleutnant zur See Oskar Kusch—Offiziere im Widerspruch." See Dieter Hartwig, 362–69.

Herwig, Holger H. "Clio Deceived: Patriotic Self-Censorship in Germany after the Great War." *International Relations* 12 (1987), 5–44.

Hillmann, Jörg. "Die Kriegsmarine und ihre Grossadmirale im kollektiven Gedächtnis." *Historische Mitteilungen* 20 (2007), 5–73.

Jahr, Christoph. "Die Militärjustiz als Steuerungsinstrument soldatischen Verhaltens in den Weltkriegen 1914 bis 1918 und 1939 bis 1945." In Bruno Thoss and Hans-Erich Volkmann, eds., *Erster Weltkrieg—Zweiter Weltkrieg: Ein Vergleich. Krieg, Kriegserlebnis, Kriegserfahrung in Deutschland*. Paderborn: Schöningh, 2002, 323–34.

Klönne, Arnold. "'Du weisst es—keine Zeichen irrten': Südlegion: Ein Bericht über Rudi Pallas und den Jungenbund Südlegion." *Puls 13—Dokumentarschrift der Jugendbewegung* Heidenheim: Verlag der Jugendbewegung, 1986.

Lehmann, Sebastian. "Der Streit um Forsteck—Zum Verhältnis zwischen der Stadt Kiel, der Marine und der Partei im Nationalsozialismus." *Mitteilungen der Gesellschaft für Kieler Stadtgeschichte* 80, no. 3 (Dec. 2000), 127–44.

Leverenz, Bernhard. "Der Begriff der Öffentlichkeit." In Erich Schwinge, *Militärgesetzbuch nebst Kriekssonderstrafrechtsverordnung*, 6th ed. Berlin: Junker, Dünnhaupt, 1944.

Messerschmidt, Manfred. "Die deutsche Militargerichtsbarkeit im Zweiten Weltkrieg." In Hans Joachim Vogel, Helmut Simon and Adalbert Podlech, eds., *Die Freiheit des Anderen: Festschrift für Martin Hirsch*. Baden-Baden, 1981.

Morio, Bert. "Oskar Kusch und der Marineschiessplatz Holtenau." Article available at: http://www.holtenau-info.de/history/kusch-oskar.htm. Accessed April 4, 2017.

Neitzel, Sönke. "Der Bedeutungswandel der Kriegsmarine im Zweiten Weltkrieg." In Rolf-Dieter Müller and Hans-Erich Volkmann, eds. *Die Wehrmacht: Mythos und Realität*. Munich: Oldenbourg, 1999, 245–66.

Orth, Kathrin. "Kampfmoral und Einsatzbereitschaft in der Marine." In Jörg Hillmann and John Zimmermann, *Kriegsende 1945 in Deutschland*. Munich: de Gruyter Oldenbourg, 2002, 137–55.

Paul, Gerhard. "Blutiges Terrain: Todesurteile und Exekutionen von Marinesoldaten in Kiel." In: *Landunter: Schleswig-Holstein und das Hakenkreuz*. Münster: Westfälisches Dampfboot, 2001, 268–79.

Peifer, Douglas C. "Commemoration of Mutiny, Rebellion, and Resistance in the East and West German States and Militaries." *Journal of Military History*. 65, no. 4 (Oct. 2001), 1013–52.

———. "The Past in the Present: Passion, Politics, and the Historical Profession in the German and British Pardon Campaigns." *Journal of Military History* 71, no. 4 (Oct. 2007), 1107–32.

———. "Selfless Saviours or Diehard Fanatics? West and East German Memories of the *Kriegsmarine* and the Baltic Evacuation." *War & Society* 26, no. 2 (Oct. 2007), 99–120.

Rahn, Werner. "Der Seekrieg im Atlantik und Nordmeer." In *Das deutsche Reich und der Zweite Weltkrieg*, Vol. 6 (Stuttgart, 1990), 175–425.

Rönnau, Jens. "Marine-Untersuchungsgefängnis: 2. Weltkrieg in Kiel: Die Geheimakte Kusch." *SHZ.de*, Aug. 30, 2014. Available at: www.shz.de/regionales/schleswig-holstein/panorama/2-weltkrieg-in-kiel-die-geheimakte-kusch-id7542706.html. Accessed March 23, 2017.

Rosenkranz, Erhard. "Aus maritimer Sicht: Von der Kriegsjustiz zum Wert der Inneren Führung." *Marineforum*, Heft 7/8, 1992, 234.

Rust, Eric C. "The Case of Oskar Kusch and the Limits of U-Boat Camaraderie in World War II: Reflections on a German Tragedy." *International Journal of Naval History* 1, no. 1 (Apr. 2002). Available at http://www.ijnhonline.org/volume1_number1_Apr02/article_rust_kusch_uboat.doc.html (accessed July 21, 2017). Translated into Spanish by Carlos Ballesta as "El Caso de Oskar Kusch y los Límites de la Camaradería en los Submarinos Alemanes en la Segunda Guerra Mundial: Reflexiones sobre una Tragedia Alemana." Available at http://www.telecable.es/personales/submarinos/kusch/kusch.htm. Accessed Apr. 4, 2006.

Salewski, Michael. "Selbstverständnis und historisches Bewusstsein der deutschen Kriegsmarine." *Marine-Rundschau* 67, no. 2 (1970), 65–122.

"Schönberg: Schule feiert ihren 100. Geburtstag." *BerlinOnline: Berlin auf einen Klick!* Textarchiv der *Berliner Zeitung*, Apr. 11, 2000. Available online at http://www.BerlinOnline.de/wissen/berliner_zeitung/archiv/2000/0411/lokales/0175/index.html. Accessed Feb. 28, 2001.

Schulze, Heiko K. L. "Reichseigenes Schuhwerk ist dem Verurteilten vorher auszuziehen . . . : Die Schiessanlage in Altenholz bei Kiel als Hinrichtungsstätte." Schleswig-Holstein, Landesregierung, Landesamt für Denkmalspflege, DM 2010, 79–84. Available at http://www.schleswig-holstein.de/DE/Landesregierung/LD/Downloads/Wissen/DM2010_AltenholzSchie%C3%9Fanlage.pdf?__blob=publicationFile&v=2. Accessed Mar. 23, 2017.

"Strasse Am Schiessstand wird unbenannt in Oskar-Kusch-Strasse." *Landeshauptstadt Kiel—Offiziell*, Mar. 3, 1998. Available at http://www.kiel.de/presse/9833154537.html. Accessed Mar. 21, 2017.

Thun, Johann. "'Hellas ewig unsere Liebe': Der Bund Südlegion," in Thorsten Carstensen and Marcel Schmid, eds., *Die Literatur der Lebensreform: Kulturkritik und Aufbruchstimmung um 1900.* Bielefeld: Transcript, 2016, 97–100.

Topp, Erich. Book review of Heinrich Walle's "Die Tragödie des Oberleutnants zur See Oskar Kusch." *Marineforum*, Heft 5, 1996, 34–35.

Walle, Heinrich, "Der Fall des Oberleutnants zur See Oskar Kusch." In Thomas Vogel, ed., *Aufstand des Gewissens: Militärischer Widerstand gegen Hitler und das NS-Regime 1933–1945.* Begleitband zur Wanderausstellung des Militärgeschichtlichen Forschungsamtes. 5th ed. Bonn: Mittler, 2000.

———. "Der Fall Kusch: Eine bleibende Mahnung an die Offiziere der Marine." *Marineforum*, Heft 7–8, 1992, 234–38.

———."Doppeltes Todesurteil: Die Tragödie des Oberleutnants zur See Oskar Kusch." Published March 22, 2005. Available at: http://www.123recht.net/Doppeltes-Todesurteil-__a12415.html. Accessed Mar. 23, 2017.

———. "Ein deutsches Schicksal: Zweimal zum Tode verurteilt. Die Tragödie des Oberleutnants zur See Oskar Kusch." *Truppenpraxis* 5 (1997), 346–50.

Welch, Stephen R. "Commemorating 'Heroes of a Special Kind': Deserter Monuments in Germany." *Journal of Contemporary History* 47 no. 2 (2012), 370–401.

———. "'Harsh but Just'? German Military Justice in the Second World War: A Comparative Study of the Court Martialling of German and US Deserters," *German History* 17, no. 3 (1999), 369–99.

WetterOnline, includes historical German weather data; available at: http://www.wetteronline.de. Accessed Aug. 31, 2006.

INDEX